FREE BORN

BEN SANFORD

STENOX PUBLISHING
Clarksburg, MD

First originally published by Page Publishing 2020

ISBN 979-8-9886249-6-7 (pbk)
ISBN 979-8-9886249-7-4 (digital)

Printed in the United States of America

ELARIA

WILDS
LAKE PICARA
POR-SHADA MOUNTAINS
KIERAN DIVIDE
MELTORIA
GORGENCIA
LORTALA
PLEVIS
ASTARIS
LA-KELAR
TOVAL
PICERO
PICERAN
CARCHA
ASTARIA
DESANTI
RES-PAR
VESTI
TOR-PAR
ONTARA
CAREA
ESTASA
LOWER IRLO
GREEN
TECTA
VOLATO
FERNARES
LAVERA
RELUSIA
CARHALSI MTS
ANTEEN
LAROSE
SARCOSA
FLEVIUM
SOVELL RIVER
ELYSIA
BENSHA
TALISSIA
VELLESIA
NATAN
CORDLESS
PORT ESTES
CORVONA
FAR POLANTIS
LODRESH
AQUALANIA SEA
DABLAS
NEAR POLANTIS
ALCONAR
CREPSOS
FREEPORT
TALNAIRA
TULAR MOUNTAINS
BASETA

MAGE   BANE

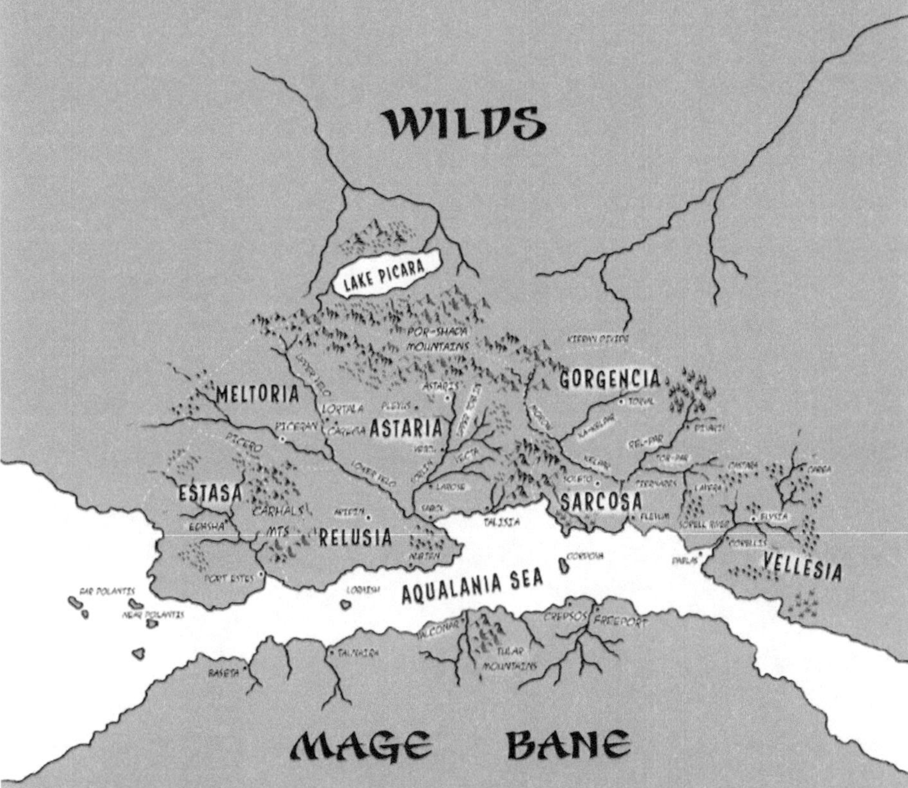

ASTARIA
POR-SHADA MOUNTAINS
UPPER VELO
ASTARIS
PLEXUS
UPPER TORLIN
LORTAIA
CAREGA
VECTA
PICERAN
VETCUS
TORLIN
LOWER VELO
LAROSE
TALESIA
SABOL

CHAPTER 1

Ethanos led his mule through the forest of pines. A strong north wind whipped through the high branches above, whispering the coming of winter along the Por-Shada Plateau. Nearing the end of his arduous trek, he took measure of his catch—a dozen beaver pelts, a bearskin, and enough venison to feed him for a month. His brown leather shirt was well-worn with several tears, and his thick brown trousers fared little better. He wore a gray cloak of wolf fur and a black buckled sword belt.

"We're late, Ethan," his large friend lamented, wary of the scolding they were sure to receive upon their return.

"What are you worried about, Krixan? I'm the one who'll get yelled at," Ethan answered, not at all concerned about his father's ire. He was accustomed to his father's wrath, and this occasion would be no different.

"I hope he only yells at you. That man scares me," Krixan lamented as he rubbed his balding head.

Ethan regarded Krixan with an odd face. Krixan was a giant of a man, standing nearly eighty-two inches with a heavy, powerful frame. He has seen his friend kill a man with his bare hands. Most people thought Ethan was large, standing seventy-four inches with a slender build and thick arms, but Krixan made him look small in compare.

"Frightens you?" Ethan said. "That bear we killed was frightened of you, Krix. How can you be afraid of my father?"

The big man raked his thick fingers through his rust-colored beard, struggling to find the words that aptly described his apprehension. "Bah!" he growled, bereft of the vocabulary needed to convey his thoughts.

"Don't worry about it, Krix. Has my father ever scolded you? Even once? No. Even when we were children, he had nothing but praise for you. He saved his wrath for me."

"Even his kind words frighten me," Krixan grunted.

Ethan shook his head, amused by his large friend's cowardice.

"I look fondly to this day's end, Ethan. A warm fire and thick walls are preferable to camping in the wilds with you."

"Well, thanks, big fella. You didn't have to come with me if you didn't want to, you know," Ethan said with a hurt look that even a blind man could see was insincere.

"Of course I had to come. Someone needs to look out for you. Besides, your mother insisted. No one else could survive your expeditions in the wild."

"I thought you enjoyed our little foray into the high country?"

Krixan snorted. "We were caught in three rainstorms. Lost half our provisions crossing that accursed stream, we were set upon by wolves that killed our horses, and I was poisoned by that rotten meat you cooked. No, I think I like palace life over the forest with you."

"And I thought we had a good time," Ethan said despondently. "At least we were able to purchase this fine animal from that farmer, or we'd have had to carry our packs all the way back to Astaris."

Krixan regarded the poor excuse for a mule trailing them. They had to pay three gold pieces for the ugly, half-lame mule. One gold piece would have bought a full warhorse with armor back in Astaris but need drove the ridiculous price.

The high pitch of a woman's scream rent the crisp autumn air. Ethan dropped the mule's reins and ran off through the forest of pines toward the source of the panicked cry, with Krixan trailing close behind. The trees quickly gave way to an open meadow of rolling grass overlooking an upper branch of the Torlin River below. There amid the dying sea of brown grass sat a finely dressed woman atop a gray palfrey. She was dressed in a bright-blue blouse over dark riding trousers. Her flame-red hair blew freely in the wind, framing her porcelain smooth face. Two men accompanied her, each were clad in mustard capes and brown mail, with a coat of arms emblazoned upon their breastplates that Ethan could not discern from the distance that separated them. Both men had their swords drawn, and Ethan could see them swinging frantically at an unseen foe. He could see a dark-gray shape lunge at one of the men with fangs bared and gnashing.

"Mountain wolves!" Ethan shouted to Krixan who trailed several paces behind. He drew his sword and ran apace across the meadow. He could see one of the men fall under dark-gray shadows that swarmed over him. Pitiful human screams greeted them as they drew nigh, mixing with the snarls of savage jaws in a disjointed melody. A look of abject horror transfixed the woman's countenance when her brown eyes met his as a large gray head sprang toward him. Ethan's blade spun in his hand as he drove the point into the wolf's mouth. The animal snarled and snapped as the blade impaled its throat. Ethan kicked the beast, freeing his blade as the wolf staggered briefly, whimpering in agony as blood filled its mouth. No sooner had the beast dropped than two others were upon him. Ethan took a fore paw with his next blow before turning on the following wolf with a slash across its muzzle. Krixan followed to his left, set upon by another wolf.

Far larger than their nearest cousins, the mountain wolves weighed more than a large man, often exceeding two hundred and twenty pounds. They were hunted to extinction in six of the seven mage kingdoms of Elaria. Ethan believed they were extinguished in his native Astaria until a pack had set upon him in the high country, killing their horses.

Ethan spun his blade, parrying one beast then another, lopping off whatever flesh they offered him. In moments both wolves' bodies were upon the ground, blood issuing from their multiple wounds. Ethan felt a great weight upon his back as another wolf drove him to the ground, sinking its fangs into his right shoulder.

"Agghh!" He screamed, rolling over as he hit the ground, trying to dislodge the wolf's mouth from his flesh. He stopped after two rolls, still facing the ground with the wolf upon him. He reached over his shoulder, grasping the beast with his bare hands, and pulled it over him, freeing its fangs from his shoulder. Ethan winced in pain as the fangs ripped muscle and tendons as he tore the creature from his shoulder. The damaged tissue quickly knitted together, healing as soon as the fangs were torn free. Ethan drew a knife from his belt as his other hand grasped the wolf as tightly as he could. He thrust his knife rapidly into the beast's belly a dozen times before slicing its throat and rolling it off him. As Ethan gained his feet and retrieved his sword, another wolf sprang forth, snarling and snapping as Ethan's sword lopped its head. He caught sight of Krixan hunched over several paces to his left, hacking away at his prey as wolf blood splattered his furs and leathers. Ethan could see several gray tails scurrying away northward, fleeing toward the Por-Shada Mountains.

"What is your name, sir knight?" the woman's voice called out, drawing his attention.

Ethan turned, regarding the woman on the horse briefly before closing on the fallen soldier who was lying moaning in the grass. "I'm not a knight," he answered her while kneeling beside the wounded man. The guard's throat was nearly ripped open but not enough to kill him just yet. He was fortunate. Ethan cut away the man's cape and pressed it against the side of his throat before checking his other wounds. His arms were mangled, and his belly was ripped open. His chain mail was shredded.

"Are you a mage healer?" Ethan asked the woman. He knew she was noble born by her bearing and rich clothing.

She gazed at him as if she were struck by a bolt.

"If you are not a knight, then you are a vassal to a local lord. If so, then you are addressing a highborn lady and should do so upon a knee with deep reverence. Am I understood?" she admonished with an icy voice.

He stood, facing her with his dark-blue eyes narrowed against the morning sun. He was incredibly handsome, so much so that it nearly took her breath. He was tall and broad of shoulder. His face was tan and jaw squared. He tilted his head, examining her in a curious way like a dog might. He was clearly not a mage-born noble by his unassuming manner. He lacked the haughty posture of mage-born pretention, yet he looked as if he were of a different world altogether. He lacked the awed humility of the common born.

"Your man here is in need of a mage healer, girl. What is your mage gift?" Ethan asked, ignoring her taunt.

"You dare address me—"

"Are you a mage healer?" he asked again more forcefully, cutting her off.

She glared at him with pursed lips as her other guard came to her defense, preparing to level a sword to Ethan's throat.

"I wouldn't do that!" Krixan growled, towering behind the fellow with his sword pressed to the man's back.

Ethan snatched the man's blade, snapped it in half, and tossed it aside.

"There are two others just over there, both dead," Krixan jerked a thumb over his shoulder in the direction he indicated.

Ethan stepped closer to the noblewoman and seized her about the waist, pulling her from her mount over her heated protest.

"Krixan, take the man with you to the palace before he dies."

"That's a good two-hour ride, Ethan. I don't think he'll make it."

"Without a mage healer he is dead anyway," Ethan said.

"There are mage healers in our party just downriver," the woman said.

"Who's in your party?" Ethan asked her.

"Members of the royal family of Astaria. Princess Arian and Princess Ceresta, along with a sizable force of mage lords and knights of Astaria. I suggest you flee before I order them to seize you. The king shall have you flogged for your impudence by addressing me so informally and for touching my person," she hissed.

"My lady, you shouldn't—" Krixan began to say before Ethan raised a palm to warn him to silence.

"It won't be the first time the king has strapped my backside, girl. You better get going Krixan."

Krixan hoisted the wounded man on the saddle and climbed behind him. Ethan swatted the horse's rump, sending it off.

"Who are you?" the woman asked, her eyes burning a hole into Ethan's flesh.

"I'm someone who saved your life. You could at least say thank you, or do they lack such manners where you're from?" Ethan goaded.

"*I am Lady Elenna Torhess*, daughter of *Lord Vegar*, vassal of King Evor Ectus of Estasa. My mother is sister to the king."

"I know most of the highborn ladies of Astaria, that's why I didn't recognize you. So why is an Estasan noblewoman in Astaria?"

"You *dare* ask such a question of me? What is your name?" she asked in a low dangerous voice.

"I'm nobody. I'm just a simple man of Astaria." He shrugged.

"The king shall have you flogged in the courtyard of Astaris for all to witness. I shall insist upon it!"

"You wound me Lady Torhess. But why would good King Bronus do such a thing?" Ethan smiled, unnerving her with his ease.

"As the *future* queen of Astaria, my word shall be law."

"*Future queen of Astaria?* King Bronus is already wed, Elenna. I don't believe Queen Gabrielle would appreciate being replaced."

She failed to slap him as he caught her hand. "I wouldn't do that, Elenna." He smiled.

"You *dare* touch me? You *dare* soil my name upon your lips? I am to wed the *crown prince* of Astaria, you *fool*, not King Bronus. I shall be your *queen*. If King Bronus does not have you flogged for this offense, be sure that Crown Prince *Ethanos Blagen* shall!" she fumed.

Her words washed over him like an ill wind. She could see the color drain from his face. She could sense his sudden apprehension and lifted her chin to press her advance.

"Ethanos Blagen is your betrothed?" he asked while backing a step.

"Yes!" she hissed, stepping forth to drive the point. "He is attending matters of state along the Gorgencian border. He is expected at the palace any day now."

"Has the crown prince agreed to this betrothal?" Ethan asked warily.

"Of course. He is rumored to be pleased with the arrangement," she said defiantly. She tried to press into his mind to read his thoughts, but her mage power revealed *nothing*, as if a barrier were placed over him. She attempted an enchantment to bend him to her will but to no effect. She chewed her lip in frustration. The excitement with the wolf pack must have impaired her mage powers.

"I don't know what you've been told about Ethanos Blagen, but you will find him very disappointing, Elenna. He would make you a poor husband."

"You dare soil his name upon your lips?"

"What's wrong with my lips?" he countered, regaining his bearing as he crossed his arms, looking down at her with an amused look playing upon his face.

"Everything is wrong with you, whatever your name is. Prince Ethanos Blagen shall make a fine husband. He is rumored to be the handsomest man in the seven kingdoms."

"He's actually quite ugly but go on."

"Why you conceited—"

"Oh, I'm not conceited, my lady. I know well my many faults."

She regarded him strangely. Despite his barbaric garb and offensive tongue, he was quite comely with a man's body and a boy's charm. His dark hair was cut very short and his dark-blue eyes projected an unsettling confidence. His leather shirt and fur cloak were torn at the shoulder where the wolf had bitten him. She had forgotten that since he acted as if he was unharmed, but she remembered the wolf clinging to his back during the fray with its fangs embedded in his shoulder. How could he have survived the encounter unscathed? She reached out to touch his shoulder, ignoring the wolf's blood staining his raiment. She parted the threads of his torn shirt, examining the flawless contours of his smooth muscled shoulder.

"You have no wound. Not even a scratch or scar. That is not possible. I saw the wolf bite you." She lifted her bewildered eyes to his. "Are you not a *mage*?"

"No, I am not a mage."

It made no sense.

"Then...who are you?"

He piqued her curiosity, but he ignored the question, stepping past her to snatch the wounded man's discarded cloak upon the grass. He wiped the blood from his blade, returning it to his sheath upon his left hip. Ethan turned back toward the tree line atop the ridge to the west.

"Where are you going?" she shouted after him.

"I left my mule in the forest to come to your aid. Hopefully, he hasn't run off with our gear and game," he answered as he continued up the grassy rise.

"What if the pack returns? I have only one guard left to protect me!" she complained.

Ethan turned on her with disgust painted across his face. "You threaten to have me whipped for failing to bow to your presumed magnificence, and then you demand that I stay to protect you? I must learn to never underestimate the presumption of the mage born."

His fierce stare unnerved her. There was something strange about this man that she could not discern. He dressed like a pauper, but his bearing bespoke an indifference to title or authority.

"You ride a mule? That seems fitting for one of your station," she said.

"A mule is an honest animal, Elenna. You would be wise to judge a man on his strength of character and the kindness of his heart rather than the weight of his purse or the greatness of his title." He turned his back to her again, walking toward the tree line.

"You may be low born, but you wield your blade like a master swordsman. If you remain to guard me, I shall forgive your poor manners and shield you from the king's judgment. And I shall pay you two silver coins for your trouble, which is far more than your mule is worth."

Ethan turned to face her once more. "I paid *three gold* coins for that mule, Elenna, after our horses were slain by another wolf pack. I don't need or want your coin. My pride is worth more than all your father's wealth and land. You needn't worry about the wolf pack, for they shall not return after we bloodied them. They'll seek easier game elsewhere. As for King Bronus, there is nothing you can do to spare me from his wrath. If you desire to see me punished, then your wish shall be granted."

"Are you oath bound to House Blagen?" she asked sternly.

"Yes," he answered after a pause.

"Then you are charged to obey my edict. I demand that you stay!"

"My knee only bends to the king and then only grudgingly. You are not entitled to my service or my heart, my lady."

"Your heart? I've placed no such claim," she regarded him carefully.

"Return to your guard. I'll return shortly," he said, turning away one last time in search of his mule.

*****

Fortunately for Ethan, he found the mule where he had left it. He feared the wolf pack might have circled back and found the helpless beast. He led the mule back to the girl and her guard. She regarded his mule with a condescending smile. He noticed her guard had four horses in tow. When the wolves attacked, the guards dismounted, and their mounts had run off.

"Had you stayed, I would have lent you the use of one of our mounts for our return to Astaris. I think this is better, for I shall take great pleasure in seeing you atop your *noble* steed." She smirked.

"I would be proud to ride this mule through the palace. He has born my burden for many days, and I'm happy to call him friend." Ethan ran his hand gently through the mule's mane.

The ground shook beneath them as scores of mounted warriors thundered over the grassy rise, riding north and west, shadowing the river below. Men in black tunics over black breeches with gray mail rode forth in columns of two, closing swiftly on their small party. Amid these warriors were several mages of varying ability and a young woman with dark-brown hair and black riding trousers and blouse. Elenna smiled with relieved satisfaction with the royal party's arrival as the mounted soldiers circled them, one column to each side, forming a protective perimeter around them.

The woman in black with lush brown hair and feminine yet discerning features stopped before them, eyeing Ethan with a look one might give an errant child. Beside the young woman sat a captain of the royal guard. He was a square-built man with graying temples and a black crest with yellow lightning centered upon it on his chest. It was the royal symbol of Bronus Blagen, the lightning lord.

"Captain Dorun," Elenna greeted him with a sweet smile. "This man speaks perdition and refuses to give his name. I…" Her smile faded as she read the captain's thoughts.

Dorun dismounted and quickly took a knee. "Prince Ethanos."

"Get up, Dorun. I told you not to kneel, especially in the field," Ethan reminded him.

Elenna turned sharply to Ethan, staring at him with a volatile mix of embarrassment and anger. "You are the crown prince?" she asked numbly.

"He is the *reluctant* crown prince, Lady Elenna," the woman atop the mount replied.

"Why did you not tell me?" she asked, her confidence suddenly shaken to its core. She remembered her place as the shock of his true identity took hold, and she began to kneel.

"Get up, Elenna. Unlike you, I don't like anyone kneeling to me, just as I don't like kneeling to anyone else."

"You're long overdue," the woman atop the horse scolded him.

"We ran into some trouble up in the high country with a pack of mountain wolves, Ceresta," Ethan explained.

"Mother is worried, and Father is furious," Ceresta said.

"Our mother is *always* worried, and our Father's *always* furious." He shrugged.

"No, *you* are the cause of all Mother's worries and the source of all Father's fury."

"He may find that I have a little fury for him," he said in regard to the arranged nuptials they had planned for him.

The soldiers surrounding them stiffened at Ethan's harsh words toward the king.

"You would do well to mind your tongue, Ethanos," Ceresta reproached him.

Elenna's romantic vision of the Astarian crown prince quickly waned. In its place was the irreverent tongued young man beside her.

"My tongue is the least of my problems, Ceresta. Did Krixan find you?"

"Yes. Arian healed Lady Elenna's injured guard. We will take you to them, and then we must make haste to Astaris," his sister said.

"All right. Do you have a spare mount? I would take one of Elenna's, but she insists I ride back to Astaris on my mule. As you can see, the poor beast is already laden with all my gear."

"Prince Ethanos, of course you may have one of my spare mounts," Elenna apologized.

"My name is Ethan, just plain old Ethan, and *no*, you were quite adamant that I would not ride one of your mounts. I'll find my own," Ethan dismissed her as he walked away.

*****

The column rode swiftly beneath the shade of outstretched limbs of the broad-leafed sorek trees. Off to their left, a steep drop overlooked the Upper Torlin snaking through the vale. The wind whistled through the boughs above, loosening the brittle stems of dead and dying leaves, raining down upon those below in showers of gold, crimson, and brown. Krixan rode beside him, his stomach growling its discontent as their dinner was postponed till they reached the palace. Krixan's heavy bulk was supported by the strong draft horse that contrasted sharply to Ethan's lighter martel bred mount.

"Might I have a word with your crown prince, Krixan?" Lady Elenna asked as she drew up beside them.

"As you wish, my lady," Krixan bowed his head, pulling upon his reins to allow them ahead of him.

Elenna drew her gray palfrey beside Ethan's dusty martel.

"What do you want, Elenna?" he asked, the annoyance clear in his tone.

"I wish to apologize for my earlier presumption, Prince Ethanos. You must think poorly of me." Her voice was weak but hopeful.

"My name is Ethan, Elenna, just Ethan. You can drop the title."

"Pardon my discomfort, my prince, but such informality feels strange upon my lips."

"If you're going to remain in my company, then you best get used to it. Don't fret too much, Elenna, if you prefer the pomp and formality of the world you were born to, that world awaits us at the palace. I'm sure you'll take pleasure seeing me kneeling before the king in humbled supplication."

"Why do you say such things, Pr…Ethan?" she corrected herself. "You are the future king of Astaria. You kneel only to your father and mother, Ethan. They desire only what is best for you. Why do you hate them so?"

He gave her a look. "I love my father and mother, Elenna. I would give my life for them if such a price were required."

"Then why do you protest—"

"I may love my father and mother, but I don't like kneeling to them, just as I don't like anyone else kneeling to me. This may be difficult for you to comprehend, Elenna, but I dream of a world where all men are free to live their lives as they see fit, to be as great or as simple as their gifts or ambitions decree. Unfortunately, no such world exists. In this world, all men are slaves."

"You speak despondently of a world that has bequeathed you such wondrous gifts, Ethanos Blagen. You are the firstborn son of the great king of Astaria. You are mage born, though you claimed not to be. You are—"

"I did not claim falsely, Elenna. I am no mage."

"How can that be so?" she asked, confused by such a possibility. Those gifted with magic were born to those of magic. If both parents were so gifted, then their children would be mage born as well in likely equal measure. If only one parent was mage born, then the child's mage power would likely be weaker. The greatest of the mage born, those with the most power, were the ruling classes of seven kingdoms of Elaria. Ethan's father was the greatest of the kings of Elaria. He was a lightning lord, the firstborn with the ability to cast lightning in over half a millennium. He could slay entire armies with lightning springing from his fingertips. Ethan's mother was a seer and an enchantress of the first order. His maternal grandfather was Lord Dragos Mortune, also a master seer and healer. Male healers were extremely rare, perhaps one born to each generation in all the seven kingdoms, giving further evidence to Ethan's rich bloodlines. Each of Ethan's siblings was wondrously gifted with multiple mage skills. How could Ethan, as firstborn, be bereft of magic?

"I am immune to magic. Did you not know?" he asked.

"There were whispers of your ability to resist magic, like an enhanced mage shield. That is all that we knew of you in Estasa."

"I have no mage shield, Elenna. I have no magic at all. I am immune to mage powers whether they are to my benefit or detriment. That's why you couldn't read my thoughts or enchant me."

"You knew?" she gasped, startled that he ascertained her intent.

"Yeah, I knew. I can tell when someone attempts to use magic against me. Perhaps that is what nature gave me to offset my lack of mage power."

"If you lack mage power, then how did you self-heal from the wolf bite?"

"I didn't use magic, my body simply heals itself. It's a unique ability I was born with. Though I am immune to magic, I am also immune to harm."

"Can you die?"

"I don't know, I never tried." He smiled. "I'm sure if someone cut off my head, then I'd be hard-pressed to grow another. Or grow another body, however it works."

He actually smiled. She sighed, that small victory easing her anxious heart. "Are there any other skills you were born with?"

"I have the strength of three men equal to my size," he lied, understating his true power.

"Interesting," she said, noting the thickness of his arms, thighs, and chest. She remembered him pulling the wolf off his back as if it were a pup. Elenna couldn't help but note the perfect symmetry of his face and the masculine way, which defined his every gesture. Most handsome men flaunted their comely looks with colorful tunics and hose and long locks. Ethan was just the opposite. He wore rugged garb best suited to the wilds. His hair was shorn, and he despised the pomp and self-importance of his fellow mage born. She smiled inwardly, contemplating how much more handsome he would look once she cleaned him up and dressed him in royal finery.

"Why do you hide such a fetching build and handsome face beneath those rags?" she asked with a lascivious smile.

"I like what I'm wearing. Unfortunately, my mother will insist I change into something uncomfortable once I arrive."

"Is that so terrible?"

"Yes, it is. Besides, who thinks I'm handsome?"

"I do. I thought so when I first set eyes on you when you saved me from the wolf pack."

"No. You thought I was a savage or a peasant. Women find power attractive, and now that you know that I'm the crown prince, you suddenly find me attractive."

"No, Ethan, I do find you attractive. I like the real you," she almost begged him to believe her.

"You met the real me when I saved you. You wanted to have the real me whipped, so forgive me if I don't believe you."

"I thought you were common born, and you acted such a bore. What did you expect me to conclude? You were the one who allowed me to believe falsely," she challenged.

He gave her a look. "That is the point, Elenna. If I were common born and I saved your life by risking my own, you would judge me on my deference to your high station. If someone saves your life, the first acknowledgment that should proceed from your lips is gratitude. You instead took offense to my lack of reverence for your high birth. You placed higher importance on such frivolity rather than the sparing of your life."

"I thought you were common," she said weakly.

"What difference does that make, Elenna? Common men's lives are just as precious as mage born."

She lifted her chin as she stared ahead, refusing to counter what she knew to be false. Debating him seemed pointless. He sensed her withdraw, and the shame she inflicted on herself for her harsh words earlier. "Elenna," he said softly, turning his head to hers. "I do not blame you for what happened between us. You are mage born, raised since birth on the belief of mage superiority and right to rule."

Instead of assuaging her guilt, his words struck her as poison. "You speak sedition, Ethanos. You deny the right of mage rule?"

"I don't deny it, but I do question its wisdom. Are mage born truly the wisest among us that we should trust their ability to rule over mankind? Just because some are born with wondrous gifts of magic does not warrant their greater wisdom."

"The world you dream of would be a dreadful place forlorn of hope."

"How so?"

"You so easily disregard the benefits of the thousands of years of mage rule that has blessed the seven kingdoms. Through magic we bring enough rain to water our crops but not enough to flood our riverbanks. We prevent the many wars that plague the Mage Bane, where magic has no effect, or the northern wilds where mages are devoured by dragons. Are the common born better served in such mage-less places? Mage healers cure common men of all ailments of the flesh, mending mortal wounds or restoring lost limbs or eyes. What fate do those similarly afflicted in the Mage Bane or the wilds suffer? Seers and telepaths can look into the minds of men to determine their guilt or innocence, where common men often judge the innocent guilty. We protect them from the natural world, from disease and from each other. It is only fitting that they acknowledge their mage rulers with gratitude and adoration."

"What are the names of your two guards that were slain by the wolf pack?"

"I am uncertain. Why do you ask?" she said, annoyed with his changing topic.

"They sacrificed their lives to protect you, Elenna, and your first thought after the wolves fled was to question my lack of deference to your nobility. Your first priority should have been to the care of those men. That is why mage rule subverts justice. Ultimate power corrupts. My father is a good and just king, but good kings will eventually beget selfish kings who care nothing for others."

"Would not nonmage kings beget tyrants as well?"

"I never claimed common men to be morally superior. They are ruled by their passions as much as we. All kings eventually beget tyrants."

"Then what do you suggest?"

"No kings at all."

She gave him a look. "Then chaos is your master, Ethanos, for such a world would bring us to ruin."

"I didn't say chaos would rule. Power should be shared by all, balanced in a way so no one man could rule without consent of the governed."

"How would such a thing work?" She shook her head, dismissing his ramblings as mere fantasy.

"I don't know. It would require men wiser than a dummy like me. I was not born with my brother's intellect."

"You are a strange crown prince, Ethanos Blagen." She gifted him a smile.

"Strange?"

"No other mage born is so self-effacing as you. Why do you think so little of yourself?" To her, Ethan had every reason to boast. He was every bit as powerful as his mighty sire but in a simpler way. Where his father could cast lightning and bring ruin to nations, Ethan could slay any individual mage regardless of their power. Being immune to magic, coupled with his regenerative powers and great strength, made Ethan a very dangerous man.

"I'm not self-effacing. I just know my limitations. I know that I lack my brother's and grandfather's wisdom and my father's mage power. I lack my mother's patience and my sisters' devotion to duty. I am good with a sword and bow, but those are warrior skills that will not aid me in ruling a kingdom. I do know that I'm ill-suited for the protocols of palace life."

"Is that why you venture into the high country, to escape?"

"Yes, it's the only time I'm truly free," he reflected sadly.

"Free? You are to be king one day, Ethanos. Who has more freedom than the king?"

"Everyone else is bound to the king, and the king is bound to his responsibility for his people. I will resent such chains. I will make a poor king, and my people deserve better than I."

"I think you would make a great king, Ethanos Blagen. You care for others and would have their best interest at heart."

"I have nothing to offer Astaria but my sword. The throne requires more than my youthful arrogance and dull wit."

The trail ahead opened up as they drew nigh the palace. Before them was Astaris, rising above the Por-Shada Plateau like an azure mountain rising above an emerald sea. The outer walls of the city jutted into the air at odd angles from fifty to one hundred and fifty feet. They were crafted of bluestone with varying hues. The walls of the inner citadel rose four hundred feet behind the outer walls, resting on the city's far northern end. Towers of even greater height twisted into the aeries above in spirals of azure and gray, each spell formed by the sky lords of old. Their long column skirted the city from the east, approaching the main gate on the city's southern face. Before the watch towers that flanked the main gate, a smooth gray road ran from the city entrance to the river valley below. The ground before the main gate provided a breathtaking view of the Torlin valley with its hundreds of villages dotting its meandering banks on either side.

Passing under the stone archway of the city entrance, they rode through the wide avenue that ran from the gate to the inner citadel two miles ahead. The main avenue divided the great city into eastern and western halves. All commerce flowed over this vital artery as vendors lined either side, selling their wares to the bustling crowds that filled the street in the late day. Men dressed in colorful tunics and hose escorted ladies in long gowns with tight bodices. Great horns sounded, heralding the royal hunting party's return. The good citizens of Astaris bowed as they passed, much to Ethan's annoyance.

"Captain Dorun!" Ethan called out over his shoulder.

"Yes, my prince," Dorun answered, drawing up along Ethan's flank.

"Send your men up ahead and tell the people *not* to kneel. Have them go about their business."

"As you command, Prince Ethanos, but I must caution you of your father's likely objection."

"When does my father *not* object to my decisions, Dorun?" Ethan grinned.

Dorun gave him a knowing smile. There was not a brave man in the entire kingdom that did not tremble with trepidation before the king, save for Ethanos. The men of Astaris were grateful that Ethanos drew all the king's wrath, sparing them his ire. Dorun rode on ahead to convey Ethan's command.

The high inner citadel towered over the city as the waning sun alighted its smooth walls of silvered blue. A spell shield covered the city, protecting Astaris's temperate climate from the changing seasons without. The guards at the citadel opened the gate as they drew near. Beyond the citadel, a great tourney field of manicured grass spread out before them. Knights in full armor paraded the grounds, plying their warcraft as men-at-arms in chain mail and archers in green livery occupied the perimeter, honing their skills. Beyond this vast parade ground was the inner palace with spiral towers rising seven hundred feet into the firmament, their azure and alabaster surfaces aping the sky above. The towering citadels were spell forged ages ago by the sky lords who founded Astaria in her dawning years. Tall crafted pillars, two meters abreast, formed a semicircle around both sides of the gate of the inner palace. A smaller courtyard awaited beyond the pillars of the gate and before the palace proper. Ethan's sisters stopped at the palace entrance as he continued on.

"Where are you going?" Ceresta asked with an eyebrow raised over a dark-brown eye.

Ethan pulled on the reins, circling his mount to face them. "Taking my horse to the stables," he answered what he thought was obvious.

"Father and Mother are waiting. The others can tend the horses," his sister Arian said as she dismounted, tossing her reins to a soldier nearest her. Her dark-red hair trailed behind her. She wore the white dress of a mage healer, and her expressive green eyes came to his as if waiting for an obstinate child.

"I'll take care of my own mount, I don't need anyone waiting on me." Ethan ignored their counsel.

Krixan rode up beside him, pushing him from his mount. Ethan's face planted painfully into the black stone of the inner courtyard. His bruised face quickly healed as he came gingerly to his feet.

"I'll tend to your horse, Ethan. Don't keep your father and mother waiting," Krixan said as he snatched the horse's reins and trotted off to the stables.

Arian and Ceresta smiled at the lovable giant for putting their brother in his place. Krixan was Ethan's best friend and the only man in Astaria who was Ethan's physical match. Krixan followed Ethan on every dim-witted adventure that piqued Ethan's interest, but Krixan would not allow Ethan to disrespect his father, no matter how trivial.

Ethan brushed himself off, scolding himself for letting Krixan catch him off guard. "I think I'll let Krix tend my horse," Ethan declared as if that was his idea all along.

"A wise decision," Ceresta bit her lip so as not to laugh.

*****

King Bronus and Queen Gabrielle awaited them in the great hall of the palace. The great hall was an expansive chamber with blue-stone walls arcing toward a cupola centered above. Mage-lit spherical lanterns hung from the ceiling, bathing the chamber in luminous light. King Bronus sat on his throne beside his queen. His steel-gray eyes matched the square jaw, trimmed beard and large build that defined the strength of the man who wore the crown of Astaria. Coal-black hair draped beneath his heavy crown, a crown he had enlarged since his ascension to symbolize the weight of responsibility that it represented. "A king must be ever mindful of the burden of his rule," he had told Ethan since he was a child. A throne should be uncomfortable, lest a man take selfish pleasure in it. Bronus Blagen was a bear of a man who towered over most with his muscled build and tall stature. He wore a black tunic over black trousers. Like Ethan, he had a disdain for the hose and bright colors that most men in the seven kingdoms wore in lieu of trousers. The two of them were more alike than either would concede. A gold streak of lightning was sewn into the chest of his tunic, the symbol of his house.

Seated upon the throne to his left was Queen Gabrielle. Her auburn hair cascaded over the shoulders of her purple gown. Her light-green eyes smiled warmly as she beheld her firstborn enter the great hall. She noted his tattered clothing and fur cloak. She had hoped he would be more presentable when he was introduced to Lady Elenna, but fate intervened. She cringed at the thought of poor Elenna meeting Ethan as he was now dressed, like a savage on a mammoth hunt. Arian and Ceresta flanked their brother while Elenna trailed several paces. They stopped short of the dais where the king's and queen's thrones rested and knelt.

"Ceresta!" the king called to his eldest daughter.

"Yes, Father?" she answered, lifting her eyes to his.

"You and Arian are excused. Clean yourselves and change into appropriate clothing for the feast this evening in honor of our future daughter, Lady Elenna."

Ceresta and Arian quickly bowed and stepped without, leaving Ethan alone with their parents and his betrothed.

"Elenna dear, rise and come hither," Gabrielle commanded softly, holding out her left hand to the young maid.

Elenna rose gracefully to her feet and glided across the mirrored stone floor. She climbed the dozen steps that ascended the dais and took Gabrielle's hand, standing beside the queen as Ethan knelt alone before the throne.

"*Stay where you are until I grant you leave to rise, boy!*" Bronus growled as Ethan attempted to gain his feet.

Elenna tried to bite her smile, gleeful to finally see Ethan put in his place.

"Where have you been?" Bronus asked with seething anger.

"I—"

"Do you know we expected you weeks ago?"

"We were—"

"Are you cognizant of the trouble you've stirred, *boy*?"

"Father, let me—"

"I have sent scores of patrols scouring the countryside, hoping to find one trace of you!"

"If you let me exp—" Ethan tried to say before Bronus cut him off again.

"Your mother has exhausted herself with worry because of you, Ethanos! Your brother has been searching for you for days with little rest!"

"Are you going to allow him to speak or continue berating him?" Gabrielle asked, admonishing her husband with her wifely look.

"Oh, why bother, I already know the boy's excuses." Bronus threw his hands up.

"Stand, Ethanos," his mother said with a warm smile.

"I'm sorry for causing you worry," Ethan said, coming to his feet. "We were set upon by mountain wolves. They killed our horses and we—"

"I know that, *boy*! Your sister's a telepath unless you've forgotten. If you desire to play in the woods like some wayward child, I suggest you limit your forays nearer the palace and never more than half a day's ride. You have responsibilities that require you here, Ethan. If you're to be king one day, you need to act it," Bronus admonished.

"I never asked to be king, Father. If I'm such a disappointment, you can place me aside for Tristan. All I ask is my freedom."

"Your freedom?" Bronus asked darkly, his gray eyes afire.

"My freedom," Ethan answered. "I kneel to no man, and no man kneels to me. It seems a fair price in exchange for a throne and crown."

"Only the grave shall grant you freedom, son. You are my first-born and heir. You are bound to *me*. I am your *king*, and you will obey me. Am I understood, *boy*?"

"Yes, sire," Ethan released a measured breath.

Elenna flinched, terrified by the king's demeanor. She suddenly felt empathy for Ethan. How he could suffer his father's rebuke without cowering was a testament to the boy's courage. She hoped to never suffer the king's wrath lest she break down in tears.

"Might we speak alone, Father?" Ethan asked.

"No, Ethanos. I do not wish to suffer any more of your foolish banter. I know you're angry and wish to vent your ire upon me, but as your *king*, I refuse you such an audience."

"If I am to be king one day and entrusted with the throne of Astaria, then I should be trusted to choose my own queen," Ethan said what he wished to keep from Elenna's ears, but his father forced his hand.

"If you desired a bride of your own choosing, son, then you would have already done so. You are past the age of choosing, so we chose for you. You will wed Lady Elenna. You will conduct yourself as befits a future king of Astaria. You will bring honor to this house."

Ethan felt the walls close around him, trapped by forces beyond his control and by a life not of his choosing. The pounding of his heart deafened his ears.

Panic gripped Elenna's heart as she beheld Ethan's despondent frown. He did not want her. *Am I so terrible to look upon?* she mused bitterly. Or was he merely displeased by her poor treatment of him when they first met? She had to do something to prove herself in his eyes.

"My king!" she spoke, rushing to kneel at Bronus's feet.

"What troubles you, my child?" Bronus placed his meaty left palm under her chin, lifting her eyes to his.

"Please show Prince Ethanos mercy, sire. His anger is caused by my insult upon him."

"How so, Elenna?" Bronus asked.

"Prince Ethanos came to my aid when my company came under attack by a pack of terrible wolves. After saving my life, he suffered my insult to his person. I was unaware of his name or true title and berated him thus. I threatened to have him whipped by your decree for his speaking so freely when I thought him common born."

"My dear child, we have all wanted to flog Ethan at one time or another. The boy is altogether impossible to live with as I can well attest. Perhaps I shall make his flogging a wedding gift for you, shall we say, *fifty* lashes. After he says his vows, of course." Bronus laughed heartily.

Elenna shook her head. "No, sire, that shan't be necessary." She paled.

Ethan rolled his eyes, knowing his father was taking great pleasure in his torment. "Since I am unworthy of a private audience with you, sire, might I be excused?"

Bronus regarded him darkly, contemplating what to do with the boy. Why did Ethan always stir his anger? He was the source of his greatest pride and greatest disappointment. "Leave us, child. We shall expect you for the feast this evening in your honor," Bronus told Elenna with a kindness that contrasted the harshness he showed his son.

Elenna bowed reverently and withdrew, stealing a hopeful glance to Ethan, who stood statue-still, facing his parents.

"You may speak freely, son," Gabrielle said as Elenna passed without.

"I'm not marrying her," he said dryly, his sea-blue eyes narrowing bitterly.

"You will do as I command, Ethanos!" Bronus roared.

"Grandfather did not choose your wife, what gives you the right to choose mine?"

"Because I am your king, boy. You are only entitled to what I allow you. I grow weary of your insolence. There is much I admire in you, son. Since you were a child, I took pride in your courage as the only one to stand up to me. You have never cowered from my wrath, nor did you cry out when I strapped your backside. I punished you often, but I was proud of you all the same. You have a warrior's courage and a kind heart, Ethan. Both are virtues necessary to a king, as are wisdom and discipline, which you lack. You're past the age of childish defiance. It is my responsibility to see my kingdom has a worthy king once my life is at an end. Every king needs a queen and heir. You will produce that heir long before you ascend the throne."

"Have I not shown responsibility?" Ethan growled. "Did I not demonstrate my ability to innovate and command on the battlefield?"

Ethan had long argued that a lighter cavalry, armed with composite bows, could outmaneuver and defeat his father's heavy horse. With a command structure based solely on merit rather than nobility, he wished to revolutionize mounted warfare. His tactics proved successful in three mock engagements with his father's royal cavalry.

"Your pretty ponies might be worthy as scouts and guarding supply chains, but they shall never replace armored knights in full regalia bearing down upon the enemy."

"I proved—"

"You proved nothing, Ethanos! I ordered Captain Marco to remove his contingent to Castle Plexus, where they can perform supportive duties. As king, you must learn to trust in the traditions that have served Astaria since the sky lords of old that established our kingdom."

"If I have displeased you, Father, then I ask that you limit your wrath to me and not on the men I trained. They are as worthy as the highborn knights that they bested on the tourney fields."

"Perhaps I shall find use for them that you deem worthy of their talents as long as you *happily* accept Lady Elenna as your bride."

Ethan sighed painfully, torn between mercy for his men and an arranged marriage to a woman he despised.

"Is Lady Elenna not beautiful, Ethan?" His mother smiled softly.

"I've seen her true nature."

"You cannot see her thoughts, Ethan, but I suffer no such impairment. Lady Elenna is fond of you. Do not judge her harshly for ill words spoken in duress. She may have spoken poorly to guard her heart. She was promised to you and did not wish her affection for a handsome stranger to come between you. Fate determined that you would be that stranger," Gabrielle said with pure empathy for his betrothed.

"I wish you had asked me before committing to this," Ethan sighed.

"If the choice were yours, Ethan, who might you have chosen?" Gabrielle asked.

"Jennifer Murtado," he answered. Of all the ladies at court, she was the one he could actually converse with freely. She was one from a small circle of his closest confidants that was not offended by his wild spirit and strange opinions. He could easily envision a life with her, though he doubted he would ever love her in the way his father and mother loved each other. Theirs was a rarity in Royal matches in that regard.

"She is a lovely girl," his mother said.

"Then why pass her over for this Estasan noblewoman who has no loyalty—"

"Enough!" Bronus roared. "Lady Elenna is the niece of Evor Ectus, king of Estasa. Your marriage will bind our kingdoms with a defensive alliance to check any aggression the Meltorians, Relusians, or Gorgencians may contemplate. Your sister Arian shall also wed Evor's heir, thus completing our union. We shall purchase peace through our collective strength. The greatest victory in war is the war not fought. You are dismissed, Ethanos. Bathe and present yourself at the feast tonight appropriately attired."

*****

Everyone in the palace granted Ethan a wide berth as he stormed through the corridors with a fearsome scowl. He passed the stairwells that led to the baths below and the one that led to his bedchamber above. He stepped passed from the inner keep, crossing the courtyard, passing the stables and guardhouses that circled the towering citadels to the seclusion of the small wooded enclave behind the keep. Amid this small grove of wooded pines were piles of logs that required chopping before they were distributed throughout the palace. An old woodcutter named Laris Yance spent his days chopping away at the piles that were deposited. Hardly anyone of note ever visited Old Yance, save for one. Ethan passed under the towering pines, tossing his fur cloak aside as he retrieved an ax embedded into a cutting stump while Old Yance looked on.

"Good afternoon, Prince Ethanos," the old woodcutter greeted him.

"Just Ethan, Yance," Ethan corrected him. Yance shook his head and grinned as Ethan set a log upon the stump and began chopping away. Ethan spent many a day helping Yance chop wood. Yance knew whenever the king berated him for Ethan would take out his anger on Yance's logs. Yance had never known a mage born who partook in common labor until Ethan. The prince was not afraid to raise a blister, though even when he did, it simply healed. It struck the old woodcutter that the palace was filled with scores of visiting lords and ladies, each careful to project their own self-importance and parade through Astaris in all their rich finery, and here was Ethan, the crown prince of Astaria no less, chopping wood at his side. Old Yance held King Bronus in high regard and respected him with awed reverence, but Ethan he loved. The boy would make a great king. Yance was a simple woodcutter, but Ethan made him feel as important and respected as a high lord of Astaria. If Ethan asked Yance to take up his ax and join him in battle against the host of the seven kingdoms, he would do so even if it meant certain death. He would follow Ethan Blagen through the gates of damnation.

Ethan spent several hours chopping firewood and talking with Yance about the high country, wolves, and women. Yance shared tales from his youth as Ethan listened while chopping away. He knew Yance was lonely, his wife having passed years ago, and his children with families of their own. There were countless others like him, toiling away in the winter of their lives with no one to talk to. Yance was a good man, in Ethan's opinion, a hardworking and honest wood-cutter whom others took little notice of. Ethan had known him for years, spending as much time with him as anyone else, except Krixan, of course.

"I thought I would find you here." Tristan Blagen grinned as he stepped through the pines to greet his brother. He was nearly Ethan's height but slight of build with sand-colored hair and an attractive yet studious face. He wore a sky-blue tunic over tan hose and a black woven sword belt. His long sword hung low upon his left hip with a jeweled scabbard. He was the epitome of a high prince of Astaria. Ethan turned to his brother's voice, smiled, and swung the ax into the stump, leaving it embedded there while stepping toward Tristan.

"I heard you've been looking for me," Ethan slapped him on the shoulder.

"Over much of the countryside, big brother. Mother was worried and Father—"

"Was furious, I know," Ethan finished his sentence.

"As your brother, I am grateful that you incur all Father's wrath, leaving me unscathed." Tristan smiled.

"I'm beginning to wonder if Father's anger is rooted in my drinking him beneath the table in front of all his high lords," Ethan recalled a fortnight past when he once again bested his sire in the palace tavern in the cellar of the inner keep.

"That could be true. Father did hold the title as the mightiest drinking man in all of Astaria until you came along. He never was a good loser. Of course, I could ill imagine his anger if he knew that you cheated," Tristan cautioned with humor in his eyes.

"Me!" Ethan touched his chest as if struck by a bolt. "I never cheated."

"You can't get drunk, Ethan. Your mind heals as quickly as your flesh. Do not tell me otherwise, for I know it true."

"It's not cheating if I'm able to do it."

"It *is* cheating, but you needn't worry, for I am the only one who has surmised that you've been faking your inebriation. Your secret is safe with me." Besides Ethan, Tristan was the only one he knew of whose mind was unreadable. His mind was immune to manipulation of any sort.

"Come," Tristan added. "Mother sent me to fetch you. She doesn't want you to be late for your—"

"My funeral."

"She's a beautiful girl, Ethan. Bear that in mind. Grandfather is eager to speak with you as well."

"What about?"

"I do not know." Tristan shrugged. "But he has been unusually excited about something of late and wishes to speak with you about it. He refuses to leave his castle at Plexus until you come to him."

CHAPTER 2

The sound of flutes, harps, and alto voices conjoined in a soft melody that echoed through the great hall into the outer corridor where Ethan waited with little desire to enter. The chorus of voices within echoed merriment and cordiality that Ethan wanted no part of. He bathed and dressed in a timely manner but passed over the silver tunic, hose, and pointed shoes his mother had instructed the maid to set aside for him. Instead, he donned black wool trousers, black shirt, and thick black boots. A long sword hung from his left hip and a short sword upon his right. A pair of axes were cross slung across his back, and three knives were sheathed behind each sword. He was greeted with odd looks from those he passed in the adjoining corridors. While everyone else was garbed in fancy dress, Ethan looked ready for battle. He took a deep breath and entered the great hall.

Merriment and song filled the festive air as he stepped within. Dozens of musicians congregated in the chamber's far southeast corner. Scores of tables surrounded the open floor in the hall's center, where the guests would dance after the feast. To every corner of the vast chamber, he beheld hundreds of guests seated for the feast. Lords and vassals in silk tunics, hose, and flowing capes accompanied ladies in voluminous gowns that swept the mirrored black floor as they walked. Ladies of upper houses wore spiraled hats with fabric woven into their cones that draped over their shoulders. The sound of hundreds of voices echoing off the bluestone walls was deafening. Basin torches lined the chamber's walls, providing light for Ethan to see, though he needed it not. May the fates have mercy upon him if that truth ever surfaced. The others benefited from mage lanterns suspended from the ceiling that bathed the great hall in ample light. Ethan's immunity to magic meant he could not use the light they offered. His ability to see in the dark was an ability he planned to keep secret for as long as possible. He let others think he had weaknesses where there was truly strength.

The hundreds of voices grew suddenly still as Prince Ethanos made his way toward the king's table. Even dressed as he was, Ethan drew many flirtatious glances from many of the ladies. Other maidens frowned, despondent over the prospect of Ethan wed to another. His eye caught Jennifer Murtado sitting amongst her house. They shared a look before he moved on to the king's table.

"Ahh, here he is now, Lord Vegar," King Bronus's voice boomed as he beheld his son approaching his table.

Ethan noted the eastern lord with a leaping fish sewn into the chest of his light blue tunic, the signet of Evor Ectus, king of Estasa. Lord Vegar was a slight-built fellow with a trimmed black beard and piercing green eyes.

"Ethanos!" Queen Gabrielle said from her place at his father's side. "Those are *not* the clothes that I chose for you!" she admonished.

Ethan feigned dismay as he examined his attire. "My apologies, Mother, I didn't realize—"

"Don't lie to your mother, boy," Bronus growled. "You see what I must deal with, Lord Vegar." Bronus lifted his open palms in Ethan's direction. "Be thankful you only have daughters. They are compliant and eager to please. Sons, on the other hand must, always test you. Where are the pretty clothes your mother placed out for you, Ethan?"

"Where are the ones she set out for you, Father?" Ethan countered, pointing out that his father's attire was similar to his own, sans the weapons hanging off his back and hips.

"I am the king, boy. I will dress as I see fit!" Bronus snorted.

"As the future king, I choose what I will wear as well," Ethan declared.

"Mind your tongue, boy. I can still take you over my knee if need be!"

No, you actually can't. Ethan kept that thought to himself.

"Sire, I believe Prince Ethanos looks very handsome in his attire," Elenna said as she arose and came to Ethan's side.

Bronus regarded Ethan with narrow gray eyes. He came carefully to his feet, skirting the table to stop in front of his son. The hall grew quiet as a tomb, every eye fixed on the king and what he would do. Bronus unsheathed Ethan's long sword and tossed it upon the table, followed by his short sword, his axes, and all his knives, stripping him of his weapons. He then placed Elenna's hand in Ethan's and pushed them onto the open floor.

"The first dance of the night shall be the beautiful Lady Elenna and my mule-headed firstborn, Prince Ethanos!" Bronus declared loudly for all to hear.

Ethan escorted Elenna to the center floor, guiding her as they danced to the melody. She gazed up at him with smiling green eyes. She wore a golden gown with a tight-fitting bodice and puffed sleeves. She stood a full head shorter than him, and her flaming red hair was swept in an updo style.

"It appears you have been disarmed, my prince. Did you think me so dangerous?" She smiled.

"Oh, you're dangerous, Elenna, but not in that way. I just wore all those weapons to annoy my mother for selecting such dandy attire."

"Was the attire similar to what your brother is wearing?" She regarded Tristan with a nod, where he sat amid his family at the king's table.

"Yes."

"I think you would look quite attractive in such raiment," she teased.

"I doubt it. So tell me, Elenna, how do you feel about marriage to a complete stranger?"

"Well." She smiled slowly. "At first I was fearful that I would wed a portly, balding, or aging lord or monarch. When my father revealed that I was to wed the crown prince of Astaria, I was pleasantly elated. Your reputation precedes you, Ethanos."

"So I've been told," he sighed, not believing it.

"What of you, my prince? How did you receive the news of our betrothal? Before I insulted you, of course, during our unfortunate meeting this morning?"

He gave her a look. "Elenna, the first I knew of our betrothal was when you told me of it."

A horrified look transfixed her face. She thought he had known before and was playing her for sport when they had exchanged such heated banter. "I…I thought you knew all along. That is why you thought so poorly of me when we first met. I am sorry, Ethan."

"Don't be sorry, Elenna. If you had your wish, I would have had my lashes then be free to live my life as I wished thereafter. Now my path has been chosen, and I am bound to obey."

"And I am that path," she said sadly. "I am sorry that I displease you so." She frowned.

"It's not you, Elenna, it's me. I…I don't…" Ethan struggled to put his thoughts to words as it felt all scrambled in his mind. "I don't belong here."

"What do you mean?" she asked, looking up into his piercing blue eyes as they moved across the floor.

"I…I don't belong here."

"You mean the palace?"

"Not just the palace but everywhere. I can't explain it, but I know in my heart that our world is not my home."

She thought that was the strangest thing she had ever heard. "You don't want to be king?"

"No."

"Why? What would you do otherwise?"

"I would be free. I would live."

"Free? Live? Whatever do you mean?"

"To go where I wish and do as I wish. To kneel to no man and have no man beholden to me, that would be true freedom."

"Could you not find happiness with me?" she asked tearfully, her moist eyes barely able to match his stare.

"Give me time, Elenna. I don't love you right now, but maybe we can grow on each other. What my parents did is still too fresh in my mind. If you can be patient with me, then I—"

She kissed him, fierce and desperate. "I can be patient. For you, Ethanos, I can be *very* patient."

They danced for a time. When they finished, others took the floor, and Ethan planned to take a seat, but Queen Gabrielle intervened and forced him to join her for another dance.

"Won't Father be jealous? He will want the first dance with his queen," Ethan said, trying in vain to make his exit from the dance floor.

"Your father hates dancing as much as you." She gave him a look. "Besides, I enjoy dancing with the most handsome man in the seven kingdoms."

"Every mother thinks their son is the most handsome," Ethan reminded her.

"You *are* handsome, Ethanos, though you dress like an ogre."

"If you hate how I dress now, wait until I'm king."

"That is why you need a strong queen, to keep you in line." She touched a finger to his nose as she smiled into his sea-blue eyes.

"Is that why Father arranged this marriage, to keep me in line?"

"No. Your father did not arrange this. I did."

Ethan sighed, biting his anger and his tongue, lest he say something he would later regret.

"One day you will have children of your own, my son. You will be forced to choose what is best for them, even if they hate you for it. I hope on that day you will then understand and forgive me." She sighed tiredly.

"Best for me? How is forcing this on me for my benefit?" His words came harsher than he intended.

A haunted look passed his mother's green eyes. It was a familiar gaze that he found disquieting, a look that meant she had a vision.

"What have you foreseen?" he asked.

She stared into his eyes for a time, the pounding of her heart deafening the sounds around them. "You *must* wed Elenna. Avow it, Ethanos!" She gripped his hands desperately as they danced.

"Why? Just tell me why she is so important?"

"I cannot tell you here. Come to my chamber later this night. Then I shall tell you my vision. Just know that what I saw will be avoided if you wed Elenna and ascend the throne of Astaria, as is your birthright."

*****

The wide spacious corridors were alit with mage lanterns, which Ethan could not see for he was immune to their magical properties. He needed them not. Even if he did, his path was well lit with the nearly full moon shining through the tall glass windows that lined the corridors of the queen's tower. Guards in black armor, with silver crescent moons and stars emblazoned upon their chests, stood post at the entrance of their queen's private sanctum. They summoned the queen's handmaid, who greeted Ethanos with a curtsy before ushering him into his mother's presence.

Queen Gabrielle sat before her vanity, combing the folds of her deep auburn hair. She gazed into her mirror, catching sight of the first strands of silver to claim dominion upon her crown. Whether it was worry or age that brought about the dreaded transition, she could not stay the hand of time. She foreswore self-pity for her life was richly blessed. She was the only child and heir of Lord Dragos Mortune, master seer and archmage of incredible power. She was the wife and queen of Bronus Blagen, king of Astaria and the first lightning lord born in over five centuries. Theirs was an unusual marriage among the royal houses of Greater Elaria, for they truly loved one another. Where the kings of Gorgencia, Sarcosa, and Meltoria proudly boasted their baseborn progenies for all to witness their virility, Bronus held only to his wife's bed, honoring his queen with his fidelity. Many whispered that she had bewitched the king with an enchantment, while others claimed the king willfully pledged his devotion due to her astounding beauty. Either way, she and Bronus were joined by the unbreakable bonds of true love and devotion.

Gabrielle was further blessed by the children born of their union. Ethanos was the perfect blend of his father's masculine power and his mother's empathy for others. Though he was slighter of build than his burly sire, Ethanos was nearly as tall and broad of shoulder, with the comeliest face she had ever seen. When they first discovered his immunity to magic, they feared it was a detriment to his ability to one day rule, but his power to self-heal and his incredible strength nearly made him invincible against any single foe. No mage, no matter their power or craft, could stand against the Astarian crown prince. Despite all his gifts, however, the boy wanted nothing more than to roam free in the wilderness like a wayward spirit. He despised the formality of court and proper attire. He was the only man in all of Astaria to incur Bronus's wrath with painful regularity. The boy's stubbornness was a gift from his father, no doubt. They were too much alike, she surmised.

Her second son possessed her husband's gray eyes, but his slighter build and thoughtful manner were eerily similar to her father, Lord Dragos. Tristan Blagen was the son who always obeyed his parents and adhered to the protocols and decorum expected of royal progenies. He was the only member of the royal household able to counsel his brother to obey their parents. Gabrielle was ever grateful that Tristan truly loved his brother and fully supported Ethan's eventual ascension to the throne. His love of books and practicing his mage craft equaled Ethanos's adventurous pursuits. A further blessing for Gabrielle was her children's mage abilities. Whereas most noble children were born with a single mage gift, and often a weak one at that, all her children, save for Ethanos, inherited multiple gifts from the potency of their parents' union. Tristan's mind was permanently shielded from any mage manipulation. Despite Gabrielle's and Dragos's wondrous abilities as master seers, neither could read any thought that came to Tristan's mind. Unfortunately, Tristan could not receive their projected thoughts telepathically either, as they were able to do with his sisters. The ability to speak mind to mind over great distances was a most helpful skill, which Tristan was helplessly immune. Tristan was a gifted fire caster, able to cast fire from his outstretched hands over tremendous distances. He was also a binder, able to touch a finger to a subject's forehead, binding their will to his command. Only the strongest of mages could resist such power.

Ceresta was her third child, but the first of her three daughters. Ceresta shared her mother's lush brown hair and high feminine cheekbones but possessed her father's fiery temper. She was her father's favorite, and he valued her counsel over any other save for his queen. Ceresta inherited the power of foresight and clairvoyance from her mother's house coupled with wondrous mental shields. She could cast fire like her brother and enchantments like her mother, temporarily bending men to her will.

Arian inherited the fiery red hair of her late maternal grandmother and the sparkling emerald eyes of her mother. Like her elder sister and mother, she was an enchantress. She could cast light as dim as a candle to illuminations that alit a moonless midnight sky. Like her mother and grandfather, Arian was an archmage healer, able to mend damaged flesh, remove disease and regenerate severed limbs or impaired organs by mere touch.

Felicia Blagen was the youngest of Gabrielle's children, inheriting the golden locks of her late paternal grandmother. She possessed her father's mage shielding, which provided limited protection from harmful mage powers. She could project ice and sound with equal potency.

Despite the richness of her life and the joy of her family, Gabrielle was plagued by prophetic visions, the current of which centered on her eldest son. Being immune to magic, Ethan was always depicted in her visions as a dark void akin to an ink spot upon a detailed picture. Her visions of late were different in that Ethan's countenance could be clearly discerned. Each vision was recurrent, a repeated telling of events that had yet to come to pass. The fact that she could clearly see him proved that his immunity to magic would be stripped away, allowing her to see him in her mage-gifted vision. Though she could clearly discern his face, to her horror, she envisioned her son suffering unbearable torment, the details of which she dare not contemplate. The visions were prophetic in nature and foretold a terrible warning of what would come to pass if Ethanos failed to heed their warning.

"Mother," Ethan's easy voice called as he stepped within.

She turned, setting her brush aside as she beckoned him forth. He came to her side, taking a knee to meet her eye to eye. Gabrielle ran her fingers over his cheeks before kissing his forehead. He felt ill at ease with her unusually strong fixation. He and his mother often shared close bonds of affection, but this was something far more than a mother's doting. He sensed great fear in her moist green eyes.

"Are you all right?" he asked.

"I am sorry, Ethanos, for forcing this marriage upon you without your consent or counsel," she said, keeping her hands upon his cheeks. When he began to speak, she placed a finger to his lips, silencing him as she continued. "You must, however, trust me in this. You *must* wed Lady Elenna."

"Why?" he asked quietly, trying to suppress the anger that consumed him over the whole affair. "You spoke of a prophetic vision concerning me. I'm here at your behest, Mother. Just tell me what you saw."

Gabrielle took a measured breath, searching his beautiful blue eyes, haunted by what she should reveal but wouldn't. She would not reveal the details of his broken body or spirit that her visions revealed so painfully clear. "Your immunity to magic will be impaired. How this shall come to pass, I know not, only that it shall. That is how I can see you in my vision."

Ethan did not relish the thought of being subject to mage power, but there was more to his mother's concern than that.

"There is more," she said as if reading his thoughts. "You suffer *terrible* unending torment. You will cry out for death to take you, but…it shall not answer." She was crying now, unable to dam the tears flowing rivers upon her cheeks.

If death could not take him, then his ability to self-heal must prevent his injuries from killing him. "How does my wedding Elenna prevent this?"

"The vision is clear on what you must do. If you enter the Mage Bane, then the prophecy will be fulfilled. But if you wed before you enter therein, then the prophecy is thwarted, even if you enter the Mage Bane thereafter."

"That doesn't make any sense." Ethan made a face. "What does my marriage have anything to do with the Mage Bane or your vision of my suffering yet unable to die? If I can't die it is because of my ability to heal, which would not work in the Mage Bane. The three of them have no correlation."

"Your suffering does not take place in the Mage Bane, Ethanos. My visions cannot penetrate that mage-less land as no magic can."

The Mage Bane rested along the southern shores of the Aqualania Sea. It was an untamed, hostile land populated by pirates, mercenaries, and barbaric peoples who sheltered within its boundaries. A handful of kingdoms occupied several of its prominent regions, carving their mage-less realms out of those untamed lands. For unknown reason, no magic would work there, as if a vast invisible curtain were drawn across its boundaries, preventing magic from entering. Strangely, Ethan himself was a small version of the Mage Bane as no magic could touch him, except his own regenerative power and strength. Ethan's uncanny ability to learn skills at a rapid pace or a new language in mere hours was thought to be a mage gift unique to him and would likely be impaired as well in such a land. Perhaps entering the Mage Bane might permanently strip away his immunity to magic once he returned to the seven kingdoms.

"How does my marriage prevent this?" he asked, believing the adherence to such visions as foolish.

"I know not," she sighed tiredly. "I only know that it does. If you wed Elenna, then this vision shall not come to pass."

Ethan slowly gained his feet and stepped toward the window. There he paused, staring up at the nearly full moon illuminating the celestial realm. He stared for a time, collecting his thoughts as he reflected on what she had revealed. "Mother, I've lived my entire life free of magic, following my own course whenever the duties of my post allowed. I do not believe in prophecy or the infallibility of magic. Despite the crown, I shall one day wear or the restrictions placed upon me by the role you and Father intend for me, I am still my own master, at least in here." He tapped his head. "I will wed Elenna as you ask. I will vow to you that I shall *not* enter the Mage Bane," he assured her before turning from the window and fixing his blue eyes to her. "Remember, Mother, that prophecies often come to pass despite actions taken to avoid them."

*****

He was up before dawn, donning light armor of boiled leather and thick black trousers with soft-soled boots. Ethan set out for the palace green in the courtyard of the outer citadel, where a cohort of king's knights and guards trained in the tourney field. Several were in full regalia, pushing their warhorses into full gallop as they bore down upon their comrades before the king's box, which overlooked the field. Other knights practiced afoot with long swords, maces, and double-bladed axes. Some sparred in light chain mail with their heads bare, while others were clad head to boot in full black armor as their sergeants barked instructions.

Ethan skirted the edge of the tourney green as the knights took notice of their crown prince. They quickly stopped what they were doing and took a knee.

"Stand up, I'm here to train, the same as you!" Ethan commanded, hating seeing grown men kneeling to anyone, especially to him. He took his place outside a fighting square to await his turn when the knights within stepped aside for him.

"Your Grace," Commander Durisk waved an open mailed fist toward the center of the square.

"Call me Ethan, just Ethan, Sir Durisk. And I'll wait my turn like everyone else."

"And you will explain to your Father on my behalf when I address the crown prince so informally, Your Grace?" Commander Durisk grinned.

Ethan always trained with the men and always asked to be called by the abridged version of his given name. Unlike the mage-born lords of Astaria, Ethan preferred to train with knights, nobles, and common soldiers with equal measure, valuing the skill and bravery of each. The men loved Ethan for he rewarded them based on merit than high birth. When he asked for volunteers to resign their posts with the king's guard to help him raise and train a force of light cavalry, a hundred knights and two thousand base infantrymen eagerly stepped forth. King Bronus was aghast, allowing only two knights and ten soldiers to do so. Ethan took those twelve men and recruited fifteen hundred more from across Astaria to form a lightly armed but swift-moving cavalry force. Ethan recruited men who were natural riders or archers, whether they were soldiers, craftsmen, commoners, or peasants. He scoured the holds of foreign ships visiting Astarian ports for galley slaves who were chained in their holds. He sought out galley slaves who were former soldiers, purchasing their freedom in exchange for five years of service with pay in his new cavalry force. Ethan outfitted his men with lightweight mail, composite bows, and small yet swift horses. They drilled night and day for two years before he tested their metal against King Bronus's heavy horse in mock engagements. Ethan commanded his light cavalry while Lord General Brax commanded the heavy horse. Ethan's asymmetrical warfare of hit and run tactics while denying his adversary his preferred direct engagement was devastatingly effective. What began as the king humoring the desires of a fifteen-year-old prince resulted in the creation of a new yet devastating cavalry force that the kingdoms of Elaria were unprepared to face. Lord General Brax, the king's highest soldier of rank and most trusted advisor, lauded Ethanos's achievement, and acknowledged his defeat in three different mock engagements. King Bronus snorted derisively, dismissive of the test and refusing to properly place them with the main army, removing them to Plexus as if they were an afterthought.

"I'll speak on your behalf, Sir Durisk," Ethan affirmed.

"So be it, Ethan," Commander Durisk said.

Ethan waited his turn before stepping forth to challenge Sir Vortez. As soon as he stepped within the square, Lady Viola Luciel, mage healer and niece of Lord Luciel, drew nigh. A mage healer was always present during training drills of king's knights so as to prevent any unnecessary death and allow the men to train to their upmost without concern to safety. Though Ethan could self-heal, his opponents were dependent upon mage healers to repair the damage wrought by the Astarian crown prince.

Ethan struck fast, catching Sir Vortez unprepared, striking emphatically before spinning around his more heavily armed foe. Ethan swept around Sir Vortez, his swing cutting into the knight's left calf with enough force to pierce the armor, slicing the knee nearly in half. Sir Vortez crumpled to the grass in pain as Lady Viola hurried forth. She lifted the thin folds of her white gown as she knelt beside the stricken knight. Closing her eyes, she pressed her glowing palms upon the savage wound, calling upon her power to mend the sundered flesh. Sir Vortez was enraptured as her soothing touch permeated his body. Within moments the wound was healed, and Lady Viola gained her feet, slightly short of breath but no worse for the wear. Healing wounds was very taxing upon young mage healers, limiting the effectiveness in healing multiple patients without rest between healings. A mature mage healer such as Lady Viola, however, could heal a dozen severe wounds without respite. The violent training on the palace green prepared both the men and the mage healers for battle by replicating the nature of warfare in realistic detail. Because there were a limited number of mage healers born in every kingdom, usually numbering between ten and thirty per realm, larger numbers of physicians were extensively trained in human anatomy and treatment. Often these trained physicians focused their efforts in keeping their patients alive long enough to be treated by a mage healer.

"Training with you is always a painful experience, Prince Ethanos," Sir Vortez said as Ethan offered him his hand, pulling him to his feet.

"You're too good to give a chance to, Sir Vortez. Last time you took my right foot, remember." Ethan grinned.

"And before that, you took both of my hands." Vortez smiled in kind.

"Only after losing my left arm at the shoulder."

"Enough, gentlemen, shall we continue?" Commander Durisk interjected. "I believe Ethan is ready for two at a time."

Ethan nodded in kind, holding his sword at the ready while taking a fighting stance. Sir Morlis and Sir Kracklaw came upon him from opposing flanks. Ethan stepped away, quickly skirting Sir Morlis, fixing his opponents in one direction by stacking them. Their swords clashed in a dizzying array as sparks burst from their clanging steel. Within moments both knights were felled as Lady Viola hurried forth to treat them.

And so it went throughout the morn as Ethan battled every man in the cohort, drawing an ever-larger audience as the day progressed. He sparred with two, three, four, and five opponents at a time. He lost two fingers on his left hand and four on his right before they regenerated instantly as he continued on. As soon as the second cohort to train caught wind that the crown prince was sparring with their comrades, they quickly rushed onto the tourney field. All the knights in the realm took pride in sparring with Ethanos, judging their skill with how they fared against the finest sword in Astaria. Ethan was adept at learning new skills, mastering swordsmanship at five years of age, and beating fully trained knights at the age of twelve. His swordsmanship increased exponentially ever since, his movements swift, fluid, and economical in motion.

*****

Ceresta and Arian accompanied Lady Elenna along the lower battlements that overlooked the tourney field, as the late morning sun reflected off the azure stone walkways ahead. They spent the early morn dining with the king and queen as the matriarch of House Blagen discussed the details of Elenna's upcoming nuptials. The ceremony was planned in a fortnight. There would be a dozen formal balls preceding the event, culminating in the grand ball, where Elenna would preside as the crown princess of Astaria. She felt giddy, elated with the beauty and grandeur of her future kingdom. Born the niece of the king of Estasa, she never dreamed of being a queen one day. If she had, the pragmatist within surmised that her king would be old or poor of countenance or both. Fortuitously, Ethan was neither. He possessed all the qualities of a fine husband; he only required a strong wife to tame his wild nature and refine his poor etiquette.

"It shall be joyous having you as our sister, Elenna," Arian sang sweetly, hooking her arm with Elenna's.

"Thank you, Princess Arian, you are most kind," Elenna gifted her a practiced smile.

"Do call me by name, Elenna. We shall be family soon enough," Arian said.

"That sounds delightful, Arian." She smiled more genuinely. "Of course I could never use such informality with the king or queen. It would feel improper to do so."

"Mother and Father would ask you to address them as such in private, for they shall be your parents for all intents, just as your father and mother shall be Ethan's," Ceresta said matter-of-factly.

"The king did not appear so informal upon our return yesterday. He seemed quite rigid in dealing with Prince Ethanos," Elenna observed.

"You shall find, Elenna, that when our brother is involved, Father's temperament becomes exponentially volatile. We must apologize for Ethan's rudeness yesterday. To you shall fall the unenviable task of taming Ethanos. We have all tried to do so, to no avail," Ceresta lamented tiredly.

"To his credit, Prince Ethanos is quite chivalrous when it comes to rescuing helpless maidens," Elenna reflected on his timely intervention when she was set upon by wolves.

"Yes, strangely for one who does not espouse the knightly vows of defending the helpless and guarding the honor of maidens, he spends an inordinate amount of time still doing so." Ceresta shook her head.

"Prince Ethanos does not hold to defending the helpless or guarding the honor of maidens?" Elenna asked.

"Oh, he does believe in their merits, he only questions the necessity of knightly vows to do so. He believes men should hold to such beliefs without vain promises to do so to their sovereign," Ceresta explained.

"Perhaps he is correct to believe so. In Estasa, our knights pledge no such vows, they merely espouse their loyalty to their lords and king, and truly there can be no greater vows than those," Elenna said.

"Ethan would disagree. He holds vows to serve nobility as an archaic form of governance." Ceresta sighed.

"Yes, I do recall him questioning the right of the mage born to rule. It will fall to me to instruct him otherwise," Elenna answered with a firm voice that failed to match the doubt in her heart. Ethan was stubborn in his convictions, but at least he was not cruel like most princes. In fact, he treated her kindly once their misunderstanding had passed. Yes, she could work with kindness and, given time, tame his willful spirit.

The clanging of steel and shouting of men drew their attention to the tourney fields below. Elenna stepped toward the rampart, gazing with disbelief at the spectacle. The normative order and discipline of the royal practice yard degenerated into a chaotic melee. Knights in black mail and armor swarmed the palace green, converging on a single foe. From this height, it was akin to a nest of hornets swarming an intruder. The king's knights converged on their single adversary, who seemed to avoid their blows with surprising swiftness. The fellow was lightly clad in black leather and spun amid their serried ranks like a dervish. She stared with a slackened jaw as the man passed among his foes, his sword taking whatever flesh they offered him. Knights in heavy mail toppled with shattered knees and ankles. Men in full armor fared little better as their cumbersome shells limited their mobility as the fellow struck at their wrists, knocking swords form hands. The man wore no helm, his short black hair visible from her vantage. He lowered his shoulder, smashing into a wall of shields, knocking a fully armored knight to the ground as he rolled over top of him, before springing to his feet. Elenna's eyes drew wide as they beheld the man's countenance as he gained his feet. "Ethan?" she whispered.

It was Ethan who passed swiftly among his father's knights, striking them down in methodical order, one foe here, two there, a sword here, a limb there. She saw him take a vicious blow to his left arm, severing it above the wrist. He ignored the wound as he spun past the man who delivered the blow, striking the man beside that fellow at the ankle. Ethan's left hand regrew as the man he struck toppled over under the weight of his armor.

"I understand not," Elenna said, unable to comprehend what was transpiring before her eyes.

"Fret not, Elenna. It's Ethan's way of training with the king's knights," Ceresta answered with disinterest.

"A contest?" Elenna was flabbergasted by the barbarity of it all, cringing as Ethan was stuck in the shoulder, nearing collapsing under the weight of the broadsword impacting his flesh. He winced in pain as he ducked, then twisted free before striking a hurried blow as he staggered away. He was soon set upon by a dozen sword tips leveled and circling him. They closed in unison, faster than Ethan could dodge their advent. They wasted little time completing their advance, their sword tips piercing his torso and limbs, trapping him in place as he grimaced in pain.

Elenna gasped as the swords pierced his flesh, her eyes closing before the awful visage.

"All is well, Elenna, look yonder," Arian assuaged, touching a hand to her shoulder.

Elenna stole a furtive glance, catching sight of Ethan rising from certain death. The melee seemed at its end as the knights and Ethan appeared to share in some sort of hearty banter. She released a heavy sigh. Was this to be her new life, wondering what foolishness her prince would partake every day? The princesses drew her away, conversing as if the events below were but a trivial occurrence. If Astaria were to ever go to war, Ethan's gifts would be certain to place him in the front of battle, while all the other mage lords were placed safely to the rear.

*****

Ethan made his way to his private chambers, his boiled leather mail battered and trousers torn to shreds, revealing more of his muscled legs than they covered. Each boot was cloven at the toe. Oddly, the only part of his anatomy that did not regenerate was his hair, which was shorn in parts where knights' swords took their measure. Luckily for Ethan, he kept his hair cut close to his skull, which made him further stand out from his contemporaries.

Ethan found a washbasin with fresh towels awaiting him in his chambers. He dismissed his personal attendants years ago, insisting he was capable of dressing and undressing himself. He hated having others wait upon him, believing men should see to their own personal needs. He stripped off his ragged clothing and washed himself with a moistened cloth, scrubbing the blood that was caked into his flesh. Ethan opened the chest that rested at the foot of his bed to remove a pair of loose-fitting cotton trousers and shirt. As he reached onto the open chest, his eye caught sight of the small stone, no wider than a thumbnail, sitting off to the side among his other boyhood treasures. At first glance, it was a simple nondescript gray rock with no distinguishing characteristic other than a smooth rounded surface. As his hand drew near, the stone emitted a dull greenish hue that intensified in brightness, the closer his flesh came to it. He took it in hand, holding it aloft as his eyes beheld the wonder of its brilliant illumination. In a world filled with magic that he mostly could not see, as he was immune to its benefits, Ethan reveled at the lone magic that he could conjure, for only he could cause the stone to glow. He told no one of its discovery, lest his father order it taken away to be studied. He knew once it was taken from him, he would never get it back, so he kept it secret. To everyone else, it was naught but a stone. In time Ethan discovered that if pressed near anyone else, it disrupted their mage ability. He would use it to play tricks on his sisters, impairing their powers at inopportune times. It would cause Ceresta to read false memories or thoughts or cause misdirection in Felicia's ice casting. He thought to try similar antics with his mother, father, or grandfather but wisely guessed they'd quickly find the source of their magical impairment. In time he grew bored with his magical stone and stored it in his chest with his other mementos. Whatever the stone was, it interfered with magic.

Ethan returned the stone to its resting place and donned his trousers, boots, and a plain pullover shirt, affixed his sword belt, and stepped without.

*****

Lady Elenna was attended by a half-dozen maids, each scurrying about her chamber to prepare her for the feast. Two combed her hair, styling and setting it in high folds while fixing a wreath of flowers upon her head. Others helped her ease into the cumbersome yet beautiful emerald gown with voluminous petticoats, tight corset, and long sleeves that shimmered in the dim light.

A knock upon her door drew every eye as she ordered a servant to answer.

"A guard, my lady," the girl said, craning her neck to her mistress as she blocked the door, awaiting her command.

"What does he want?"

"Prince Ethanos stands without. He asks if he might escort you to the feast."

"Of course," Elenna answered sweetly, though she was inwardly elated. This was an unexpected but welcome change in her betrothed. She stood, smoothing her gown and resetting her wreath ever slightly. Her maids withdrew a step and curtsied before she stepped without. She found Ethan waiting in the outer corridor, leaning against the opposing wall on his left shoulder with his arms crossed. He looked entirely too comfortable in his simple black trousers and shirt with his sword belt hanging low upon his left hip. The guards, standing post to either side of the door, stepped aside as she passed between them. Ethan smiled as she stepped forth, coming off his wall to take her proffered hand, bestowing a kiss upon it as he bowed.

"My lady."

Her eyes drew wide with his formality. *Is this the same Ethanos I have known these past days?*

"My prince," she replied, bobbing a curtsy, his politeness taking her aback.

"Shall we proceed to the great hall?" he offered her his arm.

"I would be delighted." She smiled, slipping her hand under his elbow as they walked. For any girl, it was a great transition forsaking the home of their birth for her lord husband. She was fortunate to wed into the royal house of Astaria, where queens are treated as equals to their kings. The Astarians valued fidelity in marriage and chivalry in the treatment of women. Elenna's native Estasa was protective of the fairer sex, but women were expected to be demure and gracious, sans opinion or argument. The kings of Sarcosa treated their women as little more than property to be veiled and silent with downcast eyes forlorn of spirit. The Gorgencian monarch boasted countless wives, concubines, and bed slaves to cater to his voracious appetite. Vellesia was ruled by queens, but little was known of that far-off realm. All in all, the plight of women in Elaria was problematic at best. Prince

Ethanos was irreverent, wild, and often immature, but he was not unkind, and in the end, that was enough.

"Are you finding Astaris to your liking, Elenna?" Ethan asked with genuine interest.

"The palace is beyond my imagining, my prince…I mean Ethan," she corrected herself.

He smiled at that. Perhaps he was wearing on her. Perhaps she might eventually join him in the practice yard, or the archery field? Perhaps he might talk her into a ride in the high country, or a hunting venture or a fishing trip along the Upper Torlin? Mayhap after they wed, they might spend the spring in a forest retreat far from the trappings of court. Ethan could build a cabin, and she might cook whatever game he caught. Perhaps they might set up permanent residence outside Astaris? He mused on the possibilities, thinking that he might grow fond of his future queen if they spent time together with no one else around. There were so many things he longed to share and wondered if she might join him.

"You seem in better spirits, Ethan. Has the unpleasant surprise of our nuptials given way to anticipation or resigned acceptance?"

"After we wed, would you like to live in the mountains?" He couldn't mask the excitement in his voice.

"The mountains?" she asked, finding his question rather odd.

"The mountains. We can be far from everyone, just you and me. We could hunt, fish, swim in a forest stream, watch the sunset behind the mountains while listening to wolves echoing their mournful songs," he expounded, further convincing himself what a wondrous idea it was.

Elenna thought it the oddest thing she had ever heard. Before she could form an answer, Ethan continued to rattle off his arguments in favor.

"We could raise our children outside the palace and visit only when the king required our presence," Ethan thought it a fair compromise. He could still partake his favored activities while siring the heirs his father demanded of him.

"You desire that we live in the wilderness?" she asked calmly, though her pounding heart belied the horror she felt of such a ridiculous possibility. If the decision were Ethan's, then she might as well concede to a life in the wild, but there was the one voice that could counter this idiocy without her having to object. "That sounds lovely, Ethan, but would your sire agree to such an arrangement?"

Ethan answered with silence, as he well knew that his father would never relent to such a notion. Elenna could easily sense his souring mood and liked it not. He was crestfallen, and it saddened her to see him so. If she were to ever enjoy a life with Ethan, she knew she had to at least try to make him happy.

"Perhaps if I asked your mother? And we needn't spend all our time away from court. Perhaps shorter visits to your mountain retreat would appease King Bronus?" she spoke soothingly.

"You would do this for me?" he asked, stopping midstride as he faced her with his pleading blue eyes that melted her heart.

"I shall ask, and there is no harm in that. All your parents can do is say no, and if it makes you happy, then it is worth the attempt. Besides, your parents like me." She smiled teasingly.

"Yes, they do." He rolled his eyes.

Elenna held no desire to live in the wilds, but if her future parents acquiesced to her request, she would hold greater leverage in her marriage. By ingratiating herself with the king and queen, she might obtain for her husband things which he might not receive without her intervention. Then she could expect Ethan to ingratiate himself to her. She smiled devilishly at the possibilities, thinking of all the things she might have him do for her. A more formal wardrobe would be the first concession she would extract from him.

"Prince Ethanos!" A royal guard spoke, closing swiftly upon them from the opposite direction. The guard stopped several paces before them and began to kneel when Ethan ordered him to remain afoot.

"Stand and report."

"My prince, the king requests your presence in the throne room as well as Lady Elenna."

"For what purpose?" Ethan asked.

"I know not, but the king insists it is most urgent."

*****

The throne room felt as cold as a tomb as Ethan and Elenna stepped within. They found King Bronus upon his throne, his icy countenance indicating the grim nature of the news he was about to share. Elenna's father, Lord Vegar Torhess, stood at the base of the dais, his face mirroring Bronus's sour disposition. As soon as they entered therein, Bronus commanded them hither. Ethan and Elenna stopped short of the throne and knelt before given leave to rise.

"Ethanos, you shall release Lady Elenna to her father and return to your chambers until morning!" Bronus commanded.

"Why?" Ethan made a face akin to tasting sour milk.

"Your betrothal is at an end. Lady Elenna and Lord Vegar shall be leaving Astaris tonight by order of King Ectus."

"What?" Ethan asked as Elenna stood frozen in place, too numb to speak.

"Are you deaf, boy? I said your betrothal is at an end by order of King Ectus. Remove yourself to your chambers and remain there until morning!" Bronus growled impatiently.

"Why, Father? Not a day ago, you forced this betrothal upon me without my consent or counsel, and now it's over. Why? At least tell me why?"

"You only have to obey, Ethanos. I need not give explanation. That's the benefit of being king, my son, I order and others obey."

"Spare me the platitudes of your regal authority, Father. Just tell me why."

Bronus stood from his throne, descending the dais, his heavy boots slapping the stone steps like thunderclaps. Elenna and her father backed a step, wary of the murderous look in the king's eyes, gray eyes that stared into Ethan's blue. Not many men stood over Ethan besides Krixan, but Bronus bested his son by several inches with heavy girth. The mere sight of the Astarian monarch instilled fear in the bravest of men, yet Ethan stood statue-still, awaiting the strike that was sure to come. Ethan refused to flinch, knowing full well how his father despised cowardliness.

"Elenna's maternal grandfather, King Emar Ectus agreed to betroth her to a Vellesian lord's eldest son, Mors Valnar, monarch of Vecaba, when she was born. Her grandfather since passed without sharing the knowledge of this betrothal with his son, the current king, Evor Ectus, nor his since deceased daughter or her lord husband, Vegar Torhess. When word reached Lord Valnar of the new betrothal, he immediately sent word to King Ectus and Astaris, demanding adherence to his prior claim to Elenna's hand," Bronus explained in a deadly calm voice.

The whole thing made little sense. Why did Lord Valnar wait so long to place his claim? He knew nothing of this Vellesian lord. Though he was glad to be free of this betrothal, it seemed to Ethan as if someone did not wish Estasa and Astaria joined in alliance.

"Elenna, I'm sorry," Ethan sighed before turning to leave.

She stood there, accepting her fate with all the courage she could muster, a sole tear squeezing from each eye. "Ethan."

"Yes," he turned back to face her.

"Whenever you begrudge your fate, lamenting the choices made in your name that you hold no say in, remember me this day. Give thanks that when you do wed that you shall retain the home of your youth and the companionship of your family, a family that loves you and a home of such beauty." Her voice betrayed her breaking heart.

Ethan looked upon her with pity, cognizant of the unknown awaiting her in Vecaba. He stepped near so as to speak to her ear only. "If your lord husband should treat you poorly, let me know and I'll kill him," Ethan's voice was but a deathly whisper. In that moment, they were closer than they had ever been to that point, yet it only made their parting that much harder for her to bear.

And then he was gone, his shadow passing from the throne room and out of her life.

*****

They watched from the shadows of the palace as the Astarian prince crossed the courtyard of the inner keep, their distinctive purple eyes hidden with their cowls. She smiled victoriously with the breaking of the Astarian-Estasan Alliance, though her sister seemed more reserved. Their mistress placed them in the Astarian court years ago to oversee her interests. Her first priority was always that the Astarian crown prince bears no heirs for House Blagen. The interests of her liege were intact for now. With that, they withdrew to the shadows, ever mindful that the Astarian crown prince could see through their disguise.

CHAPTER 3

He sat in the sill of his window, the pale moonlight bathing his indifference as he numbly stared at the starlit sky. He should celebrate his broken betrothal but strangely felt nothing. How could he rejoice in his apparent deliverance when all he could see was Elenna, her broken spirit playing so clearly across her face. What sort of life awaited her in Vellesia? Thinking of her plight shamed him for his own self-pity. He leaned his head back against the casing wall of the sill with his left foot resting on the opposing wall and his right foot dangling inside his chamber.

"Ethan?" a soft voice called out from the doorway. His eyes followed his little sister cross the floor. She pushed his foot off the sill, smoothing the skirt of her dress as she sat.

"I thought you would be happy." Felicia smiled. "I know you didn't like her."

"You could say that?" he said tiredly.

"Then why are you not pleased?"

"I don't take pleasure in others misery, even if they are spoiled highborn ladies. Besides, I'm sure our parents will find a similar replacement to chain me to."

"Perhaps you might like a distraction to occupy yourself in the meantime?"

"Distraction? What distraction will meet our parents' approval, baby sister?"

"One that our grandfather requires your assistance with."

"Dragos? I know he had something to discuss with me. What is it?"

"We ride for Plexus come sunrise," she said as she slipped off the sill to make her exit.

Plexus was the ancestral home of their grandfather Dragos Mortune's house, resting in the gap of Atar along the Por-Shada Plateau, some days ride west of Astaris.

"All the way to Plexus? What has he discovered?" Ethan asked curiously.

"He believes he has found a portal but requires your unique ability to facilitate it." Before she uttered her last word, Ethan came off the sill and started packing.

*****

They rode out at sunrise, Ethan, Felicia, Krixan, a score of royal guards, and Marco Valanus, a captain in the light cavalry especially trained by Ethan. Despite the unit's success in mock engagements against his father's heavy horse, his father dismissed the result out of hand and threatened to disband them altogether. Lord Dragos intervened on his grandson's behalf and agreed to maintain and quarter the new royal light cavalry at his seat in Plexus. As a captain in said cavalry unit, Marco Valanus often traveled between Plexus and Astaris on matters pertinent to the crown and House Mortune. The son of a horse groomer, Marco overcame his low birth by demonstrating his mastery of horsemanship, which did not go unnoticed by the Astarian crown prince who recruited him into his new service. Marco's stature and build were nondescript. He was plain of face with simple brown eyes that bespoke little of note. Yet he was steadfast, humble, and ever grateful for the opportunity granted him by Ethan.

They rode through the morn, crossing over the eastern feeders of the Upper Torlin. Bridges of stone or wood spanned the larger streams, while lesser creeks were easily forded. Forests of oak and maple gave way to the sparse Por-Shada Plateau. Ethan rode off with Marco to scout ahead once their line of sight expanded. Marco couldn't fail to note Ethan's better spirits the further they drew away from Astaris.

"How fares the men?" Ethan asked.

"We train every day, Your Grace. They are most diligent in improving their skills," Marco politely affirmed.

"They deserve better than banishment to Plexus. They only suffer because of the king's anger with me. And, Marco, just call me Ethan when no one else is near."

"That would be improper, my prince, but if you would have it so I shall acquiesce. As for the men, each is grateful for the opportunity to serve the Astarian throne. Most of us are of low birth and never dreamed to ride a horse, let alone own one. We owe that to you…Ethan."

Ethan had gifted each man who served in the light cavalry his own horse for five years of service. For twenty years, they were gifted with plots of land. Their pay nearly equaled the royal cavalry, a fact bemoaned by the latter but warmly received by the former. Unknown to the rank and file, Ethan arranged for their generous compensation from his own coffers, wealth that was gifted him since birth. He felt the realm would have need of his light cavalry and knew the king would never approve such expenditure from the royal treasury. Ethan assumed he could finance his beloved cavalry with his own wealth until he ascended the throne. Then he could fully incorporate them into the Astarian army. It never escaped Ethan's notice that his father often encouraged his siblings' various endeavors but always doubted his own. His mother always acted the peace broker between them. They were too much alike, she claimed, and Bronus felt the boy required a firm hand if he were to be king one day. To Gabrielle's relief, Ethan never took his father's harsh rebukes to heart. Though Bronus often berated his son, he was secretly proud how the boy persevered to test him time and again. His son had courage that even the bravest would envy, and cowards had no place upon a throne.

"I'm sorry my father doesn't see your worth, Marco. He is a stubborn man when it comes to Astarian military tradition. That's why he can't see the advantage a fast-moving, quick, striking cavalry can have on a battlefield. But war will come to our land sooner than most believe, and when it does, you and your comrades will demonstrate your worth."

"I hope to prove your faith well placed, Ethan."

"You don't have to prove anything to me, Marco. When the time comes, you'll perform as you have trained. All I have given you is an opportunity, Marco. What you do with it decides your greatness or mediocrity. But knowing your character, I am pretty sure which way you'll lean." Ethan smiled.

*****

Three days hence

The gap of Atar separated the southernmost mountains of the Por-Shada range from the foothills that meandered south and east. Between these prominent geological rises rested the gap of Atar, a flat arable land dotted with the vassal estates of House Mortune. Resting upon the steppes of the Por-Shada Plateau on the northern edge of the gap of Atar was Plexus, a massive fortification of gray stone. Citadels of silver, azure, and ebony spiraled above the outermost battlements, overlooking the lands below like an eagle perched upon the utmost peak. The castle's outer walls were the height of ten men before meeting the massive white bulwarks above. Like all the great palaces of Elaria, the castle was spell forged, with magic used in every stage of its construct.

They were met upon the eastern approaches of Plexus by a score of knights and men-at-arms of House Mortune, with the stars and crescent moons of that ancient house emblazoned upon their shields and capes.

"Prince Ethanos, Princess Felicia, your grandsire Lord Dragos welcomes you to your mother's ancestral home," Sir Vorkis greeted them, his helm raised revealing the weathered face and graying beard that betrayed his years of service to Lord Dragos.

"Greetings, Sir Vorkis. You are to lead us to the ruins where Grandfather awaits us, I presume?" Felicia gifted a mischievous smile. Her grandfather had already spoken to her, reaching out to her mind long before, telling her where they were to proceed. She hadn't told Ethan, who expected to meet Dragos at the palace. Dragos, as a master seer and telepath, was unable to speak to Ethan's or Tristan's minds, but Felicia had no such impairment.

Ethan gave her a look that wondered why she hadn't said this before. She thought it prudent to remind Ethan of the benefits of magic from time to time.

"Very well, Highness, we are honored to escort you," Sir Vorkis said, turning his gray destrier to lead the way.

*****

The ruins of ancient Charron rested in the shadow of the palace, surrounded by encircling pines that threatened to overcome the ancient holdfast of the long-extinct House Charron. Only a few foundations remained of what once was a thriving palatial city. The site was littered with broken stone and toppled columns. Several small hills circled the area, each sparsely covered in pines, maple, and chestnuts. Broken boulders were strewn about the grassy field, the skeletal remains of a long-dead civilization.

Their party passed to the far side of the ruins, stopping short of the westernmost hill. There upon its near slope was the mouth of a massive cave, wide enough for two wagons to enter therein abreast. The richness of the soil to either side of the entrance was evidence to its recent discovery. A dozen men-at-arms stood watch over the site, standing post like stone sentinels.

As Ethan drew nigh, he was greeted by a familiar face making its way down the hill. Dragos Mortune stood just shy of Ethan's height, his long silvery hair disheveled, jutting out in every direction as if he were struck by lightning, as it was prone to do whenever Dragos used his wondrous mental powers. He was dressed in the long azure robes of his mage caste, with silver crescent moons and stars sewn into their folds.

"Ethan, my boy, you have come!" Dragos grinned excitedly as Ethan dismounted.

Ethan barely had time to plant his feet before his grandfather dragged him up the hill, forgoing the embraces and salutations his grandsire was prone to grant. He had never seen Dragos so animated. Dragos spoke quickly, his words crowding together with such rapidity that Ethan could ill discern their content.

"A sudden tremor days ago shook the hillside, shaking loose the soil obstructing the entrance of the cavern. Simply extraordinary, Ethan. Extraordinary. The cavern stretches into the bowels of the hillside," Dragos explained, leading the way as Ethan, Felicia, and Krixan followed, struggling to keep pace with the elder patriarch. Ethan was dumbstruck by Dragos's behavior as he all but ignored Felicia, whom he always doted upon over his grandsons. Dragos was entirely focused on Ethan, as his eldest grandson was the only person in the known world who possessed the ability to see things obscured by anti-magic. Dragos continued to ramble on, with Ethan struggling to follow what he was saying except when he bandied about keywords like *boundary* and *portal*. Passing under the mouth of the cave, Ethan noted that only a portion of the entrance was uncovered by the ground shake, the rest had been excavated in recent days, opening the cavern to its fullest. Mage-lit lanterns lined either wall, their ambient light illuminating the cavern, stretching endlessly into the bowels of the hillside. Of course, the mage-crafted light was invisible to Ethan, as all he saw when he stared at them was their basic framework. Dragos, knowing of Ethan's impairment, ordered two men-at-arms to precede them, bearing standard torches. Little did anyone know that Ethan had no need of them as he could see in the dark as if it were day. It was a secret he kept to himself through the years and felt no reason to share such information. The less anyone knew about his abilities, the better off he would be, or so he reasoned.

After a brief walk, the cavern widened significantly, its jagged walls smoothing as they formed a circular chamber some ten meters abreast. Along the right half of the chamber as they entered, Ethan noted an anomaly along the wall's surface. Stepping closer he could see a large patch of the wall's surface, nearly five meters abreast and three meters high, ripple like the surface of an ink-black sea.

"What do you see, Ethan?" Dragos asked excitedly, hoping his grandson could tell him what was on the other side. As a master seer, Dragos could draw visions from his mage orbs, revealing images of what was, is, and will be. His visions were clear and precise, allowing him and those similarly gifted, to shape and alter future events. Upon occasion, there were dark spots to his visions, clouding his clairvoyance. In time he learned that the most common source of his frustration was Ethan. Any vision of Ethan was obscured as he was immune to magic; therefore, magic seemed immune to him. If Dragos drew forth a vision that included all the members of his daughter's family, only Ethan's visage would be hidden behind a shimmering black surface. A vision entailing the Mage Bane, that accursed land beyond the Aqualania Sea, carried the same affliction. The Mage Bane was aptly named as no magic could dwell therein. This barrier acted much the same, save that its entire surface was anti-magic, blinding him to what lay beyond. Ethan suffered no such hindrance, for whenever he gazed into Dragos's orbs, he could clearly discern what the shimmering dark blur obscured, yet everything that Dragos could see, Ethan could not. Between the two of them, they could accurately decipher any vision Dragos called forth. That was why Dragos was so intent upon Ethan's arrival as he was staring at the dark surface of the cavern wall for days, driving himself mad, trying to see what lay beyond.

"The wall appears alive," Ethan answered, stretching out his hand toward the shimmering dark surface.

"Ethan, be careful!" Felicia warned as she and Krixan stepped beside Dragos.

"What do you see?" Dragos asked again, irritated with Ethan's dumbfounded silence.

Ethan reached out to touch the strange surface, but his hand passed through the wall as if it were air. Before the others could utter a word of warning, Ethan stepped through, disappearing from their sight.

"Ethan!" Felicia cried out in alarm.

Krixan and Dragos both stepped toward the wall in disbelief, each reaching out to where the wall swallowed Ethan. To their dismay, the wall swallowed them in kind as they touched its surface. Felicia stood in numbed silence, wondering what had befallen them.

*****

Ethan emerged in a dimensional impaired chamber, where the ceiling, floor, and walls to either side were obscured in shimmering light melding with inky blackness. He could not see where his feet touched the ground or gain any sense of distance or space until Dragos and Krixan emerged from the wall behind him. Looking back, he could see out of the portal whence they came as if gazing into the cavern through a window. He could see Felicia's terror-stricken face, but the words escaping her lips were muted by the barrier between them. Her shifting eyes indicated that she could not see him as he saw her.

"Ethan, what did you do?" Dragos said excitedly, his aging eyes scanning their surroundings in awed wonder.

"I…don't know." Ethan shrugged.

"I have made many attempts these past days to breach that wall, but all I felt was an unforgiving surface, as if it shifted to solid stone as my hand drew near," Dragos explained.

"So where are we?" Krixan growled, logically concerned for their collective safety than the wonders of their discovery.

"A temporal anomaly of some sort, or an interdimensional plane, but most likely a portal," Dragos added as he explored the mysterious chamber, stroking the whitened hairs of his beard.

"A portal?" Krixan made a face.

"A portal, yes. A gateway between worlds. They were once numerous throughout Elaria in the golden age of mage craft thousands of years ago. The ancients told of their visits to sister worlds by passing through such structures. Overtime the portals fell into disuse, lost to the ages one at a time until forgotten, save for vague references in the ancient texts. To find one in working order and able to enter therein is extraordinary," Dragos marveled.

"How did they operate such a thing? You spent many days here trying to do so without result. How did they do it?" Krixan asked.

"They mentioned a key to opening the portal," Dragos answered.

"Ethan is our key. Do you think there were born ones such as him in those days?"

"I don't believe so, Krixan. There has never been mention of one born immune to magic except Ethan. The key was a physical object of some unknown property. But you're thinking, my boy," Dragos encouraged the big fella.

Felicia gasped, passing through the wall to join them. Krixan reached out, taking her hand to steady her.

"Where…" she uttered, gaining her breath as her eyes grew wide with her surroundings.

"Where? That is yet to be determined, my dear," Dragos explained. "It seems you have unlocked the portal for all of us to use, Ethan."

"Yeah, but where does it lead?" Ethan wondered when his eyes caught the outline of another portal on the opposing wall of the one they passed through. It rippled like the watery surface of a wine-dark sea as he stepped nigh, the others taking notice as he did so. A ray of bright light shone in the center of the second portal, growing exponentially as he drew near, until the portal's entirety came to life, revealing what lay beyond. The others looked to Ethan for answers as they beheld nothing, save for the portal's dark shimmering surface.

Ethan's right hand flew to his sword hilt, drawing the blade with blinding swiftness before stepping through the portal.

*****

He was saddle sore having ridden from Fort Smith to the backwaters of West Texas, but Deputy US Marshal Jake Thornton, would not relent until he reached Red Rock. The town was a good half day's ride ahead, so close he planned to ride through what remained of the day and through the night if need be. His father was the sheriff of Red Rock, and Jake feared for his safety. He rode to warn him that Sam Shade was being released from his Texas prison, and swore to kill the sheriff of Red Rock if he were ever released. Sam Shade was a fast and deadly killer who should have hung for his crimes but received prison by a favorable judge. Men like Sam Shade weren't released on their own accord. No, he had to have friends well placed in Austin to gain such an early release, and those friends most likely intended his father harm. Jake did not dare warn his father by telegraph, for if the message were intercepted by the wrong people, they would alter their plans of dealing with his father. Judge Parker warned him of all this before he left Fort Smith. Judge Isaac Parker was a shrewd man who saw what other men did not. When word reached the judge from a "friend" in the Texas court, that Sam Shade was to be released, he quietly took Jake aside and explained what that truly meant. Judge Parker was an old friend of Jake's father since the end of the war and hired Jake on as a deputy US marshal because of his father's reputation.

Jake had set out at once upon receiving the news from Judge Parker. A fellow deputy marshal, Bass Reeves, offered to cover his circuit while he journeyed to Red Rock. Jake accepted, telling Bass he'd meet up with him at Fort Sill in a month. Each Marshal was accompanied with a wagon, cook, and a posse man. Jake sent all of them with Bass while retaining his Indian guides, Long Paws and Running Wolf. Both guides were no more than boys, brothers and neither having reached their sixteenth birthday. Despite their youth, each was an expert tracker. Jake's maternal grandmother was full-blooded Kiowa, but he certainly did not inherit any tracking skills from that source of his bloodline. Running Wolf and Long Paws were full-blooded Kiowa as well and accompanied Jake to visit their native West Texas. Their kin dwelled in the village just ahead. Long Paws was the elder of the two, with long black hair that fell below his slender shoulders and expressive brown eyes that matched his younger brother's. Both wore buckskin trousers with frayed straps running the outside of each leg. Their plain tan shirts covered a thinner cotton undergarment, which Jake gifted them to protect their leather shirts from the oils of their skin. They rode matching black pintos.

Jake towered over his two companions; at six feet, four inches, he towered over most other men as well. Jake had short black hair, piercing green eyes, and a complexion that fell somewhere between his half Kiowa mother and white father. Jake wore twin Colt .45s upon either hip and a dusty brown Stetson upon his brow. He wore a black vest over a blue tucked shirt with his tin star pinned to his vest over his heart. He rode a black-spotted white palomino he named Bull.

The late afternoon sun shone brilliantly over the rock and sand terrain that straddled either bank of the Pierna Mala River. Long Paws and Running Wolf preceded him along the west bank of the river, with the rocky slopes of Johnson's Ridge overlooking their right. Bull snorted, his head suddenly shifting as if spooked.

"Easy, Bull," Jake soothed, stroking the horse's mane.

Bang!

The sound of rifle fire rang out. Jake saw Running Wolf tumble from his saddle, unable to see where he was hit. Bull reared in the air as Jake tried to draw his Winchester from its sleeve. Bull's startled movement saved Jake a bullet to the ribs as a round grazed his chest. He reacted poorly to the near miss, arching back in the saddle far enough to lose balance. Jake tumbled from his mount, striking the unforgiving ground. He heard the distinctive snap of breaking bones as his ribs struck a jutting rock. His left ankle landed awkwardly as well, pain running north along his shin. More rifle fire followed as Jake struggled to collect his bearings. He crawled into the river, using the bank for cover to shield himself from the gunfire above. From this makeshift position, he could see two or three men well positioned behind fat rocks upon the ridge above. He could not see Long Paws or Running Wolf from where he sat. His rifle remained in his saddle some meters away, where he left Bull. He winced, struggling to draw a pistol as pain ran the length of his left side.

"For all the good a pistol will do me from this far," Jake grunted. *A perfect place for an ambush and I ride right into it*, he thought sourly as another bullet nearly took him in the head, striking the water behind him.

"What the…" Jake uttered. His voice trailing in bewilderment as the hillside behind his mysterious attackers shimmered like the rippling surface of a dark sea. His attackers continued their relentless fire, oblivious to what lay behind them. Jake winced as another rifle shot struck a rock nearby, spraying stone fragments in his hair.

"Agghh!" He heard the awful sound of human suffering from the ridge above. The rifle fire abated long enough for him to rear his head. Jake's eyes narrowed in awe at the strange visage above. The flash of steel reflected the bright sunlight, wielded by strangers whose forms were obscured by the rocks above. He thought he saw swords slashing but dismissed it out of hand as impossible. Was he losing his mind? The longer he gazed, the clearer the impossible picture took shape. He spied two men hacking away at his attackers, swinging what appeared to be *swords*. He further stared in disbelief as a head sailed into the air before tumbling down the embankment. The echoes of his attackers' screams quickly faded as they succumbed to the sword-wielding strangers that seemed to materialize out of thin air. The last thing Jake Thorton saw before passing out were the shapes of the two men descending the ridge, making their way toward him at a hurried pace.

*****

"How long should we wait, Grandfather?" Felicia asked, her eyes fixed to the murky surface where Ethan and Krixan had stepped through moments before.

"Patience, my dear, and you know better than to use that endearment on me. Grandfather makes me sound old," he reproached, insisting that his grandchildren address him by his given name. Dragos sounded youthful, strong, and *handsome*. Grandfather conjured images that were far different. Despite his wrinkles, creaking bones, and silver hair, Dragos still felt as he did in his youth. His daughter and grandchildren thought the only thing youthful about Dragos was his maturity. He was as incorrigible as Bronus. It was no wonder that Ethan was so difficult to civilize, having inherited his obstinate nature from both bloodlines.

"Yes, Dragos, I shall refrain from such appellations that you find offensive." She rolled her eyes.

"Thank you, my dear." He smiled and patted her head. "You were always my favorite." Of course he said the same to all his grandchildren, claiming each as his favorite, often while the others were present.

Felicia humored him with a smile. It was part of her grandfather's charm, often acting a child and playing the fool to mask his crafty mind.

Their eyes were instantly drawn to the far wall as the shimmering surface bulged, mimicking the shape of the person attempting to pass through.

"Ethan!" Felicia gasped, coming to his side as he stepped within, carrying a man of similar size over his shoulder. The man was strangely attired and incoherent. Ethan passed through the chamber, depositing Jake on the floor of the cavern before passing back through the portal, to the interbarrier plane where Felicia and Dragos remained.

"My stars, Ethan, who was that man?" Dragos asked.

"I don't know, but he needs help. Felicia, step back through the portal and see to his injuries. I left him on the cavern floor."

Before they could utter a word in response, Ethan passed back through the portal whence they came.

*****

"Is he awake?" a voice whispered, though the language was unfamiliar. It sounded akin to some central European language, perhaps German. No, it lacked the harshness of German or the feminine softness of French. Was it Greek? Either way, he understood none of what was said.

"He needs rest," a woman answered. She sounded attractive, and Jake struggled to open his eyes to confirm if her face matched the beauty of her voice. Jake realized he was resting in a bed, not just any bed, but a very comfortable one at that. Even the boarding houses in Fort Smith did not have beds this comfortable. Where was he? Wherever he was, it certainly wasn't a dream as pain coursed the entire left side of his body.

"He's waking," Felicia said, touching a hand to his head.

"What of his injuries?" Ethan asked.

"The ribs along his left side are broken, his left ankle is fractured or sprained severely, and he suffered a contusion to the left side of his skull. It's a miracle he lives, considering our magic cannot heal him," Dragos said, standing behind them as they all stared curiously at the stranger resting before them.

"He is immune to magic like me," Ethan thought aloud, encouraged to find a fellow traveler who shared his peculiarity.

"Aye, but he can't heal himself like you can. But like you, he can impair our mage powers when we stand near him. The boy we found beside him shares his immunity. I wonder if all of them are so afflicted? Simply extraordinary," Dragos stroked his beard, pondering the implications of an entire world void of magic.

Jake's eyes eased open, adjusting slowly to the dim light. He found himself abed in a spacious chamber of gray and black stone. Torches lined the periphery of the chamber, affixed to silver brackets along the walls. His sight lowered to the strange faces staring back at him. The nearest was a young woman who sat beside his bed, leaning forward. *Am I dead?* he thought, thinking her an angel. He smiled like an idiot, unable to take his green eyes from her beautiful face. She was young, perhaps sixteen, he could not tell. Her emerald eyes matched his, and her golden hair stood out in the dark chamber. She returned the gesture, gifting him a smile.

"Thank you," Jake said, wondering if she spoke English as well as her native tongue.

"What did he say?" Ethan asked, drawing Jake's attention. It was then Jake noticed the others. The young man who just spoke was of a similar build and stature to him. He was clean-shaven, with short black hair. He sat at the end of his bed and wore a long black shirt of some sort. The fellow smiled back at him in a way that set Jake at ease. Between these two stood an older gentleman with silvered hair and beard, wearing a...*robe?* Jake shook his head, thinking his vision had gone amiss. Behind the older man was a giant, who leaned against the far wall with his massive arms crossed over his chest. His posture was not meant to intimidate, as the big man looked more bored than anything else. But men of his size needn't do more than breath to appear dangerous. Jake was no small man himself, towering over most men he knew, including his good friend Bass Reeves who stood 6'2".

"I don't know. His language is unknown to us," Felicia finally answered him.

"Now that he's awake, I might as well get to work." Ethan sighed.

Krixan and Dragos started for the door as Felicia stood, giving Jake a reassuring smile before following the others out.

"Was it something I said?" Jake laughed as they cleared the room.

"That's good. Keep talking," Ethan said, taking the stool Felicia vacated by Jake's side. They would never get the answers they sought until they learned the stranger's language, and for that they needed Ethan. For some odd reason, he could master a language in a matter of hours. Within a day, he could master accent, tense, and dialect. Whether such mastery was a mage gift or a natural talent, no one could guess. Ethan could master nearly any skill in equally short of time, once he understood its basics. He mastered the sword at the age of five, the bow at the age of six, and horsemanship at seven. He wandered into the smithy at Astaris when he was four. By day's end, he mastered the art of blacksmithing, able to shoe a horse, forge a blade, and construct a bellow. As for language, he need only learn the meaning of a word one time before he permanently committed it to memory, and with that, he started off with the basics.

"Ethan," he said, touching his chest before pointing to Jake.

The deputy marshal nodded in understanding before saying what the man wanted to hear. "Jake," he said, touching his own chest.

"Jake." Ethan smiled, offering him his hand in friendship.

"Much obliged, Ethan." Jake shook his hand.

*****

Hours had passed since they left Ethan alone with the stranger. Dragos checked on the stranger's young companions that they brought through the barrier. One had succumbed to his injuries, but the other suffered a broken arm but would live. The injuries were inflicted by the projectile weapons that the strangers used. Dragos examined the wounds of the dead boy and found the effect of the weapons devastating. Ethan and Krixan brought back the bodies of the assailants as well. They were severely disfigured by the sword strikes to their heads and necks. It was a gruesome affair, but Ethan thought it prudent to leave no evidence behind. He even brought back the stranger's horse, a smaller horse with black spots upon its white coat. The other horses had run off.

Felicia could hear their laughter through the thick oak door of the chamber as she waited without, with the serving maid in tow holding a tray of food for their guest. The girl was comely with long dark hair braided below the shoulders of her cotton gown.

"I'll take that, Melida," Felicia offered, dismissing the girl who bobbed a curtsy and withdrew. For reasons she would deny, even to herself, Felicia didn't wish to share the stranger's attention with another female. *Am I so transparent?* She kept the worry to herself as she stepped within.

Ethan and Jake's eyes drew instantly to the doorway as she entered. Ethan gave her a face as he saw the tray of food in her hands. *Was she trying to pass off the food as her own cooking?* he wondered. Ethan doubted if she had ever stepped one foot into a kitchen in her life.

Oh. He smiled inwardly as the truth dawned. "Well, Jake, look what my sister cooked up for you," he said in perfect English.

"That's right neighborly of you, miss," Jake said with his Texas drawl.

Felicia blushed, sensing his meaning, if not the strange language it was spoken in.

"You must be famished, Jake." She set the food in his lap before grabbing a stool and nudging Ethan to move his further toward the end of the bed while she sat near Jake's head.

Jake couldn't help but smile whenever his eyes met hers. She was the loveliest thing he had ever seen. He still was a little unclear about where he actually was, but at least Ethan understood him now. He was most pleased to hear that Felicia was Ethan's sister and not his wife as he first thought. She seemed content to sit beside him as her brother, and he continued their conversation.

Before they could continue, Dragos hurried through the doorway with surprising quickness for one of his advancing years, though Ethan would never mention age to his grandfather, who insisted he was still a young man.

"Our young friend is doing much better, I see," Dragos said, taking a stool before nudging Felicia further toward the end of the bed to make room for him to sit beside Jake's head.

Felicia gave Dragos a murderous look before shifting further afield. Jake stifled a grin at their antics.

"Dragos," Jake said, lifting a finger toward the older man before shifting his digit to the girl beside him. "Felicia. Did I guess correctly?" he asked.

"Not bad, Jake." Ethan smiled, then addressed his grandfather in his native Elarian. "I've been teaching Jake our names. He's got ours down pretty good, but I still have to teach him the others."

"He knows the important ones at least. So what have you learned?" Dragos asked, rubbing his hands in anticipation.

"Not much as yet, Dragos. I just learned his language, and I'll start asking him more pertinent questions," Ethan explained.

"*Umm*, this chicken is very good," Jake said, biting into the roast chicken on his tray. "Thank you, Felicia," he smiled as he chewed with his back propped up by pillows to support his broken ribs.

"He said thank you, Felicia," Ethan said. He then named the chicken, bread, and carrots on the tray in their English translation to add to their vocabulary.

"You are welcome," Felicia said in perfect English, patting Jake's hand.

"What's he thanking her for? I'm the one who ordered him fed," Dragos asked before Felicia nudged him with her elbow.

"Jake just started telling me a little about his troubles," Ethan decided to change the subject from their juvenile antics, and they all thought him the child.

"What kind of troubles?" Dragos asked.

"His father is in danger of some sort. Let him finish his story, then I'll tell you what he said," Ethan explained before turning back to Jake, telling him to continue.

Jake explained that his father is the sheriff of the small West Texas town of Red Rock. He spoke of a villain named Samuel Shade, a man that his father sent to prison, and how the villain was freed through nefarious means. He further explained how Sam Shade was on his way to Red Rock to murder his father. Ethan relayed the tale to Dragos and Felicia as Jake finished.

"He's obviously anxious to be on his way to warn his father," Ethan explained.

"Not like that, he's not," Felicia warned. "He shouldn't be moved at all, and if so, very carefully."

"What did she say?" Jake asked.

"She advises you to stay put for your body to heal properly."

"I don't care if I have to crawl over broken glass, I have to help my father." He coughed, Ethan reading the desperation in his eyes.

"What did he say?" Felicia asked, noting the pain in Jake's voice.

"His father's life depends on him reaching this place he calls Red Rock," Ethan said, keeping his eyes on Jake as he answered.

"Dragos, can you spare a contingent of cavalry to aid Jake's Father?" Felicia asked her grandfather.

"They would do little good, Felicia. According to Jake, their weapons are obsolete, and they don't speak Jake's language. Fortunately, I know a man who can help him," Ethan said with a mischievous grin.

"Father will never allow it." She gave him a withering look.

"Dad never said I couldn't visit an interdimensional realm."

"Dad?"

"That's what Jake calls his father, so in the spirit of learning our guest's culture, I should start using their terms of endearment."

Felicia rolled her eyes. "Just because Father never said you couldn't visit an interdimensional realm, doesn't mean that you can."

"Come on, baby sister, you know forgiveness is more easily obtained than permission. Besides, dear old Dad is many days ride away."

"What did she say?" Jake asked, his eyes drifting between the two of them.

"Oh, the usual, I'm a moron or something like that. She thinks you are one handsome man too," he said, giving Felicia a devilish smile as he did so.

"What did you just say to him?" Felicia snarled as Jake turned red.

"Oh, relax, I just told him that you like him. It's not much of a secret, and he likes you too."

"Did he say that?" She asked, now turning red herself.

"He doesn't have to. Have you noticed the way he looks at you?"

"It's true, my dear. You two are like lovesick wolves howling under a full moon," Dragos said.

"All right, Jake, you have three days to teach me all about your weapons, people, and history. Then I'll be going to Red Rock to help your father."

*****

Jake was pleased to learn that his Indian tracker, Long Paws, survived the ambush with only a broken left arm and a knock on the head. Regretfully, Running Wolf was not as fortunate, having succumbed to his injuries during the night. Ethan and Krixan brought Long Paws and Running Wolf through the barrier with Jake, the bodies of their assailants, Jake's horse, and the strange projectile weapons that they used. By the next morn, Long Paws was well enough to visit Jake with his left arm splinted but no worse for the ware. One look at the boy and you could see how he came about his name, as his large feet seemed too big for his body. Ethan quickly learned Long Paws native tongue while Jake educated him on basic history, government, and culture of the United States. By late afternoon, Ethan had Jake moved to the central courtyard of his grandfather's palace, where Jake instructed him on the fundamentals of the Colt .45 pistol and the Winchester .30-30 rifle. Ethan retrieved a twin holster from one of the bodies of Jake's attackers, buckling the belt tightly about his waist and tying down each holster to his thighs. Jake was dumbstruck by how quickly Ethan came to learn trigger control and sight alignment, two principles that took most men thousands of rounds to comprehend and tens of thousands to master. Ethan mastered both with less than two dozen rounds. Even more remarkable was Ethan's natural aim. He was quickly hitting every target within ten yards from the hip, each draw a little quicker than the last.

Jake leaned against a wagon for support, refusing to lie down while instructing Ethan, with a crutch under his left arm for support. The pain was nigh unbearable, but he soldiered through. When

Ethan first broached the idea of traveling to Red Rock in his place, Jake thought his good intentions misplaced. Jake knew their medieval weapons would be useless and would never send a man to certain death, especially a man like Ethan who risked his life to save him. Ethan soon won him to the possibility when he realized how quickly Ethan could master a skill, first English, then sidearms. Jake wondered what else Ethan might surprise him with. Jake also noted the deference the people who lived in the palace afforded Ethan. He wondered if his newfound friend was a feudal lord of some sort. If he was, in fact, a noble, he had a funny way of acting the part with his easy nature and disdain for the aristocracy. When Jake described the governmental system of the United States, Ethan was excited beyond belief that no kings or lords ruled the nation. When Jake revealed that their leaders were selected by the people, and only served short periods of time before returning to common life and that no man knelt to any other, Ethan's desire to travel to Red Rock grew quickly into an obsession.

By evening, Felicia ordered Poor Jake back to his bedchamber to rest, scolding her brother for having their guest tax himself teaching him how to use his new toys. Felicia was beginning to comprehend Jake's native English by Ethan relaying words to Dragos, who permanently imprinted them in her memory. Learning verb tenses was far more difficult, but she could carry on simple conversations by day's end.

While Felicia saw that Jake was fed and his injuries tended, Ethan went about finding clothes that might blend to his new environment. Using deer hides, he had the seamstress make him two pairs of leather buckskin trousers with frayed straps running the outside seams, similar to Long Paws'. He recruited the palace shoemaker to help make him a pair of moccasin boots.

When Ethan visited Jake the next morn, he was decked out in his new buckskins, moccasin boots, a tan leather pullover shirt and his twin tie-down holster. His sister was already there, feeding Jake his breakfast and doting upon him like a mother hen. He wondered if she left his side since last night.

"Well, what do you think, Jake?" Ethan asked with his arms outstretched to display his new garb.

"It's passable. Looks like what an army scout or a trapper might wear." Jake shrugged.

"Mother will hate it," Felicia said dryly.

"You'll need a knife and hat as well," Jake added.

"I'll fetch a hat once I reach town, and I have plenty of knives," Ethan explained.

"I lost my hat when I fell from my horse, but what about those men you killed, did you find one among them?"

Ethan shook his head no. The three men that he and Krixan killed were badly disfigured, and their headgears were shredded by their violent attack. Besides their bodies, Ethan and Krixan only retrieved their weapons, leaving everything else behind. Ethan brought the heads of the slain men to Jake, asking if he knew them, but Jake had never seen the men before, though their damaged faces were difficult to know for certain. Their identities, along with their motives, died with them.

"When you get into Red Rock, get yourself a good Stetson. That will keep the sun off your head. If you'd oblige and fetch my saddle pack for me?" Jake asked.

They had brought Jake's gear from his horse into his bedchamber. Ethan fetched it from its resting place along the far wall. Jake fished out a long knife with a fat blade from his pack, gifting it to his friend.

"What's this for?" Ethan asked.

"A bowie knife. You'll need a good knife and your native variety will raise suspicion."

"Thanks, Jake. I'll be sure to return this."

"Keep it. It's the least I can do for saving my hide and helping my father. I've been thinking, and I believe it best if you take my horse with you. His name is Bull, and he'll blend in better than your horses, and he is acclimated to the Texas climate."

"Sounds fair, Jake. We best get back to my gun practice," Ethan said in a perfect Texas accent.

*****

Two days hence

Ethan was saddled and ready. They built Jake a litter using Krixan's horse to take him to Long Paws' village. Krixan would stay in the Kiowa village until Jake was able to ride, while Ethan went on to Red Rock by himself. Ethan spent the previous day getting to know Bull. The usually ornery horse took a sudden liking to Ethan, which Jake found surprising. Dragos had imprinted as much of the English language as he knew into Krixan's mind. It would form a good foundation for the big man to become fluent if they lingered in Red Rock longer than they intended, though Ethan reassured his grandfather that he would not tarry across the boundary. Ethan conveyed to Jake as much of Elarian culture and history as Jake shared of Earth. His Texan friend was a little taken aback when Ethan revealed his parentage and high birth. Ethan reassured Jake that the American system of government was superior to his own backward feudal society. They cobbled together a cover story for Ethan, saying he was the son of a large landowner from Ohio, who journeyed west looking for adventure.

Once again, they entered the cavern where the boundary lay. Felicia accompanied Dragos as they bade them farewell.

"My lady," Jake regarded Felicia kindly as he sat uncomfortably upon his litter. He took her proffered hand and kissed the back of it.

"Be safe, Jake Thorton," she said with watery eyes.

"I shall, my Yellow Rose." He smiled as she gripped his hand ever tightly.

"Take care of him, Ethan," she said, not taking her eyes from Jake's.

"He'll be all right, little sister," Ethan said as the four men stepped toward the portal. Krixan brought a second horse, which carried Running Wolf's body to return it to his village. The wall's surface shimmered to life as Ethan drew near and passed through, the others following close behind. Dragos and Felicia waited for a length of time before the cavern's surface returned to its inky black form, sealing the boundary until Ethan's return.

CHAPTER 4

"Easy, boy," Ethan stroked Bull's mane, calming the spotted palomino as they skirted the river. He rode half a day, stopping several times for Bull to get a drink before continuing on. The West Texas sun bore down, narrowing his eyes with its intense glare. Brown grass covered the riverbanks as the slow-flowing Pierna Mala meandered through the valley. If what Jake said was correct, then Red Rock should be a couple of hours ahead. Sweat gathered in all the usual places as he wiped his brow with his right palm, drying it on his buckskin trousers. Even with the sun arcing behind him, the intense glare reflecting off the patches of sand stung his eyes. The arid climate contrasted sharply with the wooded pines of the Astarian high country. Jake was right about needing a hat to keep the sun off your head. He would be sure to acquire one once he got into Red Rock. He wished Jake would be with him when he reached town, but it would be painful for his friend to be dragged on his litter for that long. Long Paws and Krixan would wait for him to further heal before bringing him to town. Ethan hoped he wasn't too late to warn the sheriff.

*****

He leaned back on the hind legs of the chair with his feet propped up on the hitch post, enjoying the fresh air while the porch overhang kept the sun off his head. The town was quiet as late with few cattlemen passing through. The only other soul on the dusty main street was George Adams, the owner of the Red Rock mercantile. He noticed George crossing the street with a purposeful gait.

George paid him a visit every afternoon, while his wife tended the store. George Adams was a stick-thin man with a handlebar mustache, black hair, and graying temples. His wife was as rotund as he was thin, and Sheriff Thorton wondered what might happen if Mrs. Adams ever rolled over her husband while in bed? He was certain that Red Rock would be short one mercantile operator. Ironically, the couple did produce three attractive daughters. In this rough country, George would be fending off suitors for many years.

"Afternoon, Sheriff," George greeted him upon his approach.

"George," Ben Thorton said, touching a finger to his hat in a semi salute.

"The town's awfully quiet as late."

"Yep," Ben answered briefly.

"I expect things to get a bit livelier once Caleb Miller comes to town this weekend."

"I suppose," Ben said.

"They say he has two thousand head of cattle ready to move."

"I reckon he does."

With Ben's brief responses, most men would correctly surmise that he didn't want to talk, but George Adams chattered on, oblivious to the sheriff's disinterest.

"My missus is looking forward to the social at the Lawton ranch the Saturday after next. Shall you be in attendance, Ben?"

"I don't fancy dancin', George, but I do favor Mrs. Lawton's apple pie."

"I'm sure she'll make one just for you, Sheriff." George smiled ear to ear. "My, how things have changed these last few years."

"How so?"

"Well, when you took the job of sheriff way back then, I never figured Bill Lawton ever to cotton to a man who wore Union Blue. That was a very un-Texan thing to do. But you've done a heck of a job, Sheriff, if even a man like Bill Lawton, who speaks with reverence of John Bell Hood, can tip his hat to a former Union cavalry captain."

"Tell me, George, do you know the name of my late first-born son?"

"Samuel, wasn't it?"

Ben nodded and affirmed. "I named him after Sam Houston. You know General Houston, George?"

"Every self-respecting Texan knows Sam Houston, Ben." George grinned.

"Yes, every Texan knows Sam Houston, but how many heeded his counsel about secession? Nary a soul. Sam Houston believed in the Union, in the United States of America. The secessionists cursed him for it and called him a traitor for not following the southern states into oblivion. Texas didn't listen, and our great state fell with the confederacy. Ole Sam was right. As most men listened to hot heads, clamoring for war and secession, I heeded General Houston and fought for the Union."

"Well, when you put it that way, Sheriff, I guess siding with the Union wasn't so bad."

Sheriff Thorton was never much one to argue or waste words in idle chatter, but George Adams touched a nerve.

"What really rankles me, George, is many of those mouths clamoring for secession down in Austin, remained safely at home throughout the war, and they called me a traitor!" Ben spat in disgust. "They're the same sorry bunch who called me an 'Injun lover' because my late wife's mother was full-blooded Kiowa, yet where were they when I was fighting Comanche while I was a Texas ranger?"

"Well, you sure have lived an exciting life, Sheriff." George grinned, oblivious to Ben's meaning.

Ben scrubbed his jaw with his left hand, noting the three-day stubble on his chin. Out of the corner of his right eye, he noticed a tall silhouette upon a horse at the end of the dusty street. George turned to where Ben was looking, resting his hands on his hips.

"Looks like a stranger in town, Sheriff. I've never seen him before."

Ben noticed the stranger's large build and swagger. There was a way the man carried himself that bespoke confidence sans arrogance. He wore buckskin trousers, moccasin boots, and a plain pull-over shirt. His twin holsters were tied down to either side. He was a clean-shaven, handsome fella with short black hair and penetrating blue eyes. Ben's eyes narrowed at the spotted palomino, recognizing the familiar mount. Ben leaned carefully forward, coming slowly to his feet.

"Back away, George!" Ben Thorton cautioned.

George dropped his hands from his hips, looking briefly at the sheriff. His face grew pale as he quickly withdrew.

Ben lifted the Henry Rifle leaning against the hitch post, leveling the barrel on the approaching stranger. "That's far enough, mister!" Ben warned as the fellow stopped several yards shy.

"I'm looking for Sheriff Thorton." the man asked, carefully eyeing the barrel pointed at him.

"Well, you found him, son. Now you mind telling me how you came about *that* horse?" Ben asked, drawing the hammer back on his rifle.

The stranger noticed the sheriff's large build and the hard, leathery face. He wore a vest over a tan collared shirt. His holster was tied down on his right thigh. He wore a dusty white hat that drew down on his brow. His rough countenance reminded the stranger of his father in many ways.

"This horse belongs to Marshal Jake Thorton. He sent me to find you. He got hurt real bad about a half day's ride upstream."

"What's your name?"

"Ethan. Ethan Blagen."

"How bad is he hurt, Ethan?"

"A busted ankle, broken ribs and a knock on the head. Throw in a fever and a dozen bruises, and you'll get a better picture. My friend has tended him and set his leg. He just needs time to heal."

"If your story is true, why aren't you with him?" Ben doubted this story. His heart was pounding for fear of his son's well-being.

"He sent me along to help you, Sheriff. Can I dismount and tell you why? What I have to say is best not said in an open street."

"All right, Ethan. Get down real slow, tie your horse to the post and unbuckle your holster."

Ethan complied, letting his holster drop on the front porch of the sheriff's office as Ben waved him inside with the end of the rifle. As he stepped within, his eyes slowly adjusted to the dark, noticing the large desk sitting to one side of the front room, and a rack of rifles behind it on the right wall. A caged door on the back wall led to three jail cells in the back room.

"Have a seat!" the sheriff commanded, waving the rifle to two empty chairs facing the desk. Ethan sat down as the sheriff stood behind the desk. "All right, young fella, start talking."

"Jake said you wouldn't trust me unless I told you something that only he would know. Your wife's favorite song was the Red River Valley. She sang it to your boys to rock them to sleep when they were babies. Though you served under Phil Sheridan in the war, you favored General George Thomas."

"Anything else?"

"Oh, yeah. He said, 'God bless Sam Houston.'" Ethan gave him an infectious grin.

Ben lowered his rifle and extended a hand. "Welcome to Red Rock, Ethan."

Ethan took Ben's hand and shook it. The sheriff had a strong grip. Though he was a large man, Ethan sensed he was much larger in his youth. Now he had the settled build that came with age, but his grip felt like iron.

"Fetch your holster, son, and we can get on the trail. You can lead me to Jake."

"Jake is safe right now. Long Paws took Jake and my friend to his people. They will nurse him back to health. We have to stay here."

"Why?"

Ethan fished a folded piece of paper from his boot and passed it to Ben. The aging sheriff opened the drawer of his desk to retrieve his glasses. Ethan wondered their purpose but feared asking would alert the sheriff to his ignorance of their world, which would bring his truthfulness into doubt. He would tell the sheriff the truth eventually, but right now, he needed the sheriff to trust him and heed his warning.

"Jake says this Sam Shade fella was released from prison and he is supposed to meet up with Conrad Finch here in Red Rock. Jake said that Sam Shade has repeatedly said he plans to kill you when he gets into town," Ethan parroted the letter.

"They let Sam Shade out of prison?" Ben shook his head. "They should have hung that animal from the nearest tree. I should've never taken him alive in the first place."

"What's our plan?"

"*Our* plan? You seem like a smart kid, Ethan. This isn't your fight. I suggest you leave town. There's little point—"

"I promised Jake that I'd help you until he is healed. That's a promise I intend to keep."

Ben dropped his hat on the desk and racked his fingers through his gray hair. He sighed as he rubbed his temples with his fingers, fixing Ethan with a hard scowl. "Boot hill is filled with young men with more courage than sense. You ever kill a man, Ethan?"

"Yes," he answered carefully. He needn't tell the sheriff that it was with a sword and not a gun.

"I reckon if I tell you to leave town, you'll ignore me and stay anyway?"

"Yep." Ethan smiled.

"Aw hell, if you're gonna stay we might as well make it legal," Ben opened the drawer a second time, fetching another item which he tossed to Ethan.

Ethan lifted the item, examining it. It was a piece of metal, two inches wide and shaped similar to Jake's star. It matched the adornment pinned to the sheriff's vest.

"Raise your right hand and say 'I do!'"

"I…do," Ethan answered, not knowing what he was saying "I do" to.

"Now pin that badge on your shirt. You're now an acting deputy of Red Rock. When Skeeter gets back, I'll have him fix you a place to stay."

"Who's Skeeter?"

"Skeeter Smith. His real name is Thomas, but everyone calls him Skeeter. He's my deputy. He's out at the Miller place and won't be back till sundown. Come on!"

"Where to, Sheriff?" Ethan asked while pinning the star to his shirt.

"We're going to arrest Conrad Finch. He's been in town for a few days now with Junior Wills. No point in waiting for Sam Shade to show up and having us confront them all together."

*****

"I raise you twenty." Conrad Finch tossed the chips into the center of the table. He sneered at the man across from him as he chewed on a toothpick. Conrad Finch was a vicious, ornery fellow with yellow-stained teeth, dark beard, and a scarred, pockmarked face. His light-brown eyes mirrored the hue of his remorseless soul. He wore a black vest over a red-and-white checkered shirt. His black hat sat high on his brow, while his foul breath escaped whenever his lips parted.

"I fold," Charlie Spencer said, throwing his cards down. The two other men at the table chuckled as Charlie lost nine hands in a row.

"We best get going, Charlie. Pa will notice if we ain't back soon," his brother Bob said, sitting to his right.

"I shoulda knowd better than to played tis' game," Charlie spat in disgust.

"Your pa will skin your hide if he finds out how much you lost, Charlie," John Custis said from behind the bar. He was the owner of the Lucky Star saloon. The bar lined the back wall while a dozen round tables covered the floor. The four men occupied a table off to the right of the bar. The other tables were empty since it was only the afternoon. The only other soul in the place was Stone Grierson, a lanky lad with a tie-down holster and spurs who stared out the right front window of the saloon.

"Sheriff's comin', Finch," Stone hollered.

"What of it?" Conrad snarled.

"He looks fixin' to do something. Got another feller with 'em. A big feller just like him, but younger."

"Move back to the corner on the other side o' the door, Stone."

Stone Grierson backed to the front corner as Sheriff Thorton stepped through the swinging front doors with his Henry rifle in hand. Ethan trailed him, stepping within and standing off to the side at the front, opposite Stone as the sheriff stood in the center of the saloon. He lowered the rifle to the four men sitting at the table.

"Charlie, Bob, you boys best get home. *Now!*" Ben Thorton ordered.

"Yes, sir, Sheriff!" Their voices squeaked in unison as the two boys jumped to their feet and hurried from the saloon.

"Is there a problem, Sheriff?" the fellow sitting to Conrad's left asked.

"You men are under arrest, Junior. Keep your hands on the table where I can see 'em!" Ben's eyes narrowed. Conrad could see the menace in the old sheriff's eyes. If he wasn't careful, the sheriff would shoot him dead.

"John, come out from behind there and take their guns. I don't want any trouble from either of ya," Ben said as the bartender started to move.

"You're the one askin' for trouble, Sheriff!" Stone Grierson shrieked as he reached for his pistol.

Ethan cleared his holster in a blink of an eye, firing before Stone cleared leather. He fired three rounds into Stone's stomach and chest. Ben turned briefly to the sound of gunfire to his right, distracted by the boy's interference as Conrad Finch retrieved his right hand from the tabletop, going for his gun.

Boom!

Blood sprayed from Conrad's back, following the path of the bullet that went clean through him. He stumbled backward, crashing to the floor in his chair. Junior Wills lifted his trembling hands as his two comrades lie bleeding on the saloon floor. Smoke spewed from his barrel as Ben worked the lever-action of his rifle.

"Agghh!" Stone Grierson wailed in agony as he writhed on the floor with vomit spraying from his mouth. Piss and blood pooled beneath him. Ethan circled around him with his Colt .45 drawn on the screaming man. He reached down, removing Stone's holstered pistol, then tucked it into his own pistol belt. Killing with a sword was messy, but the power of the pistol unnerved Ethan. It was loud and violent and swift.

"Fetch Doc Wilson, John!" Ben growled.

"Will do, Sheriff," the barkeep said, rushing out the front doors.

Sheriff Thorton circled behind Junior Wills, keeping the barrel on the frightened cowhand's back.

"I'll blow a hole clean through you if you as much as flinch, Junior."

"I ain't movin', Sheriff," Junior whimpered as Ben pushed his head down on the table. He lifted Junior's pistol from his holster then stepped back.

"All right, stand up, Junior! Ethan!"

"Yeah, Sheriff?" Ethan shifted his eyes to Ben.

"Wait with these two while I lock Junior up in the jail."

"Will do, Sheriff." Ethan nodded.

"And Ethan?"

"Yeah?"

Ben regarded him for a moment as their eyes met. "Well done, son. Well done."

"My pleasure, Sheriff."

*****

"You just made a big mistake, Sheriff!" Junior Wills snarled as Ben locked him in the cell.

"I've made 'em before, Junior. Just be thankful that you were too slow on the draw or I'd have shot you too," Ben said as he turned the key, locking the cell door.

"I ain't done nothin', Sheriff! Why am I locked up fer?" He gripped the bars of his cell, his face pressed between the columns of reinforced steel.

"Why don't you tell me, Junior?" Ben lifted an eyebrow.

"I ain't done nuthin', Sheriff. I'll say it again and again. You ain't got no cause to lock me up."

"Why don't you tell me why you and Finch were waiting for Sam Shade?"

Junior's jaw slackened with his paling face, his reaction confirming Jake's warning.

"What was Stone Grierson doing there with you? Was he in on it as well?"

Stone! thought Junior elatedly. "Once Stone's pa finds out what happened, Sheriff, your life ain't worth spit. That goes for yer new deputy too. He'll kill ya. He'll kill ya all!" He screamed as Sheriff Thorton turned his back on him and walked out.

*****

By the time Doc Wilson arrived, Stone Grierson had expired. His was a painfully long death as his innards were twisted and aflame. He cried for his long-dead mother, cursed the heavens, whimpered, sobbed, and screamed in an endless chorus of adjoined, stressful emotions. Eventually he grew pale and clammy until death mercifully took him. Conrad Finch suffered no such misery. The rifle shot struck his heart, killing him on impact. Ethan surmised that Finch was the eviler of the two men, as he was older and thus guilty of more foul deeds than the much younger Grierson boy. Finch deserved a more painful death, but fate was an unjust mistress, granting mercy and judgment randomly with no regard to merit or guilt. He had been in this world less than a day, and he had already taken a life.

"Well…not much I can do for these men," Doc Wilson said, looking up to John Custis as he knelt by Finch's body.

"Stone's Father won't be pleased, I can tell you that," John said as he untied his apron and set it on the bar.

"I suspect he'll have some choice words for the sheriff," Doc Wilson said as he closed his medical bag and stood up.

"The sheriff didn't kill Stone, I did," Ethan interjected as he stood off to the side.

Doc Wilson eyed Ethan studiously. The doc was an older man with gray hair with lingering patches of brown. He had a bushy mustache with even-set brown eyes and a narrow aristocratic nose. He wore a black satin vest over a white collared shirt with his sleeves pushed up to his elbows.

"What's your name, young man?" Doc asked.

"Ethan."

"What happened here, Ethan?"

"The sheriff confronted the two men at the table when the boy you call Stone tried to shoot the sheriff in the back. That's when I shot him."

"Stone didn't leave him much choice, Doc," John Custis defended him.

"That sounds like Stone Grierson, more brash than sense. Don't make much difference now. If I were you, Ethan, I would leave town tonight. Heck, I'd leave the state," Doc advised.

"That's good advice, I suggest you heed it, Ethan," Sheriff Thorton said as he stepped through the swinging doors.

"And leave you alone? No, I'm staying, Sheriff." Ethan held firm.

"More guts than brains. Ben Thorton shook his head. "All right, Ethan, if you're gonna stick around, I need you to go to the jail and keep an eye on our prisoner."

"Will do, Sheriff." Ethan nodded and stepped without.

"That boy saved your skin, Ben," John said after Ethan was out of earshot.

"Yep," Ben said with his characteristic bluntness.

"How long have you known him? I've never seen the young man before," Doc asked.

"He just rode into town an hour ago. I never met him before then," Ben said as the other two shared a look.

"An hour?" Doc asked.

"He sure doesn't waste any time settling in," John said.

"No, I reckon he don't. John, I'll need you to come down to the jail and fill out a witness statement. Doc, if you can wait here for the undertaker, he should be along shortly."

*****

The late autumn West Texas wind swept through the open window, cooling the arid room as the sheriff poured two glasses of whiskey on his desk. It was nearly sundown and Ben thought it was time to find out a little bit more of who his new deputy was.

"Have a drink, Ethan. I think we earned one after today."

Ethan lifted the glass and downed it before realizing that in this world, he was not immune to the effects of alcohol.

"I see you're no greenhorn when it comes to the bottle." Ben grinned, refilling Ethan's glass.

Ethan didn't know what a greenhorn was but surmised its meaning. "No. I'm no stranger to fermented drinks, Sheriff."

"I reckon you're not. You're pretty handy with a gun too. Stone Grierson was fair on the draw, but with you, he never cleared leather. How long have you been shooting, Ethan?"

"A week or so, Jake taught me."

"A week?"

Ethan realized his mistake as he wondered how he would explain himself. "I am a fast learner, and Jake was a good teacher."

"He's not that good. Well, it was not a long distance between you and Stone when you fired those shots, but your speed was impressive. No matter. We'll work on your marksmanship." Ben dropped a light-brown hat on the desk. "That's for you. It's a little worn but will do the job. It's painful watching you squint all day without a hat on your fool head."

"Thanks, Sheriff," Ethan said as he tested the Stetson for its fit.

"So tell me where you hail from, Ethan?" Ben leaned back in his chair and placed his feet on his desk.

"Ohio," he answered carefully, trying to recall the cover story that Jake and he practiced.

"Good state, Ohio. The folks there are a good-natured lot and not as full of themselves like the city folk in the east. How long have you been in Texas, Ethan?"

"A few weeks is all," he said, taking another swig of whiskey.

"What do you know of our fine state?"

"Besides the Alamo, not much," Ethan conceded.

"Then it's high time you were properly educated, son."

Sheriff Thorton spent the next few hours extolling the virtues of Texas. Ethan hung on Ben's every word. He was fascinated by the whole country, let alone Texas. He could not believe a land the size of America had no kings or nobles. No man had to kneel or show obeisance to another. Each man stood proud and free and could benefit from the full measure of his labor. After a time, Skeeter returned from the Miller ranch. Skeeter was an old man, much older than the sheriff. He had shaggy gray hair, narrow eyes, and a face as worn as old leather. His right eye squinted severely, and he was missing every other tooth. Though a pistol rode his right thigh, he preferred a sawed-off shotgun due to his eyesight dimmed by age. Skeeter pulled up a chair beside Ethan while the sheriff pulled out a deck of cards. They thought it prudent to teach Ethan the nuances of poker while they drank whiskey and told tall tales of Texas into the wee morning hours.

For the first time in his life, Ethan finally felt at home.

CHAPTER 5

Ethan spent the following days learning his way around Red Rock and the names of the townsfolk. He found them a hardy, industrious lot with simple faith and fierce pride. Doc Wilson visited the jail with regularity, conversing with Sheriff Thorton at length over various topics. Ethan quickly grew fond of the doc with the time he spent with them. Jacob Steward was the town blacksmith, and Ethan spent a couple of afternoons with him learning to shoe horses with the advanced methods the Texans used. His hands quickly callused as his ability to regenerate was impaired in this world. Parson Green visited the sheriff after Sunday service, trying to return his wayward sheep to the fold as the sheriff missed another of the parson's sermons. When George Adams first set eyes on Ethan, he found the young man disconcerting. Since that day, the village mercantile operator warmed up to the boy, especially his three daughters, Emily, Sara, and Connie May. They baked Ethan meals, breads, and cobbler, giving them an excuse to visit him at the jail. They continuously reminded him of the social coming up at the Lawton Ranch, and he promised each of them a dance, though he hadn't a clue as to how they danced in Texas. He didn't want to attend the social, but Mrs. Lawton made a point of inviting him. Besides, ole Skeeter and the sheriff insisted that he attend to stay in the Adams sisters' good graces. Both men clearly wanted to continue enjoying the young ladies home cooking, and Ethan was the key to obtaining such treasures.

Besides the good sheriff, Ethan found old Judge Donovan the most interesting man in town. He was the schoolmaster, the town's stonemason, and the justice of the peace. He would converse with

Ethan into the late evening in the jail, discussing such things as history, law, politics, and hunting. The judge spent time as a trapper and grizzly hunter. He traveled the Oregon Trail and hunted buffalo throughout the Great Plains. He fought at the Battle of Buena Vista during the Mexican War. Despite the impairment of his enhanced strength and recuperative abilities, Ethan was still a fast learner and absorbed much of the judge's telling. Judge Donovan was a bear of a man with gray hair circling his balding head. He had deep blue eyes and a heavy clean-shaven face. Another evening passed with the judge, the sheriff, and Skeeter sitting in the jail with their feet up on Ben's desk while smoking cigars as Ethan listened to tales of their adventures.

"It was about an hour or so later that that grizzly circled back and came up behind us. With no place to go but off that cliff, we both jumped into the river below. All the way down, I prayed that it was deep enough for us not to hit bottom. Zeb was so afraid of that bear he forgot that he didn't know how to swim," the judge said as the others laughed.

"Well, Judge, how long you figure I can hold Junior locked up in the back?" Ben jerked a thumb over his right shoulder toward the rear of the jail.

"Well…" The judge took a puff of his cigar as he contemplated. "I can give you another day or two, but that's about it. All we have is hearsay."

"Conspiracy to kill the sheriff has to count for more than that, dag gummit!" Skeeter spat.

"That may be so, Skeeter, but right now all we have to go on is thirdhand rumors passed from some unknown witness to Jake and Jake to Ethan. If Sam Shade don't show his face in the next two days, we're gonna have to let Junior go," the judge explained.

"In the meantime, we need to be ready for when or if he does show. I'll be taking Ethan out in the morning to practice shooting," Ben said.

"He should be as good as Bill Hickok by how many shells I'm having to reload each day," Skeeter complained.

"Give the boy his due, Skeet. He's nearly as accurate as me and a whole lot faster, and he's only been shooting for a couple of weeks," Ben praised his deputy.

"If you teach me how to reload the shells, Skeet, I'll be glad to do it," Ethan offered.

"Ambitious young fella, ain't he," Skeeter grinned to the other two. "He keeps it up, and maybe he'll be sheriff, and you'll be his deputy, Ben."

"At my age, he's welcome to it." Ben gave Ethan a heartfelt grin.

*****

"Let's try three this time," Ben said as he stepped across the dry creek bed and set cans atop three fat rocks. As soon as Ben returned to his side, Ethan drew his Colt, fanning the pistol as he fired three shots from the hip, knocking each can from its perch. Ethan holstered his pistol before the first can hit the ground. Ben shook his head in disbelief. Hip shooting required natural ability and extensive practice, but no one should be able to do what Ethan had learned in just two weeks. The boy had a natural feel for the gun and the target. He was able to perfectly squeeze the trigger at incredible speed without slapping it. This, coupled with his unnatural aim, made Ethan a deadly gunfighter. Ethan was also able to take life without hesitation if need be, as he did with Stone Grierson. Ben knew that that ability was far more important than gun speed and accuracy. He had known many men that were skilled with firearms, but they hesitated in a fight, allowing lesser men to kill them. He recalled during the war young men loading one musket ball after another into their barrels without firing a shot, forgetting to fire and oblivious of their mistake. Some men are natural killers, and some men have to be conditioned to kill, while many more will never be. Ethan was a natural killer, a good lad, but a killer nonetheless.

"I think you might be as good as Jake, maybe even faster, and I spent years training him to your current ability," Ben praised.

"I'm not as good as Jake, not even close." Ethan grinned.

"Yeah, you are, and I'd hate to live on the difference. Why are you always smiling?" Ben found the boy's grin out of place, but it seemed in the short time that he had known Ethan, the boy was constantly grinning.

"Because I'm happy. Ever since I came to your great state, I am truly free for the first time in my life."

"All Americans are free, Ethan. Why were you not?"

"My father. I was expected to obey his plan for my life, and I always disappoint."

Ben wondered how any Father could find Ethan disappointing. He was a good-looking boy, broad of shoulder, brave and easy natured. He reminded Ben so much of his own son. Ethan's father's animosity made little sense. "What does your father want you to do?"

"He wants me to take over for him when the time comes."

"Take over what?"

Ethan thought how he should answer without lying completely. "My father owns large tracts of land."

"A farmer?" Ben asked.

Before Ethan could answer, a rider appeared around the bend of the dry creek bed, riding at full gallop. Ethan's hand went to his pistol before Ben raised a palm to stay his draw.

"Easy, Ethan, I know this girl."

Girl? Ethan made a face as the rider pulled her reins, stopping just yards before them, her horse's hooves kicking dust in their face as it stopped. She wore men's shirt and breeches, with a holster and dark Stetson. Her golden hair was tied off behind her, and her dark-brown eyes fixed intently on Ben.

"Sheriff! My father sent me to tell you that Sam Shade is in town. He's got several others with him," she panted.

"Where in town, Jodi?" Ben's eyes narrowed with his scowl.

"I don't rightly know, Sheriff. I came to fetch you before he reached the edge of town."

"Where's Judge Donovan?"

"He's out at the Miller place, Sheriff. He doesn't know either."

"All right. I want you to fetch the judge and then ride straight home and stay there."

"I can help, Sheriff. I can bull's-eye a rattler at fifty yards," Jodi argued.

"Men aren't rattlers, girl. You get Judge Donovan, and you get yourself home."

She touched her hat, acknowledging his order before jerking her reins and galloping off.

"Who was that?"

"Jodi Lawton," Ben answered. "Pretty gal, but she's wilder than a rabid grizzly. I pity the fella that takes her for a wife. She'd more likely gut him than kiss him."

*****

Ethan drew Bull up alongside Sheriff Thorton's dusty gray pinto as the West Texas wind blew tumbleweeds past their lathered mounts. Ben Thorton's narrow eyes studied the town below from atop the low dust swept hill. The sheriff drew his holstered Colt, spinning the barrel to ensure he had a round in each chamber before doing the same with his Henry rifle.

"We'll enter town from the southeast along the brush line there." Ben pointed out the area to Ethan.

"Why there? The jail is on the opposite end of town?"

"The brush line should conceal our approach, and the hard soil along that line will raise little dust. We best get a move on before—"

The sound of gunfire echoed from the town.

"Aw hell, come on, Ethan!" Ben kicked his heels, spurring his pinto to a full gallop.

"Come on, Bull!" Ethan clicked his tongue, following Sheriff Thorton down the dusty hill.

*****

Ole Skeeter winced as bullets flew overhead as he crouched below the shattered front window of the sheriff's office. His aged heart pounded emphatically, taxing the old deputy to his limit. He contemplated returning fire, but to poke his head up to take a shot meant certain death. He counted three others besides Sam Shade, nearly all of them ranch hands of Hank Grierson, one he recognized as Lefty McCoy. He nipped Lefty in the leg and watched him go down as the others first rushed the jail. The slug didn't kill him, though, as Skeeter recognized Lefty's nasal voice among those shouting outside.

"They're comin' to get ya, Skeeter!" Junior Wills taunted gleefully from his cell in the back of the jail.

"I'll remember you said that, Junior!" Skeeter hollered back as two more rounds struck the windowsill above his head, spewing splinters in his hair. A long minute passed with no gunfire, unnerving the old deputy until Sam Shade's baritone voice broke the silence.

"Throw down your guns, Skeeter, and open the jail and I'll spare ya. I got George Adams and Spence Lawton. I'll put a bullet in their heads iffin you don't."

If Skeeter could risk a glance, he would see Sam Shade standing across the street in front of Orson's tannery with George Adams and Spence Lawton kneeling in the dirt before him. Spence was the eldest of Bill Lawton's brood, a wiry, quick-tempered youth, whose arrogance caught him unawares by Shade's men. Sam Shade stood with the barrel of his Colt leveled at the back of Spence's head. Sam was a barrel-chested ruffian with hard hazel eyes and greasy brown hair that fell below his weathered hat. Tobacco-stained teeth filled his sneering mouth, framed by equally unkempt mustache and week-old stubble on his thick chin. His left meaty hand gripped the neck of George Adams, while Spence Lawton knelt to his right. Three years in prison thinned his robust waistline, which bulged less prominently upon his red and white checkered shirt. Off to his right, at the corner of the tannery, Willie Mann covered the jail with his rifle. Off to his left, at the corner of the mercantile, Lefty McCoy covered the side window of the jail with his .30-30. Winchester. Willie's younger brother, Dalton Mann, stood beside Sam, smoke drifting from the end of his pistol's barrel.

"Give it up, Skeeter, or we'll fill ya full o' holes!" Lefty shouted in his nasal voice.

"Shut your mouth, Lefty, before I put a second round in ya!" Ole Skeeter shouted back.

"He's under the window. Take 'em," Sam whispered to Dalton Mann.

Dalton nodded, stepping tentatively across the street. Skeeter knew something was amiss and withdrew to the main room's back door that led to the cells in the rear of the jail, crawling on all fours as quickly as his muscles would allow. Skeeter cleared the doorway with Junior Wills snarling face greeting him behind the bars of his cell. Dalton Mann's cautious approach gave Skeeter the time to take up position behind the rear door, his sawed-off shotgun leveled on the front window and doorway.

"Open your mouth, and I'll shoot you first!" Skeeter warned.

Junior Wills started to say something but closed his mouth and sat down on his bunk.

The sound of gunfire broke the air. Sam Shade turned as Willie Mann slumped to the ground, blood pooling in his shirt. More gunfire erupted behind him. Turning back, he observed Lefty McCoy cry out as he went down.

"Let them go, Sam!" Sheriff Thorton commanded, stepping into the street near Willie Mann's body with his rifle tucked into his right shoulder and pointing ominously at Sam's head.

Dalton Mann dropped his pistol into the street, pleading mercy with his hands raised.

"Go ahead and pull that trigger, Sheriff! It won't stop me from plugging these two," Sam spat as he tightened his grip on George Adams's neck.

"You aren't leaving here in one piece if you do!" Ethan said with his pistol covering Dalton as he stepped into the clear near Lefty McCoy's still corpse.

"This your new deputy, Sheriff?" Sam sneered, craning his neck in Ethan's direction. "He looks like a savage. What is he, half Comanche, Apache, Arapaho?" he snarled, twisting George Adams's neck with his pistol barrel pressed to the Lawton boy's head.

"And what if I was?" Ethan challenged.

"The only thing I hate more than the man who put me in prison is a filthy savage. Was your mother a Comanche squaw, boy?"

"Maybe she was. It's still a step above the whore that bore you," Ethan goaded.

"I came here to shoot you dead, Ben, but mayhap I'll kill your deputy instead!" Sam fixed Ethan with a murderous glare.

Ben kept the slack out of the trigger, waiting for any window to shoot without George or Spence being hurt. Ethan's goading had unnerved Sam, distracting the outlaw as he had to focus on too many sources of his anger.

"Let George and Spence be, Sam. Your fight is with me."

"Taint worth it, Sam. Livings better than dying," Dalton Mann pleaded, his hands still raised in surrender as he stood half between Sam and the jail.

"Shut your mouth, coward! Mr. Grierson will skin you once he finds out what a worthless cur you are!" he berated his comrade.

Boom!

The rifle bullet caved Sam Shade's skull. His lifeless corpse stood briefly before dropping into the dusty street. The shot caught Ethan by surprise as the smoke issuing from the barrel of the sheriff's rifle caught his eye. Time stopped in that eternal moment as if he were in a dream. His senses, which were always in tune in his own world, were severely dulled in this one.

George Adams and Spence Lawton released measured breaths, overcome with relief. The townsfolk soon flooded the street. Some were sympathetic and supporters of Sam Shade, but most were relieved, thankful, and curious.

CHAPTER 6

The day after Sam Shade was buried on boot hill, Deputy Marshal Jake Thorton rode into Red Rock in the company of a giant and a Kiowa boy. He nursed three broken ribs and a splint on his left ankle. He sat miserably in the saddle, the jarring of the trail doing him little good, but he looked markedly better than when Ethan first saw him. The afternoon sun shone painfully bright as the late autumn winds blew tumbleweeds down the street. Jake held his Winchester .30-30 across his lap, resting his right hand in the lever as his left hand held the reins of his dusty brown mare. He heard not a word of the happenings in Red Rock since sending Ethan in his place. He prayed his friend and Father were well but was ready if they were not. Krixan rode at his right, staring intently at his strange surroundings. He was expecting a settlement similar to Long Paws' village but was greeted with the odd mixture of adobe and wooden structures. His long sword felt out of place as the men he passed eyed it with curiosity. Fortunately, Ethan had the seamstress at Plexus make him a pair of buckskins and shirt to match his own. He wore a holster from one of the men they had killed protecting Jake, but it was ill-fitting for one of his size. Jake planned on finding his large friend one of proper size now that they were in town. Krixan hoped Ethan was alive and well or Queen Gabrielle's anguish would be too terrible to contemplate.

Long Paws rode to Jake's left, suffering the hostile glares of the townsfolk they passed. He tried his best to ignore them, holding his head high as they rode. He knew few of the white men's words, but he understood the word "savage," which they whispered in hushed tones.

"Jake!" John Custis shouted as he stepped through the swinging front doors of the Lucky Star.

"John." Jake tipped his hat as John came into the street to greet him.

"We heard you were hurt," John said, giving the giant who rode beside him a strange look.

"I still am," Jake answered. "Is my father well? I sent a friend along to help him over a week ago, he is—"

"Ethan," John added excitedly. "He came riding in about that time, told the sheriff how you were hurt and just yesterday helped him take down Sam Shade and his bunch. A right nice young fella."

"Ethan? Where is he?" Jake asked, his heart pounding, hoping both he and his father were safe.

"He's down at the jail with your father."

"Much obliged," Jake said before riding on.

Krixan followed Jake through the town, frustrated with his poor English. He never imagined such a handicap, likening the detriment to being deaf. At least those afflicted in Elaria could be cured by the touch of a mage healer. Fortunately, Jake was sympathetic to the big man's plight and helped him learn the native tongue, albeit at a painfully slow pace.

"Ethan," Jake said, looking at Krixan while pointing ahead. Krixan nodded. Following him in the direction indicated.

*****

"Sheriff! Sheriff Thorton!" Young Billy Wells shouted as he came running into the jail, finding Ben at his desk and Ethan sitting across from him cleaning a rifle.

"Slow down, Billy," Ben said. "What—"

"It's Jake, Sheriff. Jake's in town and riding this way. He's got an Injun boy and a giant with him!" Billy said excitedly, catching his breath.

Ben Thorton wasted little time clearing the doorway with Ethan close on his heel. He paused at the front of the jail, a grin playing across his weathered face as his son came riding down the street.

"You're a welcome sight, son," Ben said as Jake dismounted in front of the jail, using a cane to lean on as he tied his horse to the hitch post.

"So are you, Dad." He smiled, embracing his father. "I see you found your way, Ethan," he added as they parted.

"And I see you didn't lose Krixan along the way." Ethan grinned.

"He's a good man. He seems to be growing on me." Jake smiled as they both regarded the big man.

"Did you accomplish what you came here to do?" Krixan asked, his strange language drawing Ben's attention.

"Not yet, Krix. It's been pretty quiet around here in this peaceful town."

Krix snorted. He could always tell when Ethan was lying as it usually entailed his lips moving.

Ben welcomed them into the jail, sitting Jake in a chair to ease the pain in his leg. They were soon joined by Skeeter and Judge Donovan as Jake relayed all that transpired since the ambush, leaving out his time across the barrier in Astaria. It was a tale his father would never believe. He said how he and Long Paws were set upon by renegades and were spared by Ethan and Krixan's timely intervention. Skeeter, in turn, told Jake all that had transpired since Ethan rode into town. Jake leaned back in the chair with his right leg stretched out in front of him, resting his head against the far wall opposite Ben's desk. The others stood along the edge of the room. Ethan and Krixan stood near the front door with Long Paws beside Jake. Judge Donovan took a seat beside Ben's desk while Skeeter lingered near the rear door that led to the cell area.

"I reckon I missed all the action," Jake lamented.

"Sam Shade, Conrad Finch, Willie Mann, Lefty McCoy, and Stone Grierson, you've been in town little more than a week, Ethan and you nearly filled up boot hill. Any word on Hank Grierson? He sure won't take kindly to his son's killing," Jake said.

"Haven't heard a word out of him," Ben grunted, pouring himself a glass of whiskey as he sat on the edge of his desk.

"The fact that Stone was with Conrad Finch indicates Grierson's allegiance. I still don't know who sent the men that ambushed me at

Johnson's Ridge, and I don't think all these fellas you killed were working for Sam Shade," Jake said.

"Then who were they working for?" Ethan asked.

Hank Grierson was a wealthy cattle baron whose father carved out a sizable spread along the Pierna Mala. Hank took his father's ranch and grew a small cattle empire out of it, though Sheriff Thorton suspected he accomplished such a feat through nefarious means. He was rumored to rustle cattle in Mexico and selling them in Santa Fe. One of Ben's oldest friends was a captain in the Texas rangers out of El Paso. He told Ben that Mexican authorities were searching for rustlers that matched the description of several of Hank Grierson's ranch hands. If Grierson wasn't above stealing from Mexicans, he probably had no inhibitions about robbing stages or banks north of the Rio Grande. Hank Grierson held well-known ambitions to dominate access to the Pierna Mala River, knowing control of it would mean control of Red Rock. He used his amassed wealth to buy out the lands owned by the Franklins and Potters. Sam Shade should've remained in prison for twenty years. Only a man of Hank Grierson's connections could have arranged his parole.

"I have my suspicions," Ben finally answered.

"Who?" Ethan asked.

"Until we have more definitive proof, it's best we don't say," Judge Donovan warned. He and Ben had discussed Hank Grierson at length and didn't wish his name bandied about until they were certain of his culpability. And with Stone Grierson's death, they thought it best to let the situation play itself out. Either Hank would seek vengeance and blunder or would curtail his troublesome activities.

"Sheriff Thorton, may we come in?" The sweet feminine voice of Emily Adams rang through the closed doorway.

Ben gestured Ethan to open the door where he was greeted by the three smiling faces of Emily, Sara and, Connie May Adams, each holding a plate of food. Emily carried roast beef, Sara a dozen potatoes, and Connie May a loaf of freshly baked bread.

"Ladies," Ethan acknowledged, opening the door wide open for them to enter.

"Good morning, Ethan." Emily winked as she paraded past him and set the roast beef on Ben's desk.

"We heard of Jake's arrival and thought you boys would like something to eat," Sara said in her singsong voice as she and Connie May placed their plates upon the desk.

Ben shook his head, knowing full well the Adams girls didn't just whip up this meal for them. A roast takes hours to prepare.

"That is might nice of you girls," Judge Donovan said as he and Skeeter hovered over the baked treasures.

"Hi ya doin', Jake?" Connie May flirted.

"Just fine, Connie," Jake answered.

"And who is this?" Emily asked, running her eyes over Krixan's towering form.

"That's Ethan's friend, but he don't speak English," Skeeter said while stuffing a piece of bread in his mouth.

"He's learning. Emily, this is Krixan. Krixan, this is Emily, Sara, and Connie May," Jake introduced them.

"Nice to make your acquaintance, Krixan." Emily curtsied.

"Emily." Krixan bowed his head.

Ethan cringed at the gesture, wondering how Krixan could ever pass for anything other than what he was, a feudal warrior. He was even wearing his sword. Ethan hoped Jake had a good cover story for Krixan.

"Well, what language does he speak?" Sara asked.

"Russian," Jake said. "He's Ethan's cousin." Jake said Russian because he couldn't think of anyone in Red Rock who spoke it and chose the European country farthest afield.

"Oh, Jake, your poor leg," Connie May said kindly, coming to his side. "We heard tell that you were badly hurt."

"I'll live, Connie." Jake smiled politely. Connie was smitten with Jake since she was a little girl, and as she neared her fourteenth birthday, her amorous aspirations had not waned.

"He'll be fine, Connie. I'll have the Doc take a look at his leg, but I doubt he'll be up for any dancing at the Lawtons' party," Ben said.

After a time, the others started to filter out, leaving Jake, Ethan, Krixan, and Long Paws. The sheriff and Skeeter took their regular patrol around town. Jake winced as he worked the knots in his leg muscles. His right trouser leg was torn off to accommodate his leg dressings. Ethan poured him a shot of whiskey as Jake lifted his glass to toast his friend.

"Thanks, Ethan. You saved my neck in that ambush, and you saved my father."

"I didn't save your father, Jake, I only lent a hand. He don't need no help," Ethan said in perfect Texan.

"Well, I thank you all the same." He downed the glass. "What are your plans now, Ethan? I reckon you want to get back home."

Ethan released a measured breath, not having thought that far ahead. "I'd like to stay awhile and learn more about your land where men are free."

"Some men are freer than others." Jake sighed. "But you're welcome to stay as long as you like. I know my father's taken a liking to you, and he don't usually warm up to anybody."

"Then I'll stay." Ethan smiled, refilling Jake's glass. Krixan would be sure to give him an ear full about prolonging their stay, arguing rightfully so, how his father would tear him limb from limb for such an extended absence.

That's what he gets for trying to marry me off without my consent, Ethan mused, justifying his decision to stay in Red Rock. Besides, he was finally afforded what he always longed for—*freedom*. He planned to savor his time in this strangely familiar land of the free where nobles dared not dwell and men did not kneel.

＊＊＊＊＊

There's a yellow rose of Texas…

Abigail Lawton's voice carried over the festive crowd as a dozen couples danced in the grassy square. Abigail Lawton was a voluptuous woman of thirty-five years with chestnut hair and emerald-green eyes that sparkled when she looked at you. She was the wife of William Lawton and mother of their five children and possessed the sultriest voice in all West Texas.

The Lawton ranch rested along the western bank of the Pierna Mala, surrounded by two thousand acres of prime grazing land. Ethan, Krixan, and Jake sat at one of the tables brought outside as they listened to Mrs. Lawton sing and the townsfolk dance. Ethan found the song a lively tune that contrasted sharply to the drab, monotonous melodies of his native Astaria.

The days after the showdown with Sam Shade seemed to pass quickly. The sheriff replaced Krixan's ill-fitting gun belt with one his size and offered him clothing similar to his own, which the big man gladly took to blend in, though one of his size would never truly blend in. They even found him a large cream-colored Stetson that fit his thick head. Ethan refused a change of clothing, preferring his buckskins and simple pullover shirt to the garb favored by the townsfolk. Long Paws returned to his village, where Jake would fetch him upon his return to Fort Sill. Krixan missed the boy as they had grown quite fond of each other as they nursed Jake back to health. Though Krixan started to pick up English, his mastery of firearms was thus far disappointing. At this point, it might be better if he used the pistol to bash someone over the head.

"Come along, Ethan." Sara Adams took him by the hand, dragging him to the dancing square.

"I'm not much of a dancer, Sara. You might—"

"Don't be silly. A big handsome boy like you should have no problem dancing with a shy girl like me." She smiled, pulling him along.

"I don't know this dance."

"Don't fret, Ethan, I'll teach you the steps. It's time you learned how we dance in Texas."

He noticed her sister Emily take Krixan in tow and thought it might be amusing watching the clumsy giant dance to her tune. George Adams stood at the edge of the square nervously watching his girls as Judge Donovan spoke in his ear, doubtless not hearing what the judge was saying. Widow Perkins had managed to drag

John Custis from the food table to dance with her, while Sheriff Thorton and Bill Lawton struck up a conversation where Bill did all the talking.

"Listen, Ben," Bill Lawton explained in his Texas drawl. "You and I know Hank Grierson is behind this whole mess. Hell, the whole town knows it fer sure. His boy, Stone, was with that Finch Fella, waiting fer Sam. And we all know what Sam Shade was fixin' ta do. He wanted you dead, Ben. Then when he does show up, he's with three of Grierson's ranch hands. What about the two you're holdin' in the jail? Junior Wills and the younger Mann boy, I'm sure a little persuasion and they'll tell ya who put 'em up to it. I say we gather up a posse and arrest Grierson TODAY."

"I can't arrest a man on hearsay and my own suspicions, Bill. Besides, Junior Wills and Dalton Mann ain't sayin' a word."

"Dag blast it, Ben, they threatened my boy!" Bill roared. "Sam Shade put his gun at the back of Spence's head, lest you're forgetting."

"Sam Shade's dead, Bill."

"And Hank Grierson put him up to it, Ben. How long do you think he'll wait before hiring a new gunslinger to shoot you dead? He'll do for the judge, too, before taking over the rest of the town, placing his lackeys in your posts. At that point the rest of us are as good as dead. I ain't waitin', Ben. You say the word, and between the Millers and me, I can get you twenty deputies in an hour."

"Aye, we may need them, but not yet. Let Junior and Dalton's trials run their course, then we'll see what action should follow. I'm not ready to start a range war just yet."

"You're still gonna need some more men."

"I just got two, and by the looks of that big fella, you could say I found three." Ben's gaze followed Ethan and Krixan as they danced with the Adams girls.

"I hope they shoot better than they dance." Bill made a face as they both nearly stumbled over their partners' feet.

"Ethan's plenty quick on the draw. Accurate too. The giant fella, he don't shoot too good, but he's strong as an ox. He should make folks behave just by lookin' at 'em funny. They come awful cheap too."

"Cheap? How cheap?"

"Ten dollars a month plus room and board in the jailhouse. The town threw in new holsters and guns for good measure, and Jake gave Ethan Bull for saving his life. The big fella doesn't have a horse. He rode in on one lent him to him by Jake's Indian guide, so I'll have—"

"He can have one of mine. I have plenty of horses, and you'll need all the help you can get."

"That's right generous of you, Bill."

"Bah, think nothing of it. What are two fellas like them doing in these parts with no horses anyhow?" Bill made a face.

"Don't rightly know," Ben answered in a casual manner to deflect further inquiry of Ethan's origin. Ben wasn't sure where Ethan hailed from, but it wasn't Ohio. The boy spoke Krixan's native tongue, whatever strange language it was that the giant spoke, though Ben was certain it wasn't Russian. He also doubted Krixan was Ethan's cousin as he claimed. Whatever secret Ethan was keeping, Jake seemed to be privy. It all made little sense. The only thing he was certain of was Ethan's loyalty. The boy was genuine in his offer to help. If Jake trusted Ethan, then that was enough for Ben.

It was then that the craggy voice of Gus Lawton drew the ears of those gathered near the dance square. He was the grizzled elder patriarch of the Lawton clan since the passing of Bill Sr., five years before. Though the Lawton ranch belonged to Bill Junior, he often deferred to his uncle. Gus Lawton had a portly belly and gray whiskers above his dark beard. He wore his six-shooters over chaps and a gray checkered shirt.

"I ain't no match for my nephew's wife's lovely voice, but I'll give a try," Gus said with a guitar in hand as he regarded his fellow bandmates to follow his lead, plucking an old Texas cavalry song.

Ethan danced to the merry tune with each of the Adams girls, the widow Perkins, Mary Brown and her sister Lily, and Jodi Lawton, who, despite her wild beauty, complained about having to wear a dress. Ethan wondered how he ever mistook her for a boy when he first saw her, but she was no boy now.

"What are you staring at?" She growled as her brown eyes looked up at him through the gold curls that framed her young face. She wore a yellow dress with full petticoats that well displayed her feminine curves.

"You clean up right nicely, Jodi." Ethan smiled as they danced.

"Well, don't go getting yourself used to seeing me like this. My mother made me wear this stupid dress and iffin you poke fun at me, I'll whop you up side your thick head." She'd have shaken a fist at him if he let go of her hands.

"I'll keep my mouth shut for your sake, Jodi, though you do look right pretty," he spoke with a perfect Texas drawl.

She didn't know if she should blush or smack him.

"Don't be mad at your ma, Jodi. Mothers are like that. I remember countless times my ma had me dressed in ridiculous outfits whenever important people paid us a visit."

"At least she didn't make you wear a dang dress," Jodi pouted.

If only you knew, Ethan kept that thought to himself.

"I ought not be short with you at all, Ethan. You and the sheriff did save my brother's life the other day when Sam Shade had his gun barrel aimed at his head. Thank you," she said.

"The sheriff did most of it. I just helped a little by finishing off Lefty after Skeeter wounded him."

"That's a whole lot more than most folks would do. The sheriff is a brave man, but even the bravest need help. That's what my pa always says."

"He's got Skeeter. He's a lot more help than—"

"Skeeter's nice and all, but he's an old man. You're the help the sheriff needs, Ethan. You're fast with a gun. That's all the whole town is talking about, how the sheriff has found himself a deputy as fast and deadly as Jake."

"I'm just lucky to still be alive. I'm not that fast or accurate. I'm not that smart either."

"Tell that to Stone Grierson or Lefty McCoy." Jodi smiled.

"You give me more than my due, Jodi, but I'm obliged for your faith in me. You would do me a great service if you took care of Krixan for me for the rest of this fine day."

"Why? Where are ya going?"

"Back to town. Skeeter's watching the jail, and I promised to relieve him so he could ride out here and have some of your mom's apple cobbler."

"You best get going, or else there'll be none left once he gets here. The judge has already had two servings."

*****

The river road paralleled the western bank of the Pierna Mala, taking him straight into town five miles ahead. The late autumn wind blew dust in the air as tiny swirls spun along the surface of the dirt trail. West Texas was a harsh, arid, and unforgiving climate, but Ethan found it strangely appealing. But it wasn't the land that drew him to this place; it was the freedom. It was a land without kings and lords, where men were ruled by laws instead of the whims of a privileged few. It was a land where no man knelt. It was a land worth dying for. The only regret that clouded his spirit was the fact he could not stay here forever.

The last thing Ethan remembered this day was the sound of gunfire.

*****

When Ethan finally opened his eyes, he found himself abed in a poorly lit room with the small window facing him providing the only light. It was still daylight, and he wondered how he arrived at this strange place. He noticed that a blanket was tucked under his chin. He struggled to rise, but the pain in his right side would not suffer him to do so. He dropped his head back onto his pillow in frustration. He was naked under the covers, save for his undergarment that only covered his loins. He noticed his clothing and guns resting upon a small table on the room's near wall. The sunlight peeking through the window told him it was daytime still. How long had he been out? And how did he come to be here?

"You're awake."

Ethan craned his neck to the voice, finding Jake sitting in a rocking chair in the corner with his left leg propped up on a stool, and a rifle resting across his lap.

"Wh…" He tried to form words through his hoarse throat.

"Where are you? In Judge Donovan's spare bedroom where you've spent the past day and a half."

"Wh…Wha…What hap…"

"You were shot by Nate Grierson. Lucky for you, the bullet went clear through and missed your spine. The doc thinks you'll be all right but a mite sore for a spell."

"I…guess this…I guess this confirms my ability to heal is impaired in your world."

"Afraid so, Ethan. Krix wanted to take you back to the cave and return to Astaria so you could heal yourself, but you'd have bled out on the trail."

"So this is how it feels for everyone else." Ethan smiled weakly.

"Welcome to Texas. You're here two weeks, and you've already been shot. Now you can experience the healing process like the rest of we poor mortals."

"It's a pleasure." Ethan winced, shifting painfully to find a more comfortable position.

"Take it easy, Ethan, or you'll undo all of Doc's hard work of patchin' you back together. Besides the gunshot, you broke a couple of ribs when you fell off Bull's back."

"So that's what hurts so much. I guess we make a fine pair, broken ribs and all."

"I reckon so." Jake grinned. At least Ethan was taking it all in good humor.

"Where is Bull? Is he…"

"Krixan's taking good care of him, when he's not guarding the jail and watching over you like a bear-sized nursemaid."

"Where is Krixan now?"

"Over at the jail, guarding Nate Grierson and the others."

"Nate Grierson?"

"Stone's younger brother," Jake answered before further explaining. "He's the one who shot you. A number of us heard the gunshot and were able to track him down before he returned to his father's ranch. He wanted revenge for you killing his brother. His old man is out of the area tending other matters, or he'd have reeled the boy in, but now we have an even bigger mess. My father expects an attempt to free Nate Grierson, so we are keeping a tight watch on the jail, now that Hank Grierson is back from wherever he was."

"And you're guarding me," Ethan sighed, rolling his eyes.

"Just returning a favor to a certain brash Astarian prince who rescued my bacon from the frying pan. If Grierson wants you, he'll have to come over me to get to you. Besides, I'm not much use for anything else with my leg like it is." He regarded his outstretched limb with its splint.

"Thanks, Jake. Did the doc say how long I'll be..."

"At least a couple of weeks, Ethan. You might as well get used to that bed 'cause you'll be fixed to it for a while."

Panic washed over him at the thought of such confinement. *Two weeks!* How could he endure it? Ethan was used to constant activity. Moments of levity were ill-suited to his restless spirit.

"Oh, it's not the end of the world, Ethan. You'll be up and around in no time. Since you'll be laid up a bit, the judge brought you some things to read to pass the time." Jake pointed to the books stacked on the table by his bedside.

Ethan reached out, taking the bound cover of the first book into his hand. "*Ivanhoe?*" he read aloud.

"I told the judge you might fancy that one in particular. It's a fictional account of events in our long-ago past set in England. The other books are pure history, mostly of the United States, a little Roman, some medieval, and one on the Mongols."

*****

He closed the book, setting it aside and fetching another from the generous stack. The waning daylight cast lengthened shadows through the far window as Ethan devoured the first pages of the next text. For five days, he immersed himself in the history and culture of his adopted home. He read *Ivanhoe* in one sitting, struck by the familiarity of the setting and smiling as he read of Sir Wilfred challenging all the Norman knights to joust by slapping their standards as he passed. He read with great interest the founding of the United States, its very existence a repudiation of the merits of monarchy. It was a land where men aspired to greatness not upon the height of their birth, but the drive and ability of their character. The story of the American Revolution kept him on the edge of his seat throughout its telling. The ebb and flow of that conflict shifted like a pendulum, favoring one side then the other until the fates granted the miraculous victory to the colonials. The expansion and settling of the west drew the greatest interest with colorful characters like Jim Bridger, Daniel Boone, and George Rogers Clark. He marveled at the exploits of Wyatt Earp, Doc Holiday, and Bill Hickok. Jake's friend and fellow deputy Marshal Bass Reeves's exploits exceeded those of Earp and Hickok. Born a slave, he escaped his master in 1862 and made his way to the Oklahoma territory, where he learned to shoot and came to know that inhospitable land. He was later hired on by Marshal Fagan as a deputy and since then had been in dozens of shootouts, killing more men than Earp and Hickok combined. The fact that he served so many years in the most dangerous territory in the west and still lived was a testament to the man's skill and fortitude. Ethan reflected that despite all its wonder, even America was accursed with the institution of slavery. How could a republic based upon the belief that all men are free abide the subjugation of an entire race of people? He had asked this of Judge Donovan one night.

"Governments are not good or bad, they are merely instruments wielded by men," the judge had explained. "Wickedness springs freely from the heart of man, and we must forever tame our basest inclinations. To do so, we must impair the implementation of such desires. The folly of despots and monarchists resides in the false belief that said individuals are inherently good and can be trusted to rule with pure intentions. The sad truth, Ethan, is that men are inherently evil and can never be trusted with the levers of power. The authority of government *requires* a full separation of powers, with checks and balances divided among multiple parties to curb the ability of any group to suppress another. The scourge of slavery is a blight on mankind since the days of antiquity, and it could not end with just our revolution. Rather than lament its existence, let us rejoice in the difficulty expunging it from our land, for only equal suffering could ever foster its return, and that is a price none would be willing to suffer."

Ethan reflected on the truth of the judge's theory. How often had the history of his own world confirmed what the judge had spoken? The history of Astaria was replete with tales of good kings who ruled wisely before dying and passing on their power to spoiled princelings whose rule served their own self-interest. Their reigns often disintegrated into utter depravity.

Jake had stepped without as Sara Adams brought him a steaming bowl of her mother's chili. She sat and shared all the gossip in town while Ethan pretended to care. She was a sweet girl, so he endured her banter. Most of the townsfolk were a friendly sort once they accepted you in their community. Sheriff Thorton was the toughest nut to crack, and Ethan managed to win him over within minutes of arriving in town, everyone else sort of fell in line thereafter. Sara eventually excused herself as she was expected home. The judge soon replaced her, taking a chair by Ethan's bedside. Judge Donovan and the sheriff were the best of friends, but there weren't two different personalities in all of West Texas. Ben Thorton was a somber, ornery old lawman of few words, whereas Judge Donovan was a boisterous extrovert who took a liking to people with relative ease. He would talk with Ethan for hours on all matter of subjects, expounding on topics as far-ranging as scientific discoveries to ladies' fashions. Oh, how the judge loved to talk about the fairer sex. He had been wed twice, losing his first wife to typhoid and the second to childbirth. He had a daughter from his second wife, who was now wed to a gunsmith in St. Louis. His Beautiful Bonnie, he would call her.

"Find yourself a good woman, Ethan. Settle down and give her a dozen babies. There be no greater thing a man can do than to father children and see to their upbringing," he said as he leaned his heavy frame back in the chair.

"You sound like my parents, Judge. If I wasn't here, they'd be fixin' to hitch my wagon to the nearest filly they could find." Ethan grinned.

"That's how all parents are, lad. We all want grandkids someday, and some of our offspring need a wee bit o' cajoling. I was like you when I was a lad, itching to explore the world, and explore it I did. I was a cabin boy on a whalin' ship in Boston. I took my earnings when I was sixteen and set out west, looking for adventure. Those were the days, my boy," the judge's eyes fondly recalled.

"So what's going to happen with the Grierson boy that shot me?" Ethan asked, changing the subject.

"Well, I don't rightly know. I put in a change of venue to avoid jury suppression by his old man, but Hank Grierson managed to stay that request by the county. While we're waitin' to decide to proceed with a local trial, Grierson is busy hiring guns."

"Guns?"

"Luke Crawford. He's a notorious gunslinger from Abilene. A right dangerous fella, that one. Word is he'll be at the Grierson ranch by tomorrow."

*****

Two nights later found Ethan fast asleep when the sounds of rifle fire woke him from his slumber. He stumbled out of bed, barely able to gain his feet as he affixed his gun belt and made his way for the door. Judge Donovan met him in the outer room, wearing naught but his nightshirt and a shotgun in hand.

"You should be abed, Ethan. You ain't going to do much good in your current state."

Save for his loin garment, bandages, and six-shooters, Ethan was as naked as a jaybird. Ethan retrieved his Stetson from its place on the hat rack beside the front door and placed it upon his head as if that would cover his nakedness. The judge shook his head as they stepped without. Once in the street, Ethan limped gingerly, trying to keep pace with the judge as they made their way toward the jail. Once crossing over the adjoining street near the Adam's Mercantile, they spied Krixan in the front of the jail beating out flames that spread out across the wooden porch that ran the length of the jail.

The big man swung a heavy blanket, dousing the flames as they drew near.

"That's far 'nough!" Skeeter's graveled voice rang out as the barrel of his sawed-off shotgun peeked through the front door of the jail. Krixan dropped the blanket and drew his holstered Colt, before lowering it as he recognized the half-naked men.

"Dang it, Skeeter, it's us!" Judge Donovan shouted as ole Skeeter poked his head through the door.

"I'd've figured it was you sooner if I wasn't wondering what in the tar nation two naked men were doing in the middle of the street," Skeeter squawked.

"We were in a hurry to save your behind. Next time I'll let your bacon stay in the fire while I get fully dressed," the judge growled irritably. "What happened here anyway?"

"Attempted jailbreak," Ben's craggy voice echoed behind them.

They turned as Ben came up the street with his Henry rifle in hand.

"They set fire to the front of the jail before tying ropes to the bars on Nate Grierson's cell window and yanking it free," Ben explained. Unfortunately for his would-be rescuers, the sheriff had shackled Nate's right ankle to the bars in his cell door. Their attempts to shoot the shackle chain alerted Ben, Skeeter, Krixan, and Jake from the fire to the rear of the jail. Krixan put out the fire, while Jake covered the prisoners and Skeeter covered the front. Ben pursued the would-be rescuers to the edge of town where they disappeared into the night.

"You best get inside Judge before your posterior pokes out of your nightshirt. I'll have a hard-enough time sleepin' tonight without that image in my brain," Ben said tiredly as he stepped past them and entered the jail.

By that time, the street was filling up with curious onlookers. Ethan did not care to gift them a show of his nearly naked form and quickly followed the sheriff inside. The judge sent Skeeter back to his place to fetch him and Ethan their clothes. The old deputy chuckled and stepped without. Ethan leaned against Ben's desk, nursing his side as blood seeped through his bandages.

"You fool kid," Ben growled, noticing the bleeding wound.

"I'm all right, Sheriff." Ethan winced.

"Yeah, you look it," Jake chided as he sat in the chair facing the open door to the cell area where he trained the barrel of his Winchester.

"I best have Skeeter fetch Doc Wilson when he gets back. He might have to sew you up again," Ben said, scrubbing his face with his left hand.

"What now do we do?" Krixan struggled with the words as his English progressed as well as could be expected.

"Tomorrow I'll ride out to the Lawton and Miller ranches and tell them to stay put and tell the other ranchers the same. Jake, you send word to El Paso. Tell them to send whatever Marshals they can spare and move the Grierson boy out of Red Rock. Meanwhile, we should all stay close and keep our eyes open."

CHAPTER 7

The Grierson ranch, eight miles southeast of Red Rock

Cole Grierson stood in the great room of the ranch house with his head bowed as his father berated him for his clumsy attempt to free his brother from jail. Hank Grierson towered over his slight-built fifteen-year-old son, the youngest of his brood. At sixty-nine inches and gray overtaking his dark-brown hair, Hank Grierson had seen more winters than he cared to remember. He was one of the first settlers along the Pierna Mala and planned to stake his claim to the entire valley when a score of homesteaders sprouted up along *his* river before he could do so. If not for the damnable war of Northern Aggression, he would've achieved his goal, but the carpetbagging Yankees imposed taxes, which drained his cash flows. After that, he felt no qualms about rustling cattle from his neighbors and selling them across the border and vice versa. Nor did he raise any moral objection to order the robbing of stages and trains.

He amassed great wealth, which he planned to use to eventually buy out his neighbors, using the softer tactics to coerce them, preferring the carrot to the stick. Most refused to sell, however, so he employed ruffians to raise hell throughout Red Rock Township, making life in town intolerable, the first of his many plans to increasingly force them to sell. This plan went quickly awry as the townsfolk hired a Yankee-loving sheriff who brought his men to heel and sending Sam Shade to prison. Sheriff Thorton never traced the men back to Hank Grierson, allowing him to operate without the law breathing down his neck. Using his connections throughout the state, he arranged the release of Sam Shade, who would rid him of the meddlesome Sheriff Thorton under the guise of revenge for having thrown him in prison. The sheriff's US marshal son was to be killed first, with the sheriff none the wiser until Sam Shade showed up in Red Rock to finish him. With the sheriff dead, chaos would ensue as he carefully planned, then he would step in to restore order after many of the larger landowners were killed. He would purchase their defunct holdings on the cheap and establish an apparent cattle empire until the true wealth of the Pierna Mala was revealed. The valley contained a rich silver vein that was unbeknownst to all but Hank Grierson and his foreman Emmitt Cobb. He refused to mine it, fearing a silver rush would drive up the price of his neighbors' property. He would wait until he owned *all* the surrounding land before exploiting his find. He could then build an empire to rival the Vanderbilts or the Morgans.

Alas, all his plans were foiled by the sheriff's new deputy, Ethan Blagen. He saved Jake Thorton from the men Hank hired to ambush him and arrived in town in time to warn the sheriff about Sam Shade. He killed his eldest son and helped the sheriff kill Sam Shade. His second son took upon himself to kill the deputy, and now he was held for attempted murder. That left him his last son, Cole, who risked his fool life trying to free his brother.

"I told you to stand clear!" Hank Grierson growled. "You're as dense as your fool brothers. You'll stay here at the ranch until I'm finished with Sheriff Thorton and his new deputy."

"You gonna kill 'em, Pa?" Cole asked.

"Yes, I'm gonna kill 'em, but we have to tread carefully. When I move on Sheriff Thorton, it'll be swift and thorough."

*****

The town was on edge in the weeks leading up to the trial of Nathaniel Grierson. The Red Rock bugle was strangely silent on the events surrounding the confrontation with Sam Shade and the arrest of the Grierson boy. The editor of the small newspaper, Carl Wheeler, was a close friend to Hank Grierson, and there were whispers that his editorial prerogatives were compromised. Judge Donovan was struggling to find an attorney to prosecute the case as his first choice, the Honorable Thomas McCade, had gone missing. The advantage of the passing of time was Jake and Ethan's recovery. Ethan was back on his feet and had recovered his gun speed while improving his accuracy. Jake was getting by with the use of a cane, but it didn't hinder his gun handling.

It was a late autumn day as the sun hung low in the clear western sky when Judge Donovan ordered Nathaniel Grierson to appear. The courthouse was actually the schoolhouse where Judge Donovan also served as the town's schoolmaster. He sent the children home at noon, before ordering Nate Grierson brought before him. The judge's plan to change venue was denied by the county and his appeals to the state had received no response. He had no attorney to prosecute the case, and there was no word from the Grierson patriarch. Did the boy's father plan to provide a defense? Hank Grierson was a hard, ruthless man, but he was ever loyal to his blood. Judge Donovan couldn't conduct an adequate trial in Red Rock, and the state court system was blocked. He had little choice but to remand the case to the federal court, but he had to first officially order the defendant to remain in town custody until arrangements could be made to surrender him to the US marshals. Jake couldn't transport the prisoner by himself, so he would wait for reinforcements. The judge figured thirty days would be sufficient until transport could be arranged.

Ethan and Ben escorted Nate Grierson from the jail, leaving Krixan and Skeeter to guard the other prisoners. The court was two blocks from the jail, along the same street. Nate's hands were chained in front of him, and a long shackle connected his ankles, providing him ample stride to walk but not run. Jake was already at the court with Judge Donovan and Mayor Dale McDonald, who would witness the proceeding. Ben noticed the front doors of the Lucky Star closed and barred off to his right. John Custis never closed the saloon, and that cautioned the craggy sheriff's usual steely nerve. In fact, there wasn't a soul in sight as every door was locked and shades drawn as the autumn winds blew tumbleweeds along the dusty avenue.

"Get back to the jail, Ethan!" Ben growled, leveling his Henry rifle on Nate's belly, motioning him to turn about. No sooner had

Nate turned, then a dozen men filed into the street, blocking them from the jail. Ben recognized one as Emmitt Cobb, Hank Grierson's foreman. He was a portly, snarly fellow with a pockmarked face and a right-handed draw. He was average height at five foot nine and wore a plain tan shirt, black vest, chaps, spurs, and a deep brown Stetson that hung below his brow, shielding his cruel brown eyes. Emmitt stood beside a cocksure youngster with twin tied-down holsters. He had greasy, unkempt black hair that framed the virgin beard that failed to mask his baby face. He was a bit young, but Ben Thorton knew a hired gun when he saw one. The others were a mixture of Grierson ranch hands and men he did not know.

Ethan stood at Ben's side, his hands hovering over his pistols, his breath holding in the narrows of his throat as his pounding heart thumped audibly in his ears. Twenty paces separated them as Ben held his rifle at Nate's back. Any move and he wouldn't hesitate to blow a hole in Hank's boy.

"Release the boy, Sheriff, then clear town. Take yer deputies and son with ya, and we'll let ya live," Emmitt said with a mocking sneer.

"A sheriff don't run like a whipped dog, Emmitt. You boys best walk away," Ben warned.

"Sheriff's resign all the time, old-timer. You just be real smart like and resign right now. Don't worry about the town, Mr. Grierson will hire himself a new sheriff," the baby-faced gunslinger mocked.

"You're long on mouth and short on brains, son. You best clear out. I won't say it again!" Ben growled.

"I ain't yer son, old-timer. My name's Robert *Crawford*, mayhap ya heard of me." He grinned menacingly as if his name held great import.

"Never heard of you," Ben said.

"No?" Bobby Crawford's voice raised two octaves. "Well, mayhap you heard of my brother *Luke*? He's just outside yer courthouse with Mr. Grierson."

Ben's eyes narrowed at that statement. Hank Grierson was rumored to have hired Luke Crawford, a fast draw and known killer, and if he was outside the courthouse, that put him behind them.

Ben could ill afford to steal a glance behind him with twelve men threatening his front.

"Here he comes now." Bobby grinned, his eyes briefly leaving Ben and Ethan, fixing over their shoulders and up the street.

Panic took Ethan's heart. They had to deal with the threat in front of them before the others closed in behind. Once Bobby Crawford shifted his eyes, Ethan made his move.

Emmitt Cobb's confident sneer fell as Ethan cleared leather with blinding speed. Before Emmitt's finger grazed the handle of his holstered Remington, Ethan's first bullet took Bobby Crawford in the chest. His second struck the man beside Bobby in the gut. The third took Emmitt in his gun arm, just above the elbow.

Ben shifted his aim to the men on Emmitt's left, working the lever of his Henry rifle in rapid succession, dropping three before something stung his right thigh. His adrenaline drowned the pain as he continued to fire. He saw Krixan and Skeeter emerge from the front of the jail, shooting into the back of the line of men, driving off those that remained standing.

Ben and Ethan turned, catching sight of a dozen other men coming up the street behind them, smoke obscuring their blurry image. Ben clubbed Nate Grierson with the butt of his rifle, knocking him to the dirt before emptying his last shot at the approaching threat. He tossed the rifle aside and drew his pistol as Ethan struggled to reload one of his six-shooters. Rifle fire echoed further up the street as Jake, and Judge Donovan took up aim from the courthouse, catching their opponents in a cross fire. Ethan had two shells remaining in his left Colt while he fumbled, reloading the other.

Ben stumbled to his knees as he lifted the barrel of his pistol, fixing a blurry silhouette in his sights before firing off a round. He could see the figure drop, the man's body flopping in the street. His vision faded briefly, then returned enough to find Hank Grierson's hawkish brown eyes fixing him in the sights of his double-barrel twelve-gauge. The twin barrels loomed ominously as Ben struggled to lift his aim to Hank, when he saw the elder Grierson topple over.

Ethan shifted his aim from the older man he just shot, who he correctly guessed was Hank Grierson, to the wiry built fellow with pale-green eyes and a vicious scar running the left side of his face. His greasy black hair and lean face looked similar to the gunslinger he shot first, the one calling himself Robert Crawford. This was likely his brother Luke, whom Ben spoke of as a dangerous killer. Ethan lost sight of him as gun smoke obscured his line of sight. Deafened by gunfire, Ethan could poorly discern the muffled shouts that echoed all around them. As the smoke cleared, Luke Crawford was gone, along with Emmitt Cobb and a dozen others. The still bodies of Hank Grierson, Bobby Crawford, and several others littered the street. The screams of gunshot men rent the air in a morbid meld of uncomfortable moans to gut-wrenching agony. He noticed Krixan and Skeeter move among the fallen, kicking guns away from the wounded. Rifle fire sounded in the distance, though Ethan couldn't ascertain their direction. He moved to Ben's side as the aged sheriff lie upon the ground, blood pooling in his right pant leg, oozing through the brown wool. He quickly stripped the shirt off Bobby Crawford's still form and rushed back to Ben, binding the material around his leg.

"You done good, Ethan." Ben winced painfully as if his leg were on fire.

Ethan nodded, patting Ben's shoulder as Krixan and Jake approached from opposing directions. Others filtered into the street, helping Skeeter and the judge gather up weapons and seeing to the wounded.

"Help me move him inside," Jake said as he struggled to bend down on his stiff leg.

"We'll move him, Jake. You fetch Doc Wilson," Ethan said as he attempted to lift Ben. Krixan pushed him aside and scooped Ben up into his arms as if he were a wee babe and carried him into the jail. Ethan and Jake shook their heads and smiled for Ben Thorton was a large man.

*****

Jake and Ethan waited in the parlor of Mrs. Anderson's boardinghouse when the door to the bedroom finally opened, and Doc

Wilson called them in. Stepping within, they were greeted by Ben's sleeping form on the bed, wearing naught but a nightshirt and thick bandages wrapped around his leg. "Why don't you boys open up that window over there? The chloroform is a bit strong in here," Doc said as he washed his hands in the bowl on the dresser.

"How's he doing, Doc?" Jake asked as Ethan opened the window.

"He's fine. I dug the bullet out and stitched him up. He'll be a mite tender for a while, so he'll need to be abed a few days. Of course, like I was worried with both of your injuries, we must watch to see if infection creeps in. I cleaned the wound and applied some molds that are favored by your Indian friends, just like I did with you, Ethan. So we'll just wait and see," Doc Wilson explained, wiping his hands with a towel.

"Fat chance of keeping him in bed," Jake snorted. "He'll insist on walking out of here as soon as he wakes."

"We'll just have Krixan sit on him. That oughta keep him still." Ethan grinned.

"If that's what it takes," Doc said. "I figure Skeeter can be acting sheriff for a few days."

"He'll enjoy that," Jake chuckled.

They left Ben resting and returned to the jail to meet with Judge Donovan. Hank Grierson and Bobby Crawford were confirmed dead, along with two of Grierson's ranch hands and another hired gun. Several others suffered various wounds, two of which might be mortal, but time would tell. Luke Crawford, Emmitt Cobb, and a dozen others fled town. Skeeter filled out wanted posters on each of them. Before nightfall, they would gather a posse and set out to find them.

CHAPTER 8

Red Rock returned to relative calm over the proceeding weeks. The dead were buried, the wounded tended, and the trials of Nate Grierson and the others finally proceeded without the political roadblocks thrown up by the deceased Grierson patriarch. Several posses returned empty-handed as Emmitt Cobb and Luke Crawford simply disappeared into the backwaters of West Texas. Jake departed soon after; his body healed enough to resume his duties. Bass Reeves was probably wondering when he would show up at Fort Sill. Before he bade farewell, he took Ethan out of town to assess his gun speed and marksmanship and to hone his skills. Ethan's speed and accuracy matched his own, and Jake felt he was equal to the task of facing Luke Crawford should the gunslinger return. Jake wondered when Ethan would return to Astaria, but his friend seemed content to stay in Red Rock for the foreseeable future. Returning to town, he packed his horse and said his farewells. The Adams girls baked bread and cakes for him to eat on the trail. They stood beside his father, who leaned on a crutch as his leg healed, waving their goodbyes in front of the jail. Ethan offered to return Bull to Jake, but he refused, claiming that the spotted palomino belonged to Ethan now. Ethan repaid his friend with several gold pieces from his saddle pack that he brought with him from Astaria. Jake refused the gift, saying that the Marshal Service would replace his mount. Besides, Bull took a liking to Ethan, and Jake was loath to separate horse from man.

"When you do finally go home, give that pretty sister of yours my regards," Jake tipped his dusty cream Stetson before turning his horse and riding on.

"Will do," Ethan smiled as his friend disappeared down the avenue.

The following Sunday found the sheriff, Ethan, and Krixan in church at the behest of Parson Green, who badgered poor Ben for weeks to attend. Refusing to suffer alone, the sheriff dragged his two young deputies along to share in the fun. Krixan understood little of the sermon as he continued to struggle with the Americans' language. Ethan found the Americans' religion surprising considering their independent nature. The parson spoke of their deity washing the feet of his followers, as if their God were a servant, the same God who rose up the weak to triumph over the strong. Such a religion would be met with resistance in Elaria by the ruling mage born who saw their power justifying their dominion over lesser men. Ethan found such a revelation riveting and attended church every Sunday thereafter.

With the Christmas season soon upon them, Ben and Skeeter spent their evenings in the sheriff's office, whittling wooden horses, toy guns, and dolls to gift the poorer children in town when the twenty-fifth of December rolled around. Ethan and Krixan were soon recruited in the endeavor, helping to build and paint toy soldiers and deliver cloth and cotton to the Adams sisters to sew clothing and hair on the dolls they made. Come the eve of the special day, they followed Ben around town, helping him set out the treasures under the decorated trees in each home. Ethan found the festive season as inviting as the winter solstice celebration in Astaris. Several ladies of Parson Green's congregation visited each home, singing carols as passersby greeted each other with heartfelt good wishes. Ethan spent one afternoon gathering up blankets, canteens, and cookware, traveling to Long Paws' village to deliver the gifts. His young friend was off with Jake, but his kin insisted upon a fair exchange, offering Ethan another set of frayed leather trousers and two leather pullover shirts.

The trial of Nate Grierson received little fanfare considering the chaos his arrest first caused. The jury found him guilty, and the judge sentenced him to twenty years for attempted murder, leaving Cole Grierson as the sole heir of the once-powerful clan. Having suffered three shootouts in a short time, Red Rock received little notoriety from its violence as the story was little reported. Ben Thorton found it strange that the gunfight at the OK Corral made the eastern papers when only three fatalities resulted in that melee. His battles with Grierson's bunch far exceeded that total, and it barely registered a blurb in the El Paso papers, much to Mayor McDonald's delight. No officeholder wanted their town to be considered a lawless frontier post.

The last Saturday before Christmas found them at the McPherson ranch attending the annual Christmas Cattle Ball. Gabe McPherson's barn was decked out in holly and mistletoe with tables filled with varied dishes brought by the town's ladies and a roasted steer cut from his herd. A large dancing area was cleared in the center of the barn with fiddlers plucking lively tunes. Ethan was dragged onto the dance floor more than once as the Adams sisters, Laura McPherson, and Agnes Miller each took a turn at him as "The Yellow Rose of Texas" repeated in the background. The Texans surely loved that tune, and Ethan found it to his liking. He always hated dancing in the formal galas in Astaris but found them strangely enjoyable in West Texas. The Americans reveled in freedom, and it manifested itself in all their activities, especially their dance and their music.

Another month would pass, and Krixan urged his wayward friend to return home as they were long overdue. Ethan rightly feared that once they returned to Astaria, that his father would forbid him from crossing ever again. Knowing forgiveness was more easily obtained than permission, he decided to write a letter reassuring his sire that all was well and that he was attending important matters on this side of the barrier. Using paper from Judge Donovan's desk, he wondered how it would be received as it was unlike the rolled parchment used in his native Astaria. Ethan rolled his note around a long stone to weigh it down. He and Krixan journeyed to Johnson's Ridge, where the barrier rested upon the rocky hillside. As Ethan drew nigh, part of the rocky cliff face transitioned into a shimmering dark surface. Ethan dismounted, leaving Bull's reins with Krixan as he stepped into the barrier while keeping one foot on Texas soil. Once his head and upper torso were within, he could see the outline of the barrier upon the far wall of the mystic chamber. He tossed the weighted message toward the opposing wall, where it disappeared into the murky surface of the far portal. Once he saw it pass from sight, he returned whence he came, stepping firmly atop Johnson's Ridge.

"Your father will be displeased," Krixan mumbled as they drew their horses away.

"I'm sure Dad will forgive me in time. I am his favorite, you know." Ethan smiled weakly, trying to lighten the big fella up.

"No, he won't, and I wouldn't go calling him Dad if I were you," Krixan warned.

"Relax, Krix. We are performing a great service for all mankind. Men haven't passed through the barrier in hundreds of years. We owe it to posterity to further explore this wondrous land. Our names will be written down in texts that shall be read for thousands of years by young boys who dream of such adventures. The time spent here is a small price to pay for such renown."

"Posterity? Bah, you just want to extend your freedom as long as possible, even if it lands you in a cage once you finally return."

If I return, Ethan kept that thought to himself.

*****

By late March, news reached Red Rock that Luke Crawford had killed a Texas ranger near Laredo. The governor ordered a $2,000 bounty on his head, and the Texas rangers were scouring the state from Brownsville to El Paso searching for the hired gun. There were rumors that Crawford, Cobb, and a dozen others had crossed south over the Rio Grande, where only bounty hunters would follow. Sheriff Thorton could only sit and wait for them to come to him, and that could take years. Meanwhile, Ethan and Krixan continued to hone their shooting skills with both their Winchester rifles and Colt .45s. Skeeter showed them how to reload their shell casings. Ethan spent an inordinate amount of time with Jacob Steward, the town black-smith, where he further learned the intricacies of the superior horse-shoes the Americans used. Ben Thorton shook his head in wonder at this. Upon first meeting Ethan, he never thought the Midwestern boy would be so skilled at marksmanship, let alone metalworking. The boy was also learning to play the guitar, practicing each night in the jail. Anything he put his mind to, he was able to quickly master—everything, that is, except for poker.

Ethan constantly picked Ben's brain on his time in the war, where Ben lauded the advent of the repeating rifles used by the Union cavalry over their confederate counterparts' slow muzzleloaders. Ethan spent even more time with Judge Donovan, siphoning every bit of knowledge the judge had whether it was sailing the North Atlantic, exploring the frontier, history, politics, science, or the countless stories the judge loved to tell. The judge was fond of sharing crass jokes that would make a Pinkerton blush.

An early summer evening found them in the jail gathering around Ben's desk playing poker, Krixan, Ethan, Ben, Skeeter, and the judge. Though he understood the game, Ethan lacked the ability to hide his emotions, making him easy prey to the stone-faced judge and craggy sheriff. Krixan played surprisingly well, even taking the majority of the winnings on occasion. Usually Judge Donovan took the pot, having spent time riverboat gambling along the Mississippi. This night belonged to Skeeter, who managed to bluff Judge Donovan on a large pot with only a pair of threes. Ethan was nearly out, down to his last ante when the judge offered everyone a cigar. Krixan took one happily, taking huge puffs as if he were born to it. Ethan politely declined as the darn things made him turn green. Ben chuckled at that, wondering how a fast draw killer like Ethan couldn't stomach a cigar.

"Ante up, boys!" Skeeter said with his cigar clenched in the side of his mouth.

Ethan sat with his chair turned backward as he rested his thick forearms on its back while staring at his mismatched cards. His hat rested high on his brow as he released a pained sigh, knowing this was his last hand.

Ben smiled wryly at his young deputy's comical expression. He reached under his desk, pulling out a bottle of whiskey and refilled their glasses. Once everyone called, folded, or raised, the judge took the pot ending Ethan's night.

"You've many talents, Ethan, but I don't reckon poker to be one of 'em," Ben said, eyeing the jack of clubs, nine and six of hearts, and the deuce and three of diamonds that Ethan dropped on the table. Besides the fact that he couldn't bluff a blind man, Ethan had to have the worst luck in cards Ben or the judge had ever seen. After playing half the night, Ethan's best hand the entire evening was a pair of sevens.

"Ben's right, Ethan. You have the worst luck at cards than anyone I've ever met, including Lucky Ned Johnson.'" The judge laughed.

"If he was terrible at cards, why was he called Lucky Ned?" Ethan asked.

"That's a good question, lad," Judge Donovan began in the subtle excited tone he always used when he started to tell one of his stories.

Ben shook his head as he started to deal out the cards. He had heard this particular story a half-dozen times but kept silent as the judge told the tale.

"It was during the California gold rush back in forty-eight. Ned Johnson had found himself a small stake in what he thought was a major find, having dug up a couple of good-sized nuggets. Ned couldn't keep himself from the card tables and gambled away his nuggets along with his claim. The fella who took his stake moved into the small shanty he had erected on the site. A freakish storm struck out of nowhere the next night, smashing the makeshift hovel to pieces and killing the man who won it the night before. The unclaimed land was returned to the territory, where it passed onto new claimants who hoped to follow up on Ned's early success. They found nothing on the property as the nuggets Ned found led to no others. Ned meanwhile was forced to find work and save for a new claim, which he did after several months. His new claim seemed a barren patch of useless earth. Just when Ned was about to give up and go back home to Virginia, another freakish storm struck, shattering his new shanty to pieces, but Ned survived. He climbed out of the rubble and found that a runoff of stormwater had revealed something glistening upon the ground. He found himself another gold strike, only this time it was atop a deep vein. If he hadn't been so lousy at cards, he would've stayed with his worthless claim, and that is why we called him Lucky Ned," the judge explained.

"One incident doesn't make a man lucky," Ethan said.

Ben grinned for he knew what the judge was going to say next, for he made the same observation when he first heard the tale.

"That you might claim, but Ned was in San Francisco one night and ate himself a fine steak. It happened perchance that the meat was tainted. He spent half the night in the privy when a fire swept the boarding house he was staying, killing everyone inside except for Ned. Another time he booked passage on a ship to take him back to Virginia in order to wed his sweetheart he left behind to find his fortune. Well, Ned's horse pulled up lame along the way, and he missed his boat. The ship happened to sink on its voyage near Cape Horn. His girl thought him dead and married another. Ned was crestfallen when he heard the news. A year later, the girl was enraged with her husband and planted a kitchen knife into his heart while he slept. They say she was a bit touched, and the judge sent her away to a sanitarium for the insane. Ned's lame horse spared him a sinking ship and a crazed bride. You must remember Ethan that your ill fortune at cards may well be a blessing that you now cannot see."

"Does that mean you're going to give back my money?" Ethan laughed.

"Now you sound as crazy as ole Ned's intended," the judge opined.

Ethan shook his head and fetched his guitar as his friends continued to play. His fingers moved nimbly over the strings as he played "The Streets of Laredo" and "The Yellow Rose of Texas."

*****

It was mid-July when Sheriff Thorton and Krixan were out of town, transporting a prisoner that was wanted by the sheriff of El Paso. It was late afternoon as the sweltering Texas heat blurred Ethan's line of sight as he rode back to town from the Miller ranch. Caleb Miller called for Ethan to come to the ranch. A number of his cattle had gone missing, and two of his ranch hands were found dead on the edge of his vast spread. Ethan investigated the grizzly scene, promising to relay the information to Sheriff Thorton once he returned from El Paso.

Ethan sensed a disquiet as he rode into town as something felt strangely amiss. "Easy, boy." Ethan stroked Bull's mane as even he sensed danger. Ethan found no one in the street. As he drew near the Lucky Star saloon, the source of his unease manifested itself as a nondescript man wearing a blue-and-white checkered shirt, dark vest, and brown trousers stepped through the swinging front doors of the saloon and into the street. Dark hair peeked below the rim of his gray Stetson, and he wore a tie-down left-handed holster. He was clean-shaven with pale-blue eyes that stared through Ethan as if he were translucent. The man's face held no distinguishing features as if he were a generic human specimen. Ethan drew back on the reins as the fellow stepped into the street, fixing his eyes to Ethan's.

"That's far enough, Deputy!" The man called out, his face void of expression. Ethan could now see that he was a well-built fellow, just shy of six feet. The man's left hand hovered over his holstered Colt as Ethan slowly dismounted and stepped clear of Bull.

"You know me, but who are you?" Ethan asked as his right hand hovered over his pistol as well.

"The name is Stanton. Miles Stanton," he said evenly with no inflection in his voice to give away any sense of emotion. The man was obviously a hired killer sent to exact vengeance for either Hank Grierson or Bobby Crawford. Miles wasted no more breath, his left hand going for the draw.

Ethan drew and fired before Stanton cleared leather, emptying his Colt into the stranger's body. Ben told Ethan to always continue shooting until your opponent stopped as often one bullet failed to slow someone before they did equal harm in return. Ethan holstered his right-handed pistol while drawing the left as Miles Stanton's riddled body toppled to the ground, his blood soaking the dirt where he fell.

With the gunslinger's death, Ethan's legend continued to grow. Most of the townsfolk called him their guardian angel while the

Grierson men and the Crawford gang referred to him as the Devil's Deputy.

*****

By late summer, Ethan visited the barrier two more times, tossing messages through the portal to reassure his family that he was well and would return by the winter festival. Krixan insisted that they return immediately, but Ethan always found a reason to linger in Red Rock. Early September found him accompanying a posse led by a US marshal into the New Mexico Badlands searching for George Spencer, an associate of Luke Crawford that escaped the gunfight at Red Rock that felled Hank Grierson and Bobby Crawford. The badlands were the most inhospitable terrain Ethan had ever seen. The days were hot and the nights bitterly cold. After some time, they cornered George Spencer but were unable to bring him in alive as he fought to his dying breath in a shootout that lasted half a day. They had the advantage of numbers as well as smokeless powder, whereas the outlaw's shots betrayed his position in the rocky terrain. Ethan returned to Red Rock by early October from his New Mexico foray.

Rumors circled town that Luke Crawford and Emmitt Cobb had returned to the Grierson ranch, but several searches by the sheriff revealed nothing. Other rumors circulated concerning Ethan and Krixan. Some suspected that they had found a silver mine as Ethan had spent some of the silver pieces he had brought with him from Astaria. That, coupled with their mysterious forays downriver where the barrier resided, only fueled the rumors.

*****

The second night after his return to Red Rock, Ethan was visited by unsettling dreams. He awoke suddenly, sweat pouring off his forehead as he struggled to find his bearing. In his vision, Astaria was going to war. The dream was entirely too real to ignore. He could not rest until he knew the truth of it.

Ethan spent the morning packing his things. He had purchased another horse to carry his excess load. He had hundreds of rounds of ammunition, several bowie knives, an extra Colt .45 with holster, two pairs of buckskins, and moccasin boots with braided leather straps along their seams. He packed his guitar and several days of hardtack. Saying his farewells to Sheriff Thorton, Skeeter, and the judge was more difficult than he thought. They were like family, and he promised to return as soon as he was able.

Ethan stood at Ben's desk as he removed his star, handing it back to his friend, but Ben refused.

"Hold on to it, Ethan. The job's yours again once you return." Ben gifted him a rare smile for his weathered face as he stood from his chair to stand beside him.

"Thanks, Ben. That means more to me than you know."

When Ethan first told Ben that he had to leave, he asked him why? Ethan revealed his dream that his family was in great peril. Ben thought it strange but had come to trust Ethan's instincts. He loathed seeing the boy go. He was so much like his own son that he often caught himself calling him Jake.

"You take care of yourself, boy." Ben's voice broke with emotion. He'd have given Ethan a hug but feared he might burst.

"I fear more for you, Ben. Luke Crawford is still out there, and—"

"I'll handle Crawford if he shows himself, Ethan. Never you fret none. He doesn't have Hank Grierson's political machine shielding him anymore. Everyman in town will back my play if need be. You just worry about your kin and see that they are safe."

"Thanks, Ben. When you see Jake, tell him—"

"I'll tell him goodbye for you. Now get along, or you'll squander a half day's riding."

Ethan stepped without where Krixan was already atop his mount. George Adams and John Custis greeted him, and the Adams girls tearfully bade them farewell. Ethan climbed into the saddle, and lifted his hat in the air, saluting his friends as he rode away, wondering if he would never return again.

*****

It was near dusk when they reached Johnson's Ridge, where the portal shimmered to life as they drew nigh. Ethan's focus centered on his terrible vision and the need to cross the barrier to find the truth of it. That same determined focus dulled his otherwise dependable instincts. Had he approached the portal more cautiously, he might've discovered the dozen pair of eyes trailing dangerously close. Ethan and Krixan dismounted at the bottom of the ridge before leading their mounts afoot up the rise and through the dark shimmering surface, disappearing from sight.

*****

They were greeted by torchlight as they emerged from the shimmering portal. The flames lined the length of the cavern, leading to the mouth of the cave some distance above from the bowels of the hillside. The air was stale and dry in the subterranean chamber.

"Hold!" A nervous voice echoed with uncertainty. There standing post along the opposing wall of the circle-shaped chamber was a guard dressed in the azure tunic and gray armor and leggings of House Mortune. Even the dim light could not mask the boy's young face and diminutive stature as he leveled his drawn sword in their direction.

"Put the sword down, friend. We are here to see Lord Dragos," Ethan said with measured calm.

"Who are you?" the soldier asked.

"He is Crown Prince Ethanos Blagen! Now put away your sword and let us pass before I bash in your fool brain!" Krixan growled.

"Pr…Prince Ethanos!" the lad stuttered, dropping to his knees. "My apologies, my prince."

"Get up, kid. I hate talking to a man on his knees," Ethan said as the boy seemed frozen in place.

Ethan rolled his eyes, then took the young soldier by the hand and lifted him to his feet. "Why are you in this cavern?" he asked.

"We are here for you, Highness. Ever since you disappeared a year past, we have stood guard awaiting your return. I would have regarded you with due deference if you were not so strangely garbed," the soldier answered with downcast eyes.

The sound of armored feet striking the cavern floor echoed along the chamber, growing louder as they drew nigh. Within moments a score of knights clad in black with a silver orb emblazoned upon their chests, filed in around them. They were the queen's guards, and Ethan wondered their purpose until the feminine silhouette emerged from the darkness, torchlight bathing her face with the familiar high cheekbones and regal airs. The woman wore a silver gown that shimmered even in the darkness like a million stars sparkling in the night sky.

"Mom?" Ethan's eyes alit.

"Ethan." She rushed into his arms, forsaking any queenly propriety. He held her in his warm embrace as she basked in overwhelming joy. She clung to him fiercely, lest he disappear like a cruel vision that taunted her with her deepest wants and then snatched them away. The tighter she held him, the firmer he felt, and she knew he was truly home. After several minutes of savoring his embrace, she pulled slightly away so as to see his beautiful face. He was strangely dressed with frayed leather trousers and a plain shirt, with strange metal objects tied to either leg. An odd-shaped hat rested low upon his brow. She removed the hat and tossed it to the ground so as to see him more clearly. She ran her fingers through his short hair, which was obscenely short, even by his ridiculous standard.

"Where have you been?" she finally asked with more concern than ire.

"In Red Rock, helping Jake and his father."

"Who?"

"The man Ethan rescued and brought through the portal," Dragos answered, stepping into the chamber from the cavern passageway.

"Grandpa," Ethan smiled past his mother as his grandsire drew nigh. Lord Dragos wore the azure robes of his mage craft with silver stars and crescent moons sewn in their folds.

"Now, now my boy, you know better than to address a young fellow such as myself with *that* appellation," Dragos playfully scolded.

"How did you know that I was going to return today?" Ethan asked, bewildered by the irony.

"We didn't, we only knew that Krixan would since you are invisible to our foresight," Dragos explained. "Come, there is much we must discuss, and I prefer the comfort of my holdfast to a cave."

"What about the war?" Ethan asked, his question taking his mother and grandfather by surprise.

"How do you know of that?" Gabrielle asked, her eyebrows knitted together in concern.

"You're not the only ones who have dreams," Ethan said before following them without with the reflective pool of the portal still shimmering in their wake.

*****

The palace of Plexus was a half of an hour's ride from the mouth of the cave. Dragos left a small contingent to guard the mouth of the cavern against anyone who dare enter unbidden. Soldiers in blue mail with bright azure capes stood post upon the lowered drawbridge of the fortress as Dragos led the procession into the castle upon his dusty gray palfrey. The banners bearing the coat of arms of House Mortune, a crescent moon and silver stars upon a field of blue, blew proudly above the battlements.

Within moments, they were ushered into Dragos's inner sanctum, a secluded, windowless oval-shaped chamber with a massive oak table in its center. Upon the table was a map of Astaria, depicted in rich topographic detail.

"We received word a fortnight ago that Ortovan Marvo, king of Meltoria, led a vast host across the Upper Velo, crossing over into Western Astaria here." Dragos swept his hand over the map, jabbing his finger into the realm's northwestern province of Laratia, home of House Jarvo.

"How vast a host?" Ethan asked as he studied the map.

"Our reports indicate fifty thousand to a hundred thousand. They have invested the palace at Lortala." Lortala was the seat of House Jarvo, which overlooked the Velo some one hundred leagues north of the converse of the Picero and Velo Rivers.

"Is Lord Jarvo still there?" Krixan asked.

"No," Dragos answered. "He ordered his entire household to Carega, before the Meltorians invested the palace. He left three thousand defenders to hold the fortress and withdrew with the rest of his host. He should be with your father's host by now."

"And my father is marching posthaste to engage the invaders?"

"Aye, that he is, my boy," Dragos regarded him keenly for he knew well the look in Ethan's eye.

"And how many men did our king take with him?" Ethan asked, not relishing the answer that he could already guess.

"Ten thousand royal infantry, his personal cavalry, and the vassals of Houses Torrent, Jarvo, and Luciel, as well as those houses' noble cavalry."

"That's all?" Ethan lifted his alarmed eyes to Dragos's, wondering why his father called upon just three of the nine great houses of Astaria.

"Yes," his mother interjected. "There was little time to wait for the houses east and south of Astaris to marshal their levies. Your father gathered what forces he could most rapidly deploy."

"Then he took the light cavalry that I trained before I left," Ethan said, hoping them to confirm it.

Dragos shook his head. "Your father has little use for them. Though I counseled him to take them, he refused, stating he wouldn't fritter precious provisions on your *pretty ponies.*"

Ethan sighed in frustration. His light cavalry were invaluable in scouting the enemy, cutting their lines of communication and supply, and harrying their advance. They had demonstrated their worth in the mock engagements against his father's heavy horse, using Ethan's unconventional tactics to defeat them. His father dismissed the result as an exercise in *pretend* warfare. The kingdom spent precious resources developing the light cavalry at Ethan's behest, but it seemed his father dismissed their potential without Ethan present to defend their worth.

Ethan ran his right index finger over the map, stopping at Lortala, the last known location of the Meltorian army. It all made little sense. If the Meltorians stormed Lortala, what was their next move? Surely they would know that Astaria would counterattack. They could not hope to defeat the Astarian forces led by a lightning lord, unless…

"How many of my light cavalry are here?" Ethan asked excitedly.

Dragos drew away a step as Ethan's tone transformed from inquisitive to alarm. "Perhaps fifty, maybe more."

"That's all? Where are the rest?"

"Garrisoned at Far Point, Newcore, and Tallich," Dragos answered.

Ethan quickly scanned the map, running his finger from Plexus to the points Dragos indicated. Each was a half day's ride west and north from his grandsire's palace.

"What troubles you, Ethanos?" Gabrielle stepped nigh, touching a hand to his shoulder.

"Dad's walking into a trap," he answered with a deadly serious look in his ocean blue eyes, a look that sent ice down her spine.

"A trap? Are you certain?" Dragos asked.

"Ethan, how can…" Gabrielle began, but the words escaped her.

"Dragos, muster all your forces, especially your cavalry, and march toward the Velo posthaste. Do not wait for your infantry. Order them to follow, but do *not* wait upon them. Send out riders tonight to muster the light cavalry that my father foolishly left behind," Ethan commanded.

"Do not speak ill of your father, my son. His is the burden of leadership that you have shamelessly shunned," Gabrielle scolded him.

"No man is above the trappings of our species, Mother, not even my father. Father made a mistake leaving behind the light cavalry that I trained, out of spite for my absence," Ethan shifted his tired eyes to Krixan. "Come on, Krix, we best get moving."

"Where are you going?" Gabrielle asked.

"We'll gather every light mount in the palace and start heading west before sunrise. Hopefully, we can counsel the king to take more prudent actions."

Dragos, Krixan, and Gabrielle shared a look, knowing that Bronus would not be swayed by anything his wayward son would counsel. If Ethan were to say that it was day, with the sun at its highest, then Bronus would believe it to be night.

"How many cavalry can you muster in a day's time?" Ethan asked.

"With your light cavalry included, I would hazard a guess of three thousand. Your brother is marching from Astaris with a host of one thousand more mounts and six thousand foot."

"Order him to dispatch his cavalry and join you en route."

"What are you planning to do, Ethanos?" Gabrielle asked, her voice choked with worry.

Ethan removed his Stetson, sweeping it across his body as he bowed, fixing his mother with a mischievous grin. "Well, ma'am, you don't have the Texas rangers or the US cavalry, but you have the next best thing, you have ME. Krix and I will just have to serve up some Texas justice to Ortovan Marvo and the Meltorian army." He put his hat back on his head and stepped without.

CHAPTER 9

The early fall wind slapped his face with relentless fury. Ethan leaned forward in the saddle, scanning the valley floor below from the grass swept hilltop. The grunt of the brown chestnut mare beside him alerted him to Krixan's overbearing presence. His large friend was never far afield.

"Your father awaits, my prince. Shall we proceed?" Krixan's rough voice boomed in the crisp air.

Ethan shot his large rust haired companion a disgusted look. "Don't call me that, Krix. You know I hate that title."

"But that's what you are." Krixan scratched his red beard, giving little heed to his comrade's objection. Ethan was ridiculous at times and was even worse these past days since their return from Red Rock.

Ethan shook his head. No matter how many times he reminded Krixan not to call him by his title, the large ruffian said it with greater emphasis. Probably just to annoy him out of mere amusement. Ethan had become accustomed to a world without titles, lords, and kings, dwelling across the barrier for the past year. He lamented the end of his freedom but looked with hope to return to his friends once he knew Astaria was safe.

Narrowing his sea-blue eyes, he scanned the valley floor, where the army was encamped. Thousands of tents and barricades in ordered rows lined the valley green. Pavilions striped in the red and white of House Torrent lined opposing the blue and white of House Luciel. Pavilions striped with the green and yellow of House Jarvo occupied the far end of the vale. Ethan shook his head, dumbfounded that his father planned to go to battle with just these three houses in his muster.

"Krix, you best stay here with the boys. If I'm not back by dusk, that means I wasn't able to turn my father from this folly. If that's the case, you need to ride to Tel-Ar and gather up as many mounts as you can. Dragos should be there by now. Tell him of our contingencies. He'll know what to do."

"Will you take any riders with you?"

Ethan craned his neck in the saddle, looking at the column behind them. Five hundred riders all armed with composite bows and riding swift, slender mounts. He had organized and drilled these men since his fifteenth birthday against the advice of his father. *What good are so poorly protected riders?* His father had barked, deriding his efforts though allowing his son the leeway to continue the endeavor, thinking it best for Ethan to learn from his failures. But Ethan didn't fail, not in his own eyes anyway. He argued the value of swift-moving cavalry over the expense and weight of a heavy horse. True, his men would not stand up to the charge of his father's royal cavalry, but they could do so much more. His father thought so little of them that he left them behind at Plexus. Thinking on Krixan's question, he correctly surmised that anyone he brought with him when he treated with his sire, his father would merely assign them some mundane task not befitting their skill.

"I'll take one squad. The rest keep with you."

"As you wish, Prince Ethan." Krixan grinned.

"The next time you call me that I'll take that hammer of yours and bash in your skull." Ethan smiled.

Krixan removed his helm, slapping his balding head with his left palm. "I have a hard skull, Ethan. You might need a couple of swings."

"A hard head and dull wits is no way to fight a war of words, big fella."

"You're not so swift of wit yourself, Ethan. You're not so little either," Krixan observed.

"I am when standing next to you, Krix." Ethan was larger than most men but looked a child next to Krixan's massive bulk. His short dark mane and tan complexion further contrasted to Krixan's pasty skin and red beard.

"Ethan, you sure you do not wish to change your clothes before meeting your father?" Krixan suggested. He had already changed out of his western garb for dark trousers and tunic while retaining his six-shooters and a sword and hammer with them.

"No. Why? What's wrong with what I'm wearing?" Ethan countered with a hurt look upon his face.

Krixan took in Ethan's buckskin trousers, brown leather moccasin boots, his tan leather shirt and his Stetson bending low upon his brow, and the twin Colt .45s tucked into the holsters of either hip with the holster straps tied to his thighs. "Well…nothing…I just thought you might like to look more…more noble."

"Who cares, Krix. We're not exactly going to a palace ball."

"I think you'd dress the same even if we were."

"Maybe next time I will. I don't care much for palace ball's anyway."

"I could be scented with lavender and roses, and you could be covered in swine dung, and the ladies would still claw each other to dance with you," Krixan said.

"Those ladies want to dance with the crown prince, not me, Krix."

"No, they want to dance with you. If you don't see it, you have no cause to question my wit."

"I'll see you tonight." Ethan smiled before riding on into the vale, wondering what reception awaited him below.

*****

Riding through the forward pickets, he was not quickly recognized. Before long, the shouts of "Prince Ethanos" heralded his approach, much to his chagrin. Men arrayed in red and gold tunics over dark breeches greeted him with fists to chests. Pikemen in black and archers in forest green bowed as he passed. Knights in mail lifted their visors, revealing broad grins as they beheld Ethanos Blagen riding in their midst. A hundred yards ahead, he spied the black banner with gold lightning centered upon its field, rippling in the wind before a grand pavilion. It was the coat of arms of his father, King Bronus Blagen, the lightning lord.

"Ethan!" the sweet high voice of a woman called out to him over the wind.

His right eye caught sight of her standing before a pavilion of House Torrent. Silky auburn hair framed her delicate feminine face, masking the strength of the woman herself. Large brown eyes smiled as he recognized her in a long black dress.

"Ceresta!" He smiled, pulling on his reins and steering Bull in her direction before dismounting in a flourish and lifting her off the ground in a fearsome hug.

"Where have you been?" were the next words to escape her lips as he finally set her down. It was a question he was already sick of answering. He gazed down at her as she crossed her arms, lifted an eyebrow, and tapped her foot as if he were an insolent child.

"You know where I've been, little sister. I didn't exactly keep it a secret."

"We haven't heard from you for over a year. Mother is distraught, and Father is furious. He's waiting for you. He knows you are here."

Ethan shifted his eyes to the black pavilion in the camp's center. "You can read his thoughts this far away?"

She nodded.

"You're getting better. You need to teach me that trick."

"Magic doesn't work on you, Ethan, you know that. The only person in the world immune to magic and immune to good sense as well," she reproached.

"And the only one in our family who doesn't have it either," he added.

"That's not true. You have that gift where you master any skill with minimal effort, and your other gifts as well, such as your recuperative powers and superior strength. And with all those gifts, you didn't see the need to send us word that you were safe. We all thought you must have perished."

"I sent word many times."

"We never received it," she answered.

"That's what Mom said," he sighed.

"*Mom?*"

"I'll say Mother if it makes you feel better."

"It does." She shook her head at his informality. Had he been living in a barn for this past year? "And *what* are you wearing?" Her nose wrinkled at the sight of him.

"What's wrong with what I'm wearing?" He shot her the hurt look he gave Krixan.

"We haven't the time for a proper assessment. Father's waiting."

*****

Bronus Blagen stood before his pavilion with his thick arms crossed over his chest. He wore dark mail over black tunic and trousers. His cold gray eyes narrowed at his son's approach. Like a silhouette carved from granite, his imposing form projected the authority of the realm. His coal-black hair draped beneath his silver helm while his square jaw clenched tight as if it would snap.

Ethan eyed his father carefully as he slowed Bull to a trot, stopping several yards before him before dismounting. He noticed Captain Clovis of the king's guard standing before a contingent to his right. "Captain, could you see to my men while I speak with the king?" Ethan asked, cocking his head to the dozen riders trailing him. "Perhaps a place along the perimeter, where we can conduct reconnaissance."

"As you wish, Prince Ethanos," Captain Clovis bowed his head, regarding him.

"Thank you," Ethan said gratefully.

"Belay that order, Captain!" King Bronus commanded sternly. "I will decide where this *boy's* men are placed and what assignments he is worthy."

"As you wish, my king," Clovis quickly answered before backing a step away from the king's wrath that was sure to rain down upon poor Ethanos.

The others cloistered nearby backed away as well, sensing the coming storm and wishing no part in it.

Ethan let out a measured breath before stepping forth. Removing his hat, he took a knee before his father. Bronus's breath grew heavy as he looked down at his son. Ethan expected Bronus to grant him leave to rise, but Bronus kept him on his knee.

"Where have you been, boy?" the king asked with a deathly quiet.

"I—"

"Your mother has cried herself tearless in her worry over you!" His voice grew ever harsher, ever louder.

"I was—"

"A *year!*" he roared, standing over Ethan as if to strike him. "A year and not a word, not a letter. Nothing!"

"I sent—"

"You show yourself now. Why now, Ethan?"

"I—"

"I know why, boy. You heard of the battle to come and wish for a chance of glory. These brave men here with me have honored their codes and oaths. They have done all the tasks required to get us this far, all the tedious tasks you take for granted. Tell me, boy, how did we feed this army en route? How did we transport the horse feed and tools to keep us equipped? You think of warfare as riding off on a gallant charge without any appreciation for the preparation before or the consequences after. Now I suppose you think I should open my arms to my firstborn and let him lead this attack? Let him cover himself in glory unearned. You are an insolent child, Ethanos Blagen!"

"Dad, I'm sorry. But I didn't—" His words were cut off as the king's gauntlet caught him across his face. He spat out the blood that filled his mouth and wiped his split lip with the back of his right hand. The wound quickly healed, leaving no trace of the blow.

"You will address me as 'Father,' 'king,' 'Your Grace,' 'Your Highness,' or 'sire.' Do *not* ever speak to me informally before my men."

"Yes, my king," Ethan gave up. There was little point in offering explanations until his father was finished venting. At this rate, it might take all day.

"For once you *shall* do as you are bid. You shall stand where I tell you, sit when I tell you, and go only where I tell you. Disobey me, boy, and I'll slap you in irons, drag you back to Astaris, and throw you in the blackest dungeon in the palace. Don't look to your mother for mercy. If it were her choice, she'd have you in chains already, locked away until she found a suitable bride for you to wed and sire her the grandchildren she so desperately wants."

Ethan waited patiently as his father continued ranting, recalling every transgression his wayward son ever committed as well as a few that he didn't. Bronus Blagen, king of Astaria, let out a heavy sigh, his brain finally empty of words. He reached out his left hand and placed it upon his son's head.

"What am I to do with you, boy?" he asked himself aloud while shifting his eyes to the gray skies above.

"May I speak, sire?" Ethan asked carefully, not to again spark his father's ire. Those dark-gray eyes came back to him, but the storm in his gaze relented, and Ethan saw something different that he hadn't expected: his father looked tired.

"Come," Bronus said.

Ethan came to his feet and followed his father into his pavilion. The king's pavilion was richly designed but sparsely furnished. It was ten meters abreast and five meters high at its center post, and it had small cots to either side and a map table in its center. A tall man dressed in black leather and chain mail stood by the table. He had brown hair, which grayed at his temples. Dark-green eyes under bushy eyebrows shifted with the man's face from the small table to the tent entrance. His lean muscled form seemed naturally tense, as if the man was born to duty.

"King Bronus," Jorus Brax regarded his liege.

"Lord General," Bronus replied.

"Prince Ethanos." Jorus smiled tightly as his eyes shifted to Ethan.

"Ah, Jorus, don't call him that lest he take offense to the word. Our proud young Ethanos would like nothing more than to be rid of his birthright and me as well." Bronus waved an open hand to Ethan, mocking his magnificence.

"Never you, Father. I'm proud to be your son."

"Proud to be my son but not my heir?" Bronus half asked, half declared. "Bah! Say what you came to say, Ethan."

Finally! Ethan could now say what he had ridden for days on end to share with his father.

"You're walking into a trap," he declared.

"Is that so?" Bronus asked, more annoyed than amused.

"How so, Ethan?" Jorus asked. Jorus Brax was a seasoned commander who questioned every detail of any plan. He respected Ethan and took seriously any misgivings the crown prince voiced.

"The Meltorians want us to attack. They wouldn't have crossed the Velo unless they had a plan to deal with your magic." Ethan looked calmly into his father's gray eyes, hoping to see if he was believed.

"What magic can they hope to conjure to match a lightning lord?" Jorus asked.

Lightning lords were a rare occurrence. Once or twice in a millennium, a mage was born with the gift to cast lightning. Bronus Blagen was a weapon unto himself, able to strike down mage-less armies at will. Even a mage gifted to cast a shield would not be strong enough to protect himself from Bronus's lightning for long. Eventually, the lightning would work its way around a shield mage's protective barrier.

"I don't know," Ethan confessed.

"You don't know!" Bronus admonished him. "Is this the counsel you offer to turn my hand, *boy*!"

"I know little about magic, Father, but I know tactics. Lord Brax just asked what magic they could conjure to match your lightning? They know your power. Does it not concern you that they have crossed the Velo to face such power? They have openly challenged you because they have found the answer. We are marching blindly into a battle against a foe whose strength we do not know."

"If what you say is true, then what course do you believe we should follow, My prince?" Jorus asked.

Ethan stepped toward the map table in the pavilion's center, eyeing the Velo valley richly depicted on the ancient scroll. Ethan jabbed his finger to the map. "*Here!*" he declared emphatically, his digit pressed to the crossroads of Tel-Ar, twelve leagues east of their current position.

"Tel-Ar?" Brax asked curiously.

"Withdraw the army to Tel-Ar. There we hold the high ground while we have Dragos's troops at Plexus join us there, as well as any other house we can muster. From there, we can assess the Meltorians strength before striking them in force."

"And forsake our lands west of Tel-Ar to our Meltorian foe?" Bronus nearly choked on his words. "I think not, Ethan. If we concede this ground to an upstart like Ortovan Marvo, then the Gorgencians will be sure to challenge our eastern border as well. Once that transpires, then the other mage kings will pluck our feathers one by one."

"But—"

"I reject your plan, Ethan! We stand and fight come the morrow. We win or die here on this battlefield!"

Ethan relented. He tried his best to reason with his father, but his sire's anger and passion clouded all reason. "Very well, sire. If that is your intent, I will do my part to see us through. With your leave," Ethan regarded his father as he turned to leave.

"And where do you think you're going?" Bronus's harsh tone froze him at the entranceway.

"To see to my men. I plan to scout the Meltorian positions. It is one of many tasks my light cavalry can perform better than your heavy horse."

"*Your* light cavalry?" Bronus growled. "Those riders are *my* light cavalry, not yours. I am their king, not you. As my heir, you shall one day place such a claim but not today. You have forsaken your sacred duty this past year. I hope your time there was well served, or was it merely a chance to live as a god among mortal men?"

"What do you mean?" Ethan's mood soured with the accusation.

"Mind your tone, boy. I am still your king and your father!"

"My apologies, Your Grace, but do you truly believe I spent my time across the barrier bathing in glory with no regard for those I left behind?"

"Why else, Ethan? For one such as you, who can easily recover from mortal wounds, what else could keep you in such a place? Any foe could easily be dispatched by your skilled hand, while your recuperative powers could nullify their fiercest blows. What foe could've kept you there? None. You remained in their land to revel in the glory of your power in a mage-less realm."

"I've never sought power, Father, you know that," Ethan answered sadly, hurt by his father's inference.

"I didn't say power, Ethan. You seek to befriend every hopeless cause, bringing victory from certain defeat and having the downtrodden praising your name. True leaders can't afford such vanity, son. The burden of a crown forces them to make hard decisions for the greater good and living with the consequences of those decisions. In this you are still a child."

"I thought you knew me." Ethan frowned. "I've never sought glory, only justice. If you believe, otherwise, there is nothing that I can say to sway you. As far as my absence, if you were with me across the barrier, then you would know why I stayed there so long. If you can't forgive me for that, at least acknowledge that I am here when you need me most."

"Need you? You may be immune to magic, Ethan, but you have none as well. You are strong and skilled with arms. You can heal yourself. These gifts only make you a glorified foot soldier, not a mage lord of great renown."

"If I am a foot soldier, then I'll take my place in the line of battle as a common soldier."

"Nay! You will command my light cavalry and provide security to our lines of communication and our baggage train. That seems the best use for those pretty pony riders you trained."

Ethan held his tongue. This was his father's way of hurting him for his long absence from Astaria.

"As you wish, Father."

"It is my wish, Ethan. The baggage train seems an apt place to deny you the glory you seek. 'Tis the proper punishment for the vanity of a spoiled princeling."

"I don't care about glory or war. I'd rather have peace. As far as the glory you think I sought beyond the barrier, I was only a mortal man there. Magic cannot work there, not even mine. I stayed because a good man needed my help. It is the same reason I will go back once Astaria is safe."

Bronus marched across the pavilion and struck Ethan across his face with his gauntleted fist. Ethan's head snapped back from the emphatic blow, his blood splattering across the pavilion wall. Ethan's severed lip quickly healed as his blue eyes met his father's vicious scowl.

"Your healing power is hindered across the barrier, *boy*?" Bronus's spittle sprayed Ethan's face as he drew near. Ethan had never seen his father so enraged.

Ethan nodded.

Bronus struck him again. "You risked your life for a childish adventure?" He was on the verge of apoplexy.

Ethan said nothing.

"Lord General!" Bronus commanded.

"My king," Brax answered.

"Once this battle is concluded, you shall assign twenty men and deliver the crown prince to Astaris in chains. Inform the queen of his…poor judgment. She will select for him a suitable mate. Perhaps he shall grant me a grandson who is more worthy to rule my kingdom then he is."

"Yes, my king."

*****

Bronus's breath hung heavily in the air as Ethan stepped without, tortured by visions of his son dying in some forsaken far-off land. "I love that boy, Jorus, but how he tests me!" Bronus growled, his eyes fixed on the entryway as Ethan stepped without.

"Yes, sire."

"Bah, Jorus! You've been my dearest friend since we were boys. Call me Bronus when no one else is present." Bronus had to often twist his lord general's arm to loosen his devotion to courtesy. Ethan could never see that his father hated the pomp and formality of court as much as he.

"Very well, Bronus."

"Ahh, that's more like it." Bronus smiled, clapping Lord Brax on his back before retrieving a jug of wine and two flagons from beneath the table. He filled both cups and offered one to his comrade. "Drink up, Jorus."

"As you wish," Jorus downed his cup.

"Now tell me what weighs your mind, old friend? You think I deal too harshly with the boy, don't you?"

"I do. Ethan is many things, my friend, but a glory seeker he is not. If he lingered beyond the barrier, where his healing power was impaired, then I believe he had good reason to do so. You should trust your son, Bronus."

"Bah! I trust him to gray my hair, that's what I trust him to do. He has a duty to Astaria that he has forsaken. His wanderings must cease if he is to be king one day."

"Ethan does not wish to be king."

"It is not his place to deny his duty or forsake his birthright. He *will* be king one day."

"Of course, he doesn't want to serve a king either," Brax said more to himself than Bronus as his eyes drifted out of focus.

"Either he is a king or he serves a king," Bronus declared.

"You misread my intent. There is an ancient legend that foretells the birth of the one born free."

"Free of what?"

"Of everything," Brax sighed recollecting what he remembered of such texts and where he had read them. "Does it not strike you odd that Ethan is free from magic? Has there ever been born one such as that? I've never heard told of such. And his ability to self-heal in mere moments. He is free from harm and disease. But even more remarkable is his mind, the way he thinks," Jorus marveled, his voice but a whisper.

"The way he thinks? The boy talks madness!"

"The way he thinks," Jorus emphasized. "There is no one like him, not in all the seven mage kingdoms, the wilds, or the Mage Bane. He desires freedom form mage rule and from the titled aristocracy. He desires that all men stand on their own merits. He desires no man to bow to another. Strange, is it not, for a crown prince of the greatest mage kingdom to hold such beliefs? I believe Ethan is *Free Born*."

"Free Born?"

"Yes, the prophecy of the one born free. I believe it to be him."

"And what, pray tell, is the destiny of this Free Born?"

"To usher in a free world. He is a catalyst bringing about a great transformation."

"Jorus, that is a lousy interpretation. Whether he is or is not this…this…free-born person, what am I supposed to do?"

"Nothing. If it is his destiny to bring about such transformation, it would avail you naught to aid or deny him. He will fulfill his destiny regardless, whatever that destiny might be."

"He can't fulfill his destiny here if he dies across the barrier."

"Regardless, destiny shall guide his path. Remember a year ago you tried to wed him to the niece of the Estasan king? Destiny intervened as her Grandfather had promised her to another."

"Was it destiny or just dumb luck?"

"Does it matter? The result was the same: Ethan is yet free. My point being in all this, my old friend, is that I believe Ethan's destiny is setting the path he will follow, regardless of his father's wishes. Do not worry yourself about your son's future, for it shall only aggrieve yourself and the boy you claim you love. Enjoy the years you have left to each other and not fritter them in useless squabbles."

Bronus drained his cup as he pondered Jorus's words.

*****

Ceresta found Ethan sitting on his saddle beside a cook fire as his horse was tied to a hitch post behind him. He hooked his elbows around his knees as he stared into the crackling flames. He was alone as everyone avoided him as per the king's instructions. His squad of light cavalry was reassigned, and he was stripped of all command. He retained his mount and his strange weapons because they did not realize their deadly potential and overlooked them. After the battle, they would likely rectify that oversight. Ceresta smoothed her skirts as she sat on the ground beside him.

"You might want to step away, Ceresta, before Dad sees you in my company. As angry as he is with me, he might take it out on anyone who even speaks to me."

"I can deal with Father, Ethan, but must you test him so?"

"Test him? All I have to do is breathe, and I send him into the fits."

"You've been absent for a very long time, dear brother. What did you expect?" she said incredulously.

"I…I thought he might listen to reason before leading our army into this trap."

"You truly believe that?"

"Yes."

"Ethan, we can sense any mages within Astaria. We can sense the number of mortals in the Meltorian army to a man. We know their strength and disposition."

"If what you sense is true, then we will prevail."

"But you don't believe it is?"

"No, I don't," he sighed.

"I see," she said quietly, not sure if he were mad for believing so or if she were mad for ignoring his warning. She reminded herself that Ethan knew almost nothing of mage power and was thinking only of tactics.

"What did father say besides stripping you of command?" she asked.

"After the battle, I am to be returned to Astaris in chains, thrown in the dungeon, and wait there until Mom can find a *suitable* mate for me to wed. Then I will give them the grandchildren they so desperately want," he said quietly as he stared into the flames.

"Give Father time, Ethan," she rubbed her hand over his thick shoulder. "He loves you more than you could ever know."

"Yeah, and I wish he knew how much I love him and that my actions are for reasons other than the glory for which he thinks I'm drawn. What difference does it really matter now? Either we all die in battle if I am right, or I am wrong and we win, and I spend the remainder of my days a prisoner in Astaris."

"And if Mother chooses Jennifer Murtado as your bride, would that be so awful?" She smiled.

"She didn't choose her last time."

"Perhaps I can bend her ear."

"That would make my cage a little more tolerable, I suppose." He returned her smile.

"You better sleep, Ethan. Good night." She kissed his forehead before stepping away in the dark.

CHAPTER 10

The fall wind swept along the upper vale, bending the rust-stained grass like waves rippling upon a golden sea. King Ortovan Marvo of Meltoria led his vast host across the frozen Velo. As a weather lord, he could freeze rivers or melt ice by simply outstretching his arms and casting his power. He could affect the environment by calling forth limited rainfall or scattering clouds but lacked Bronus's ability to command lightning. His army numbered eighty thousand infantry, three thousand knights mounted, and two thousand afoot. All the lords of Meltoria answered his muster, leading their cohorts in bright golden mail over black tunics and leggings. They aligned from the east bank of the Velo to the eastern slopes of the vale. The heavy horse paraded in the front left flank, their lances raised as they trotted forth through the waving grass.

King Bronus sat astride his black warhorse with his dark-gray visor lifted above his brow, as he surveyed the enemy host drawing nigh. Pikemen arrayed in the red and white of House Torrent aligned to his left, nearest the river. The blue and white of House Luciel occupied the Astarian center. The infantry, dressed in yellow mail over green tunics of House Jarvo, held the right. They numbered forty thousand infantry and two thousand noble cavalry. Behind the Astarian center, ten thousand of the king's infantry waited in reserve. The king's heavy horses waited on the far right, numbering four thousand. Though outnumbered eight to five, the Astarians had superior cavalry and the lightning lord as their chief mage.

*****

Ethan waited with the baggage train, far behind the king's infantry. He leaned forward in the saddle, his arms resting on the pommel as he watched the massive wall of soldiers marching forth. A dozen king's knights surrounded him, tasked with shadowing his every move. With no sword, they thought him defenseless. Fortunately, neither his father nor his guards knew what his pistols or rifle could do. Ethan felt a strange sensation creeping the length of his spine. He turned carefully, circling his mount as he stared south over the rolling sea of autumn grass that blanketed the vale. There along the horizon, he could see two dozen pairs of horsemen lined east to west and evenly spaced covering the length of the field of battle and riding slowly toward him. Beyond these horsemen, a massive wall of infantry followed in their wake on foot. Sunlight reflected off their shields and swords like thousands of flickering stars. The blood drained from Ethan's face as his father's folly came to light. This was the Relusian army as a dozen banners of differing Relusian lords led their cohorts into battle. How could they have approached unseen? There appeared to be eighty thousand to one hundred thousand men. Only a shade mage could mask a small troop movement. By the size of the Relusian host, it would take a score of shades to conceal their advance, and there might be only one shade mage in all of Relusia and Meltoria combined.

"Sir Tarns!" Ethan shouted while pointing southward.

Tarns turned in his saddle, looking southward where Ethan was pointing. His eyes quickly swept south before returning to Ethan's alarmed scowl. "Something troubles you, Prince Ethanos?"

"Can't you see them?" he shouted, waving his hand toward the approaching Relusians.

"See who?" Tarns made a face, gazing south again while straining his eyes to find what Ethan was speaking of. He stared blankly at the matted grass that ran beyond the horizon.

"Tarns, the *entire* Relusian army is marching right for us! Tell me you can see them!"

"The Relusian army?" Tarns repeated as if Ethan were mad.

"Tarns! Go to my father and tell him one hundred thousand Relusians are directly behind us. I will tell Lord General Brax to face our reserves southward."

"Prince Ethanos, the king has ordered us to keep you here."

"Tarns, if we stay here, we *die*. Now go!"

*****

Bronus lifted his gauntleted right arm into the air as his men looked to their king atop his black warhorse at the head of the army. He lowered his gauntlet, and the men of Astaria shouted a war cry as they marched north. The two thousand cavalry of his noble houses, paraded before him as he signaled them forth. The morning sun flickered off their lances as they charged upon the Meltorian center. Far off to the Astarian right, the king's heavy horse mirrored the charge of the noble cavalry, shaking the ground as they sallied forth to meet the Meltorian cavalry along the valley's edge.

Lucious Tarns broke through the pikemen of House Luciel as he rode through their serried ranks to reach the king. "Sire!" he shouted over the din of battle, slowed only by the dozen king's knights that surrounded his liege.

Bronus turned in his saddle, irritated by any distraction at this critical juncture. He needed to release his lightning before his cavalry reached the Meltorian center. "Blast it, Lucious, you are supp—"

"Sire! Prince Ethanos says the Relusians are upon our rear!" he shouted frantically.

"What?" Bronus scowled, trying to comprehend what he had said.

"The *Relusians*, sire!" Sir Tarns pointed south as he drew up beside him. "Prince Ethanos says the Relusians are upon us!"

Bronus looked over his shoulder toward the south but could not discern anything from his vantage point. He was tempted to growl at Sir Tarns for spreading Ethan's wild tales but realized the boy might be right.

"Have Lord Brax verify if it is so. Go!"

"Yes, sire," Sir Tarns bowed his head and sped off.

Bronus returned his gaze to the enemy at hand. His eyes fixed on the Meltorian center where row upon row of pikemen awaited the Astarian cavalry. Bronus extended his arms toward the enemy host. His gauntlets only covered the back of his hands, leaving the flesh of his palms and fingers free. Lightning erupted from his fingertips in unchecked fury, arcing over his cavalry and sweeping the Meltorian center. The Astarian noble cavalry broke into a full charge as the lightning passed over their heads. They would strike the Meltorian center, where the lightning had struck, providing a double blow to split their army in half. The cavalry would cut through the center and reform in the enemy's rear before striking them again from behind. Most of the work would be done by the lightning, leaving only pockets of soldiers where the lightning passed or shield mages provided limited protection. Even a shield mage could not resist the power of lightning for long, unless there were multiple shield mages to help them form a larger shield formation. Ortovan Marvo, the Meltorian king, would have brought all the shield mages in his kingdom, but they were lucky to field as many as the fingers on one hand.

The lightning arced through the firmament, spilling into the Meltorian host before dissipating against a number of interlocking invisible bubbles. At the center of each bubble, a shield mage lifted their outstretched arms, protecting those around them from the lightning lord's fury. With a number of shield mages congregated at the Meltorian center, Bronus shifted his tactics and swept the rest of the enemy line with his deadly conjuring. Bronus's eyes widened in alarm as his lightning was absorbed by a score of shield mages throughout the Meltorian formation. How Ortovan Marvo acquired so many shield mages, he could only guess.

Mage fire erupted from the enemy center, spewing forth upon the approaching Astarian cavalry.

"Recall them!" Bronus shouted to Ceresta, whose cinnamon mare waited behind him.

She reached out to Veglan Luciel, commander of the noble cavalry, relaying the order to his mind. Lord Veglan turned his mount as the wall of fire slammed into his forward ranks. Men and horses tumbled to the ground, tripping those who followed as fire swept over them. The screams of burning men rent the morning air as they struggled to strip their heated armor. Others ran in circles with flames leaping over their flesh. Horses fled, with fire dancing along their backs and tails. Hundreds fell as the charge faltered under the weight of the flames. Meltorian archers followed with deadly volleys as the remaining cavalry turned and fled, racing toward the safety of the Astarian lines.

Bronus poured his lightning into the Meltorian ranks, but too little effect as the number of shield mages blunted his power. His army would now bear the brunt of the attack, but they were out-numbered two to one unless he committed his reserves. Realization struck him like an arctic gale, Ethan was right. The Relusians were upon his rear.

*****

"Lord Brax! The Relusians are upon us!" Ethan shouted again, trying to sway the lord general to turn south to face the threat, but how could you argue a point when what you claim is invisible?

"I cannot commit our reserves to a phantom army when the Meltorians are drawing nigh!" Brax countered.

"Phantoms?" Ethan was crestfallen. The Relusians would soon be upon them, and he was talking into the wind. He looked once more upon the pairs of riders some distance ahead of the Relusian host and wondered their purpose. Understanding suddenly washed over him, they were pairs of shades and shields, the shades to mask the army and shields to protect it. How the Relusians acquired two dozen shades and shield mages was beyond him.

"Brax! Ask my father to withdraw to the rear and commit our reserves to hold the front!" Ethan drew his twin Colts to make certain each of their chambers were loaded, spinning each cylinder before holstering them. He took another loaded pistol from his saddle pack and stuffed it into his pistol belt. He then took out his Winchester, racking the lever-action to load a round into the rifle's chamber.

"What are those things, Ethan?" Brax asked.

"They are special gifts from Samuel Colt and the Winchester Corporation, Lord General! After this day, you, too, will praise their blessed names, if we live to tell the tale. Lend me your sword." Ethan extended his right hand.

The lord general hesitated to surrender the blade, but the certainty in Ethan's eyes forced his hand. He placed the black wired hilt into Ethan's hand. Ethan tucked it into his pistol belt and hurried off. Ethan's guards started to follow after him but were stayed by Jorus's command.

"Leave him be!"

"Lord General, the king commanded us to follow him," one knight pleaded.

"I will answer to the king for this, not you," Jorus Brax assured them.

*****

Magnus Delmarin, king of Relusia, ran his tongue over his dry lips with heady anticipation. He was a master shield mage of the highest order. He sat astride a heavy brown charger with a shade mage beside him. To either flank was a dozen similar pairings. Together they formed an interdependent system to mask the army's movement and to protect it from magic. The Gorgencian king had lent him the shade mages and many of the shield mages that he and his Meltorian allies required. Once the Astarian king was slain, the Gorgencians would attack Eastern Astaria and their age-old enemy would be finished. As a master shield mage, Magnus's power was essential to join the shields and shades at the line's center. Once upon the enemy's rear, the shades and shields would withdraw safely to the Relusian rear.

"King Magnus," the shade accompanying him said.

"Yes, Fario?" Magnus regarded the young man, dressed in brown robes at his side. Fario was the eldest son of Baron Vencil, a high lord of Gorgencia. He was an attractive lad with dusty-blond hair and even set brown eyes. He was high enough born to be a suitable consort for Magnus's daughter and heir, Crown Princess Shandara

Delmarin. Since the Relusian crown princess was only twelve years, he had a few years to still find her a suitable match. Of course, he needn't worry about such if any of his wives would bear him a son, but until that day, the eldest of his six daughters was first to inherit his throne.

"Your Grace, look yonder," Fario lifted his chin to their far left as his arms were outstretched above him to project his shade over himself and those behind him. The closer they drew to the Astarian line, the higher he had to lift his arms. At this point, his arms started to ache severely, and he looked with anticipation for the slaughter to commence so he might rest his arms.

Magnus shifted his blue eyes toward the direction Fario indicated, where a lone rider galloped forth from the Astarian line. The rider wore a strange hat and sand-colored leather garb while brandishing a strange metal object in his right hand and his reins in his left. The rider broke sharply toward the Velo on Magnus's far left, riding straight for the shield and shade mages paired closest to the river.

"Do you think he is a scout or messenger, Your Grace?" Fario asked.

"It matters little his purpose, Fario. He shall soon discover, to his great surprise, that he is riding into our vast host. He cannot see us yet. Once he does, it will be too late." Magnus's condescending grin matched his pompous bearing. He was a slender built man with long dark hair framing a narrow, delicate, almost feminine face. He wore thin leather armor, rather than a warrior's steel. He carried no sword and left the fighting to his vassal lords. He considered it enough that he provided a shield for his men, and they had no need for his sword.

The shield mage upon the Relusian far left paid little mind to the strangely dressed rider in barbaric garb that closed swiftly upon them. The mage shield would prevent a single mortal man from entering its protective bubble. The rider would be unhorsed if he struck it directly. Even masses of infantry could not bend the contours of a well-crafted mage shield. The rider would most likely pass to either side of their pairing before running headlong into their wall of pikemen waiting some distance behind them, where he would meet his end. With the shade mage beside him, the shield mage smiled, knowing the approaching rider could not see them. He would be their first victim this day. Concern quickly reversed his smile to a frown as the rider fixed his gaze upon them.

Ethan broke through the protective aura of the shield as if it were empty air. Shock transfixed their faces as he lifted his rifle to his shoulder, putting a bullet in the heads of both mages. The shade and shield mages fell from their saddles as the terrible sound of the rifle echoed over the battlefield, drawing many eyes to its source. Ethan wasted no time as he kicked his heels into Bull's flanks and raced off to the east, where the next pair awaited.

Two more rounds exploded from his rifle as two more mages fell from their saddles as Ethan continued his desperate ride along the Relusian line.

*****

Lord General Brax's doubts melted away like snowflakes beneath a summer sun as the Relusian host emerged along their southern flank. Ethan's ride was akin to a giant curtain being drawn across their line of sight, revealing the enemy behind it as he felled their shades in detail.

"Elise!" Brax called out to his telepath mage who sat astride a dusty mare beside him.

"Yes, Lord General?" the young maiden replied. Each general had a telepath mage close at hand to coordinate with their commanders.

"Inform the king to come posthaste!"

*****

The king's heavy cavalry smashed their Meltorian counterparts along the eastern flank, driving them off in a full retreat. Unlike their unfortunate noble cavalry that met the Meltorian center and were greeted with fire and slaughtered at the outset of the battle, the king's cavalry had no mages to contest their advance. They charged desperately as they knew it was faring poorly for their brothers along the Astarian line of battle. Their commander suddenly ordered them to return southward rather than turning into the exposed Meltorian left flank. As they bemoaned such a squandered opportunity, they quickly realized the peril emerging to the south.

*****

The cool fall wind pressed upon his face as Ethan fixed his eyes on the next pairing. Confusion, awe, and fear among the Relusian ranks were his great advantage as they were slow to react. Those furthest behind him, now lumbered forth, fully cognizant of what he had wrought. Stray arrows sped past, sailing hopelessly astray. He sheathed his rifle and drew one of his Colts as he pierced the next shield's bubble. He fixed the sight on the wide-eyed shield mage and squeezed off a round. The bullet pierced the mage's skull. A second round struck the shade mage before the shield mage's body slipped from the saddle. Ethan barely slowed as he continued on. Angry shouts echoed from his right as the Relusians cursed him. Despite the varying colors of the Relusian houses, this day they were all uniformed in golden mail, black helms, and scarlet capes.

*****

The Meltorian infantry slammed into the Astarian ranks, their swords slashing between interlocked shields. Their mage shields withdrew to their formations' center, allowing the fore ranks to move freely. Arrows arced over the din as swords met flesh. The Astarian line buckled under the weight of the Meltorian numbers but surrendered ground grudgingly. Lord Brax deployed his reserves, blunting the Meltorian surge and slowing their advance.

Vancel Torrent survived his fated charge with the noble cavalry, though dozens of his kinsmen fell to the terrible mage fire wrought upon their ranks. He saw Lord Luciel go down in a heap with a score of others and doubted he survived the swirling flames. The surviving riders rallied to him as he led them through their infantry and to the Astarian rear. He did not know how many survived, but by the numbers in his company, he counted a mere three hundred mounts. Drawing close to Lord Brax, his eyes fell on the unfolding horror to the south as if the gates of damnation were about to be unleashed. Vancel's vision was drawn to Ethan riding across the Relusian front.

"What is he doing?" Vancel thought aloud. The answer came as he saw his friend slay two more mages, thus revealing what had been hidden behind them. Ethan needed help as the Relusians were now surging forward. Vancel Torrent lifted his sword ready to lead the remnant of the noble cavalry to aid his prince when a strong hand grasped his arm.

"No, Vancel," a grim voice commanded.

Vancel turned to meet the face of his king beside him.

"Sire! We must help Ethan!"

"He is too far afield, lad, for you to aid him. Gather your men and be ready," Bronus said, his voice masking his worry laden heart. Bronus rode beyond the southernmost of his men and dismounted, his heavy armored boots imprinting in the soil. He drew upon the anger festering in his blood and screamed his fury as he cast his rage upon the exposed Relusians. Lightning erupted from his fingertips, streaming swiftly southward and passing unhindered into the Relusians serried ranks nearest the River. Soldiers shook emphatically as the charged energy streams rippled through their cohorts. Blood issued from gaping mouths and exploded from ears, eyes, and noses. With no mage shields for protection, the Relusian left flank was helpless as tens of thousands crumpled to the ground from the Lightning Lord's Fury.

*****

The men closing on Ethan, staggered as lightning riddled their ranks, sweeping from the west like a river of death. Ethan swerved between a scattering of pikemen, dodging left, then right as sword tips swung at empty air. He stayed his trigger, saving his chambered rounds for the next mage pairing. The task was growing more difficult as the Relusian infantry were aligning with their mages. Relief washed over him as lightning erupted overhead, clearing his path as he drew close to the next pairing. A dozen Relusian knights charged forth afoot to defend the two mages ahead. Ethan quickly noticed the dark hair and narrow frame of the mage. It was the Relusian king, Magnus Delmarin.

Magnus fixed a nervous eye upon Ethan's approach, as he outstretched his arms to shield himself from King Bronus's lightning. Realization dawned on him as he recognized the son of Bronus Blagen and why the man had been able to see their formations. Ethan pulled back on Bull's reins, rearing the horse into the air as several knights blocked his way to Magnus.

Ethan emptied two rounds into the knights, then drew another pistol and felled six more before chasing the others from their king. Magnus lowered his arms, releasing his shield as he attempted to flee. Ethan circled close, reaching out a hand and snatched Magnus Delmarin from his saddle, dropping him on the ground. Ethan felt his neck jerk suddenly, nearly jarring him from his saddle. Reaching his right hand to his neck as he shifted his pistol to his left, he felt the feathered end of a bolt protruding from his neck, just below his ear. The wound instantly healed around the barbed arrow. He quickly wrapped his fingers around the protruding end and yanked it free, reopening the wound as he did so. He quickly healed a second time as another shaft struck his right arm. Lifting his eyes, he saw a dozen crossbowmen and archers with notched arrows trained upon him. At twenty paces, they were deadly close. Scores of pikemen and swordsmen rushed toward him, determined to protect their king, who lay upon the grass beside Ethan's mount.

He couldn't waste this opportunity. Ethan emptied his pistol into the soldiers rushing to engage him. Holstering his pistol, he leaned low in the saddle, reaching out his right hand as his left gripped the pommel. Wrapping his fingers around the collar of Magnus Delmarin's leather tunic, he yanked him into the saddle and kicked his heels.

"Come on, Bull!" Ethan shouted in his ear. The horse snorted in understanding as it kicked its hind legs, bounding northward as arrows and bolts showered their retreat.

Lightning crackled around him, passing left, right, and above as its deadly bright streams struck those trailing him.

*****

Bronus unleashed his full power upon the Relusian center and right. Only nine or ten shield mages remained, congregated on the enemy right. With his full fury pressed upon them, they slowly succumbed. First one and then another tumbled from their mounts, their bodies shaking helplessly before exploding. It was too much. Soon the entire mage line broke and ran or stayed and died. Lightning now streamed unhindered along the entire Relusian front. With all the Astarian infantry deployed north, to face the Meltorian host, only the remnant of the noble cavalry and Bronus's lightning protected the Astarian rear.

Bronus lost sight of Ethan amid the chaos as his lightning lit the firmament above with blinding brilliance. He dared not relent, for if he did, his kingdom would fall to ruin. He silently prayed that Ethan's immunity to magic held, for it was never so dearly tested. Ghastly screams echoed from the Relusian ruination, screams that cut to the bone and nerve, shaking even the grimmest of warriors. Bronus poured out his soul upon the Relusian center, wrapping his anger around the terrible power that flowed from his fingertips.

"Look, sire!" Lord General Brax shouted, his voice conflicted between hope and fear.

Ethan emerged through the glow of the lightning, silhouetted before its incredible brightness. Scores of Astarian noble cavalry broke ranks. They galloped across the matted grassy field, closing fast to protect their crown prince. From this distance, they could see him struggle as he swayed unnaturally in the saddle. He had something slumped over his horse in front of him. Ethan drew near as Vancel Torrent and his comrades filed in around him to guide him to the king.

"Ethan!" Ceresta cried joyously as her brother closed the distance that separated them before stopping several paces before the king and dropping the limp body of Magnus Delmarin at his father's feet. Ceresta's smile reversed as the horrific image contorted her face. Ethan slipped from the saddle, his feet painfully planting in the ground. A dozen arrows protruded from his back, several more embedded in his legs, three from his arms and two in his neck. He looked a giant tortured pincushion.

Bronus ceased his lightning as his heart went to his throat. He and Ceresta rushed to Ethan's side as Ethan's hoarse voice whispered inaudibly. Ethan reached behind his neck and yanked out the arrow that hindered his throat. The reopened wound sealed instantly, clearing his voice.

"Help take these out!" he whispered as loudly as he could.

"Vancel! Lend a hand!" Bronus commanded as he started yanking the bolts and arrows from Ethan's body. Ethan grimaced with each painful rip, reliving the agony that they already rendered. Within moments he was free of the impediments.

"Well done, Prince Ethanos!" Lord General Brax praised him.

Bronus eyed the boy with pride and anger. "I probably should yell at you, son, but I can't bring myself to do it." He shifted his eyes to the quivering Relusian king, who was now awake and kneeling in the soil before them. Several king's knights seized Magnus and clapped him in irons.

"Whatever survives of your army after this, I suggest you order them to surrender!" Bronus waved his right arm southward as the Astarian royal cavalry paraded across their field of vision nearly four thousand strong. They sped swiftly along the southern edge of the Astarian army with lances raised. The sun shone upon their steel-tipped lances, contrasting their black armor with gold lightning emblazoned upon their chests. They dressed to the right, aligning their formation as Bronus released another volley of lightning throughout the listless Relusian formation. The lightning ceased as the king's royal cavalry surged forth, their hooves pounding the earth like thunderclaps.

Vancel Torrent rallied the remnant of the noble cavalry, extending the line of the royal cavalry and riding forth to meet the Relusian host. The field was ablaze as lightning ignited scores of fires amid the Relusian ranks. Spirals of smoke drifted above, obscuring the battlefield in shades of black and white. The Astarian lances lowered as they drew near, passing through the smoke-choked air to whatever awaited beyond.

Beyond the din and haze the Astarians found tens of thousands of Relusians strewn upon the battlefield, their bodies twisted, burning, and scorched. Others flopped painfully like tortured fish, trying to twist their crippled bodies from the encroaching flames. Once the shield mage line crumbled, they were helpless against the lightning lord's fury. The Astarian cavalry swept over those still standing in the fore ranks, driving through the Relusians like wet parchment. Those still in ordered formations broke under the weight of Astarian lances. Smaller groups and individuals still standing fell to the broad swords of the cavalry. With their king missing and their mage wall broken, the remaining Relusians broke asunder, half fleeing and half raising their arms in surrender.

As Bronus returned his attention northward, cognizant of the Meltorian threat, he noted his son's absence. "Where is Ethanos!" he growled.

*****

Ethan wasted little time reloading his rifle and pistols before guiding Bull through the tightening ranks that separated him from the Meltorians. He caught sight of a Meltorian fire mage casting flames upon the Astarian fore ranks. Lifting his rifle to his shoulder, he fixed the red-robed figure in his sights and squeezed off a round. The sound of the rifle overcame the din of battle, the cries of the dying, and the clang of metal, bewildering the men of either side. The Meltorian fire mage slipped from his mount, his listless corpse dropping like a weighted sack. The mages always kept back from the forward ranks, using a line of steel to shield them from the enemy while they cast magic upon their foes. The mage casters sat on horseback to see over the heads of their fellows, while protective mages hid within the ranks afoot, with little need to see the enemy.

Ethan worked his way through the serried ranks, targeting any Meltorian mage he could find. Those mounted were easy targets as he took careful aim. Within minutes he slew two fire mages, an ice mage, a blinder, and two shield mages. The shields were difficult to find, standing afoot among the infantry. He dismounted and worked his way into their ranks. Ethan found a shield mage with his arms outstretched, shielding those around him from both mage craft and warcraft. Arrows would bounce harmlessly astray, and sword points would be thrust as if into stone.

Ethan fixed his rifle on the Meltorian forward infantry, emptying his rifle into their mass, each round a head shot. He sheathed his rifle in his saddle, dismounted, and sent Bull to the rear before drawing his pistols. The strange echo of gunfire and the falling soldiers frightened the Meltorians and allowed Ethan to advance on the shield mage. Once within his line of sight, Ethan leveled the barrel of the Colt on the head of the mage. The bullet pierced the mage's skull, splattering brains and blood upon its exit. Ethan withdrew the pistol, keeping it close to his body, lest someone attempt to snatch it away.

A soldier swung a short sword, but Ethan sent a round into his skull. He felt others closing in upon him. Holstering his pistol, he drew Lord Brax's sword. He blocked a blow from his right, spinning around the block and chopping the man's leg. Another came at him from behind. Ethan parried the blow with unnatural swiftness, then delivered a devastating thrust. He kicked the man's chest to free his blade from his heart. The emphatic blow pierced the fellow's armor as if it were wicker. Yanking the sword free, he spun upon another, parrying the man's blade, then thrusting his sword into the Meltorian's neck. Another came upon his left. Ethan ducked, swinging his blade upon the fellow's knee. He stumbled away as the man crumpled to the ground. He dodged another hasty blow, taking an offered arm at the elbow. No longer chasing mages, he now fought whatever enemy was near, spinning like a dervish as he tore through their formation. He felt a sword pierce his back, before spinning on his attacker, forcing the fellow to lose his grip on the hilt. Ethan cut down the now unarmed foe as his wound healed around the embedded blade that jutted from his back.

He continued on, his shirt stained with blood and torn with the dozens of wounds he had thus far suffered. He tore into the enemy like an apparition conjured from their darkest nightmares. He looked the part of a savage wounded animal with intense wild eyes staring through a blood-splattered face with a sword protruding from his back. Slash. Thrust. Parry. Thrust. He felled three more, driven by instinct and guided by skill. He lost track of time and place, thinking only of the nearest foe. He felt a spear tip in his left thigh. He took the head of the one who dealt the blow. His thigh healed as a crossbow bolt struck his right cheek. He quickly gripped the projectile and yanked it free as a half-dozen swords closed around him. He drew his pistol with his left hand, dropping four of them in quick succession. Holstering his empty pistol, he moved on the others. His lungs were taxed repeatedly but regenerated to full health as quickly as they were drained. He stumbled upon another shield mage, the fellow's frightened brown eyes fixed upon him with his arms helplessly outstretched. As the soldiers protecting the mage gave way, Ethan stepped forth, driving his sword into the mage's heart.

Lightning followed Ethan's path, ripping through the shield break in the Meltorian ranks. With lightning and arrows passing overhead, he felt another sword pierce his back. As he was fighting off that attacker, three more arrows struck his legs and back. Swinging his blade blindly, he felt it strike flesh before a shattering pain slammed into his skull. He rolled on the ground as the sound of lightning crackled above along with the echoes of men shouting someone's name.

"Dragos! Dragos!"

The words were the last thing Ethan remembered before the world went dark.

CHAPTER 11

Was he dead? The world was eerily quiet as he lay there, pressed into the ground by a great weight. He wondered if he were in a grave, and the weight he felt was soil piled upon his back. His fingers on his left hand twitched. Ethan released a shallow breath, trying force in fresh air. A slick fluid coursed his face as he felt armored mail imprinting on his left cheek. His left hand came to life as he attempted to draw it close to his chest in order to push himself off the ground, but something attained it, trapping the hand away from his body. Running his fingers blindly down his palm, he found a thin shaft piercing his palm and embedding it to the ground. He tried lifting it off the ground to no avail, for there was too much weight upon it. He closed his eyes as the slick fluid oozed down the bridge of his nose. Ethan tested his right hand, which felt under greater duress than his left, but it was free of impediment. He wiggled his hand closer, inch by inch, drawing it under his chest with great effort. He pushed his body upward far enough to bring his knees to his waist. With his head planted painfully in the ground, he brought his right hand across his body, reaching out for his left, then yanked the trapped hand free.

Snap! He heard the arrow break as severe pain gripped his left hand. The wound healed before he retrieved it to his body. Once upon all fours, Ethan lifted his back, coming slowly to his feet as the corpses atop him fell away.

"Sergeant!" He heard a soldier cry out as his head emerged from the pile of corpses that littered that piece of the battlefield. As the waning sun lingered in the western sky, he wondered how long he had been unconscious. A dozen Astarian bowmen, clad in green livery, trained their arrows on him as he tossed bodies from the pile, further freeing himself. The bodies of the slain were piled neck high all around him. The bowmen's eyes grew fearfully wide at the sight of him. He stood amid the corpses piled to his chest, his leather shirt stained dark from his countless wounds, and his blue eyes shining through his blood-smeared face like a ghostly apparition rising from the dead. Arrows protruded from his neck and back, and his shirt was torn from the scores of stab wounds he suffered. Their faces lit with recognition as they knew only one man that could suffer such duress and yet rise on his own accord. They lowered their bows in unison.

"We've found him!" The cry went out across the field of battle, reverberating like thunder as it grew unabated.

*****

"Let us fetch a litter for you, Prince Ethanos," the sergeant pleaded as they escorted him toward his father's pavilion.

"I'll walk," Ethan grunted hoarsely. He stopped suddenly and lifted an open hand to halt the procession. He pointed to the arrow protruding from the base of his neck. "Can you take it out?" his scratchy voice asked.

"I will try," the sergeant said uncertainly. He wrapped his tentative fingers around the feathered shaft and weakly tugged.

"Just rip it out, I'll be all right," Ethan said.

The sergeant tried to yank more forcefully, but the arrow would not yield.

Ethan winced as the tip reopened the wound. "*Harder!*" his gravelly voice commanded.

The sergeant placed his left palm on Ethan's back to push him away as his right pulled on the embedded shaft. The barbed point came free as Ethan stumbled forth a step, his neck healing instantly.

"Much better. Thank you," Ethan tested his voice. He still walked stiffly with a score of arrows impaling his back, arms, and thighs. The waning daylight illuminated the carnage of the battlefield. The pitiful cries of wounded and dying men echoed over the Velo like the melodies of disembodied spirits. The aqueous soil beneath his moccasin feet was soaked in blood. Severed limbs or crowns littered the ground, not allowing one to take two paces without stepping upon a missing limb or digit. Ethan was grateful that his pistols remained holstered, for he would have hated to dig under the piles of corpses to search for them if they had fallen. He didn't recall when or where he had lost his Stetson, but he wouldn't likely find it before nightfall.

"How goes the battle, Sergeant?" Ethan inquired as they continued on.

"Victory is ours, Your Highness," the sergeant said elatedly.

"Ethan, just call me Ethan. After the day I just had, I think I have earned it."

"Of course, Your High…Ethan," the sergeant corrected himself as he shook his head. Ethan was the only noble in the seven kingdoms who received being addressed by his title as an insult.

"We won the battle?" Ethan asked. "How?"

"Your grandsire, Lord Dragos, swept behind the Meltorian host with thousands of cavalry and light horse. They struck just as King Bronus ripped apart the enemy center where you pierced their wall of mage shields."

Ethan smiled inwardly as the revelation that Dragos had dealt the killing blow. He had sent for him to join them before he had first treated with his father. At least his grandfather heeded his counsel.

In every direction, soldiers were busy tending the multiple tasks that demanded attention, but no matter the urgency of their task, every eye was drawn to their crown prince, who walked among them as if arisen from the dead. They said not a word as they stared at him with silent appreciation until one soldier shouted his name: "*Ethanos!*"

Others followed in kind, echoing his name until it reverberated through the ranks like deafening thunder. The serried ranks quickly gave way to a score of heavy horse.

"Make way!" Knights of the king's guard shouted as they heralded the king as he drew nigh. The knights' horses circled Ethan and his escort as King Bronus's heavy mount towered before Ethan. The escort and the soldiers nearby took a knee before their sovereign.

Ethan eased himself to the ground as he knelt with great difficulty. Bronus stared at his son for a long moment, his emotions a volatile mix of fierce pride and festering anger.

"Damn you, boy!" Bronus growled. "Fetch a litter!" he commanded.

"I can walk, Father," Ethan offered, despising the idea of being carried.

"You'll be carried, or I'll break your fool neck myself, boy. That's an order."

"I need to find Bull. I don't kn—"

"I've already found him, along with your silly-looking hat, Ethanos. They await you at my pavilion. Now shut your mouth and do as you are bid."

*****

"Ethanos!" Ceresta gasped as he was brought into the king's pavilion upon the litter. She rushed to his side as they set his litter upon the ground.

"I'm all right, just help me pull these arrows from my backside," he pleaded. He had already dislodged three of them while he was being carried.

"I'll help you, Princess," Krixan's deep voice echoed.

"Krix?" Ethan lifted his head, fixing his gaze to his large friend who stepped from the map table in the pavilion's center where Lord Brax, his grandfather Dragos, his brother Tristan, and a dozen generals and aides-de-camp were gathered. Their collective attention was drawn to Ethan's prone form since he first entered their midst. Krixan immediately went to work, pulling arrows from Ethan's back and thighs as he lay face down on the litter. Dragos, Tristan, and Lord Brax quickly joined the endeavor. Within moments Ethan was free of the shafts and his wounds knitted closed. As Ethan gained his feet, he noticed his father standing in the entryway, staring at him with his steel-gray eyes. The others stared as well, each regarding the Astarian crown prince with wonder.

"Why are you all staring at me?" Ethan asked warily.

The others backed a step, save for Dragos, as Bronus stepped forth and placed his meaty hands on Ethan's shoulders. "I thought we lost you, boy." His voice betrayed the worry that had gripped his heart. Bronus wanted to say that he was sorry. He wanted to thank Ethan for saving the army and his life, but his voice betrayed him, breaking with emotion. He wanted to yell at Ethan for such reckless abandon, but his boldness was what carried the day. Any less on Ethan's part and the Astarian casualties would've been in the tens of thousands.

"You turned certain defeat into complete victory, my boy." Dragos smiled broadly, slapping his grandson on the back.

"I wondered what purpose those things you and Krixan carry on your hips serve? I surmise that your visit across the barrier was most productive, Prince Ethanos," Lord Brax said as he ran his fingers through his trimmed beard.

"Yes, they are quite dangerous," Ceresta added, "and I suggest you do not make Mother aware of their devastating potential."

"You look well used, big brother." Tristan grinned.

"I'm as good as new," Ethan said, though his face was caked in blood, and his shirt was so torn that it revealed more than it covered.

"Yeah, you look it," Tristan rolled his eyes.

"Ceresta," Bronus called to her.

"Yes, Father?" She turned to his piercing gray eyes.

"See to your brother. The rest of us have duties to attend." He shifted his eyes to Ethan. "Once you've cleaned up and changed out of those rags that you are wearing, we shall talk."

The others followed their king as Dragos lingered a moment, rubbing Ethan's head affectionately before following the others.

*****

Ethan changed into a spare set of buckskin trousers and tan shirt. His moccasin boots were blood splattered but still functional and fit to wear. He reloaded his pistols and rifle, fixed his holster around his waist, and tied down both holsters to his thighs. It was late in the evening when he found his father standing before the mage healers pavilion, staring out at the cook fires that stretched across the battlefield like stars upon a clear night sky.

"Are you all right?" Bronus felt a warm hand upon his shoulder. He turned, finding Ethan standing to his right.

"I'm fine, son. Here, this is yours," he handed Ethan his well-worn Stetson.

"Thanks." Ethan smiled, placing it on his head.

"Where did you find that silly looking thing anyway?" Bronus scrunched his face at the sight of it.

"Sheriff Thorton gave this to me my first night in Red Rock," he fondly recalled.

"Who is Sheriff?"

"Sheriff is his title. His name is Ben Thorton. His son was the man I brought back across the barrier."

"Yes. Dragos spoke of him. This sheriff you speak of, is that a title of nobility in their land?"

"No. They have no nobility or kings. A sheriff is a man trusted by the people to enforce the law in the village that he serves. Ben Thorton is the sheriff of Red Rock, and I was his deputy," Ethan said proudly.

Bronus bristled at the thought of his son serving as second to a village leader when he was the crown prince of Astaria. It was far beneath him, but he kept such thoughts to himself.

"Tell me why you lingered in this Red Rock for so long?"

Ethan told his father all that had transpired during his time away. Bronus did not share the boy's enthusiasm about Earth's mageless properties but found Ethan's adventures exciting, nonetheless. Tales of villains, heroes, desperate battles, and desperados piqued Bronus's imagination. The boy spoke fondly of the times he spent with Sheriff Thorton. He could easily discern Ethan's admiration for the man. Bronus felt a tinge of jealousy of the sheriff for the close relationship the man shared with his son. The sheriff lacked the burden Bronus carried when dealing with Ethan, the burden of being his king before being his father. Bronus could not afford the luxury of being Ethan's friend. He spent the boy's entire life trying to instill in him the responsibility that being king entailed. Bronus reproached himself for such self-pity. He should be glad that his son could enjoy such freedom before ascending the throne for once that occurred, such times would be sparse.

"And that's why I have to go back," Ethan explained. "Luke Crawford is still alive, and he plans to kill the sheriff. Ben is getting old, and he needs help."

"It seems you've already done enough, son. Your sheriff friend has his own son to help him. I need my son to help me."

"I thought I just did." Ethan smiled.

"You did." Bronus smiled in kind. "It felt good to have you by my side, Ethanos."

"It felt good to be by your side, Dad." He grinned.

"Dad?" Bronus lifted an amused eyebrow, no longer offended by that endearment.

"It's not an insult," Ethan shrugged innocently.

"No, it is not. I shall allow it after what you did this day," Bronus said before adding with a finger in Ethan's face, "as long as you refrain applying such appellations in the company of others."

"All right," Ethan agreed. "So what now?"

"You, my wayward, insolent, disobedient child, shall return to Astaris at first light."

"Dad, I'm fine. Let me help you. My wounds are—"

"Your work here is done," Bronus cut him off. "You accomplished what you set out to do, son. You saved your fool of a father from his prideful ignorance. Your mother longs to see her firstborn, and I'll not have her suffer your absence another day. When you see her, be sure to not reveal that Earth acts the same as the Mage Bane. She need not know that her mule-headed son spent this past year living recklessly without his ability to regenerate."

"She'll not hear it from me."

"Nor I, but Krixan shall never keep such facts from your mother, so I suggest he remain with me."

"Am I still to be escorted in chains and thrown in the dungeon ere I return?"

"The idea has its merits, but I surmise you have redeemed yourself to some measure, son." Bronus clapped him on the back.

"Then I can again escape the marriage noose." He sighed in relief.

"I wouldn't make such boasts when you see your mother, boy, or she'll have you wed at sword point. I suggest you find an acceptable girl and wed her before your mother takes matters into her own hands. What about Lady Murtado? I thought you fancied her?"

"I do. I will wed her in time, but I still have much to attend before then."

"Aye, but your next trip across the barrier shall be brief, or I swear I'll wring your neck till your head pops off. Let's see if you can regenerate from that. You will also bring with you a dozen king's guards with you for protection."

"All right," Ethan yielded the points. He wondered how he'd explain a dozen Astarian knights accompanying him back to Red Rock? Maybe they could pass as a traveling circus or a troupe of actors? He quickly shook such silly notions from his head. No matter what they did, they would all blend in as well as Krixan in Parson Green's church choir. Ethan said his good night and stepped away.

"Ethan?" his father called him back.

"Yes?" he turned, facing his sire with war-weary eyes.

"Thank you, Ethan."

"You're welcome, my king." He smiled.

*****

They knelt in the muddy war-torn soil, with their hands bound behind them and their eyes downcast. There were nine shield mages, seven shades, and a dozen other captive mages of varying abilities. All the shades and most of the shields were Gorgencian, proving that the Relusians and Meltorians did not act alone. Kneeling before the line of trembling men were Magnus Delmarin and Ortovan Marvo, the kings of Relusia and Meltoria. The glare of the morning sun shone painfully in the mages' eyes, dimming their vision, but affording Magnus and Ortovan a clear view of the judgment to follow.

Hundreds of Astarian knights and men-at-arms stood in disciplined ranks surrounding the enemy captives. Bronus lowered a gauntleted fist, signaling the executioners to begin. One by one, the captive mages were dragged before their fellows, with their necks placed upon the chopping block. Nary a sound escaped their lips as they stared dull-eyed as the first head rolled. The process continued until only the two captive monarchs remained. They would be brought to Astaris to bind themselves through oaths to never wage war upon Astaria again, oaths bound in magic. With so many shield mages fallen in this battle, it was doubtful that enough remained in all of Greater Elaria to ever again challenge King Bronus's supremacy. Having lost so many shades and shield mages, Gorgencia was now defenseless against his lightning power. With victory at the Velo, Astaria had effectively neutralized three of their neighboring realms.

After the executions, the men went about their grim duties. There would be time for celebration upon their return to Astaris. For now, they had dead to bury, wounded to heal, and a battlefield to set right.

CHAPTER 12

"Hail Prince Ethanos!" The smallfolk hailed as the column paraded through the village. The streets were lined with the populace kneeling as he passed. Workmen in leather jerkins and trousers knelt beside silk-clad merchants, women in homespun dresses, and landed peasants in wool tunics and hose. They ignored his order to rise and simply stared in awe at the Hero of the Velo, as some were beginning to call him. Others called him King Saver or Mage Slayer. Had the Meltorians won, each of these villagers would've been enslaved or slain. Now they remained safe, thanks to the glorious return of their crown prince. He hoped none would recognize him in his strange garb. Dressed in buckskins with six-shooters and Stetson, he looked nothing of their world. Since his return, he felt as alien to Astaria as he appeared to it.

"Must it bother you so to have our people acknowledge their crown prince?" Ceresta reproached, riding at his side.

"I tell them not to kneel, and they do it anyway. I tell them to rise, and yet they still kneel," he lamented, weary of it all.

"They kneel to the throne, Ethan, not you, a throne that shields them from the dangers of our world."

"It is unnecessary, just a humiliating formality steeped in tradition," he made the same complaint with every village they passed through since leaving the Velo, three days past.

"They honor you, brother, for your bravery and fell deeds. They do so because they are grateful and have manners, unlike a certain crown prince I know."

"You think me ill-mannered? You wound me, Ceresta." He smiled.

"Of course you are ill-mannered. Look at how you are dressed? I suggest you don more fitting attire before presenting yourself to the queen when we attain."

"What's wrong with how I'm dressed?" He gave her his hurt look.

"Nothing is wrong with your attire if you plan to wrestle a bear or ride a mastodon, but I suggest you rethink your presentation when treating with the queen."

"The queen? Why don't you just say *Mom*?"

"You have been remiss in your duties as a prince and as a son, Ethan. Our *mother*, the *queen*, has been distraught over your extended absence. We feared you had perished across the barrier."

"Yeah, I feel bad about that. I never meant to—"

"You never mean to cause harm, Ethan, but you often act before you think. If mother is curt, be mindful that you are its cause."

"I did apologize when I saw her at Plexus when we returned. She seemed more forgiving then you are making her seem. When I go back across the barrier, I'll be sure to return more frequently to assuage her anxiety."

"Neither Father nor Mother will allow it, Ethan. You are to remain in Astaris from now on," she reminded him.

"What do you mean?" Alarm rang in his voice. "I thought after the battle that Father's anger was—"

"The battle only changed the manner of your return to Astaris, Ethan. Just because you are heralded with awe and glory instead of chains does not change the nature of your return. You are to enter the palace and publicly apologize to the queen for your prolonged absence. Then you shall select a bride that the queen approves."

Ethan was crestfallen. He had come back to save his family and the realm and was rewarded with a cage. "Father raised no objection to my returning to Red Rock, why is it now forbidden?"

"Father rules the realm, but mother rules House Blagen."

"And the only thing I wish to rule is beyond me."

"What is that?" She regarded him.

"Myself."

*****

The gates of Astaris opened with great ceremony as their procession passed within the blue walls. Throngs of people lined the Main Avenue, casting petals in the air, heralding the return of their prince and princess. Cheers of "Ethanos!" rang out in the midday air. Knights of the city garrison paraded to the fore and flanks, their bright silver armor resplendent with the sun playing off their raised lances. The people of Astaris greeted them dressed in their finest raiment. Rank upon rank of women dressed in flowing gowns and tight bodices stood beside tunic-clad merchants with hose and pointed shoes. Lesser lords and ladies lined the way, shielded by their vassal swords. Every noble daughter in the realm seemed to be presented with the hope of catching the prince's eye. The avenue ran from the outer gate, through the city proper, to the gates of the inner citadel.

"Even commoners and peasants are better dressed than you," Ceresta chided. Ethan wore the same shirt he wore at the Velo, with its scores of holes from arrows and swords having been stitched. He wore one of his other leather pullover shirts these past days, one not covered with stitched holes and tears, but for some reason, he decided to don his war-battered garment. She wondered if he would have done so if she had not nagged him to dress more appropriately. She should have known better as Ethan always did the opposite of what she advised.

They passed under the raised portcullis of the inner citadel, where the host of Astarian nobility was assembled upon the tourney green. Every member of the great houses gathered to greet the first cohorts of their victorious army. The only missing faces were those lords still en route from the Velo. Each of the great houses stood below their banners where their coat of arms was proudly displayed. Though each was overly proud of their own signet, they were all bound by rich bloodlines joining them through marriage over the centuries. Observing the differing banners, Ethan acknowledged his lineage to each, as he was a direct descendent of the lords of each house. Of course, such kinship didn't prevent the high lords from pushing their daughters to Ethan in hopes of refreshing their blood ties to the throne. If the commoners and lesser nobility were well dressed, the greater lords and ladies thus assembled were adorned far richer by comparison. Each of the ladies wore long silken gowns that flowed in shimmering perfection. high lords in rich doublets, silken trousers, and billowing serge capes stood beside sons in tunics and hose. The mage lords and their houses were aligned on opposing sides of the tourney green, allowing Ethan and his escort to pass between them.

Queen Gabrielle awaited them at the north end of the green, standing atop a raised dais overlooking the assemblage. Princess Felicia and Princess Arian stood to either side, each dressed in golden silk gowns and smiling at their wayward brother's return.

Ethan noticed Lord Torrent standing before the red and white colors of his house, off to his right. He clicked his tongue, guiding Bull to his right, breaking free of the formation.

"Lord Torrent!" Ethan hailed as he drew up before him.

"Prince Ethanos," Lord Torrent spoke as he started to kneel.

"Stand, please." Ethan smiled as he pushed his hat further back on his brow as he leaned forward with his hands resting on the pommel. "I thought you should know that Vancel is well. He fought bravely and has brought great honor to your house and Astaria."

"It is kind of you to say, my prince," Lord Torrent said with a hint of pride in his brown eyes. Lord Torrent often chided his first-born son, reproaching the boy for his dull wit and oafish manners. He was a prideful, cunning lord who did not suffer fools lightly. His son's friendship with Ethanos was one of his boy's notable achievements. Having sired only sons, Lord Torrent lacked a daughter to present to Ethan for a bride. Having known Ethan's nature, he knew it a useless gesture to tempt the boy with something he was loath to accept. He snickered inwardly at the other great houses' attempts to make their daughters into the future queen. How little they knew Ethanos.

"Ethanos!" Ceresta hissed, annoyed with his diversion and for keeping their mother waiting.

Ethan touched a finger to his hat, granting Lord Torrent an informal salute that Sheriff Thorton was prone to use, before turning Bull's reins. He galloped to the base of the dais, dismounting in a single bound and climbed the steps to greet his mother.

Queen Gabrielle's heart beat emphatically at the sight of her son. How she longed for this day through the months of anguish of not knowing if he lived or died across that accursed barrier. Their brief reunion at Plexus was bittersweet with the uncertainty of war, but now her entire family was safe. Her startled eyes drew wide as Ethan ignored protocol and wrapped his thick muscled arms around her, lifting her off the dais and twirling her around in a fearsome hug. Ceresta face-palmed as gasps rippled throughout the assemblage. Ethan finally set her down and took the expected knee before his queen.

"I'm sorry," he said with a sheepish smile, masking a wolfish grin.

"Oh, Ethanos," she sighed, not knowing what to do with the boy. She placed both hands upon his cheeks and kissed his forehead before taking his hands in hers and helping him to his feet. "We have much to discuss, my son, but for now, we shall partake in the festivities," she said, turning him toward the crowd and lifting her hands to the gathered nobility.

"My lords and ladies of Astaria, we welcome the return of Crown Prince Ethanos Blagen and the vanguard of our victorious army."

An uncharacteristic cheer rang through the highborn crowd, a tribute to the fell deeds of their native sons and the prince who led them. The danger that loomed over their realm, like a dagger to the throat, was lifted. Now they could reap the rewards of victory and peace and partake in the first of many festivities that would continue apace until the king's arrival. Once King Bronus returned to his capital city, Astaris would host the great celebration, the first of what would become a holiday of the realm.

*****

Ethan tugged at the stiff collar, hating the rich doublet, tunic, and hose his mother insisted that he wear for the ball she organized in the great hall. Arches of bluestone angled to the ceiling, above a floor of mirrored black stone. Lanterns hanging from the ceiling, cast images of celestial bodies upon the azure stone walls in varying colors. Each image was cut from the lanterns' sides and covered with colored glass. Musicians armed with flutes and harps were perched upon a raised dais in a corner of the chamber as soprano voices echoed in song. Ethan felt naked without his buckskins and pistols. He didn't even have a sword as his mother deemed it inappropriate for the evening as she paraded every highborn lady of Astaria before her wayward son, forcing him to dance with everyone.

He gifted the first dance to his sister Felicia, holding her close as they moved across the floor. She asked about Jake, and Ethan gave her his regards. She was glad to hear that he was yet unwed, and Ethan offered to take her with him the next time he crossed the boundary, if he was able to slip their mother's attention. Ethan danced with countless others as the night progressed, looking to make his exit when he was able.

"Prince Ethanos." Lady Lucia of House Gadera curtsied before him.

Ethan sighed inwardly, hoping in vain for a reprieve from the next dance, but smiled politely to the young golden-haired maiden and took her hand.

"If I crush your feet, I apologize, my lady. I am quite the klutz and have stepped on the feet of three ladies already this evening." He smiled as he led her across the floor.

"I was forewarned about your poor dancing steps, my prince, but you move with the care and grace your high station demands."

"Grace?" Ethan lifted a brow. Oh, how Sheriff Thorton and Skeeter would never let him live that assessment down if they had heard it or fail to comment on his ridiculous attire.

"You are very graceful when you choose to be, my prince. I believe your clumsiness on the dance floor is a clever act to avoid an activity that you abhor."

"Lucia, call me Ethan." He smiled.

"That would be wholly inappropriate, Prince Ethanos. I did not venture onto this dance floor to win your favor but to thank you for saving our army at the Velo. As vassals of House Jarvo, my father, brother, uncles, and cousins fought there, and we owe you their lives."

"We all owe each other, my lady. Being a soldier is a symbiotic relationship, with the man who fights beside you. I owe my life to the army as much as they owe me." He smiled sadly, reflecting on how many of his countrymen had perished at the Velo. The last count exceeded six thousand.

"You were the catalyst of our victory, my sweet prince. Most of us know how you hate formalities. You should know that many mage born find your casual demeanor enduring, and not every maid is desperate to win your hand."

"Not even you?" he asked, intrigued by the girl's odd manner.

"No, my prince. Sorlan Carn has already asked for my hand, and my family has accepted."

"Then why dance with me?" he asked, intrigued further.

"I already told you, to thank you for your deeds at the Velo and," she added in a whimsical drawn-out voice, "for delaying your betrothal for as long as you have."

"Delaying my betrothal? How has—"

"By delaying your betrothal, you have kept alive the hopes of nearly every highborn lady to be your queen, leaving us less discerning maids our pick of the many young lords of the realm." She smiled.

"Well, you're welcome, my lady." He inclined his head to her. "But I fear my delayed betrothal has come to an end. The queen insists I make a decision soon."

"Hmm," Lucia mused. "I thought you might use your royal request to bargain for more time."

"Royal what?" he asked.

"Your royal request."

"What's a royal request?" he asked, taken aback.

"You truly don't know?" She lifted her brows above her emerald eyes.

"If I did, I wouldn't be asking."

"A royal request is an acknowledgment from a sovereign to a subject who has saved said sovereign, their heirs, or the realm. You have achieved all three and maybe entitled to multiple requests."

"What kind of requests?"

"You must formally ask the king for a royal request and explain *why* you are so entitled. He then shall either grant or deny your request, but if your deeds are true, he cannot refuse to receive your request. You then state your request, and the king will decide whether to grant it or not."

The wheels in Ethan's mind started to spin. He had never heard of this, perhaps because he could not recall a royal request ever being granted. Of course how often did a mage king or his heir require rescuing? Or how often could one man make such a difference in a battle that decided the fate of the realm? That was rarer still. He wondered why his father or mother hadn't mentioned that he was entitled to a royal request. Did they fear what he might ask, or were they merely as ignorant of the tradition as he was?

"I can see your confusion in this. Perhaps you should study on the nature of royal requests before you decide what to ask for. You must be patient with your lord father, however, for the last royal request was granted hundreds of years ago, and he may be as ignorant of it as you."

"What can I ask for?"

"I am unsure, but it should reflect the value of the services rendered. And it should be more than merely choosing your own wardrobe." She smirked, regarding the formal costume he so visibly despised.

"I already choose my own clothes, but while I bathed, someone absconded with my clothes and left me with this," he snarled distastefully.

"You are quite handsome, my prince." She smiled teasingly.

"My friends would laugh me into the grave if they saw me dressed like this," he thought aloud, thankful that Ben, Jake, and the judge were on the other side of the barrier and that Krixan was still en route from the Velo.

"I believe our dance is at its end, Prince Ethanos." She stepped back, curtsied, then withdrew.

Ethan's eyes came alive, eager to depart the great hall and begin his research on the nature and limitations of royal requests. But where would he first look? *Dragos*, was the first thought that sprang to mind. The archives in his grandfather's tower here in Astaris included countless volumes of ancient texts. Ethan enjoyed reading but never more than exploring the physical world to which he committed most of his energies, but he was not ignorant of the deeper intellectual pursuits either. If knowledge was power, he meant to be well armed.

"My prince." Jennifer Murtado stepped nigh and curtsied, bringing Ethan's thoughts back to the present.

"Hello, beautiful." He smiled. She was the only lady he truly wanted to dance with, even though he didn't want to dance. Then he realized if he didn't want to dance, then why should he? After the Velo, he shouldn't have to do anything if he didn't want to. "Jennifer, walk with me." He held out his hand.

She smiled warmly, placing her hand in his as he led her out of the great hall. Queen Gabrielle regarded them carefully. Had Ethan attempted to leave the ball alone, she would have denied his exit, but she noted the way his eyes alit in Jennifer's presence. She was his childhood friend from the years she fostered with the royal house in Astaris. Gabrielle lamented not choosing the girl a year before, instead of betrothing Ethan to Lady Elenna before King Ectus rescinded the engagement. Ethan wouldn't have been able to cross the barrier and…Her thoughts trailed before realizing that without going across the barrier, then the Velo might have turned out less favorably for Astaria.

*****

Ethan led Jennifer to the upper levels of the great keep, stepping out onto the balcony overlooking the courtyard below. It was a half-circle-shaped platform of dark-gray stone, with a low blue wall lining its outer curved edge. Starlight painted the night sky above as they breathed the cool night air. Ethan faced her, lifting her chin with a finger as he stared into the emerald pools of her green eyes. Jennifer reflected the warmth of his smile, which matched the tenderness of her heart. She was a kind, beautiful woman. Kindness was a rare trait among the mage born and an attribute that Ethan favored strongly.

"You look lovely in that dress," he regarded the rich azure folds of her skirt and the tight bodice that accentuated the swell of her bosom.

"You would too if you wore a corset as constricting as mine," she teased.

"I think not. My outfit is embarrassing enough," he said, turning her around.

"What are you…" she started to ask, but the answer came as he immediately loosened the ties in the back of her bodice. He undid them enough to ease the tension in her torso.

"Ethan!" She gasped at his audacity. They were always comfortable in each other's presence. He loved that she called him by name when they were alone.

"Feel better?" His blue eyes smiled as he spun her around to face him.

"Much. Though my mother will be distraught over my comfort." She gifted him a smile.

"That's a mother's job, ensuring of their grown children's discomfort. Look at me, and you'll know you're not alone in that regard."

"I think you look quite fetching, Ethanos Blagen."

"Don't get used to it, 'cause I'm never wearing a tunic, doublet, or hose again. If I'm going to be king someday, then I should be trusted to dress as I damn well please."

"Like the strange garb you wore when you arrived this morning?"

"Yes, and as the future king of Astaria, I will wear my buckskins, hat, and six-shooters every day, regardless of what anyone thinks."

"Actually, I thought they were becoming on you." She smiled up at him as she cupped his cheeks with her hands. "Of course you would probably look better without them," she whispered.

"Maybe someday you will see what I look like without them."

"Don't make promises you cannot keep, Ethan."

He turned his lips into her hand, kissing her palm as he placed his hands over hers. "I'll make you this promise. I will wed you before any other maid in the kingdom. But do not begrudge me if I can delay it awhile longer."

"I can never begrudge you anything, Ethan. If we are destined to be wed, then I trust the fates to make it so."

"I still have much left undone across the barrier. If I can slip my mother's eye, I will need to return to Red Rock. My friends need my help."

"I don't know which will be more difficult, helping your friends or escaping your mother?" She laughed.

"My mother," he answered all too quickly. "Thank you, Jennifer. You've always been here when I needed you."

"And I always shall. I love you, Ethan."

He smiled. Taking her into his arms, he pressed his lips to hers. They lingered in a tight embrace below the starlit sky. Ethan found contentment in her embrace and thought sharing his life with her agreeable.

She observed the happy couple from the shadows, wearing a cowl to shield her face and amethyst eyes from those who could recognize their origin. The crown prince's sudden return and apparent rapid betrothal were of keen interest to her liege. Events were unfolding apace and unforeseen in a dangerous mix. Extreme measures would have to be taken if events unfolded as they seemed to be flowing. Lady Lucia had unwittingly played her part to undo the damage the queen had rendered, even if her thoughts were not her own. Her mandate was clear; Ethanos Blagen must *not* sire the future heir of Astaria. Just as she had done a year ago with the breaking of his betrothal to Lady Elenna, so she would with his next.

*****

The following morning found Ethan in the library of his grandfather's tower. He spent the better part of the morn ascending the little-used spiral stairs that ran the length of the tower. The citadel of Lord Dragos ascended seven hundred feet above the courtyard of the inner keep, its azure walls spiraling into the firmament in omnipotent glory. Everyone, save poor Ethan, could easily attain the heights of the tower with the lift, a two-meter-square stone that ascended or descended the citadel. Since the lift was mage powered, Ethan's magical immunity rendered it useless to him in ascent. Strangely, however, the lift would allow him its use in descent. The library was more than halfway up the tower, which consumed much of his time climbing the endless stairs.

Once there, he piled countless books upon the long oak table centered in his grandsire's library. To his utter frustration, Ethan could only read the newer texts that were written by hand or in rare print, none of which were older than two centuries. All the ancient texts were mage spelled in their construct and preserved through the ages by equally powerful spell craft. The words contained within their countless volumes might as well be blank parchment as far as Ethan was concerned, for he could not read them. Once again, his magical immunity rendered him blind to their content, nor could he read the titles that ran along the bound archives.

Ethan growled in frustration, pounding his fist on the oak table. He needed someone to read the texts aloud for him, but he wanted no one to know what he was searching for, for if his mother discovered his intent, she would ban him from her father's tower. He had no choice but to seek help. Dragos was his preferred choice, he would help his grandson without question as he often partook in Ethan's schemes, but unfortunately, he was still days away with the army. He couldn't ask Ceresta. Telling her was the same as telling their mother. In fact, Ceresta was worse. When he was king one day, she would still reproach him for his countless misdeeds, of that he had no doubt. No, he knew who would help him, but they were a matched pair, and he would be forced to confide in them both.

*****

Ethan grunted as he ascended the tower stair, balancing the tray with both hands and two bottles of wine tied around his neck. He cursed his displeasure with every level he passed, lamenting the pitiful state of servitude he was reduced to in order to appease his "helpers." Quite a pair they were, Arian and Felicia, each cheerfully reviewing grandfather's texts while Ethan fetched their supper.

"Oh, you're here," Arian chirped happily as Ethan entered the library.

"What took so long?" Felicia teased, smiling from her chair on the opposite side of the heavy oak table from Arian.

"Unlike you, I had to take the stairs," Ethan growled as he set the tray of steaming food upon the table.

"Might I remind you, dear brother, that we are working tirelessly at your behest. You are unable to read these mage-spelled texts. All we ask is that you facilitate our endeavor by doing the simple tasks that we ask." Arian smiled sweetly. "You may serve our dinner now."

"You're enjoying this too much," he grumbled as he set their plates full of steamed roast beef, carrots, and broccoli beside the open texts in front of them.

"Of course we are enjoying this. How often are poor helpless maidens served dinner by the crown prince of Astaria?" Felicia giggled. "Wine, please." She held out her goblet.

"Helpless maidens? You two are about as helpless as a cave bear in a field of sheep," he said, dutifully pouring their drinks.

"And you would do well remembering that," Arian said as she turned another page of the ancient text with her left hand while eating with her right.

If only Dragos were here, Ethan lamented. His grandsire would've already discovered what he sought, and without the homage, his sisters extorted from him. At least they agreed to help, he reminded himself. There were few mages in all the realm who could shield any thought from the queen. If his sisters discovered anything of note, they could keep it from their mother for a time. Eventually the queen would not only discover *what* they sought but *why* they were doing so.

"Have you discovered anything yet?" Ethan asked with his foot on a chair with his right hand resting on his holstered Colt, while the other rested on his knee as he leaned forward, looking over their shoulders.

"Put your foot down, Ethan. This is an archive, not a barn," Arian scolded him. Arian's parental personality always manifested when Ceresta and Mother were absent. When they weren't, she mimicked Felicia's playful spirit, but when they were, she was a stern taskmistress.

Ethan humored her by setting his moccasin clad foot back on the floor and dropping his Stetson on the table as he scratched his head. He hadn't cut his hair in weeks and longed to rid himself of its cumbersome length, though it was little more than two inches.

"We have discovered that the traditions of royal requests reach as far back as the reign of Astar the Great, nearly three thousand years. The tradition is not exclusive to Astaria either. It dates back even further in Gorgencia and Estasa, and only less recently in Sarcosa and Meltoria, let alone Relusia and Vellesia," Arian explained.

"What do they entail?" he asked.

"They're an award for 'exceptional' service to the crown or realm," Felicia said.

"Define exceptional," he asked.

"From what we have read, it is no less than saving the life of a crown royal, one in the direct line of succession," Arian explained.

"Or saving the realm," Felicia added.

"Which is extremely difficult and explains why royal requests are exceedingly rare. They are so rare, in fact, that the last royal request granted by an Astarian king was over three hundred years ago," Arian said.

"So I'm entitled to one?" he asked hopefully.

"You saved father and the realm at the Velo, Ethan. You are entitled to one, but whether Father grants one to you is his prerogative," Arian tempered his enthusiasm.

"If Father denies Ethan his request, then he threatens the foundation of our sacred mage laws," Felicia warned.

"Yes," Arian answered slowly, "if the request is weighed in equal measure to the service rendered."

"So what can I request?"

"Patience, Ethan. We are still researching that." Felicia smiled, tilting her head toward the stacks of tomes piled on the table. It was going to be a long night.

*****

"Where is your brother?" Queen Gabrielle asked Ceresta as they dined alone in her private chambers.

"I haven't seen him since this morn. He is probably chopping wood with Yance, or up to some other mischief."

"Hmmm," Gabrielle mused. "I believe you are correct. He is most likely indulging his reckless pursuits, savoring the last morsels of his freedom. Your father shall arrive four days hence. We have much to prepare for the celebration upon his arrival. Lord Drevlin shall oversee the preparations throughout Greater Astaris, and Lord and Lady Celembar shall oversee the preparations throughout the inner citadel. You, your sisters, and I shall arrange the festivities within the inner keep. By the way, where are Felicia and Arian?" Gabrielle inquired, lifting her goblet of wine to her lips.

"I haven't seen them since this morn." Ceresta shrugged.

*****

"Listen to this!" Felicia said excitedly, drawing Arian and Ethan to look over her shoulder as she read from the ancient tome. "The receiver of the *gift* shall not attain that which belongs to another's domain, save only the bonds that bind one to the other may be severed or redefined. As such, a slave or vassal's service is the purview of his master or lord, his value therein may be reclaimed as his own but not another's. The receiver of the *gift* may sever or redefine the bonds that bind him to his master, lord, or his...*king*."

"What if a king refuses the request?" Ethan asked.

"If the request is weighed in fair measure to the service rendered, the king must acquiesce, or..." Felicia's voice trailed off.

"Or what?" Ethan asked.

"Or risk the unraveling of the mage power of the royal line."

CHAPTER 13

Queen Gabrielle stood regally upon the dais, overlooking the sea of faces assembled upon the palace green. The towering azure walls of the citadel rose imperiously around them as they gathered upon the tourney fields, awaiting the king. The banners, displaying the colors of the great houses of Astaria, were arrayed along the fore ranks of the assemblage. The lord of each house stood forward of their colors as their kin and vassals aligned behind them. The green and gold of House Jarvo was posted furthest east. As Gabrielle surveyed the might and majesty of the realm, her eyes stopped at the gray and black of House Murtado, posted the furthest west. The way before the dais was open, allowing the king's procession to pass freely between the gathered hosts. Gabrielle wore a golden satin gown with glistening silver sewn into the edges of her cuffs and collar. Her crown nestled firmly in her auburn hair, as her emerald eyes sparkled with anticipation for the advent of her lord husband.

Thousands were gathered upon the palace green, each dressed in raiment worthy of royalty. Ladies in silken and satin gowns adorned themselves with necklaces of gold, silver, or rare gems that matched the color of their eyes. The greater lords wore rich doublets, serge capes, and tunics over thick trousers. Lesser lords and the younger heirs of the great lords donned tunics, thin hose, and cloaks in their houses' colors. Two hundred knights sworn to House Blagen, aligned upon either flank, their black armor resplendent with the gold lightning of their king emblazoned upon their chests. Behind the queen, and upon the dais, were scores of mages and archmages sworn to House Blagen, wearing the traditional robes of varying hues, designating their unique magical gift. The palace steward, the captain of the guard, the monarch of Greater Astaris, and countless others were posted upon the dais along with Princesses Ceresta, Arian, and Felicia.

Gabrielle sensed unease in her two younger daughters that fit not with the celebratory mood of the palace. She would investigate the source of their misgivings once the ceremony was concluded or perhaps even latter as she wished not to dampen her spirits. Today would be joyous, for she would finally have her family whole after a year apart. She was giddy, excited for the ceremony to commence and partaking in the celebrations that follow. She regarded Jennifer Murtado standing behind her lord father and imagining her as Ethan's queen one day. She was a bright and beautiful lady with the tender heart Ethan needed to calm his restless spirit. Once that marriage was sealed, Gabrielle could look to her other children. She felt a pang of guilt for neglecting their betrothals as her concern for Ethan consumed much of her time and worry.

She was yet plagued by dreams of her firstborn suffering. The dreams were prophetic, as she was so gifted, but what was unusual was the fact that she could see Ethan at all in them. They were the same dreams that plagued her for over a year now. Prophetic dreams were manifested through her mage gift, and whenever she beheld a vision of which Ethan was included, he was represented by a blurred dark image as he was immune to magic. The dream revealed her son in clear detail, suffering terrible agony as if his magical immunity was impaired or simply stripped away. The dream was a warning of the consequences if Ethan ever entered the Mage Bane. What was most odd and disturbing was that Ethan was not in the Mage Bane in her vision. Yet entering the Mage Bane would eventually lead to his suffering.

Gabrielle shook such foul visions from her head as her eyes beheld a score of knights in blue armor with the moon and stars emblazoned upon their chests, signet of her father's house. Lord Dragos broke from their midst as he passed through the main gate, galloping forth to the base of the dais as his gray destrier reared into the air, billowing his dark-azure cape behind him with its alabaster moons and stars sewn into its folds.

Gabrielle beamed proudly as her father dismounted in a flourish, his blue armor resplendent in the midday sun. His silver beard contrasted the bright azure of his helm. He still cut a dashing figure at his age, and Gabrielle loved him dearly, wishing her mother yet lived to partake in his company. As father of the queen, Dragos was the only great lord of Astaria not required to bend the knee, as his flesh was so closely bound to the throne. He ascended the dais, stopping before his daughter as he took her hands in his and pressed them to his lips.

"My queen," he greeted her with sparkling eyes.

"Welcome home, Lord Dragos," she said, failing to conceal her glee.

"Your boys have done well. All *three* of them." He winked. Dragos stepped aside, taking his place beside his granddaughters, sharing a curious look with Arian and Felicia as he did so. They looked one to the other, wondering how he knew what they had been up to.

It's my tower. I know all *that transpires there*, he whispered in their thoughts. *You needn't worry. Your secrets are safe with me.*

*****

Ethan spent his morning brushing Bull's back and repairing his shoes. Torg, the master blacksmith of Astaris, urged him to allow him to shoe his horse, but Ethan insisted to do the work himself. The old smith shook his head and grunted. It was useless to argue with the boy as he hated others waiting upon him. No lord or lordling tended their own horse, let alone a crown prince of the greatest realm in all of Elaria, yet Ethan was like no other. As the palace green was filling up with guests throughout the morn, Ethan tended his horse, chopped wood with Old Yance, and cleaned his pistols and rifle.

Torg was quite busy himself, hard-pressed by the hundreds of knights needing his services before the Grand Review. Ethan spent the better part of the morning helping Torg and the other smiths shod horses and repair armor. Many a knight gave strange looks upon entering the forge, seeing their crown prince hard at work and tending to their requests. Torg had never seen Ethan so happy as if he hadn't a care in the world. He whistled a merry tune while hammering away. Ethan was always jovial and easy natured, but not to this extreme.

Ethan lifted the battle-worn shield, setting it upon the bench, and began hammering out the dents. The shield belonged to Sir Loris D'avlar, a sworn sword to House Torrent and good friend to Vancel Torrent. Sir Loris was aghast when he asked Torg to see to his shield, only to have Ethan step from the shadow of the smithy, slap him upon the black and take the shield in hand to fulfill the request. Sir Loris began to protest the impropriety of the crown prince performing such a task for a lesser knight, when Ethan told him to relax and let him do his work.

Ethan noticed a mop of dirty blond hair peeking over the end of the stone bench, observing his work with unassuming green eyes.

"Don't hide back there, Nathan. Come around and help me." Ethan waved the boy hither. Nathan was a stable boy whose mother was a scullery maid and cook and his father a chimneysweep in the palace. He wore a plain brown tunic and threadbare leggings, yet was a well-fed, fairly clean, and good-natured youth of nine years. He had often heard rumors of the crown prince performing layman's work but did not believe it until he saw with his own eyes. He circled the bench as ordered and began to kneel when Ethan stopped him.

"None of that, Nathan. We have too much work to do, and today you are my apprentice. How does that sound?" Ethan winked at the startled boy.

"Truly, Your Grace?" he asked excitedly.

"Yes, but only if you call me Ethan. Now hand me that smaller hammer over there." He pointed to the tool hanging upon a rack behind him.

"Yes, Prince Ethanos," Nathan obeyed, retrieving the smaller hammer and placing it in Ethan's hand.

"What did I say about calling me Ethan?" he said as he took the hammer and began pounding out the smaller dents.

"My apologies, Prince…Ethan, but my mother says to be mindful of my betters." He left unsaid what could be higher than the royal family.

"Betters, huh." Ethan gave him a look as he rotated the shield to work on the other side. "You know something, Nathan? Your mom works very hard in the kitchens making delicious meals for the people that live in the inner palace. And your father works equally hard cleaning out the chimneys so we all can have clean operating hearths. I don't know what is better than hard, honest work?"

"Truly?" Nathan scrunched his face.

"Yes. It's true, even if certain gentry or nobility fail to recognize it, it's still the truth."

Nathan grinned as Ethan ruffled his hair. The boy helped him throughout the morn until the queen discovered Ethan's whereabouts and sent Sir Cabor of the queen's guard to fetch him, summoning him to the palace green.

Ethan wiped the ash and grime caked on his hands with a rag, then tossed the soiled cloth on the bench.

"Come on, Torg. If I'm going, then so are you."

"That would be improper, Ethan. There be thousands of lesser knights and vassals gathered in Greater Astaris, with no place for 'em on the palace green, let alone a common smith," Torg protested.

"There's nothing common about you, Torg, or any other smith. You work your own magic with ore, iron, and steel. There's a place for you on the prince's square," Ethan offered while lifting his holster off his workbench and buckled it around his waist. He tied down the twin holsters to both thighs before adjusting his trail worn Stetson. "Be sure to bring your men with you."

"Aren't you changin'?" Torg asked, noting Ethan's buckskins and moccasins.

"No," he answered in a drawn-out response. "I think I'll dress as I please from now on." Ethan grinned before stepping without, where Bull was tied to a hitch post in front of the smithy.

Torg shook his head as he untied his leather apron and set it aside before calling his fellow smiths to gather themselves for the grand review. Few had ever stepped onto the tourney green, let alone stand upon the prince's square. Now they would be placed in the fore ranks of the realm to witness the grandest of spectacles.

"Come on, Nathan. You ride with me," Ethan called out to the boy as he climbed in the saddle.

"Me?" Nathan asked with wide eyes as he lingered near the entrance of the smithy.

"Yeah, you." Ethan grinned, pointing a finger at the dazed youth. "You've been promoted to squire for the day. Of course, I'm not a real knight so don't get too full of yourself over the appellation."

Nathan grinned, running to Ethan's side as the crown prince lifted and sat him behind him.

"Ever been on a horse before, Nathan?"

"No, Pri…no, Ethan, I haven't."

"Just hang on. Bull's no warhorse, mind you, but he's one of my dearest friends."

With that, Ethan clicked his tongue and turned the reins, guiding Bull to the palace green.

*****

Lord General Jorus Brax paraded along the tourney green astride his grey destrier, his mount skirted with black wool. A silver sword with lightning woven along its length was emblazoned upon either flank of the horse's wool skirt. The lord general had identical markings emblazoned upon his black armored breastplate. His visor was lifted, revealing the trimmed beard and dark discerning eyes distinctive to the solemn, well-spoken commander. A plume of blue feathers ran along the center of his helm and down his neck. He dismounted at the dais before kneeling to his queen.

"Rise, Lord General." Gabrielle waved an open palm to her far left, where Lord Brax posted himself upon the dais.

Gabrielle was not surprised then when two knights of the palace guard escorted the motley band of smiths around the assemblage to the prince's square, adjacent to the dais, guests of Ethan, no doubt. Nor was she caught unawares when she spotted her firstborn astride his spotted horse at the back of the crowd with a peasant boy for a companion. Of course, he hadn't changed, wearing the strange savage garb that seemed as a part of him as his own skin. She was slightly miffed that he lingered in the back of the assemblage when his place was upon the dais at her side.

Tristan was next to enter the citadel, riding forth upon a snow-white charger, sans armor, lance, or shield, and dressed in a deep crimson tunic and trousers. He regarded Ethan with a knowing look, before shaking his head and moving on to take his place upon the dais.

The triumphant lords and knights made their way to the tourney green one by one, each parading before the reverential crowd to kneel before their queen and take their place of honor just below the dais. Vancel Torrent was accompanied by a dozen knights of his lord father's cavalry, each bedecked in the red and white of House Torrent. Krixan followed last, his towering form weighing upon his poor destrier. Unlike Ethan, he exchanged his Texan garb for dark wool trousers and shirt but retained a single six-shooter on his right hip, and his Winchester sheathed upon his saddle pack. Amusement rippled through the ranks as Ethan's friend knelt before the queen, yet his head still remained above hers.

Gabrielle smiled warmly as she bade Krixan to rise, placing a motherly kiss upon his right cheek and ordering him to stand beside Tristan, and among her family.

Traitor. Ethan smiled, shaking his head. Krixan might be his best friend, but he was hopelessly wrapped around his mother's finger. He was the son they wished they had, save for the bald head and the foul gas he was known to pass at times.

Ethan felt his mother's eyes trained on his over the heads of the gathering, scolding him with her silent stare. He was expected to take his place upon the dais to formally receive his father, but Ethan needed his father to precede him.

The sound of trumpets heralded the advent of Bronus Blagen, the Lightning Lord, the Bane of Meltoria and Relusia, and Mage King of Astaria. Flanked to either side by Kings Ortovan Marvo and Magnus Delmarin, who were brought to pay homage and seal their passivity in magic, he rode astride his black destrier. His heavy warhorse suffered equal duress to Krixan's weary mount as the heavily built king rode forth. He wore plain black mail over similarly hued tunic and trousers with his great sword at his hip, sans helm or lance. His steel-gray eyes met Ethan's blue upon clearing the pillars that circled the main gate in an arc. A vast column of king's guard, mages, and commanders of rank trailed the king. He broke from the formation, ordering the others to stay in place. His heavy warhorse clopped the soil, leaving ruts in its wake as he closed on Ethan.

Ethan removed his Stetson and swept it across his chest, bowing as the king drew nigh. Young Nathan clung tightly to Ethan's back, burying his face from sight.

"Welcome home, sire," Ethan greeted his father, lifting his eyes to his.

"Shouldn't you be up there with the others, son?" Bronus jerked a thumb toward the dais.

"I would, but I'd like a formal audience if you could oblige?" Ethan asked.

"A formal audience?" Bronus lifted a thick brow over a skeptical gray eye.

"Yes," Ethan said, ever hopeful.

"Shouldn't you be dressed formally then? Perhaps one of those ridiculous outfits your Mother purchased for your misery and my amusement?" Bronus's booming laugh broke the stillness in the air.

"I think I'm old enough to dress myself," Ethan said with a pained smile.

"Bah! After the Velo, boy, I guess you earned it. Who's that behind you?"

"My honorary squire for the day. Meet Nathan."

Young Nathan dared a glance at the king before quickly lowering his gaze. "Good afternoon, Your Highness," he said shyly.

"Nathan? Ahh, the stable boy. Hmm, well, you keep an eye on Prince Ethanos, Nathan. He is apt to misbehave at least a dozen times a day."

"Yes, Your Highness." The boy blushed.

"All right, Ethan, you'll have your audience, though I'm certain no good will come of it." Bronus drew away, steering his warhorse along the pathway that divided the crowd. Gabrielle smiled at her lord husband's approach. The sight of his trimmed black beard over his thick square jaw made her heart swoon just as it did when she was but a maid. No match in the seven kingdoms paired two as dissimilar as Bronus and Gabrielle. He was coarse, large, and rough, where she was elegant, refined, and slender. He was blunted steel, and she was polished gold. He was strong ale, and she was sweet wine. He was boiled leather, and she was the finest silk. He was the tempest storm, and she the gentle breeze. Bronus's heart quickened as his gray eyes beheld his beloved. He could face any test or challenge with her by his side. He was the most feared man in all the land, but in her arms, he was a mere puppy. He loved her above all else, more than his kingdom, his children, or his life. Their children were more important than either of them, and he would sacrifice his or her life for them, but he did not love them above his queen. What he loved most in his children was that they were a symbol of their union, a part of her and him, flesh, and soul.

Bronus Blagen dismounted at the base of the dais, his armored boots imprinting in the soil as the entirety of the assemblage knelt in unison as well as those gathered upon the dais, save for Dragos and Gabrielle. The knights along either flank stayed a horse but lowered their lance tips to the ground.

Ethan dismounted and helped Nathan down before taking a knee at the back of the crowd. The king's procession followed him to the dais, each dismounting and taking a knee, including the mage kings Ortovan Marvo and Magnus Delmarin.

Bronus ascended the dais to receive his queen. The ladies of the realm blushed, and the lords and knights chuckled as King Bronus lifted his queen off her feet and twirled her around, pressing his lips to hers with a hungry kiss. Gabrielle caught her breath once they parted, fixing her emerald eyes to his steel-gray as she feigned outrage with his boldness. He was as incorrigible as Ethan, but it was useless to tame the untamable, so she yielded a smile, and he kissed her again.

"Welcome home." She smiled as their lips parted again.

He grinned like the overgrown child that he was and embraced her as he winked at his three daughters over the queen's shoulder. Arian and Felicia blushed and giggled with delight, while Ceresta tried to scold him with a broken frown that quickly morphed to a laugh as well. Ceresta could never deny her father a smile when he emitted such mirth.

Bronus regarded Dragos, Tristan, and Krixan before facing the assemblage.

"Rise!" he commanded.

That took long enough, Ethan grumbled to himself as he gained his feet. He swore that after this day, he would never kneel again or be knelt to, if his father was just.

"My brave people," Bronus's deep voice echoed like rolling thunder, clear and emphatic through the still air. "We set aside this day forevermore to honor our fallen at the Velo. The blood of six thousand sons of Astaria stains that river's eastern bank, sacrificing their full measure. Their lives have purchased peace along our western border for generations. A peace now to be sealed." Bronus regarded Ortovan Marvo and Magnus Delmarin, signaling them to ascend the dais. The two monarchs were richly dressed in robes of gold and crimson, with their majestic crowns set firmly upon their brows.

Ethan could clearly see the two monarchs ascend the dais before kneeling to his father. Lord Dragos drew nigh to the king, speaking the incantations into Bronus's ear for him to repeat. He could have done so telepathically, but Bronus hated anyone in his mind, unless in the battlefield. Ethan watched impatiently as his father spoke aloud the incantations, binding the royal houses of Relusia and Meltoria. Neither realm could wage war or raise arms against House Blagen. Each monarch repeated the vows of affirmation, sealing their obedience to the terms in magic, and should they violate said terms, the magic would consume their bloodlines, striking dead all who shared their blood. From this day forth, the monarch of Astaria would regulate commerce between the kingdoms, oversee treaties between the kingdoms and outside parties, and approve all marriages of the royal houses of Meltoria and Relusia, as well as their vassal lords. Only an aggressive act by Astaria could negate the terms or the willful violation of the code of mage law by the Astarian monarch. With the conclusion of their vows, the two monarchs arose and withdrew.

"My good lords, ladies, and subjects of Astaria," Bronus declared. "The honors I bestow upon the heroes of the Velo are too numerous to acknowledge individually in one day. So great was the sacrifice and the valor displayed by so many, I would be remiss to bestow praise carte blanche upon their entirety. Nay, I believe such heroism should be acknowledged to the individual by their sovereign as I shall do so over the coming days. This day, at this time, however, we shall set aside to honor the greatest among the heroes, for their selfless sacrifice postmortem or fell deeds most grand."

Ethan listened as his father called forth Lords Torrent, Luciel, and Jarvo for their houses' sacrifice, their vassals forming the majority of the army he led at the Velo. Grenar Luciel was honored postmortem for leading the noble cavalry in their ill-fated charge upon the Meltorian center. His eldest son and heir, Grevar, now stood in his place before the king. Vancel Torrent was acknowledged for leading the remnant of the noble cavalry after the death of Lord Luciel, displaying rare courage when the battle was most dire. A pikeman named Yotar Fulgent, who personally slew a sound mage, two commanders of rank, and six soldiers, was knighted in the king's royal guard and gifted with ten gold pieces, a destrier, and full suit of armor. How he was able to kill a sound mage, who could pierce skulls up to a dozen paces with their voice, Ethan could only guess. Half a dozen men were knighted for similar acts of bravery.

Ethan smiled proudly when his father called forth Marco Valanus for leading the decisive charge alongside Lord Dragos that decimated the Meltorian rear. Marco proved, as Ethan had often argued, that the light cavalry could move swiftly around the battlefield yet strike an emphatic blow when needed. Had Marco's contingent consisted of only heavy horse, they would never have reached the battlefield in time. Marco was awarded a captaincy in the royal guard, passing command of his light cavalry cohort to Tarlis Korsh. King Bronus's plans to scrap Ethan's *pretty ponies*, was squashed after the Velo. Ethan suppressed the urge to say "I told you so," though he so desperately wanted to. Such boasting would be wasted, however, for his father would only growl and strike him if provoked or taunted. Bronus was never a good loser. Besides, Ethan had to keep his focus on what really mattered, at least to him anyway.

Finally Krixan and Dragos were both acknowledged for their significant contribution before Bronus paused, his steel-gray eyes fixed on his firstborn. Father and son looked one to the other, each one half of the true saviors of the realm. Without Ethan, the enemies' shield mages would've carried the day. Without Bronus's lightning, the break in the shields could not be exploited. There was no honor Bronus could bestow the boy to fully reward his service, but Ethan asked for a formal audience for some purpose, and Bronus relented.

"Lastly, I summon Ethanos Blagen, Crown Prince of Astaria, Savior of the Realm and Hero of the Velo. He has requested a formal audience before the throne in full view of the lords of the realm. Ethanos, come hither!"

Ethan climbed into the saddle before reaching down, offering Nathan his outstretched hand and lifting the boy to sit behind him. He clicked his tongue, guiding Bull along the pathway between the assembled lords, ladies, and vassals of the realm gathered on the palace green. Ethan received a mixed greeting by the noble assemblage. Many offered fake smiles, concealing their disdain for his strange attire and poor choice of a squire. Every noble house had repeatedly offered their firstborn sons to squire for the crown prince, only to have their requests dismissed by Ethanos. Now, during the pinnacle ceremony of the realm's greatest triumph, he awarded that place of honor to a mere servant boy, one who was dressed as poorly as the prince. Others greeted him fondly, grateful for his timely intervention at the Velo, knowing he saved their collective lives with that brave act. Many others simply acknowledged him with the reverence his title was due.

Ethan stopped short of the dais and dismounted before helping Nathan down. "Here, hold these," he said, handing Nathan Bull's reins. "And take good care of this," he added, placing his trail worn Stetson on the boy's head.

"Yes, Pr...yes, sir," the boy corrected himself as Ethan grinned before ascending the dais and kneeling to his father.

"Rise, boy," Bronus's rough voice couldn't mask the pride he had for his son. "You asked for a formal audience, and so I have granted it."

"My king," he spoke, regarding Bronus with the formal appellation. "My queen," he greeted his mother with equal reverence.

"Spit it out, boy!" Bronus growled impatiently, suddenly cognizant of just how uncomfortable Ethan sounded when he spoke within the confines of proper decorum. The boy would have to overcome that when he became king.

"I…" He paused, trying to gauge how his parents would respond to what he was about to ask.

Gabrielle stepped nigh, touching a hand to his cheek. "Go on, Ethan. Speak freely." She gifted him the warmest of smiles.

He shifted his eyes from one to the other. He felt strangely nervous, an emotion that was alien to his nature. Ethan collected his thoughts before again kneeling at his parents' feet. A cold chill ran the length of Gabrielle's spine. Ethan was acting out of character, and it unnerved her. Warning bells rang through her mind as she retreated to Bronus's side.

"I formally ask for a royal request for my services to the realm and my king."

"A royal what?" Bronus made a face.

Dragos lifted a curious eyebrow and nodded with approval. Gabrielle paled, realization washing over her. She then heard the quiet thoughts of Felicia and Arian. She craned her neck, staring intently at her younger daughters as they attempted to suppress the memories and thoughts that would confirm their collaboration in this scheme.

"I formally ask that I be granted a royal request," Ethan restated while lifting blue eyes to gray.

"What is this royal request you speak of?" Bronus's voice was harsher than he intended, but Ethan always tested his patience.

"A royal request is granted to those who save the life of the ruling monarch or their direct heir or save the realm. The request is asked formally of the monarch and granted to the subject. The nature of the request is weighed to the measure of service rendered," Dragos explained.

"What do you want, boy?" Bronus asked.

"My life," Ethan said.

"Your *life?*" Bronus lifted a heavy brow over a gray eye. "You ask for what you already have. Does blood not flow through your veins? Does air not fill your lungs?"

"I live, but my life is not my own, and I would have it so," Ethan countered.

"And how would you have it?" Bronus growled.

"Free me. Free me from the bonds that bind me to the throne. Grant my birthright to Tristan and set me *free*. Let me kneel to no man forevermore or be knelt to ever again."

"And why would I do so?" Bronus asked.

"Because I have earned it, and I *request* it."

"A request is merely that, a request. Should I choose to reject it, it is within my right." Bronus's voice was dangerously low.

"The boy has the right of it," Dragos interrupted. "Royal requests are far more than their namesake. They represent the proper reward for services rendered. If the request is reasonable, they cannot be denied. To do so could unravel all bonds of magic within the realm." *As well as undue the magic binding Kings Marvo and Delmarin to the vows they swore to House Blagen*, Dragos thought silently.

Bronus snorted irritably as Gabrielle paled with Ethan's words. Those further afield struggled to hear the words quietly spoken upon the dais. Magnus Delmarin overheard enough to know that Ethan desired to forsake his birthright. His feelings were uncertain on the matter. As much as he despised the boy, would it not be better for Relusia if a nonmage sat the Astarian throne? Ethanos might be immune to magic, but he was dangerous in different ways, and as long as Bronus lived, the two of them formed a near-unbeatable tandem.

"Oh, Ethanos," were the only words Gabrielle could utter with her breaking voice and moistened eyes.

Bronus could not assuage his own sense of rejection with his son's request. Ethan's greatest desire was to throw all that he bequeathed him back in his face. Ethan would inherit all that Bronus possessed, one day sitting the throne of the greatest kingdom of Elaria, yet he wanted none of it. The pain of his son's denial struck at his very core until he could bear it no longer. "You would forsake your family as your reward?" Bronus spat angrily.

Ethan was taken aback by his father's hurt. He came to his feet and reached out to his sire, placing his hands upon his father's large shoulders. "I would never forsake my family or exchange the love I hold for you for a mountain of gold or any treasure of this world. I shall forever wear your name with pride, Father. I am Ethan Blagen, and I swear to defend my house until my dying breath, but I am no mage. If you search your feelings, you will find the truth in my words. I was meant to be free. Free from any throne or lordly obligation. If I truly wanted, I could have forsaken my house and fled to the wilds or the Mage Bane and embraced my free-born right. But to do so would have meant forsaking my home and family, whom I love. Please, Father, grant me my freedom, while allowing me to retain my bonds to our family."

Ethan's heartfelt appeal deflated Bronus's ire, rendering him crestfallen. Bronus looked toward the heavens, his unfocused eyes catching sight of lonely clouds passing over azure walls and below blue skies. Ethan was right; if he listened to the whispers of his heart, he could see the truth clearly. Bronus released a heavy sigh, returning his weary eyes to Ethan.

"So be it," he relented. "Take a knee, my *son*."

Ethan again knelt as Bronus placed a meaty hand upon his head before speaking in a mighty voice.

"Prince Ethanos has been granted a royal request for saving the realm and the lives of his father and people. Ethanos has requested his *freedom* from the bonds of royal obligation. Forthwith he is *free* of the Astarian throne, which shall now pass to his brother, Prince Tristan, when I am no more. Ethanos kneels to no man, and no man kneels to him. He is equal to every man as all are equal to him. Though free to make his own way in this world, he retains his bond as *my son*. Arise, Ethanos, *freeman of Astaria!* And never kneel again!" Bronus proclaimed.

Ethan gained his feet and embraced his father. Bronus was taken aback by the boy's affection, struggling to recollect the last time Ethan offered such heartfelt gratitude. Gabrielle covered her mouth as tears squeezed from her eyes. Tristan shook his head, not surprised by his brother's action or pleased by his own ascension. A thirst for regal authority was not of his nature, a rare trait among mage-born princelings. Had Tristan displayed a hint of haughty arrogance that was akin to so many, Ethan would've never gifted him the throne. For the sake of others, Ethan would've retained his birthright.

Tristan will make a far better king than I, Ethan reflected, easing the weight of his decision. Tristan was guided by logic and reason and would rule in kind. Whereas Ethan took after their sire in many ways, Tristan seemed a more somber version of their maternal grandfather. Dragos nodded with approval, regarding Ethan with a knowing smile. Of all his kin, Dragos was the most understanding and indulgent of Ethan's adventurous spirit and thirst for freedom. Dragos often counseled his daughter and son-in-law to loosen their parental bonds, allowing Ethan a measure of freedom he longed for. Dragos knew Ethanos was never meant to be a king or vassal. He was a stranger to this world, as if born out of place and time by the fates as a cruel jest. By his deeds at the Velo, Ethan was finally able to correct that oversight. Ceresta gave her brother a scolding look that she was apt to offer Ethan for his misbehavior. Arian and Felicia gifted him their knowing smiles, having shared in his mischief over the previous days, a fact that the queen would soon discover and chastise them for. He owed them a great debt for that, and he was certain they would extort some reward from him for it.

"Ethan, that is your reward for one royal request, but you are entitled to *two*, one for my life and another for the realm. Have you considered another worthy request?" Bronus asked.

"I haven't." He shrugged, having considered little beyond his freedom.

Bronus placed his thick hand upon Ethan's shoulder. "Would you trust me to state the terms of your second request?"

Ethan was again taken aback, uncertain of his sire's intent. He hadn't thought of a second royal request and couldn't think of anything he wanted. He was free with a world to explore, and the possibilities were endless. He held the power to heal and the ability to learn whatever he desired, what more could he ask for?

"I trust you, Father," he relented.

"*Krixan!*" Bronus summoned the big man forth as he ordered Ethan to stand aside.

Krixan stepped forth, taking a knee before his king.

"I would not have my son venture into the perils of this world alone, as his freedom now allows him. Will you join him wherever his stubbornness may lead him?"

"I doubt he can place his boots on the right foot without my advice, my king," Krixan grunted. "Aye, I'll do it."

Bronus slapped Krixan on the shoulder. "Truer words were never spoken, Krixan. I grant you the same freedom as my mule-headed firstborn. You are herewith free of lordly obligation. You kneel to no man and no man kneels to you, Krixan, son of Kraxan."

*****

The highborn mages, lords, and ladies of Astaria gathered in the great hall for the celebrational ball. The ladies of the court wore billowing gowns with layered petticoats as they floated across the mirrored stone floor with practiced grace. They were attended by lords and lordlings in rich doublets over silken shirts and colored breeches. Musicians played their cultured melodies that reminded Ethan of droning monotony. The dull music was a far cry from the lively tunes that his friends back in Red Rock favored. Ethan stood off to the side, dressed casually in his buckskins and six-shooters, enjoying the gaiety of the crowd while dressing as he pleased, much to his mother's displeasure. He looked on with great amusement as his mother forced Tristan to dance with every maiden in attendance. Tristan smiled and politely took each girl in hand, praising their charms as they danced across the floor. Tristan showed the ladies nothing but smiles while throwing Ethan dirty looks.

It's your turn, little brother. Ethan smiled, lifting his goblet to Tristan, who shook his head in return.

"You're enjoying yourself too much, my boy," Dragos said as posted at his side. Dragos wore the azure robes of his mage craft with the silver crescent moons and stars sewn into their rich folds. He tucked his hands into their opposing sleeves, with his disheveled hair sprouting unruly in each direction. It was strange how quickly Dragos transitioned from a seasoned warlord in resplendent blue armor to the robes distinctive to a master seer. Dragos spent the previous hours in his tower, immersed in his mage craft. The use of his gift disordered his silvered hair, contorting it in a tortured myriad, akin to a man struck by lightning.

"Nonsense, Grandpa, I'm just acknowledging my brother's happiness. Look at him move across the dance floor. He makes a dashing prince, far worthier than the clumsy imbecile who preceded him." Ethan couldn't suppress his grin.

"Hah, even you don't believe such drivel, and don't call me Grandpa. It makes me sound old. Call me Dragos or nothing at all."

"Okay, nothing at all," Ethan smiled.

"Don't let your newfound freedom go to your head, Ethanos. You can still suffer my wrath if you vex me much."

"Come on, Dragos, you know I mean no affront. Besides, you're my only family member who approves of my decision."

"You were born to be free, Ethan. I have seen your wild and willful spirit since you were a babe tugging on your mother's skirts and knew then that your destiny lies beyond the trappings of court. Your mother and father will come to understand in time. I am also not the only member of our family who supports you. What of your coconspirators?" Dragos cast a knowing glance toward Arian and Felicia.

"How did you—"

"How did I know? I know all that transpires in my tower. I suspected what your intentions were with the texts you and your sisters were reading. Every page you turned was known to me once your sticky fingers touched them. Of course, you only opened a few before remembering that you could not read them at all and recruited your younger siblings to aid in your nefarious activities. Being the tolerant and empathetic elder member of our household, I kept my silence and forgave your trespass into my tower."

"Thanks, Gra—Dragos," Ethan corrected himself.

"How did you come to know about royal requests in the first place?" Dragos inquired.

"Lady Lucia," Ethan regarded the fair maid dancing with her intended.

"Hmm, she is to wed Sorlan Carn," Dragos observed.

"I suppose," Ethan spoke in a Texas drawl, forgetting himself.

Dragos shot him a queer look.

"Sorry, just a mental lapse." Ethan shrugged as his eyes drifted to the lonely form of Jennifer Murtado standing beside her brother Javier as she stared longingly at the dance floor. "Excuse me, Grandpa. I have to attend to something."

Ethan skirted the periphery, avoiding the attentions his presence often drew. Unlike in the past, when every high lord with a marriageable daughter pushed their comely progenies into his view, now they shielded them from his sight. A marriage to Ethan would no longer gain them the throne. He still caught more than a few longing glances from highborn maidens who snuck a peek from behind their father's shoulders, but most ignored him, pining for the attention of the *new* crown prince. Ethan cared not. He knew the true ambitions of most highborn lords and maidens, and he was glad to be done with it.

"Would you care to dance?" he asked, offering Jennifer a hand.

She gifted him a smile and her hand as he drew her out onto the floor.

"Hello, beautiful," he said, gripping her closer than Astarian norm, reverting back to his time in Red Rock, where they held tight to their dance partners.

"Ethan." She smirked. "I thought you had forgotten me after forsaking your birthright?"

"Forget you? All I said was I did not wish to marry right away."

"More like *not at all.*" She raised a skeptical brow.

"I wouldn't say that, Jennifer, but there are things I must attend to. I have friends back in Texas who need my help. Once things are set straight there, I'll be sure to return home and pursue more personal matters."

"And if another suitor fills the breach in your absence?"

He thought on that for a moment before answering. "We'll leave it to fate, and then if we are meant to be, then we are meant to be."

And if not? she thought sourly.

They danced for a time before she commented on his eldest sister standing beside his mother. She had not danced the entire evening, while Arian and Felicia shared their time with every lordling in the realm. Ethan kissed Jennifer's hand before withdrawing. He approached Ceresta and dragged her onto the dance floor over her protest. Gabrielle gave her son a curious look as he danced with his sister.

"Ethanos!" Ceresta ground her teeth.

"Relax, little sister. I'm not the only one who noticed that you haven't danced all night."

"I doubt my improprieties can be judged by the likes of you."

"Easy, girl. I didn't call you improper, only frigid. Every young lord in the kingdom is scared to death of you. I'm just trying to thaw you out a bit so you'll smile more. Then maybe, they'll start asking."

"You're incorrigible," she huffed as he spun her around as if they were dancing in Bill Lawton's barn.

"You only think that because you're just like Mom."

"Mom?" She scolded him with her eyes.

"I'm free now, Ceresta, and I can call our mother Mom if I want to. It's not an insult, you know."

"Perhaps not, but it is hardly proper and wholly inappropriate. Despite your newfound liberation, she is still queen, and you should treat her as such."

"I'd never disrespect our mother, but she is not my queen."

"Only because of your selfish request," she retorted.

"Selfish request?"

"Yes, selfish!" she admonished. "Father honored you before the whole realm, and you reward him by throwing your birthright away. You might as well have spat in his face."

"I don't want to be king, Ceresta. I only wanted my freedom. I earned it. Is it so wrong to claim what you earned?"

"If it so hurts the ones who love you, then yes, it is. One valiant deed does not justify forsaking your duty."

"At least Dragos thinks well of my choice."

"That is hardly a sound endorsement. Grandfather has always indulged your restless spirit as if he is reliving his childhood through your eyes."

"Come on, Ceresta, lighten up a little." He grinned as he again spun her about before bringing her back into his arms. "Life is too short to gloomily reflect on the few dark clouds of a sunny day. I'm not throwing my life away on childish adventures. I actually have important matters to attend back in Red Rock. You should come with me. A fine-looking girl like you could get married right quick in West Texas. I know a few Texas rangers that would take a fancy to you, ma'am," he said with a thick Texas accent.

Ceresta just looked at him as if he sprung a second head. "You're hopeless." She rolled her eyes, trying to bite off the smile he was forcing upon her. How she had missed him. The palace was a dull place sans Ethan's carefree spirit.

"I know I am, aren't I?" He smiled.

"At least you admit it," she laughed. "Grandfather brought a few things along that you left at Plexus when you returned from the barrier. He had been dragging them across Astaria in his baggage train, hoping to return them to you. When Father sent you back to Astaris after the Velo, Dragos's baggage train was still miles off. I had them placed in your room."

"Thanks, I was in a hurry and couldn't bring my pack animal to the Velo." The packhorses carried hundreds of rounds of ammunition, several bowie knives, another holster with a single Colt, several pairs of buckskin trousers and shirt, and his guitar. *Maybe I can play "The Yellow Rose of Texas" at the next ball*, he thought happily.

"I assume Mother shall receive your next dance?"

"Yeah, if she'll have me." He shrugged.

"Of course she'll have you, though she often would like to strangle you, just as most of our household does. She still loves very much, Ethanos. Go to her."

"And what about you?"

"I have a new dance partner in mind." She smiled and kissed his cheek before crossing to the opposing wall, where she found Krixan standing alone. He wore a nondescript gray linen tunic over thick dark trousers. Unlike Ethan, he tastefully left his six-shooters in his bedchamber. She took his massive hand and led him onto the floor. His pale, balding head blushed as crimson as his rust-colored beard. He was as much a brother to her as Ethan and Tristan and stood high in her parents' regard, her mother's especially. Like Ethan, he was now free but continued to treat the royal household with great formality, unlike her wayward brother.

Ethan approached the dais, where the king and queen sat overlooking the gala. Taking off his well-worn Stetson, he swept it beneath him as he bowed at the waist, before rising to address the queen. "Would you care to dance, Queen Gabrielle?" He grinned devilishly.

"Ethanos," she regarded him with a bemused countenance before rising from her throne. She stepped down as he tossed his hat upon the dais and led her to the center of the floor.

"Thank you, Ethanos, you look much nicer without that hat." She smiled.

"I like my hat." Ethan gave her his hurt look.

"My dear son, you like everything that is improper or poor in taste."

"Come on, Mom, do I look that awful?"

"You are very handsome, Ethan. I just wish your attire matched the handsome boy that I raised. You now have the freedom to do as you wish, but as your mother, I shall always offer you my counsel, whether you heed it or not."

"Fair enough. I meant what I said earlier. Even though I forsook the throne, I am still part of this family. If you ever have need of me, I will come with all haste from wherever I am," he assured her as they continued to dance.

"Oh, Ethan, I know you shall. Do not misinterpret my misgivings on your decision with disappointment. I am proud of the man you are and all that you have done for Astaria and your father. I would speak falsely if I said I was pleased with your choice, but it was made with a pure heart. I will not begrudge your happiness, but as a mother, I worry for you."

"Worry?" He lifted a curious brow. "I'm fine, Mom. Nothing can hurt me, well, not permanently anyway."

"Now you listen, Ethanos Blagen." She fixed him with a terrible gaze. "No matter where you venture in Elaria, you *will not* enter the Mage Bane. *Avow it!* Avow it, or as queen of Astaria, I will see you locked in the dungeon!"

"I'm free, Mother." He smiled uneasily, not certain how to respond. There was great fear driving her warning, and his mother was never one easily frighten.

"You're free from the throne and the realm, but you are never free from being my son, and I will always protect my children whether they wish it or not!"

"All right, I promise, just as I promised last year before I crossed the boundary. I will not enter the Mage Bane," he reassured her.

Gabrielle's breath eased, but her terrible vision of Ethan suffering unbearable torment still plagued her. She was certain that if he entered the Mage Bane, the visions would surely come to pass. The fact that she could clearly see his image suggested that his magical immunity would be impaired or stripped away. The strangest part of her vision was that his suffering took place outside of the Mage Bane but was the result of his entering therein at an earlier time. She lifted her hand to his cheek, running her fingers along his face. How she loved him, her precious boy. The very thought of any of her children suffering in agony or dying rent her heart. It was a fear men would never comprehend, for it was rooted in a mother's love.

Gabrielle's train of thought was broken by strong voices in the outer passageway. Soon the entire great hall grew silent as a dozen king's knights passed through the doors of chamber, dressed in their black battle armor, not the ceremonial lighter armor of their sworn brothers who were posted along the periphery. Gabrielle stepped from Ethan's arms, returning to her place upon the dais as the crowd parted for the approaching knights. The knights stopped well short of the dais, their captain stepping forth and inclining his head to their king. The guardians of the king did not kneel when in direct service to their sovereign as they were to never be off their feet. A subtle dip of the head was all that was required of their deference.

"Sir Glaver, what urgency presses at this hour?" Bronus's rough voice boomed to every corner of the great hall as every ear in the vast chamber was attentive to Sir Glaver's next utterance.

"My king, messengers await your audience on matters most urgent. Shall I admit them?"

"Bring them forth!" Bronus commanded, his gray eyes narrowing as two figures passed under the high arch of the entrance. One was a commander of rank, a knight bearing the green and black of House Varo. He was a tall, well-built man and dark of hair with streaks of gray on his trimmed beard. Beside him strode a young boy in a blue tunic and gray hose, with the crescent moons and stars of House Mortune emblazoned upon his chest. All in House Blagen recognized the boy as a squire to Sir Dunston, a knight of Dragos's house. The gray-bearded knight and the young squire approached and knelt to be received by their king.

"Arise, Sir Knight and young Milo," Bronus acknowledged them.

"Your Grace," the knight said, gaining his feet. "I am Sir Thacran of House Varo. I bring ill tidings that dare not wait. I apologize for disturbing the gaiety of this austere assemblage, but what I have to say—"

"Out with it, sir!" Bronus growled impatiently, annoyed with the flowered speech that wasted his time.

"Yes, Your Grace. One of my sergeants came upon this young squire—"

"Milo," the king regarded the youth. "We know him well. A fine lad in service to Sir Dunston."

Ethan and Dragos stepped close to the dais. Sir Dunston was charged with guarding the cavern entrance at Plexus that held the gateway across the barrier. What was young Milo doing in lands sworn to House Varo far to the south?

"My sergeant came upon young Milo during a patrol of our lands. Most of the knights and men of House Varo had marshaled and marched for Astaris once you had called for our banners. I remained with few others to hold our lands in our lord's absence. I am the sworn sword of the fire mage Marcel Varo, brother of our lord, Ledder Varo, high lord of Astaria."

"This is so," the deep voice of Lord Ledder echoed from the assemblage, confirming Sir Thacran's identity.

"My lord," Sir Thacran regarded his liege before returning his gaze to the king. "King Bronus, young Milo here"—he placed a hand upon the squire's shoulder, who stood nervously beside him in the king's presence"—came to us, having escaped from a band of ruffians who were strangely garbed and armed with powerful weapons of terrible potency. It is he that should begin this tale."

Ethan's pulse quickened as he noticed Milo's reaction when the boy's eyes stared at his six-shooters. Something was terribly amiss, and if he was taken captive, then what of the knight he served who was charged with guarding the barrier?

"Go on, Milo. Speak freely, my child." Queen Gabrielle gifted him an encouraging smile.

The young boy swallowed nervously, deeply afraid of the royal court and the high lords and ladies that encircled him. "Your Graces, I...I bring ill tidings. Lord Dragos entrusted my liege, Sir Dunston, and Sir Corlis with the guarding the sacred caverns of Plexus. They, along with their squires and fourteen men-at-arms, guarded the cavern entrance. After Prince Ethanos and his party departed for the Velo and Lord Dragos for his encampment west of the palace, a band of strangers caught us unawares. They slaughtered Sir Dunston and Sir Corlis and all our men, including Sir Corlis's squire, Willhelm. They even slew our baggage servants, cooks, and foragers. They were terrible to behold, Your Grace. They killed everyone." Milo nearly cried in the telling.

"How could they take an entire detachment by surprise? From where did they assault the cavern?" Bronus asked.

Milo lifted his watery eyes to his sovereign. "They did not assault the cavern, sire. They attacked *from* the cavern, armed with weapons akin to Prince Ethanos's." Milo lifted a finger, pointing to Ethan's twin Colts.

The blood drained from Ethan's face.

"They took me captive as their guide, demanding that I reopen the gateway. I told them that only Crown Prince Ethanos was able to do so. They asked if Prince Ethanos was Ethan Blagen. I answered that he was, and they cursed his name, referring to him as the Devil's Deputy. They spoke many words that I did not understand. Lord Dragos had imprinted in the minds of all those charged with guarding the barrier, as much of the strangers' language as he had discerned when the stranger passed through a year ago. I knew enough to speak simply with the men but little else. They bound me hand and foot and remained at the cavern for the better part of two days, trying to open the gateway, but to no avail. Upon failing, they decided it best to leave, not wishing to remain in a land sworn to House Blagen. Having examined the maps that were in Sir Corlis's keeping, their leader decided to make for the sea."

"Who was their leader?" Bronus asked.

"Luke Crawford," Ethan said as the look the boy gave him confirmed. "He had a scar running the length of his left cheek, with fierce pale-green eyes and a thin muscled build?"

Milo nodded.

"Who is this Luke Clawfard you speak of?" Bronus fixed Ethan with his steel-gray eyes, trying to recollect all that Ethan had told him about his time across the boundary, but needed reminding which villain this Luke Clawfard was. There were so many names that Ethan threw at him, he wondered how he would ever get them all straight.

"Luke Crawford," Ethan corrected him. "He's an outlaw wanted by the Texas rangers, the sheriff of Red Rock and the United States marshals. He's the reason I needed to return to Red Rock. He's as fast on the draw as Jake or me, and Sheriff Thorton needs my help."

"Not anymore. This villain is now loose in *our* lands!" Bronus growled.

"He shall not tarry long in Astaria, my king," Sir Thacran said as Bronus's eyes shifted intently back to his.

"Go on!" Bronus commanded impatiently.

"When young Milo came upon us, Mage Marcel Varo ordered us to intercept the strangers near the southern end of the Corsis Valley. We aligned ourselves to either side of Mage Marcel as the bandits came upon us. Mage Marcel spewed fire upon the strangers to no avail. They merely rode through the walls of flame untouched. Not even a hair on their heads was singed. They are impervious to magic, Your Grace. Once they passed through the wall of flame, we attempted to stay their advent with our steel, but they unleashed magic of their own with their foul weaponry. Mage Marcel Varo was struck in the chest, a mortal blow that felled him instantly. Others followed in quick succession, including a dozen knights of House Varo. A mere handful of our number escaped along with young Milo. We rode to Astaris in all haste to relay this tale, my king."

"You were wise to come here, Sir Thacran. I'll have the steward see to your men. You may join your liege, Lord Ledder, and his retinue." Bronus regarded the lord of House Varo, who stood among the gathered lords, his countenance pale with the news of his brother's demise.

"My gratitude, Your Grace." Sir Thacran bowed and withdrew.

Bronus called forth one of his captains of his guard. "Send word throughout Astaria, warning every vassal and holdfast of these outlaws. I shall reward ten thousand pieces of gold to any that bring me this Luke Crawford dead or alive!"

"They're probably at the coast by now. Have your people avoid contact at all costs. Leave Luke Crawford to me," Ethan said as he ascended the dais and retrieved his Stetson.

"You do not command here, boy!" Bronus growled. "As king, I shall mete out justice in *my* realm. You will stand clear!"

"I don't command here, but you don't command me either," Ethan countered, placing his hat upon his head as he made for the exit.

"Where are you going, son?" Bronus called after him.

Ethan paused in the middle of the hall, the guests parting as he approached. He craned his neck over his right shoulder, facing his father, who leaned forward upon his throne with his fingers gripping its arms.

"I'm going to do what I failed to do in Red Rock. I'm going to kill Luke Crawford. Even if I have to chase him to the ends of Elaria."

CHAPTER 14

She found him in his bedchamber, packing only what he needed and little else. Ethan filled his saddlebags with hundreds of rounds of ammunition, salted meat, and spare buckskins, undergarments, and shirts. He set aside his single holstered belt, placing it in his chest at the foot of his bed. Before closing the lid, the emerald glow of the small stone he found so long ago sparkled with life as his hand drew near. He never told anyone of its discovery or strange properties, using it to play mischief with his siblings as it interrupted their mage powers whenever he placed it in their proximity. It was time he shared its discovery with Dragos, and allow him to investigate its mysteries, but alas, that would have to wait for another time. He ran his fingers over its smooth surface, the stone glowing brighter the closer his flesh connected with it. He drew his hand away, the stone's glow fading as he did so. He quickly regarded the holstered Colt he left in his chest before closing the lid.

"Must you leave so soon?" Gabrielle finally asked as she lingered at the doorway.

"Mom." He gifted her a smile before stepping near, drawing her into his embrace. Ethan placed a kiss to her forehead before taking a step back. "I have to face Luke. I am the only one who can."

"Can what…die?" she asked.

"No, defeat Luke. He can't heal himself as I can, and no one else can best him with one of these, except me," he patted the Colt .45 resting on his right hip.

"Must you tempt fate, Ethan? Let others take up the cause of justice. Haven't you done enough?"

"What other choice have we? Let him run out of bullets, and then take him down? How many of our people would have to be sacrificed for such a strategy to play out? Fifty, one hundred, two hundred? No." He shook his head. "I must do this. Crawford is here because of me. He followed me to Astaria, and I must correct my mistake."

"Might you at least wait until morning before rushing out in the middle of the night?" she pleaded.

"I don't dare wait. I figure I can put twenty miles between Astaris and me before bedding down for the night."

"Your Grace," a soft feminine voice beckoned from the outer corridor. Ethan caught sight of a young serving maid standing at his doorway, holding a tray of steaming chicken, fresh bread, and carrots.

"Come, Millie," Gabrielle ordered the servant hither.

The young girl curtsied, stepping nigh, placing the tray upon the bed before curtsying again and stepping without.

"What's all this?" he asked.

"You left the hall before the feast. You need a warm meal before taking the trail."

Ethan smiled and shook his head with wonder at the love of a mother. "Thanks."

"You're welcome," she said, cupping his chin in her delicate fingers, fixing her green eyes to his blue. "You just remember your promise, my son. *Do not enter* the Mage Bane under any circumstance, do you understand?"

"I promise. If Luke Crawford goes that far, I'll wait him out or leave him to his fate. Even he won't live long in that foul place."

Her eyes softened with his reassurance. "Very well." She patted his thick chest. She then noticed the strange stringed instrument leaning against the wall. She found it odd that he possessed such an item knowing his resistance to any musical lesson she had foisted upon him throughout his childhood. "Is that some strange mandolin?"

"No, that's a guitar. I wouldn't be caught dead playing a mandolin like a foppish minstrel," he said indignantly.

"And you *play* this instrument?" she inquired curiously.

"Well…yeah…but I'm not very good."

"Show me!" she commanded.

"Mom…I—"

"Have you played for others?"

"I…Yes," he sighed.

"Then you can play for me."

Ethan knew when he was beaten. Retrieving his guitar, he sat on the edge of his bed and gifted her one of the few melodies he picked up in Red Rock. He preferred "The Yellow Rose of Texas" or "The Streets of Laredo" but wisely chose a more appropriate selection for the moment, "The Red River Valley."

Gabrielle swooned over the rich timbre of his voice, a perfect blend of boyish charm and masculinity. She shook her head, despondent over his refusal to demonstrate his musical prowess throughout his childhood. All this time, he hid his voice, professing his disdain for the musical arts and robbing Astaria of his talent. Of course, she should not have been surprised about this hidden attribute as he always mastered anything he set his mind to. Unfortunately, he often set his mind to skills that reinforced his reckless nature.

"Why, Ethan?" she sighed.

"Why? Why what?"

"Why do you hide your gifts, denying us the beauty of your voice?"

"I have a lousy voice, and I don't like to sing. Besides, it's one of the few songs I know, and it reminds me of home." He cringed as he said it, wishing he could take back that last word that contorted his mother's gentle smile into a hurt felt scowl.

"Home?"

"I meant to say—"

"No, your heart merely spoke before your mind, Ethan. So Red Rock is your home now?"

"Astaria is my home." His reply sounded insincere even to him. "I…I just feel…at ease in Texas."

She pursed her lips, her emotions in turmoil over the confession of his true feelings, which merely confirmed what she long suspected.

"Since I was a boy, I know you had the highest aspirations for my future. You and father envisioned a crown upon my brow and a princess in my bed, with grandchildren born of my blood for you to dote upon. Such are the expectations for a firstborn royal. But…your dreams were my chains. I have always had this inner voice whispering of greater possibilities, free of responsibilities and obligations of my birthright. I yearn for freedom, Mother."

"Your freedom sounds like a life of loneliness, son. Do you not yearn for a family of your own?"

"Someday," he said defensively. He would never admit that all the maidens in the land had little effect on him, not even Jennifer, who was more a friend than the object of marital ambition. Strangely, his male urges came alive beyond the barrier, though he did not act upon them. When he returned to Red Rock, he would be hard-pressed not to court Sarah Adams.

Gabrielle's unspoken fear was Ethan sating his male urges upon whores or women of loose moral character once he ventured beyond Astaria. Many of the other kingdoms held more liberal views on the act of fornication. In Astaria, however, it was severely punished outside the bonds of marital union. Some believed Ethan sought his freedom merely to sow his seed far and wide, partaking in the pleasures of the flesh that highborn princelings and lords in other lands enjoyed. Even Gabrielle, like everyone else, did not suspect the truth that Ethan had yet to know a woman.

*****

Ethan met Krixan in the inner courtyard, where they bade their farewells to Ethan's family and friends, before setting off into the dark of night. Bronus placed his right arm around his wife's shoulders, drawing her close as her moistened eyes followed Ethan's shadowed form as he passed from sight. She had repeatedly asked for Ethan's reassurance to never enter the Mage Bane. "I promise" were the last words he spoke to her before attaining his mount and riding away. Her other children stood beside them to see him off, while Dragos waited upon the veranda above, observing his grandson's departure with grave misgivings. Something felt amiss, and the wizened seer struggled to know its source. He had spoken earlier with Lady Lucia, inquiring how she came to know so much concerning royal requests. She stared at him with wide curious eyes, bereft of understanding. Reading her thoughts revealed the truth of her ignorance. She held no such converse with Ethan. Was Ethan lying about where he learned of royal requests? If so, then why? Though he couldn't read Ethan's thoughts, Dragos knew when he spoke falsely. There was no lie in Ethan's voice. Lady Lucia did tell him of royal requests, which made her thoughts untrue. How was that possible?

*****

She stood in the shadows of the outer courtyard as Ethan and Krixan passed without, the cowl shielding her amethyst eyes from Ethanos, lest he see her as she truly was. Her sister stood at her side, similarly concealed for only the firstborn of House Blagen could see through their mage-distorted faces, revealing the purple of their irises and revealing their origin. Their monarch would be pleased with the indefinite delay in Ethanos Blagen's betrothal and his renunciation of the Astarian throne. Such a fortuitous turn of events allowed their monarch to implement other contingencies.

*****

The proceeding weeks found Ethan and Krixan following Luke Crawford's corpse-strewn path all the way to the sea, to the port city of Talesia, where rumors abounded concerning Luke Crawford's destination. The most reliable sources spoke of the gunslinger forcing passage on a swift merchant ship bound for the independent isle of Cordova, centered in the heart of the Aqualania Sea, and a short distance from the Mage Bane. Ethan booked passage on the fastest ship in port, hoping to catch Luke before he could slip away.

CHAPTER 15

The Isle of Cordova rested in the center of the Aqualania Sea. Fifty miles abreast at its greatest width, it curved around Shark's Bay, forming a natural harbor on the isle's eastern shore. The harbor shared the same name as the isle, as it was Cordova's center of power, culture, and commerce. The city held no allegiance to any of the seven mage kingdoms. It was ruled by numerous free mages and a plutocracy of a dozen merchant families, who built vast fortunes facilitating trade among the seven mage kingdoms, the western hinterlands along Elaria's northwestern coast, the Mage Bane, and the isles of Near and Far Polantis.

Spring came early to Shark's Bay as a warm tropic wind pressed upon his face as he looked out over the water. Ethan and Krixan followed Luke to Cordova, spending the past day seeking him out in the bustling port city. The eastern sky glowed with the coming dawn, illuminating the tranquil waters of Shark's Bay. Ethan stood along the wharves with Bull's reins in his left hand as he observed the beauty of the tropic sunrise. He wished his family were here to share in the wonders he beheld. *You only have one life*, Ethan mused, *and you should live it to its fullest*. He looked at the sunrise over the sea with the same wonder as the Astarian high country or the exotic terrain of West Texas. Though the wharves were bustling with sailors, merchants, and laborers scurrying in each direction, no one else savored the moment to enjoy the dawn. It was not surprising, for those who dwell in paradise to take such grandeur for granted. It was no different in Astaris, where no one ever joined Ethan atop the walls of the palace to gaze at the tall northern pines carpeting the

Por-Shada Plateau from the Upper Torlin to the foothills of the Por-Shada Mountains.

"Where to today, Ethan?" Krixan asked while stretching his back.

"Krix, what are you doing?" Ethan admonished.

"I'm stretching my aching back, Ethan," he stated the obvious.

"I know you're stretching your back, Krix, but you're missing the sunrise. Look!" he said, throwing his open hands toward the rising sun.

"Yes, it's very lovely," Krix yawned. "But I'd rather be in bed. In fact, I'd still be asleep if my best friend hadn't dragged me out of bed to witness it!" he growled.

"And where would you be, without me dragging you out of bed, big fella?" Ethan goaded.

"I'd still be asleep like a normal person!"

"Who wants to be normal when you can be us?"

Krixan shook his head. It was pointless to argue with his thick-headed friend. He might as well *enjoy* the sunrise.

Ethan's eyes shifted to a half-dozen men clad in brown leather tunics and gray mail, brandishing crossbows and closing upon them along the wharf. Craning his neck in the opposite direction, he noticed four more behind them. There was no official garrison of Cordova, just freestanding militias and hired mercenaries. He saw two of the men training their crossbows on Krixan. He took a step, blocking their aim as they released their bolts. Ethan drew his Colt with blinding speed. One bolt went astray, passing over his left shoulder and into the bay. The second struck true, embedding into Ethan's hip as he fanned his pistol, sending a bullet into each man, then turning upon the men behind him with his other pistol, and sending a round into each of them. Krixan stormed across the white stone wharf, putting a bullet into the heads of the four men behind them. Ethan had struck each in the chest or abdomen. Though lethal, they still lingered, twisting upon the white stone surface in agony. Ethan closed on the other six, finishing off those still alive, save for one.

The last man moaned as blood oozed from his stomach. His insides felt on fire as he lifted his pleading green eyes to Ethan's towering form.

"Who sent you?" Ethan asked as he reloaded.

"Go ahead and kill me!" the man moaned.

"Tell me who sent you, or I'll do something *far* worse." He leaned close and whispered, "I'll let you live."

The man's eyes grew wide. There were no mage healers in Cordova, and his continued existence would be measured in degrees of agony without respite until he eventually succumbed.

"Cornan Thune. Our Patron is Cornan Thune," he moaned.

"What kind of mage is he?" Ethan asked.

"A...a fire caster and a..."

"A what?"

"A binder." The man coughed blood.

Ethan drew back at the mention of a binder mage. A binder was one of the rarest of mages. His brother Tristan was so gifted, yet rarely used his great power. Cornan Thune was a dangerous foe.

"Why did your master order you to attack us?" Ethan frowned.

"Because of your comrades."

"What comrades?"

"Ten or eleven men carrying similar weapons as yours left the harbor a week ago. Our patron's attempts to join them in his house proved ill-fated. The strangers were immune to his mage gifts."

"Your master wanted their weapons." Ethan shook his head. Being a binder was not enough for Cornan Thune, he wanted their guns to further enhance his power.

"When word reached him of your"—the man winced in pain before continuing—"of your coming, he ordered us to take your weapons."

"Where did the other men who carried weapons like ours go?"

"We...we don't...know."

Ethan leveled his pistol on the man's head and fired. After gathering whatever shell casings they could find, they decided to pay a visit to one Cornan Thune.

*****

Arnos Pagge stepped out of his carriage, as his servant shielded the morning sun with an umbrella. His sandaled feet stepped onto the cobbled stone that led to the entrance of the grand estate. Palm trees swayed in each direction as he turned, surveying the harbor below. The estate was a vast structure of marble and granite, with statuesque pillars, cavernous halls, and gardens of breathtaking diversity. The estate overlooked Cordova as it rested among the hillsides that surrounded Shark's Bay. From these heights, he could see the white stone columns of the harbor forum centered in the city below. The forum was the dominant landmark of Cordova, resting along the bank of the Cordela River, towering over the center of the city like a mountain of crafted stone. The city grew along both banks of the Cordela River that fed into the bay. Structures of stone or wood lined the avenues that branched from the riverfront. Ships laden with cargo traversed the tranquil waters of Shark's Bay. Arnos Pagge looked one last time at his native city, before taking a breath and stepping toward the estate. He smoothed the folds of his maroon robes before reaching the front atrium of the estate.

Arnos was met at the front atrium by a woman with brown hair with silver gracing her temples. Her face was homely and nondescript. She wore a simple brown dress over her diminutive form. Her eyes were downcast, and an iron collar circled her neck. Arnos's manservant folded the umbrella and stepped forth to address the woman as his patron refused to consult with a slave.

"Welcome to the House of Cornan Thune," she greeted them with a deep curtsy and bowed head.

"Inform your master that Arnos Pagge awaits him," the servant stated dismissively as the woman was beneath his status as a free servant.

"Of course, sir. Please step within," she offered, before hurrying off to address her master.

Arnos stepped within the front atrium accompanied by his manservant and three free swords of his personal guard. The men were impeccably attired in scarlet tunics and polished steel breastplates and greaves. Like most men of Cordova, they wore knee-length tunics sans hose or trousers due to the temperate climate of the isle. Arnos examined the tapestries that adorned the stone walls of the atrium. Cornan Thune may be a demon-spawned extortionist, but his tastes were quite refined. He ran his hand over his rotund girth that stretched his robes to their limit, wondering if his host was planning to feed him on this visit.

"Master awaits," the woman's voice softly echoed from the adjoining hall.

"Proceed," Arnos's manservant commanded her.

They followed her through several vast corridors lined with life-size statues cast in marble and depicting the human form in detailed perfection. Each was worthy of the royal palaces of Elaria. They passed a half-dozen guards posted throughout the estate, each eyeing the visitors warily. They were at last ushered into a brightly lit vast central atrium with an open roof above a shallow pool. Their host awaited them at the chamber's far end, sitting behind a low table covered with various platters of food.

"Welcome Arnos, my dear friend," Cornan Thune said in his sickly-sweet voice laced with conceit. Cornan sat behind the table with the practiced posture of mage-born nobility. He had shoulder-length blond hair framing a narrow feminine face. His sky-blue eyes appraised Arnos's glutinous form with veiled disgust. Cornan wore an ankle-length azure tunic and golden robe that cascaded behind him, spilling onto the floor. A woman, who matched his youthfulness, sat upon his right. She wore a gossamer scarlet gown with lace bodice, which barely concealed her spilling cleavage. Her dark-brown eyes lacked the mirth of her upturned lips. Her deep red hair framed her attractive, porcelain face. Upon his left sat an older man with a pudgy face that poorly matched his waif-thin body. He wore a simple gray tunic. His sandy blond hair was cropped short, and he paid the visitors little regard as he nibbled the fruits and pastries that filled his plate.

"Come, Arnos, sit," Cornan waved an open hand to the opposite side of the table.

"My thanks," Arnos said as he sat upon the floor cross-legged behind the low table. His cushion poorly supported his girth, a fact that amused Cornan, no doubt.

"Oh, before we begin, my friend. Lady Forbis, would you mind," he addressed the woman seated to his right.

"My pleasure, Lord Cornan." She smiled, narrowing her dark eyes toward Arnos and his entourage.

"What?" Arnos shrieked as darkness clouded his vision. His guards and servant gasped similar reactions as they were so afflicted.

"As you can surmise, Lady Julia Forbis is a blinder," Cornan said, coming to his feet and circling the table, stepping into their midst.

"Sleep!" he commanded as he touched the foreheads of Arnos's guards, one by one. They fell to the floor as he touched them, obedient to his will. He finished with Arnos's manservant, before retaking his seat opposite his frightened guest. "That should suffice. You may release our *esteemed* guest, my dear."

Lady Julia released a bated breath. As a blinder, her power was taxing to maintain when applied to multiple individuals.

Arnos's sight instantly returned as the spell was lifted. He craned his neck behind him, horrified by his guards' incapacitation.

"You needn't worry, Arnos, they are merely asleep. You may collect them when you leave. Before we begin our…negotiations, I should formally introduce *my* council. The beautiful woman to my right is Lady Julia Forbis. She is a telepath, and of course a *very* gifted blinder. As the daughter of the former archmage of our fair city, she has returned to serve her father's native isle. This"—he regarded the fellow to his left—"is Torz Jova. Torz is a shield mage, which protects our small council from suffering what your entourage has just endured."

"Was that necessary?" Arnos asked unhappily.

"A mere demonstration, my dear Arnos. Surely a man of your supreme understanding of the nature of our great port's complex and interdependent ruling apparatus can appreciate the subtle reminder of what a powerful mage can do. We are grieved by the recent demise of your former council of free mages, which afforded your ruling plutocracy the magical protection that an independent harbor such as Cordova requires."

"Demise?" Arnos bristled at the reference. "They were *murdered*! Murdered by savages who were ill-affected by their magic." Arnos recalled the horrific scene where Luke Crawford and his band arrived in Cordova, then swept into the mage council's inner sanctum, killing the nine free mages that protected the city.

"Yes, it seems the strangers possessed some ability to shield themselves from your mages' power. They also possessed projectile weapons of unknown origin. Weapons that are beyond the capability of any in the seven kingdoms," Cornan added while biting the smile forming upon his lips.

"Their weapons were too advanced for such barbarous men. They are no doubt pawns of a mage king or a mage lord of great ambition." Arnos's accusatory statement was obviously directed to his host.

"You believe I am their patron?" Cornan smiled falsely while touching a hand to his chest in mock indignation. "I assure you, my dear Arnos, that their arrival to our fair city was as much a surprise to me. It is unfortunate that they slew your mage council, but I have surmised that they are *not* in the employ of any mage lord or king. The place of their origin is a mystery, but no conspiracy with a house of Elaria is likely. I believe your council fell victim to a mere theft and nothing more. The strangers slew your mages, stole their gold, and then sailed away toward the Mage Bane. It seems two of the strangers have foolishly returned *alone* to our fair city. I have dispatched a squad of men to kill them and bring me their weapons. They should be returning as we speak."

"The men you speak of do not appear to be any of the strangers that slew our council," Arnos countered.

"If they did not actively participate in the raid, they are still most assuredly compatriots of the men, as they carry similar weapons. It matters not, soon I shall have the weapons of these two men and will use them against their comrades whenever they return," Cornan explained.

Arnos merely nodded as Cornan continued.

"Which brings us to your current…dilemma," he said after a pregnant pause. "With no mage council to shield you from the ambitions of any wayward son or daughter of a mage king or high lord, you are helpless against those who wish to claim lordship of Cordova. The mage kings allow your current independence because collectively they prefer your independence over you falling under the dominion of one of their peers. But I doubt they would care if you fell under the dominion of a wayward mage who held no allegiance to any of the seven kingdoms."

"Like you," Arnos snarled bitterly.

"Is not magic the currency of our world?" Cornan spread his hands as if instructing a child. "In this regard, you are a pauper."

"What do you desire?" Arnos asked, dreading what the man might demand.

"Unlike your mage council, who only asked for a meager percentage of your transactions, I already possess vast holdings on your isle. For protecting your interests from those with magical gifts, and from incursions from the Mage Bane, I simply ask for favorable agreements in the conduct of my business."

"Such as?"

"As head of House Pagge, you own the stone quarries upon which our masons and artisans are dependent. You shall only provide stone to those projects commissioned through me."

Arnos suspected such. Cornan Thune had forced similar agreements with House Purciel and House Floren, who controlled the city's iron ore and timber. He would no doubt bind all the merchant houses to his will, replacing their free markets with Cornan Thune's managed economy that was captive to his ambition. The free guilds of masons, artisans, cobblers, blacksmiths, bakers, shipwrights, and craftsmen of scores of varied specifications, would be displaced by

Cornan's slave labor. Cornan first arrived in Cordova the previous autumn and had since used his binding ability to secure vast holdings and wealth. With the recent demise of Cordova's mage council, he quickly filled the vacuum, extorting the merchant families to acquiesce to his outrageous demands. Within the fortnight, Cornan Thune would be the de facto king of Cordova. As both a binder and a fire mage, no mortal man could stand in defiance of his power.

"House Pagge shall abide your terms," Arnos relented.

"Most wise, Arnos." Cornan smiled wickedly. "Of course, there is *one* more provision I require of you."

"And that is?" Arnos could only ponder the darkest of possibilities that lurked within the man's evil mind.

"If our fair city is to emerge upon the world stage and be recognized by the great kingdoms with the respect we so richly deserve, we shall need a lord Regent who can speak with the kings and queens of the seven kingdoms on equal footing. I shall expect your full backing for such a naming."

"You wish to be our king?" Arnos poorly hid his disgust.

"I *shall* be your king, my dear Arnos, and I expect your fealty. You can demonstrate your loyalty by kneeling before me and pledging your life to my service."

Arnos swallowed past the lump in his throat, wondering what he…

"Halt!" The panicked shouts of guards echoed in the outer corridors, followed by sounds of struggle. *Boom!* A deafening sound repeated itself several times. Alarm transfixed the usually calm face of Cornan Thune. All their eyes stared intently as a large dark-haired man dressed in tan leather trousers and shirt stormed through the entryway and across the central atrium. His dark-blue eyes swept the conscious occupants with terrible intensity, focusing on the man centered behind the table.

"Are you Cornan Thune?" the man asked.

"I am," Cornan said cautiously, eyeing the strange weapons hanging upon the man's hips.

The stranger drew his weapon upon the confirmation and squeezed the trigger. Cornan Thune toppled over as the bullet pierced his skull.

Lady Julia fixed her power upon the stranger to no avail. Her eyes grew wide, alarmed by her power's ineffectiveness.

"That doesn't work on me, girl," the stranger said, shifting his aim to Torz Jova as he attempted to rise. The shield mage toppled backward as a bullet punctured his forehead.

"Please." Arnos Pagge shielded his face with his hands, cringing before the stranger.

"Who are you?" the stranger asked.

"Ar…Arnos Pagge."

"Are you a friend of Cornan's?"

"No! He and these two others demanded my fealty so he might be our king."

"Why would you make him your king?"

"He demanded it. Our mage council was murdered by your friends, and we were helpless against him."

"Your mages were killed by Luke Crawford?"

"I…I do not know their names, my lord, only that they carried weapons such as yours."

"They are no friends of mine. In fact, I've been hunting them. Stop cringing. My name is Ethan," he said, holstering his pistol.

"Of course, my lord."

"Ethan. Just Ethan. I'm no lord."

"As you wish, Ethan," Arnos whispered with downcast eyes.

"Stand up, Arnos. I don't like talking to anyone on their knees. Men belong on their feet," he said, extending his hand to the Cordovan merchant.

Arnos tentatively accepted Ethan's hand, wary of the stranger's intent as Ethan pulled him to his feet. Standing fully erect, Arnos was still a head shorter than Ethan. "It appears even standing I am looking up to you. I surmise everyone looks up to you." Arnos smiled nervously.

"Not him," Ethan jerked a thumb toward the larger man passing through the entryway. He stood a full head higher than Ethan with rust tinted beard and a balding crown. The man carried a blood-stained ax and wore dark leathers with jagged metal guards on his thick forearms. He carried similar weapons as Ethan upon his hips.

"How many did you kill, Ethan? I only heard two shots," the giant asked.

"I shot those two, Krix. These other fellas were like this when I got here." He pointed out Arnos's unconscious guards and servant.

"They are my guards. Cornan Thune put them to sleep after Lady Julia blinded them," Arnos explained.

Ethan gave Lady Julia a cold look. "That wasn't very nice of you, was it?"

"You have made a grave mistake, peasant!" she said icily.

"What else is new." He smirked. "Your boyfriend made the greater mistake when he sent his goons to kill us."

"Mage Thune was neither my mate nor paramour. I suggest you be mindful of your tongue when speaking to your betters!"

"Luckily for you, *Julia*, I don't kill girls, but you are testing that conviction."

"By slaying Mage Thune, you have rendered Cordova defenseless. With no mage to protect the city, Cordova's fall is now inevitable." She glared.

"If Cornan Thune was so powerful, how did I kill him so easily? He couldn't have been that special." Ethan made a face as Krixan rolled his eyes, knowing Ethan was enjoying this too much.

"You mock the mage born at your own peril, peasant!"

"If an ignorant, dim-witted moron like me can kill two mages in as many seconds, what does that say about you?"

"I wonder, by what measure, your courage shall wane when a host of mage born sweeps into this city?" she asked.

"Maybe we'll just stick around and great them with the same hospitality we gave Thune."

"Why you arrogant—" she protested before Krixan cut her off.

"My lady, it is pointless to argue with him. I suggest you gather your things and depart Cordova before nightfall."

"I'll have your name before I take my leave," she snarled.

"I'm nobody, just a poor ugly peasant who doesn't know his place." He shrugged.

She doubted that. "Ethan! You said your name was Ethan. There is more to your name than that."

"His *full* name is Ethanos Blagen, former crown prince of Astaria, my lady." Krixan smiled with his arms crossed over his massive chest.

"Thanks," Ethan glared at his friend as Arnos's and Julia's eyes grew wide.

"Your Grace, we are honored—" Arnos began to kneel.

"Would you stand up!" Ethan growled. "I'm no prince. I traded the throne for my freedom. I kneel to no one, and no one kneels to me."

"You forsook the throne?" Julia gasped.

"Yes."

"Why?" she asked.

"I didn't find it to my liking."

"But you are a mage-born crown prince. Why would you forsake such a claim?"

"I'd rather be *free* and live among those who are, but in the near term, I'm seeking a man named Luke Crawford. He is wanted by the people of Red Rock, the State of Texas, and the United States government. Here's what he looks like." Ethan fished a folded parchment from his pouch, handing it to Arnos. It was a likeness of Luke drawn by Ethan, akin to the wanted posters that circled West Texas.

The glutinous merchant's eyes lit with recognition at the image.

"I know this man. He was the leader of the men—"

"Who killed your mage council," Ethan finished his sentence.

"Yes. We thought you one of his companions. That is why Mage Thune set his men upon you," Arnos said.

"It's a mistake Thune won't repeat. Where did this man go?" Ethan said, tapping the paper in Arnos's hand.

"We believe he fled for Free Port in the Mage Bane," Lady Julia interjected.

That is what Ethan was afraid of. It was the one place he could not enter or would not enter without breaking his promise to his mother.

"Mage Thune falsely believed that you were comrades of the man you seek. He planned to use your weapons against him when he returned," Lady Julia explained.

"You believe Luke Crawford is coming back?" Ethan's eyes alit at the possibility. If so, it would make his task easier.

"A man such as him cannot resist the easy treasure that he so effortlessly plucked upon his last visit here," Arnos said.

Ethan's eyes narrowed in contemplation as an idea took root. "Arnos, gather the heads of the ruling merchant families of Cordova and the masters of each trade guild. I have a proposal to offer them."

"I shall gather them in the harbor forum this evening," Arnos agreed.

"Julia." He smiled at her.

"Your Grace." She nodded in kind.

"Ethan. Just Ethan," he reminded her.

"Ethan," she said uncomfortably.

"If you wish to remain in Cordova, and help this city as you claim, perhaps you would accept a position as the archmage upon the new mage council of Cordova?"

"I would be honored," she whispered, not believing her ears.

*****

The city forum of Cordova rested on the Southern bank of the Cordela River, where its mouth opened into Shark's Bay. Pillars of winter gray and alabaster spiraled to the massive roof above, each the height of four men. Wide stone steps descended from each face of the edifice, allowing the good citizens to enter from any direction. The forum was the largest public works project the port city ever constructed, even costlier than the stone wharves and docking facilities that were ancient yet maintained through the centuries. The central forum was a circled stone platform centered in the bowels of the massive structure's interior. Rows upon rows of stone benches rose in concentric circles in each direction so those seated further back could see clearly the happenings below.

Hode Purciel stood beside Arnos Pagge on the circled stone. He was the head of House Purciel and owned the iron ore mines that supplied the city. He was a heavyset, bullnecked man with a powerful build. He wore a white belted tunic over dark cotton trousers. Ethan noted that the man was probably the only other man, beside Krixan and him, who wore trousers in the tropic port. He was a boisterous, loud-spoken man who lacked patience for fools.

"Cornan Thune is *dead*!" Hode Purciel declared to the congregants in the forum. His dark-brown eyes swept the assemblage seated in the circled rows above. "He planned to make of himself our master, transforming our collaborative governance into his mage-ruled fiefdom. But our tribulations are not ended with his demise. We are now vulnerable to any mage-born lord who would make himself our king. We may have an answer to that dilemma. The man who removed the tyranny of Cornan Thune has an offer to present us. Ethan!" He called the former Astarian prince forth.

Ethan and Krixan descended one of the three stairs that divided the stone seated rows. Some of the congregants knew his true lineage, but most were seeing him for the first time. Ethan removed his hat as he stepped into the stone circle.

"My name is Ethan Blagen. I am the son of Bronus Blagen, king of Astaria. By saving my father's life at the Battle of the Velo, I earned a royal request, which I used to free myself from the throne. I kneel to no man and will have no man kneel to me. I spent nearly a year across the barrier that divides our world from Earth," he began, hoping they understood something of the world on the other side of the barrier. "When I returned, I was followed by a dozen desperados who were wanted for crimes against the people of Texas. I followed them to your fair city, but I was too late to save your mage council. When I was across the barrier, I served as a deputy to the sheriff of a place called Red Rock. A sheriff and his deputies are tasked with upholding the laws of the cities and villages for which they serve and protect the citizens from those intent to do them harm. I am willing to serve your city in a similar role. Krixan and I *will* protect you when these men return, and from any rogue mage born intending to subjugate your people."

"And what price would you claim for such service?" several of the guild masters asked in unison.

"Ten gold marks per month for myself, and ten for Krixan, plus expenses. I also want thirty silver marks for any deputies we hire, and ten gold marks for every mage we hire to replenish your council," Ethan said.

Though ten gold marks was a hefty sum, it was far less than their former mage council demanded.

"It is a fair price for our new mage chancellor!" Arnos declared.

"I'm no mage chancellor. If I take the job, I will be your sheriff. I will uphold the laws of your city and protect your people and property. Before you decide, you must know that I will not enforce your slave laws or return any slave that slips your chains. I despise slavery and will not abide it, though I will not interfere with your slaves either."

They debated his proposal at length before agreeing to his terms.

CHAPTER 16

They spent the remainder of spring establishing their presence in Cordova. Ethan had a tin smith forge tin stars for him, Krix, and a dozen deputies he had enlisted. It was a novel concept for the citizenry of Cordova, who observed Ethan's role of sheriff with bemused curiosity. He recruited his deputies from the hardiest stock in Cordova. Each was a master swordsman or archer and was of the sort to yield to no man. He armed them with crossbows and long swords and outfitted them with gray cotton shirts and brown leather trousers and boots. He forbade them to wear tunics, capes, or hose of any kind. They acknowledged no man their better and treated all citizens equally before the law. Ethan displayed no favoritism, recruiting deputies native to all the seven mage kingdoms, Cordova, or the Mage Bane. Much of their work thus far had been breaking up drunken brawls that spilled into the streets from the night time crowds that filled the waterfront taverns.

Ethan renovated a sizable one level wooden structure near the harbor's Central District, outfitting the layout to conform to Sheriff Thorton's jail in Red Rock, but with a dozen holding cells to accommodate Cordova's larger population.

Lady Julia helped Ethan recruit mage gifted for the new mage council, but after two months, they only found two. One was an ice mage, and the other a light caster. Both were expatriates of Estasa who were born outside the lines of inheritance and fled the free isles of Far Polantis.

The early morning found Ethan sitting behind his desk, reviewing the arrests made the night before, each detailed on the unrolled parchment. The five deputies on the night shift had an eventful evening with two murders, a stolen horse, and a dozen brawls. Krixan found an empty cot in an open cell in the back. His snoring echoed painfully to the front of the jail. Ethan tried to block out the distraction but to poor effect. It was no use berating the slumbering giant; Ethan surmised that even a ground quake probably wouldn't wake him. Instead, he suffered in silence along with his deputy Nils Purciel. Nils was the barrel-chested temperamental younger brother of Hode Purciel.

"Blast, is he going to sleep all day?" Nils asked, leaning on the desk, reading the parchment over Ethan's shoulder.

"Don't worry, he'll wake for lunch." Ethan grinned.

"Then sleep all afternoon till dinner," Nils added.

"Most likely," Ethan set the parchment aside and unrolled the map of Cordova over the desk. "This is where I want to focus our patrols." He tapped the map, indicating the lower harbor district.

"I agree. Half the brawls and nearly four of five murders take place there." Nils nodded.

"We'll start tonight. I'll join you on the night shift."

"I welcome your company." Nils slapped him on the back.

"All right, you've been up all night. Go get some sleep before you fall over."

No sooner had Nils stepped without than Lady Julia passed through the doorway, accompanied by another woman dressed in a loose flowing white gown, with dark-brown hair and discerning green eyes. "Good morning, Sheriff," Julia greeted him with a winsome smile.

"Julia," he greeted, touching a finger to his forehead in a casual salute that Ben Thorton was apt to give, as he leaned back in his chair. His eyes drifted to the other woman who stood beside her with her chin up, mimicking the proud carriage of a highborn lady. Ethan disliked her already.

"Ethan, this is Lady Thela Corval. She is an archmage healer. She heads a contingent of twelve Vellesian mage healers. They have come to Cordova on an errand of mercy to treat our sick and infirm." Julia beamed proudly.

"Sheriff Blagen, such a strange title," Lady Thela said with uncontained mirth.

"The title means I keep the peace in our fair city, ma'am," Ethan said with his Texas drawl.

"Your legend precedes you, Prince Ethanos. How strange to find you performing such service in Cordova of all places," Lady Thela said.

Ethan gave Julia a hard look. He asked the ruling families and guild masters to not reveal his lineage.

"Now, Ethan, do not give me that hurtful look. Lady Thela already knew who you were," Julia countered.

"My sister mage healers are ignorant of your true identity, Prince Ethanos. You need not worry," Thela assured.

"The name is Ethan, just Ethan. How long will you be staying in Cordova? The city has gone a long while since a mage healer has visited here."

"Queen Valera has sent us here to offer Cordova the goodwill of the Vellesian people. We plan to spend at least forty days in your city. That should suffice to see that all of the people on the isle are healed."

"That is very thoughtful of your queen. Be sure to convey to her Cordova's gratitude," he said.

"Of course, Prince Ethanos…"

"Ethan, just plain ole Ethan," he corrected her.

"Ethan." Her mirthful grin remained. "Our queen would appreciate your assistance in safeguarding our mage healers while they see to your people."

"Didn't you bring protection with you?" Ethan asked, not imagining so many mage-born healers venturing far afield without a heavy host to guard them.

"We have a score of our queen's personal guard, and several ships of her majesty's fleet, but I worry they may not be enough should our guild be assailed by sterner foes than mere brigands," Thela said.

"We have few mages to protect you, and I only have a dozen deputies to cover the entire city. Even then, that leaves a handful per shift. There's not much we can do for you. I suggest you keep your girls together and conduct your healing near the city forum and in broad daylight. There you can concentrate your guards more effectively."

Julia cringed with Ethan's reference of "Girls." For one born of royal blood, Ethan's manners and speech were akin to a barbarian's. He noted the genuine look of disappointment painted upon the women's faces, paining him with guilt.

"All right, I'll see what I can do." Ethan sighed. He never could disappoint a woman with a sad, pleading face, unless she was trying to drag him off to the wedding bed.

*****

Ten days hence

Ethan avoided the Vellesian healers, delegating a few deputies to augment their guards, while he patrolled elsewhere. Hode Purciel managed to form a governing council to manage the city, which included the patriarchs of the dozen wealthiest families and the masters of each trade guild. They were pleased with Ethan's efforts to quell the raucous atmosphere that permeated the port city. The late spring breeze rolled off the waters of the bay, cooling his heated brow. The waning sunlight bounced off the water's surface as it settled beneath the western hills that circled behind Cordova. Ethan patrolled the wharves each night, ever watchful for ships that might return with Luke Crawford. The governing council hosted a grand reception to honor the Vellesian mage healers in the home of Arnos Pagge. Ethan was expected to make an appearance shortly, but not before attending his allotted rounds along the lower harbor district. Krix and four of their deputies were to be patrolling the troubled area, but Ethan had not yet found them among the bustling streets, serried with drunken sailors.

"Evening, Sheriff," one fellow burped as he staggered passed.

Ethan regarded him briefly before continuing on. He crossed several alleys before noticing a commotion up ahead.

The Dead Man's Anchor was an oft-busy tavern of ill repute. Salt-worn timbers overlapped along its outer walls, with slate-gray tiles covering its slanted roof. The structure had burnt to the ground four times in the past one hundred years and was quickly rebuilt each time. As Ethan drew near, he was greeted by the sight of people fleeing the tavern amid the sounds of shattered glass and breaking timbers.

Ethan approached the tavern door, took a deep breath, and stepped within. Several bodies crashed into his legs as he cleared the entrance. He stepped to his left as an errant fist just missed his jaw. The entire floor of the tavern was a chaotic melee of drunken sailors, free swords, and laborers. In the back-east corner of the room, he saw one of his deputies with his left arm around one fellow's neck, while he punched him in the face with his right. Fists flew in every direction, and the fighting appeared to have no reason or sides, just a mob of crazed loons. Ethan caught a fist with his left hand and twisted it behind its owner's back before tossing the offender through the front door and into the street. He quickly turned, sensing another patron approaching his back side. He caught a sandaled foot in his right hand and yanked the man from his feet, sending him crashing to the floor. A chair smashed across his back, breaking apart with the force of the blow. Ethan turned upon his next attacker, grasping the fellow's tunic collar and punching him full in the face. He heard the man's nose break as he connected. He had little respite as other combatants crashed into him, knocking him to the floor. Before he regained his feet, he spied a large silhouette filling the front entrance.

"Enough!" Krixan's deep voice reverberated across the tavern floor. Everyone stopped momentarily, eyeing the giant with curiosity before continuing their melee. Ethan smirked, observing Krixan's face contorted in rage. Krixan stormed across the floor, his fists slamming atop of one head after another like a bear swatting pups. Two other deputies followed in his wake as bodies flew in all directions, displaced by his large friend's emphatic blows. The deputy in the corner fought his way off the wall to join his comrades. Ethan grinned, making his own path through the crowd. He grabbed one fellow by the scruff of his neck, tossing him across the tavern near the entrance. Whenever he caught a respite blocking punches, he'd grab another drunken patron and toss them toward the front door. Some gained their feet and fled the establishment, while others moaned among the ever-growing pile that Krixan and Ethan were making.

When they finally finished, Ethan, Krix, and their deputies gathered around the bar and raised their cups to another fight broken up. Drunken brawls were a nightly occurrence when they first started but now were down to one or two a week.

Krixan downed his ale in a single gulp and slapped the cup on the bar before releasing a thunderous belch. "Well done, boys. I miss the times when we broke up fights on a nightly basis. Gone are the days," Krix bemoaned the progress they achieved these past two months.

"Gone are the days with good riddance!" Geron Plortes said with wads of cloth stuck up his bleeding nose and his right fist swollen.

"Bah! When we're old men, you'll tip your cup fondly recalling these days." Krix slapped Geron on the back. "You best get a move on, Ethan. You are expected at the reception about now," Krixan added with a grin, knowing how Ethan loathed attending such functions.

"After we lock up this bunch." Ethan jerked a thumb toward the half-dozen drunks they had bound, sitting against the far wall.

"Leave those fellows to us. You just worry about showing your pretty face to that highborn crowd, since they're the ones paying our salary," Krix added.

"That should be part of my next contract, not having to attend these gatherings," Ethan growled.

"At least they don't expect you in formal attire like a tunic," Hors Dragger said.

"If they did, I'd take this badge and tell them where they can stick it." Ethan tipped his hat, bidding them adieu as he stepped without.

*****

Ethan brushed off the dirt on his sleeves and straightened his holster as he dismounted and tied Bull's reins to a circled hitch post before entering the home of Arnos Pagge. The guards at the front gate nodded politely when he rode up, allowing him to pass within the outer walls that circled the estate. Attendants rushed forth to tend his horse, but he insisted on Bull staying near the entrance in case he needed to hastily depart. He walked up the steps of the elaborate home, passing between the massive marble pillars that circled the entrance before passing within.

The home of Arnos Pagge was a vast single-level plaza of interconnected stone chambers, joined by open-roofed atriums with large circular fountains and richly detailed sculptures that befitted royalty. Servant girls in brief white tunics hurried throughout the halls, granting him curious stares for his strange attire.

The unmistakable voice of Hode Purciel echoed from the adjoining hall. Ethan passed within, lingering in the back of the crowded feasting hall as Hode addressed the esteemed assemblage. The hall itself was a vast, well-lit chamber with wide windows that overlooked the bay from the hilltop estate. The lights of the harbor sparkled in the distance as the image of the full moon flickered off the bay. Hode rambled on and on, lauding the new governing coalition of Cordova, and heaping nauseous praise upon every constituency. He repeatedly thanked the visiting Vellesian mage healers and their benevolent Queen Valera. Ethan wasn't really listening to his unending drivel. He liked Hode personally, but whenever leaders spoke, whether they were mage kings, generals, or politicians, he knew it was all flowery crap. He stared over the sea of heads, observing the mage healers centered in the great hall. They wore the traditional white dresses, distinctive to their craft. They were the image of serenity and charm, each impeccably groomed and comely, with bright eyes and sweet smiles. They gathered around their chief matron, the archmage healer Thela Corval. Though they were all very beautiful, one stood above the rest with striking black hair that shone brightly in the torch-lit chamber. She was tall, nearly seventy inches with glowing olive skin. He was awestruck, unable to turn away until her eyes shifted gently to his. His mouth grew dry as he stared into the depths of her golden eyes, spellbound by her strength sand beauty.

"Ethan Blagen!" Hode Purciel called out to him, jarring him from her spell as he shifted his eyes to the thick-necked patriarch of House Purciel, standing in the midst of the grand reception hall. The girl turned her eyes from Ethan as he stood dumbfounded as much by her charm as to the content of Hode's statement that preceded the utterance of his name.

"Sheriff Blagen, come forth my good fellow!" Hode smiled, waving him hither.

Ethan groaned inwardly, hating undue attention in such settings. Hadn't he told the ruling council that he would serve as sheriff but to exclude him from public light? It was hardly Hode's fault, for Ethan's notoriety spread like wind-driven flames. He had liberated Cordova from the tyranny of Cornan Thune. He was the hero of the Velo, the breaker of mage kings, and the prince who rejected a crown. He dressed as he pleased and looked nothing like a mage-born royal. Men wanted to be like him, women adored him, and mage-born lords trembled at the mention of his name.

She watched Ethan make his way through the parting guests, stopping at Hode's side as he removed his Stetson. The brief glance they exchanged took her breath, sending her heart racing with abandon. He was *not* what she expected. He wore the garb of a savage, with blood staining his shirt and trousers. He carried the strange weapons on his thighs that were the source of great rumor. There were whispers of their mystical properties, perhaps mage-forged weapons of unknown origin, but she doubted that. They were obviously of anti-mage construct, built by the hands of men from the other dimension that he visited. They seemed to fit his character, adding to his distinct individuality. He was rumored to be very handsome, but she was not prepared for how understated that belief proved to be. She never found any man to her liking until his dark-blue eyes found her amid the crowd, drawn to her as she was drawn to him. She kept her eyes on the other man, Hode Purciel he was called, so as not to draw Ethan's attention. She expected him to exert the proud carriage of a mage-born prince, but he seemed anything but. He looked natural standing before the esteemed gathering, though she could discern that he did not wish to be there. He had acquiesced to Thela's request of providing added protection to their guild during their stay in Cordova, often assigning most of his available deputies to supplement their own guards. Ethan had not joined in any of the protection assignments, tending other duties rather than treating with the Vellesian mage healers.

"When our former mage council was slaughtered by the nefarious pirates of Luke Crawford, our fair city was vulnerable to the ambitions of Cornan Thune. Our new sheriff not only rid Cordova of Thune's threat, he restored the protection from mage dominion that our former council once afforded. My fellow citizens and visiting dignitaries, I present Ethan Blagen, sheriff of Cordova." Hode slapped Ethan on the back, formally introducing him to the assemblage.

Ethan surveyed the surrounding crowd, briefly noting the girl he saw in the midst of the Vellesian delegation, before passing on. He held his hat in his left hand while his right rested on the grip of his holstered Colt.

"I came to your city seeking Luke Crawford and his men. They are wanted by the sheriff of Red Rock, where I served as deputy. These men are extremely dangerous and immune to magic. After raiding Cordova and slaughtering your mage council, they fled across the sea to the Mage Bane. Knowing Luke, he will quickly tire of the sparse pickings there and seek easier riches. Since Cordova is the closest port within the Mage Zone, he will return. I didn't come here to be your guardian or sheriff. Since Cordova is the *only* patch of dirt within the Mage Zone that serves no king, I feel a kinship with you. I despise monarchy and despots and trust no man to rule with honor when there is no restraint to his power. Power should be shared and diluted, and laws should apply equally to all whether peasant, lord or merchant. As long as Cordova holds to no monarch or despot, I will stay. As sheriff, I will enforce the laws of your city, save for the subjugation or apprehension of slaves. I do not abide that institution and *will not* enforce it. I extend my gratitude to our visiting Vellesian healers for their time tending our people. I hope you are satisfied with the protection provided by my deputies. Now, if you'll excuse me, I have duties to—"

"You are leaving already?" Hode Purciel asked.

"Well, I have matters that—"

"Surely your deputies can handle whatever tasks that need tending, Ethan?" Hode pushed.

Ethan released a tired sigh, relenting to Hode's perseverance. He discretely withdrew to the back of the atrium, seeking a quiet corner to escape the festive crowd. A few younger men gathered around him, begging tales of his adventures. Ethan relented, retelling of his gunfights in Red Rock and his time in the New Mexico Badlands, though the boys wanted to hear of the Velo. Ethan sighed, again relenting to their pressure, and retold that awful battle. They were expecting tales of adventure and glory, but Ethan gifted them the terrible truth of death and war. He told of sons, brothers, fathers, and husbands dismembered and torn apart, never to return to those that loved them. So great were the mortally wounded, that even a thousand mage healers could not have saved them, and they only had a handful.

"Most wars spring from the ambitions of the highborn, but the low born bear the brunt of it," Ethan reminded them. "It's their sons who die, their homes that burn, and their daughters dishonored, and for what? So some lord might expand his domain? There are only two reasons to fight a war."

"What are they?" one lad asked.

"To defend your land or fight for your liberty."

"Liberty? Have men ever fought for such?" the same lad asked.

"Yes, they have." Ethan smiled. "Let me tell you about George Washington."

She caught sight of him, stealing one last glance before retiring from the atrium. She froze as his eyes met hers across the crowded chamber. Then she was gone. Those gathered around him listening to his tale did not catch the long pause in Ethan's telling or the pounding of his heart. For the first time in his life in Elaria, Ethan felt a stirring in his loins.

CHAPTER 17

The next morning found Ethan patrolling the northern avenues of Cordova. With most of his deputies guarding the Vellesian mage healers, he took over more of their primary duties, most especially patrolling. He took everything north of the Cordela River, while Deputies Fass Volun and Cres Arton handled everything south. Nils Purciel oversaw the protection of the mage healers, while Krixan commanded the jail. Krixan was most likely asleep, Ethan sagely surmised. At times Ethan wondered if Krixan were part bear, hibernating most of his days. *He's large enough to be a bear.* Ethan shrugged. Ethan couldn't begrudge him too much; for the first time in nearly two years, Krixan had time to rest and was taking full advantage.

The port grew eerily silent the further north Ethan patrolled. Where nearer the wharves, street vendors crowded either side of the avenues; here he was lucky to find one on any given street, as markets gave way to residential structures. Most of the homes in the tropic port were two-level structures, constructed of brick and mortar with slate roofs to withstand the salty air. Most of the lesser streets were little more than alleyways, barely wide enough for two men to walk abreast. The larger avenues, those wide enough for two wagons to pass in opposing directions, were sparsely placed either circling the harbor or jutting outward like the spokes of a great wheel. It was upon one such avenue that Ethan walked, his line of sight stretching northeast where the gray brick of the road blended with the green tropical foliage at the city's limit. Ethan stopped in the middle of the street, craning his neck, staring south and west where the street ran straight to the water's edge. Even from this distance from the wharves, the city was relatively flat, its elevation rising no more than mere yards above the harbor center. Beyond the edge of the city, the elevation rose significantly as palatial estates dotted many of the surrounding hillsides.

He was asked to pay special attention to this quiet sector of the city as a plague of robberies were noted here of late. The attacks were being made by one or two men, their faces covered as they targeted travelers afoot, often coming upon them from an adjoining alleyway. He doubted they would attempt to rob him as his reputation would prove that task to be suicidal, but it couldn't hurt to have a look. Sheriff Thorton had beaten in his head the importance of patrolling the streets of Red Rock, not just for the deterrence of crime, but to know the people you protect. If you earn the people's trust, they would come to trust you in return, often sharing information that you could never discover on your own. He hadn't realized how much Sheriff Thorton taught him about being a peace officer until he started mentoring his own deputies, then all of Ben's lessons came flooding back. He missed Red Rock terribly and had hoped to have already returned, but Luke Crawford had to be dealt with first. He wondered what Ben, Skeeter, and Judge Donovan were doing at this very moment? Probably sitting in Ben's office playing poker and wishing he were there so they could take his money. Ethan laughed at the memories of his feeble attempts to learn the game. He fondly recalled all the late evening's playing cards while listening to Ben, Skeeter, and the judge's stories. He wished he could take his father and grandfather there with him. He could picture his father trying to drink the judge under the table and wondered who might win such a contest. He missed his friends terribly and hoped they were well.

His thoughts returned to the girl he had seen the night before, the Vellesian mage healer with golden eyes and olive skin and hair so black it shone with torchlight reflecting off its silky strands. She was the loveliest thing he had ever seen. Beautiful seemed a poor description of her, lacking the full effect that her countenance projected. Looking into her eyes nearly took his breath. He felt his lungs constrict and pulse quicken, robbing him of all sense and reason. Even now, a day later, he could not shake her vision from his mind.

Who was she? No mere mage healer should manifest such duress or obsession in his heart, could she?

"Help!" a panicked voice cried out, shaking him from his thoughts. He looked around, seeking the source of the frantic plea.

"Help me!" the voice called out again, drawing Ethan to the side alleyway just ahead upon his right. He ran apace, his moccasin feet pounding the brick-lined street as he cleared the corner. There at the end of the alleyway, a slightly built man in a gray tunic cowered beneath two men clad in brown tunics with their faces covered with white scarves wrapped around their heads. Ethan stepped forth, closing upon the assailants without hesitance, his blue eyes focused intently upon them. Before taking his tenth step, he knew he had made a grievous mistake.

Ethan looked up as the massive net descended, too late to react as it draped over him. The three men in the alleyway, the assailants, and their supposed victim ran toward him with swords drawn. He felt the tug of the netting as his ankles were drawn taught, jerking him from his feet, dragging him in the direction whence he came. He twisted futilely, trying to gain his bearing, his grunts drowned out by the shouting of his assailants. He struggled working his hands in the constricting net, bringing them to his chest as he was dragged into the wider street, with the men trailing him jabbing their swords through the net, stabbing him repeatedly. Most of the blows were simply a nuisance, piercing a shoulder or arm. They were painful but healed quickly. Several landed in more sensitive areas, especially one that drove deep in his chest through his collar bone. The three men repeatedly jabbed him as their fellows dragged him in the opposite direction for some unknown purpose. Their slashes and jabs were meant to keep him off-kilter, distracting him from what awaited in the street ahead. Ethan managed to grip the netting with both hands, ripping it open as he stretched his arms apart.

"We'll have none of that," he heard one of his attackers' snarl before chopping the fingers of his right hand.

Ethan howled in agony as the fingers regrew. His effort was not in vain as a gaping hole was rent in the net. With room to maneuver, he worked his right hand to his holstered Colt. Looking over his head, he aimed the pistol on the nearest target, the man in the gray tunic that played a convincing victim. The fellow stabbed at him, his face contorted in desperate rage. Ethan squeezed the trigger, striking the gray tunic in his left breast. The man staggered, the color draining from his stricken face before stumbling to his knees. Ethan shifted aim to the other two while he was hopelessly dragged, still caught in the net. Ethan emptied his pistol into the two men, one dropping like a sack, a bullet to the throat, the other slowing with three bullets in the chest and belly. With his trailing assailants neutralized, Ethan started swimming his way out of the net, keeping a hold on his pistol as he squirmed free. With just his left foot still twisted in the netting, he was dragged clear of the narrow alleyway and into the wider street where dozens of swordsmen awaited him.

"Not the neck, we need him alive!" He heard one of them shout.

Alive? Ethan thought sourly, wondering who these men worked for.

They closed ranks, ready to drive their swords into his limbs before he worked the Colt in his left holster free. He fired off a round before the first blade fell. The serried mob paused, startled by the deadly reputation of Ethan's weapon, before pressing on. Ethan emptied his Colt, dropping several closest him, their writhing bodies an obstacle to those behind them. His leg was still caught in the netting, but he was no longer being dragged. He spotted a sword upon the ground, fallen from the hand of one of those he shot. Reaching out to snatch it, he felt the cold steel pierce his back. Doing his best to ignore the pain, he stretched desperately for the blade's hilt, before another chopped his wrist, nearly severing it in two. He retracted his mangled left arm as it quickly healed. The blade in his back lingered as the fellow who stabbed him held it in place. Ethan's wrist healed as his right hand reached his bowie knife behind his right holster. He thrust it over his left shoulder, striking the fellow who stood over him in the inner left thigh. Ethan tucked his left shoulder and rolled to his back, knocking the fellow over and snapping the sword that impaled his back in half. The man lay beneath him, blood draining from his mangled artery. The blow was mortal, and Ethan well knew the man would bleed to death in moments. Others pressed upon him, jabbing at his thighs and arms, but keeping a small distance between them so as to avoid the others' fate. With the netting still wound around his left foot, Ethan could not gain his feet. The blade in his back was still a nuisance as it pierced his lung. He drove his back down upon the ground, driving the tip of the blade out of his chest. He pinched the sword tip with his fingers, pulling it free, but not before receiving a dozen more wounds. He managed to cut the netting free of his foot, suffering repeated jabs in the process.

Alarmed by Ethan's freed limbs, his attackers stepped closer, discarding their quick jabs for deeper thrusts.

"Stick and hold! Don't let him move!" their leader desperately commanded.

They lacked choreography in their movements, several landing blows before the others. Ethan let the blows land where they may, expending his efforts on only one of his attackers, letting him drive his sword into his hip while slashing his throat with his knife. He retracted the sword as the man's hands went to his severed throat, trying to hold back the spurting blood as he went to his knees. Ethan pulled the sword free as three others impaled his back and thighs.

She waited nearby, her countenance hidden beneath the dark cowl. She felt sudden apprehension when the Astarian prince freed himself from the netting and dread when he gained his feet. Her enchantments drove the free swords onward, stripping them of fear as they pressed their attack, though their natural survival instincts would overwhelm her enchantments at times, forcing her to reassert its effects several times.

Stick and hold! she whispered the command that others echoed. They must each drive their swords into his flesh and hold them in place until he was completely subdued, then and only then, could they bind him in ropes and chains, strong enough to contain even one of his strength.

Dread filled her heart as Ethan's hand found a sword. He jabbed at his gathering foes, cutting down those nearest him, their piling corpses a hindrance to those further back. From afar, it looked a huddled mess, with dozens of men converging upon that single foe, swarming over their brethren to land whatever blow that they may. Ethan discarded his sword for his bowie knife again, using its shorter blade to maneuver within the crowd. A dozen swords impaled his flesh, but most of their masters had fallen to Ethan's fell hands. One fellow drove his sword into Ethan's shoulder. Ethan twisted free, driving his knife in the fellow's eye. He retracted the blade before another attempted to pierce his chest, slashing the man's sword arm at the elbow as the fellow's hasty strike went amiss. The thrusting blades of his attackers ebbed enough for him to begin dislodging the blades impaling him. He wasted little time removing two swords from his stomach, one from his left thigh, and two from his left hip.

Attack! the enchantress commanded desperately.

"Attack!" the men chorused in unison as her command screamed in their minds.

Ethan again grasped a sword, slashing and jabbing his way free as the men mounted one last desperate charge, driven by the command of the mage whispering in their captive thoughts. For every blow they landed, Ethan took a life, moving through their breaking ranks with an economy of motion. A sword pierced his left shoulder. He spun free of the blade, gutting the attacker from hip to hip, his innards spilling onto the street before Ethan moved on. He cut, slashed, received a blow, cut, jabbed, removed a sword, slashed again, gaining strength as he went.

The attackers finally broke, what few remained, fleeing the madness as the enchantress commanding them lost her hold, desperate to flee herself.

Ethan cut them down from behind as they fled, emerging from the pile of dying flesh, caked in blood like an avenging spirit risen from the grave. His eyes swept the carnage, catching sight of her as she turned away, attempting to escape. Her foot caught on her dress, tripping her as she fell onto the unforgiving gray bricks of the street. The blow stunned her briefly. She struggled to her knees, panic coursing her mind, retarding her basic motor functions. She cried out as a heavy foot struck her back, driving her into the ground.

"Stay down!" Ethan snarled, dropping to a knee before flipping her over, tearing her cowl from her head. Long dark hair unfurled, spilling on the ground as her amethyst eyes met his dark blue. Her eyes grew wide, trying to avert his terrible gaze. Ethan was soaked in blood from head to boot, his clothes torn to shreds, and his foul mood radiating like a bursting star. He stared at her for an eternal moment, his eyes softening with recognition.

"I know you," he said.

Impossible! her thoughts screamed. She was certain that he had never seen her, at least not close enough to discern her features.

"I've seen you at Astaris," he said. He had seen her several times through the years, her amethyst eyes difficult to miss, often catching sight of her when she thought he wasn't looking. She looked to be in her early fourth decade, with an olive complexion that further stood out in these tropical waters. "Who are you?"

The sound of sandals slapping stone echoed behind him. He craned his neck, catching sight of his attackers regrouping and running toward him, with swords raised and shouting war cries to stiffen their resolve. Ethan left her upon the street, turning upon his attackers with a sword in hand, blood dripping from its tip. There were only a dozen left, precious few to challenge him as he cut the fore ranks to pieces with practiced ease. Rage gave way to deathly calm, their blades failing to touch him as he moved within their midst. They came upon him haphazardly, like men without a sense of preservation. They were obviously enchanted, but by whom? His proximity to the enchantress should have hindered the furtherance of her enchantment upon them, unless there was another. Beyond this, what sort of enchantress could affect more than one at a time? A very powerful enchantress, no doubt, one of such power to come but once in a hundred years. But there must be more than one, for these men came at him with abandon, sans armor or leather of any sort, their flesh exposed to his taking. He took what they offered, be it hand, leg, finder, or more vital flesh, slashing then moving on.

No sooner had Ethan felled his eighth man than the others broke again, scattering to all directions. Ethan cared not, ignoring the fleeing mice as he turned back to claim the cat, but when he did, she was gone.

*****

Krixan rode through the city with Deputies Volun and Arton beside him, following the direction where the last gunshot was heard. Curious citizens filling the street, jumped clear as Krixan's horse barreled past, refusing to ease his pace.

They found Ethan standing amid the dead, digging his pistols from beneath the piles of flesh, tossing corpses aside as if they were pups. He reloaded both pistols from bullets slotted in the back of his belt, then holstered them as Krixan pulled back his reins, his horse's hooves planting in the street before him.

"You look like crap," Krixan snorted. Ethan stood there, drenched in blood, his shirt and trousers torn and ragged. His lashes blinked the blood away that ran into his eyes and covered his face.

"I'm fine, Krix. You should never judge a person by how they look." Ethan gave him that hurt look he was prone to use.

"I had a dog once when I was a child. The dog found a rabbit one day and chased it all over the countryside until he caught it. He tore into it, ripped it to shreds, and dragged the bloodied corpse back home for all of us to see. I've never seen a more wretched-looking carcass in all my life until now, looking at you." Cres Arton grinned, shaking his head as he regarded Ethan.

"I'm glad to humor you, Cres. I'll keep that in mind when I fill out your upcoming roster assignments." Ethan smiled, giving as good as he got before ducking into the alleyway where this whole mess stated to retrieve his Stetson.

Krixan leaned forward in the saddle, his eyes scanning the carnage littering the street. He counted at least thirty dead and two others barely alive with their guts ripped open, and a third with his legs missing below the knees.

"Ethan did all this?" Fass Volun asked in disbelief. He was the last deputy that Ethan hired on, having served less than a fortnight. He was the youngest deputy at eighteen years but made his reputation as a hired sword due to his rugged build and skill with a blade.

"Yep," Krixan understated, having grown accustomed to Sheriff Thorton's abbreviated answers during his time as his deputy.

"I have heard rumor of his deeds at the Velo, but thought them tales stretched a bit thin," Cres added his voice to the chorus of disbelief.

"Most rumors are lies, but when Ethan is involved, they are usually understated," Krixan said.

"I did not know you used words that big?" Cres grinned, taken aback by Krixan's prose.

"I'm not as dumb as you look." Krixan snorted before catching sight of Ethan stepping back into the street from the adjoining alleyway, hat in hand. "What happened here, Ethan? These men attacked you without armor or mail of any kind?" he asked, making little sense of the scene.

"They were enchanted," Ethan said, crossing the street to the wounded man with no legs.

"Enchanted? All of them?" Krixan asked. An enchantress could cast a spell on one person for a brief time and for a simple task or charm them for affection.

"All of them at once," Ethan answered, kneeling beside the wounded man, tying a strip of cord from the lining of a cape around the man's left leg, forming a tourniquet. The fellow wailed weakly, having lost a great deal of blood.

"How many enchantresses were there, and where are they now?" Krixan asked, looking to and fro, unease playing across his face.

"At least two that I know of, though I only saw the one. She was black of hair, maybe thirty or thirty-five years, olive skin and purple eyes."

"Which way did she flee?" Cres asked, a grimace erasing his usual grin.

"I don't know, but don't go looking for her. Any mage powerful enough to do what she did is too dangerous for any of you. I'll have to find her and her coconspirator. First things first, though, we need to get these wounded men to the Vellesian healers before they die without talking," Ethan said as he finished tying the tourniquet to the fellow's other leg.

*****

Lady Julia Forbis met Ethan at the jail with Lady Thela by her side. He sent Cres to fetch them as he and the others moved the three wounded men to the jail, though one had expired in transit. Julia passed through the doorway, her eyes drawing wide at the terrible sight before them. Three men were laid out upon the dusty wood floor, two with their guts ripped open and a third missing his legs below the knees. One of those with his stomach slashed open had clearly passed, his vacant eyes staring at nothing.

Julia gasped, regarding Ethan standing over the men, his face unrecognizable beneath the blood dried to his skin and clothes. His shirt was nearly torn from his body, rent in a dozen places.

"Prince Ethanos?" Lady Thela asked in alarm.

"What happened here?" Julia asked, collecting herself.

"I was ambushed on the north side of the harbor. I need these men healed immediately!" Ethan had no time to spare, for neither man looked long for this world.

"Of course," Thela said. The Vellesian mage healer knelt beside the man without legs. Had the strike been higher, he would have already died, but even now, it was probably too late. No sooner had she touched her hands to his thighs, his breath had ceased.

Ethan sighed, frustrated as the man's legs grew anew, only to wither at his ankles as he expired. A mage healer could only regenerate damaged tissue of the living. Once a patient dies, they are unable to animate their sundered flesh, even for appearance's sake.

Lady Thela sighed tiredly as her efforts went for naught, moving swiftly to the last man still living.

The last man lived longer than he had a right to, his pale, clammy flesh and blue lips indicated the moments of his young life were few. His early cries of torment gave way to an eerie silence as his hands rigidly held his innards from spilling further. When Lady Thela touched her hands to his chest, she could not spark the slightest response, for he was dead as well.

*****

"This is clearly a move against Cordova. If these mages partaking in this attack are as powerful as Ethan believes, then his removal is necessary before they can assail the city in force. They must be hunted down and killed. Let their heads decorate Touler's Point, overlooking the harbor entrance. Let them herald any who visit our fair port, proudly declaring the price of conspiring against our autonomy!" Hode Purciel pounded fist into hand as he addressed the ruling oligarchs and their diminished mage council, who gathered in the city forum. The attack upon Ethan that morn had shaken the stability of Cordova that was nursed and rebuilt following the raid led by Luke Crawford. It was a not so subtle reminder of their collective fragility.

Their current mage council consisted of a blinder and telepath in Lady Julia, an ice caster of modest ability in Vulanus Cromar, and a light mage in Tana Portavis. The latter two additions to their council were of Estasan heritage. Both were cousins and the children of free mages that were outside the lines of inheritance and fled Estasa for opportunity and fortune in the free isles of Far Polantis. If Ethan's summation on the power wielded by the purple-eyed enchantress proved correct, Cordova's collective mage council would be hopelessly outmatched.

"What you say is true. An attempt on Ethan's life is a likely precursor to a greater attack upon us all. She must be found," Arnos Pagge declared, his girth stretching the waist of his tunic. The others were seated upon the stone benches that surrounded the circle of the city forum. The circle was cast in mirrored white stone, surrounded by curved benches that rose in each direction akin to a giant bowl, providing ample view of the speaker below to the small gathering seated upon the lowest tiers as of now, or larger gatherings of hundreds during full attendance.

"If she can be found?" Julia said, doubtful of their chances to do so. Mages of such power were not beaten by inferior mages. "Let this serve as a warning to those among us who do not see the urgency in replenishing our mage council. We must place the utmost of our energies in the recruitment of mages to fill our council."

"Hah!" Hode Purciel snorted derisively. "Had you your way, we would all have bent the knee to Cornan Thune."

"I did what I believed best in Cordova's interest. After the decimation of our council, what choice had we? Better to serve the tyrant in our midst than a monarch in a far-off land. With Thune, we could have at least influenced his decisions. We would suffer no such voice with a foreign potentate. We need magic to fight magic," Julia defended her actions.

"Or one immune to it," Arnos sagely opined.

She gave him a look. "Yes, Ethan's arrival was most fortuitous, but we mustn't burden him with our collective defense. There will be times when he is absent from Cordova. We must prepare for those times while we benefit from his protection. We *must* replenish our mage council," Julia strongly affirmed.

"Julia makes good sense, fellas," Ethan said as he entered the forum through one of the arched entryways on the levels above. He donned a fresh pair of buckskins and shirt and bathed, washing the blood that soaked his skin.

"Ethan!" Hode smiled as his young friend descended the stone steps to stand in their midst. "We are glad to see you alive and whole."

"Well, I'm alive and kicking. That's a phrase my old friend Judge Donovan would often say." Ethan slapped Hode Purciel on the back while gifting Julia a reassuring smile. "Julia is right to be concerned, and you should place all your efforts on replenishing your mage council. They are the true defense of Cordova. I can defend you in the interim, but there will be times when I am absent."

"But what of this enchantress we are seeking?" Arnos worriedly asked.

"Leave her to me," Ethan said.

"You mustn't face her alone, Ethan. She is far too dangerous, and her attack on you is part of a larger conspiracy against Cordova," Hode argued.

Ethan doubted a conspiracy against the city but kept that thought to himself. He had seen the enchantress at Astaris several times through the years now that he reflected on it. The last time was during the Estasan delegation's visit, when he was briefly betrothed to Lady Elenna. He regarded the new members of the mage council, Vulanus Cromar and Tana Portavis, each of Estasan descent. Could they be part of a cabal against him? The fact that the enchantress was at Astaris meant that he was the intended target, not Cordova. He kept this fact to himself as well, at least until he captured the enchantress and uncovered her motives.

"What do you plan to do?" Julia asked.

"I am riding out tomorrow for North Point," he answered. North Point was a small inlet on the northern shore of the isle, nearly ten miles north by northwest.

"North Point? But why?" Lady Tana Portavis asked.

Ethan regarded the light caster carefully, wondering about her true loyalties. She was a waif of a girl, barely sixty inches and thin as a stick, with deep red hair and pale-blue eyes. "One of the men I slew today mentioned the inlet as the place they were to take me."

"For what purpose?" Hode asked.

"They had a ship waiting to take me off the isle. Where to? I do not know." For all Ethan knew they might have planned to toss him overboard once they were out to sea or take him to the Mage Bane where they could be certain of his death.

"What do you hope to find?" Mage Vulanus Cromar asked.

"I don't know, but anything we find is more than we currently have. I'll take Krixan with me. We should be back by nightfall."

*****

Krixan grumbled as they rode beneath the still palms in the sweltering heat. The road connecting Cordova to North Point was a cobblestone trail that meandered the narrow vales and tropic jungle of the isle. Ethan stripped his leather shirt, wearing the cotton pull-over shirt in its place, sweat soaking this garment as well.

"What do we hope to gain in this village we are going?" Krixan growled irritably, ducking his head to dodge another low-hanging branch. He was certain this trail was built for dwarves.

"Probably nothing but we have to try. They were going to bring me here for some purpose. They had a ship waiting…"

"Bah! That ship is long sailed. We'll only find empty water." Krixan snorted.

Krixan's prediction proved true. By midday, they reached North Point, which was a sparsely populated inlet surrounded by two dozen wood-framed structures. The small port was empty, water lapping its quiet wooden piers. The locals claimed that there was a ship docked the past several days but that it lifted anchor in the middle of the night. They claimed the ship was crewed by dark-skinned Sarcosans, including their captain, who boasted a strange headdress and thick dark beard. The locals mentioned others wearing long cowls to hide their faces and forms. Whether the mage he sought was among them, he could only guess.

Late afternoon found them halfway to Cordova when they were met by three riders with lathered mounts. Each wore light brown tunics, sandals, and a short sword. Ethan recognized them as members of Hode Purciel's household guard.

"Sheriff!" The men shouted in unison when coming upon them.

"Kliven, Torun, and Ulan," Ethan greeted, recalling each of their names. There was a nervousness about them that set him on edge.

"Sheriff. We were sent to fetch you!" Ulan shouted excitedly, short of breath with terror-filled eyes.

"What troubles you, *boy*? Out with it!" Krixan growled.

"The harbor was attacked! Seven ships, admiralled by the pirate Noris Greybar, sailed into port this morn, in the company of Luke Crawford and his companions!" Ulan panted.

"Crawford is in Cordova?" Ethan asked.

"Nay! He fled with Captain Greybar after they raided the city."

"What did they take?" Ethan asked.

"Not what, but who," Ulan said cryptically before answering further. "They captured the Vellesian mage healers and sailed away with the poor girls bound and chained. The mage's powers were ineffectual against them," Ulan added.

"What of the Vellesian escort? They had a flotilla of ships guarding their mage healers?" Ethan asked.

"All sunk but three, and one of those is badly damaged. The pirate Greybar devastated their small fleet at port, catching them unawares."

"What of our deputies guarding the Vellesians?" Ethan asked, dreading the answer.

"Nils Purciel lives but was wounded by the kind of weapon that you carry. Three other deputies were not as fortunate, and with the Vellesian mage healers captured, there is no one to heal them."

Ethan's mind went to the golden-eyed mage healer he saw that night in Hode's villa, two days prior. The thought of her in Luke's clutches raised the bile in his throat.

"Where did they take them?" Ethan asked, though he knew the answer.

"We believe they will sail for the Mage Bane. Captain Greybar is a sworn vassal to Gervis Tomaz, warlord of Palacia," Ulan explained.

"Of course they'll flee to the Mage Bane," Ethan shook his head, his promise to his mother weighing heavily upon him. "How long ago did they set sail?"

"They were just underway when our Lord sent us after you. Even then they were still within the bay," Ulan added.

"Then we might have time," Ethan grunted, kicking his heels in Bull's flanks, hurrying apace down the cobblestone trail.

*****

The sight of burning and listing ships greeted them as they rode into port. Smoke twisting in spirals of gray and black drifted above the harbor like tortured spirits. The sound of cracking timbers echoed over the waves as another listing ship's hull snapped at the bow before slipping beneath the surface. The bodies of dead and dying men bobbed amid the surf, their blood drawing the namesake of Shark's Bay to feed. Fires along the piers spread to the adjoining structures along the waterfront. Thousands flooded the piers, forming bucket chains to douse the festering flames.

"Ethan!" Julia cried out to him as he and Krixan raced along the piers. Bull slowed as Ethan turned him to where she stood amid the crowd gathering along the waterfront.

"Julia, what's happened?" He asked as Krixan pulled up beside him.

She stood with people crowding around her seeking protection that they hoped she could provide. Her rich gown was bloodstained and torn as she had moved among the wounded who seemed everywhere. But she was no healer and could offer little to aid them.

"Luke Crawford returned. He came with the Pirate Lord Noris Greybar. Four of your deputies were killed trying to protect the mage healers as well as hundreds of Vellesian sailors and the Vellesian admiral who commanded their expedition. Nils Purciel is terribly wounded, though he might live if we can find a mage healer to tend him," she said with a broken heart and watery eyes.

"How did this happen?" he asked impatiently.

"They sailed into port disguised as merchant ships. Their lead ship had disembarked before their intentions were clear. Crawford and his men spearheaded the assault, striking where the Vellesian mage healers were gathered. We tried to retaliate, but our mage skills are useless against those men," Julia said with her voice breaking with emotion.

"Did we manage to kill any of them?" Krixan asked.

"One of Luke's men and four of Greybar's ships met their end. The Vellesian admiral accounted well of himself before his flagship went under. Greybar escaped with his Vellesian captives and three vessels. The Vellesians ranking captain is preparing to sail after them, though what he can do against Luke Crawford's terrible weapons I do not know. It seems a voyage doomed to fail," Julia lamented.

"No, it's not," Ethan said before riding on to seek out the Vellesian captain.

CHAPTER 18

Ethan stood at the prow of the *Righteous Wind*, sunlight reflecting off the blue of his eyes as he fixed his sight to the horizon. The song of sea birds echoed over the lapping waves, the beauty of their ancient melody contrasting the grim task that lay ahead. He craned his neck, gazing skyward as their tall white sails caught the full wind, driving their bow through the surf. Ethan nearly lost his footing as the ship lurched forward.

Krixan stood beside him, gripping the bulwark with a desperate hold as he leaned over the ship's side, depositing his breakfast into the sea. Krixan lifted his head, wiping his mouth with the back of his hand while fixing Ethan with a disgruntled scowl. For someone red of hair and fair skin, Krixan looked a little too green as he took poorly to life at sea. Captain Lorelo said it takes a few days aboard ship for some to gain their sea legs, but Ethan recalled their voyage from Astaria to Cordova, where Krixan was as sick at the voyage's end as he was at the start. Ethan squirmed under the scrutiny of his large friend's glare.

"Why are you looking at me like that?" Ethan grinned.

"Once again you managed to involve ourselves in a matter, we have no business in, and there you stand, relaxed and unaffected while I throw my guts up on this cursed ship!"

"You fared better than I in Red Rock," Ethan countered. "I'm the one that got shot."

"Bah! As much as you threw yourself in front of every gunslinger in West Texas, you should've been shot twenty times. And if you got your fool self killed, where would that have left me? I'll tell you where…

stuck! Only you can cross through the barrier and bring others along. Not that I'd want to come back and have to explain to Queen Gabrielle that her thick-headed son got himself killed. You never did tell her that your ability to heal was impaired in Texas, did you?"

Ethan gave a guilty shrug.

"I didn't think so. Now we're chasing those ships ahead filled with a dozen gunslingers and scores of barbarians, mercenaries, and cutthroats, hoping to catch them before they set ashore in the Mage Bane. If you haven't forgotten, the Mage Bane is that foul place you promised your mother that you would *not* enter!" Krixan growled.

"And we won't. We'll catch up with them and free the Vellesian captives *before* they reach the Mage Bane coast, even if Luke Crawford and his gang get away. We can always turn back shy of the coast and return to Cordova to wait them out. Luke will come back at some point, he can't help himself."

Krixan snorted, dismissive of Ethan's childish optimism. Nothing ever went smoothly as Ethan claimed.

"Prince Ethanos!"

Ethan turned about as Captain Lorelo marched across the foredeck, his high leather boots slapping the weathered planks as he drew near. Ethan shook his head at the man's attire. He wore puffed white trousers tucked into his high black leather boots. The ruffles of his white blouse peaked at the edges of his red doublet, with gold tabards upon his shoulders, indicating his rank. A rapier graced his left hip. A long blue serge cape billowed in his wake. Ethan noted that all the ship's officers were uniformed in a similar fashion. The common sailors assigned to the ship wore loose linen shirts over knee-length trousers and soft seal skin shoes. Captain Lorelo was a tall, lean fellow with a trimmed brown beard, piercing gray eyes, and hawkish nose. He was entirely void of humor or mirth, and Ethan doubted he ever smiled, even when tickled as a babe. Despite his calm veneer and apparent serious adherence to protocol and duty, Ethan sensed a great trepidation in Captain Lorelo bon his entire crew, as if a blade were dangling above their collective necks.

"Cap, how many times do I have to tell you to call me Ethan, just plain old Ethan. I'm not a prince anymore."

Lorelo stiffened at the good-natured rebuke. "You are the son of King Bronus of Astaria, Prince Ethanos. In Vellesia we demonstrate proper deference to nobility."

"Well, I don't favor being called Prince. I earned the right to be called by name without that pompous title. Since Krix and I came along on this little voyage to help you retrieve your mage healers, you might want to oblige such a small request."

"As you wish, Ethan," Lorelo relented as if he swallowed a bee.

"Thanks, Cap'n." Ethan smiled, slapping him on the shoulder. "Can you catch those ships before they reach the Mage Bane?" Ethan jerked his chin beyond the bow, where the silhouettes of the three vessels graced the horizon.

"We shall forfeit our lives to do so, if necessary," Lorelo stated firmly.

"That's awful noble of you, Cap, but I don't think the fate of a dozen girls is worth the lives of your entire crew."

"My queen would see it differently. She told Admiral Varo to safeguard her mage healers at all cost. They represent nearly two in three of the entirety of their guild."

Ethan wasn't surprised. The mage healers in Astaria never numbered more than a score. What Ethan didn't understand was why Queen Valera of Vellesia sent so many of her healers to Cordova? Was it simply to curry favor with the populace for some reason known only to her? Were they simply a cover while other Vellesian agents spied for a future invasion? Or were they what they wished to be seen as, a simple act of generosity on behalf of the Vellesian throne? Something about the Vellesians never sat well with Ethan. Their realm was shrouded in mystery. Few Vellesians ever emigrated from their native land, and fewer still spoke ill of their lives there. What they couldn't conceal was their fear of their queen, as if her very name could strike them down half a world away. Regardless of their monarch, Ethan couldn't help thinking of the comely mage healer with the golden eyes that seemed so familiar. The thought of her suffering at the hands of Luke or the others was insufferable. For one who seldom favored the power of his mage-born brethren, Ethan sorely wished they had a wind mage with them now. He hoped Captain

Lorelo's confidence in his ship to catch the pirate rabble was not misplaced. At least his Vellesian comrades were taking the risk seriously as they crowded the vessel with an extra five dozen soldiers from their sister vessels. The rest of the Vellesian ships would make way once they affected their repairs. Captain Lorelo confirmed that an entire Vellesian fleet was underway from Brelar and en route to Free Port. How Lorelo knew this was beyond him.

"You just get us close to those ships, and we'll help you rescue your Vellesian girls," Ethan assured him.

*****

She winced as the unforgiving manacles chaffed her wrists. They were secured behind her back with nary a link between them. Her ankles were similarly bound as she sat upon the deck beside one of the strangely attired men who wielded the same mysterious weapons as the Astarian prince. She heard his fellow conspirators refer to him as Jeb. His scraggy mustache and unkempt brown hair gave him an older appearance than his youthful countenance suggested. He wasn't as cruel natured as his comrades, but neither was he kind. If she protested her ill-treatment, he would kick her to silence. A queer aura surrounded the man as well as his comrades, which shielded them from magic. 'Twas the same as the Astarian prince. Unfortunately if a mage were in close proximity to them, it completely blocked their mage powers; thus, each of her fellow healers sat beside one of these ruffians. Clearly they were aware of their effect on the mage born as Jeb kept within a foot of her at all times. She cursed his discipline, for if she could only access her powers for a brief moment, she could escape this cursed confinement. She could only wait and hope an opportunity presented itself before they reached the Mage Bane. If she only had use of her hands, she'd lift the hood of her dress over her head to conceal her beauty from these vile men.

Their leader, a lean, cool-tempered fellow, whose trimmed beard poorly hid his apparent youth, eyed her with a terrible mix of lust and violence. His fellow travelers used his name liberally, and she committed it to memory—Luke Crawford. It was a name she would never forget, and if the fates were just, she would have her vengeance. He wore a black shirt that buttoned down the center, with black trousers and a wide-brimmed hat whose sides bent up and rear leaned down. It was of similar fashion to the one the Astarian prince wore, though his was dusty brown, while Luke's was coal black. While Jeb was her apparent jailer, Luke kept Thela Corval constantly at his side. He had freed her ankles but wrapped a collar and chain around her neck, leading her across the deck as he attended his business. Lady Corval appeared well used and morose as Luke dragged her behind him. When they were first taken, she gave each of the mage healers a reassuring smile, but now her broken spirit had nothing to share but hopeless misery. Thankfully, none of them were violated as of yet, but she doubted these men's moral proclivities were the reason. They were taken for some purpose, and only a fool would doubt these men would eventually take such liberties.

"They're drawing a little too close for my liking, Grubber!" Luke snarled at the ship's portly captain.

"My name is Greybar," the man corrected him again, indignant with Luke's purposeful mangling of his name.

Noris Greybar was a broad-shouldered bear of a man, with a rotund belly and black beard that had surrendered much of its luster to gray and age. He was a notorious slaver and privateer, who spent the past three years in the sole employ of Gervis Tomaz, warlord of Greater Palacia. Palacia was a desert kingdom that dominated the northern coast of the Mage Bane from the foothills of the Tular Mountains to the western approaches of Free Port in the east. As a native Gorgencian, Noris Greybar was born the fourth son to a lesser mage house. His only mage gift was his linguistic proclivity, in which he could master any tongue, dialect, or accent within a day. Unable to inherit his lord father's lands, title, or wealth, Noris left his home at fourteen years for life at sea, where his linguistic skills proved invaluable. He started as a third mate on a merchant vessel, learning the workings of a ship and the languages of all the major ports of call in Greater Elaria. By seventeen, he commanded his own vessel.

He was later drawn to the more dangerous but lucrative slave trade, where he earned his fortune. Most men participated in the slave trade for profit, but Noris Greybar took wicked delight in that vocation. A sense of inner pleasure washed over him when he closed manacles around the limbs of former free men and women, as if their very souls were drained of their essence. Of course, there was no greater satisfaction than the enslavement of highborn captives, especially mage born. But mages were usually too difficult to collar. Many mages could bring ruin to his entire flotilla, so capturing mage born was nigh impossible until Noris Greybar stumbled upon Luke Crawford. The strangely attired and rough-speaking Texan was the perfect partner for Noris Greybar's grandiose ambitions. The Texan's ability to render mages powerless, coupled with the safe haven afforded them by the Palacian warlord Tomaz, opened endless possibilities for one Noris Greybar. Unlike his Vellesian counterpart, Greybar dressed in more practical linen trousers and shirt that cooled his body in this tropical climate. Before battle, he would don armor of boiled leather and studded gauntlets. He wore a row of daggers across his belly.

Noris planned the first raid on Cordova, where Luke Crawford's men slaughtered the city's mage council and looted the treasury. Since rumor spread that a delegation of Vellesian mage healers were visiting the harbor, Noris could not help himself and organized this second raid. Unlike the first, when they tested Luke's men's ability to simply kill mages, this raid attempted something far more difficult—capturing mages and delivering them to Gervis Tomaz.

"The sun is soon to set," Captain Greybar pointed to the sun hanging low in the west, where the sea stretched to the horizon. "They shan't catch us tonight, and we'll be along the coast by late tomorrow morn."

"And if not?" Luke asked.

"They have but one single vessel. If they draw close, I'll dispatch the *Brand* to stay their advance, while we slip away," Noris said. Noris named these three ships the *Brand*, the *Whip*, and the *Chain*. The *Brand* was the smallest but most maneuverable vessel in his flotilla, with a sleek hull and a single mast. The *Chain* held his heaviest ordinance, her decks laden with catapults, boarding ramps, and large crossbows. The *Whip* was his flagship and was a comfortable balance between speed and weaponry.

"Let's hope your ship is up to the task. I ain't fixin' to waste more bullets than necessary," Luke snorted. Though his men usually carried a heavy supply of munitions, they expended a great deal throughout their trek across Astaria and their raids upon Cordova. Once their bullets were spent, their position in Elaria would become precarious.

"My ships are up to the task, Luke. You needn't worry on that. Once we reach the warlord's palace, all our endeavors shall be thusly rewarded. We needn't share all our catches with Gervis Tomaz to reap great profit." His lecherous eye drifted to the girl chained at Jeb's feet.

Luke followed his eyes to the girl in question. Her slender face and full lips were impossibly perfect. Her defiant golden eyes bespoke a deep intelligence that appraised them as if they were bugs beneath her feet. Luke stepped across the deck, dragging poor Thela behind him, before stopping at the girl who sat at Jeb's feet.

"What's your name, girl?" Luke asked.

"Allie," she answered without reservation. If she were lying, he couldn't discern.

"Well, Allie, our good captain has taken a shine to you. He thinks he might keep you for himself rather than sell you to Warlord Tomaz. I think you're trouble, and I'd just as soon slit your throat now and be done with you. You remember that if you try to stir trouble. I'm not above killing women or feedin' their carcasses to the sharks." Luke spoke in broken Elarian as Greybar had taught him much of their language in so short of time. Allie understood him all too well.

"I'll be sure to remember that, Luke Crawford," she said, her eyes staring through his with terrible intensity.

*****

The morning sun was veiled with gray overcast painting the sky. Throughout the night, the *Righteous Wind* closed on Greybar's flotilla, drawing within eight ship lengths of the trail vessel. Now that they were near enough to discern faces on the ship ahead, Ethan and Krixan drew cloaks over their heads. They weren't certain if Luke knew they were aboard, and if not, they planned to keep that fact a secret as long as possible. The other two ships in the pirate flotilla were just farther ahead of the trailing vessel, and Ethan knew the likelihood of their survival if all three ships engaged the *Wind* simultaneously was precarious at best. The rocky coast of the Mage Bane rested just beyond the bow of the lead vessel, making every second precious.

The ship nearest them suddenly turned hard to port as her crew scurried across her deck, preparing for battle.

"Lower masts!" Captain Lorelo ordered, standing upon the foredeck as his crew prepared for battle.

"We don't have time, Cap!" Ethan argued. "If we lower masts, we'll lose your healers to the Mage Bane."

"And if we don't, they'll burn our masts and rigging to ash!" Lorelo shouted over the wind as he regarded the spirals of dark smoke drifting above the braziers fixed to the deck of the opposing ship.

"Turn into her. Grant me one pass before surrendering our speed," Ethan pleaded.

Lorelo had scant time to weigh his options, and both were fraught with peril. To do as Ethan advised, risked his ship's rigging, thus losing their pursuit altogether. If that transpired, they would never find them. If he lowered his masts, he risked losing the other ships anyway.

Ethan climbed the foredeck, fixing Captain Lorelo with an intense stare while placing his hand upon his shoulder. "Trust me."

Captain Lorelo's icy resolve melted under Ethan's assurance. The Astarian prince was certain in his choice of action, where Lorelo was shaky with the alternative. "So be it," he relented. "*Full mast! Hard to port!*"

The oarsmen on each vessel responded to the beating drums, their bodies straining under toil and lash as each ship drove upon the other. Ethan strapped his satchel over his shoulder, which contained a water pouch, a hundred rounds of Colt ammunition, his Stetson, and a spare box of ammunition for his Winchester. He slipped his retaining straps over both holstered Colts, racked the lever-action on his Winchester, and placed it in its sheath over his back.

"Come on, Krix!" he shouted, starting his ascent up the ship's center mast.

"You've got to be kidding?" Krixan growled, knowing the answer and wondering if his friend was trying to get him killed.

*****

Noris Greybar observed the action between the dueling ships from the starboard stern of his flagship. Luke Crawford stepped beside him with the captive Thela in tow as the Vellesian ship turned sharp to starboard, then to port, drawing alongside the *Brand* as a figure swung from the upper mast of the Vellesian vessel, passing over his ship's side and onto the deck of the *Brand* through a hail of arrows.

"Blagen!" Luke snarled. If he lived a thousand years, he would never forget that face, even with the distance that separated them.

*****

Ethan swung from the upper mast as the ships drew close, sweeping over the other ship's deck as the opposing crew loosed arrows. He dropped in their midst, his left ankle breaking upon landing as two arrows struck true in his thigh and chest. The wounds healed before he gained his feet with pistol drawn. He emptied his first pistol, fanning the hammer with his left palm. Two swordsmen nearest him fell in quick succession, and a third stumbled, taking two rounds in the chest, but still moving. Ethan holstered his Colt, snatching a sword fallen on the deck by the first man he killed.

Ethan ran across the deck, cutting down crewmen where they stood. Another arrow stuck true, embedding in his left arm before he claimed the archer's head that sent it. Krixan followed, swinging from the lower mast of the *Righteous Wind* before crashing upon the deck of the *Brand*. No sooner had he done so than the ships pulled apart,

Captain Lorelo unnerved by the *Brand*'s crew loading fire munitions into their catapults.

Ethan yanked the arrows from his chest, thigh, and arm after finishing another archer. He closed on the crewmen tending a brazier, catching an upraised arm at the elbow. The pirate screamed as his arm gave way. Ethan's second stroke split his belly, his innards spilling upon the deck as Ethan moved on to the catapult beside them, finishing the crewmen posted there.

Krixan gained his feet, storming across the deck with his double-bladed ax, smashing skulls or knocking men aside like gnats buzzing a bear's nose. He and Ethan finished at opposite ends of the deck, Ethan at the stern and Krixan the bow, with his ax embedded in the captain's skull. Krixan stomped his foot on the captain's chest, holding the body in place while yanking his ax free, the blade slick with blood and brain.

As soon as Krixan set foot upon the *Brand*, the *Wind* turned hard to starboard, pressing toward the *Chain* and *Whip*, and leaving Ethan and Krixan to deal with the *Brand*.

Luke Crawford lifted his rifle, fixing Krixan in his sights as he squeezed the trigger. The round went astray with the lurch of the ship. Krixan dropped to the deck after the bullet struck the rigging some feet above him.

Ethan swept the stern, his sword taking limbs or vitals wherever they were carelessly offered. He took a gash to his arm, which healed as the blade's arc left his flesh. Ethan thrust his sword tip through the offender's leather breastplate, the dull crunch of bone and tissue echoing poorly through the din. Ethan kicked the pirate's corpse in the chest, freeing his blade before another approached behind him with sword swinging. Ethan ducked, dodging the hasty arc of the blow while bringing his sword to guard his face and drawing his other pistol with his left hand and plugging the fellow with a bullet to the chest. The man stumbled, his eyes drawing wide, staggered by the blow. Ethan holstered his Colt before taking the man's head.

The sound of rifle rife rang over the sea as he turned, catching sight of Krixan dropping to the deck as Luke's first shot struck the rigging of the ship. Before he could find the source, Ethan staggered as Luke's second shot struck true, piercing his left arm, before passing through. Ethan winced as the wound closed. He dropped to the deck, unsheathing his Winchester from his back and taking aim as he lifted his eyes just above the bulwark. The rocking of the ship hindered the steadying of his sights as Luke's third shot punctured the bulwark to his left. Ethan squeezed the trigger as his front sight hovered in Luke's general vicinity, knowing he wasn't likely to get a perfect sight picture. Ethan's shot missed Luke, instead striking the man beside him—Captain Greybar.

Noris Greybar stumbled to the deck, holding his hands over the blood pooling his boiled leather cuirass.

Emmitt Cobb and John Fuller joined Luke, taking aim with their rifles just as Ethan's second shot struck George Middleton in the chest. Middleton stood just beside Jeb, who stepped toward his comrade as he fell.

No sooner had Jeb taken two steps, then fire erupted from Allie's fingers. The flames swept skyward, igniting the ship's sails and forecastle. Jeb turned back, staring in wonder as Allie stood, free of her bonds with fire spewing from her outstretched fingertips. He quickly recovered, suddenly cognizant of why they kept their captives close at hand. He quickly tackled her, driving her shoulder into the deck as he landed atop her. She cried out with the force of his body pinning her to the deck.

Luke Crawford cursed the Devil's Deputy for his misfortune as flames engulfed the bow of the *Chain*, and Captain Greybar dying beside him. He needed Greybar to communicate with the savages of this feudal world. He then remembered the mage gift of his captive.

"Fix him!" He kicked Thela toward Noris, allowing her to briefly lie just beyond the aura of his magical immunity.

"My hands?" She pleaded, twisting her back to him, revealing her bound wrists.

"You don't need your hands in front of you. Just touch him!" Luke commanded, crouching below the bulwark, lest Ethan's next shot find him.

Thela twisted her body, stretching her hands toward Noris Greybar's chest, grasping his hands with hers. Once she was free of

Luke's crippling aura, she felt rapture as magic flooded her veins. A bright orange glow filtered from her palms, bathing the stricken captain with ethereal light. She drew the bullet from his chest before mending the damaged tissue.

Ethan spied Emmitt Cobb upon the deck of the *Whip*. Hank Grierson's former ranch foreman lowered his rifle, distracted by the fire engulfing the front of his ship. Before he could squeeze off a round, Ethan felt feet pounding the deck. He turned just as a sword swung to meet him. He raised his rifle to block the hasty strike. The sword struck the butt of the rifle, taking the first two fingers of his right hand. Ethan barely felt the wound as he was awash with adrenaline. His fingers regrew as he drove the butt of his rifle into his attacker's gut, then smashed his skull before leveling the rifle on another pirate emerging from the stair to the lower hold.

Boom! The sound of the rifle rang out as the bullet caught the fellow in the throat, sending him tumbling down the stair.

*****

"*Full ahead!*" Captain Lorelo commanded, his eyes fixed over the bow as he beheld the fire spreading unchecked upon the deck of the *Whip*. His pulse quickened, knowing the lives of the Vellesian mage healers rested in the speed and might of his vessel. Before he could close on the burning wreck, the third ship in Greybar's flotilla lurched forth, blocking his advent.

"*Full masts! Pound the oars!*" Lorelo commanded, meeting the *Chain* head-on.

The two vessels sped apace, their oars cutting the surf as they drew nigh. Flaming arrows spewed from their bows, arcing over the chop as balls of flame joined their volleys from catapults mounted to the forecastles of each vessel. The foremast of the *Righteous Wind* burst into flame as a fire munitions punctured its center. Balls of fire struck the bow of the *Chain*, spreading their gelatinous flames across the forecastle. The *Wind* was similarly afflicted; her portside bow was ablaze as sailors from either ship leaped into the sea, their clothing alit. The ships passed starboard to starboard, the oars of either ship snapping like brittle twigs against the hulls of the opposing vessels. The bow of the *Wind* twisted to starboard as she reached midship of the *Chain*, smashing into the center bulwark of the pirate galley. Boarding ramps dropped onto the *Chain*, with iron hooks fixed to their far ends, which caught the starboard bulwark of the *Chain*. Vellesian soldiers swept over the ramps as archers fired into their midst. Several stumbled from the gangplanks, falling between the two ships into the sea. Several ramps twisted under the strain of the two vessels shifting apart before snapping, spilling more soldiers overboard. Nearly forty Vellesians swarmed the *Chain*, intermingled with pirates brandishing an odd mix of scimitars, short swords, knives, and axes. A few pirates still manned the catapults, hurling balls of flame onto the *Wind*. Screams of dying and wounded men rent the air, their bodies strewn across either deck beset by blades or flames lapping their flesh.

*****

Ethan was torn between searching below and the chaos engulfing the other ships. He couldn't discern the happenings aboard the *Whip*, which drifted perilously close to shore as the rocky coast of the Mage Bane drew near. Smoke obscured his line of sight, blinding him to the battle betwixt the *Wind* and the *Chain*. The vision of the golden-eyed girl aboard the flaming wreck of the pirate galley, consumed his thoughts. He possessed an overwhelming urge to go to her and protect her from such a cruel fate, but greater need guided his path as he chose to go below.

*****

No sooner had Lady Thela healed Captain Greybar than Luke Crawford stepped beside her, drawing her within his mage-less aura, rendering her powerless. Luke kicked Greybar's foot, stirring the groggy Captain.

"Get up, Noris. We ain't the time!" Luke barked.

Noris's vision slowly cleared, his body still awash with the euphoric residue of Lady Thela's healing power. As he gained his feet, his eyes transfixed to the horror surrounding him. His flagship drifted to shore, fires spreading across her main deck. The ship's rigging and masts were engulfed in flame. Behind him, he could see the terrible carnage wrought as the *Chain* was joined to the *Wind*, her mighty decks poorly contested by his men, fighting hand to hand against the Vellesian boarders.

"We must set ashore!" Luke shouted over the panicked cries of the crew.

"We cannot land here. We'll rip our hull on the rocks," Noris cautioned.

"Better than burning!" Luke countered. "Give the order!"

Noris relented, knowing they had little choice now.

*****

The oar master slashed at him with his short sword as he descended into the lower hold. Ethan jumped back, his sword deflecting the errant strike while his left hand went for his Colt.

Boom! The oar master staggered a step, unaware of what had transpired. The man was massively built with grease-stained beard and foul breath spewing from his mouth. He was bare-chested with dark trousers and a whip coiled upon his hip. His dull blue eyes drew vacant as blood pooled internally. Ethan knocked his sword from grasp and thrust his blade through the wretch's throat, then kicked him, his corpse slapping the floor of the lower hold. Ethan stepped into the dim light, finding himself between two rows of oar benches that ran to either side, with slaves chained to the benches by their ankles and to the oars by their wrists. They stared at him with the sunken eyes of broken men. They wore little more than ragged tunics. Their ankles and wrists were swollen and chafed by the irons that bound them. The stench of the lower hold tortured his senses.

"Where are the keys to your shackles?" he shouted.

They spoke not, only staring blankly at him, not understanding his question.

"The keys to your shackles? Where are they? Do you want to be free or not?" he asked firmly, desperate for any sign of life among these poor wretches.

"Not here," the nearest fellow coughed, his emaciated form nearly a skeleton. His filth, hunger, and scraggly beard masked his true age.

"Then where?" Ethan stepped toward the fellow for an answer.

"They are not on this ship. We are chained in place until voyage end, then rotated to the opposite side."

Ethan shook his head, holstering his pistol and casting aside his sword before taking the chains that bound the men's wrists to the oars, snapping them with ease. He did likewise to the long chain looped through the rings on their ankles. They were awestruck by his strength.

"Do you want your freedom?" he shouted.

"Yes," most answered.

"Then arm yourselves and help man this ship!" he commanded.

"Aye, we shall," several answered, the spark of hope rekindled in their weary eyes.

"You'll find my friend above deck. His name is Krixan. Now go while I free the rest of you." He waved the four men he freed toward the stair while moving on to the next bench and the one after that, snapping chains with his bare hands as he went.

*****

Fresh air greeted him as Ethan emerged from the bowels of the ship, cleansing his nostrils of the noxious stench of the lower hold. The top deck was littered with the dead, dying, and wounded crew that Ethan and Krixan struck down. Nearly forty of the freed oar slaves joined him upon the deck, brandishing whatever weapons they could scour. They were an emaciated, filthy rabble, their breath was foul, and they were poorly used, but they were free and looked to Ethan with awe and gratitude, and most importantly, direction.

"Who are you?" one fellow asked. He was taller than the rest, with broad shoulders that even now held great power despite the hunger that robbed him of his once-great bulk. He had even set brown eyes and long golden hair with gray tainting his locks. Age began to lessen his height, yet he was still a giant of a man, standing somewhere between Ethan and Krixan's height.

"The name is Ethan, and you?"

"I am Jorus Darcannon, first sword to my brother Lagas Darcannon, the sea lord of Valconar."

Valconar rested along the northwestern shores of the Mage Bane, just beyond the Tular Mountains. Valconar was an age-old enemy of Palacia and a dominant sea power, whereas the warlord of Palacia depended upon privateers such as Noris Greybar in order to project his influence beyond his desert kingdom.

"Are you the leader of these men?" Ethan asked, his eyes scanning the men gathered around.

"I'll speak for them if they'll have me, but it is you we look to friend." Jorus grinned, clasping forearms with Ethan.

"So be it, at least until we are all free of these pirates," Ethan answered. "Let's first rid this ship of their stinking corpses."

"Aye! That we shall do. You heard Ethan, boys. Let's set things to right!" Jorus shouted, waving his scimitar over his head.

The men shouted their agreement before stripping the dead of their weapons and clothing. They tossed the pirates overboard whether they were dead or wounded. Scores of dorsal fins circled the ship, drawn by the bloodstained water as the sharks took their fill. Krixan stood beside Ethan at the ship's stern, their eyes drawn toward the *Righteous Wind* and the *Chain* still locked in their macabre dance, smoke, and flame billowing from their serried decks. Farther afield, they beheld the *Whip* run aground upon the rocky shore, fire sweeping her once proud deck from bow to stern. He could make out the harried forms of Luke Crawford, Emmitt Cobb, and the others wading through the surf with their captives in tow. He counted all twelve mage healers among them as they gained the beach, along with ten Texans and a score of others clad in mismatched attire of the ship's crew.

"They reached the Mage Bane," Krixan growled as if to say *I told you so.*

"Yeah," Ethan sighed tiredly, despondent over his failure. He didn't kill Luke or save the mage healers. He counted only ten of Crawford's gang, meaning they likely killed one.

Luke crossed over to Elaria with twelve, himself included. Yet despite crossing the length of Astaria and conducting two raids upon Cordova, he lost only two men. If he could've caught them on the high sea, his regenerative power would've evened the odds, but now—now they were within the Mage Bane, where he could die like any other man. There was also his promise to his mother not to enter therein, warning of great suffering should he do so. Despite all that, he could not dismiss the golden eyes of the alluring mage healer. The very thought of her in Luke Crawford's clutches, or any other man's, chilled his blood.

"What of our fellow travelers?" Krixan asked, lifting his chin toward the other interlocked vessels.

Ethan looked back toward the flaming wrecks, a cursory glance confirming there was nothing to salvage but survivors. Both ships were doomed, drifting perilously toward the coast. He could see Captain Lorelo upon the forecastle of the *Chain*, sword in hand and dispatching another foe. Despite his pompous attire, the man could wield a blade.

"Jorus, how many of you are still below deck at the oars?" Ethan asked.

"Near twenty. Most of those can't walk, but they can still pull an oar."

*****

The *Brand* drew alongside the *Wind*, her oars retracting as she approached. Ethan kept a fair gap between them, lest the *Brand* meet a fiery end as well. They called out to the Vellesian crew, urging them to forsake their vessel. A few immediately forsook their doomed ship, the rest following soon after, jumping clear of the flames and swimming to the safety of the *Brand*.

By the time they pulled the last survivor from the sea, they counted fifty-three Vellesians, including Captain Lorelo and three prisoners.

*****

"You'd risk what remains of your crew for the lives of those twelve girls?" Krixan snorted.

"Aye," Lorelo answered without pause. He could not return to Vellesia without Queen Valera's mage healers without forfeiting his life and those of his wife and children. The same threat loomed over every member of his crew.

Ethan regarded Lorelo uneasily. There was more to the man's urgency than perhaps even the good captain was aware. Having rescued Lorelo's crew, the *Brand* withdrew from the tangled vessels, staging offshore within view of the coast. From there, they observed Crawford's men attain the rocky shore, holding a strong position upon a low, rock-strewn ridge just above the beach. Much of the coastline from Free Port to the east and the Tular Mountains in the west was inaccessible by miles of shallow waters with jagged rocks jutting from the seabed. There were only a few port villages along that stretch where a small number of ships could disembark. Craven's Nest rested forty leagues to the west. It was a vassal of Palacia and the obvious intended destination of Noris Greybar's flotilla, and the nearest source of supply and reinforcements for Crawford's men. The small port had enough moorings for a dozen galley sized vessels.

Jorus Darcannon unfurled the map across the table in the former captain's cabin. The others gathered around the table, following the Valconar lord's finger as he detailed the lay of the land before them.

"We are here." He jabbed his finger to the point offshore where their ship was anchored. "They were likely headed for Craven's Nest...here," he said, running his finger west along the coast, stopping at the small port before returning his thick finger to their current position. "They are well positioned upon this ridge but cannot stay there indefinitely. A thin line of scrub brush and cacti line the coast, but further inland is league upon league of endless desert where nothing lives. The nearest Palacian outposts are many leagues beyond the coast, positioned along a line of oases. Another twenty leagues beyond them, a larger Palacian city rests with large tracts of arable land. The most accessible port lies twenty leagues further west of Craven's Nest, where the Shazar River empties into the Gonar Bay." The Palacians moored their meager number of warships there and fortified the harbor to withstand the superior Valconar navy. Palacian settlements ran the length of the Shazar, connecting Gonar to the larger Palacian strongholds in the south.

"What do you suggest we do?" Captain Lorelo asked.

"Logic suggests but one course…here!" Jorus jabbed the map, indicating the small coastal village of Lupen's Cove, four leagues east of their current position. Lupen's Cove was a small fishing village of little note, surrounded by dangerous reefs and shallow approaches, save for a narrow path through those perilous waters known to few other than the fishermen who dwelled there.

"How are you certain of our current location? What sets this part of this blasted coastline apart from any other?" Krixan growled.

"You would be correct to believe so as the northern coast looks much the same from the western approaches of Free Port to the foothills of the Tular Mountains, but there are landmarks of note if you observe carefully. When next you step outside, pass a gander to our east, and you'll spy a queer shaped hilltop that stands apart. Its forward slope drops steeply into the sea, and its reverse slope rises at a near-impossible angle for a man to crawl, let alone walk to attain its summit. That hilltop is aptly named Vulture's Perch. 'Tis from there those foul carrion gather, feeding off the ships that break themselves upon these rocky shores, and no waters are as dangerous as those that surround Lupen's Cove, which lies just east of that hill," Jorus explained.

"And to whom do the good people of this cove owe allegiance?" Lorelo asked.

"Only themselves. There be naught but a half-dozen wells in their small village, enough to support them and their kin, but little else. The surrounding land possesses a wee patch of vegetation to supplement their sea harvest. Beyond that, little grows. They are not hostile to strangers, nor are they welcoming. They are cautious but fair-minded folks," Jorus added.

They'll be more cautious and less fair-minded once they cross paths with Luke Crawford, Ethan thought sourly.

"Can you navigate the approaches to Lupen's Cove?" Captain Lorelo asked hopefully.

"Nay. I wouldn't risk our only ship unless I was better versed in these waters. I think it best to go east to Free Port. There are never fewer than a dozen vessels bearing the flag of Valconar there. They shall rally upon my word, and I'll bring them to port here," Jorus indicated a mining colony some leagues east of Lupen's Cove.

"Crepsos?" Ethan read the name aloud.

"Aye, Crepsos. They have a small accessible harbor surrounded by deep tranquil waters. 'Tis a mining colony rich with ore and salt. They have no allegiance but to coin. Fill their purse with gold, and they'll gladly join your cause," Jorus said.

"While we sail for Free Port, we leave the mage healers to the mercies of those *men*," Lorelo nearly spat that last word, shaking his head in disgust, dismissive of the plan.

"I can sail to Free Port and return within days. I can disembark a landing force at Crepsos, order them to take the fairly safe overland route to Lupen's Cove while we position our fleet off the coast, blocking the port. They have nowhere else to go, lest they staged men and ships somewhere close by, but that I doubt," Jorus advised.

"I cannot risk it. Set us ashore, and we can part ways," Captain Lorelo said.

"Luke Crawford holds the ridge overlooking the beach. It's suicide to set ashore here," Ethan pointed out.

"Perhaps so. Perhaps not. Either way, we shall do as we must," Lorelo said.

Ethan stared at the map, his thoughts running in opposite directions. The life of the girl who consumed his thoughts weighed against his promise to his mother. His duty as sheriff of Cordova weighed in the balance as well. The Vellesian mage healers visited Cordova on a mission of mercy, rendering great service to the people of his new adopted home. Their safety was his responsibility as well, and he needed to see them safely returned.

"Cap, you needn't risk all your men to save your mages," Ethan offered.

"How so?" Lorelo asked, everyone suddenly looking at Ethan, especially Krixan, who was already shaking his head.

"I have a plan."

CHAPTER 19

They came ashore with the waning light of day with the sun slipping below the western sky. They were a near-even mix of Vellesian sailors and soldiers. They waded ashore with their crossbows, bows, and swords held above their heads while forsaking any equipment or armor that might weigh them down and provided no protection from bullets. Some lost their footing under heavier waves, the force knocking them below the surf before they regained their feet.

Gunfire rang out from the ridge above as bullets rained in their midst. They struggled through the chop and surf as the beach lay far afield. The shallows along the coast ran hundreds of yards in places, exposing them to the withering fire of the Texans' terrible weapons as they trudged step by grueling step. Captain Lorelo planted his feet into the hard seabed as another wave pressed upon his back. He jumped as it passed, allowing him to ride the wave a meter or so. He led his men from the front and center as they spread around him in a broken line. He caught sight of a soldier far to his left take a bullet in his chest, his body slipping below the surf with his flailing limbs. When another moved to aid their fallen comrade, Lorelo admonished his effort, for the man was doomed and to not waste the living on the dead. Another two were similarly stricken off his right, yet each kept their feet for a time, before being driven under the lapping waves. One never resurfaced, while the other eventually attained the shore, only to die upon the beach. Further off his left, another sailor was thrice struck, with wounds to his arm, chest, and neck. His lifeless corpse now drifted with the current amid his pooling blood.

"Hold your fire till they draw closer, ya fools! Bullets are worth more than men, so use only one per target, and let nature take her course!" Emmitt Cobb reminded his fellow Texans as he paced behind them upon the ridge.

"One bullet per soldier. If you might miss, then wait for a better shot!" Luke echoed Emmitt's command.

The Vellesians bravely trudged along, fighting waves, fatigue, gunfire, and nightfall as they reached the shore. Thirty men went into the water, yet only twenty crawled ashore. There they held, huddling behind whatever cover they could find on that rock-strewn beach.

And there they waited.

*****

They shuffled along in the dark, their hands bound in front of them in fetters and a rope connecting them neck to neck. Allie led the coffle, the tug of the rope scratching her throat whenever the slack drew taut. Her captors eyed her warily. Luke had instructed them to kill her if any trouble or mischief arose throughout their trek. Luke wanted to kill her for setting their ship ablaze, but Captain Greybar argued that Gervis Tomaz would pay her weight in gold. Luke relented for the time but knew he would have to kill her eventually for her affront and to keep the others in line. 'Tis a pity, for she was most fetching, though she had a look of a woman not to be trifled with.

Some time had passed since they heard gunfire coming from the ridgeline. Once her countrymen came ashore, Luke Crawford ordered their captives taken inland to begin their trek to Lupen's Cove. It was a suicidal gesture on the Vellesian captain's part, and she cursed his stupidity. A wiser choice would've been to withdraw and set ashore further east where the nearest ports lie. The only positive in the bloody affair was that eight Texans remained upon the ridge, along with the dreadful Captain Greybar and a dozen of his men. Once they had come ashore, they no longer guarded their captives so closely as the Mage Bane blocked their powers. No longer having to place one of his men beside each mage, Luke sent only two of his men, Terrance Wheeler and Jeb Cullen, to herd their captives along, as well as eight of Greybar's men to guide them. The Vellesian captives may have great powers, but here they were only women, chained and helpless. What danger could they possibly pose? Luke ordered them to move apace in the cool night air, to close the distance to Lupen's Cove. Traveling at night would allow them to best husband their water through the arid trek. Once the Vellesians' landing at the beach were neutralized, Luke would catch up with them as the captives moved far slower than men not so encumbered.

Without her Mage gifts to protect her, she had to rely on her wits. Fortunately, Greybar kept his better-disciplined men with him, sending the complainers and shirkers to guard them. The two Texans were more observant, but there were but two of them, and each lingered in the rear of the column. Luck again favored her as the pirate leading their coffle was a dull wit. She lifted his dagger from the sheath on his hip. He still had not noted its absence or observed her holding the blade beneath her chin, where she slowly cut the rope binding her to the others. The only ill fortune to befall her was the light of the quarter moon illuminating much of the surrounding terrain. She waited until they passed within a field of boulders before cutting the last strands of rope with the lead fellow but two paces to her front. She stepped forth, reaching her bound wrists to the side of his head and drove the dagger deep into the side of his neck. Before the others realized what she had done, she withdrew the blade and slipped away in the dark.

*****

She hid behind a fat rock, drawing the dagger close as the shouts of the men chasing her drew near. They'd expect her to flee into the night, a hapless maiden frightened of their masculine superiority, though she was taller than most of them. She cursed the fetters binding her hands, greatly limiting her options with the knife. The clarity of her vision in the dim lunar light was akin to an owl's, revealing the rugged terrain in splendid detail. Her hearing was attuned to the labored breath of the heavyset pirate in their small party, a grossly fat and foul-tongued ruffian who boasted his sexual charms. The mere sight of him sickened her. She waited patiently for him to clear the rock she was hiding behind before striking quickly, slashing him across his right elbow. He jumped back, screaming in octaves too high for one of his gender. His sword fell from his weakened grip as his forearm hung limply at his side. Before she could land another blow, he swatted her away with his other hand while shouting their location.

They were soon upon her. She slashed at them in vain as she felt pairs of hands upon her, disarming her while throwing her to the ground.

"I should've killed you back on the ship!" Jeb spat, standing over her with pistol trained on her head, his finger beginning to work the trigger. Her pounding heart muffled his voice as she stared into the barrel of his Colt. She never imagined her end to be as this, upon an insignificant patch of dirt far from home and at the hands of men of such poor measure. She undertook this journey at her mother's behest. Her mother spoke of destiny and the good of the realm. She believed with all her entirety in her family's prophecies and foresight and could not fathom their fallacy. But now, *now* she realized the blindness in her family's vision as death drew nigh.

Bang!

Gunfire rang out in the darkness as Jeb's gun hand fell, his body collapsing as three others either dropped dead around her or writhed in agony. Two of the three yet lingered with gunshots in their torsos. She wasted little time reaching for her fallen dagger. Before she could plunge the blade into her wounded captors, another man stepped from the shadows with a long knife in hand. He gripped the first wounded pirate by the hair, running the thick blade over the fellow's throat with enough force to nearly separate head from neck. He wasted little motion before doing the same to the other, whether dead or not, making certain to leave nothing to chance before approaching her. She tensed as he drew near until his face shone clear in the moonlight.

It is him! Her heart pounded emphatically as gold eyes fixed to blue.

"Are you all right, miss?" Ethan asked, squatting in front of her with his elbows resting on his knees, holding his bowie knife loosely in his right hand.

"It's you," she whispered, not trusting her eyes.

"Yeah, it's just me, Ethan. I remember your face from Arnos Pagge's villa that night in Cordova, but I never caught your name."

"Allie," she answered after a brief lapse as she stared into his eyes. When she first set eyes upon him, he had taken her breath, but now…now that they had finally spoken one to the other, she found it beyond her imagining.

The sounds of gunfire and clanging steel echoed nearby, followed by the screams of dying men.

"Come on Allie, we best get moving," Ethan smiled easily, offering her his freehand while sheathing his knife with the other.

She couldn't help but return his smile, overcome by a strange sense of familiarity as she placed her hand in his. Ethan's smile eased slightly as their hands touched, a jolt running the length of his arm before filtering throughout. His breath caught briefly in the willowy narrows of his throat as if bewitched, though no magic dwelled in this mage-forsaken land. It felt as if he had been here before in another life not his own, but his all the same, as if she were with him for a thousand lifetimes, reliving this moment time and again, drawn one to the other.

He had saved her when all seemed lost, she reminded herself. That fact dampened her smile as the realization sunk in. She would be dead if not for him.

"Come on, Allie," he said again before snatching Jeb's pistol belt, gun and satchel of ammunition. He led her to where her sister mage healers stood, surrounded by a dozen men bearing the signet of Vellesia upon their chests, a golden rose on a field of black. They wore black leather mail over golden tunics and leggings and were armed with short swords. Allie noticed with satisfaction the bodies of her captors upon the ground, blood pooling beneath their warm corpses. The Vellesian soldiers were searching the dead for the keys to the girls' fetters but to no avail.

"You needn't bother, Sergeant," Allie called out to the soldier of rank.

"My lady?" He bowed his head, regarding her.

"The keys to our bonds are with their leader, Captain Greybar."

"Blasted pirates!" The sergeant cursed their ill fortune.

"Where's Krixan?" Ethan asked.

"I'm over here, Ethan," Krixan said before the sergeant could answer. He stepped forth carrying the pistol belt and satchel of ammunition that belonged to Terrance Wheeler. Krixan's rifle fire killed the Texan before the Vellesian soldiers rushed forth to slay the remaining pirates.

"How many did we lose?" Ethan asked.

"Two. One dead and the other dying with his belly split open," Krixan growled bluntly.

"Then finish him but make it quick, Sergeant," Ethan said.

"What of the bonds binding our mage healers?" the sergeant asked.

"See to your men. Krix and I will take care of your girls."

The Vellesians collectively stiffened at Ethan's use of the term "girls." He shook his head at their childishness. Apparently their gratitude for his help did not outweigh his disrespectful tongue.

Oh well, what else is new? Ethan shrugged before lifting Allie's hands, examining her bonds. The manacles were fairly well made with thin iron rings linking them together. Not overly strong but enough to hold women or men of average strength. Placing his hands upon her left manacle and the chained links, he pulled with all his strength. When he came ashore, he felt his enhanced strength and regenerative powers fade, just as they had when he first stepped upon Texas soil. He still retained his knowledge, his skills, and his own considerable physical prowess, evidenced when the center link in Allie's bonds bent apart, freeing her.

"How?" Allie asked in wonder. Ethanos Blagen was renowned for his immunity to magic, his regenerative power, and his enhanced strength. The Mage Bane was supposed to block his strength and ability to self-heal. She knew the oppressive nature of the Mage Bane as it blocked her powers, rendering her nearly helpless.

"These are thin chains, Allie, designed to hold women. Greybar probably thought heavier chains would slow you down," Ethan explained. "Krix, just yank them apart!" he shouted to his friend.

Krixan snorted, grabbing hold of the nearest mage healer and wrapping his massive hands around the links and pried them apart with ease.

"You don't have to make me look bad, Krix. At least *pretend* to struggle with it." Ethan scowled.

"Bah!" Krix snorted again, ignoring Ethan's taunt as he went down the line, freeing the mages of their bonds. A couple of Vellesian soldiers attempted to aid in the endeavor but could not avail the chains.

Allie wondered if Ethan was strong enough to bend chains with his normal strength, how much stronger was his mage-enhanced power? His mage-gifted strength was rumored to be three times that of his natural strength, but who could truly measure such? He could be ten or one hundred times stronger than the average man for all they knew.

"Gather up your people, Allie. We have to move. Luke will be pounding feet to get here after hearing our gunfire."

*****

They marched throughout the night, placing as many miles between Crawford's men and themselves as they could. Allie learned that Captain Lorelo and thirty of his crew had thrown themselves at the Texans holding the ridge overlooking the beach. It was a diversion for Ethan, Krixan, and a dozen Vellesian soldiers to come ashore further east to attack Crawford's men from the rear. Such was their intent until they happened upon the coffle of mages marching east from the ridge.

Allie spent the better part of the night walking beside Ethan. She was never one to need comfort or reassurance from others, but she found Ethan's presence strangely inviting. She had heard much of the fabled Astarian crown prince through the years. Some spoke of his magical immunity, his great strength, his ability to self-heal, or his comely features. What struck her as most surprising was how unprincely he truly was. He seemed overly comfortable and relaxed, even though he must be dead upon his feet from exhaustion. Queen Valera, the monarch of Vellesia, often spoke despairingly of the Astarian prince, considering him an arrogant princeling who forsook duty for his own self-interest. The queen thought him little more than a dull-witted, selfish youth who used his charming looks to gain friends and favors. Allie now laughed at such assumptions. Ethanos Blagen was clever, as his plan of attack proved. He was selfless as he risked his own life entering the Mage Bane on their behalf, for no great gain that she could see. And his looks? It seems he tries to hide his handsome features beneath his barbarian garb and the strange hat that rested upon his head. Even his hair was cut short, forgoing the flowing locks favored by the young lords of the mage realms.

"What of Captain Lorelo and his men?" she asked of him, wondering what fate awaited her brave countrymen.

"I don't know. We planned to attack Luke from both front and back, but we agreed that if we could free you, then we would set out for Lupen's Cove. Your captain said he would follow the coastline to the port if we failed to attack the ridge. Luke has little choice now but to follow us. That should buy your friends time to get off the beach without suffering further."

"We are both on our own then," she summarized.

"For now? Yes, but we're both headed in the same direction."

"As is your friend Luke," she added.

"And what a friend he is," Ethan sighed.

"Where did you gain his acquaintance?" she asked, looking over to him in the waning dark as they walked.

"It's a long story, Allie."

"We seem to have plenty of time for the telling," she stated the obvious.

So Ethan told her, beginning with his brief betrothal to Lady Elenna and all his journeys thereafter. She listened attentively to his wondrous tales, favoring the rich timbre of his voice as it carried softly in the quiet night air. It was masculine yet soothing and set her mind at ease despite all their troubles. She listened to every detail of his story, learning all she could of his past.

"And what of you?" he asked. "I grow weary speaking of me," he said.

"What do you wish to know?"

"Everything," he answered all too quickly. "Your family, friends, your life growing up? Where is your home? What are your dreams?"

"I fear my answers would bore you." She sighed pleasantly, her sultry voice enthralling him even in a sigh, stirring feelings he had never known.

"Why not? You listened to my boring tale."

She rolled her eyes in the dark. "You have many attributes, Prince Ethanos, but boring is not among them," she admonished playfully.

"Then you must not have been raised at court. Life there would bore a tree."

"I imagined that life in Astaris would be filled with intrigue, excitement, and splendor. Am I remiss to believe so?"

He laughed.

"Are you laughing at me?" she asked darkly.

"Me? I would never think to offend a lady of such beauty." He smiled.

"Again you jest. Do you ever answer truthfully, Prince Ethanos?"

"Call me Ethan. Just plain ole Ethan, and I did answer truthfully. You *are* beautiful, but I figured you already knew that."

"Hmmm…Ethan." She tested his name on her tongue. "Very well. I shall do as you wish, and you may call me Allie."

"Sounds fair."

"As far as beauty is concerned, many women are beautiful, but not many are in your eyes."

"What makes you say that?" he asked.

"Come, Ethan. You are a handsome Astarian prince whom every maiden in your realm dreams to wed. You have found *none* to your liking?"

"I find most of them attractive but not enough to wed them."

"Or bed them?" She lifted a curious brow.

"Not that either. I'll only bed the woman I love."

"The name of said maiden?"

"Which maiden?" he asked, confused by her inquiry.

"The maiden that you love, of course. The one that has captured your heart?"

"I haven't found her yet. Perhaps you know of one that I might like?"

"I doubt you need my aid in such endeavors…Ethan." She smiled mischievously.

"You might be surprised how much help I actually need. I am quite hopeless in managing my life. At least that is my family's opinion."

"And you forsook your birthright to escape your horrible family?"

"*No.*" Ethan was taken aback. "I love my family. I love them more than myself. I'd give my life for them."

"Yet you have forsaken them?"

"I forsook the crown, not them. I would never forsake them."

"And yet you dwell in Cordova and far from home."

"I came to Cordova seeking Luke Crawford. He must be brought to justice. And just because I live in Cordova doesn't mean I can't return home."

"And when do you plan to return to Astaris?"

"I'll go home for the winter festival. It's a joyous time with lively music, warm fires, games, and families gathered around tables filled with delicious food." His mouth watered at the vision. He had eaten little but dried meats and stale bread for days.

"It sounds delightful."

"It is to me, but what of your homeland? What holidays do your people celebrate?"

"Holidays?" she thought aloud. "We have no such festivals as you describe. We do celebrate Queen's Day during the summer solstice."

"Queen's Day?" He made a face, not liking the sound of it.

"It is a sacred time where we offer praise and gratitude for the benevolence and protection our queen provides."

"What has she accomplished other than being born to warrant such praise?"

"Our queen protects the realm, she attends our needs, she—"

"She drains the joy of life," Ethan added.

Allie pursed her lips, wondering how to respond to his derision. "Monarchs are not charged with our entertainment in Vellesia. Are they so charged in Astaria?"

"Absolutely!" Ethan said in all seriousness. "King Bronus is a barrel of laughs. He drinks with the knights and men and is a good loser when I best him at the cups." Ethan couldn't help but chuckle, unable to keep a straight face.

"Your assessment of King Bronus fails to match his reputation. You ought not to lie, Ethan, for you are not very good at it." She smiled.

I better improve my lying or my mother will know where I've been, he thought sourly, wondering how he'd pull that one off.

"Yeah, I'm a lousy liar, but I'm lousy at a lot of things, unlike you," he added.

"Me?" She raised a brow over a golden eye.

"Yeah, you. You're a mage healer and a fire caster, and you are exceptional at avoiding questions by asking questions of your own."

"That is because I find your answers more entertaining than your questions," she teased.

"Well, it's nice to know that I amuse you. Perhaps if my stint as sheriff of Cordova doesn't work out, I can find work as a fool."

"Motley doesn't suit you." She smiled.

"What about you?" he asked. "You still haven't told me about your family or home. Are you avoiding the question or prefer keeping your life a mystery?"

"A woman needs a little mystery to gain a man's attention, Ethanos, lest you quickly tire of our company."

"I'm not much for mysteries, Allie, just be yourself."

"Hmm," she mused aloud. "You appear honest, Ethan, but mystery surrounds you, even if you intend it not."

"Ethan," Krixan's deep voice echoed as he drew up alongside him.

Allie regarded the large man with mild curiosity. She knew he was a close friend of Ethan's, but he rarely spoke a word.

"It's nearly sunup," he reminded him.

"All right, keep 'em moving, and I'll catch up," Ethan said.

"You are leaving?" Allie asked, wondering his purpose. They had marched through the night, skirting the coastline south of Vulture's Perch. The strange landmark loomed ominously to their north, its jagged, uneven slopes and foul habitants, a grim reminder of their peril.

"I won't be long, Allie. Just keep Krixan out of trouble while I'm gone." He tipped his hat before retreating to the rear of the column. She found the gesture odd but endearing.

*****

Ethan sought higher ground as he slipped away from the column, finding an outcropping of boulders to his south. He scaled a house-sized rock before lying prone upon its surface as he gazed west, looking for any sigh of Luke or his gang. Ethan wagered that Luke was too clever to expose himself when facing the rising sun. He would be nearly blind to Ethan's rifle. The sun broke the horizon, illuminating the rugged terrain that stretched endlessly to the west. It was a desolate, barren landscape with rolling dunes, jagged crevices, and boulders strewn about in no particular pattern. The land appeared to have been visited by a hellish apocalypse or dragon fire. Ethan felt helpless, having to await the sunrise in order to see afar. The one ability he possessed outside the Mage Bane that he had never revealed was his ability to see in the night as he could in the day.

Ethan's patience finally bore fruit as he noted movement just north and west. At first, he spied a dark blur amid the sea of sand and stone, then a head appeared moving eastward, the man's body obscured among a field of boulders. More followed, some could be seen from the waist upward, while others he could only descry the tops of their heads bobbing above thick rocks. Half the man wore Stetsons of varying hues, but only one wore black. Crawford was foolish enough to continue his pursuit at sunrise. Ethan was surprised at Luke's careless decision and soon found what he sought. There amid the quarry, he found Luke's black Stetson. He lifted his Winchester, fixing his sights to his target before squeezing the trigger. Perhaps he could end the danger of his mother's prophetic vision by slaying his greatest enemy right here.

The sound of the rifle broke the eerie stillness of the desert morn as the bullet struck the head of his target. Luke's black Stetson tumbled in the air, confirming the kill. Ethan quietly withdrew, sliding down the boulder's face as a score of heads dropped to the ground in unison.

That should slow them awhile, Ethan thought as he moved eastward to rejoin his comrades. He had sought Luke Crawford for the better part of two years. To kill him in so nondramatic fashion seemed strangely amiss. Of all the emotions he expected to consume him at this pinnacle moment, indifference was not among them. Yet Ethan felt only apathy.

*****

By late morn, their weary column reached Lupen's Cove. The cove was little more than a small inlet surrounded by swaying palms and adobe dwellings. A stone wharf ran along the water's edge, large enough to moor a handful of vessels. Unfortunately, no ships were in sight, and the only villagers to greet them were old men, women, and children.

They regarded Krixan and the Vellesian men with obvious trepidation, stealing furtive glances from windows or doorways. The men and women were similarly dressed in linen tunics that fell below their knees, with sharkskin moccasins for footwear. The villagers tended several gardens that supplemented their fish-heavy diet. Krixan counted no more than two dozen adobe structures of varying size in the village. There was no sign of horses and minimal livestock, as the village held no means to feed such beasts. Krixan let the Vellesians treat with the villagers, excusing himself to search for Ethan, who had not caught up with the column since they separated. He heard sporadic gunfire throughout the morn, sometimes near and other times afar, proof that his friend still lived. Ethan most likely followed their obvious trail, stopping periodically to delay Luke's men whenever practical. Though the sound of continued gunfire proved Ethan was still alive, it also meant that Crawford's men were close by as well. With no ships to escape by sea and no horses available to outpace their pursuit, Lupen's Cove might as well be a dead end. The only alternatives left to them were to stand and fight or flee afoot to Crepsos. He advised the Vellesians to be ready to depart once he returned.

He found his friend some miles south and west along their route of travel. Ethan favored his left ankle, hobbling along in visible discomfort when Krixan found him. He twisted it running through a large crevice some time ago. His mild sprain now festered with his misuse as he ran thereafter to escape Luke's pursuit. Now he was nearly crippled. Krixan scooped him up, throwing him over his shoulder, ignoring Ethan's protest, and raced back up the trail.

When Krixan returned to the village, the Vellesians had eaten, dressed their wounds, and resupplied. The village blacksmith removed the broken manacles from the mages' wrists. The mage healers replaced their less practical footwear with the moccasins favored by the villagers. They retained their white dresses that reflected the intense heat of the southern sun. Nearly all of them had blistered feet and suffered from lack of sleep and nourishment.

Krixan set Ethan down in the village center as Allie stepped forth, greeting him.

"Ethan, what happened?" Her smile eased as she regarded his discomfort.

"I—"

"He turned his ankle then ran on it," Krixan answered for him. He'd have called him a damn fool but knew Ethan had no choice in the matter.

"Are your people ready to move out?" Ethan asked. "You need to leave town before Luke's men get here. Put as much space between you and them as you can."

"They are ready. We refilled our water pouches and ate what we could. I'll have Sergeant Letaro construct a litter for you," she said.

"Don't bother, I'm staying."

"Like hell!" Krixan growled.

"We won't leave you, Ethan," Allie said firmly.

"I'll only slow you down. I can find a home to hide in while you slip away. Even if they find me, I'm far from helpless." Ethan patted his holstered Colts. "Besides, I killed Luke. Without him the others are far less dangerous."

"Then I'm staying with you!" Krixan bellowed.

"Allie and the others are going to need you in case Luke's men catch up to them. You're the only gun they have."

"And what do I tell Queen Gabrielle when I leave you to die?"

"Tell her I made my own choice and would not be deterred. Besides, if I die here, then her prophecy of my endless suffering will not come to pass. No one's taking me alive," Ethan said darkly.

"Agghh!" Krixan growled, rubbing his balding head in frustration, knowing Ethan would have his way.

Prophetic suffering? Allie pondered Ethan's words. Queen Gabrielle was a known seer with a gift of visions. Allie's own mother was well versed on the mage abilities of all the royal and noble houses of Greater Elaria. Did Queen Gabrielle foretell a dire fate for her son? The thought of Ethan dying or suffering filled her with dread. He would not suffer such a fate if she could help it.

CHAPTER 20

Ethan leaned against the dusty clay wall with his Winchester in his hands as he stole a careful glance out the second level window. Krixan and the others slipped out of the village hours ago, yet Crawford's men made no attempt to enter the cove. Ethan worried that his friends were spotted departing along the coastal trail and intercepted. But if that had transpired, he would've heard gunfire by now. They placed him in a vacant dwelling whose owner was out to sea. The structure was narrowly built of adobe and clay, with a ladder connecting the levels through a three-foot square hole in the back of the floor. They couldn't conceal his presence from the restless natives of Lupen's Cove, but they did disguise his location by pretending to place him in a similar vacant structure facing the one he occupied.

The distinct sound of creaking wood drew Ethan's attention to the ladder behind him, his rifle barrel following his eyes to the opening.

"Ethan?" a familiar feminine voice called out from below, barely above a whisper.

Ethan eased off the trigger as Allie's head cleared the opening. Her raven-black hair was tied in a long ponytail, and she wore the simple gray tunic worn by the locals, revealing her shapely muscular legs that peaked below the brief hemline.

"Allie, what are you doing here?" he growled, meeting her mischievous gold eyes. His heart pounded, fearful for her safety as danger waited without.

"Don't use that tone with me, Ethan Blagen," she scolded as she stepped clear, tugging a pack that she set down beside him.

"It's not safe here, Allie!"

"It's not safe anywhere, especially if you stand alone. What were you thinking staying behind?"

"I can't walk fast on my ankle, so it's better to stay and hide, or fight if I have to, rather than slow everyone down. I'm not helpless, Allie. I can probably take them all now that Luke's dead. If not, then I will take a lot of them with me. That should buy the others time to escape. I was hoping it might buy *you* time to escape, but *here* you are."

"Yes, here I am…with you. Is your life worth less than the others? I won't let you stand alone, Ethan."

"Allie, your mage powers don't work here. What do you—"

"I know well my limitations in this forsaken place," she cut him off while snatching the extra pistol he had lifted off Jeb. She opened the cylinder, checking each chamber to be sure it was loaded, before closing it. Ethan's jaw slackened as she handled the weapon like an old pro.

"How did you—"

"I am very observant. I saw that imbecile Jeb handle his weapon repeatedly. It doesn't require a dazzling intellect to operate this," she hoisted the pistol, extending it in her outstretched hand.

"Easy there, Wyatt Earp," Ethan put his hand over hers, lowering the pistol to the floor. "You might want a few pointers before you blow your fool head off by mistake."

"Wyatt Earp?" She lifted a curious eyebrow, not comprehending the reference.

"Never mind, he's a famous lawman on the far side of the barrier. Look, if you're gonna shoot a pistol, use both hands and hold it at eye level." He hobbled on his throbbing ankle, stepping behind her as he reached around, his hands bracing her shoulders as he whispered in her ear. Allie felt a shudder as his breath played across her neck.

"Aim at the center of your target, keeping the front site, that's the raised bead on the end of the barrel, focused. When you're ready to shoot, lock the hammer back like this," he said softly, pulling the hammer through its series of metallic clicks. "Hold the front site on your target and squeeze the trigger in a continuous even pull without yanking your finger. If you squeeze smoothly and keep your sites aligned, the bullet will go where you aim it," Ethan eased the hammer back into its safe position. Being this close, Ethan realized how tall Allie was. At nearly seventy-one inches, she towered over every woman and many men. Her arms were not large but toned and held considerable strength unusual to her gender. Her eyes revealed a strange confidence, which permeated her entire bearing. She masked these obvious male attributes with effortless femininity. Her sultry voice, flowing curves, and disarming smile were overwhelmingly feminine.

"If you can shoot that thing as well as you handle it, I might have to hire you on as a deputy when we return to Cordova. That's if we survive all this," he added.

"Or maybe I can be…what do call yourself? Oh yes, Sheriff. Maybe I can be sheriff and *you* can be my deputy." She bit her smile, keeping her face as serious as she could.

"That wouldn't work because I don't take orders from girls."

"Girls?" She smiled, though it failed to reach her eyes.

"Don't take offense, Allie." He raised his hands, expecting her to strike him. "I don't take orders from men either."

"Girls and men? I'm certain you meant *women* and boys?" she challenged.

"Come on, Allie, I thought you were a better sport than that. Don't tell me I hurt your feelings?"

"My feelings?" she questioned innocently, touching her free hand to her heart. "I only fear offending your tender sensibilities."

"You little stinker." He shook his head. "And I thought you Vellesian mages were a dull insufferable lot. Not you, you're just insufferable."

"Then we are evenly matched." She poked his ribs with her finger.

The sound of hooves pounding soil drew their attention to the window. Ethan pulled her behind him as he pressed his back to the wall, keeping to the shadows while stealing a glance at the village square below. A handful of riders, clad in white tunics and headdresses, flooded the village center. Their horses were lathered and spent. The men had deep olive skin with trimmed beards and black hair peaking below their white headdresses. They carried curved scimitars on their hips and long spears in their strong hands. Ethan counted five in total and wondered their origin. They were not in Luke Crawford's small contingent, but their leader seemed well animated as he called out the villagers of Lupen's Cove. The man appeared a head taller than his fellow riders with a loud, boisterous voice that boomed as he spoke. He could ill discern the man's countenance from his vantage point, save for the hard scowl that seemed permanently affixed. One of the village elders stepped forth to greet him, a silver-haired fisherman with a well-weathered face and clad in a loose brown robe.

Ethan could not make out what they were saying beyond their initial greeting. The village elder pointed eastward, seeming to indicate Krixan and the others' route of travel. The riders seemed highly interested in the whereabouts of Krixan's group, and Ethan started to doubt their neutrality. Any doubts of the riders' allegiances were swept away when Emmitt Cobb and his fellow travelers entered the village alongside the horsemen. Ethan noticed the pirate captain, Greybar, among them, with a half dozen of his crew. Ethan paled as he beheld Luke Crawford amid the gathering, wearing a gray checkered shirt and a brown Stetson. He must have switched clothes with one of his fellows, fooling Ethan into shooting the wrong man.

"Ethan, what troubles you?" Allie whispered.

"I didn't kill Luke. He must've switched his shirt and hat with another to throw me off. If that's not bad enough, these riders that suddenly appeared out of thin air seem to be working with him."

The name Luke Crawford filled Allie's mouth with bile, and she lamented his continued existence in this world. She well knew that their very lives depended on the villagers not revealing their presence to these villains. She regarded the riders carefully, discerning their origin and sudden appearance at this inopportune time. "The men on horseback are Palacian. Most likely a patrol sent from one of the oasis' south of here. They were probably drawn by your gunfire last night," she surmised as she looked over his shoulder through the window.

"How do you know they are a mere patrol and not scouts of a larger contingent?"

"They are too far afield for a planned expedition. If they intended to advance this far from their post, they would've brought camels. Their intervention seems unplanned, as the nearest oasis is likely five to ten leagues south of here."

"Planned or not, the Palacians are aligned with Greybar and Luke," Ethan scowled. "Our only hope is that the villagers tell them we are in the adjoining house. That might buy us time to—"

"The villagers will not reveal our presence, Ethan," she assured him.

He leaned his back against the wall with his eyes fixed to hers. "They won't, huh. How do you figure that?"

"I can be very persuasive." She shrugged innocently.

"You know, cute and innocent don't work for you."

"They don't?" she feigned indignantly.

"They only work for little girls with big sad eyes, not beautiful, tall women with massive…curves."

"Oh." She bit her lip to mask a smile.

*****

Luke Crawford rubbed the stubble of his chin as he stared into the hearth. He was anxious to continue their pursuit, hoping to finally settle his score with Ethan Blagen, and retrieve his prized captives. He'd probably have to kill a couple of mages to remind them the price of defiance. Perhaps he'd kill only one, the taller, comely girl who burned their ship. Some of his men would argue against it, claiming she was far too fetching to kill, but that was a perfect reason to do so. If her fellow mages saw her perish, despite her beauty, then they would more quickly learn their place and realize that their own beauty would not purchase their lives. It was their good fortune that the Palacian patrol stumbled upon them, but they possessed only a half-dozen horses, not enough for their company. Luke wanted to pursue Ethan's group once they entered Lupen's Cove, but Greybar and the Palacians counseled against it. They argued that the Vellesians were afoot and would be long to reach Crepsos. They would spend the night in Lupen's Cove and continue their pursuit at dawn.

Before they entered Lupen's Cove, the Palacians dispatched riders south to gather as many reinforcements as they could quickly muster, ordering them to converge on Lupen's Cove, Crepsos, and all points in between. Other riders were sent west to Craven's Nest to gather what ships that were positioned there. They planned to surround the fugitives by land and sea, leaving little to chance. Luke relented, reluctant to stay his hunt, but willing to heed their counsel. It was nightfall, and most of the men were asleep, save for those standing post.

"You worry too much, Luke. We'll catch 'em come sunup," Emmitt Cobb's gravelly voice echoed as he stepped beside the gunslinger.

"Blagen always finds a way to cheat death. I'll believe him dead when I see his wretched corpse. Then I'll piss on him and leave him for the buzzards."

"If in we kill 'em, we'll be stuck in this world. They say he's the key to opening the portal," Emmitt cautioned.

"There ain't nothin' to go back for. We're dead men unless we stay south of the Rio Grande, but here…" Luke paused to gauge their surroundings. "Here we can live like kings. All we need to do is rid this world of Ethan."

"They say his ability to heal himself is impaired here in the Bane. He can't have gotten far on foot, and we have eight guns to his two."

"He's overcome longer odds before," Luke recalled that fateful day in the streets of Red Rock when Ethan and Sheriff Thorton slew his brother, Hank Grierson, and so many others. He'd been on the run ever since, hunted like a mangy cur. That ended here on the morrow when he planned to put a bullet between Ethan's eyes.

"*Luke! Luke!*" Colm Conroy shouted excitedly as he burst through the doorway.

"What is it?" Emmitt asked as he and Luke regarded the intruder.

"The horses…they're gone!"

"Gone?" Emmitt scowled.

"Plum gone, and the Palacian guarding them is dead. We found him with his throat cut. We found another Palacian cut nearly in half on the outskirt of the Cove's east side."

Blagen! Luke growled bitterly, knowing somehow that he was the one responsible.

*****

The cool ocean breeze soothed his face as they rode east along the coastal road. They spoke little since escaping Lupen's Cove with the Palacian mounts in tow. She rode upon his left, with a tether connected to a trailing mount, while his tether was similarly affixed to the other two. Moonlight played along her face, and the exposed flesh of her legs as the saddle pushed the skirt of her tunic high upon her thighs. Ethan found her state of dress distracting as he tried so hard not to stare. She knew the effect she had on him and did nothing to conceal herself.

Stinker! Ethan thought, knowing she did so on purpose, probably to torment him. He'd known many a fair maid and women of renowned beauty, but not a one stirred the slightest longings in his loins, not even Jennifer Murtado. Perhaps that was why he avoided the marriage noose for as long as he did, somehow doubting his ability to perform as expected. It wasn't until he crossed the boundary that he began to feel the urges that every other man attempted to sate since puberty. The Adams girls were the first to stoke his fires, but those urges were nominal in comparison to the firestorms that Allie ignited. He found it odd that in all of Elaria, Allie was the only woman that stirred his blood.

"You know, Allie, in Astaria we don't teach our mage healers to slit throats like you did back there," he recalled as she had approached the Palacian guarding the horses from behind and ran her dagger across his throat. Ethan planned to dispatch the man himself but stared dumbstruck as Allie moved with all the skill of a trained assassin.

"I have trained in all forms of combat since I could walk at my mother's insistence. You think it unbecoming for a mage healer to do so?"

"It's unusual, not unbecoming. I shouldn't be surprised, because nothing about you is usual."

"As I said, a woman needs a little mystery. I would not wish to bore you."

"Hardly. I used to live a quiet life until you came along," he said. She laughed.

"I believe you have that reversed, Ethan. I lived a quiet life until I met you."

"So this is my fault?"

"Of course not, but turmoil surrounds you. Perhaps it is your destiny. You are a transformative figure, manifesting great change wherever you tread. You did save my life, Ethan, and I am in your debt." Her voice sounded almost sad, acknowledging his fell deed.

"You don't owe me anything, Allie. My sister is a mage healer, and I'd like to believe if she were of similar need, that someone would step forward to safeguard her life and virtue."

"Perhaps so, or not. Either way, I am still in your debt, and I will see it repaid," she said with an air of determination.

"Why does it matter so much to you. I would never demand of you a favor to balance the scale. It's the same if you saved my life twice over. I would not feel I owed you another. That's what friends do, Allie, they help each other. I've lost count of the times Krixan, Ben, or Jake saved my life, or how many times I saved theirs."

"I am your friend, then?" She smiled.

"After all we've been through? Yes, I'd say we are friends."

"Very well…friend, but I shall still seek to repay the debt."

"Why? Can't you just accept a kind act without reciprocity?"

"My mother insists that we are to never be beholden to any, save the Royal House of Vellesia. Our loyalties must never be in conflict."

"How does my saving your life threaten your loyalties to your queen?" It made no sense.

"You are not of Vellesia, Ethan, you cannot know," she said sadly.

"Thank the fates for that. This queen of yours sounds like a wicked witch. If we manage to escape this land, why not take up permanent residence in Cordova? We'll tell your queen that you quit. You can be free and make a decent life for yourself. The city could use a mage healer. You could even serve on the mage council that helps defend the city. You can cast fire as well, which comes in handy sinking attacking ships. You can be free like me, Allie."

"If it were only so," she lamented. "I am bound to the queen by blood magic, Ethan. It binds the loyalties of all Vellesians to the throne. I must return to Vellesia. My mother—"

"What of your father, Allie? You speak as if your mother's will were law."

"My father died long ago," she sighed sadly. "It is my mother who rules our house and serves the throne."

"What house do you serve?" he asked, wondering her surname.

"Mage healers in Vellesia forsake their family name. They serve only the throne."

"What if we stayed here, in the Mage Bane? You could be free then."

"Our powers are impaired here, Ethan. What life could we hope to build in such a savage land?"

"What good are mage powers if you are a slave to the whims of a tyrannical queen? Wouldn't you rather be free?"

"I couldn't forsake my family for my selfishness."

"Maybe my father could help you. He is a lightning lord. Perhaps your queen would listen to—"

"She would not release me, even at his behest."

"This queen of yours sounds like a real treasure." He rolled his eyes. "Maybe I should have a talk with the old bag and set her straight."

Allie stifled a laugh as the vision of Ethan haggling with Queen Valera came to mind.

"Or we can invite her to Astaria, and I'll show her the boundary. Maybe I can take her across and leave her on the other side. Perhaps she can find honest work there as a schoolmarm or a dance hall girl."

"You mustn't speak so," Allie cautioned.

"Why not? Is your queen a goddess? No, she is flesh and blood like you and me. Besides, I'm not Vellesian, and she is not entitled to my loyalty."

"In Vellesia, any disdain of superior mage blood is punishable by death," Allie shuddered.

"Mage blood is no more precious than common born. To raise one man above another based upon no merit other than birth is asinine."

"But we are both mage born, Ethan."

"Allie, the only benefit of my gifts is that they help shield me from the tyrannical whims of other mages. Your mage power ordains you to help others by selflessly sacrificing your life to heal their wounds or deformities. Mage healers are different from their fellow mages in that regard; they often forsake the trappings of power for the benefit of the common man."

What Ethan said was often true, as mage healers were almost always female and foreswore marriage until their twenty-fifth year, dedicating their prime years to healing the populace of their realms. Some would stay within the capital, attending the royal family and any who journeyed there for treatment. Most others, however, journeyed throughout the land, healing those who were unable to travel. Upon their twenty-fifth year, mage healers would wed, often a lord or highborn vassal, in order to pass on their gift to future generations. Where most mages were feared, mage healers were revered by the masses. Male healers were extremely rare, but not unheard of. Ethan's maternal grandfather was a gifted healer, among his many other mage powers. His daughter inherited many of his gifts, thus leading to the royal family seeking her to wed Prince Bronus in the days of Ethan's paternal grandsire's reign. Mage's with multiple powers were highly sought after for brides or consorts of the ruling nobility, in hopes of strengthening the mage potency of their future heirs. Since Allie could cast fire as well as heal, each a complex and rare gift, she would likely wed a high lord or prince when her time of service was at end.

"You truly hate the mage born?" she sadly asked.

"I don't hate them, Allie. I just think they make poor rulers. Heads of state should be selected based upon merit and ability, not the fortune of birth."

"And how would you determine such merit or ability? And once a man or woman attain such status, what guarantee can ensure their wise rule or that of their heirs?"

"Let the people vote for their leaders. Whomever they chose can serve for a limited time, and then the people can choose another. If a leader is cruel or incompetent, you can limit their mischief to a brief period rather than a lifetime."

"Perhaps you are right, Ethan, but the mage-born rule the seven kingdoms and will not abide your beliefs."

"I don't plan on converting them. I will encourage democratic governance in Cordova and the Mage Bane, establishing a nation where men can live free and prosper by the sweat of their own brow, a land where no men kneel or address men with titles unearned. The mage born can keep their wretched kingdoms. When our lands prosper, all shall know the mage born offer little to their people but chains and servitude."

"The mage born claim that only mage rule can safeguard the peace and protect their people," she countered.

"A wise American once said that those who sacrifice their liberty for security shall have neither. And where is this *great* peace you speak of when every mage kingdom conspires against their neighbors, coveting their wealth and land despite their own plenty? Power only makes them greedier."

"Even your own father?"

"No," he sighed, conceding the point. "My father is fair and just, if not ornery. He forbids slavery and holds mage born and common equally before the law, but the fairness of Astaria is dependent upon his will. What happens when the crown passes to those future kings who care not for such fairness?"

"Had you not forsaken your birthright, you might have safeguarded your sire's wise reign."

"I would have, for a time, but once I passed, what assurance would I have that my son or his son after him wouldn't undo all that

I had labored for? Even wise men beget morons and looking at the royal houses of Elaria, you know this to be true."

*****

They found Krixan and the others just after sunrise along the coastal road. The Vellesians were surprised by the horses that Ethan and Allie had found. Their elation soon soured once Ethan informed them of the Palacian patrol. That meant that others would likely come to supplement Crawford's and Greybar's contingent. They also lacked enough mounts for everyone to ride to Crepsos. Eventually they decided that Ethan would ride ahead with four Vellesian soldiers, who would share their mounts with four mages. They would ride ahead several miles and dismount. Ethan would then return for the others, leading the four empty mounts and repeat the process again and again, collecting everyone. They would continue the process throughout the day, leapfrogging to place as much space between themselves and Crawford's men as possible. Krixan was disappointed that Luke still lived, and everyone was worried that another mounted force might overtake them before Crepsos.

Ethan found it odd how warmly Allie was received by her fellow mages, including Thela, who embraced her as might an older sister or aunt. No one admonished the young healer for abandoning the group to aid Ethan. This contrasted the many times his father treated him harshly for his adventurous spirit.

By late afternoon, they came upon a few thatched huts surrounding a single well. The lush foliage of the coastline began to press deeper inland the further east they traveled. Several tracts of arable land surrounded the small community, which one could not consider even a village. It was as good a place as any to water their horses and rest as the endless flight since they had set ashore had drained their weary party. Ethan was the first to approach the well, with Allie seated behind him as he rode forth. The other four mounts filed in around them as the inhabitants of the small community greeted them cautiously. A dozen men and women gathered about clad in simple wool tunics of light brown and gray that hung to their knees. Some wore trousers beneath, others not, regardless of their gender. Some were bare of foot, while others wore sandals of varying constructs. They seemed extremely slight of build and diminutive in stature, a testament to their arduous labors and malnourished diet. An elder couple with silvered hair and weathered faces stood forward of the others, obviously to speak on behalf of the group. Neither of the pair brandished weapons of any sort, though some of the men further back held sickles or axes in case trouble erupted.

Ethan dismounted, leaving Allie on the horse while gingerly stepping toward the couple, favoring his sore ankle. If the man was frightened, he showed it not, greeting Ethan with a stern but not unkind face. The woman was equally brave, standing firmly before the towering stranger. Ethan respectfully removed his Stetson before speaking.

"Sir, ma'am," he greeted them, touching a finger to his head in an informal salute, though they did not recognize the gesture. "My name is Ethan."

"Welcome, friend. I am Cornelus, and this is my wife, Denella. How may we aid you in your travels?" the old man asked.

Ethan mentally shook his head in wonder. These people were dirt-poor farmers, dwelling in one of the most inhospitable climates in all of Elaria, and yet they offered aid to complete strangers. Such was the code of these desolate lands where people depended on each other in order to survive. Ethan explained their plight, the urgency of their trek, and *who* followed in their wake. They had need of their well and would move on as quickly as they could. He stepped toward his mount and fished several silver anchors, the official currency of Cordova, from his pack and offered them to the couple. They refused at first, prideful and stating that travelers are always welcome to use their well. Eventually, Ethan's insistence weakened their resolve. He argued that their willingness to tame this land eased their travel along the coastal road and that the silver coins were a fair payment for their efforts.

Allie was taken aback by the kindness and respect Ethan showed to these peasants. He spoke to them with a respect he refused to offer high lords or mages. He treated them as his equal, though he was a prince of Astaria. *My name is Ethan,* he simply said, greatly understating his place in the world.

Ethan waved the others to dismount, to drink, eat, and rest while he gathered their mounts and departed to fetch the others. Allie could see the weariness in Ethan's posture. He hadn't slept in days, catching what little rest he could for minutes at a time. He hobbled on his tender ankle as he tied the mounts one to the other, before climbing into the saddle of his own mount. She came to his side, placing her hand upon his thigh.

"Ethan, let one of our soldiers ferry the next group, you *must* rest," she pleaded.

"I'll be fine, Allie." He smiled warmly as if the light of her eyes renewed his strength. "Take care of your people, Allie, and yourself while you're at it. Don't worry about me, I'll be back before you miss me." He tipped his hat to her and rode off toward the west.

Allie watched as he slipped from sight, wondering when he would fall from the saddle in complete exhaustion. Ethan was the most stubborn male she had ever met. He threw himself in harm's way with reckless abandon. He thought nothing of entering the Mage Bane to affect their rescue, even though doing so impaired his regenerative powers. Without his ability to heal, it would take an army to keep Ethan alive if he lingered any longer in this foul land.

Did he even care if he lived or died? she wondered. He was nothing like she expected. The rumors coming out of Astaria often depicted a brash, cunning warrior prince who felled mages in battle as if they were straw. He captured kings, toppled armies, and refused his own crown. The real Ethan, however, was almost childlike, with a naïve understanding of the world. She certainly did not expect to find any connection between them, nor did she intend it, but since that evening in Cordova when she first set eyes upon him, she yearned to be in his presence. Her mother warned her about forming emotional bonds with the former Astarian crown prince, but she was caught in a current which now guided her destiny.

*****

It was dusk when the last of their group reached the small settlement. They were utterly spent and forsook their plans to ride through the night, deciding to rest until dawn. Ethan and Krixan were the last to enter the makeshift perimeter they established just north of the well, a small outcropping on a cliffside overlooking the sea. The others had started a fire after gathering driftwood throughout the day from the beaches below. They set their mismatched bedrolls around the fire, made from whatever they could muster from the saddle packs and the men they had slain. The men mostly went without, ensuring the ladies had enough to keep them warm. Allie was startled when Ethan returned, dropping two large snakes at her feet, until she realized that they were headless. Their scales were copper and gray, and each was near five feet in length.

"Cook 'em up. They're better than the vittles we've been eatin' the past couple days," he said after she gave him a curious look, wondering the snake's purpose.

"You desire to *eat* these?" she asked, taken aback, ignoring his Texas drawl, which he reverted to at times.

"Snake's good eatin', Allie. It's not a steak or roast boar, but when you live in the desert, you learn to make do."

After tending his horse and checking on the guards posted outside the perimeter, Ethan found Allie struggling with the cumbersome serpents. She obviously did not know how to cook a snake.

"Here, let me help," Ethan said, kneeling by her side as he drew his bowie knife from behind its sheath behind his left pistol.

"My apologies, Ethan, I don't know how to—"

"Cook a snake? Don't worry, Allie, I'll show you."

"Actually, I don't know how to cook anything." She shrugged.

"I thought all girls learned how to cook?" He made a face.

"I am mage born, Ethan. The palace provides our basic needs, freeing us to tend our craft. Do princes in Astaria learn to cook?"

"Not in the palace, but in the wild, I learned how to cook what I killed. It was either that or go hungry. I've been hunting and tracking since I was a child."

She watched as he cut into the rear of the snake, running his knife along its length. He separated the skin from the meat, stripping it away before removing the innards. He wound the meat around a stick and set up a spit over the fire. He repeated the process with the second snake carcass as the Vellesians observed him as if he had grown a second head. The soldiers treated the mage healers with great deference and were visibly uncomfortable with Ethan's blunt speech and lack of decorum. They spoke not against him, however, for they depended upon him and Krixan against Crawford and his men. They certainly didn't like him, this he could discern by their humorless faces and rigid demeanor. The other mages smiled politely whenever Ethan addressed them, but they only gazed at him briefly and spoke sparingly.

"I don't think your people like me very much," Ethan said, offering Allie a piece of cooked snake.

She regarded him curiously before partaking. The meat was tastier than she would've guessed, and she devoured the many portions he offered thereafter. "This is very good, Ethan."

He smiled, offering her another piece, which she gratefully accepted. "They don't dislike you, either," she continued while chewing. "They do not know how to treat with you. You are an Astarian crown prince—"

"Not anymore," he corrected her.

"Deny it all you wish, Ethan, but royal blood still courses your veins. In Vellesia, royalty is honored with great reverence and none more so than our queen. To gaze upon her unbidden is punishable by death. Her word is law, and she suffers no insolence or disrespect. Pray that you never fall under her dominion."

"So your friends are frightened of me because of my royal lineage?"

"Frightened? No. Wary? Yes."

"What about you, Allie. Are you wary?" He asked, lifting his Stetson higher upon his brow as they sat before the crackling fire.

"I should be, you're a very dangerous man, Ethan Blagen."

"Dangerous? I'm a broken-down wreck," he moaned as he shifted painfully, beset with aches and bruises throughout his body.

"Oh, Ethan, I quickly forget how you have suffered for our sake," she inched closer, touching a hand to his shoulder.

"I'm all right. I've felt worse, believe me," he said, offering her another piece of snake.

She found his statement odd for one who was immune to harm in the mage lands whence he came. "How so? I thought you were immune to physical harm?"

"I can heal from any wound, Allie, but I'm not immune to the pain." He yawned.

Her eyes grew wide at that revelation. "You've felt the pain of every wound you have suffered?" She thought of the Battle of the Velo, where Ethan was rumored to have received hundreds of wounds.

"No one's immune to pain, Allie. At least none that I have heard tell of. Why does that surprise you?"

She was caught unaware by the question, her thoughts elsewhere until bringing herself back. "I…thought that since you are able to heal, that you were immune to pain as well. There have been mages who were so gifted. It is a rare gift, but not unheard of. Of course, it has been over two hundred years since we have heard tell of a mage with this power."

"Being immune to pain is one mage power I wish I had." Ethan smiled tiredly. "It would've saved me a lot of…pain."

"You sound very tired, Ethan," she wondered how he managed as well as had. He was beyond exhaustion, beyond reason, beyond whatever limit one could ever ask. He needed to sleep, or he'd be dead in the saddle come the morn, but how she loved the timbre of his voice as the night grew still. She could imagine going to sleep beside that voice every night and to wake up beside that voice every morn. She shook the vision from her fancy. She needed a clear mind, and Ethan had a way of jumbling her thinking.

"Look over there, Allie," Ethan lifted his chin toward the moonlight playing upon the sea. Allie followed his eyes to the horizon, where the heavens met the darkness of the sea as celestial light lit the watery surface. He gained his feet, offering her his hand to join him. She accepted as he brought her to her feet and guided her toward the edge of the sea cliff, drawing away from the others.

"It is lovely," she sighed, rarely taking the time to enjoy the wonders of the world. Her mother and grandmother had instilled in her duty, discipline, and perfection, often overlooking the basic human desire to play, and to relish the beauty that surrounds them. Her father always found delight in the simple pleasures of life, the song of birds in the evening sky, the morning dew on a forest pine, the smell of bread baking in the hearth, or the beauty of the mountains that circled the palace, piercing the clouds above. Her father reveled in all of these and often took her by the hand to reveal whatever wonders that the new day beheld. Part of her missed him dearly, the part that was yet a young girl who favored her father's company. He had been gone so long now that she often forgot how much she missed him. She wondered if her mother longed for his company. If she did, she said it not, often remarking on his many shortcomings and imperfections. Her mother had not loved her father, so she doubted if she missed him. She wed him out of duty to the realm and for Allie's betterment. Allie selfishly thought what if she could marry out of love. Must love and duty forever be in conflict? If she was to wed, would not duty spoil any such affection? Did love even exist? Were not such feelings simply lust, desire, and reciprocity wound as one?

"What are you thinking?" he asked as she stared for a time, lost in thought.

She returned her face to his, firelight dancing across her golden eyes. Ethan thought they were the most beautiful thing he had ever seen. "Do you ever consider your destiny when following the leanings of your heart?"

"I don't believe in destiny, Allie," he said quietly, his kind eyes softening as he regarded her.

"You believe not in your own destiny?" She spent a lifetime receiving her mother's teachings about her destiny, that to believe otherwise seemed strange.

"We make our own destiny, Allie. I see no value in chaining ourselves to a predetermined outcome."

"Do you believe your coming to our world was mere happenstance? You are immune to magic, Ethan. Such a thing portends a great destiny."

"My great-grandsire, Dorgus Mortune, spoke to me of my destiny when I was a child, just before he passed."

"And what did your grandfather say?"

Ethan released a tired laugh, shaking his head at the memory. "He said my destiny would manifest a great transformation or some similar nonsense."

"What sort of transformation?" His answer intrigued her.

"He said I was *Free Born*, and that I would bring lasting peace and freedom to *all* of Elaria." He never spoke of his great-grandsire's prediction to any, not even Dragos or Krixan, but for some unknown reason, he felt compelled to share his innermost secrets with Allie, as if she were an extension of his own flesh.

"Free Born!" Allie gasped. The Free Born was a legend known to a few of the houses of Elaria. Queen Valera had extinguished the lesser houses of Vellesia that adhered to the prophecy, fearing belief in any prophecy that countered her visions of her royal house's predestined omnipotence. Could the Free Born be true? And if so, was Ethan the source of the storied legend? If Ethan was the Free Born, then how could Queen Valera's visions come to fruition? Two truths that proved the other false could not coexist.

Ethan could see her mind working, trying to comprehend what he had just revealed. "Don't waste your thoughts trying to make sense of my grandfather's ramblings, Allie. It's all nonsense."

"How can you disregard his visions so callously?"

"Because they do me no good. He revealed no path I must travel to achieve these great aims, offering no counsel on how they could be achieved, nor any guidance that was useful in any way. To further his madness, he said that in order to fulfill my destiny I had to *lose* to my greatest enemy. How does that make any sense?" He shook his head.

"And which enemy was he referring?"

Ethan shrugged tiredly. "My only guess is Luke Crawford. He's been my greatest enemy and has alluded me for nearly two years now. I thought I killed him south of Lupen's Cove, but he pulled the old switcheroo with his hat and shirt. I don't know how losing to Luke Crawford will free the world, and what does freedom mean to the world anyway? If I struck the chains from every slave and serf in all of Elaria, just as many would be enslaved within a generation of my passing. That's why I don't believe in prophecy, Allie."

"What do you believe in then, Ethan?"

"Freewill. I go where I feel myself led, not following some predetermined course set by others. Besides, if destiny is predetermined, then it will come to pass regardless of my actions."

"Not true, Ethan. Destinies are precarious things. They are set in prophecy in order to guide their source to fulfill their meaning. If they were predetermined, then there would be no need for the prophecy in the first place. Your grandfather's vision is meant to guide you, and for you to be mindful of your destiny, lest you fail to attain your purpose in this life."

"And what of love? Is that predetermined as well?" he asked.

"Love," she started to answer but closed her lips, struggling to answer honestly. *What was he thinking?* she mused as his blue eyes stared intently into hers. "No."

"No?" He lifted an eyebrow at her bluntness.

"Nothing is entirely predetermined, not even love. However, I believe there is *one* person that you are intended to find, and if you fail to do so you shall live a life of regret," she explained.

His silence was deafening. He simply stared into her eyes, unnerving her usual calm. It irritated her how he so easily made her feel like a lovestruck girl. This was not what she intended, and it made her angry. Just as she was about to recant and claim that love was a fraudulent hoax propagated to instill hope in forsaken hearts, Ethan surprised her again.

"I agree."

"You…you agree?" She narrowed her eyes.

"I believe each person forms one half of a larger heart, with jagged ridges along its center like the demarcation line along a puzzle piece. It can only be whole when joined with its other half. People spend much of their life looking for their other half. Many fail to find it and live out their days in loneliness. Others join with a close fit, though always cognizant that something is amiss that whispers doubts in the recesses of their minds. Finally, there are those who find their missing half, and for them, they reap love's full reward."

There, under the moonlight overlooking the sea, they kissed.

CHAPTER 21

They continued their arduous trek the next morning, leapfrogging with their horses to find defendable terrain while ferrying the others to join them in small groups. The clear skies bode well for their travels, and the thicker vegetation along the coastal road afforded the weary travelers some respite from the sun. By dusk, they found themselves camped beneath a grove of swaying palms atop a rise overlooking the coast. With desert sands far off to the south and sparse vegetation to either flanks, they could observe far afield in any direction. Krixan and Ethan took turns ferrying each group. Ethan and Allie watched as Krixan's towering form passed from sight to fetch the last of their group. Once his friend was beyond sight, Ethan went about setting a cook fire for his daily catch, which consisted of another snake and a golar. The golar was a predatory reptile that measured half the length of a man. Its jaws were sharp as knives, and their mouths were filled with venom. They could tackle much larger prey with jagged claws that sunk into flesh, not relenting until the prey was brought down. Ethan's catch was just under three feet. Once again, he lopped the heads, knowing that such creatures could still release their venom even after death. The Vellesian soldiers, who at first scoffed at his choice of delicacy the night before, started to warm to the idea after quickly tiring of their tasteless rations. Allie found it odd how comfortable Ethan looked tending a fire and cooking, considering his royal birth.

"I never knew a man that enjoyed cooking; perhaps you could work in my mother's kitchen. She is constantly searching for a better cook. I think you would look most fetching in an apron serving me dinner." She smiled, taking wicked delight in teasing him.

"Very funny," he growled. "With that smart remark, you can help me skin these." He handed her his knife while fetching another from his pack.

She at first thought to feign ignorance in the task, hoping that he might do the work himself, but he knew her aptitude more than capable. She shrugged and smiled, joining him in the endeavor.

"You don't take teasing well," she said while biting her smile.

"Oh, I can take all the taunts you wish to throw, girl, just don't get used to me cooking for you." He smiled, cutting into the golar.

"Such a pity. A woman could become accustomed to having the former crown prince of Astaria as her personal servant. I'd be the envy of every maiden in Greater Elaria."

"With the way servants are treated in your kingdom, I think I'll pass. Of course a poor fella like me could get used to looking at a pretty girl like you, Miss Allie." His voice transitioned into a Texas drawl.

Allie thought it strange that Ethan mimicked the accent and style of dress from across the barrier, forsaking his native culture. He had a habit of feigning a naivety that some would mistake for stupidity or ignorance, but it was clearly a mummery, fooling others to underestimate his cunning. Oh, he was naïve and ignorant of the workings of the royal courts of Elaria, refusing to play a game he was very much a part of. His intelligence was considerable, often taking her aback with the breadth of his knowledge on so many topics, far exceeding mages renowned for their intellect. Yet even this gift he refused to use to its fullest as he was dismissive of the world he was born to and ignorant of the dangers the mage born presented to all he held dear. Having come to know him, she could not fathom his royal upbringing. He clearly felt at ease around laymen and peasants rather than lords and mages. Though he championed the cause of the lowborn and downtrodden, he certainly was not one of them. His irreverent tongue and free spirit set him apart from all castes and classes. He was a nation unto himself, though he was apparently gaining converts to his cause in the port city of Cordova. If his revolutionary ideas spread beyond the tropic isle, the wrath of the mage kingdoms would surely descend upon him and his fellow visionaries.

"Does this meet your satisfaction?" she asked, holding the skinned snake in her outstretched arm.

"Not bad, Allie. I might make a cowgirl out of you yet."

"Cowgirl?" She lifted a dark eyebrow.

> She's the sweetest rose of color this cowboy ever knew
> Her eyes were bright like diamonds
> They sparkle like the dew
> You can talk about your Clementine
> And sing of Rosa Lee
> But the Yellow Rose of Texas
> Beats the belles of Tennessee.

She struggled to make sense of the lyric of his little song, but how she loved his voice.

Ethan went onto explain about cowgirls, cowboys, the history of Texas, and the Yellow Rose. He spoke at length about his time in Red Rock and the adventures he had or those told to him by Sheriff Thorton and Judge Donovan.

"Maybe when I return to Red Rock, you might come along. Maybe I'll set aside my tin star and take up ranching. I know of some land along the Pierna Mala that might be for sale. I can learn you to lasso steers and shoot coyotes, maybe even teach you the guitar so you can sing the cattle to sleep."

"Or you can follow me to Vellesia. I could teach you how to dance as well as other skills a handsome young man like yourself should know for courting a fair maid." She smiled flirtatiously.

"I don't think your queen would appreciate my company," Ethan said, placing the golar upon a spit. He left unsaid the hard truth that lay between them, that if they survived the Mage Bane, they would return to their separate worlds. She was bound to a realm that he would never abide.

*****

329

The sound of hooves clapping the ground echoed in the pre-dusk air as Krixan led the last group into the encampment, but he returned with ten horses instead of five. Among the new arrivals were Captain Lorelo and four of his crewmen. The steadfast Vellesian captain looked worse for the wear as his doublet was missing and linen shirt torn in ragged strips. His feet were bare, and his puffed trousers frayed at the knee. He was received by Archmage Thela Corval, who stepped nigh to greet the weary captain.

"My lady," Captain Lorelo bowed upon dismounting.

"Captain Lorelo? How—" Lady Thela began before the good Captain responded.

"Lady Thela, I must have a word with Prince Ethanos," Lorelo said as his eye caught sight of Ethan, Allie, and several others gathering round.

"Cap'n," Ethan said. "It's good to see you're still among the living. How'd you come about your horses?" Ethan eyed the mounts that looked similar to the ones they commanded.

"We ambushed a detachment of Palacians near Lupen's Cove. We came upon a dozen riders. We slew half their number before the rest returned whence they came."

"Lupen's Cove? What of Luke Crawford and—"

"They took ship, fleeing the Cove before our arrival, leaving a handful of Palacians to await their comrades. We dispatched the former, learning what had transpired and where you had gone, and then we ambushed the latter, taking five of their mounts."

"A ship?" Lady Thela asked. "What ship and to where did they sail?"

"A fishing vessel that returned to the Cove just after Ethan absconded with their horses. Whether they sailed east or west, I know not," Lorelo explained.

"Are these four the only men you have left?" Ethan asked.

"Nay. I left over a dozen afoot at the Cove in order to catch up with your party."

"That's not all, Ethan. Tell him, Lorelo!" Krixan snorted as he towered in the saddle behind the Vellesian Captain.

"The Palacians claim that they have another contingent heading for Crepsos," the captain said.

"How many?" Ethan asked, not wanting the answer.

"They claim one to two hundred," Lorelo said.

"Wonderful," Ethan sighed tiredly as he removed his Stetson and scratched his head. "If I was a betting man, I'd wager Luke is sailing straight for Crepsos to cut us off while his Palacian buddies drive us right to him."

"We could turn back to Lupen's. Perhaps another fishing vessel has returned that we could make use of," Allie added.

"The fishing boats won't do us much good, Allie. They have to stay close to shore and would never make it to Cordova. If we come across one of the Palacian privateers, we would be outmatched," Ethan explained.

"Once offshore, our mage powers will be restored. We can set ablaze any ship that draws nigh," Lady Thela advised.

"The magical impairment of the Mage Bane juts out to sea for many miles in different places, Thela. Allie was lucky with her fire casting because the spot we set ashore, the Mage Bane barrier stopped at the water's edge. At Lupen's Cove, the barrier stretched several miles north," Ethan explained, just as Jorus Darcannon had explained to him before they set ashore.

"I say we push on for Crepsos. I doubt these Palacians have made up much ground as us, and we might just beat Crawford there," Krixan said.

"If so, then we must depart posthaste. We can ride through the night if need be," Lorelo declared.

"No. Our horses need rest, or they'll start dropping, and without them, Luke will be the least of our troubles. No, we stay put till morning, then continue on as fast as our mounts can take us," Ethan said. "I suggest everyone get some shut-eye. Morning will be here soon enough."

*****

Krixan found his friend staring off to the east at the edge of their encampment as the others bedded down. From their hilltop, they could see the coastal road shadowing the shoreline as it snaked its winding course ever eastward, disappearing into twilight.

"It's not often I find you alone, Ethan. Allie has been attached to your hip since we found her. You ought to see her scowl whenever it's your turn to ferry the next group. She's taken quite a shine to you," Krix said thoughtfully.

Ethan craned his neck, stealing a glance to their campsite behind them. He could see Allie setting up her bedding and speaking quietly with another mage healer of similar age, a young girl brown of hair with Allie's deep olive skin.

"Allie's a nice girl." Ethan shrugged innocently.

"You like her," Krixan stated. It was not a question.

Ethan looked up to his friend's dark eyes, his right hand resting on his holstered Colt while his left hooked into his belt. "Yeah, I like her. She's a good friend."

Krixan slapped him upside his head, knocking his hat ajar. "Not like that, dummy! You *like* her," Krixan pushed, trying to drag the truth out of his thick-skulled friend.

Ethan removed his hat with his left hand and scratched his head with his right, wondering how to answer. "I reckon I favor her company if that's your meaning."

"Favor her company? That's what you say about your horse, not a girl like that," Krix jerked his head in the direction of the encampment.

"Yes, I like her. She's pretty and kind and easy to talk to, but what difference does it make? She's bound to serve her rotten queen and I'm not. Once we escape this land, we'll go our separate ways," he said tiredly.

"I doubt that. For two people supposedly going in different directions, you both find excuses for walking together. When we left you back at Lupen's Cove, she insisted on staying behind to help you. The odd thing is her people didn't argue with her. They just nodded and continued on their merry way. For some reason, she is hell-bent on saving your life."

"Bah, she just wants to pay me back for saving hers. It's some sort of familial honor thing."

"It's more than that, Ethan. She's got all her people committed to keeping you alive, and they're going along with her. It seems the life of Ethan Blagen is very important to her. You aren't much different. How many times have you stuck your neck out on her behalf? Hell, you even broke your promise to your mother in order to save her. I've never seen you act this way with any girl, not even Jennifer Murtado."

"Allie may find me agreeable, but the rest of them would just as soon see me gone once we escape. When that day comes, Allie and I will part ways."

"If she's the one you desire, then you'll find a way."

"If there's a way, I don't see it. Besides, we have more important business to worry about right now, like how we are going to get out of this country alive."

*****

The mining colony of Crepsos rested in an inlet bay, surrounded by the hills that encircled the settlement on three sides. The center hills, resting due south of Crepsos, were dotted with mines upon their sea-facing slopes. Some were burrowed into the hillsides, while most were open quarries where salt, ore, and rock were extracted. Hundreds of stone structures circled the diminutive bay, connected by a series of gravel roads that formed half rings around the bustling port. Other roads ran due east, west, and south, jutting from the harbor like spokes inside a wheel. Strangely, several ore-laden transports sat anchored in the middle of the bay. Spires of gray smoke drifted above the smithies in the port's near side. From his vantage point overlooking Crepsos from a western hilltop, Ethan could spy a score of vessels moored along the stone wharves in the port's center. Whether Luke Crawford was present, he could not ascertain from afar.

The neighing of a horse echoed in the morning air as Captain Lorelo drew up alongside him, staring intently at the mining port below. Ethan leaned forward, resting a forearm on his pommel with his Stetson shifted high on his head. They were the first group to reach the hilltop, and Ethan intended on ferrying the next group but discovering Crepsos altered his plan. The others in their group waited some distance to the rear, shielded within a grove of swaying palms.

"You know what sounds good about now, Cap? A thick steak, well done with all the trimmings and a tankard of cold brew." Ethan's eyes projected the heavenly vision before him, his mouth-watering with the image.

"Aye, a lord's feast," Lorelo answered politely, though wondering why the Astarian prince would be thinking such with the task at hand.

"A what?" Ethan made a face.

"A lord's feast."

"What the hell is a Lord's feast? I was talking about a thick steak and all the fixings, not a stinking noble's gluttonous meal."

"In Vellesia, what you speak of is food only befitting highborn."

"That's because your kingdom's run by morons, Cap. No offense."

Lorelo bristled at the insult, but Ethan ignored him as he continued.

"That's not how things run in Texas. If we happen to survive this, I'll take you across the barrier and treat you to Mrs. McPherson's steak dinner and Mrs. Lawton's apple cobbler. The best food you'll ever taste. In fact, I think I'll open my own pub in Cordova. I'll graze me some cattle and have some pretty gals serve up steak and potatoes to sailors as they make Cordova a port of call. You can visit and bring your crew with you. The first meal is on me."

Captain Lorelo looked at Ethan as if he grew a second head.

"Why do you all look at me like that?" Ethan asked, noting the Vellesians collective bewilderment and annoyance with his manner of speech.

"You speak unlike any mage born I have ever known. You denigrate the authority of mage rule, yet here you are in a savage land, risking your life for a dozen mages that bear you no kinship or loyalty. You are an irreverent, rebellious young man who would be put to death in Vellesia for the disrespect you bear our queen, yet I cannot help but regard you fondly for saving our lives and standing at our side in such a dire time."

"I'll take that as a compliment, Cap'n. you're not so bad yourself." Ethan gave him a half-cocked grin that looked out of place on any native Elarian save the former Astarian crown prince.

"Do you intend to ferry the next group as you planned?"

"Now that we found our destination, I best keep an eye on things. Have one of your boys bring up the next group."

"Aye. I'll have mate Toulous attend to it." Lorelo regarded Ethan before withdrawing to see to his people, but not before Ethan handed him the reins to his horse. Ethan had removed his pack before doing so, not wishing to be parted with his extra knives, guns, and ammo. Before long, Allie emerged from the campsite to join him.

*****

She sat beside him throughout the morn, still wearing the borrowed tunic that she first donned at Lupen's Cove. Far briefer than her long mage gown, it afforded her freer movement, though it did tend to rise unseemly high when she sat, gifting Ethan an envious view of her legs. He pretended not to notice as he sat beside her, but she smiled more than once as she caught him stealing a glance when he thought her looking elsewhere. Allie had never sought the attention of boys, often consigning their entire gender to a category of juvenile simpletons. Her mother schooled her at length on the trappings of romantic love, which held no relevance to the greater aims of her house. Duty to family was placed above such individual fancy. What would her mother say if she could see her now? Allie had never questioned her mother's teachings, ever the dutiful firstborn daughter of her house. Ethan had a way of making her forget duty and obligation, filling her head with other possibilities. She enjoyed his attentions, the way he talked, the touch of his hand upon her shoulder, the desire in his eyes as they met hers. Unlike the lustful stares of Crawford's men, which felt soiled and degrading, Ethan's desire was pure and invigorating. She welcomed his affections as if they were meant to be as if it was right to do so. But she took the greatest pleasure in his company, just feeling his body next to hers, or listening to the sound of his voice as he spoke just above a whisper, and his smell. He smelled just right.

How odd, she thought of the many ways that Ethan pleased her, it was the small details that one often overlooked. *I wonder what he looks like without his clothes?* She shook the distraction from her mind, struggling to retain control of her emotions, which grew difficult in Ethan's presence. *There is a time and place for all things,* her mother often said, and so it would be with her and Ethan, but now was not that time.

Ethan tried to concentrate despite Allie's distraction, struggling to keep his eyes upon the port below. Krixan had already come and gone, leaving to ferry the last group as Ethan kept watch. As he examined Crepsos from afar, something struck him that was strangely amiss. The port was unnaturally quiet. There was little activity along the wharves, and the heavily laden transports waited in port throughout the morn with no apparent urgency to move their cargo.

He suddenly descried a line of ships bearing from the east, sleek triremes with their white sails full with the wind, closing upon the harbor's mouth. They waited for a time before flags upon their forward masts were near enough to discern, displaying the *Red Falcon* on a field of gray, the coat or arms of the sea lord of Valconar, Lagos Darcannon.

"Jorus." Ethan grinned as the man was true to his word.

"The brother of the Valconar sea lord?" Allie asked.

"So he claims. He sailed for Freeport to rally any Valconar ships that might be anchored there. Looks like he found five."

"You saved his life, and now he returns the favor," Allie said somberly, wishing that she could do the same.

"Why are you so intent on saving my life, Allie? With the way we feel about each other, what difference does it make?" he asked, touching a hand to her chin.

"It doesn't," she conceded, gifting him a smile.

Pop! Pop!

The distinct sound of distant rifle fire echoed dully in the west.

*****

Ethan ran back to their encampment, bursting into the grove of palms with Allie close behind. The Vellesians were on their feet, all eyes drawn to the west where the shots were fired. Since the last group was smaller, that left them a few mounts remaining. Ethan wasted little time climbing into the saddle of the nearest horse.

"Ethan," Allie touched a hand to his knee, her golden eyes pleading him to caution as she stood at his horse's side.

"Stay put! No adventures on your own, Allie," he reproached as he pulled the reins, turning about.

"And you? You plan to ride off alone, facing who knows what? I'm coming with you."

"No!" he growled harsher than intended. Allie withdrew her hand as if bitten, though her startled eyes quickly narrowed in indignation at his rebuke. "It's bad enough that Krix is in danger, don't make me worry for you as well." His tone softened as he regarded her. "Please stay put and allow these men to protect you."

"Riders coming!" more than one voice shouted.

Ethan eased his horse to the edge of the grove, staring of to the west as a trail of dust drew nigh. He could discern a handful of riders with a mountainous man upon the lead mount.

"*Yaw!*" he shouted, urging his horse down the hill to meet his comrade. At the base of the hill, he drew his rifle, holding it in his right hand and the reins in his left as he urged his horse on. Within moments he pulled back on the reins, holding place as Krixan and the others drew close.

"What were those shots?" Ethan asked.

"A Palacian cavalry force right on our tail! I slowed them a bit, but there's too many. I took a couple with my rifle, that should give them reason to pause but not for long. We best keep moving."

"We'll hold them at the hill, come on." Ethan pointed the barrel of his Winchester to the grove where the others awaited them.

*****

No sooner had they attained the hill than more gunfire erupted from the east. They crossed to the opposing side of the grove, stealing a glance to the port below, where the Valconar flotilla occupied the harbor. Flashes of gunfire erupted along the wharves, riddling the approaching ships. They spied several bodies drop into the sea from the vessels' serried decks. Projectiles of varied sorts spewed from the Valconar armada. Balls of flame arced overhead, some falling short, sputtering into the water, while others splashed upon the docks, spreading flames where they struck.

Ethan pondered their good fortune as the Valconar fleet exposed the trap Luke Crawford planned to spring had they attempted to enter Crepsos while fleeing the Palacians. Luke must have caught favorable winds to have reached Crepsos before them. Ethan then wondered if Luke was merely expecting them at some time or knew they were waiting just outside the port? Either way, the Valconar fleet revealed Luke's location, drawing his attention to the docks, where they attempted to land. The only question was, did Luke keep any-one back to guard the western approaches into town? Either way, it mattered not, for he had to act.

"Krix! Keep an eye out to our west for the Palacian cavalry," Ethan said, working the lever on his Winchester, loading a bullet into the chamber. He removed a .30-30 round from his pack and topped off the rifle.

"Where are you going?" Krixan asked, though he knew the answer.

"It ends today, Krix. Keep Allie safe." Ethan tipped his hat before kicking his heels into his horse's flanks and sped off toward the port city below.

"Where's he going?" Allie asked, catching her breath as she ran from the opposing side of the grove.

"To get his fool head shot off!" Krixan growled as Ethan sped down the winding trail, his steed's hooves pounding the dusty surface, illuminating his approach for miles around.

Allie heard little more, her ears deafened by the emphatic pounding of her heart.

"He won't stand alone!" Lady Thela declared, standing at Allie's side. Allie turned as Thela placed her hand upon her shoulder. Allie returned the reassuring gesture with a knowing glance.

*****

He could taste the salty air of the seaport below, pushing his lathered mount to its utmost, his eyes searching the structures at the village edge for any sign of Crawford's men. He cursed the barren landscape that circled the port, affording him little concealment as he drew nigh. The swaying palms dotting the surrounding hilltops belied the naked landscape below. The clear blue of the sea stretched endlessly to his left, aping the azure infinity of the clear sky above. The sound of gunfire and the screams of the wounded echoed distantly ahead from the center of Crepsos.

He raced his steed at full gallop, closing upon the village, which grew larger in his line of sight. The small port was well ordered with roads either circling the bay or running straight from its heart. The structures at the village edge were modest homes of the harbor's citizens, simple one-room constructs of stone mortared walls and clay roofs.

Ethan burst into the village, his horse kicking up gravel as he went. Not a soul was in sight. Doors were locked and windows shuttered, as the good citizens of Crepsos hunkered down until the conflict subsided. Ethan crouched low in the saddle, speeding through the empty streets, with the reins in his left hand and rifle in his right. Plumes of billowing smoke blotted the sky ahead as he drew closer to the port's center. Gunfire echoed along the waterfront as he pulled back the reins, easing his mount to a trot before dismounting.

*****

Ignoring the intense heat of the festering flames, he steadied his aim upon his intended target, a well-built Valconar sailor with a broad chest and chiseled jaw, standing upon the forecastle of the lead vessel. Luke squeezed off the round, catching the fellow full in the chest. He didn't wait for the man to drop, shifting his aim, passing over many faces, conserving his precious rifle bullets for only the choicest of targets. Logan Curry stood far to his left, and Emmitt Cobb further right, taking careful aim. The others were interspersed along the wharves, picking their targets as they saw fit. Greybar's men stood beside them with swords and bows to counter any Valconar that might set ashore. Thus far, they held their ground, catching the approaching armada by surprise. Luke cursed his misfortune, having the Valconar fleet ruin his plans of ambushing Ethan upon his approach. Of course, Ethan might yet be miles off and nowhere near Crepsos for all he knew.

They only reached the mining port themselves the night before, thanks to favorable winds. The mining colony easily acquiesced. Luke demanded nothing more than their inaction until he dealt with Ethan, Krixan, and their Vellesian comrades. The miners were not pleased seeing their ships laden with cargo sitting idle in the bay, but Luke demanded that no vessel leave port else word might spread of their presence. But alas, his plan was now in ruin as the damnable Valconar fleet sailed into port. Captain Greybar pointed out the sigil of House Darcannon displayed upon the lead vessel, the *Red Falcon* on a field of gray. The slaver captain cursed, his eyes finding the tall, golden-haired Jorus Darcannon standing at the prow of the second vessel in line. Jorus took cover before Crawford could pick him off, diving below the forecastle as a bullet passed overhead. That had been at the battle's start, and he still remained below the bulwark of the vessel, ordering his men to do likewise. The orders were difficult to relay, as the crews in the other ships remained at their posts, easy prey for Crawford's men.

"Full ahead! Archers, stand on my command!" Jorus shouted over the din. He mustered a handful of bowmen who crawled below either bulwark, making their way to the forecastle. Once the ship drew within a dozen yards of the wharves, he would give command, certain of his bowmen's ability to hit their target at that range. Meanwhile the Valconar flotilla advanced painstakingly slow, their oarsmen driving their prows through the lapping waves as Crawford's Texans picked off their crewmen.

Luke slowly backed away as the ships drew perilously close, keeping his barrel trained upon the lead ship's deck. He could feel the wooden pier give way to the gravel road that ran behind it, as he backed to the street.

"Agghh!" He heard a terrible scream to his left. He turned, catching the gruesome sight of Logan Curry flailing upon the wharf, gunshot in the back. Confusion gave way to unchecked rage as his eyes trailed further behind his fallen comrade, to the unmistakable form of Ethan Blagen, the Devil's Deputy, running along the harbor road, working the lever of his Winchester as he shifted his aim to Luke.

*****

Moments before

Ethan approached the wharves afoot, making his way to the sound of gunfire. Reaching the last line of structures that ran nearest the docks, he spied a Texan with his back to him, firing at the Valconar ships. Lifting his Winchester to his shoulder, Ethan squeezed the trigger, his bullet punching a hole in the center of the man's spine. Ethan stepped into the clear, working the lever-action as the man cried out, his body dropping like a sack of wheat. As he set foot in the open, the battle unfolded before his eyes like an unfurling portrait. The wharves were lined with Greybar's pirates, Luke's Texans, and a number of Palacians, with weapons drawn and trained upon the Valconar ships, which drew ominously close. Fires spread unchecked along the docks, their trails of black smoke shifting with the wind, obscuring his brief, clear vision. His eye drifted right, catching sight of the unmistakable silhouette of Luke Crawford. Ethan lifted his rifle, fixing his site to target as Luke's pale-green eyes found his across that deadly space.

Ethan felt something amiss, catching sight of a swinging blade arcing nigh as he shifted, dodging the hasty blow, rolling to the ground while bringing his barrel to his attacker's gut.

Boom!

The Palacian warrior's gut exploded, spraying Ethan with blood and innards as the mortally wounded man stumbled forth, bringing his sword down upon him. Ethan shifted to his right, blocking the weakened strike with his rifle, then kicking at his assailant with his right foot as he lay on his left hip. One forceful strike toppled the bleeding man off his feet. Ethan rolled over, seeking Luke's position through the din and smoke.

Luke again cursed his misfortune as Ethan slipped from sight, his view blocked by the Palacian warrior who suffered a gutshot at close range. The warrior stumbled before dropping upon the gravel street, obscuring his view of Ethan. Luke shifted aim, fixing the blurred image beyond the dying Palacian. A primary rule of gun-fighting that Luke Crawford lived by was to aim center mass at the exposed target area, whatever that might be. If you gave him a leg, he'd aim for the knee. If you gave him an arm, he'd take the elbow. From this range, he could ill discern what lay beyond the wounded Palacian, as the fellow flopped in the road like a fish thrown upon the beach.

"Fire!" Luke heard, just as he squeezed the trigger, sending his bullet off target. He cursed angrily before catching the disconcerting sight of the Valconar ships in his periphery.

Jorus Darcannon stood at the prow of the *Falcon's Claw*, commanding his archers to rise and fire. They arose in unison, losing their shafts upon their foes.

Luke's eyes grew wide at the sight of a line of archers in tan livery standing shoulder to shoulder upon the forecastle of the Valconar ship just shy of the wharf. Luke ducked as arrows whizzed past, his left shoulder aching as he struck the unforgiving gravel. He quickly recovered, tucking the butt of his rifle to his shoulder as he lay upon the ground, finding an archer in his sites and firing before the second volley was loosed. The bullet caught the second archer in the line in the left shoulder. The archer screamed as the round shattered his joint and shredded muscle and ligaments. He stumbled to the deck in agony as his fellows kept their aim, loosing another volley as the hull of the *Falcon's Claw* slammed into the wharf.

"Charge!" Jorus commanded, his crew rising from the deck of his vessel, brandishing shields and short swords. They bounded over the bulwarks and onto the wharf, storming the colony in force. All along the waterfront, the other Valconar ships followed the *Falcon's Claw*'s lead, disembarking Valconar soldiers and sailors along the wharves.

Luke emptied his rifle into the charging mass, working the lever in rapid succession as he gained his feet. One of Greybar's men stepped forward, guarding his left flank as the Valconarans swarmed the dock. Before the fellow could raise his sword, he stumbled with a bullet passing through his ribs before exiting his right lung. Luke didn't need to look to know that Ethan fired that shot. That was doubtless intended for him. Luke dropped his rifle, drawing his twin Colts as he withdrew, shooting any who blocked his path or drew too close.

*****

"Blast!" Ethan cursed, smoke obscuring his vision as Luke passed from sight. Gaining his feet, he was met by another Palacian with his arm outstretched, bringing his sword toward Ethan's neck. Ethan ducked below the hasty strike, driving the butt of his rifle in the fellow's chest, knocking him to the street as another came up behind him. Ethan pivoted, squeezing the trigger as the barrel aligned with his attacker's head. The man's jaw exploded, his body dropping like a weighted sack.

"Oh, come on!" Ethan moaned as a dozen men encircled him, an odd mix of Palacian cavalrymen, Greybar pirates, and several free swords that were now in the hire of the slaver captain.

*****

Allie gasped, her breath catching in the narrows of her throat as she cleared the last street that lined the waterfront. Her eyes betrayed her racing heart as she beheld Ethan beset on all sides. She had commandeered a mount once Ethan had left the hilltop, hoping to aid him in any way she could. Krixan drew his lathered horse up beside her, struggling to keep pace throughout their ride. A half-dozen Vellesians filed in around them, including Captain Lorelo, who came at Lady Thela's insistence to protect the headstrong mage healer. The others remained atop the hill, keeping watch for the Palacian host that waited to their west. Allie was determined to save Ethan's life, returning the favor he rendered her.

Allie stared spellbound as Ethan worked the action of his rifle, dropping two assailants in as many seconds, emptying his rifle into their standing corpses. The one nearest him fell backward, losing his grip upon his sword. Ethan dropped his rifle, snatching the hilt of the falling blade before it hit the ground. Allie looked on in disbelief as Ethan moved amid his foes, his sword dancing like a dervish as they fell to his blade. His movements flowed with noble grace, as if the men before him were statues. She had never seen Ethan this way, so swift, so serene, so *pure*. He parried an emphatic thrust, bringing his blade down upon the offender's wrist before moving on, leaving the stricken sell-sword to his anguish. He spun, blocking another high strike meant for his head, his foot kicking the Palacian's groin while stepping aside, his sword following through, taking the fellow's sword arm at the elbow.

Allie wondered how it was possible? Ethan's great strength and recuperative powers were impaired in the Mage Bane. Even rendered mortal, he seemed an army unto himself. Some of his attackers fled, leaving their remaining comrades to their fate. Ethan finished the last of them before a host of Valconar soldiers emerged through the shifting smoke that covered much of the waterfront.

Gunfire rang out. Allie craned her neck sharply to the right as one of her Vellesian guards slipped from his saddle. Another slumped forward over his pommel, blood oozing from his lips. Krixan lifted his rifle, seeking the source of the attack before his horse bucked wildly, its hindquarters struck twice, throwing him into the street.

"Behind us!" one of their men cried out as she circled her horse around to see. There in the middle of the street behind them stood two of Crawford's men, one with a rifle in a red and green checkered shirt over brown chaps and the other with a pistol and wearing a sand-colored shirt and gray trousers. Allie suddenly felt a strong arm around her waist, yanking her from the saddle as bullets sped where she sat, just missing their target. She felt the impact as they tumbled to the street, her rescuer protecting her from the gravel by bringing her down atop of him.

"Who—" she started to say before meeting Ethan's familiar blue eyes staring up at her as she lie atop him.

"Agghh," he moaned, nudging her off him. "Why am I not surprised?" he growled, gaining his knees while drawing his pistol. "I left you behind to keep you safe, Allie," he grunted, favoring his back as he crouched behind the jumpy horses.

"We came to help you," she protested, following as he maneuvered amid the disorder. Krixan had crawled to safety to the south end of the street, while Captain Lorelo and the others struggled to gain their bearing.

"Getting yourself killed isn't helpful, Allie," he said, taking her by the hand and sprinting to the street corner where Krixan covered their movement, staying Luke's men's gunfire with his rifle.

"Thanks," Ethan grunted as they passed behind Krixan's shoulder.

"Where's your rifle?" Krix asked, squeezing off another round while aiming around the corner of the building.

"I didn't have time to fetch where it dropped. I was too busy running over here to help." He lost his Stetson somewhere along the way, as well as his horse pack and extra ammunition.

Krixan pulled back as a bullet struck the corner of the building just above, showering them with powdered stone.

"You know, Krix, gunfights aren't the same without Ben, Skeeter and the judge."

"If we live through this, I'll be sure to tell them how they missed out on this wonderful experience!" Krix snorted, not sharing Ethan's nostalgia at this time.

"Don't worry, big fella, I got this. Just keep 'em busy for a moment," he said, slapping his friend on the back. "And you stay *put!*" Ethan touched a finger to her nose, trying to scowl his disapproval, but his anger melted away as he lost himself in her eyes. "Just stay with Krix, please." With that he turned, racing along the waterfront and disappearing around the opposite corner of the building.

Within seconds the sound of gunfire echoed down the street in the direction of their assailants. Krixan stole a glance around the corner, catching sight of Ethan dashing across the street over the bodies of the two Texans while snatching a rifle that lay near their warm corpse, before disappearing to the opposite side of the street.

"Damn fool!" Krixan growled as Ethan slipped from sight, obviously intent on finding Luke somewhere east along the next avenue.

Allie could easily discern the source of Krixan's ire. She quickly raced around the corner into the street whence they came, where several of her brave Vellesians lie dead or wounded beside their mounts. One who was wounded cried out, holding his lower abdomen while writhing in pain. She could spare him no time as she raced up the street with Captain Lorelo and Krixan close behind. She snatched a pistol from one of the dead Texans before turning east along the second street that circled the harbor.

*****

Scores of Palacian cavalry swept around the Vellesians entrenched upon the hilltop that lay west of Crepsos. The Vellesian soldiers and mage healers observed helplessly as the Palacian host swept down the slopes of the hills that rested due south of the port. They dispatched two mounts to warn Captain Lorelo of the enemy bearing down upon them, but the Palacians were certain to join the battle before that warning could be raised.

*****

Krixan grunted as his heavy boots pounded the gravel streets. Oh, how he hated running, it was an endeavor suited to those of slighter builds and defter feet, but he trudged along, chasing the sound of gunfire that always seemed just a street away. They found a dozen corpses littering the avenues, an odd assortment of Palacians, pirates, sell-swords, or citizens of Crepsos who were caught in the cross fire. Whenever they reached the next street, they found it empty as Ethan kept one step ahead. They were soon joined by Valconar soldiers and sailors, who at first mistook them for foes until Jorus interjected, recognizing Krixan's mountainous form and Captain Lorelo's nondescript face that stood out for its extreme blandness. They reached an accord none too soon as the ground suddenly shook with the thunder of hooves.

*****

Palacian cavalry flooded the street, sweeping deep into Crepsos before their advance was contested.

Krixan snorted a few choice obscenities as he descried the distinctive Palacian breastplates and helms adorning the cavalry as they turned onto the street, their horses' hooves kicking up stones as they raised their swords to match their war cries once they spied their Valconar foes.

Boom!

The sound of Krixan's rifle greeted the Palacians, the lead rider tumbling from the saddle, striking the ground before the trailing riders trampled him underneath. Krixan emptied his rifle into their serried mass, striking man or horse in equal measure, but even rifle fire could not stay their charge. Krixan began to reload as Valconar soldiers swept past him to give battle.

Men afoot were poorly matched against mounted warriors. The brave Valconaran soldiers met the charging Palacians, struggling to land a blow as horses knocked them aside, their massive weight breaking the Valconarans formations like a hammer striking clay. Men were cut down, trampled upon, or thrown aside. Others broke and fled as Palacian scimitars lopped heads and limbs with practiced efficiency. Krixan managed to load three shells before a Palacian rider fixed on him. Krixan quickly tucked his rifle's butt into his shoulder and fired off three shots into the charging desert warrior. Two rounds tore into the horse's breast, the third striking the rider in midtorso, sending horse and man astray. Another rider followed, fixing his ire upon the towering Astarian giant. Krixan went to his pistol, emptying his Colt as Allie stepped beside him with the pistol taken from the dead Texan who ambushed them. Their combined fire unhorsed the rider and another that followed.

Jorus Darcannon rallied the fleeing Valconarans, leading them back into the fray. Soon the sound of cheers rang out among the Valconarans as scores of their countrymen swarmed the adjoining avenues, shouting war cries as they flooded the streets, surrounded the Palacian mounts, and tore their riders from their saddles.

Krixan, Allie, and Captain Lorelo took advantage of the occupied Palacians and pressed their search for Ethan.

*****

"Stick yer head out again, and we'll blow a hole clean through it, Ethan!" Emmitt Cobb hollered. The former Grierson foreman's dusty gray Stetson rested high on his brow as he stood by the doorway of a vacated dwelling. Luke stood post at the window to his right, while Ned Stiles and George Carson were out front, positioned behind each front corner with rifles trained across the avenue where Ethan jumped back behind the northwest corner of the opposing structure. Colm Conroy stood behind the window to Emmitt's left. The adjoining buildings were occupied by Greybar and a dozen others, a mix of his crewmen, Palacians, and free swords in their employ.

A growing number of Valconarans gathered along Ethan's side of the avenue. A few adventurous souls attempted to cross the deadly open space between the factions. Their bullet laden bodies littering the streets attested their foolishness. The others quickly wizened to the folly of such bravado and held position behind the thick stone walls of the structures that lined the avenue.

Though he had cut Luke's number in half, Ethan was still outnumbered five guns to one. Without his ability to regenerate, he was unlikely to survive a straight-up fight while Luke's men were so entrenched. Out of his periphery, he sensed movement to his rear right, behind the back corner of the structure to his direct right. There, standing behind the stone corner was Krixan. Ethan nodded to his friend, acknowledging his presence.

Five versus two, he reminded himself, the odds doubling to his favor. Ethan's elation was short-lived as he spied Allie's head poking around Krixan's girth with a pistol in hand. He couldn't determine its make or condition and wondered if she even knew how to reload it once it ran dry. Even if she did, he doubted she had any spare ammunition to do so.

Ethan could see Valconaran soldiers crossing over the contested street some distance to the west, where the road's curve mirrored the waterfront. They were met with hurried shots that failed to hit. Luke had to know that his position would be soon compromised.

"Luke!" Ethan shouted, keeping his back flat against the wall of the building.

"What do ya want, Blagen?" Luke hollered back, stealing a careful scan from behind the window of the vacated dwelling they occupied.

"There ain't much point in anyone else dying today! How 'bout we settle this ourselves, you and me, in the open! Have your people back off, and I'll do the same!"

"Too thin, Ethan. We seven guns to your two. If you want us, come and get us!" Luke shouted back.

"You have five guns, Luke! I killed two of your boys a few streets back. I don't have to come get you. I can stay put as the Valconarans surround you. They outnumber your Palacian friends. Once they attack, you'll drain your ammo right quick, keeping them at bay. Once you run dry, all I'll have to do is stroll across the street and put a bullet in your brain. Even if you come out of this alive, you'll most likely waste most, if not all, of your ammo, and then what? Without your guns, you'll have little to offer Gervis Tomaz than your magical immunity, and without me, there's no going home."

"Home?" Luke snarled. "We got no home, thanks to you, Blagen, not with our faces on every wanted poster from the panhandle to the Rio Grande!"

"I can always back away, Luke! Make my way to the ships, sail away, and wait for you to stick your neck out of the Mage Bane, where I can regenerate. What chance would you have then?"

Luke rubbed his jaw, thinking on Ethan's words. He had to finish Ethan while he was in the Bane. Somehow he knew it would come to this.

"All right," Luke snorted. "You back your boys up two blocks to the west, and I'll do the same, with mine to the east. Then I'll meet you in the street."

*****

Krixan took Allie by the arm, ignoring her protest as he dragged her away. She vehemently opposed Ethan's harebrained idea, but the die was cast. Krixan was none too pleased with this plan and even less so with what Ethan made him promise to do. Ever cognizant of his mother's vision of him suffering, Ethan asked Krixan to put a bullet in his brain if Luke won their duel, and he was injured and not slain. Krixan knew if he was to kill Ethan, even out of mercy, then he could never return to Astaria sans shame or guilt. Curse Ethan for coaxing such a promise out of him.

The rattle of Luke's spurs contrasted the quiet deftness of Ethan's moccasin boots as they stepped into the clear. The midday sun hung high in the firmament, favoring neither as they faced with Ethan to the west and Luke to the east. Ethan could see past Luke's shoulder, where Emmitt Cobb, Noris Greybar, and the others waited two blocks behind their comrade, just as Krixan, Allie, and the Valconarans held position an equal distance behind him.

Luke's tan shirt and black vest were stained with blood. He once again wore his black Stetson that he made one of Greybar's crew wear days earlier in his stead when Ethan killed the man, mistaking him for Luke. It was a clever trick, though the dead fellow would beg to differ. A mere ten paces separated them, and Ethan could see Luke's almost-boyish-looking clean face. He most likely had shaven that morn, probably bathed as well, which contrasted Ethan's soiled leathers and days old stubble and stench. Though Ethan was a lawman and Luke an outlaw, it was Ethan who looked the savage and Luke the gentleman. Luke appraised him with cold pale-green eyes that offered no pretension. Many evil men could mask their natures with feigned courtesies and fake smiles, but Luke Crawford either could not or would not. He wore his contempt like a badge of honor, his sneering lips holding all the joy of curdled milk. Even the shade of his Stetson failed to dim the fire in his eyes that glowed like emerald flames. It was strange for two men that despised each other so intensely to be so unfamiliar. The mutual dislike was based entirely upon their reputations and fell deeds committed against the friends and allies of the other. In fact, before his foray into the Mage Bane, Ethan had only met Luke one time on that fateful day in Red Rock when he slew Hank Grierson and Bobby Crawford.

Ethan wished he hadn't lost his hat but was fortunate that the sun's blinding glare was directly overhead and not staring him in the face. There were no choice words or witty remarks shared between them. Ethan vowed to kill Luke for his crimes and the threat he posed for Elaria as well as Sheriff Thorton. Luke vowed to slay Ethan for killing his brother, slaying his friends, and spoiling his carefully laid plans.

They drew in unison, Luke going for a full draw while Ethan squeezed off a round just as the barrel cleared leather, his left hand fanning the hammer after the first bullet sped to target.

Luke's dead hand squeezed off a round in the dirt as Ethan emptied his Colt, the bullets pummeling Luke's torso, while one drifted higher, striking the base of his neck. Luke collapsed like a puppet whose strings had been cut.

Ethan felt something punch his left shoulder, followed by crippling pain. The sound of rifle fire rang out as smoke spewed from Emmitt Cobb's rifle. Ethan dropped to the ground, his shattered shoulder aching as he did so. He struggled drawing the pistol in his left holster with his right hand, while his left flopped uselessly at his side. Bullets crossed overhead as Krixan responded in kind, firing off rounds from the corner of a structure behind him. The sound of shouting and feet slapping gravel grew audibly as Ethan struggled to work the pistol free with his opposing hand. He felt it come free after needless duress, extending his draw while lying upon the street, searching for Emmitt over the pistol's sites, but the outlaw was nowhere to be found. A score of Valconarans swarmed past him, with blades raised and arrows notched, seeking out Emmitt, Greybar, and the others before they could slip away.

"What were you thinking?" Allie's voice reproached as she rolled him to his back, her eyes red with worry.

CHAPTER 22

Ethan sighed, gazing over the portside of the *Falcon's Claw* at the retreating coastline as the Mage Bane shrank from view. They did it. He and Krixan managed to go ashore, rescue the Vellesian mage healers, along with many others. They even slew Luke Crawford and most of his men, without getting themselves killed in the process. Emmitt Cobb escaped however, along with three of his fellow Texans, Noris Greybar, and a handful of free swords and scores of Palacian cavalry, disappearing into the desert waste. With Luke dead, Emmitt would be wary to repeat the bold actions that led to their current state. Ethan doubted Emmitt would be warmly received by the Palacian warlord upon their return, but the Texan's immunity to Magic was still a valuable asset that Gervis Tomaz would be sure to make use of. For the time, however, Cordova had found a new ally in the sea lord of Valconar. By saving Jorus Darcannon from the hold of Greybar's ship, Ethan had earned the man's gratitude and friendship. As Ethan was the sheriff of Cordova, Jorus extended his friendship to the city as well.

"How fare's your shoulder?" Allie asked, standing beside him. After finding him wounded, lying in the street, Allie bandaged his shoulder and had him escorted to the *Falcon's Claw* and set sail posthaste. Once the ship passed beyond the magically immune barrier that hovered just offshore, the wound healed instantaneously, the bullet squeezing from his shoulder as the tissue closed behind it. Ethan's entire body tingled, every ache and bruise dissipating as the wondrous rebirth of his power washed over him in euphoric splendor. Once offshore, Allie insisted they remain so, waiting for the others to eventually join them. Jorus oversaw establishing order to the suffering port, while Krixan searched for Ethan's pack while gathering the guns from those they had slain. Captain Lorelo oversaw the evacuation of the remaining Vellesian healers, bringing them aboard the following vessels as well as whatever wounded they could gather.

Once they breached the magical barrier, the mages made short work of healing the wounded. Men with mortal wounds that would have lingered in agony until death finally claimed them were spared such a fate by the healers' touch. Several of the severely wounded succumbed before the ships broke the barrier. One fellow with his belly ripped open, held on with his innards in his hands, his cries unnerving even the hardiest of souls. Once free of the Mage Bane, Lady Thela Corval pressed her palms to his chest, bathing his flesh with her magical power. His organs repaired themselves, retracting to their proper place, his skin stitching together, concealing the mended tissue beneath.

With their wounded healed and men gathered, the Valconar armada set sail, promising to return their new friends to the safety of Cordova.

"My shoulder's fine, though I can't say the same for my shirt," Ethan said, running his fore digit through the bullet hole in the left shoulder of the garment.

"Your garment? If the projectile drifted slightly right, it would have pierced your heart!" she admonished, her voice rising higher than she intended. The bullet actually struck his chest before angling through his shoulder, missing his heart by the narrowest of margins.

Ethan smiled, gazing into her eyes over his right shoulder as his forearms rested on the bulwark of the ship. "You're awfully cute when you're angry, Allie."

Cute? she mused irritably. No one ever called her that, save for her father when she was a wee child. "You could have been killed, Ethan. Does your life mean so little to you that you'd risk it needlessly?"

"Needlessly?" He gave her a hurt look.

"We could have surrounded Luke and waited him out. Why did you take such a risk? Why did you place false trust in Luke's men to not intervene?"

"Their chicanery didn't work, Allie, I'm still alive. That's more than Luke can claim."

"If Emmitt's aim drifted ever so slightly, you would be dead. Fate has favored you by the slimmest of margins. Does this not trouble you?" she pleaded, hoping he would see the recklessness of his actions.

"It had to be done, Allie. I couldn't risk Luke escaping. I've spent the better part of two years tracking him down, and I'll waste no more time on the likes of him. I owed it to Sheriff Thorton to bring Luke to justice."

"Why do you owe him? He is safely on the other side of the barrier, where Luke could not return. If the sheriff is the kind of man that you claim, he would not have approved the risk you took."

Ethan turned to fully face her, placing his hands upon her shoulders. "I swore an oath when Ben gave me the badge, an oath to protect the citizens of Red Rock and to uphold the law. Those men that kidnapped you were outlaws in Red Rock, and I am charged with bringing them to justice."

"But you no longer serve Red Rock," she argued.

"I'm still Ben's deputy, and I swore an oath."

"Oaths to common men are just words in the wind."

"I swore an *oath*, Allie. It is just words, but words that I stand by. What use is a man whose word counts for nothing?"

"Do you always keep your promises?" she challenged.

The question gave him pause, his broken promise to his mother coming cruelly to mind. "I keep my promises unless I have good reason not to," he said kindly, leaving unsaid that she was the reason for his breaking his promise. They stared one to the other, each searching the other's eyes, bereft of words.

"Ethan!" The booming voice of Jorus Darcannon broke the stillness between them. Jorus placed a meaty hand upon each of their shoulders, a broad grin pushing the corners of his graying blond beard. His large frame started to fill out after two years of captivity and deprivation. His ragged tunic was replaced with gray boiled leather mail, over tan linen tunic and trousers, with the *Red Falcon* of Valconar emblazoned upon his chest. Gold braids adorned either shoulder, symbols of his rank as admiral. A broad sword rode his left hip and a short sword his right. His large feet sounded audibly when he paced the wooden deck despite his soft seal skin boots.

"Jorus." Ethan grinned, greeting the larger man who nearly rivaled Krixan in height and soon in girth. "You seem in good spirits."

"Aye, lad. Good spirits indeed. I've spent the better part of two years slaving in the hold of Greybar's wretched hold, pulling an oar. That cur went to great lengths, ensuring my survival while others lasted mere months under similar duress. I'm free now, thanks to a certain Astarian prince."

"I'm no prince, Jorus, just a freeman of Cordova. Besides, we owe our lives to your timely intervention."

"Hah! You see, Allie, what a humble fellow Ethan is? He saves my life and says we're even when all I have done is to sail into Crepsos to battle our mutual foe."

"If you hadn't arrived when you did, I'd have run into Luke's trap. I'd have ridden into Crepsos and been greeted by a hail of bullets from every window around me. Instead, you revealed Luke's presence and drew all his attention to the wharves while I slipped into the port unseen."

"So say you, Ethan, but I don't believe it. You are kissed by fate. We all owe you our lives, and I intend to balance the scales. We sail to Cordova to return you to your people, though I wish for us to sail to Valconar where my lord brother could receive you properly, but I know you desire it not, so we'll sail for Cordova instead. But I will return to Cordova again with a Valconar armada to offer your city the gratitude of our kingdom and perhaps form a friendship that is to our mutual benefit. Meanwhile, allow me to offer a small boon, Feris!" Jorus commanded a sailor standing midship to come hither.

"I believe this is yours." Jorus grinned, taking the object from the sailor's outstretched hand.

"I thought I lost it for good this time," Ethan smiled, taking his dusty, worn Stetson from Jorus and placing it upon his head.

"I thought you might want it back, though it's strange to behold a royal prince favoring such ill-used garments." Jorus's broad smile was revealing several missing molars in the outer reaches of his mouth.

"I'm not a prince, Jorus. I'm the sheriff of Cordova in Elaria and a deputy of Red Rock on Earth."

Jorus still did not understand what Earth or Red Rock was, and whenever Ethan tried to explain it, he merely nodded, pretending to listen. It was a lousy habit, one that his dearest wife accused him of whenever she babbled on about some topic that seemed trivial, but ended up being important to her as his latter ignorance caused her apoplexy. He could ill imagine what she might say to him after a two-year absence? Did she think him dead? Did she invite another man to her bed? *Nay*, he reminded himself. She had born him four sons and five daughters and, at the twilight of their lives, would never entertain such possibilities. She was a good woman, even if she often lumped him upon his head with a ladle.

"Jorus, step this way," Allie softly commanded, drawing the boisterous lord several paces away from Ethan, stepping outside Ethan's anti-magical aura. She cupped her hands to his large face, bathing him in luminous hues of orange, crimson, and golden light, restoring his teeth to their full glory. The aches in his joints dissipated as well, as her healing powers renewed him.

"My lady." Jorus was bereft of words. He had not received a healer's touch since he visited Loraish twenty years ago.

"A gift, Lord Darcannon, on behalf of Vellesia. A small measure of gratitude for your gallantry at Crepsos."

"It was my great honor, my lady." He smiled, running his tongue over the perfectly formed teeth where moments before were only gums.

Ethan regarded her. Once again, she surprised him with a kindness that was uncharacteristic for a mage born. She was tired and spent after suffering such duress, yet she did not overlook a small ailment such as Jorus's missing teeth, gifting him their renewal. It was a small act of kindness but far from insignificant. It defined her empathy, tenderness, and devout sense of duty.

Jorus smiled and stepped away, leaving Ethan and Allie to themselves. Even a blind man could see their fondness for each other, and Jorus knew their time was drawing to a close.

"That was kind of you. Maybe you could fix Krixan's bald spot as well." Ethan smiled as she returned to him.

"I already offered, but he refused."

"Refused?" Ethan lifted a curious eye, feigning ignorance. He didn't tell her that his sister often offered to heal Krixan's scalp, but he refused her offer as well, claiming the fates made him as he was and thought it unlucky to change it.

"You needn't act surprised, Ethan, he told me he refused your sister's similar offer…repeatedly."

"Oh, I forgot about that," he gave her his look that was half puppy-dog and half-feigned ignorance, but she well knew it was all an act.

Liar, she thought, smiling inwardly at what a lousy liar he was. It was a favorable trait in a man that he was a poor deceiver; it helped a woman keep track of his actions and allowed her to intercede when he planned to make a poor decision, which men were apt to do.

Ethan's gaze returned to the receding shore, his thoughts suddenly elsewhere. He was strangely silent as if a great shroud descended between them.

"Ethan?" she asked, touching a hand to his shoulder.

"Uh, I'm all right, just thinking." He sighed.

"Of what?"

"I spent so long hunting Luke Crawford, and…I thought I would feel more fulfilled with having finished him, but I don't feel anything."

"What were you expecting?"

"I don't know." He shrugged. "I guess I should look to enjoying my freedom without the specter of Luke Crawford hanging over me."

"Your *freedom*," she reminded herself.

"Yeah, maybe I can start making the world into what it should be. At least in the small part that I occupy," he smiled weakly.

"Your freedom sounds lonely."

"Lonely?" He hadn't thought of that. All those years he yearned to be free of the path set before him, to make his own choices. He never considered if it would bring him happiness. Happy or not, it felt right. He was born to be free. Why couldn't she join him? To hell with her duty and her queen. "I wouldn't be lonely if you stayed," he said, looking into her golden eyes that radiated like a thousand stars, eyes that seemed to see straight through him as if his soul were translucent. Her ebony midnight hair framed her achingly feminine face. Despite her disarming beauty, he felt strangely at ease around her, as if she were a part of him, an extension of his own flesh.

"If only the choice were mine," her voice was but a whisper.

"Your queen." He tried to mask the venom in his voice. He despised the rules and oaths that bound men and women to their mage lords and sovereigns.

"My queen," she affirmed. "She would not release me from my oath to Vellesia. All Vellesians are bound to our queen and the crown princess."

"Princess?" This was the first he heard mention of the queen's progeny. "What is she like?"

"Few have ever seen her. She often remains in the shadows while the queen rules. Some mistake her quiet role for passivity, but they would be remiss to do so. The princess is even more cunning and dangerous than the queen."

"She doesn't sound so scary." Ethan tried to lighten the mood. "I mean she is just a girl, right?"

Allie gave him a dark look. "Believe so at your own peril, Ethan."

"What's she going to do, beat me up?" He grinned.

"Men." She smiled, shaking her head.

"What?" he asked, enjoying her sudden gaiety.

"Is that how you measure a threat? By the physical power it represents?"

"Yes," he bluntly answered.

She gave him a look.

"Words can't hurt me, Allie," he further explained.

"Words are not her weapon, though her tongue makes good use of them."

"Then why is she dangerous? What mage power does she possess?"

"She has many, as does the queen. They can cast ice and fire with equal measure, bind the will of others, and foresee any threat with the gift of prophecy, to name a few. Nothing escapes their sight—*nothing*."

"If that is true, Allie, then why didn't they foresee Luke capturing you and the others? Or are they not concerned with the meager lives of their mage healers?"

Allie was uncertain how to answer. "I…I don't know. Perhaps the Texans' magical immunity blocked their prophetic visions." She lowered her eyes shyly.

"Or maybe your wonderful queen knew what would happen and planned to use the pretense to wage war upon Palacia."

She brought her eyes back sharply to his. "She wouldn't do that. We twelve represent the majority of our guild in all of Vellesia. She wouldn't risk our loss over a petty kingdom in a desert waste."

"Don't underestimate the greed of the mage born, Allie."

"We are mage born, Ethan, both of us," she challenged.

"I'm no mage, Allie, I'm simply immune to them, and you… you are a healer. You use your power to heal others. That sets you apart from most," he said with sincere passion. Allie was pure and good. He loathed her subjugation to her wicked queen and princess.

"I am glad you think well of me." She blushed.

He lifted her chin, losing himself in her golden eyes. "You stood by me when others would've run. You came to Cordova to heal the sick. I've seen you tend our wounded even with your powers impaired. You are brave, selfless, and kind, Allie, of course I think well of you. Come with me. Stay with me," he pleaded.

"I…I wish…but I can't," she said through watery eyes.

"Your queen," he sighed in defeat.

"My family," she corrected. "My mother would never allow it, and I cannot leave her to the mercies of the throne."

"Then I'll rescue her, get her safely beyond Queen Valera's reach."

"She would not go with you, Ethan, not if you could find her, which you could not. What if you came with me? The queen may allow it if you adhere to the laws and protocols of Vellesia."

Never, he told himself. He spent a lifetime breaking free of Astaria and would never submit to another throne. Being a prince and heir of Astaria was bad enough, he could ill imagine being a vassal to the queen of Vellesia. "There has to be another way."

"If so, then we shall find it," she reassured him. "Perhaps we are destined to be together after all."

"Forget destiny, Allie. My mother foretold unspeakable suffering if I entered the Mage Bane, yet here I stand, free and whole. We'll make our own destiny." He took her into his arms and kissed her fiercely.

"Ships!" the sailor in the crow's nest shouted below, his right hand stretching northward to the horizon.

Ethan and Allie followed the others atop deck to the starboard bow. There upon the horizon were scores of warships, their black masts full with the wind as they drew nigh.

"The royal fleet," Allie whispered as the banners adorning the lead vessel came into view, a golden rose upon a field of black, the sigil of House Loria, the royal house of Vellesia.

*****

Before treating with the Vellesian admiral, Jorus drew alongside the ship carrying Lady Thela and Captain Lorelo, bringing them aboard the *Falcon's Claw*. The Vellesian fleet numbered six score, each sleek hulled for speed yet laden with infantry. It was a fleet meant to cross the sea swiftly and bring as much land force to bear as their speed would allow. As yet the Vellesians were unaware that their mages were aboard the Valconar ships but agreed to Jorus's parlay. Jorus proceeded cautiously for with only five vessels in his flotilla, the Vellesian admiral would think nothing to smash his ships enroot to the Mage Bane.

The *Falcon's Claw* broke from the formation, drawing to that vast open space between the lines of ships, where the Vellesian flagship awaited them.

*****

Alexar Loria stood at the forecastle of the *Golden Rose*, the flagship of the Vellesian fleet. He was broad of chest and narrow at the waist, with long graceful limbs. His coal-black hair flowed below his gray admiral's cap with gold stitching along its narrow rim. He wore a long gray silk coat with similar stitching and silver lapels upon each shoulder. His white breeches were tucked into black knee-high boots. His face was slightly chiseled and square, with a delicate symmetry of boyish attractiveness, which belied his advancing years. Alexar Loria was the uncle of Queen Valera and grand admiral of the Vellesian navy.

The *Falcon's Claw* drew up alongside the Vellesian flagship with Jorus standing at the prow, flanked by Lady Thela and Captain Lorelo. Though clad in threadbare garments that bore no semblance of his standard crisp uniform, Lorelo projected the proper demeanor of authority that his rank demanded. Ethan shook his head, standing at amidships. Lorelo could be naked as a jaybird and would still present himself as if nothing were amiss.

"Prince Alexar," Lady Thela greeted the Vellesian grand admiral, kneeling upon the deck of the *Claw*. Captain Lorelo knelt in kind as the two ships rested side by side, while sailors from either vessel tied off the lines, connecting them at bow and stern. Scores of Vellesian guards stood post, surrounding Admiral Alexar. They wore white tunics with pleated kilts and silver breastplates and shin armor. Ethan wondered if their manner of dress was the uniform of Vellesian infantry or the royal guards since Alexar Loria retained the title of prince and admiral. Ethan was never one to notice a man's attractiveness, but the Vellesian guards looked entirely too pretty, from their smooth olive skin to their perfect white teeth and boyishly symmetrical faces. If the guards appeared overly handsome, they seemed as swine compared to their prince. He seemed the epitome of human perfection, though Ethan thought he tended more feminine than a true man should. Before Alexar uttered a word, Ethan took a dislike to him as the man's arrogance shone in his entire bearing. Ethan guessed that Alexar and Jorus of similar age, but by appearances, Jorus looked twice the years of the Vellesian Prince.

"Rise," Alexar said dismissively, his left fore digit mimicking the order ever so slightly as Thela and Captain Lorelo gained their feet.

"Prince Alexar, may I present Jorus Darcannon, brother to the sea lord of Valconar. It is he whom Vellesia owes a great debt for our deliverance," Lady Thela declared, stepping aside as the two men faced one another from the decks of their respective ships.

"I extend the gratitude of Queen Valera for the return of her subjects," Alexar declared, regarding Jorus with a forced smile. "Are all our mage healers in your keeping?" he asked, though he already knew through a telepathic link with Lady Thela.

"We are honored to return *all* twelve of your mages with their lives and virtues intact, though I fear many of your countrymen under Captain Lorelo's command have sacrificed their lives in achieving this aim," Jorus's rough voice echoed, empathetic for the loss of such brave men.

"Unfortunate, though 'tis a small price for the safe return of our mage born," Alexar replied, unmoved by the loss of common born.

"Boy, this guy's a ray of sunshine," Ethan whispered in Allie's ear as she stood beside him amid the crew.

"Shhh," she reproached, hoping he would not draw unwanted attention.

"Permission to board?" Jorus asked his Vellesian counterpart, who ordered his men to stand aside, allowing Jorus to cross over the ship's side. Jorus motioned Lady Thela and Captain Lorelo to follow. Prince Alexar stole a furtive glance at Ethan, his dark-brown eyes staring into Ethan's blue, before turning sharply away. Ethan drew back a step, unnerved by the strange gesture. The look the prince gave him was not one of idle curiosity. It was a look one used to size up a foe. Ethan knew it well, for men used it whenever meeting someone new, but often in a subtle manner if the stranger posed no immediate threat. The look the Vellesian prince gave him indicated something else entirely; it was a measuring of a man you intended harm. The hairs on the back of his neck bristled as his right hand went to his holstered Colt.

"Ethan?" Allie turned to him, concern playing across her face.

"Something's not right, Allie."

Her concern turned to panic as she saw his hand grip the handle of his pistol. "Ethan, please. We are in no danger," she pleaded, placing a hand over his. Her mere touch immediately eased his racing heart. He wasn't sure what was more perplexing, the panic that the Vellesian prince wrought in his heart or the power of Allie's touch to take it away? Her power over him was not magical, as he was immune to magic and its properties. It felt more personal, as if she and she alone held sway over the trepidations of his heart.

Jorus and Alexar exchanged pleasantries before Lady Thela spoke at length to her prince pertaining to all that transpired since their abduction at Cordova.

Allie suddenly stepped away before one of Jorus's crew stumbled to the deck, coming swiftly to his side. She touched a hand to his forehead, reviving him instantly. Alexar and Thela cast a wary glance in Allie's direction before returning to their converse. Ethan came swiftly to her side to help her but backed away as he remembered that his proximity impaired her powers. The crewman gained his feet, feeling well but embarrassed by his sudden collapse.

"My thanks, my lady." He bowed.

"You are most welcome." Allie gifted him a smile.

"Is he all right?" Ethan asked, stepping to her side.

"Yes, he is faint by lack of water. He need only drink to restore himself." She assuaged the sailor's fears.

"Ethan!" Jorus's booming voice called out to him. "Come aboard, lad."

Ethan could see his friend waving his arm, beckoning him forth. Ethan sighed, wanting nothing to do with the pompous prince. "Come on, Allie, let's go."

She stopped. "Oh, Ethan, it would be inappropriate for a mere mage healer to come before a prince unbidden."

"Nonsense. You're with me." He smiled, dragging her along despite her protest. They climbed over the ship's side, stepping before the prince as his Vellesian guards withdrew several paces. Ethan found their behavior odd. If they were charged with protecting their prince, should they not remain close? It was as if they were aware of his unease. Or could they have originally intended him harm, but now changed their mind? But for what purpose would they attack? He had done their queen a great service in rescuing her mage healers. Perhaps his instincts were confused by his ordeal in the Mage Bane, but they had never led him astray, not even in Texas.

"Prince Ethanos, your legend precedes you," Alexar greeted him cordially. Ethan guessed the man couldn't fake a smile, so he hadn't bothered.

"Ethan, just plain ole Ethan, Alex. I gave up my title. You should do the same and join me in Cordova. We could always use former mage lords on our mage council. You could forgo all the pomp and ceremony of court. Kneel here, kneel there! It's all a bunch of nonsense if you ask me."

Alexar bristled uncomfortably. Ethan's referring to him as Alex was off-putting enough, but to suggest he foreswear allegiance to the throne was outright treason. Any other man making such bold declarations would be slapped in irons, but Alexar's instructions were clear—Ethan Blagen was to be granted a wide berth.

"'Tis a tempting offer, Prince Ethanos."

"Ethan," Ethan corrected him.

"Ethan." Alexar smiled tightly. "'Tis a tempting offer…Ethan, but my loyalties to Queen Valera preclude me from entertaining such selfish pursuits. I am, however, not above gratitude for your fell deeds on behalf of Vellesia. Queen Valera shall know of your brave intervention on our behalf."

"If your queen wishes to thank me, she can do so by seeing to the families of her men who lost their lives under Captain Lorelo's command. I doubt any of us would've survived without their sacrifice."

"Vellesia shall provide for the widows and orphans of our soldiers and sailors, as is our wont. Is there any boon you desire from the throne beyond this? Perhaps an audience with our queen could be arranged?"

Ethan shook his head. "No offense, Alex, but I don't fancy the company of royals, so I doubt I'll be paying your queen a visit in this life or any other."

Instead of taking offense, the Vellesian prince smirked as if privy to some jest that Ethan was unaware, but quickly corrected himself, his smirk swiftly transforming into stoic indifference. Despite the man's posture, he seemed out of sorts, as if death stared him in the face.

"So be it. We shall collect our people and make way for Brelar," Prince Alexar said.

"You still have some of your people at Lupen's Cove. You might—" Ethan said before Alexar interjected.

"Lord Darcannon and Captain Lorelo have already spoken of the matter. I shall dispatch a squadron to retrieve them and deal with any Palacians they find there."

Ethan's earlier panic transformed into bewilderment. The prince's queer behavior only proved that something was amiss, but what? Except for Allie, the Vellesians were an aloof and off-putting people. Even Captain Lorelo acted as if a great wall was erected between them. A younger Ethan would just assume they were a collection of nincompoops, but he knew better now. Something was not right, and he was certain that it centered around their rotten queen. They were deathly afraid of her for some reason, and even Allie seemed loath speaking of her, and when she did so, it was in hushed, carefully worded utterances.

Queen Valera, he thought sourly, his instincts screaming dire warnings at the mention of her name. An unsettling thought struck him, would Queen Valera punish Allie for her friendship with him? The thought of Allie suffering under her queen's cruel tyranny twisted Ethan's stomach. He wished to take her away to Cordova, freeing her from Queen Valera's dominion, but her devotion to her family would not allow it. There had to be another way, and he vowed to find it.

*****

The Vellesians collected their people from the Valconar ships and exchanged pleasantries before departing. Captain Lorelo offered a brief yet polite farewell to Ethan and Krixan, as did Lady Thela. Ethan drew Allie aside before returning to the *Falcon's Claw*.

"I don't know when our paths shall cross again, Allie, or what the fates intend, but I know we'll meet again. I don't know how or where, but my gut tells me this is so, and my instincts are never wrong," he said, holding her chin with a finger and thumb while staring into her bright golden eyes.

"I believe so as well," she gifted him the most beautiful smile, genuine and heartfelt, as if she knew it to be true.

"Be wary of your queen, Allie. If any harm befalls your family, make your way to Cordova. I will protect you. Your queen has no power over *me*."

"My family has endured in Vellesia for thousands of years, Ethan. I shall be safe. You just promise me that you shall return safely to Cordova, and no more adventures in the Mage Bane," she teasingly scolded, touching a finger to his nose.

"Yes, ma'am." He tipped his hat to her. "Besides, the only time I'll be leaving Cordova is during the winter solstice when I visit my family."

"I am pleased family means so much to you, Ethan."

"I love my freedom and the life I live, but I would give everything for my family."

She stared at him for the longest time, reflecting on his words while losing herself in his sea-blue eyes. "As would I," she said.

There, upon the deck of the *Golden Rose*, he took her into his arms and kissed her farewell.

CHAPTER 23

They were received with great praise upon their return to Cordova. Word had preceded them, relaying tales of their deeds in the Mage Bane. Before they traversed the tranquil waters of Shark's Bay, their legends and deeds far exceeded the truth. News spread through the tropic Port that Ethan faced down Luke's entire gang in the streets of Crepsos, killing them all before they could draw. Others told of Krixan tearing a shark apart with his bare hands as they gained the beach near Lupen's Cove. Others told of them both rescuing the Vellesian healers in the dead of night from an encampment of a thousand Palacian cavalry. Each retelling grew their deeds to omnipotent proportions. The entire city seemed to greet them upon their return, serried in thick ranks upon the stone wharves that lined the waterfront. The crews of the Valconar ships matched the zeal of the cheering throngs, thumping their chests and raising their scimitars in the air.

Ethan sighed, resting his forearms over the portside forecastle of the *Falcon's Claw*, surveying Cordova as if for the first time. He smiled slightly to the gathered crowds, tipping his hat to them at times, though they were unfamiliar with the gesture. The simple act, like most of his mannerisms and carriage, was entirely Texan. He was born in Astaria, lived in Cordova, but Texas was his home.

"A grand welcome!" Jorus's voice boomed, slapping Ethan's back while standing at his side.

"A right friendly people," Ethan conceded.

"Aye, lad, that they be, but wait until you visit Valconar. My people will put this reception to shame." Jorus grinned.

Ethan smiled at that, enjoying his new friend's jovial spirit. After suffering two years in the filthy hold of Noris Greybar's ship, Jorus had earned a lifetime of joy and good living. Of course he didn't have the heart to tell him that he could never return to the Mage Bane, even if it were the friendly city of Valconar. He thought on his broken promise to his mother. She was wrong about his suffering if he entered the Mage Bane, but it would serve no purpose to tempt the fates.

Soldiers in gray mail and gold tunics held back the crowds as the *Falcon's Claw* docked along the wharf, they were the personal guard of Arnos Pagge and would escort Ethan, Krixan, and Jorus to the city forum. The three men disembarked along with a dozen others, making their way through the cheering throngs. It was a brief walk from the wharf to the city forum. The long columns of gray and alabaster spiraled to the granite roof above, towering over the lower harbor like a mountain reigning over a weathered plain. Arnos Pagge, Hode Purciel, and Lady Julia awaited them atop the steps of the north face of the forum. Hode stood between the other two, his barrel chest, dark beard, and gruff manner belying his jovial nature. He looked as out of place as Ethan, wearing gray trousers and shirt, with black mail and gauntlets. He looked more warrior than oligarch. Arnos Pagge stood to his left, his rotund belly stretching the limits of his tunic and robes. Lady Julia posted to his right, her dark hair and bright eyes brought to life by her shimmering blue gown.

"Welcome home, Ethan!" Hode Purciel greeted him as they ascended the wide stone steps.

"Hode, Julia, Arnos." Ethan nodded to each of them. "May I introduce—"

"Jorus Darcannon." Hode grinned, interrupting Ethan's introduction.

"Hode." Jorus stepped forth, embracing his old friend.

Ethan and Krixan shared a look.

"Do you know each other?" Julia asked.

"Aye, my lady. Jorus's lord brother has purchased more iron from my mines than all the seven mage realms combined. Much of my wealth is credited to Valconar gold," Hode explained.

"It appears the benefits of our association continue with your champions' intervention on my behalf, Hode," Jorus said, placing a hand upon Krixan's and Ethan's shoulders.

"So we have been told," Hode regarded them with pride. They had freed Cordova of Cornan Thune's tyranny, established law and order, and rescued the Vellesian mages, and thus preserving peace between Queen Valera and the tropic port, they eliminated the threat of Luke Crawford and rescued Jorus Darcannon, earning Cordova the eternal friendship of Valconar.

"Perhaps this shall herald a new golden age for Cordova. A time to strengthen old friendships and partake the bounty of peace," Julia declared. She still recalled her unfortunate first interaction with Ethanos, mistaking him for an unlearned peasant. She regretted her temporary alliance with Cornan Thune, though at the time, he was the only hope Cordova possessed to retain their independence. Ethan changed all of that like a strong wind cleansing foul odor from still air. He swept into Cordova like a comet across a midnight sky, transforming their world before their very eyes. Despite her aiding Thune, Ethan offered her forgiveness and a purpose in restoring justice and security to the city. Looking out over the gathered assemblage, she couldn't help but see the hope and gaiety that shone upon every face. They were freemen, and Ethan instilled pride in them for that. She felt pride in that, to be part of something grand. Ethan's mere presence stayed the hand of any mage king intent to move against Cordova and allowed the city time to replenish its mage council. Free mages across the seven mage kingdoms rushed to Cordova not to conquer but to join in its defense.

"Citizens of Cordova!" Arnos Pagge spoke aloud in a deeper voice than any thought he possessed. "Let us rejoice this day in our victory over the Palacian monarch who would make himself our master. Let us rejoice this day the death of the cur who slew our mage council, Luke Crawford. Let us celebrate the destruction of Greybar's squadron at the hands of our sheriff and his chief deputy. Most of all, let us rejoice in the preservation of our vital bonds of peace with Vellesia and the friendship of Valconar. Today we celebrate..."

Arnos continued to espouse the virtues of their city and the blessings bestowed upon them as if so ordered by a higher power.

She stood amid the crowd, her amethyst eyes masked within her cowl as she observed the Astarian prince upon the high steps of the forum. Her monarch was wroth. Their prey had eluded them once again, foiling destiny and ruining their carefully laid plans. For now she was to merely observe, interceding only to eliminate potential problematic eventualities. Otherwise, she would wait for her monarch to reveal their next move.

*****

The summer months passed quickly. Cordova was always a center of change and the exchange of ideas, as it rested in the middle of the Aqualania Sea, straddling the trade routes that connected all of the seven mage kingdoms and the realms of the Mage Bane. Any news entering Cordova exited the city to every corner of Elaria. Word spread that a former Astarian prince took up residence in the tropic port as its prime defender, igniting the mage realms with wonder, euphoria, hope, and fear. Over the following months, dozens of free mages flocked to the city to join its mage council. Many were second sons or daughters of lesser houses, drawn to the freedom that Cordova offered. Most mage born were spellbound to serve their monarchs and higher lords, but lesser mages often were not spellbound until they reached maturity. These fortunate few were able to flee their households to join those of like mind in Cordova. It was an oversight that many kings would rectify by forcing the spell bond upon the mage born at an earlier age. In the interim, however, Cordova gained dozens of mages of varying gifts. With Ethan shielding the new mage council from more powerful mage lords, the council was nigh invincible. Lady Julia presided as the archmage of the council, though Ethan insisted she use the title of president, which she found strange but obliged him.

With the mage council rebuilt and strengthened to levels not seen since the golden age of Cordova's glory, Hode Purciel oversaw the expansion of the city's trading empire. With renewed ties to

Valconar and free port, the city elders reached similar accords with Vellesia and Estasa. By late summer the city welcomed the sea lord of Valconar with great celebration. The ruling oligarchs announced a holiday, and the city streets were filled with drunken revelry for two days. Lord Darcannon joined Ethan and Krixan in toasting their new friendship, draining casks in every tavern along the street of ale. The man was even larger than his brother, nearly as tall as Krixan with Jorus's graying gold mane. Ethan and Krixan relayed their adventures in Red Rock and Astaria while the sea lord spoke of his days of youth, sailing the length of the Aqualania Sea. They drank through the night, listening to his lively tales of shipwrecks, mutinies, pirates, and fair maidens. In the wee hours of that summer night, the sea lord slapped each upon the shoulder, thanking them for saving his brother from the wretched hold of Greybar's ship. The moment reminded Ethan of those nights in Red Rock when they gathered around Ben's desk playing cards and listening to Judge Donovan's tall tales. He missed his friends and planned to visit them after the winter festival in Astaris. He promised his family he would return to celebrate the winter solstice. He wondered how he'd be received now that he took up residence in Cordova. Unlike the other mage kingdoms, which responded to Cordova's ascendency with curiosity, ambivalence, or open hostility, Astaria was silent. Perhaps his father wished not to intervene in his son's life, gifting him the freedom he so longed sought. No matter his father's reasons, he would know his mind when he returned home.

Though he missed his friends in Red Rock and his family in Astaris, Ethan savored his freedom and looked to each new day with wonder. The only regret clouding his mood, however, was Allie. He dreaded returning her to her queen, wondering how she fared in that oppressive realm. He felt something amiss among the other Vellesians, something he could not discern, but his instincts told him was wrong. Wrong was perhaps too light a word, his instincts *screamed* in alarm in the presence of the Vellesian prince. Upon their return to Cordova, the Vellesians sent emissaries to treat with the ruling oligarchs, offering favorable trading terms and exclusive navigation rights for Cordovan flagged vessels. Though the city greeted the

Vellesians' offer with expected elation, Ethan liked it not. He knew they had ulterior motives, which he could not discern. He gave little voice to his misgivings, with nothing to sway opinion other than his base instinct. What he found even more disconcerting was his interaction with Vellesian commoners. Cordova was filled with countless ex-patriots from every mage realm save Vellesia. Former commoners from Gorgencia, Estasa, Sarcosa, Relusia, and Meltoria relayed heart-rending tales of the oppression in their homelands. They spoke of mage lords claiming bed rights to the wives of their subjects, often forcing men to raise their by-blows. Some lords claimed 90 percent of their subjects yields, leaving poorer farmers with little to feed their families.

One mage lord stood out from his contemporaries in his cruelty, the crown prince of Gorgencia, Prince Borcose. Like his father, he possessed the ability to spellbound animals to his will, but he also was gifted with molten hands that alit at will, emitting heat powerful enough to melt steel. Prince Borcose would wield his mage gift with impunity, taking wicked pleasure in chastising his subjects for trivial offenses real or perceived. He was known to maim those who failed to quickly bow in his presence or did not avert their eyes swiftly enough. He would brand their flesh with his bare hands, perhaps disfiguring their faces or blinding their eyes. He might melt hands or feet or leave painful burns along their limbs. Sometimes he would do such things for mere amusement, or out of boredom. His father, King Gregor, did nothing to curb his son's depravity. If there were any reason to doubt the mage born's fitness to rule, then Prince Borcose was it.

Despite the countless tales of mage-born cruelty, Ethan heard nary an utterance from those born of Vellesia. None spoke against their queen or realm. At first glance, it was expected as those he conversed with were merchants and sailors still serving under Queen Valera's sigil. What struck Ethan as strange was he could find no one among the thousands of ex-patriots that took up residence in Cordova who hailed from Vellesia. It was as if no one ever left that far-off land. Of the Vellesian merchants, tradesmen and sailors that visited Cordova, not a one spoke ill of their kingdom or queen. Only

Allie had spoken freely, and only when they were in the Mage Bane, where magic held no sway upon her tongue. She spoke of the queen's cruelty and mysterious powers.

Ethan's misgivings about the Vellesian queen only intensified in late summer when word reached Cordova that Queen Valera sent a small flotilla to Estasa, commanded by her uncle, Prince Alexar. The small fleet was to tour the Upper Aqualania Sea, making ports of call to each of the coastal mage realms.

Alas.

Those plans went amiss when the Vellesian flagship, the *Golden Rose, exploded* while anchored in Talesia, the chief port of Astaria, with Prince Alexar aboard. It was grounds for war between Astaria and Vellesia, unless diplomacy could prevail. As yet, no banners were called or armies mustered. If war were to erupt, Cordova was certain to be affected as it lies at the center of the trading routes connecting the two kingdoms. Despite the affront to their honor, the Vellesians presented no hint of hostility toward Astaria. Soon an accord was reached to negotiate a lasting peace, the details of which would be settled at a later time. Many in Cordova released a grateful sigh. Wars had a tendency to destroy those in the periphery as well as those in the battle's path. The oligarchs of Cordova preferred to build their fortunes through peacetime trade rather than the volatility and risk that wars incur.

Ethan was perhaps the only one displeased. He trusted the Vellesians not and almost preferred war. If war broke out, he would return to Astaria and help his people. He proved at the Velo how he and his father working in tandem, could defeat any mage-led army in Greater Elaria. With his father beside him, and he beside his father, Ethan knew they would prevail, and only war could unveil the Vellesian threat that his instincts screamed to him to be wary of. It mattered little now as it seemed peace would prevail. He was struck by something Sheriff Thorton once told him: peace is not the absence of war but the liberty of all people.

CHAPTER 24

"Damn that woman!" King Bronus ground his teeth as Dragos relayed the missive.

"Her uncle, Prince Alexar, was killed, Bronus. You had to expe—" Dragos began to explain before his daughter's husband cut him off.

"And what does her uncle's death have to do with us? His blasted ship exploded in *our* port. If we were to blame, why would we put our people at risk?" Bronus growled, pacing his private sanctum like a caged bear.

"She hasn't placed blame upon us, Bronus. But she mustn't ignore the offense, lest she lose face before the other kingdoms and her own vassals," Dragos said.

"By her suggestions, she is most certainly assigning blame. If we are innocent of this crime, why must we parlay to negotiate a truce?"

"She understands our position," Dragos answered, tucking his hands into the sleeves of his azure robes.

"What is it Queen Valera wants, then?" Bronus asked.

"A joint parlay to include *all* the monarchs of the seven mage kingdoms to meet in Astaria before the winter solstice," Dragos explained.

"The winter solstice!" Bronus thundered. "Why in the blazes of creation would I ruin our holiday by filling the palace with the royal asses of Elaria! For what purpose would we invite the crown heads of the seven kingdoms to Astaria?"

"She has two reasons. The first is to gather the mage royals of Elaria to create a forum through which the realms can settle their disputes through negotiation and compromise, rather than war, with the other mage monarchs mediating."

"As if I'd trust other mage kings to be honest brokers in any dispute!" Bronus growled. "What's her second reason?"

"To have all seven mage realms bear witness to a lasting peace between our two kingdoms, to demonstrate how such mediation would work."

"But what does she want?" Bronus snorted irritability, his temper ready to explode.

"She asks for a consort for the crown princess of Vellesia from one of our noble houses." Dragos sighed.

"Tristan is my heir and I'll not part—"

"Queen Valera states that she makes no claim on our crown prince. She asks that you invite the sons of your high lords to Astaris during her visit. They must come of their own free will, and the princess will make her choice. Second or lesser sons of your high lords are to be given equal consideration."

"That's all she wants? A stud for her daughter's bed?"

"Must you be so crass?" Gabrielle finally spoke as she stood by the window. Only the three of them held counsel, and she had held her tongue while her father and husband discussed Queen Valera's terms. He would have to curb his base language if they were to host the mage royals of Elaria. Bronus often complained about Ethanos's willful nature and coarse tongue, but he was a mild wind to his father's volatile tempest. She found it humorous that Bronus complained insistently about the very traits in Ethanos's character that most resembled his own.

"Why would the Vellesian queen ask for a son of a lesser house from a foreign realm? Why not a second son of a royal line or one of her own noble houses to strengthen the ties in her own kingdom?" Bronus wondered.

"To diversify their bloodline, most likely. There hasn't been a joining of House Loria to any Astarian house in recorded memory. She will choose the strongest mage blood available, no doubt," Dragos surmised.

"She tried that before," Bronus reminded them.

"Aye, that she did, but now she aims lower." Dragos narrowed his eyes. Queen Valera approached Bronus when Ethan was an infant about a match to her daughter, but Bronus refused to surrender his heir. Of course that was *before* anyone other than Bronus, Gabrielle, and Dragos knew that Ethan was void of magic or else the Vellesian queen would not have made the offer. Soon after she asked for Tristan's hand, once it was known that he possessed strong mage gifts worthy of a royal consort. Any other mage king would gladly see their second son so placed, ensuring their grandchildren would rule two of the seven mage kingdoms, but Bronus again refused. Valera never asked again for a son of Astaria—until now.

"Tell her we agree to her terms. Inform our lords of what is expected of them," Bronus declared.

*****

Two months hence

Astaris was alive with activity. Evor Ectus, king of Estasa was first to enter the Astarian capital, leading a great van of courtiers, nobles, and mages of his kingdom. He was slight of build with silvered hair and trimmed beard. He wore bright azure mail with a leaping fish upon his crest. Two score of his personal guard followed in columns of two, passing underneath the towering walls of Astaris.

Magnus Delmarin, king of Relusia, followed thereafter, wearing light armor hued in gray and gold. He was loath returning to the place of his utter humiliation after his defeat at the Velo but agreed to meet on equal footing with his fellow monarchs. Ortovan Marvo followed, equally loath to return, but hopeful that a new paradigm of cooperation might negate the advantage that Astaria held since the Velo.

Gregor Vorhenz, king of Gorgencia, brought the largest contingent to the gathering of kings, leading a host of hundreds, including his son and heir, Borcose. The Gorgencian crown prince rode beside his father wearing a rich burgundy doublet and puffed trousers. He was gold of hair, large of build with a plump, childish face that did not fit his stature. King Gregor was slim of build and tall of stature, with a mocking sneer that appeared permanently affixed. As he was able to bind the will of animals, two spotted leopards preceded his black destrier as if they were tame as kittens. King Gregor wore gray mail over green livery, with a stallion emblazoned upon his crest, the sigil of his royal house.

Karl Lorga, king of Sarcosa, followed two days after, his caravan laden with gold, gems, and carpets of his tropic kingdom. His guards were clad in flesh-colored tunics and golden mail. Scores of Sarcosan merchants in desert robes accompanied the royal retinue. The Sarcosan king wore silken robs of azure and purple, forgoing armor for comfort. He had dark-olive skin, a lean build, and black curly hair that peaked below the cowl of his robes.

Bronus and Gabrielle greeted each arrival with the formal dignity that was due a visiting crown royal as they waited upon the palace green between the inner keep and the towering walls of the citadel. Scores of the king's knights lined either side of the palace green, standing beside their mounts with resplendent black armor that matched the hue of their horses. Ceresta, Arian, and Felicia stood behind their parents, each adorned in silver gowns with ebony sashes. Tristan was absent, sent to the northwestern border under the guise of inspecting the fortifications at the conjoint of the Gorgencian border and the wilds.

The Vellesian delegation entered last, led by two hundred royal knights in gold mail over red tunics, riding underneath a black banner with a gold rose centered upon its field. The Vellesian knights passed under the portcullis of the citadel, parading to either side before dismounting to stand beside their mounts. They were followed by scores of mages, both male and female, adorned in the robes of their mage caste. The mages filed to either side, dismounting as a dozen richly decorated carriages followed. Each carriage stopped one by one upon the palace green as two footmen stepped down from the back of each carriage, lowering the step below each door and bowing as their passengers stepped without. Each carriage carried members of Queen Valera's high council, each a mage of utmost ability.

The last carriage to enter was drawn by eight bronze coated horses. It was thrice the size of the preceding carriages, plated in gold with silver inlays and four footmen instead of two. It was flanked by a dozen queen's guards wearing silver breastplates over snow-white tunics with pleated kilts. Silver greaves protected their nearly naked legs. Their helms covered their upper face, with wide slits for their eyes to scan afield. Large circled shields hung upon their backs, and silver gauntlets graced each forearm and hand. They dismounted in unison as a dozen squires hurried forth to take their reins. The guards circled to the left side of the carriage that faced the dais, forming two facing lines to either side of the carriage door. The footmen lowered the step and opened the carriage door, bowing low as a young woman stepped without. Dark auburn hair was woven into a high weave that touched her narrow shoulders. A thin silver crown nestled in her hair, lined with gems, rubies, and sapphires along its face. Her flawless olive skin shone a healthy glow. Her golden gown matched the hue of her eyes. Her gown hung off her shoulders, baring her neck and upper bosom while wrapping tightly to her corset before its full skirts billowed freely below her narrow waist. Stepping down upon the firm grass, she lifted her golden eyes, surveying her surroundings with curious apprehension. The queen's guards and footmen knelt in unison as she stepped down from the carriage, dropping to both knees with heads bowed. As the girl's eyes swept the prestigious assemblage arrayed to either side of Bronus and Gabrielle, the Astarian court gasped at the beauty of the girl. Her high cheekbones, flush olive skin, small upturned nose and exquisitely feminine charms took the breath of any man to set eyes upon her. She gifted a smile that failed to reach her eyes before stepping to the side and kneeling as a footman laid a cloth beneath her so her dress would not be soiled.

The next occupant of the carriage stepped without, a woman wearing a dark burgundy gown similar in fit and design to the first. She was taller than the girl by half a head, with midnight black hair rolling to her shoulders and a crown resting upon it. The band of the crown was wider than the girl's, forged of pure gold with large diamonds set along its length. The woman was quite tall, nearly seventy inches, with dark almond eyes that bespoke an older age than her younger face revealed. At first glance, she appeared no older than two decades, but her eyes revealed a darker truth. Her skin was olive, and her sharp cheekbones and feminine countenance were entirely similar to the girl, indicating their kinship.

As the woman stepped fully onto the palace green, the entirety of the Vellesian delegation, knights, mages, and courtiers, knelt with heads bowed in deep reverence to their queen, Valera.

Valera smiled with a warmth that radiated as she passed between her column of kneeling guards as the first girl gained her feet to follow.

"King Bronus," she greeted as she drew nigh, appraising the monarch with feigned interest. "And Queen Gabrielle," she regarded the Astarian queen beside him.

"Queen Valera, welcome to Astaris," Bronus greeted her with as genuine a smile as he could muster.

Gabrielle stepped forth, taking Valera's hands into hers. "Queen Valera, we are most honored by your visit. May you find Astaris suitable for your stay. We know you have journeyed long and are most weary. My stewards shall see to your peoples' lodging."

"You are most kind, Queen Gabrielle. I am certain to find Astaris a welcome respite from my travels. May this gathering herald a new age of cooperation and civility between the mage realms of Elaria, and thus an end to pointless bloodshed. To peace, my sister." Valera smiled, her eyes sparkling with sincerity.

"Perhaps…if all realms were ruled by queens in place of kings, then wars would be properly rendered obsolete," Gabrielle whispered for Valera's ear only before gifting her a mischievous wink.

"I have been told that Astaria has a wise and gracious queen. It is good to know that my advisors are well informed. May I introduce my daughter, Princess Amanda." Valera retrieved her hands from Gabrielle's loose grip, stepping aside to allow the Astarian king and queen a view of the comely maiden in the blue gown. "Come forth, Amanda!"

The Vellesian princess stepped froth, dropping into a deep curtsy before her mother, and the Astarian king and queen. "It is an honor to be so received, Your Graces," Amanda said.

"You are most lovely, Princess." Gabrielle smiled, taking Amanda's hand in her own. "You will make one of our young lords a fortunate man." Gabrielle thought it a pity the girl was not a second daughter of Valera, for she would make a fetching bride for Tristan.

"You are most kind." Amanda curtsied again.

"I would like you to meet our own daughters, Ceresta, Arian, and Felicia. Come hither, girls," Gabrielle commanded as they each in turn stepped forth, offering deep curtsies.

"Your daughters are quite fetching. 'Tis a pity my son, Prince Raymar, was unable to accompany us. He would have been pleased to make their acquaintance," Valera complimented.

"An equal misfortune that our sons are absent and unable to see your lovely daughter," Gabrielle offered in kind.

"Prince Tristan is absent?" Valera asked, unable to mask her disappointment.

"He is attending delicate matters of state that require his deft hand. Ethan, however, has assured me that he would return before the winter solstice," Gabrielle said.

"Ethan? Oh, yes…Ethanos, your firstborn. 'Tis a shame he has forsaken his royal privilege and is void of magic, if the rumors are to be believed," Valera said. "But he is not without honor. My mages spoke of his timely intervention on their behalf during their visit to Cordova."

At this Gabrielle perked. "What did they say?"

"I only know that he saved them from men who possessed strange projectile weapons. He was most helpful, and you should be very proud."

"We are." Gabrielle smiled.

"I am told you have a number of suitors of proper suitability for my purview?" Valera asked. "Of course, Amanda will desire one fair of countenance while I wish for a choice strong in magic and mind. A man of dull wit will likely sire a child much the same."

Amanda blushed at her mother's coarse tongue.

"Come," Gabrielle offered, inviting Valera and Amanda forth. The young suitors from the noble houses of Astaria awaited behind their king, each standing rigidly as if under military review, dressed in their finery. Gabrielle and Bronus led the Vellesian queen and princess down the line, introducing each suitor by name and house.

Before stepping forth, Valera signaled her people to rise, allowing them to gain their feet.

Allie lifted her head from her place along the line of mages, several ranks behind the royal guards. She desperately searched the crowd in vain hope of finding Ethan. It was for naught as her eyes swept the assembled lords and ladies that loitered along the periphery to witness the first meeting of the Vellesian and Astarian royal families. She recognized several royals of other mage houses among the onlookers. Princess Serena Lorga of Sarcosa stood between the crown prince of Estasa and Crown Prince Borcose Vorhenz. Even from afar, she could see the superior airs those princelings projected, as if their station was above all others. Allie knew them for fools. Ethan was their better, even without his crown. She would choose him above all others if the choice presented itself.

She sighed in exasperation, her hopes of finding Ethan in Astaris dimming with her spirit. He often spoke of returning home before the winter solstice. Was he delayed? Did he change his plans?

There are still twenty days until the winter solstice, she remembered, scolding herself for her negativity. She would use this time to know Ethan's home. Her mother promised her as much free time as she wished, to explore the palace and would make good use of that freedom. The higher placed mages would be required to attend the queen throughout her stay, but the lesser mages would be rarely required. She sorely hoped Ethan would come, or this visit would be intolerable.

*****

He leaned back, using his saddle for a pillow with his hands tucked behind his head as he stared into the campfire. Bull was tethered to a nearby tree, and Krixan was off to his right, using his saddle for a chair as he rubbed his aching feet. Fortunately for Ethan, he was upwind of his friend's awful foot odor, but the stench was often such that it made little difference. They had set ashore leagues east of Talesia, in the small port of Tornada, avoiding the major causeways and cities along their journey, for Ethan's presence caused a stir wherever he went, and they hoped to avoid as much delay such fanfare incurred. He would journey home to Astaris but by a route of his choosing. Ethan circumvented the population centers and well-used thoroughfares, skirting the Lavarnum Ridge and the Moro River.

"Would it have pained us to spend at least *one* night in a comfortable inn?" Krixan complained.

"And miss spending these cool autumn nights under the stars? We should enjoy this while we can, big fella. Once we get home, it will be nothing but soft beds, hot food, and warm blankets," Ethan said as if those were bad things.

"You're right, Ethan. What was I thinking." Krixan rolled his eyes. He often wondered if his friend was hit on the head one too many times. *Enjoy the night air*, Ethan had said the first night on the trail before they were drenched in a downpour while they slept. Three days out of Tornada, they came upon an apple tree and Ethan insisted on feeding some to Bull, knowing full well that it caused the beast to pass gas. The stench was so noxious that it trailed for miles. A skunk would make for a better-smelling companion. Ethan hadn't voiced any complaint about Krixan's foot odor, and if he did, the big man would be sure to counter with Ethan's feeding Bull those apples.

"I wonder how Nils is handling his promotion?" Ethan wondered aloud. Nils Purciel, the boisterous, rough-speaking younger brother of Hode Purciel, was the first deputy Ethan had hired as sheriff of Cordova. With Ethan and Krixan absent from their duties for at least two months, while they visit Astaris, they put Nils' name forward before the ruling council as an acting sheriff. They approved the appointment, and Ethan left a pair of pistols, a Winchester .30-30 rifle, and a score of spare rounds that he had taken from Luke's men. He had similarly outfitted two other deputies from the weapons taken from Luke's men, leaving Cordova well equipped to deal with Emmitt Cobb or the other Texans should they return. With a rebuilt mage council and a functioning sheriff's department, as well as a dozen private small armies, he doubted Emmitt would chance a return to Cordova any time soon.

"If he handles the job the way you play cards, we're all in deep trouble," Krix mumbled loud enough for Ethan to hear as he removed his other boot.

"That hurts, Krix. I'm not that bad at cards," he responded in a tone that didn't even convince himself. He brought three packs of cards with him from Red Rock, gifting one to Lord Darcannon upon his visit at Cordova. He bitterly recalled the late summer night when Lord Darcannon, Krixan, Nils, Hode, and two of his deputies gathered around his desk as he taught them poker. Ethan wrongfully thought they'd be easy game as he was used to playing with experienced players like Ben, Skeeter, and the judge. Alas, it was not to be as each was a quick learner. Ethan didn't win a single hand and finished the night down a month's pay. Lord Darcannon lauded the game and vowed to reprint copies of the deck Ethan had gifted him and bring poker to his fair city. Nils Purciel managed to win a second deck off Ethan and vowed to similarly spread the game in Cordova. Krixan grinned inwardly, knowing it was driving Ethan mad when he confronted a skill he couldn't master. Ethan was lousy at poker because was a lousy liar, and he wondered how he'd manage keeping his little visit to the Mage Bane from his mother. Krixan, of course, would never lie to Queen Gabrielle, and even if he did, she would merely read his thoughts anyway. Of course, Krixan wouldn't reach Astaris until after the solstice festival as he would be visiting his own family in Vectus, which was a good two days ride ahead. Ethan would go on alone for the last leg of the journey, and Krixan hoped his friend could manage it without getting into some sort of mischief. Krixan planned to continue on to Astaris after the holiday, spending no more than a day collecting Ethan before journeying to Plexus, to again cross the boundary. Sheriff Thorton and Judge Donovan would be happy to know that he and Ethan still lived and that Luke Crawford did not.

*****

I hope this plan of yours works, Queen Valera spoke wordless, her mind linked through telepathy as she stared out the window of her chamber. The waxing moon cast its pale light upon her face, lighting her countenance in otherworldly light.

It shall, Mother, just as we have foreseen. The pieces are aligning as required.

There are too many working parts, all moving independently, for me to be assured of success, Valera said doubtfully.

The many parts are little cause of worry, Mother, for we can mold and direct their course with ease. There is but one *part that is beyond our control, and we must trust our prophecies in delivering him into our hands.*

A part that is wild, dangerous, and highly unpredictable, Valera warned.

But necessary, and upon which our house has waited for countless centuries. Waiting patiently as we bide our time, gathering the power to ourselves as the other mage realms warred one upon the other through the millennia. The time of our ascension is at hand.

And all of Elaria shall fall under our dominion if…if that one, *unfettered, volatile force, of which we have no control, follows the path we have laid before him.*

Control? No. Influence? Yes. Magic alone is not our only weapon, Mother, and should our plan fail, there are alternatives.

*****

The city of Vectus straddled either bank of the Torlin, resting mid-distance between Astaris and Larose. The city walls, thrice the height of a man, circled the ancient city in a band of ivory, resplendent in the autumn sun. Towering citadels in a myriad of hues, spiraled above the surrounding edifices, their smooth walls and massive bulwarks testament to their spell-forged origin. Stone structures hued in crimson, emerald, purple, beige, gold, and sky blue, dotted the city, interspersed with oak and maple trees along the avenues, their summer green yielding to autumn gold and brown.

Ethan and Krixan passed through the city gate, gathering a crowd as they traversed the streets that led to the fortress keep of Kraxen Kraglar, arms master of Vectus, commander of the city guard, and friend of Bronus Blagen. Having passed through the city on their way to Cordova half a year before, Krixan and Ethan were unmistakable in their six-shooters and Stetsons. Servants attended their horses as they were ushered into the keep, where Krixan's Mother, Lara, greeted them with warm hugs and a kiss upon their cheeks. She was a well-built woman, tall yet shapely, with hints of gray in her long brown hair, betraying her true age. She had birthed nine healthy children, including six sons, each of which stood broad of shoulder, bald of head, and each taller than Ethan. Yet none of Lara's children were as large as her firstborn son, Krixan. He had fostered since his sixth year in the royal house of Astaris, returning to his home keep each autumn with Crown Prince Ethanos. Ethan grew to manhood considering Kraglar's keep his second home, and Lady Lara like a doting aunt.

"You are a sight for a mother's eyes." Lara teared as she cupped Krixan's heavy chin.

"Agghh, Mother, I'm all right."

Ethan grinned, seeing his large friend's sheepish reaction to his mother. The mere sight of a nearly seven-foot giant being coddled by his mother made him chuckle.

"Krixan, Ethanos!" the booming voice of Kraxen Kraglar sounded as his heavy boots slapped the stone floor.

"Father," Krixan regarded his sire.

"Mr. Kraglar," Ethan said respectfully. For one prone to call men by their given name and expect the same in return, Ethan could never refer to Krixan's father than anything other than *mister* or *sir*. Kraxan stood near to Krixan's height and equaled his girth, with steel bands wrapped around his massive arms.

Several of Krixan's brothers and sisters filtered into the main hall, each embracing their long-absent brother and Ethan, whom they had come to accept as part of their family. After a brief exchange of hugs, greetings, and back-slapping, the family retired to the dining chamber, where Lady Lara and her daughters served food. They brought out platters of roasted chicken, beef, carrots, corn, warm bread, and flagons of ale. It was enough to feed an army, but the Kraglar clan cleaned them bare in minutes. Ethan had long ago learned to take his fill when given the chance or he'd likely starve.

"We were hoping to see you boys soon. Started to wonder when you would show," Kraxen said, stuffing a fork full of chicken in his mouth.

"It's been an eventful last few months, sir. If It weren't for Krix, I would have been dead many times over," Ethan said.

"Dead?" Krixan snorted. "I couldn't keep you alive no matter how hard I tried with the way you throw yourself in harm's way. It's a miracle we're still breathing."

"Let's hear it. What happened since you left?" Kraxen asked.

Ethan proceeded to tell their tale, expounding Krixan's heroics and deemphasizing their time in the Mage Bane. He inwardly cringed knowing that the Kraglar clan would eventually inform his mother of his broken promise, whether they spoke of it offhandedly or she read it in their thoughts. At the tale's conclusion, the Kraglar patriarch slapped the table in approval, wishing he were younger and reliving his adventures he shared with Ethan's sire. Kraxan told the boys of Bronus's renowned drinking ability and that he was the only man to best Kraxen in the cups.

"I hear tell that you've bested your sire on repeated occasions, Ethan," Kraxen added.

"Yeah," Ethan said slowly. "I hate to boast, but—"

"He cheats," Krixan snorted. Ethan had finally admitted such to his friend during their time in Red Rock. Thankfully his mother, Dragos, and his sisters hadn't picked that information from Krixan's thoughts while they were last in Astaris.

"Hah! I wondered how a lad of your stature bested the mighty Bronus Blagen. I wish I could see him on the day he finds the truth. If I were you, lad, I'd head for the high country before he swats you." Kraxan grinned.

"He's swatted me before, I'm used to it," Ethan mumbled.

"You tell your father I'll accept his invite to Astaris after the winter solstice. You tell him I'm still up to a challenge if he provides the kegs."

"I'll do that." Ethan smiled.

Kraxen's jovial mood suddenly darkened with deadly seriousness. "Many strange happenings going on in Astaris, Ethan. I received a missive a fortnight ago, from Lord Dragos informing me that a large number of foreign dignitaries would be traversing the road to Astaris through Vectus. He said we are to see to their accommodations as they pass through and to speak not of what we see. There have been countless caravans ferrying high lords from Estasa, Sarcosa, and Vellesia, all traveling to Astaris for some purpose we can only surmise," Kraxen warned.

"High lords from foreign lands are gathering in Astaris?" Ethan made a face, wondering their purpose. The thought of the palace filled with pompous foreign lords during his visit made him ill. Why would his father invite them during his visit? "Which foreign lords?" he asked.

"No one knows." Kraxen shook his head. "They would name only the kingdom they hailed from, not their titles or the houses they serve. Very strange indeed."

Ethan wondered if his father sought a foreign bride for his brother. That would explain his inviting foreign lords to Astaris, but if that were so, why invite so many? Wouldn't those not chosen be insulted? Or did he seek matches for his sisters as well, arranging all his children's betrothals at once? No, he reminded himself, his father would have sent word to him if he intended such an important announcement.

"We've heard other rumors from the east and west, news that similar caravans were making their way to Astaris from Meltoria, Relusia, and Gorgencia. Magnus Delmarin was rumored to be among them."

Representatives from *all* the mage kingdoms of Elaria ruled out betrothal arrangements for their primary purpose. Something was afoot, perhaps a council of kings to parlay peace since the incident at Talesia.

Ethan rested poorly that night, his mind trying to decipher the information. He needed to leave come sun up. Something was amiss in Astaris, and his father would have need of him, even if he were too proud and stubborn to admit it.

*****

Ethan bade Krixan farewell the following morn, his friend following him to the northwest gate. Krixan promised to follow the day after the winter festival. He knew Ethan was eager to return to Red Rock to share the news of Luke Crawford's demise and assure the sheriff and the judge that they were still alive.

Just beyond the city gate, Ethan circled his mount around to face his friend. He rested one hand on the pommel, lifting the rim of his Stetson with the other. "Enjoy your time with your family, Krix. I'll look for you at Astaris."

"Aye," the big man grunted.

"I never say this often, big fella, but thanks. You've always been there for me, no matter what trouble I managed to get us into."

"You're a good man, Ethan, but you're a better friend," Krix rarely spoke in so many words or so fondly. Often the affection they felt for one another went unsaid.

"You'll always be my brother, Krix, and I couldn't imagine any of our adventures without you."

"Bah! Life would be dull without your adventures, Ethan. I reckon I'll tag along on our next one," he said in a perfect Texas drawl, surprising Ethan after struggling for two years with his native accent.

Ethan extended his arm, shaking Krixan's hand before turning Bull about and heading north.

"Try to keep out of trouble while I'm gone!" Krixan hollered as Ethan passed from sight, his silhouette disappearing in a grove of pines that straddled either side of the road north.

CHAPTER 25

He rode swiftly through the vale along the Upper Torlin, keeping the river to his right as a brisk autumn wind swept down from the Por-Shada Mountains. Avoiding the river bottom, where villages dotted either bank of the Torlin, Ethan kept to the hillsides. Riding through a forest of oak and maple, he looked up at their autumn leaves painted in crimson and gold. He loved the fall with its changing colors and cooling winds. He longed to see his family and join in the festivities of the winter solstice. It was always a time of sharing, music, and laughter. This would be his first festival as plain ole Ethan, not prince or lord, merely a man free of title and obligation. No man knelt to him and he knelt to no man. He wondered if his father had forgiven him his royal request?

The valley green soon gave way to the Por-Shada Plateau. In the distance, rising above the plateau and overlooking the Upper Torlin valley, was Astaris. From the foot of the plateau, he saw its azure towers spiraling into the heavens and the smooth gray road that wound its way up to the palace. Drawing nearer, he could see the spelled walls of silver blue rise in sheer vertical angles in varying heights of fifty to one hundred fifty feet.

As Ethan neared the main gate, with its watchtowers rising to either side, he wondered how he would be received. He promised his mother that he would return for the winter festival, but he had been away for a very long time. He was also alone, having bid Krixan farewell at Vectus. Ethan took a deep breath and approached the main gate.

*****

"Prince Ethanos?" The guards at the main gate heralded, recognizing their former crown prince.

"Just Ethan. If you boys call me prince again, I'll whop you upside your heads." Ethan grinned.

"Welcome then, Pr...Ethan." The captain of the gate returned the lighthearted grin.

"How goes it in the palace, Captain?"

"Crowded, Ethan. I heard you would return for the winter festival, but I thought you would wait until *after* the wedding."

"What wedding?" Ethan asked, leaning forward in his saddle with his hands on the pommel.

"What wedding! You truly do not know?" The captain shook his head.

"Enlighten me, then. It's not my brother or sisters, is it?" he asked. Though Ethan hated weddings as well as all formal ceremonies, he would attend if it were one of his siblings.

"No. The Vellesian crown princess is choosing a consort from the noble houses of Astaria. Lords of all our great houses have gathered, each offering their sons for the Vellesian princess's purview. The princess has yet to choose. All the high monarchs of the seven mage kingdoms have gathered to enforce the terms of the treaty."

"What treaty?" Ethan's brain was struggling to sort all that the captain was saying.

The captain gave Ethan a timeless look as if he had fallen from the sky or passed through another barrier. "The treaty to appease Vellesia of the death of their admiral, Prince Alexar. It seems the Vellesian crown princess has yet to wed, and her mother, the queen, has requested Astaria to provide a suitable candidate as recompense. Your father agreed, and the invitation went forth to high lords of the noble houses of Astaria for those willing to volunteer. It seemed a fair price to prevent a war."

It seemed the nobles traveling here for that purpose kept the reason for their visit a secret as Kraxen was unaware of the nature of this gathering. But why keep it a secret?

"A wedding or a war," Ethan said.

"Everybody wins."

Ethan shook his head sourly at that last comment. "Not everybody. Whomever the princess chooses will rue the day he wed her."

"How so? He shall sire the future queen of Vellesia. That is a great honor," the captain explained.

"To give up one's whole life for such a vainglory is too high a price, Captain. Life is short enough as it is. You need to take all the joy you can from it, for it's the only life you'll ever have."

"It is easy for you to mock the life of a Vellesian consort, Ethan, for you were born to a life of privilege. Every man I know would be overjoyed to wed and bed such a woman."

"Have you ever been to Vellesia, Captain?"

The man shook his head no.

"Neither have I. Every Vellesian I have known dares not speak ill of it, save for one who spoke only when free of its magic. She told of an oppressive realm where all served their queen with slavish devotion. You say the princess is beautiful, then answer me this? If she is *so* beautiful, why does her mother have to persuade the king of Astaria to offer up one of the lesser sons of his noble houses to wed her? If the life she offers is such a prize, then why haven't the kings of the other mage kingdoms offered their second sons to take her hand? The answer is that what she is truly offering is a cage. A beautiful jailer is still a jailer. I would caution any man before offering himself to such a union."

The captain was silent for a moment as he thought on Ethan's words. "Perhaps you are right. I had not thought of that," he conceded.

Ethan did not like the news the captain gave him. Something was amiss. The Vellesians must want something more than a consort for their princess, but what? Hopefully, his father was as suspicious of their intentions as he was. What really soured his mood was all the visiting dignitaries. The entire palace would be filled with pompous nobles and royal halfwits. This was supposed to be a time for food and good cheer, but now it would be formal balls and fancy-dress diners. Hopefully the Vellesians would finish their business and depart before the winter solstice. It seemed the Vellesians were determined to ruin his holiday. Ethan reminded himself that even the Vellesians were not all bad, not Allie anyway. He wondered where she was. The last he saw of her was on the Vellesian flagship off the coast of the Mage Bane. Her soft golden eyes were moist with tears at their parting. In her eyes, he knew she wanted to stay with him, but her duty to her queen surpassed the desire of her heart. No, that was not true. The desires of her heart were negated by the magic binding her to her queen. He and Krixan saved the lives of the Vellesian healers, but he doubted their queen even cared. A horrible thought then struck him. What if Allie was aboard Prince Alexar's ship when it was destroyed? The thought was too terrible to think about.

"Do you ever regret forsaking your birthright, Ethan?" the captain asked, shaking him from his thoughts.

"No. Once you taste freedom's kiss, you'll serve no other mistress. You could always join me if you wish, Captain," He knew the captain would never do that. He was too comfortable in the life he had at the palace.

"What you say would be treason if spoken by any other."

"True, Captain, but that was before the Velo." Ethan smiled before riding on through the gate.

*****

The wide central avenue of Astaris greeted him upon passing the main gate. Twenty meters abreast, the main avenue ran straight from the main gate to the inner citadel four miles north. Made of silvered fitted stones, with tall oak trees lining its flanks, it reflected the natural beauty of the Astarian capital. People crowded the main avenue as well as all the adjoining streets, with men dressed in bright tunics and hose and women in long fitted gowns of every color. Vendors hawked their wares along the avenue as knights paraded in polished mail, hoping to catch the eye of a fair maid. As Ethan made his way toward the inner citadel, the citizenry began to take notice of the strangely dressed rider. Only one man wore the buckskin garb with the strange hat and weapons that rode his hips.

"Ethanos!" the cries went out as he passed.

He tried lowering his Stetson over his eyes, to avoid recognition, but to no avail. Ethan could not hide who he was. He wished he could sneak into the citadel without ceremony, but such was not his fate.

*****

The blue walls of the inner citadel rose four hundred feet. Spell forged by the sky lords of old, they had never been breached. The main gate of the citadel gave way to a vast courtyard of short grass that constituted the palace green. Any hope of Ethan entering the citadel unnoticed was quickly quashed as he was met by the sight of thousands gathered around the palace green. Skirting the edge of the palace green, he was noticed by many, though most were attuned to the spectacle in the center green.

King Bronus's standard was raised in the center stands, overlooking the courtyard. A banner with gold lightning on a field of black descended from his box seat. Queen Gabrielle sat his right, while Queen Valera of Vellesia sat his left. Around them sat King Gregor Vorhenz of Gorgencia and King of Magnus Delmarin of Relusia. Seated beside Queen Valera was the Vellesian princess, her soft auburn hair rolled to her shoulders in soft satiny folds. She had bright golden eyes and delicate feminine features. Her eyes danced gaily over the gala before them. Mounted knights in full armor paraded before the royal box.

A lanky fellow dressed in a red tunic and silver hose stood before the royal box. "May I present to our royal audience, Vancel Torrent of House Torrent!" the tourney crier declared.

Vancel Torrent paraded before them in silver armor upon a cream tourney horse. The red and white of House Torrent bedecked the length of his lance.

"I present his challenger, Xavier Murtado of House Murtado!" the crier announced.

Xavier's slender silhouette, dressed in polished purple armor, sat astride a brown destrier. The horse trotted forth with the blue and gray of House Murtado decorating Xavier's lance.

Both riders moved to their positions on opposing sides of the tourney field with the crowd forming a large circle around the perimeter.

"Watch his right shoulder, Vance," Ethan thought aloud.

The Vellesian princess smoothed the folds of her light crimson gown as she gained her feet. Clenching a red scarf in her right hand, she extended it over the edge of the royal box. The horses clopped their front left hooves into the ground, preparing to charge while spraying sod behind them. The young lords charged as the scarf slipped from the princess's grasp, its shimmering red cloth fluttering in its descent. The powerful mounts thundered forth, their hooves chopping the aqueous soil as they closed upon each other on opposing sides of the tourney barricade that ran the length of the tourney field and kept them from crashing one into the other. Xavier Murtado eyed Vancel through the slit in his visor as the heir of House Torrent closed fast. Xavier raised his shield high in his left hand, squaring on the tip of Vancel's lance. Before receiving the blow, he dipped his right shoulder, bladed his shield, and drove his own lance under Vancel's shield. Vancel's lance slipped off Xavier's shield while Xavier's lance slammed flat into Vancel's torso, lifting him from his saddle. The air squeezed from Vancel's lungs as his mount continued without him, and his armor-laden body slammed into the ground. Xavier's lance broke asunder upon delivering the blow. He tossed the ruined weapon aside and lifted his visor to the cheering crowd as the afternoon sun played upon his purple armor.

Ethan pushed Bull through the crowd, making his way toward Vancel's prone form as mage healers rushed to check on the dazed lord. Palace guards dressed in black mail moved to stop him, before recognizing their former crown prince, then relented. Whispers rippled the crowd as Ethan dismounted near Vancel. Two mage healers knelt beside the wounded Lord as Ethan squatted over his friend and lifted Vancel's visor.

"You all right?" Ethan snapped his fingers above Vancel's wandering eyes.

"Ye…ye…yes," he answered hoarsely. "Hel…help me to my feet. I…must try again."

"I'm not sure that's a good idea, Vance."

"Ethan?" Vancel then recognized his old friend.

"Yes, it's me."

"Oh, Ethan," he coughed. "It is good to see you. Help me up. I must try again. I can't…let Xavier best me."

"How bad is he?" Ethan asked, cocking his head to the healer.

"His ribs are broken, and he is bleeding within, my prince." The young girl bowed her head reverently.

"Aisa, it's me, Ethan. I'm not your prince anymore."

"As you wish, my prince," she said demurely with downcast eyes.

"Ethan, just call me Ethan."

"Yes, Prin…Yes, Ethan," Aisa barely whispered.

Vancel tried to rise, despite the pain until Ethan forced him back down with his left hand. "Getting people to call me Ethan is as difficult as getting you to quit."

"I must remount," Vancel said in desperation.

"Not today. Your ribs are busted." The mage healers could not treat Vancel until the match was decided as per the jousting rules of Astaria.

Ethan pried the gauntlet from Vancel's right arm, over his friend's protest.

"Does he yield, Prince Ethanos?" Xavier asked loudly as he rode nigh with a fresh lance raised into the air.

Ethan gained his feet and tossed Vancel's gauntlet upon the tourney ground. "You got him, today, Xavier, and don't call me Prince."

Xavier laughed with a wide grin and bright teeth. "As you wish, Ethan. It is well to see you."

"And you." Ethan smiled.

"My sister will be pleased to see you, I'm certain," Xavier said.

"I figured she had found another by now," Ethan recalled Jennifer Murtado and her dark-brown locks and smiling green eyes.

"Not likely."

Aisa knelt closer to Vancel, struggling to undo the straps of his armor. Her slender fingers worked nimbly, freeing enough space to place her palm against the flesh of his chest. Her eyes went out of focus and her head bobbed weakly as she released her magic into him. The fissures in his broken bones and damaged organs knitted together, healing him. The flow of her magic was intoxicating, and Vancel loathed its ending. Every nerve in his body was alive with the soothing sensation. Aisa removed her hands as she finished, her head spinning before fainting upon the field.

Ethan scooped her up in his arms. "Lorna, can you bring my horse?" he asked the other healer as he carried Aisa from the tourney field.

"Yes, Ethan," Lorna answered, helping Vancel to his feet.

"Come on, Vance, hurry it up," Ethan goaded him as the crowd was eager for the next bout to commence.

"Ethan!" Xavier shouted from atop his mount. "The king demands your presence."

Ethan looked over his right shoulder toward the royal box, centered in the viewing stands.

"Tell him I'll be with him after I find Aisa a bed in the mage healers pavilion."

"He shall not be pleased with that answer," Xavier knew well that when Bronus Blagen demanded an audience, he meant immediately.

"I'm sure he won't." Ethan smiled as Xavier shook his head.

*****

The mage healers' pavilion was just off the tourney grounds. Fourteen meters abreast and white as freshly fallen snow, it dominated the foregrounds of the courtyard. Ethan found an empty cot to set Aisa upon. Mature mage healers could heal wounds quickly and with repetition. Aisa was barely a girl. At thirteen years of age, she was still developing her power and required rest between healings.

"Thank you, Ethan." She smiled weakly as her eyes fluttered open before closing again.

"You did well, kid." He patted her head.

"I'll tend to her, Ethan," Lorna offered. She tied Bull to the post outside before following him within.

As Ethan turned to leave, a young woman with dark-red hair and bright green eyes stood before him. She wore the white fitted dress of a mage healer.

"Hello, Ethan," she said, placing a slender hand upon his cheek.

"Arian." He smiled, lifting her off the ground and twirling her around in a fearsome hug before setting her back on her feet.

"I've missed you," she said, hugging him tightly.

"I've missed you too." He hugged her just as tight.

After a moment they came apart and her eyes came up to his. "We have much to discuss, but I know Father is waiting for you."

"I know, I wager it's about our *guests*?"

"The Vellesian queen?" she said.

"Yeah, that one."

"Yes. She is shrouded in mystery. Father grows weary of her company. Do keep that in mind if he is short with you. I know he is eager to finish his negotiations with Queen Valera and enjoy the winter festival and to spend time with you. He thinks of you constantly, Ethan."

"He has a funny way of showing it. Every time I see him, he growls and yells and calls me a complete disappointment."

"That's because he loves you, you stupid oaf." She slapped his shoulder and shook her head. "Men! You are all *idiots*."

"Yes, we're idiots, but you are bigger idiots for falling in love with us." He laughed.

"We do our duty to ensure the survival of our species, Ethan. Do remember that."

"I'll keep that in mind. When I heard there was to be a wedding in Astaris, I thought it was to be one of my siblings. Why haven't you chosen a husband yet?"

"So eager to see my married off, big brother?"

"I just thought you might throw an enchantment on some poor unsuspecting boy and drag him off to wedded bliss," he teased.

"Am I so ugly that I must enslave a man with an enchantment to entice him to my marriage bed?" A sharp brow rose over her left eye.

"See, my mouth gets me in trouble whenever I open it. But I thought an enchantment might be a wise move before every available bachelor in Astaria offers himself up to this Vellesian princess."

"No bother, for enchantments are short-lived and so is our guests' time here."

"Not short enough. I don't like this Vellesian queen, and I haven't even met her yet."

"Be respectful when you see her, Ethan, for Father's sake. She is quite kind, actually, so that should not be a problem."

"I'll show her the same respect she offers me, how's that? As far as her being *kind*, I met a Vellesian mage healer a while back who speaks of Queen Valera in a far different tone. I tend to believe the girl who's been raised under the wicked queen's rule than someone who has only seen her diplomatic side."

"You met a Vellesian girl? Was she pretty?" Arian perked at the comment.

"Very pretty, but so are a lot of girls, what of it?" He scowled.

"Nothing, you sound protective of her, though. Perhaps you'll be the one to be first wed after all." She grinned. Oh, how she missed teasing him.

"Not likely. I better go see Dad before he decides to break my neck for keeping him waiting."

*****

"Easy, boy." Ethan patted Bull's neck. His palomino was restless, unnerved by the vast crowds serried on the palace green. He skirted the crowd, avoiding as many people as he could, while circling close to the king's box. He waited at the edge before pushing his way through the crowd, waiting for the conclusion of the next match. Ethan gazed as the sun shone through the spell shield overhead. The shield allowed in the sun's warmth while blocking the early winter winds and chill from touching the summer kissed palace.

"The winner, Geoff Jarvo, heir to House Jarvo!" the tourney crier declared over the cheering crowd.

With that, Ethan moved forth, guiding Bull carefully through the crowd so as not to hurt anyone. Once their eyes spied his approach, the people parted, granting him space. Ethan felt all the eyes in the king's box, and every eye in the gathered host riveted upon him like ten thousand stars shining upon one point.

At twice his height, the king's box held a commanding view of the tourney field. Ethan stopped short of the stands, craning his neck upward with his hands resting on his pommel. His eyes first met his mother's. Queen Gabrielle smiled warmly, relieved to see her son safe and at home. His father came next, his hard gray eyes staring intently, regarding him with a strange mix of rage and pride for his firstborn. He couldn't mistake the heated glares of King Magnus Delmarin of Relusia or the pompous smile of King Gregor Vorhenz of Gorgencia. But it was the dark almond eyes of Queen Valera that he found disconcerting. Her eyes were fixed upon him in a way that made his skin crawl. She had coal-black hair and a haughty bearing that bespoke her ancient nobility. Ethan knew she was taking his measure for some purpose he could not guess. That was fine, for he was measuring her as well.

"Welcome home," Queen Gabrielle greeted him.

"Thanks, Mom. It's been a long year and a hard ride," he probably shouldn't have said that. If she knew where he had been, he'd never hear the end of it. He made a sworn vow to her to never enter the Mage Bane, yet he broke that vow to save Allie. If he had kept his promise, then Allie would've been raped and murdered, so what choice did he have? What did it matter, whenever he tried to do what was right, someone ended up angry with him. He resigned himself to the fact that he would have to tell her eventually, for the tale of his entering the Mage Bane was now well known in Cordova and would inevitably spread to Astaria in time. Unfortunately, the Vellesian queen certainly knew he had gone there to rescue her people. She might've shared that information with his mother, but the fact that his mother was not scowling meant that that hadn't happened—*yet.*

"I promised your mother to not berate you upon your return, boy. We have much to discuss once my matters at hand are concluded. We also have food to eat and casks to empty." Bronus's harsh tone softened to good humor. Ethan had earned his father's respect and the king started to realize that the man Ethan became was greater than the king he hoped his son would become.

"Thanks, Dad. I'll try to stay out of trouble until you're finished with your"—he regarded the monarchs seated on each side of his father—"friends."

"So this is Prince Ethanos," the high sweet voice of Queen Valera said.

"Ethan," he corrected her. "I've earned the right to forgo such frivolous titles." He returned her stare, finally able to look upon her other than through his periphery. She was quite striking, with almond eyes, high cheekbones, and smooth olive skin. She had the look of a much younger woman, though she had to be in her fourth decade, if not older. Her dark penetrating eyes bespoke her true age, and they projected a dark mystery.

"Titles are not frivolous, child. They are necessary to separate men from their betters." She smiled joylessly at him.

Ethan shifted in his saddle, facing up at her. "I didn't catch your name, miss?" He knew her name, but there was no need for her to know that.

"Ethan, this is *Queen Valera*, monarch of Vellesia," Bronus chided him, hoping the boy would show her the respect her title demanded.

"Valera, that's a pretty name." He smiled at her. Taking off his Stetson he bowed his head in mock deference. "Lady Valera, I'm Ethan Blagen." He quickly brought his eyes back to hers. "If there's anything I can do to make your stay here at Astaris more accommodating, let me know. Perhaps I could grant you a tour of our beautiful countryside or—"

"That's enough, Ethan!" his father cut him off. "As your king, I've granted you the freedom to speak and do as you wish. As your father, I reserve the right to strap your backside if I have to."

"I can fight my own battles, King Bronus." Valera smiled sweetly at Ethan. No man had ever spoken so boldly to her. "You pride yourself on kneeling to no man, is that so, Ethan?"

"I kneel to no man, and no man kneels to me. That seems fair if you ask me, Valera."

"If no man kneels to you, then do you see yourself the equal of peasants?" she challenged.

"Well, I've met thousands of peasants in my life, and I can't claim to be better than any of them. But I can tell you one thing," he added as his eyes swept the prestigious faces arrayed before him, "I know I'm better than the kings I've known, save for the one that sired me."

"Why you arrogant—" Magnus Delmarin erupted to his feet, his face red with indignation.

"Easy, Magnus." Ethan smiled. "I've already embarrassed you at the Velo. You don't want to challenge me again, do you?" Ethan knew he shouldn't be making enemies of all the monarchs of the seven mage kingdoms, but he couldn't help himself.

"You are quite arrogant," Queen Valera said, her smile painfully wide.

"Of course I'm arrogant, Valera. It's a hereditary trait among *all* royal bloodlines. The only difference between us is I don't take myself as seriously as you do."

Bronus put his hand to his face in embarrassment.

Ethan realized he went too far, but needling pompous royals was too much fun. For his father's sake, he would back away. "Since my mere existence probably offends all of you to no end, I'll make myself as invisible as possible during your stay." With that, he started to turn away when Valera's unmistakable voice stopped him in his tracks.

"Perhaps you kneel to *no* man while you dwell in Astaria, the wilds, or our southern seas, Ethanos, but if you ever find yourself within the boundaries of Vellesia, your knees will bend like any other man. I look for that day, child." Her unnerving smile raising the hairs on his neck.

He knew he should just turn away and ride on, but Ethan couldn't help himself. This woman made him angry in ways he couldn't understand.

"If I find myself on my knees in Vellesia, it's because you're on all fours in front of me." Ethan smiled in return, then rode on, turning a deaf ear to the gasps, shouts, and thunderous whispers rippling in his wake.

*****

The king's palace towered over the inner citadel. Spiraled towers, seven hundred feet high, pierced the firmament above, their blue surfaces melding with the clear sky. The high peaks circled the innermost tower, which rose from the palace center, its apex reaching eight hundred feet. There atop the grandest work of spell craft was a floor walled with mirrored glass. From there, Dragos Mortune eyed Ethan's entry through the palace gates.

"My foolish boy," Dragos thought aloud, the folds of his azure robes twirling as he turned from his looking glass to glance again into the clouded orb behind him. He needed to see his grandson posthaste. Stretching his weathered left hand over the head of the murky orb, he called out to Ceresta.

*****

Her heart pounded emphatically, nearly leaping from her chest. She felt her blood racing and breath tighten as her eyes beheld him. He rode through the palace gateway astride his spotted mount. He sat tall in the saddle with his thick arms and square jaw. His bearing was so masculine yet unassuming. She ached to touch him, to run her fingers through his hair, over his face, or the contours of his torso. His penetrating blue eyes swept toward her, catching her off guard. She jumped back behind one of the pillars, circling the foreground before the gate.

He's here! she thought with relief. All her hopes and plans depended on him to come home as he said he would. Her courage quickly returned, and she peered carefully around the pillar. He already passed through the center pillars that circled the gate in a semicircle arc. She followed by moving within the arced circle, spying him as he rode slowly into the palace proper. With his back to her, she could see he still wore the tan leather breeches, moccasins, and pullover shirt that he wore when she first laid eyes upon him. He still wore the pistols and holster. They seemed so strange to her when she first saw him, but they saved their lives many times in the Mage Bane. Despite the power emanating from him like light from a star, it was the kindness in his eyes and the warmth of his smile that made her weak in the knees.

A woman wearing a black dress greeted him as he neared the stables. She thought her quite beautiful with lush brown hair and delicate feminine features, yet her eyes and bearing denoted an iron authority. *His sister.* She recognized Princess Ceresta.

*****

"It never takes you long to stir trouble, Ethan," Ceresta greeted him with a forced frown. She couldn't grant him a smile after what he just did, that would only encourage him.

Ethan bounded effortlessly off his saddle, dropping to the ground beside her.

"I haven't seen any royals in a long time. At least I haven't lost my touch." He smiled, kissing her forehead.

"This is very serious, Ethan." She pushed him back with her left palm upon his chest. "You have done grievous harm to all the work Father has done to bring us peaceful terms with the Vellesians."

"She started it." He almost smiled, but her dour look convinced him otherwise.

"She started it? Is that the excuse you'll give Father?" she reproached him with her hands on her hips.

"I don't trust her."

"You mean to say you don't *like* her?"

"That either."

"Ethan. Personal trusts and likes are irrelevant in the affairs of kingdoms. After the incident at Talesia, we are on troubled ground with the Vellesians. Father is trying to avoid a needless war. The least you could do is stay out of it."

"If Valera—"

"Queen Valera," she corrected him.

"If Valera wanted war, then she would have already committed to it. She wants something else."

"She does. She wants a consort for her daughter. By asking for something significant yet painless, she saves face for Vellesia and Astaria."

"No," he said slowly. "She wants something else."

"What?"

"I don't know, I just got here, but I'll find out."

"No, you won't. You need to stay away from her!"

"Oh, I plan to stay away from her. As far away as I can, but I'll still find out what she's after."

"And if you cause a war?"

"If she wants war, I say we give it to her."

"We? You mean us. You gave up the throne, brother. You are a nation unto yourself now. Is it all you hoped it would be?"

He could see the hurt in her eyes, as if he betrayed them all by forsaking the throne.

"If Astaria goes to war, I'll go with her."

"That's a brave boast for a man who cannot die," she chided.

"I can die, and I'm sure Valera has found a way to do it. As far as giving up the throne, I left the future of Astaria in more capable hands. Tristan is thoughtful, smart, and even-tempered. He'll make a great king. Speaking of my little brother, where is he? I'm sure he has as many reservations about this Vellesian Queen as I do."

Ceresta paused before answering. "He is treating with our commanders along the Upper Morow."

"Why isn't he here?" He knew she was hiding something.

"Grandfather thought it wise to reassure our regional lords during these tenuous negotiations. All is well, Ethan. You need only concern yourself with staying clear of Queen Valera and her entourage." Her eyes shifted away.

"You didn't answer my question, Ceresta. Why isn't Tristan here?"

"Because Grandfather sent him there," she brought her eyes fiercely back to his. "And he wants to see you, now!"

Ethan craned his neck, staring up at the Tower of the Stars. "Up there?" He pointed to his grandfather's private sanctum atop the tower.

"Yes."

"That will take me a while."

Everyone else could merely use the lift, which was powered by magic. Ethan's magical immunity also made him immune to those things in magic, which were beneficial as well. Except for the magical gifts he was born with, all other magic had no effect upon him. It would be easier if Dragos simply came to him, but there was no point in asking, for his grandfather would simply ignore the request.

"Let me take care of Bull, and I'll start making my way up there."

"We have stable attendants for that," she reminded him.

"A man should groom his own horse. Besides, Bull is not just my horse, he's my best friend." He gave her that mischievous smile he was born with while leading Bull to the stables.

Ceresta rolled her eyes. He was hopelessly incorrigible. "Ethan," she called after him.

He looked back to her over his right shoulder.

"You need a bath, and you look like you haven't shaved in days."

"Three actually."

"I would do it soon."

He sniffed his sleeve. "Do I smell that bad?"

"Yes," she said.

"I love you too." He smiled.

*****

Dragos peered intently into the orb, his eyes transfixed with visions playing one upon the other with increased rapidity. He beheld ships burning, kingdoms rising against kingdoms, war, pestilence, and famine. Each vision was displaced by more hellish illuminations. To a wizened seer, the visions were not often disconcerting, for they represented what was, is, and *may* become. But Dragos was filled with a grim disquiet for these visions were stronger than any he felt before. The stronger the vision, the more likely they were to come to pass.

As Ethan neared the final steps, he stepped quietly, trying to catch his grandfather unawares. He needn't bother.

"Welcome, Ethan," Dragos said in a bored, distracted tone, denoting his arrival with little fanfare.

Ethan found Dragos with his back to him, and his long silver hair pointed every which way from the use of his power.

"How do you always know when it's me? I was very quiet in my ascent, and your magic cannot detect me?" he asked, clearly miffed by Dragos's uncanny abilities.

His grandfather turned from the orb, gazing into Ethan's blue eyes with a bushy eyebrow raised over his left eye.

"I knew it was you, Ethan, for three reasons. One, I called for you. Two, only you need to take the stair. Three, I heard your heavy feet pounding on my stone stairs through most of your climb. My stars, boy, you sound like a heard of mammoths trampling over dry leaves."

"Well, what do you expect. When was the last time you took the stairs?" He gasped with his hands on his knees to catch his breath.

Dragos stepped closer and brushed dust off Ethan's shoulder. "You need a bath, Ethan."

"You too, Grandpa? Ceresta just said the same thing."

"She is a perceptive girl, and don't call me Grandpa! It makes me sound old. Just call me Dragos as I always ask you."

"All right, Dragos. Why did you need to see me so urgently?"

"I need your help, Ethan. Come." He gestured him forth, returning his eyes to the murky orb.

To Ethan, the orb was a simple glass ball eighteen inches in diameter, resting atop a gray metal frame with strange engravings along its sides. Besides Dragos's looking glass, which was affixed to the smooth black floor and pivoted three hundred and sixty degrees, the orb was the only furnishing on the floor. Surrounded on all sides by a circled glass wall, which afforded Dragos a clear view of the lands surrounding Astaris, the entire chamber was a simple sterile chamber.

Dragos placed both palms upon the orb, conjuring the vision that haunted him since he first beheld it. Translucent light shot from the orb, spraying images to the mirrored glass walls in panoramic detail. The orb shimmered, shaking in Dragos's hands with emphatic reverberations. His eyes clouded over as the projected images took shape before him as the glass wall transformed into the familiar countryside of Astaria. The lush green forests, jagged mountain peaks, rippling blue waters, and rolling farmlands and vineyards sprang to life in breathtaking beauty.

The white stone avenues of Vectus came into focus as seen from above through the eyes of some omnipotent majesty that dwelled in the heavens above. The faces of vendors, tradesmen, washerwomen, and all the good people of that grand city were seen from every angle. Their cheerful greetings and warm smiles grew in size, overwhelming the landscape around them. They were quickly replaced with the warm port of Sabol, with the sun reflecting over the rippling waters of the bay at sunset.

This vision quickly waned as the azure walls of Astaris rose up in majestic splendor, its spiraled towers piercing the clouds like giant spear tips. Each of the images of Astaria replayed themselves with each ending in smoke and ruin. The lush forests were replaced with a scorched landscape twisted and black. Sparkling rivers were choked with mud and debris. The streets of Vectus were littered with broken edifices and corpses rotting wherever they fell. The port of Sabol was littered with listing vessels and sunken wrecks. Astaris was last, always last, its mighty walls reduced to pitiful rubble. Its towers were halved as if giant hands descended from the firmament and snapped them in two, leaving jagged, broken tops. The broken towers presided over the decimated palace with nary a wall still standing. Piles of rubble, scorched black with fire, were all that remained, a morbid tomb of the House of Blagen.

Above each scene of carnage loomed a dark shadow, blurred yet bold and frightening. Dragos could not see the shadow, yet knew it was the cause of Astaria's ruin. Yet despite all his knowledge of foresight and skill as a master seer, he was blind to the shadow that plagued his visions.

Whenever Dragos had visions with parts obscured by shadow, only Ethan could see what he could not, though Ethan himself was blind to everything but the shadow. The blurred shadows in his past visions were often Ethan himself, though much smaller than the massive blurs in the visions before him now. Could these visions still be of Ethan? Dragos feared they might be again. And if they were, was Ethan himself the bane of Astaria? Was it something he might do that would cause the kingdom's ruin? Or was it something he might *not* do? But these shadows were far larger and more potent than any that represented Ethan. Like Ethan, they were obviously immune to magic.

"What do you see, Ethan?" Dragos asked.

Ethan stared at the mostly blank glass, wondering what projection that spewed from the orb disturbed his grandfather so profoundly. He tilted his head sideways in curiosity as the blurry image Dragos described came boldly into focus. Red scales in overlapping rows of plated skin formed a terrifying image. Black razor claws and red demon eyes with black diamond pupils stared back at him. The body of the great beast was as large as three mammoths, with sinuous wings that stretched as wide as the throne room of Astaris.

"What do you see, Ethan?" Dragos asked again.

"A dragon."

CHAPTER 26

"What do you see, Ethan?"

"A dragon," he shrugged, unconcerned about the significance. "Why? What do you see?" He asked, his eyes drifting to Dragos.

The blood drained from Dragos's pale face. His answer came slow and tired as each word painfully escaped his lips. "The ruination of Astaria, my boy."

Ethan turned back to the dragon staring intently into his eyes. "Can a dragon destroy our entire realm?"

Dragos removed his weary hands from the orb, the vision disappearing as he did so. The color slowly returned to his green eyes as his mind cleared.

"A dragon," Dragos mused, stroking his trimmed silver beard with the thumb and fore digit of his left hand. "Yes, a dragon could lay waste to a kingdom, but—"

"But what?"

"Well, dragons are animals. They hunt for food and fight only to defend themselves. They care nothing for the fate of kingdoms. They are drawn to magic, however, and will attack mages of any kind on sight. That was the reason the mage lords of old erected the barrier stones separating the seven mage kingdoms from the wilds. They were erected to restrict the dragons to the wilds. What I saw in the vision was very personal. A dragon would have no reason to do such a thing."

"Why not, all our cities have spells woven into their construct. The dragon would be drawn to them as much as a mage. The more important question is, could a dragon do what your vision reveals?"

"Yes," Dragos answered. "Hypothetically, of course, it could. But I doubt one dragon could manifest such carnage without being slain in some manner."

"What are dragons like?" Ethan asked, for he had never seen one. No one in Astaria had seen one in ages. The sky lords of old chronicled their battles with dragons thousands of years ago, but no other reference was noted in the archives of Astaris.

"Dragons are immune to magic. They wield tremendous power. They fly swift and strong. They belch fire from their mouths, scorching large swaths of land with a single pass overhead. Their claws are like swords and teeth like knives. It would take an army to fell one."

"You say they're immune to magic?"

"Yes."

"So am I," Ethan said.

Dragos shook his head. "Ethan, we know your immunity to magic extends to the air around you for a few paces. Dragons probably function the same, but on a larger scale. If you fall within their magically immune aura, your ability to regenerate may be impaired."

"So might the dragons"

"No one has ever been able to kill a dragon since the ancient days, Ethan. They are invincible. Only ancient spell craft has created barriers to keep them at bay."

"If they are immune to magic, how does spell craft keep them at bay?"

"The ancients knew how to blend the properties of magic with the essence of immunity that coursed a dragon's blood. Their knowledge has since been lost, and we have no means to kill a dragon and retrieve their blood to repeat the process."

Ethan stared down at the Colt .45s in his holsters and wondered.

"Where do dragons dwell now?" Ethan asked.

"Only in the wilds, north of Vellesia and Gorgencia."

"Vellesia," Ethan whispered. Whether it was Allie, Valera, or the mention of dragons, he could not escape that name.

"For now, Ethan, I think it best if you do not speak of what we have seen. Not until I have time to study it further."

"Not even my father?"

"Especially your father. He has enough matters to attend for the nonce."

*****

Ethan's descent was far quicker than his ascent. For reasons his grandfather could not explain well, the lift would take him down the tower, but never up. It had taken him the latter half of the morning to climb up the stairs. Thankfully his descent was completed in moments. The base of the tower opened near the entrance to the king's hall. The central courtyard was a field of polished silver stone surrounded by the dark-azure structures that rose imperiously around it. The courtyard was serried with rank upon rank of dignitaries from the seven mage kingdoms. Knights in brown mail with capes emblazoned with the coat of arms of House Lorga loitered near the palace entrance. They were the sworn protectors of King Karl Lorga of Sarcosa. Their skin was light brown and their superior dexterity and quickness offset their diminutive stature. The tempest was the symbol born on their coat of arms, the sigil of Karl Lorga, a renowned weather mage. Their king was nowhere to be seen and was probably in the palace.

Near the stone pillars that formed a semicircle around the entryway, were the knights of Gorgencia and Estasa. The dark-gray mail of Gorgencia with the stallion emblazoned on their coat of arms, contrasted sharply with the light blue mail and leaping fish of Estasa. King Evor Ectus of Estasa marched toward the king's hall with his knights escorting him through the courtyard. Ethan noticed at least fifty ladies of various noble houses amid the crowd. Lesser lords and ladies of countless houses moved among the crowd, enough to make him dizzy trying to catalog their differing significance.

Why bother, he reminded himself. He only wanted to get away from them all. They were all mage born and arrogant. They each labored to better their station, never satisfied with the gifts and privilege they were born to. They thought him arrogant for turning from his birthright, as if the throne of Astaria was not good enough for him. He only wished to be free of titles, nobles, and kneeling. At times like these he longed for Red Rock. He missed old Judge Donovan and Sheriff Thorton. They were tough, grizzled men, hardened by their world, yet it was the honor that flowed from them that made him proud to call them friends. Besides his father and grandfather, there was no one he respected more. He wondered what they would think of all the dandies parading before him now? More importantly, he wondered what this congregation of fools would think of them? They would see them as little more than peasants, even though the greatest of these gathered lords weren't good enough to clean their boots. Ethan only needed a place to hide until this Vellesian mockery was ended.

"Ethanos!" His father's harsh voice cut through the air like a sharp blade.

Bronus seemed to appear out of nowhere form his left, which was no small feat for a man of his size. His black cape, with gold lightning running diagonally from shoulder to opposing hip emblazoned upon it, rippled in his wake. His jaw was clenched, and his gray eyes were ablaze.

"Father," he greeted him cautiously as Bronus halted inches from his nose. A dozen knights of the king's guard fanned out around them.

"I've spent the better part of my morning undoing the damage your flippant mouth has wrought, boy!"

"You summoned me to your box, and she insulted me first. What should I have done? Just stand there and take it?" Ethan growled back.

"Don't raise your voice to me, son! I'll break your neck if I have to!"

"Go ahead, it's right here," Ethan craned his neck to its side, exposing it to his father. "It'll just heal, and we'll be back arguing right here where we started."

"Blast you, Ethan. Don't you know the damage you've done?"

"It doesn't make any difference, Dad. Valera—"

"Queen Valera!" Bronus corrected him.

"Valera isn't going to war with us no matter what she claims otherwise. Think!" He jabbed his fore digit to his skull. "She's after something more than a stud for her daughter's bed. Something is wrong, I can feel it."

"Your hatred for nobility is blinding your reason, Ethan. A choice for a royal consort is a preferable alternative to war or tribute. Both our realms save face. That may all be undone now because of your arrogance."

"My arrogance? Have you noticed what surrounds you in your royal box? Those monarchs have no love for us. Have you taken no notice of what their rule has wrought in their own kingdoms? Those unfortunates who find themselves under the collective yokes for our royal guests find themselves in a living hell where no one is guaranteed protection for their property, their wedding bed, or their life. You are the only one of the seven who sees his crown as a burden of responsibility. Not them! No, they see it as their right as if all those under their dominion are so placed to serve their own selfish desires. I have no respect for them. *None!* To hell with the lot of them. If they want war, then let's give it to them. They fear you, Father, and you know what? They fear me too. I can see that in their eyes."

"You assume much, Ethan. I love you, boy. Do not doubt that. Not ever. But tomorrow evening in my hall you *will* apologize to Queen Valera."

"Never!" Ethan shook his head emphatically.

"You will, Ethan, or you will leave the palace until my guests depart."

"If I leave, I won't be coming back."

"That is your choice, son. My desire is to be finished with this business and enjoy the holiday with my family, especially you, Ethan. If you wish to not return to punish me, then so be it, but that would be very selfish of you." Bronus walked away, leaving Ethan with his anger and guilt.

*****

He raised the ax over his head and swung again. The wood split clean, the two halves falling to either side as Ethan set a fresh piece on the stump. Old Yance watched as his King's son chopped the firewood that he was supposed to chop. Ethan often came here behind the palace to chop wood whenever he had anger to vent or things on his mind. Old Yance hadn't seen much of Ethan these past two years as he was away.

Ethan stripped his shirt off, setting it atop a cord of stacked wood as he continued to work. Sweat rolled off his chest and shoulders, ambling along the contours of his muscled arms and torso. She watched him from the surrounding trees that circled them. It was perhaps the only place within the inner palace that had any trees. It was also the only place most of the guests had little interest in seeing. Most of the young lords congregated in Astaris, favored the comforts of palace life. Ethan, she knew, loved the outdoors. He loved the trees, the wind, and the open spaces. He was here to visit his family, not the palace. She watched the sweat glisten off his tan muscled back. His dark hair was longer than she remembered but not long enough to her liking. His face was obscured from this angle, but she would never forget what he looked like. He was perfect, a healthy blend of rugged masculinity and boyish charm, tempered with kindness.

Ethan froze. Someone was watching him. He swung the ax into the stump, its handle jutting into the air as he turned, his right hand hovering close to the grip of his holstered Colt.

"You can keep working, Ethan. I'm actually enjoying the view." She smiled, stepping from the trees. She stood there before him with her hands crossed at her waist and her white mage healer's dress clinging perfectly to her curves.

"Allie?" His blue eyes perked.

She stood before him, the curls of her black hair peeking from the edge of her white cowl. Her bright golden eyes sparkled mischievously as her deep olive skin flushed perfectly. She was the most beautiful woman he had ever seen.

"Yes, it's me, Ethan. Or should I call you Prince Ethanos Blagen?" she teased.

"You know better than that." He smiled, stepping toward her.

"Not prince?" She lifted a brow. "It is one thing to refer to you as 'plain ole Ethan' in the Mage Bane but quite another in your sire's place."

"Just Ethan, I gave up that title a long time ago." He couldn't stop smiling at her.

"That's good. You don't look like a prince anyway. You look *much* nicer." She smiled ever wider.

He was close enough now to touch, but he stopped at arm's length, just staring at her. "I'd give you a hug, but I'm covered in sweat and stink."

She grabbed him and hugged him tightly as he wrapped his arms around her.

"I was hoping you would come. It's nice to see a familiar face," she said as she pulled briefly away.

"What are you doing here, Allie? I didn't expect this."

"Are you disappointed that I came?" she asked with a false pout.

"What do you think." He smiled again, though his mood quickly soured as realization sunk in.

"What troubles you, Ethan?"

"Oh, Allie. If I had known you were here, I would've kept my mouth shut." He rubbed his temples with his left thumb and fore digit. "You better go away before any of your queen's people tell her you were with me."

"Yes, I heard what you said to her. That was unwise. But you saved my life, Ethan, my life, and the others. I will not forget that, not ever."

"Allie, I don't want her to punish you for our friendship."

"Do not fret. I am not without friends at court. My mother has enough influence to protect me should the queen chastise me out of pure spite."

"I've seen your queen. Don't underestimate her, Allie. She is pure evil. I could see that in her eyes. Now she has my father wrapped around her finger with this nonsense about finding her daughter a husband. I don't believe it. She wants something else. I don't know what, but she does. Now my father says I must apologize to her or leave the palace."

"If she makes you this angry, then you should leave the palace as your father says. At least until my people depart," she said sadly, lowering her eyes. She left unsaid that they would not see each other if he did.

"Will you leave with me?"

She brought her moist eyes back to him. "I…" The words were caught in her throat. "I cannot. I am bound to my oaths to the queen, oaths that are sealed by magic. Only she can release me."

"Damn the magic, and damn her!" he growled bitterly.

"You shouldn't say that, Ethan. It only makes it worse. What else troubles you? I know it is more than my queen?" She touched the side of his face, drawing his eyes to hers.

"I don't know. I…I thought when I gave up the throne that I'd give up all the worries that go with it. But now that I'm free to roam the world, all I do is find trouble and enemies wherever I go. Your queen hates me, the Meltorians and Relusians despise me for what happened at the Velo. I've made countless enemies in the Mage Bane. Emmitt Cobb is out there somewhere, waiting for a chance to kill me. There is this business with my father and your queen. I feel he is in great danger, though I don't know why. There's D…" He stopped himself from revealing Dragos's vision.

"Is that why you gave up your title and throne, to free yourself from such worries?" Her voice was soft and soothing.

"That wasn't the reason, but it should've been a benefit."

"Oh, Ethan. You can only be free of such worries if you don't care. But you do care…about your people, your family, and your friends. We live in a world fraught with danger and worry. You cannot escape it."

"I wish I didn't care," he lamented, though he didn't mean it.

"No." She smiled. "I know you well enough, Ethan, to know that is not true. But I want to know why you forsook your birthright. Since I've known you, you've placed yourself in harm's way for the sake of others. Couldn't you help others more from the throne of Astaria?"

"As I told you before, I didn't merely choose to give up the throne. I had to win the battle at the Velo and save my father's life in order for him to *free* me of the throne. It was his dream for me to succeed him, but I never wanted it."

"Why?"

"I don't like kneeling to any man, not even my father. And I don't like any man kneeling to me."

"As you said repeatedly, but why? Kneeling is merely an acknowledgment of authority, Ethan. Why does it bother you so?"

"Remember when you asked me where I found my pistols and rifle?"

"Yes, Red Rock, across the barrier," she recalled his adventures that he share with her those nights in the Mage Bane.

"I told you of my time there, but not so much of their realm."

"A little," she conceded.

"In Texas, there were no lords or kings, no magic. Just men, and nearly all of them carried these." He slapped the handle of his Colt.

"How could men organize themselves without kings or mages?" she asked.

"Each man has an equal voice in their government. They each have the freedom to build their own wealth and power without the government seizing it out of spite or greed. Some fail and are impoverished, but collectively they are wealthy beyond your imagination. Without magic as a crutch, they use their minds to create wonders to dazzle your senses. That is what freedom does to men, true freedom, anyway. That is what I am trying to do at Cordova. Perhaps even the Mage Bane could be transformed from a wild and savage land into a place where freemen can gather themselves to build a better world, a place to escape the tyranny of mage kings."

"What you speak of is treason, Ethan. But if it is, I wish I could be free. Free to choose my own destiny."

"Is there no way to free you from your queen?" He would give nearly anything to free her.

"Only her word can free me, Ethan."

Perhaps his father might have arranged her freedom if he hadn't insulted Valera for all the seven kingdoms to hear. If he could've kept his mouth shut, or if he had met with his father in private, he might have avoided Valera altogether.

"I'll apologize to the witch," he threw his hands up in frustration. It might not free Allie of Valera's rule, but it might spare her the queen's wrath.

"Apologize for your father's sake, not mine, Ethan."

"My father will be fine. He is the king of Astaria, after all, and a lightning lord. That makes him the most powerful man in the world. No, I'll apologize only for you. But heed my words, Allie, if your queen harms you in any way, I'll kill her."

"You must not speak of such things, Ethan. If you wish me well then please do not threaten Queen Valera."

He saw the terror in her eyes, and it pained him. She was right. His words soothed his rage, but it was those like Allie that would suffer for them. "I'm sorry, Allie. I'll keep my mouth shut. I'll apologize to Queen Valera tomorrow night as she wants." He could just see the sneering smirk on Valera's face when he apologized before all the lords of Elaria.

"Ethan, do not feel shamed by what she is asking of you. Remember her debt to you as well. You saved a dozen Vellesian mage healers. That is more than half our guild. My people would've been dealt a severe blow had we been slain. The queen must know of this. If you must apologize for your poor words, then she must show gratitude for your brave deeds."

"Allie!" His eyes lit up. "That's it. She owes me a favor. If I saved twelve of her mage healers, then she can at least free one as a reward for my bravery."

She looked at him with large hope-filled eyes. "You would do that for me?"

"You came after me at Crepsos. You risked your life to help me against Luke Crawford and his band. I wouldn't have made it out of there without you."

"Thank you, Ethan. You don't know what it means to me for you to feel that way. But I doubt the queen will free me, even for such a deed."

"I can try." He smiled, lifting her chin with his right hand as they gazed into each other's eyes. She pressed her lips to his, briefly tasting what she desired for so long.

He returned her kiss with equal passion, taking her in his arms as their lips merged deeper in an emollient embrace. He felt as if lightning might erupt from their lips as they touched. Was it ordained by some unseen presence that two people were to be joined? Was it fate that brought them together, or happenstance? All he knew was that her lips fit his as if they were made for each other.

"I…I shouldn't be doing this," she said, pulling briefly away as she clutched her shoulders and turned her back.

"Why?" he asked gently, missing her in his arms.

"Because. Because you are a prince."

"No, I'm not. I gave that up, Allie."

"You can't give it up, Ethan. It is in your blood. You are the true heir of Astaria."

He grabbed her by the shoulders and spun her around, staring intently into her eyes. "I can give it up, and I did. There is no such thing as royal blood. Blood is blood. Mine is no more precious than yours or Krixan's or Tristan's, and Valera's is no more sacred than mine. Once you remove these artificial titles, we are still just people, Allie."

"You could choose to be with me even if I was not of royal blood?"

"Royal blood would be a detriment, not an asset, Allie." He smiled though she seemed uneasy with that remark.

"I'm sorry, Ethan. My emotions are running in so many directions. I didn't come here to throw myself into your arms. I only wanted to see my friend and thank him for all that he has done."

"A kiss from a pretty gal is the best way to say thank you."

"You think I'm pretty?" she asked, hooking her hair behind her right ear.

"Allie, you're the most beautiful woman I've ever known."

"You're being kind." She blushed shyly.

"I'm telling the truth. You're far prettier than that Vellesian princess everyone is fawning over. I mean she's not ugly, but she doesn't seem real. But you…" He paused, taking in the swell of her bosom and the symmetry of her face. "You're all woman."

"Why, thank you, Prince Ethanos."

"Just Ethan. Here I give you a compliment, and you respond with an insult."

"I only call you prince because I know how it irritates you. You are adorable when you get that hurt look on your face," she teased.

"Don't make it a habit."

"How about a deal? I'll stop calling you prince if you take a bath?"

"You too, huh?"

"Well," she said slowly, running a finger down his chest, "I like how you smell regardless." She walked behind him, tracing her finger over his shoulders and back before stopping at his opposite shoulder. "But I think the queen will more likely agree to your request if you smelled a little cleaner," she whispered in his ear.

"Take a bath, Ethan, and maybe she'll kiss you again!" Old Yance hollered, standing beneath a nearby oak.

They both turned in his direction and laughed. They had forgotten about him, and he was watching them the whole time.

"All right, I'll get cleaned up. Hopefully the steam baths in the palace aren't overrun with guests. I'll see if someone can wash my clothes.

*****

After helping Old Yance finish chopping wood and getting a steam bath in the bowels of the palace, Ethan stood in his bedchamber, waiting for his clothes to dry. All of his spare buckskins and shirts were stitched up in several places, while the set he was awaiting were his one good set. Wearing a thick robe over a fresh loin garment, he stared out the portal of his room, surveying the courtyard below. His chamber was exactly the same as he left it. His bow and quivers hung from one wall, while his collection of bladed weapons adorned the opposite. His wardrobe lined the wall beside his bed, filled with clothes he would never wear, with silk tunics, pointed shoes, hose, and leggings of the sheerest quality, shimmering capes and hats of varying sorts, shirts and trousers of linen and wool. A full suit of armor and a suit of silver mail were displayed over iron mannequins, each polished as if ready for use. The only outfit he would be caught dead in was a shirt and trousers of black cotton with a leather sword belt. The rest he would never wear again if he had a say in the matter. He would wear the black outfit tomorrow night when treating with Valera.

Gazing out the portal with his right hand resting on the stone wall above the window, he observed the comings and goings below with disinterest. Once Allie was free of her queen, if he was successful, then he'd be free himself to be away from the gathered nobility until they departed. Perhaps he'd take Allie fishing in a mountain stream or teach her archery or swordplay. He might even teach her how to shoot. *She might be a faster draw than me.* He laughed at the thought. He noticed his guitar leaning against the corner to his right. He brought that back across the barrier and only played it once, for his mother. *Maybe I'll teach her that*, he thought. *I bet she can sing beautifully with that silken voice of hers.*

"Ethan," his mother's voice echoed behind him.

He turned as Queen Gabrielle passed through his doorway. She wore a jade gown that fitted snuggly about her torso before flowing freely below her waist. The light slipping through the portal hit her directly, bathing her auburn hair and highlighting the tints of red that sparkled with the sun. He realized how beautiful his mother truly was. She fought the effects of her age well. Her skin was quite smooth and feminine. It was not just her beauty that had smitten his father. Her intelligence was captivating. It was of a kind that Allie possessed as well and drew Ethan as much as her beauty.

"Mom." He smiled as she came into his arms while he kissed her forehead.

She hugged him fiercely. He was the only one of her children who called her mom. The others called her mother and queen, not Ethan. His time with the Americans had changed him in so many ways. The American's informal manner merely reinforced his casual personality. Though Bronus often scolded the boy, she knew he found Ethan's way of speaking endearing.

"It warms my heart to see you well, Ethan. When you left, I feared you might venture into the wilds or the Mage Bane. But you promised you would not. You are good as your word." She smiled as she looked up to him with moist green eyes.

"It's good to be home. About the Vellesian queen, I wi—"

"I know. You are going to apologize to her tomorrow evening."

"Word spreads quickly around here. Yes, I'll apologize to the witch."

"I might advise you, son, not to refer to her as a witch during your apology." Gabrielle laughed.

"I'll try, but she doesn't make it easy. The hard part is to stop talking after I apologize before my mouth gets me into more trouble."

"I'm sure you'll do fine, son."

"I'll try, but I don't like Valera, and I don't trust her. I don't believe her story about only wanting a consort for her daughter. She wants something else."

"It is possible, but I sense no dishonesty with her. Finding a suitable mate for her daughter has been her obsession for some time. She even approached your Father concerning you when you were a child."

"Me?" Ethan was taken aback. "Why would she want a child?"

"For her daughter." She gave him a dumbfounded look as if the answer was obvious. "She would have reared you in her household until you were old enough to wed."

That thought sent chills through Ethan's brain. What kind of dreary childhood might he have had, had his parents given him away? "What did she offer for me?"

"Three million gold pieces, the equivalent of our entire treasury. But your father would not give up his rightful heir. That is how much your Father loves you, Ethan."

Ethan never knew. He thought of all the times he was angry with his father, and his father was angry with him. Ethan knew it was always out of love, but knowing this made him love his father all the more.

"She never asked again?"

"No. You were two years when she first asked. As soon as word spread of your magical…peculiarity…"

"My magical immunity?"

"Yes. As soon as word spread of your nature, she never asked again. When Bronus declared unequivocally that you were his firstborn and rightful heir to Astaris, she asked for Tristan. Your father refused this offer as well."

"Why? Why was she adamant about a child from the House of Blagen?"

"I don't know, Ethan. All mage lords try to find their children mates who are of mage blood. The stronger the magical ties, the more likely their offspring would be mage gifted."

"Is that why Tristan is absent from Astaris? To protect him?"

"Perhaps, in a way. It was a precaution that Dragos recommended. Anyone the princess chooses must also accept her offer, but Dragos thought it wise to remove any…possibilities. You, of course, are protected by your immunity and your freedom."

"No mage queen would wed her daughter to someone immune to magic lest her heirs be born with no magic at all," he said bluntly.

"That is so, Ethan."

She conceded the greatest fear of any mage king or queen was to have an heir born with little or no magic. It was a death knell to any house or realm.

"Then why does she want a son of a lesser House of Astaria? Why not a second son of another mage king?"

"We do not know. Perhaps her line has already wed a number of other houses, whereas nowhere in the chronicles has it shown a link of any sort between Astaria and Vellesia." Gabrielle shrugged.

"Of all the suitors of Astaria, who is Dad's closest blood relation?"

Gabrielle made a face. "Why?"

"Just tell me who, if you know?"

"Geoff Jarvo. His mother is your father's sister. Why do you ask?" Her interest was piqued.

"I think this Vellesian princess will choose Geoff." It all made sense to him now. Allie said it was in the blood. His blood was tainted, and Tristan was not available, so the nest available male was Geoff.

"Why, Geoff?" she asked.

Ethan gave her a hard look. "Valera wants her heir to be a lightning lord."

"Ethan, a lightning mage is rare. One or two might be born in a thousand years. A child or nephew of such a mage would not likely receive their gift."

"Then Valera has found a way. If there is any trace of the gift in Geoff's blood, then I would guess she knows how to enhance it. Remember how little we know about Vellesia. When was the last time Vellesia faced invasion?"

"Four hundred years ago," she answered uneasily as Ethan's reasoning was winning her over.

"Yes. Four hundred years ago, a Gorgencian and Sarcosan alliance invaded Vellesia with one hundred thousand men. They were never heard from again. How were they destroyed? What magic do the Vellesians wield that we are unaware of? Tell Father to be *careful*. Once I apologize to Valera, you won't see me until our *guests* have gone home."

"Prince Ethanos," a young girl's voice interrupted.

They both turned as the young servant girl entered the chamber with Ethan's clothes.

"Just Ethan, Mari," he reminded her.

"Of course, my prince. I washed and dried your clothes." She placed them on his bed, curtsied, and turned to leave.

"Wait." Ethan stopped her as he fetched a silver drebett and placed it in her hand. It was a handsome sum and equaled a month's wages for her.

"Oh, no, Prince Ethanos, I am a paid servant to the royal household. I cannot acc—"

"Well, I'm not royal, so waiting on me doesn't count. Here, take it, and don't call me Prince. It's Ethan, just Ethan."

"Yes…Ethan." She curtsied deeply, nervous about addressing him so informally.

"And don't curtsy to me either."

"Yes, Ethan." She blushed and withdrew.

Gabrielle swatted his thick shoulder. "Did you see what you did to that poor girl? She was blushing."

"She wasn't blushing because of me. She's just shy."

She gave her think headed son an incredulous look. "All the girls blush when you speak to them, Ethan. They always have. You're not exactly hard on the eyes, son."

"They used to fawn on me when I was their crown prince. Now I'm just Ethan."

"They still gaze upon you with puppy eyes, Ethan."

"No, they don't. Nearly every girl I have seen today in the palace barely acknowledged my presence. I even saw Jennifer Murtado below when I was coming up here after my bath. I told her good afternoon, and she didn't even look at me."

"She's probably trying to gain your attention by ignoring you. We women have used that method since the dawn of time."

"Don't believe me then, but it's true. Women are drawn to power. Why else would Gregor Vorhenz have an entourage of female courtiers following him wherever he goes?" Ethan removed his robe and pulled on his buckskin trousers.

Gabrielle relented. It was pointless arguing with the boy. He was always oblivious to the effect he had on the female gender. She often had to nag him to keep his shirt on during weapon training sessions on the tourney green, lest half the maidens in Astaris line up to watch him drill like panting ponies.

"The queen's ball is in three days, Ethan. It is a chance to put your flawed theory to the test."

"What do you mean?" he asked, pulling a plain cotton shirt over his head, followed by his plain leather one.

"Since it is *my* ball, the women are the ones to ask the men to attend. All the maidens in the palace are free to ask any man they choose. I would wager a hefty sum that you shall be selected rather quickly." Once a man accepted a maiden's offer, he would wear her favor, usually a scarf or hair ribbon, around his left wrist until the night of the ball. Thus, a maiden would know which men were free to ask, and which had already accepted another maiden's favor.

"No, I won't, because I'm not going. They can ask all they want, but once I make my apology, the last place I want to be is in the palace, let alone at a ball." He buckled his pistol belt and tied down the holsters to his thighs. He removed the Colt from his right holster and downloaded the bullets and carefully disassembled the pistol.

"What are you doing?" she asked.

"Cleaning my guns. The trail was pretty dusty," he said as he placed all the parts on his bed and fetched a bore rod, wadding and bore cleaner from saddle pack.

"I don't like those things." Gabrielle shuddered, looking at his pistols and the Winchester rifle sticking from his saddle pack.

"They're the weapons of a free people, Mom. The Americans say 'God made man and Sam Colt made him equal.'" He grinned, slapping the pistol on his left hip.

"Couldn't you at least change your clothes and wear a sword when you treat with Queen Valera?"

"Why? The only difference between a pistol and sword is that a pistol is more efficient. *A lot more efficient.*"

*****

"Can you do it, Torg?" Ethan asked the head smithy.

Torg stood over his worktable, examining the various molds. Despite swaths of gray overtaking his temples and sagging cheeks, Torg's mind still had the youthful sharpness his body lacked. He was a full head shorter than Ethan with meaty hands and a thick neck. Torg's work counter was centered in the smith shop with a dozen firepits circling it and a score of smiths and apprentices tending varied tasks.

"How many of these do you want?" Torg lifted one of the molds to his eye, examining the fine detail and craftsmanship. It was a figurine of a soldier nearly the length of his hand, holding a small sword and shield. Other figurines included an archer, a maiden, and an ogre.

"Several hundred."

"Several hundred!" Torg's craggy voice raised two octaves. "That would take a lot of material and time. I can spare neither with every lordling in the seven kingdoms here at the palace demanding their armor and blades repaired for their jousts and tourneys. I can't invest my resources on toys. Why do you want them, Ethan?"

Ethan placed his right hand on Torg's shoulder. "Torg, the Americans have this holiday after the winter solstice to honor the birth of their God. They celebrate it by exchanging gifts. On the eve of this holiday, the children hang a stocking by their fireplace, and a mystical agent deposits toys in their stocking while they sleep. Their parents actually are the ones who place the toys there, but when the children awake the next morning, they believe their mythical benefactor has bestowed their gifts upon them. They spend their day playing with their treasures. I saw with my own eyes how happy those children were. I thought to myself, why couldn't we do that for our children? We don't have time to give toys to all the children or Astaris, but we could give one to every child in the inner palace. I mean *every* child, Torg. How many children are the sons and daughters of scullery maids or stable attendants? They have never had a toy of this quality. I'd like to see their eyes when they wake on the morning of the winter solstice with a wondrous toy to play with. If I get you the metal and materials and paint, can you help me make them?"

Torg looked Ethan in the eye and shook his head in wonder. Astaris was crowded with lords and ladies, who paraded in rich finery and demanded of his time and labor to fix and repair their weapons and possessions so they could win tourneys and bathe in glory. Here was his king's firstborn, who thought only of the happiness of children and wanted something for them to play with. He couldn't make sense of the boy. He defeated the kingdom's enemies in battle and saved the king's life, and the reward he asked for was to be free of the throne, a throne that would have been his. Now with every noble within several hundred leagues gathered in Astaris to compete for their own betterment and station, here was Ethan thinking only of a bunch of poor children who have so little joy in their lives. Where the nobles see their food, Ethan thinks of the cooks who prepared it and the maids who served it. Where the nobles see a bed, Ethan thinks of the servant who washed the bedding and made the bed.

Damn you, Ethanos! Torg thought bitterly. *Damn you for forsaking the throne and leaving it to lesser men.* Most mage kings were a petty and vicious lot, but Torg would have followed Ethan into the bowels of hell itself. He would have been a great king, and he lamented what now would never be.

"I'll do it, lad," Torg sighed. "At least the children will appreciate my craftsmanship more than our 'guests.'"

"Thank you, Torg, you won't regret this." Ethan smiled, slapping the old smithy on the back.

"All right, all right. Don't get sentimental on me, Ethan." He growled.

"I'll have the materials we'll need here by morning."

"You just fetch the materials, Ethan, me and the boys will make them. You'd just be in the way here, but we'll leave the painting to you."

The sounds of shouting and pushing disturbed their conversation, drawing their attention to the open double doors of the smith shop. Torg strode forth, wiping his ash stained hands on his leather apron as he closed on the doorway. Ethan followed, letting Torg handle the situation. If the old smithy needed his help, he would be close by.

"Your work is subpar, and you *dare* give my excuses, peasant!" a young lord in gray chain mail shouted.

Torg and Ethan were met with a gathering crowd surrounding the dark stone pavement in front of the blacksmith shop. A young Lord was shouting at a young smith who lay upon the ground with blood oozing from his cut lip. The lad wiped his mouth with the back of his left hand. He was no more than sixteen years and slight of build. His sand-colored hair was speckled with ash and his light green eyes were fixed to the ground so as not to offend his tormentor.

"Is there a problem, my lord?" Torg asked, pushing his way through the crowd.

The lord's narrow set blue eyes swept angrily toward Torg. He was of thick build, but only a few inches taller than the old smithy, but his face projected the softer feminine features of pampered aristocracy.

"Do you not know who I am, blacksmith?" he spat.

Torg was taken aback, careful not to quickly venture upon unknown ground. "Pardon my ignorance, your lordship, but there are countless lords from many lands in Astaris for the gathering. I do not know your name or title," his graveled voice answered through his clenched jaw.

"I am *Prince Borcose* Vorhenz, crown prince of Gorgencia." His voice squealed. "In Gorgencia a prince is addressed accordingly as sire, Highness, or Grace. Is that beyond your cognizance, peasant? Or are you simply ill-mannered?" Borcose sneered.

"My apologies, Prince Borcose. Might I ask what offense young Lufen is guilty of?" Torg regarded the young lad sprawled upon the ground before the Gorgencian Prince.

"How *dare* you, blacksmith? I needn't explain his crime or my judgment to the likes of you!" Prince Borcose shrieked hysterically. At the snap of his fingers, two burly guards stepped forth and seized Lufen by the arms, dragging him to his feet as Borcose raised a glowing right hand bathed in a bright crimson glow, intense heat flowing off its surface. He held it to the lad's face.

"I'll punish his incompetence as I see fit!" he gloated as the heat emitting from his palm and fingers intensified as they drew near Lufen's wide-eyed face.

Quicker than thought a powerful hand wrapped around Borcose's glowing palm and twisted it forcefully away from Lufen's face. Borcose screamed as Ethan twisted his arm behind his back. "Who *dares*—"

"You've done enough talking, Princess. Tell your men to let the boy go!" Ethan growled in his ear.

"I'll see you flayed for this, peasant! I'll—owww!"

Ethan twisted the arm painfully, sending Borcose to the brink of tears. He could still not see his attacker as Ethan stood behind him. "My name is Ethan, not peasant. My friend is named Torg Larios, not blacksmith. This boy you attacked is named Lufen. They are not peasants, they are tradesman of Astaria, and we are grateful for their craftsmanship. Even if they were peasants, they would rank above your lazy noble *ass*! Now let's try this again, Princess. Tell your men to let the boy go!"

"Release him!" Borcose pleaded. "Release him now!"

They released Lufen, who staggered a step before collecting himself. He stepped behind Torg.

Ethan jerked his head, instructing Borcose's guards to withdraw while still gripping the Gorgencian prince.

"Now you can apologize to my friend Torg for your rudeness."

"My apology, Torg Larios," Borcose quickly said.

"Apology accepted, Your Highness." Torg regarded the Gorgencian crown prince with a stone face that masked his inner glee.

Ethan tossed the Gorgencian prince into his entourage behind him. Borcose's personal guard closed ranks around him, guarding their prince with raised blades and crossbows.

"*Shoot him!*" Borcose commanded once safely within his circle of guards.

Three burly guards, dressed in gray mail and black leggings, stepped forth with crossbows trained on Ethan. They released their volley in unison, each dart speeding to target as Ethan drew the Colt on his right hip. With blinding speed, he drew and fired into Borcose's men, sending two bullets into each crossbowman as the bolts struck him two in the chest and one in the thigh. The dull pain staggered Ethan briefly as he drew the Colt holstered on his left. Two of the men he shot stumbled then dropped, but the third came on with sword drawn. Ethan riddled him with three more rounds as the man's rage drove him through the fatal blows punching into his chest in quick succession. The space between them was too close for bullets to the chest to kill him before he struck Ethan with the blade. Ethan finally dropped him with a bullet through the eye, his body crashing at his feet. The pain of his wounds festered briefly, giving way to the itchy healing sensation as the severed tissue knitted together around the embedded shafts. With only three rounds left in his second Colt, Ethan didn't have time to reload. Still griping the pistol in his left hand, he quickly holstered his right-handed Colt and retrieved the sword from the dead man at his feet.

The sound of Ethan's pistols reverberated throughout the palace, startling those who were unfamiliar with the weapon as well as those who were. Borcose's remaining guards were unmoved, stayed by fear of Ethan's pistol. They formed an uneasy circle around their crown prince, with blades drawn and eyes nervously fixed on Ethan.

Torg stepped beside Ethan, brandishing a heavy hammer in his meaty hands. All the blacksmiths quickly followed, forming up on either side of them.

"Kill them! Kill them all!" Borcose shrieked, but his men moved tentatively, unnerved by Ethan's weapon, by his ability to stand unmoved with three darts protruding from his torso, by the blacksmith standing with him and the uneasy crowd surrounding them. Before they could carry out Borcose's desperate order, palace guards flooded into their midst with sword points leveled to their throats and arrows notched. Each wore the silver chain mail and greaves of the palace garrison.

"Lower your weapons!" their captain commanded, staring down Borcose's guards. He was a nondescript soldier with no discernable feature other than an intense adherence to duty.

They stood unmoved, nine against two score of Astaris's finest.

"Only our prince commands us," a thick-necked bull of a man answered. He stood in front of Borcose, gripping his long sword with both hands.

"You have assaulted the former crown prince of Astaria, Ethanos Blagen, firstborn of the king. If you do not lay down your arms, you shall die to a man, including your *prince*!" the captain said, his eyes narrowed like a hawk about to sweep down upon its prey.

"My prince?" the bullnecked man asked Borcose.

"Lower your weapons," Borcose relented. He wasn't prepared to die.

The clanging of falling swords rang out in the afternoon air as the captain in his shining helm and mail turned to Ethan. "Sergeant, fetch Ethan a mage healer."

"I'll see to him," a distinct feminine voice answered.

Both men turned as Allie made her way through the crowd, coming to Ethan's side.

"Very well, my lady," the captain regarded her.

Ethan gave her an easy smile before shifting his eyes to the captain of the guard. "Thanks, Marco, but I'll be fine. What are you going to do with our 'friends' over there?" He jerked a thumb toward the Gorgencians.

"They shall be detained until the king decides their fate."

"I have a better idea."

*****

Allie tended the men that Ethan shot. She insisted on treating him first, but he reassured her that Torg would be of more help than her. Torg took Ethan into the smithy shop while she went to the wounded men. The first was already dead with a bullet in his brain. She quickly stepped past him to treat the other two. She placed her hands over the wounds of the next she came upon, kneeling at his side. The misshapen metal of the bullets rose from the tortured flesh into her glowing hands before the damaged flesh knitted closed behind it. The man stirred as his eyes fluttered open, his pain abating as he bathed in her magic. She moved on to the last man and treated him as well. As the last man awoke, he looked up into her eyes.

"Thank you, my lady," he whispered in awe.

"You may thank Prince Ethanos, for he insisted that I heal you before seeing to him."

Behind them, Borcose and his men stripped off their armor and mail, piling them in a great heap in front of the smith shop. They were allowed to go free if they surrendered their armor. They cursed Ethan's name, slamming their armor onto the pile while glaring at Ethan through the doorway of the shop. Ethan leaned back against a worktable as Torg placed his left hand on his shoulder while his right yanked the dart embedded in his right breast. Wrapping his calloused fingers around the feathered end of the shaft, he pulled tentatively.

"Just yank it out, Torg." Ethan winced.

"Are you sure about this, Ethan?"

"Do it."

"All right, here goes," he said, ripping it straight out. The jagged barbs along the tip reinjured the healed flesh as the shafts came free. The dart was caked in fresh blood as it made a sickly slurping sound as he drew it from Ethan's chest.

Ethan clenched his teeth as a fresh cavity was made in his chest. The excruciating pain quickly eased as the wound healed.

"That's one. Ready for the next?" Torg asked as Ethan raised a hand to stay his friend and catch his breath.

"Ethan, are you all right?" Allie asked as she passed through the entrance, concern etched across her face.

"I'm all right. It just hurts like hell because the barbs reopen the wound when we rip them out."

"What can I do to ease your pain?" She rushed to his side, placing the palm of her left hand upon his brow.

"I'll be fine once Torg takes out the other two." He nodded to Torg to continue.

The blacksmith gripped the second dart protruding from his right breast, just inches lower than the first. It took all his strength to tear it free as Ethan winced in agony, his chest twisting with the stubborn dart.

Allie took his right hand in hers, squeezing it tightly. She hated seeing him in such anguish and recalled the wounds he suffered in the Mage Bane. But his powers to regenerate were hindered there. Though he could heal himself, he still felt the pain, a fact she never realized until he told her that night in the Mage Bane.

"That's two," he answered hoarsely. "Just take the last one out before I have time to think about it, Torg." Ethan never remembered arrows or swords hurting this much.

His old friend wasted little time tossing the second dart on his workbench and grabbing hold of the third that was deeply embedded in Ethan's thigh. He couldn't get more than a couple of fingers wrapped around it, cursing his frustration. "Blast it, Ethan, it's buried too deep. Turn around."

Ethan complied, revealing the barbed tip protruding from his leg. Torg put on a heavy glove and wrapped his fingers around the jagged barbed tip and pulled it through. Ethan squeezed his eyes as the pain rippled his torso, catching in his chest before dissipating.

"Are you well?" Allie asked, cupping his face with her warm slender fingers.

He swore her voice was as smooth as silk, tender, and soothing. He stared deeply into her bright golden eyes, wondering how a woman so beautiful could walk through the palace without drawing the attention of every male who saw her. By the look, Torg gave her when she stood beside them proved at least that his eyes were working.

"I'm better now." He gave her that mischievous smile that defined his carefree nature. She had never met anyone like him. She didn't think a person like him existed. It was as if he were dropped into her world from another dimension. He talked differently and dressed differently from anyone else. To some he was a novelty, an odd quirk of nature who would live out his days and pass on, leaving little impact on the world around him. To some he was the manifestation of a hope long thought extinguished. To the noble houses of the mage realms of Elaria, his mere existence was dangerous, a threat to the very foundations of their power. She knew they were all wrong, for Ethan's destiny was far more significant than their petty hopes and fears.

Captain Marco stepped within, his eyes adjusting to the dim light. "Ethan, what do you want done with the armor and mail we gathered from Prince Borcose and his men?"

"Give it to Torg. I owe him some scrap metal for a little project we are working on."

Torg gave him an incredulous look. "You want me to melt down the armor of Prince Borcose's personal guard?"

"Yeah, that's the general idea. They're not going to need it. I spared them a dungeon cell, so they owe me for that and the three darts they so generously gave me."

"The king shall not be pleased with these events, Ethan," Marco said.

"Don't worry old buddy, I'm sure he'll tell me all about it."

"I pray you speak well, Ethan, or I shall be Sergeant Marco Valanus when next we meet."

"I always look out for my friends, Marco. You'll be fine," Ethan reassured him as he stood and clasped forearms with his old cavalry commander. Marco was one of the heroes of the Velo, receiving his promotion to the king's royal guards. Bronus would never punish him for protecting his son. Ethan craned his neck toward Torg. "Is that enough metal for our project?"

Torg nodded.

"Good. That's one less thing I have to do tonight." He smiled as he turned to Allie. "Are you free this evening, Miss Allie? Or does your queen have you occupied?"

She smiled, offering him her arm.

*****

The early winter air of Astaris hung crisp above the spell shield above, but cold could not be kept at bay completely. A slight cool air tickled his nostrils as they traversed the narrow back streets of Astaris. Ethan led her along the winding cobblestone pathways of the city's southwestern district. He had his guitar strapped over his back, with a pack alongside it. Two- and three-level structures of treated wood or white stone lined the avenues to each side. The higher levels of the structures stood out over the floors below. Streetlamps, powered by mage spells or torches, lighted the way.

"Where are you taking me, Ethan?" Allie asked, wary of the unnatural quiet of the street.

"There are not many places in Astaris that I can go without being lauded as royalty. I'm taking you to one of those."

"Why do you not partake in the festivities in the palace? There are banquets every night and dancing and music. You are still a son of the king. He would welcome your company."

"Because I hate formal gatherings. There is little joy in them, at least little joy that is genuine. I've been to countless balls and galas through the years, and they are filled with fake smiles and stiff smug greetings. I prefer spending my time with real friends. Besides, I hate dressing up."

"You don't have to dress up, but you might wish to change your shirt. That one has two holes in front, and your pants have one in front and back," she teased.

"I didn't think you noticed. Are they difficult to see?"

"You're right, I don't think anyone will notice." She rolled her eyes.

"Maybe you could sew them for me latter?"

She stifled a laugh, humored by how little he knew her. "I think your horse would do a better job of it than I."

"You can't sew?" he asked as they walked.

"No."

"You can't cook either," he remembered her confessing such when he showed her how to cook a snake.

"No."

"What kind of girl are you?" He made a face, teasing her.

"Do you sew or cook?"

"Not very well, except over a campfire."

"Then what kind of boy are you?"

"The kind not very good at doing girl's work." He laughed.

"Really?" She raised an admonishing brow. "So the brave and mighty Ethanos Blagen, who champions for the equality of the common man, thinks himself superior to we poor women?"

"I didn't mean it that way, Allie. I just...I...well women and men are...we're different," he stammered with his twisting words.

"You might wish to stop while you can, Ethan. Remember, your mouth always gets you in trouble." She gave a flirtatious wink.

"This is why we get along so well, Allie. Most people I insult, whether I mean it or not, get upset with me. You just give it right back as good as you receive."

"You will do well to remember that, Ethanos Blagen."

"Oh, I'll remember it." He smiled. He then stopped, holding out his right hand toward the building before them. "We're here."

*****

The lords and ladies of the seven mage realms gathered in the king's vast dining hall. Hundreds were seated at the long tables that ran the length of the vast chasm of bluestone. Giant hearths lined opposing walls and lighted globes rotated above, casting-colored frescos upon the upper walls above. Musicians played soft, delicate melodies with flutes blending with soprano voices. King Bronus sat at the head of the center table with Queen Gabrielle beside him. The kings and queens of the seven kingdoms joined him, seated to either side.

The lords and vassals of each monarch sat in descending order along each table. Servants wearing brown livery and hose hustled to and fro, filling goblets and fetching platters of food from the kitchens. King Bronus stood before his high-backed chair and lifted his goblet.

"My honored guests! I present a toast to the seven mage kingdoms and the monarchs that rule them. Welcome to Astaris!" His voice boomed with authority through the great hall. "And to Queen Valera, may your visit to our fair city be fruitful and pleasant!" He regarded her before taking a sip. The guests shouted their approval and began to feast as Bronus sat down to join them.

"I am most honored, King Bronus." Valera regarded him with her sweet voice as she sat along the table to his right. Her daughter, Princess Amanda, sat her left. "We hope not to burden your household any longer than is necessary. The crown princess shall make her decision in three days," Valera announced.

"Which of our young lords has caught your eye, Amanda?" Queen Gabrielle inquired.

"It will be a difficult choice, Your Grace. There are so many handsome and brave men in Astaria who have offered their hand. A few have stood apart from their brethren. I would be remiss if I revealed which has gained the most favor, lest the others forsake their hopes to be chosen. It is yet a close affair, and I like them to be on their toes so to speak," Amanda said, taking a sip of wine.

"Yes, men are best behaved when we keep them on edge and wanting to please," Queen Valera added, smiling sweetly to the kings seated around them.

"I must concur," Queen Lucieanne Lorga whispered loudly from across the table. "Husbands dance the merriest tunes when the wife cracks the whip."

Karl Lorga gave his wife a sour look, but she just smiled at him, unfazed by his disapproval.

"We have no need for whips. We women have other means to tame our husbands," Queen Gabrielle added while gazing into Bronus's gray eyes, giving him a playful wink.

"Pity the lad who is chosen." Bronus shook his head.

"Do be gentle, Princess Amanda, I would hate to think we are sending one of our noble sons to a torturous fate." Gabrielle smiled.

"Whichever son of Astaria the crown princess chooses shall be treated according to their station. You have my word as Queen of Vellesia," Valera said in a deadly serious tone. "Though we jest of such things, the boy the crown princess chooses, and who accepts her offer, shall be highly honored as the father of a future queen of Vellesia."

"And what if he sires a son?" King Evor Ectus asked, seated beside Princess Amanda.

"The firstborn of the Royal House of Loria have always been female. So it shall be with the crown princess," Valera said before shifting her gaze to the Astarian king. "King Bronus!"

"Queen Valera," he answered.

"Though such things are arranged with less formality and ceremony in Astaria, the selection of a royal consort in Vellesia is treated with utmost care. It must be bound in magic with assurances of devotion and commitment. I shall discuss the details of the crown princess's selection with you and the monarchs of the five other kingdoms tomorrow."

"Very well," Bronus acquiesced. He was all too happy to be done with Valera, her daughter, and his "guests." Three more days and he could enjoy time with his family and friends and celebrate the winter festival.

"King Gregor, something vexes you?" Valera asked the Gorgencian monarch, who sat beside King Ectus on the opposing side of the table. He sat sour-faced with a murderous glare in his eyes.

"I am not pleased," he snarled bitterly.

"And what is it that displeases you?" she asked.

"His son vexes me!" he said, rising to his feet and pointing his fore digit toward Bronus.

Bronus bristled at the Gorgencian's remark, his eyes glaring like blazing embers, dressing down Gregor.

"Your son Borcose is not without guilt in the matter, *King* Gregor. Perhaps you should see to the discipline in your own house before questioning it in mine."

"And when have you disciplined Ethanos, Your Grace?" Gregor asked, still standing and struggling to cull his rage.

Bronus slowly came to his feet, fixing his eyes upon Gregor. "Ethan has defied me when his conscience leads him elsewhere. It has *always* been with a concern for justice. Justice for those who hold little voice in our mage ruled lands or no voice at all in your land. Borcose defied the generosity of his host by attempting to mete out selfish 'justice' upon a poor blacksmith. Be grateful Ethan stopped the lad from harming Lufen, for if I were there, he would be cinders in the space of a thought!" The congregation of kings grew nervous as Bronus's hands crackled as if lightning might erupt from his fingertips. Gregor sat down, his eyes nervously fixed on Bronus's clenched fists.

Valera smiled, unmoved by the lightning lord's power. *He truly loves his son*, she mused. His pride for Ethanos was as bright as a thousand suns.

"Bronus," Gabrielle said, wrapping her fingers over his, her soft voice calming her husband's rage.

"I will defend my son when he is right and chastise him when he is wrong. Queen Valera," he said, turning to meet her sparkling eyes that betrayed little of the woman behind them. "Ethan will apologize for his offense of your person."

"Your love for your son is no less than the love I have for my own children, King Bronus. I will accept the boy's apology if it is sincere, but he must be made aware that the penalty for such an affront of royalty is *death* in my realm."

"He knows, but Ethan has earned the right of autonomy from the protocols of court. He earned his freedom on the field of battle," Bronus said.

"He has such freedom only by your leave, King Bronus," King Evor Ectus countered. "Such leniency does not extend to our realms. "If the boy spreads his sedition in Estasa, I will see him dead."

Before Bronus could reply to Evor's threat, Queen Valera spoke in his defense. "My dear Evor, it was I who was offended by Prince Ethanos, not you, Your Grace. I believe It is ill-advised for any of the monarchs of the seven mage realms to kill each other's children.

If Ethanos should be found spreading his sedition in your realm, it would be prudent to *seize* him. I am certain that King Bronus would pay the ransom you require. Ethanos would have to renew his oath to the throne of Astaria in exchange for his life. Such an alternative would be better than war, would it not?"

"Ethan sees any oath to the throne as a chain of servitude. I would never ask that of him, not even for a treasury filled with gold," Bronus said, retaking his seat, reminding her of the bounty she once offered for him.

"The choice, of course, would be yours, King Bronus. The rest of us must be content that the boy has thus far kept himself from our lands. He seems most content within the confines of Cordova, and..." She paused, her eyes trailing to Gabrielle, gauging her response. "And territories outside our purview. I see the discussion of your son troubles you, King Bronus, so let us discuss a merrier topic. The crown princess will make her decision three days hence. We desire to announce their union at the queen's ball, if Her Grace, Queen Gabrielle, would acquiesce?"

"That would be acceptable," Gabrielle said.

"Splendid." Valera smiled joyously. "We should have our stewards coordinate the details of such a conjoined affair."

"Of course," Gabrielle said graciously.

*****

The crowd of the Broken Lance sang the Yellow Rose of Texas off tune, but at least they remembered the lyrics as Ethan had spent the better part of the night teaching them the words. The tavern floor was serried with tradesmen, soldiers, ruffians, and mercenaries. Ethan knew many by name as they knew him. The Broken Lance was a two-level wooden structure with a bar running the length of the back wall, opposite the double front doors of the tavern front. Round tables of varied sizes littered the open floor, with enough space for serving wenches to ply their trade. The patrons were a raucous lot, spilling their ale as their sobriety waned throughout the night. Ethan had barely walked through the front doors before a crowd gathered around him, begging for tales of his recent adventures. He told of his duel with Luke Crawford and Sheriff Thorton's battle with Hank Grierson. Their eyes grew like saucers as he described the horseless wagons that rumbled over tracks with puffs of smoke that belched from their chimneys. He told them how Luke Crawford, Emmitt Cobb, and their gang followed him to Astaria, and his pursuit of them through the Aqualania Sea, leaving out any mention of the Mage Bane, of course.

Allie never left his side. She marveled how others gravitated toward him, and why wouldn't they? She gravitated toward him. He was so different from everyone else. He would talk with anyone, no matter their station or importance, hanging on their every word, lest he miss some detail. He found the common people more interesting than the mage born. He enjoyed their stories and seemed to understand their plight.

The patrons asked him of his strange instrument and if he picked up any songs across the barrier. So he taught them "The Yellow Rose of Texas," and it was unlike anything they had ever heard. It was cheerful and up-tempo, which contrasted with their mellow or dreary ballads and chants. Allie clapped her hands, going along with the crowd. She couldn't imagine the court musicians of Vellesia playing such a scandalous tune. Queen Valera would be red with rage if Ethan ever taught them such a melody. Ethan had lent the stringed instrument to Jollo the Minstrel, and she could see him in the center of the crowd, plucking away at the strings. Ethan gave him basic instruction on its use, and Jollo listened attentively, quickly picking up the instrument. The patrons were now singing without Ethan's help. He stood at her side, watching the crowd with a bemused look on his face.

He shifted his eyes to hers. He was worried that she might feel uneasy with this rough crowd, but she betrayed no hint of apprehension. He scolded himself for doubting her. Of course, she wouldn't be frightened after all they faced together. He had never had such a friendship with a girl before. He smiled at her as she nodded to him in kind, a hint of glee in her eye that her lips fought to contain. Before she knew what was happening, Ethan scooped her up into his arms with one arm under her back and the other under her knees as he spun her around.

"Ethan!" Her eyes grew wide and uncertain. She had never been handled in such a way.

"I'm not letting you down without a kiss." He grinned, staring into her golden eyes.

"Ethanos Blagen!" she called out his name with her gold eyes narrowed like thin rays of sunlight. "Is this how you treat guests in Astaris? By holding them hostage in your muscular arms to extort kisses from them upon your handsome lips?"

"I don't treat our guests this way, just *you*."

"Well, I'm not kissing you because I don't want you to put me down, but if you grow weary, you can kiss me *first*."

"All right," he said, kissing her as he spun her around.

*****

The following evening found Ethan in an outer corridor of the inner palace facing the arched doorway of the great hall. The entryway was the height of three men, with twelve-inch-thick oak doors that were swung open. Bluestone arced overhead, and every torch and mage lantern was lit within the great hall as light flooded through the entryway, illuminating the outer corridor. He passed Allie in the adjoining hall. They shared a look, but nothing more, lest his attempt to free her fail. As a mage healer, she would only be allowed to enter the great hall at the invite of a higher ranking guest. She would wait for him on the outer ramparts of the inner palace.

Ethan's sisters Arian and Felicia greeted him outside the great hall, Arian dressed in a turquoise gown with silver lace at her cuffs and collar, and Felicia similarly adorned in a silver gown with black lace. The light from the great hall played across the reddish strands of Arian's hair like sparkling tinsel. Felicia's golden tresses framed her porcelain face and bright-blue eyes. Each of their dresses had narrow bodices and full flowing skirts that billowed below their waists.

"Ethan!" They said in unison, each hugging him tightly.

He smiled as he beheld their lovely faces. He had missed them terribly. "At least somebody is happy to see me tonight," he said as they released him.

"Everyone is happy to see you, Ethan, at least our people anyway," Felicia said.

"The rest are here to see my humiliation," he grumbled.

"Is it truly humiliating to have to apologize, Ethan?" Arian admonished.

"Apologizing to Valera is," he shot back.

"*Queen* Valera," Arian reminded him as she brushed lint off his shoulder. "Well, you look much better tonight, but would it have pained you to wear a formal tunic and hose? Or even a cape?"

"Yes, it would have," he quickly answered. He wore his thick black trousers and pullover shirt, with black ankle-high boots and a sword. He left his pistol belt in his bedchamber. This outfit was compromise enough. If Allie's freedom didn't hinge on his performance tonight, he would've worn his earth garb. Then again, if Allie's freedom was not in play, he wouldn't apologize at all.

"I might as well get this over with." He took a breath and entered the great hall.

Resting upon the opposing side of the inner palace from the king's dining hall, the great hall was a mirror image of the former. Entryways with stone arches gave way to an expansive interior with azure stone walls arcing toward a cupola canter. Mage-lit spherical lanterns hung from the vaulted ceiling, rotating slowly, casting-colored frescos along the blue walls above. The floor was mirrored silver stone that reflected the images above in perfect symmetry. The walls were lined with lords and ladies and mages of high rank. Each king retained a score of personal guards. Seventy meters abreast and across, and twenty meters high at its center apex, the great hall was a cavernous chamber where a sizable host could be swallowed with room to spare.

Ethan made his way through the crowd, cognizant of the stares of those he passed. Even without his buckskins and pistols, he was dressed far more casually than everyone else. His hair was shorter as well, unlike the flowing locks favored by the young lords. He was bathed, shaved, and scented so as not to offend Queen Valera's nose.

Dozens of young lords and ladies were paired in the center floor, dancing at arm's length with proper court etiquette as harpists plucked soft melodies. Ethan skirted the center, recognizing many faces. He spotted Jennifer Murtado dancing with Crown Prince Erik Ectus of Estasa, her dark hair lying over the shoulders of her golden dress with its billowed skirts and tight bodice. Her blue eyes were fixed to Erik's green. He was slender and graceful and glided across the floor, holding her hand high as they moved. Her brother said she was looking forward to seeing Ethan, but it seemed she had found a new romantic interest. Ethan didn't care. He always knew most women desired a man of position and power. They fawned over him all his life as he was the heir to Astaria. By giving up the throne, he knew it would reveal who truly desired him and who did not. He thought Jennifer was different, though. She was the only girl in Astaria he had ever kissed. She chased after him since they were children and one of the few who wished him well when he left Astaris after he forsook the throne. Now she didn't even look his way. She acted as if he were invisible, even when he called her by name the day before. He was suddenly struck by something his father once said, "No woman who wants you to crawl after her is worth the effort." He thought of Allie. She didn't care about lands and titles. She liked him for who he was, nothing more. She was more beautiful than all the highborn ladies gathered in the great hall. Besides, she stood by him in the mage bane when any other girl would have run away.

He found his father at the far end of the hall, seated upon his throne with Queen Gabrielle seated beside him. Before the throne, the Vellesian princess danced with Xavier Murtado. Vancel Torrent, Geoff Jarvo, and a dozen others waited nearby for their turn to dance with Princess Amanda, hoping to demonstrate their grace and coordination. Ethan was amused, picturing Vancel Torrent attempting to dance with the Vellesian princess. He'd probably break her feet with his first step. Ethan thought the suitors looked ridiculous in their tunics, hose, and pointed shoes, especially Vancel, who towered over his companions by a good half a head. He liked Vancel and hoped the princess would choose another. He would be ill suited to a life as a royal consort. The title was just a glorified slave, obliged to walk behind his bride and serve her every whim. Of course that seemed to describe marriage in general. Even women born without mage power could entice a man to do her bidding, let alone beautiful mage-born ladies, who would use every arrow in their quiver to render a man prostate. *Not Allie, though*, he reminded himself. She could've escaped with her sister mages in the Mage Bane but chose to help him. He might not have survived had she not disobeyed his command. She wasn't like other girls. He could talk to her like an equal. She was a friend in every sense of the word. Marriage was not for him, but if it were, she would be the one. Perhaps he would marry her anyway, if he could free her of the magic that bound her to the Vellesian throne.

The soft golden eyes of the princess found Ethan in the crowd. Her lush auburn hair shimmered in the ambient light. The folds of her scarlet gown fluttered smoothly as she danced.

"My lord, Murtado," she spoke, stepping briefly away.

"Your Highness," Xavier bowed, stepping away as his turn ended.

Geoff Jarvo awaited his turn, but the princess approached Ethan, reaching her slender left hand to him.

The musicians paused as the surrounding crowd grew quiet. Off to the side, Queen Valera stood stone-faced, betraying little emotion as she oversaw every step the princess made.

"Ethanos, would you dance with me?" Princess Amanda asked.

King Bronus looked on from his throne. *For once, boy, just shut your mouth and do as you are asked*, he thought.

Ethan looked to Queen Valera, whose eyes betrayed no malice. They betrayed no warmth either.

"Are you certain, Princess? I'm not a candidate for your hand," he reminded her. Looking in her eyes, he realized how pretty she was. She had bright warm golden eyes, which seemed genuine, unlike her mother's. She rivaled his sisters' beauty, but he still felt Allie was far prettier. She looked much younger than her supposed eighteen years.

"Come." She smiled as she pulled him into the dancing circle.

"I don't dance this way," he said, lowering one hand to her waist and the other holding her hand. He led her as they moved across the floor. The suitors stood with arms crossed in disapproval as shocked gasps and whispers echoed through the assemblage.

"I'm not sure we should be doing this since your mother hates me, Amanda?" Ethan said, though he wasn't shy about accepting her offer and dancing far more familiarly than others deemed appropriate.

"It is I she will be cross with. How strange it is to be called by my name."

"Sounds good, doesn't it? I know it does to me when I hear others call me Ethan."

"You are so strange." She shook her head, amused by his speech and manner.

"How so?"

"Well…you dress simply. You care little of power since you forsook your birthright. You stand in defense of the common born. Despite all of this, your arrogance angers nearly every lord in every kingdom. Do you relish their venom? I have never seen my mother so furious in her life."

"I have that effect on people. Most mage lords are offended by any arrogance that interferes with their own. As far as your mother goes, I wish I hadn't said those things to her. I'm a lot like a dog, if you pull my tail I'll bite."

"Yes, I think Mother knows that now." Amanda laughed.

"Just tell her not to feel too offended. I've caused my father more grief than anyone."

"Yes, I notice how he cringes whenever you speak."

"You're very observant, Princess."

"Oh, not really. Even a blind deaf-mute could reach the same conclusion."

"You're probably right," he conceded. "So…have you made up your mind yet?" he asked, observing her suitors standing off to the side, anxiously waiting their turn.

"Not yet, but I am very close."

He shook his head.

"What amuses you, Ethan?"

"Do you *want* to be married like this? To a stranger you have just met? What advantage is there to being the ruler of your kingdom if you can't wed who you want? Had I kept the throne of Astaria would have married who I want, whether she was mage born or common."

"The crown princess of Vellesia shall marry who she wants." She smiled, though it failed to reach her eyes.

"I'm certain you'll make him very happy since you're easy on the eyes, Princess."

"As are you, Ethanos Blagen."

"Do you know your mother tried to arrange our nuptials when you were born?"

"No. I did not know," she said, looking into his eyes.

"My father refused, of course, but she persisted until she discovered my immunity to magic."

"How fortunate for her. You would have been insufferable," she teased.

"Nah, I'm harmless and lovable. In time I could've won her over."

Amanda nearly burst in laughter. "I doubt that. There is a rumor that you are here to apologize to her."

"It's true," he sighed.

"That does not sound like the Ethanos Blagen we have all heard tell of. Why the change of heart?"

"I have my reasons," he answered carefully, observing Valera standing amid her entourage. A dozen mages of varying guilds attended her with a score of personal guards wearing silver armored cuirasses over white tunics with pleated kilts. Valera wore a scarlet high-necked gown and a golden tiara that circled her head like a celestial arc.

"I believe our dance is at its end, Ethan. Queen Valera awaits you." She raised her hand as he kissed it.

"Wish me luck." He smiled.

Amanda's countenance darkened as she met his eyes. "Ethan, leave the palace tonight. Do *not* return until we are gone. Do not tell *anyone* I told you this, or I will suffer greatly for it." Her face brightened into a heartfelt smile as she stepped away.

Her remark distracted his train of thought as he approached Queen Valera. Was it a warning about her mother or some other danger of which he was unaware? Perhaps it was a trick to remove him from the palace while they strike their intended target. The other mage kings had plotted against his father for years, and Ethan feared for his safety. Amanda's warning was meant for him, though, not his father. But was it genuine? Besides, what harm could they do to him? He could slay the lot of them with relative ease.

The queen's guards blocked his way as he drew nigh.

"I would speak with your mistress," he said.

"Let the boy approach," Valera commanded.

Ethan stepped forth, his gaze meeting the Vellesian queen's.

"Why are you here, child?" Though her condescending tone irritated him, he would not let it show.

"Queen Valera, I wish to apologize for my rudeness yesterday morning at the tourney. Please forgive my…insolence."

She looked at him with cold appraising eyes as if she were measuring him for some unknown purpose. "Why should I forgive you, child?"

Child? If Allie's life were not in the balance, he would run her through with his sword for calling him that.

"The granting of forgiveness is the prerogative of the offended, but I *am* sorry, and though I have angered you with my tongue, I have done a great service to Vellesia with my actions."

"And what service would that be, child?"

"I rescued twelve of your mage healers when they were held captive in…near Cordova," he caught himself before mentioning the Mage Bane. It was a difficult dance to ask for a reward for service to one queen without another knowing about it.

"Yes, I was informed of your…bravery," she said as if suddenly recalling what she clearly knew.

A long uncomfortable silence followed as she could sense his growing unease. Oh, how she liked to see him squirm. This was going to be great fun.

"You wish me to absolve you now, Ethanos? No, you have *not* come to me for forgiveness. What would Ethanos Blagen care about forgiveness? You have repeatedly declared your disdain for mage lords and ladies. What is it you seek?"

"A request, Queen Valera. I saved twelve of your mage healers and I humbly ask a request."

"What would you like, Ethanos? I do not grant requests lightly, and never until I know what is requested. So, Ethanos, what do you *desire* of me?" she asked in a seductive whisper.

This was not going well. Ethan didn't expect it to be easy, but the queen had a way of unnerving him. He might as well just ask.

"There is a mage healer bound to House Loria. She is one of the twelve I rescued. I would like her freed of her oath to Vellesia."

"*Free of her oath?*" Valera asked as if shocked by his audacity.

"Yes, Your Highness. I *did* save twelve of your mage healers. Would not the freedom of one be worth the other eleven?"

"My dear Ethanos." She smiled like a cat playing with a mouse. "Only a *royal* request could free a mage of their oath to Vellesia."

A royal request was only granted when saving the life of a monarch or crown royal or saving a realm from a significant threat. Of course a monarch could grant a royal request for lesser acts if they so chose.

Ethan released a defeated breath. He knew it was a fool's errand and turned to leave.

"I might grant you a royal request, Ethanos," she said, freezing him in place.

He turned back cautiously.

"What is the girl's name?"

"Allie."

"Allie?" She pretended to struggle recollecting her. "Oh yes. A very gifted healer and very beautiful."

"And you would grant me a royal request for saving your mage healers?" he asked warily.

"Oh, Ethanos," she said in a soothing feminine voice as she stepped close, whispering in his right ear, "I will grant you a royal request to free *any* subject of Vellesia from their bond if you ask it of me...*on your knees.*"

Ethan paled. The thought of kneeling *to her* made him ill. He stepped back, uncertain.

"Is your pride worth more than Allie's freedom, Ethanos?" Valera asked. "The choice is yours. Of course such an act of reverence would require a worthy audience."

Ethan knew he could only purchase Allie's freedom with his own humiliation.

"All right, I'll do it."

A wide smile grew from her lips as she took a step back. They already had the attention of half the great hall. Few could hear their exchange of words. King Bronus and Queen Gabrielle watched silently from their thrones.

"*Let it be known!*" Valera's voice echoed through the cavernous chamber. "Ethanos Blagen has formally apologized for his offensive remarks directed to my person. It has also come to my knowledge that Ethanos Blagen saved the lives of twelve Vellesian mage healers some months ago. He has made a request of me that I can only grant for a royal request. Because of my generosity, I shall grant Ethanos a royal request if he formally asks for it in full view of the mage kings of Elaria!"

Ethan observed the familiar faces of King Ortovan Marvo of Meltoria and King Magnus Delmarin of Relusia. Gregor Vorhenz, Karl Lorga, and Evor Ectus stepped forth, each surrounded by a small entourage. He could see their curious eyes and unmasked glee as they observed his humiliation.

Valera held out her right hand. Ethan stepped forth, took a knee before her, and then kissed the back of her hand.

"I beseech your mercy for a royal request, Queen Valera," Ethan declared.

"Your request if granted?"

"The freedom of the mage healer Allie. That she be freed of her bond to Vellesia."

"As queen of Vellesia, I formally grant Ethanos Blagen, former crown prince of Astaria, a royal request to free any subject of my realm. Ethanos Blagen, I ask again which Vellesian subject do you wish to free from their bond to Vellesia?

"The mage healer Allie."

"The mage healer Allie is released from her oath to Vellesia. She is free to choose her own path and serve whichever realm she desires," Valera declared. "Does this fulfill your royal request, Ethanos?"

"Yes, Your Highness," he answered.

"Very well, you may rise, child. Find Allie and share your news with her."

Ethan gained his feet. He had sworn to never kneel again, yet a lifetime of freedom for Allie was worth more than a single act of humiliation. When he turned, he did not see Princess Amanda or many of her suitors. What he did see were the condescending smirks of the mage kings. Magnus Delmarin's smile was wider than the Velo. Of all the mage kings, he despised Ethan the most.

"Ethan! A word," Bronus ordered, crooking a finger to beckon him forth.

Ethan approached the dais, stopping short of the throne.

"We seem to have much to discuss, son," Bronus said.

"Yes, Father."

"You did well to apologize, Ethan, but who is this girl that you bent your knee for?"

"A healer," Ethan answered. He just wanted to leave. Kneeling to Valera made him disgusted with himself. She revealed how petty and cruel she truly was, yet no one else seemed to notice.

"You bent your knee for a Vellesian girl?" Bronus asked in disbelief.

Ethan bristled at his father's judgmental tone. "I exchanged a moment of humiliation for a lifetime of freedom for a *woman* who is more worthy to be a queen than any who hold that title save the woman who bore me."

"I would very much like to meet a woman who instills such passion in my firstborn." Gabrielle smiled down at him. She had waited for what felt a lifetime for some girl to stir Ethan's blood.

"As would I," Bronus added. "You shall formally introduce her."

"I will after the Vellesian delegation departs. Until then, I plan to stay as far away from our 'guests' as I can." Ethan bade his parents good night and exited the hall.

CHAPTER 27

He found her atop a battlement of the inner palace, staring out at the surrounding countryside north of Astaris. Tall oaks and maples towered over the diminutive sorek and lichen trees. They stretched endlessly north along the Por-Shada Plateau and over the Upper Torlin. The snow caps atop the jagged gray peaks of the Por-Shada Mountains ran northward along the western horizon like the white surf of a giant wave. The setting sun slipped beneath their colossal peaks, casting long shadows over the eastern foothills.

Allie took in the beauty of this strange country, wondering what sort of land produced a man like Ethan. She could see him as a child playing in these forests and swimming in these streams. She wished she had time to speak with his mother and ask what he was like as a boy. She knew he must have tested her patience to no end.

"Beautiful," Ethan's voice carried softly on the wind as he stepped across the wide built platform that ran within the battlements, stepping close and resting his forearms on the rampart at her side.

"It is a beautiful country." She regarded him warmly.

"I wasn't referring to the scenery."

"Oh." She tried to swallow her smile but couldn't. He had that effect on her.

"Oh? Is that the only word you can muster for the man who just freed you from your queen?"

His words took time to filter, then her eyes shifted sharply to his. "What have you…How?"

"Don't ask how I did it. The only thing that matters is you are free, Allie. Free to live where you wish and how you wish."

"How could you free me? I am oath bound to the Vellesian throne." Her eyes searched his, moonlight playing upon his face.

"She granted me a royal request, and I used it to free you."

"You were granted a royal request?"

"Yes, for saving the lives of you and your sister mages."

"Now I am twice indebted to you," she threw her arms around him, kissing his cheek, his chin, his nose, and mostly his lips.

"You owe me nothing, Allie. Your life is yours. You're free now, so enjoy it."

"You claim no favor of me?" she asked.

"If I claimed a favor, you'd only be trading one master for another."

"Oh, Ethan, thank you." She kissed him fiercely. Her lips lingered on his, savoring his taste and the emollient caress of his mouth.

"What will you do now?"

"I don't know. I never thought it possible."

"If you like, you can stay in Astaris as long as you wish. My parents are eager to meet you."

"Astaris? I thought you were planning to return to Cordova?"

"I am, but there is something I must do first, a place I must go."

"When are we going?"

"You're not going, it's far too dangerous."

"Of course I'm going, Ethan. I have nowhere else to go. Besides, my place is with you." She looked up at him with her bright golden eyes.

"Allie, the Mage Bane was risky enough for you. I will not risk your life for where I'm going. I would like you to stay here until I return. Can you wait for me?"

"Where are you going?" She ignored his question and asked her own, her tone changing from soft to harsh. She raised an eyebrow as if admonishing a child who just spilled his drink.

"I can't tell you, Allie. I promised my grandfather not to tell anyone."

"Ethan, you have trusted me with your life. Can you not trust me with this? Will you tell me if I promise not to follow?"

Ethan stepped briefly away, turning his back while scrubbing his face with his hands as he debated whether to tell her or not. Turning back to face her, he gently gripped her shoulders as he looked into her eyes.

"My grandfather had a vision, Allie, a very ominous one. I am not sure if I can prevent it, but I know I am the only one who can. I need you to trust me, Allie. I have to do this."

"What was the nature of this dream?" she asked, fixing her eyes to his as the weight of the question and the hold of her gaze forced his tongue.

"Dragons," he answered, defeated by her beautiful eyes that seemed to tear any veils he placed to hide his thoughts.

"Dragons?" she growled lowly, cupping his cheeks tightly with her hands. "Ethan, dragons are immune to magic."

"So am I."

"You won't be able to heal yourself. They will kill you. Only spell shields created by the mage lords of old can keep them at bay. Where do you plan to go to find dragons? The wildlands?"

His silence confirmed her guess.

"The wildlands! You test your luck too often, first the barrier, then the Mage Bane, and now the wilds. You play with death like she is your lover. Be careful, Ethan, for death plays for keeps."

"I went to the Mage Bane for you, remember? And don't speak of it too loudly or my mother will find out. I'm not going to the wilds because I want to. If I don't go, then Astaria will be destroyed, so tell me, Allie, what choice do I have?" he said with a heavy heart.

His sea-blue eyes did not sparkle like she was accustomed. He looked tired. "Ethan," she said softly. "You take the weight of the world upon yourself. You speak fondly of freedom, yet you do not reap the glory of it. I don't wish to burden you further. You have saved me in so many ways, and you have shown me such kindness. Let us enjoy the time we have."

"Thank you, Allie. Everyone else gives me grief for every decision I make, even when the decision is best for everyone. I know you're not pleased, but you understand."

"I understand, Ethan. I am also very fond of you and fear losing you. You could die out there in the wilds, and we would never know."

"I'll return. I promise." He smiled.

"I'll hold you to it." She wrapped her arms around him.

*****

The heavy rain slapped the roof of his pavilion as he stood over the map table in the large tent's center. Tristan Blagen surveyed the map's depiction of Astaria's northeastern approaches and the Gorgencian frontier. He wore a black tunic and trousers with a medium sword upon his left hip. Though he was a son of Bronus and now the crown prince of Astaria, he cast a slender silhouette, unlike his father's stocky build. He bent his keen eye to the rich details of the Gorgencian border. The early intelligence that the Gorgencians had advanced to their border in force was proving to be correct, but to what end? Their king and crown prince were guests in Astaris. If they attacked Astaria, their lives would be forfeit. He lacked his father's lightning power or his brother's bravado, but Tristan had gifts of his own, he was cunning.

"We've spotted two legions encamped here and one more here," Lord General Brax said, running his finger over the map as he relayed the information.

"Three legions," Tristan repeated to himself.

"Aye, and the supporting elements that accompany an army. Wagons laden with grain, water, metal, and rum stretch beyond the horizon. If this is a Gorgencian feint, they have me for a fool, my prince."

All logic pointed to a Gorgencian attack, but something gnawed in the back of his mind that suggested otherwise.

"Something troubles you, my prince?" Brax asked.

"It is too obvious. I sense deception. The true target lies elsewhere, I can feel it."

"Very perceptive, Prince Tristan," a stranger's voice interrupted.

Tristan and Brax looked quickly up, finding a man masked in a gray cloak standing at the entrance. His build and stature matched Tristan's modest frame. His eyes were deep purple, and strands of ebony hair peeked at the edge of his hood.

Tristan and Brax drew their swords.

"Who let you in?" Brax asked with his sword tip at the man's throat.

The man was unmoved. He raised his outstretched palms in supplication. "I mean no harm, Prince Tristan. I am gifted in evading sentries and men of common blood. Even mage born have difficulty spying my movement."

"Who are you?" Tristan asked, placing the point of his sword to the stranger's throat as well.

"I shall not reveal my name with Lord Brax present," the stranger said.

"Lord Brax is Astaria's lord general and my most trusted advisor. He shall have your name the same as me."

"My dear Prince Tristan, I mean not to offend, but Lord Brax's thoughts are transparent, and our mutual enemies will learn of my actions by simply reading his memory. If a certain queen were to learn of my indiscretion, my life would be forfeit."

"And if you're an assassin who plans to kill Prince Tristan?" Brax growled.

"If I were an assassin, Lord Brax, wouldn't I have simply killed your crown prince instead of announcing my presence?"

"Lord Brax, would you please step outside for a moment," Tristan commanded.

Brax drew his thick cloak over his head and stepped without.

"And now your name and purpose?" Tristan demanded.

The stranger drew back his hood, revealing a black mane over dark olive skin and a handsome face. He looked almost too perfect.

"I am Prince Raymar, son of Queen Valera of Vellesia. My purpose is to warn you of treachery afoot in Astaris. It was I who gave your grandfather the warning to send you from the city, to send you here where we could meet."

"For what purpose? If you had words of warning, why not give them directly to Dragos rather than leading me here?"

"You can shield your thoughts, Tristan, but your grandfather cannot. Unfortunately, your shield prevents you from receiving my thoughts as well, so we had to meet face to face."

"My grandfather is a master seer and telepath. No one can read his thoughts without his knowing it."

"My *sister* can."

Tristan found that thought troubling. "Is she the enemy you speak of?"

"We have much to discuss, and time is fleeting. Let us hope we are not too late."

*****

"Who is she?" Gabrielle asked, overlooking the ramparts through the portal in her private chamber in the queen's tower.

Ceresta stepped beside her, looking down at her brother and the Vellesian girl below.

"She is a mage healer. Ethan apparently saved her and eleven other healers from Luke Crawford and his men. The details of the rescue are still a mystery for some reason."

"What have you learned from her?"

"She is as she claims. She is a gifted healer, perhaps greater than Arian. Her name is Allie."

"What are her intentions with Ethan?"

"She cares for him."

"How much?"

"Very much. I've never felt so strong a bond."

Gabrielle gave her daughter a disbelieving look. "Greater than your Father and I?"

"Yes."

"I wish to meet her."

"When?"

"After the queen's ball. I am certain she will be staying after her queen departs. That should afford me the time to take her measure.

If Ethan fancies her, then what she lacks in titles she will counter with kindness. What have you learned about Father's meeting with Ethan?"

"Nothing. Grandfather guards his thoughts well, and Ethan is saying nothing. I would guess Grandfather had a vision."

"And he trusts Ethan's council on the matter over ours?"

"Ethan can see things that are obscured in Dragos's visions. There would be no other reason for his insistence to see Ethan when he first arrived.

Gabrielle found her father's intrigues disconcerting. It was he that discovered the portal that Ethan used to visit Earth. That misadventure led to Ethan's prolonged absence with nary a word from her son for almost a year. Her father enabled Ethan's wanderings and emboldened his independence. That directly led to his forsaking the throne for *freedom*. She shook her head, disappointed with what might have been. Ethan would have made a fine king, but he always answered the seductive call of danger. She was thankful for his power to heal himself, but she worried nonetheless. The Mage Bane represented the greatest danger outside the wildlands, but Ethan would have no need to venture the wilds, and he promised her to never enter the Mage Bane. He was not immune to death, however, despite what many believed. He was *not* immune to pain, either. She recalled her vision that tormented her waking hours. Dragos told her it was a prophetic dream, meant to warn by intertwining an action with a consequence. She envisioned Ethan entering the Mage Bane, his image shifting eerily like an aberration. The vision faded then transformed, manifesting into a horrific image cast from her darkest fears. She saw Ethan chained and tortured, suffering agony without end, agony that would kill mortal men, but he would simply heal enough to prolong his torment indefinitely.

The painful vision sent a cool shudder across her shoulders. She hugged her trembling arms as the sensation coursed her flesh.

"Something vexes you, Mother?" Ceresta asked.

"Your brother is the source of nearly all my restless nights. A Mother's burden never ends."

*****

"It is agreed!" Queen Valera declared before the mage kings of the seven mage realms. They sat around the stone circle table centered in the secluded chamber deep within the bowels of the inner palace. A domed mage lantern hung above the table's center, bathing the chamber with ample light. Only the mage kings and Queen Valera were present. It was the first such gathering in one hundred years. It was a council long overdue, and Valera suggested the calling as a backdrop to settle the affront committed against Vellesia. Of course, no wrongdoing was assigned to their Astarian Host, but the marriage pact allowed both sides to save face and calm the calls for vengeance among the Vellesian vassals.

"The crown princess will make her decision tomorrow?" Evor Ectus asked.

"Yes," Valera answered.

"And the one selected shall respond in agreement by accepting her invitation," Bronus added. "It is reasonable."

"He shall have a full day to rescind the offer, but once the queen's ball commences, he is committed. The vows of marital union shall be concluded on the apex of the day following the queen's ball. Failure to comply with the sacred vows shall invoke the judgment on the groom's house as agreed," Valera explained.

"I shall inform each of the suitors and their lord fathers," Bronus said.

"You shall, of course, inform them of the dowry owed the house of the boy who is chosen. Five hundred thousand gold pieces," Valera said.

The other mage kings stirred in disbelief. Such a sum would make the chosen House wealthier than some of them, but Bronus seemed unmoved by such a gift. As for them, they would feel ill at ease if one of their vassals wielded such a sum. Only magic bound the lords of any kingdom to their mage kings and queens. With such a sum, Queen Valera could nearly purchase whichever of Astaria's noble houses that she desired. Such a house would also be bound to the Vellesian throne by blood. Such facts must certainly have caught Bronus's attention. If not, then he was a fool.

"I shall also inform them of *all* the parameters and assurances that we have agreed," Bronus added.

"Of course." Valera smiled.

*****

"So where are we going?" Allie asked.

The morning sun broke through the trees above as they rode north, leaving the azure towers of Astaris behind them. Their breath caught in the crisp morning air, making smoky vapors when they exhaled. She was awoken that morning by a chambermaid who brought her breakfast upon a silver tray with fresh fruit and flowers. The maid said they were compliments of Prince Ethanos Blagen. The maid begged her not to tell Ethan that she referred to him as prince. Allie laughed and swore not to tell. The maid also presented brown leather trousers, boots, and lady's blouse for riding. Her mother would be aghast seeing her dressed in such garments, but she donned them and met Ethan at the stables. He presented her with a snow-white mare for her mount and led her from the palace.

"I'm going to show you the most beautiful place in the world," he looked over to her with that infectious smile of his. "And I'll show you how to shoot."

"Interesting," she mused. "I hope to be a good student."

"Well, if you're not, I'll have to spank you," he teased.

"Then maybe I should be naughty." She smiled lasciviously.

"See, I can't win, you'd just enjoy it."

"I enjoy any attention I receive from you, Ethan. This mare is quite lovely, did you borrow her from your father's stables?" She stroked her palfrey's mane, running her slender fingers through its silken hair. "She is so soft."

"I borrow nothing from my father. I bought the horse with my own coin. She's yours, my gift to you to celebrate your freedom."

"Ethan, I cannot accept this. She must have cost a small fortune, and you have worked so hard for your own coin."

"I can earn more gold, but you need a horse." Ethan took pride in earning his own way. She knew that his gift was a product of his labor, not the indulgent excess of a wealthy prince.

"But any horse would do, Ethan. This mare is breathtaking. In all my travels, I've never seen her equal."

The horse was bred for royalty, with perfect symmetry, manner, and lush white coat. She was bred by a private trainer whose specialty is the finest horseflesh for only the highest-born ladies and royals. Ethan procured her for a wealthy price.

"You deserve a mount that befits your beauty, Allie. All you have to do is name her."

"Then I shall name her Glynderelle, after the first queen of Vellesia."

"As long as it's not Valera," he said as they continued on beneath the falling leaves of oak and maple.

"You truly do not favor my queen, do you?" She smiled.

"I'd rather swim Shark's Bay with four bleeding limbs then spend any more time with that one. I don't know what Amanda's suitors are thinking, but they're vying for a life of humiliation and torment."

"You don't truly believe that?" she said quietly.

"I do," he answered quickly. "The princess is kinder than I thought, but her mother has all the charm of a pit viper."

"Why do think the princess is kind?"

"We talked last night."

"Where did you talk?"

"In the great hall, while we danced."

Allie pulled back her reins, gliding her mare to an abrupt halt. "You danced with her?" she nearly shouted before regaining her composure.

"Briefly, yes, right before I spoke with Valera. Are you jealous?" He almost grinned until he saw the indignation in her face. He pulled up on his reins, circling Bull in front of her palfrey.

"Why?" she asked.

"Because she asked me, and I wanted to stay in the queen's good graces until I could free you."

"Not you. Why did *she* want to dance?"

Ethan was unsure how to answer. Amanda warned him to leave Astaris until after the queen's ball. She also asked him not to tell a soul that she warned him."

"She told me I had upset her mother. She seemed in good spirits, though. Allie, what is wrong?"

"Nothing. I just didn't expect the princess to act so impulsively." Her eyes shifted uncertainly before coming back to his. "My mother told me what you did, Ethan. How the queen made you beg for my freedom. That you would humble yourself for me warms my heart. Thank you," she said with moistened eyes.

"You're welcome. Now let me show you why I brought you out here."

*****

They stood on the precipice, overlooking the vale from the southern cliffs that stretched above the river below. The Upper Torlin snaked through the valley below as sorek trees pressed upon either bank. Far to the west the river dropped swiftly into the vale in a cascading fall nearly a thousand feet high. Beams of sunlight broke the clouds, angling perfectly through the vale, bathing the falls with their ethereal light. The morning mist yielded to the clear air, revealing the bright autumn colors of gold and crimson mixed with pines of green. Flocks of red-winged morla birds passed from one bank to the other.

Ethan rested his forearms on his pommel and lifted his hat above his brow. "Well, what do you think?"

"It's beautiful." Her eyes were wide with wonder. She had seen mountain lakes in Vellesia that were majestic, but they paled to the timeless beauty that lay before her. "Ethan, I do not understand?" she asked without taking her eyes from the vale below.

"What don't you understand?"

She turned her eyes to his. "Why do you travel the world when there is such beauty in your homeland? Your family loves you, your people love you. Everyone is overjoyed when you visit or greet them. Astaris is aptly named the Sky City, and there is no finer city to dwell, and you are surrounded by sights such as this. Why aren't you happy?" she wondered if anything could please him.

"I am happy, Allie. There is beauty everywhere if you look for it. Cordova at sunset, with the sun flickering over the tranquil waters of the bay, is a sight I'll never forget. There were countless places that Sheriff Thorton showed me while I was across the barrier. Even the Mage Bane had sights that I hadn't even imagined. I'm better for having seen them. You know what is more beautiful than all those places? Watching men rise from their knees to taste freedom. To watch those same men follow the passions of their hearts, to build a better world. I've seen that in America and now in Cordova. I look for a world where no man is born the slave of another. Where no man has to bend his knee to another because one is born to magic and one is not."

"Yet you bent your knee for me."

"I bent my knee one time so that you would never have to bend yours again, that's different. I'll never kneel to anyone again, Allie, so make my humiliation worth it by enjoying your life."

"My mother says you are quite handsome." She smiled again, knowing the remark would make him uneasy.

"She was there last night?" Thoughts of her mother slipped his mind when he spoke with Valera. He now recalled several of her entourage that might be Allie's mother. There was a raven-haired woman with bright green eyes wearing a blue gown. There were two with black hair, like the queen's, one with hazel eyes and the other blue. There was a portly matron with dark-red locks with tints of gray, but she looked nothing like Allie.

"Oh, she was there, and she found you very easy on the eyes. She would like to see you again."

"Unless she plans on staying after her queen departs, that's not gonna happen. Tell her I'm sorry."

"What if you attend the queen's ball with me?" she asked hopefully. "I received an invitation this morning to attend by Queen Gabrielle."

"My mother invited you?"

Allie nodded excitedly.

"Allie, I hate these balls. I'll accompany you somewhere else, anywhere you want. I just do not wish to see your queen again."

"Oh," she lowered her eyes sadly, the look on her face, paining him with guilt.

"Why do you want to go, Allie? Those people care nothing for you."

"I…I've never been invited to a ball before," she said softly, looking down at her hands. "For once I just wanted to see what it was like to eat, dance, wear a fancy gown, and live like a highborn lady for one night. Would you come with me, Ethan?" she asked again, lifting her golden eyes to his.

"Allie," he sighed dejectedly, rubbing his temples with his right hand. He felt cornered. She spent her entire life subservient to the Vellesian crown. Now she had a chance to spend a night as the equal of any woman. Would he deny her that?

"I'm sorry, Ethan. It is a selfish thing to ask of you. You have shown me so much kindness. When I first saw this valley, I thought how romantic it was, and it reminded me of the queen's ball. I was struck by a fancy of walking through the palace with you beside me while we danced with the high lords and ladies of the seven mage kingdoms. But now I realize how much it would pain you, and I feel very selfish."

"You're not selfish, Allie. You're the most unselfish person I know."

"Thank you, Ethan," she said, his kind words mending her heart. "I just want to enjoy our time together you before you go off chasing dragons."

There it was, the thought struck him with a brick of guilt. He was leaving soon, and he was asking her to stay behind and wait for him, and all she wanted was to spend a night in his company attending a ball that he hated, but that she truly wanted to attend.

"All right, I'll go with you." He sighed in defeat.

"You will?" Her face alit.

"Yes. Just don't expect me to wear any fancy costume."

She twisted in her saddle, straining her neck to kiss him. He stood still as she pressed her lips to his. She lingered on his mouth, savoring his taste for a time. Her eyes opened warmly as she withdrew.

"Thank you," she said.

Looking into her eyes, he knew she was the most beautiful woman he had ever seen. If they were strangers, he would be spellbound by her beauty alone, yet other men paid her no heed. Did they not see what was so obvious to him?

"Come on," he said, pulling on Bull's reins. "I'll show you the path to the valley floor."

*****

"Why did you call for Ethan, Father?" Gabriele asked. She stood in Dragos's chamber in the Tower of Stars.

"Did Ethan speak of this with you, Gaby?" His green eyes studied her face as she stood before him with arms crossed and eyebrow raised.

"He did not speak of it, which implicates both of you in hiding secrets from your queen."

"And I shall tell you in time, but for now, you should focus your concern on the matters at hand."

"Such as?"

"The Gorgencian king. His armies stand upon our eastern border. He waits for any failure on our part to placate Vellesia. He has come to Astaris to take measure of our strength. I sense great treachery afoot."

"As do I," Gabrielle agreed.

"I cannot reach Tristan, either. Lord Brax said he met with a stranger, whose name he did not share, then he disappeared with a half a dozen horses."

"Tristan is missing?" Gabrielle shouted, unfolding her arms.

"It would appear so."

"Can you not reach out to him through any of his companions?" she pleaded.

"He has taken no such companions for me to contact, and like Ethan, his mind is protected from detection or manipulation of any sort. We are blind to his whereabouts until he decides to show himself."

"Bronus must be told," she argued.

"Nay, Gaby. Let Bronus focus his attention on the task at hand. We must trust that Tristan knows what he is doing. It is the Vellesian queen that concerns me most. I have little insight with her. Her thoughts are too simplistic, as if she had the power to conjure false memories and present them to those peaking within."

"I've never heard of such mage ability. Is that even possible?" she asked.

"It is either that or…my power is fading with age. There are holes in my visions that I cannot fill."

"I have faith in you, Father."

"Faith that is misplaced if I cannot find the truth."

*****

"Squeeze slow. Slower. Slower," he spoke softly in her ear as she pulled back the trigger of his Colt. The pistol nearly shook in her hand as she squeezed, her eyes fixed on the site of the gun as Ethan had instructed.

Boom! The pistol's barrel lifted as the bullet sped forth, catching her by surprise. The round struck just off center of the target, a notch in a tree some seven meters away.

"Not bad." He slapped her on the back.

"Can I shoot faster now?" she asked, craning her neck over her left shoulder to face him.

"Don't get ahead of yourself, Allie, you're not Doc Holiday yet."

"Who's Doc Holiday? Is he a mage healer?" She never heard of a male healer by that name.

"Never mind. Just remember, smooth is fast. The speed will come naturally like this." His right hand cleared his holster as he stepped to his left, shooting three rounds in rapid succession. All three struck center of the notch in a fraction of a second. The vision of his fight with Luke Crawford flooded her memory. Had Ethan's skill been any less, the rogue would have slain him. The thought of Ethan dying that day still haunted her.

"I could practice for years and never shoot like that. Didn't your sheriff friend tell you that you had a natural gift?"

Ethan shrugged. Learning new skills always came easy to him, though he often didn't realize *how* easy. Sheriff Thorton did claim that Ethan was a natural gunslinger. In fact, only the sheriff's son Jake exceeded Ethan's gun speed. Even the gap between them narrowed as Jake Thorton taught Ethan ways to improve his speed and accuracy. Jake was a deputy US marshal and assured Ethan an appointment as a deputy marshal if he wanted it. Having heard of Ethan's exploits in Red Rock, Federal Judge Parker, and US Marshal Fagan let it be known that Ethan had a badge waiting for him at Fort Smith whenever he chose to accept it. The only deputy marshal that rivaled Ethan's deadliness was Bass Reeves, the former slave turned tracker turned deputy US marshal who had killed more men than Wild Bill or Wyatt Earp. Ethan let the offer stand before he returned to Astaria. He loved serving as Ben's deputy. He only left that post to save his father at the Velo when he dreamed of the coming war with Meltoria and Relusia. He had been gone so long he wondered how Sheriff Thorton and Judge Donovan were faring. He sighed as if burdened with great weight, thinking that he needed to tell them that he was well and that Luke Crawford was dead.

"What troubles you, Ethan?" Allie asked.

"I just remembered I have to go back across the barrier before I venture to the wilds."

"Why?"

"I owe it to Ben. He needs to know I will be gone for a while longer and that Luke Crawford is dead."

"A while longer?" She could not veil the alarm in her voice. "Are you planning to visit there at length?"

"I had planned to anyway after the winter festival, before I discovered the threat the dragons posed. They are my friends, Allie. I can bring you with me if you wish," he offered, wondering the source of her concern for him. She started to sound as worried as his mother.

"Isn't your ability to heal impaired on Earth?"

"Yes, all magic is."

"Then why risk your life? Does your mother know you are planning a return to Earth?"

"I haven't told her, but I will," he said defensively.

"She made you promise her that you would not enter the Mage Bane, but she is indifferent to you crossing the barrier?" It made no sense unless... "She does not know that Earth is a larger version of the Mage Bane, does she?"

Ethan shifted uneasily. "I...I never mentioned it one way or the other."

"But you let her believe a falsehood. It is the same as lying, Ethan."

"Mom's gonna love you." He smiled, shaking his head.

"How so?"

"Because you're just like her. You both whip me with guilt to make me do what you want."

"No. you only *pretend* to do what she wants, while you do as you will, like entering the Mage Bane."

"To save you, remember. When you do meet my mother be sure not to mention that."

"I won't lie to your mother, Ethan, but I won't tell her unless she specifically asks. Fair enough?"

"I'll have to live with it. I guess I'll have to be sure your visit with her is brief as possible and that I am beside you or she'll simply read your thoughts anyway."

"Then you ought not leave me in Astaris at length while you traipse through the wilds and across the barrier. After too much time alone with your family, I doubt I'll be able to resist their probing whether it be direct or subtle."

"That sounds like blackmail, Allie." He smiled.

Allie fired two quick rounds, each striking center of the notch. She returned the pistol to his holster and wrapped her arms around his neck. "That's not blackmail, Ethan, that is the cold truth."

"How did you do that?" He stared to his left, dumbfounded by her speed and accuracy.

Grabbing his jaw with her right hand, she shifted his face back to hers. "I am a quick learner."

"Nah, I'm just a good teacher," he teased her. He thought she might hit him, but she only smiled as she looked up into his blue eyes. The rippling sound of the swift-flowing Torlin echoed behind him as he pressed his lips to hers. The scent of her hair and the feel of her flesh tantalized with promise, alluring him with their seductive whisper. He withdrew but a moment, gazing into her eyes with her soft breath upon his face.

"I've never felt this way before, Allie." He tried desperately to describe what he was feeling.

"Shut up and kiss me," she commanded, crushing her lips to his.

*****

They returned to Astaris as the setting sun slipped below the mountains in the west. The guards at the main gate greeted Ethan but paid little heed to his comely companion. Passing under the arched entryway, they were greeted by bright illuminations bursting in the pre-night sky throughout the city.

"Why the celebration?" he asked a sergeant in dark mail who commanded the gate.

"The Vellesian princess has made her choice, Ethan." The man grinned through his trimmed red beard.

"Who did she choose?" he asked.

"The king's nephew, Geoff Jarvo," the sergeant answered.

Ethan wasn't surprised. "Damn fool," he mumbled under his breath.

"Come now, Ethan. The princess is quite fetching, and House Jarvo shall receive a handsome gift from Queen Valera," the sergeant added.

"What gift?" Ethan's eyes narrowed with suspicion.

"Why five hundred thousand gold pieces."

"That's a lot, but it's not what I would have asked for. Good evening, Sergeant," Ethan said. "Come on, Bull." He clicked his tongue, urging his spotted palomino on. Allie followed at his side.

"What would you have asked for?" she asked curiously once they were out of earshot of the gate.

"Five hundred thousand gold pieces mean little to a queen as rich as I believe Valera to be. I would choose something she loves."

"What does she love?"

"Power. So I would ask for the freedom of ten thousand slaves."

"But how would that enrich your family?"

"I didn't claim it would. It is what I would've chosen. Of course, I would've never agreed to wedding a princess under such terms anyway, even if she were pretty as you."

*****

They met in the shadows of her bedchamber as the crescent moon shone dully through the portal. Taking great pains to ensure no one overheard, they spoke without words.

All is progressing as we planned.

Are they so ignorant of what is unfolding around them? the other asked.

It appears so.

We must continue to keep them occupied. It is best if they do not meet until the queen's ball.

The king will be quite distracted tonight and tomorrow, the queen as well. You are responsible for the guest of honor. See that he is unaware, and all I promised shall be yours.

How could they be so ignorant of what they possess?

Our house has prepared for this day for thousands of years. Take solace in their ignorance, for it shall aid us in taking what they possess, thus ensuring their doom.

What of the other mage kings?

Like useful fools, they play their part. They focus their ire on Astaria, unaware of their true foe. They fear the lightning lord and despise his son, though the boy is their only *hope. Once he is* removed, *their fate is sealed.*

They shall quickly celebrate his fall, of that I am certain. Why do they hate him so?

The boy is arrogant and he can't help but offend their delicate sensibilities. They anxiously await his demise.
Then let us not disappoint them.

*****

He cursed the wind and driving snow as he rode on through the night. He killed three horses in a day, driving them to exhaustion before mounting the next in tow and continuing on. With three mounts to spare, it would be a close affair if he could reach Astaris in time. This storm caught him unaware, and if not for it, he would surely have arrived with time to spare. At this pace, however, he could lose all his horses this night. Tristan had little choice but to push on.

*****

Ethan hoped to speak with his father, but Bronus was occupied with matters of state. His mother and sisters were nowhere to be found. He asked Marco to join him at the outer ramparts of the citadel. Even with the spell shield above, the crisp early winter wind still swirled about the heights of Astaris. A winter sky covered the eastern approaches with thick, ominous clouds stretching east and north.

One more day, he thought, and the mage kings and queens would be leaving. He wished he hadn't promised Allie that he'd accompany her to the queen's ball. How he hated such functions, but if it made her happy, he would do it. Something about the ball nagged at the back of his brain. Something was amiss, but he didn't know what or why.

"You wished to speak with me, Ethan?" Captain Marco asked as he came to his side, resting his hands flat upon the bluestone rampart overlooking the city below.

"I thought we might have more privacy up here."

"This might be the only place to find privacy while the palace is full of our guests. What is it you wish to ask of me?"

"I have a bad feeling about tomorrow."

"How so?"

"I don't know, Marco. I just feel it."

"Some of the men have similar misgivings. What would you ask of me?"

"How many men are you planning to use during the queen's ball?"

"Two hundred, give or take."

"Double it. Double the city watch as well. Tell Commander Torlis that I advise it. I'm not his crown prince anymore, but tell him to trust my instinct."

"You'll always be our crown prince, Ethan. If you advise it, then we shall see it done."

"Thanks, Marco. We need to send out patrols in all directions. I will lead one myself in the morning."

"You fear an attack upon the city?"

"I fear an attack. I'm just uncertain if it's from the outside or from within."

"Do you believe one of our guests is behind this?"

"I know it doesn't make sense, but I think Queen Valera and the mage kings are here for something more significant than her daughter selecting a consort."

"And if they are involved with treachery?"

"Then I'll kill them all, Marco. Every last one."

*****

Allie awoke, stretching her limbs out in the large soft bed as her eyes opened to the promise of the new day. Ethan had her moved to the king's tower. She spent a restful night dreaming of the coming day. All her dreams were within reach. She was struck by a memory of Ethan. She remembered the first time she beheld him in the Mage Bane. She remembered her heightened vulnerability when she was taken to that cursed land. For the first time in her life, she felt what her life would be like without magic. A woman without mage power was only a woman. Despite this, it was still only a physical vulnerability. When she first saw Ethan in the villa of Arnos Pagge in Cordova, she felt vulnerable on a far different level, one far deeper and fraught with peril. She knew then that any future without him would be one of profound loneliness.

A soft knock came upon her door, followed by a young maid who brought her breakfast on a tray.

"Good morn, my lady." The girl curtsied, setting the tray beside her.

"Good morning to you." Allie smiled.

"Prince Eth…Ethan asked me to give you this note." She handed her a rolled parchment.

Allie felt ill at ease with such a gesture. Notes often portend ill news. It could mean many things and few of them good. It most likely meant that Ethan was not in the castle to speak the words for himself. She unrolled the parchment and began to read.

My dearest Allie,

I hope you rested well. Enjoy your breakfast.

I asked my sisters' dressmaker to visit with you and fit you for a gown.

I paid her handsomely, and she is at your service for the entire day.

I know you are wondering where I am. I am not in Astaris.

There are matters of state that I must attend, even if my father is unaware.

I will return before the gala, so do not fret.

Few know where I have gone, and I would like you to keep my absence to yourself.

Ethan

Allie's fingers nearly trembled. Where was he? Would he truly return in time?

"My lady, are you well?" the young maid asked, concerned by the hurt etched across her face.

"Leave me, now!" she ordered.

"As you wish, my lady." She curtsied and withdrew.

*****

It was late afternoon when Ethan rode through the gate of the inner citadel with a small patrol of three knights. His companions were all dressed in dark mail and heavy furs. Ethan wore black bear furs over his buckskins. The men were soaked from cold rain and looked a hungry, miserable lot. Before they entered the city proper, King Bronus was made aware of their approach. He met them at the steps of the king's tower, catching them before they passed on to the stables. Bronus's steel-gray eyes bore into his son with a heated glare. His thick arms were crossed over his chest, indicating his foul mood. Ethan knew that look well and dreaded what was to follow.

"Father." Ethan smiled wryly. Calling him anything other than Father might cause Bronus to explode.

"I'll have words with you, boy! Inside!" he commanded.

"Just give me a moment to take Bull to the stables and—"

"*Now*, Ethan! See to Ethan's mount, Sir Blackar," Bronus commanded the knight nearest them.

"Yes, my king," Sir Harken Blackar said.

"Thanks, Harken. Take good care of Bull." Ethan tossed Sir Blackar his reins. He dismounted, retrieved his rifle from his saddle and followed his father.

Bronus entered the first chamber on his right, a sparsely furnished guard room with a wooden table in its center. Two men-at-arms were posted within. They regarded their king and stepped without as Bronus closed the door. Ethan set his rifle on the table and took off his soaked fur cloak.

"Where have you been, Ethan? Who gave you authority to order *my* guards from their posts to join you on your misadventure?"

"We patrolled the approaches to Astaris. I can show you on a map everywhere—"

"Who gave you authority to order *my* guards from their posts?"

"I couldn't risk anyone knowing our whereabouts."

"Who gave you the authority?" Bronus growled.

"No one," Ethan sighed.

"You are the one who vacated the throne. You desired nothing more than to rule your own life, a kingdom of one. If you wish to traipse across Astaria from one end to the other, then do so, but you no longer command any men sworn to this kingdom. I do. Tristan does. Not you. You gave up that right, son. You are always welcome in my home. I look forward to one day seeing your children sitting on my knee before a warm fire. You are always foremost in my heart, boy. But you assume much."

"I'm sorry, Father. I needed to see for myself what is out there, and I asked Marco for help. I also asked him to double the guard for the queen's ball."

"Why?"

"Something's wrong. I don't know what, but my instincts are screaming in my ear."

"Why didn't you tell me before sending my guards out on a fruitless search?"

"I couldn't."

"Why? Damn it, Ethan. Spit it out!"

"I think Queen Valera can read your thoughts. Dragos's too."

Bronus was taken aback. Was it possible? Perhaps, but Ethan despised the Vellesian queen to the point of obsession. His suspicions were growing wearisome.

"It is odd for you to claim such. The entire palace is in an uproar over your little adventure. Many now fear an attack by a 'phantom army.' Who can blame them when my firstborn makes such claims?"

"I know I'm right. If not an army at our gate, then a mage attack at the queen's ball is a real threat. I patrolled our approaches in case an army was nearby concealed by magic. I found nothing. That leaves a mage attack most likely."

"You think I'm blind to such possibilities, Ethan? You ride in here a few days ago after nearly a year's absence and assume the kingdom is about to topple unless you save us all? All you have done is alert our potential foes that we are on guard and force them underground or to attack in force."

"You suspect something as well?" Ethan's eyes alit.

"I am the king of Astaria, Ethan. It is one thing for my enemies to underestimate my power but another for my son."

"If Valera can read your thoughts, Dad, then she knows any contingencies you have made."

"Ethan, after your recent behavior, all the mage king's demanded that you remain out of sight until tomorrow. They desired your expulsion from Astaris altogether. Queen Valera spoke in your defense. She told of your rescuing her mages in Cordova. Since your apology, she has repeatedly stated that we should show you leniency. She desires no animosity between our houses and thinks excluding you from the queen's ball would be a petty useless gesture. I agree, and if there is a mage attack tonight, then our enemies would not want you present since you are the bane of any such attempt. In fact, I believe our true enemy is one who desires your absence." Bronus left unsaid that Gregor Vorhenz was the most vocal in opposing Ethan's presence.

Ethan had little more than his own suspicions, and he did not wish to burden his father any more than he already had. "All right, Dad, I'll do whatever you want of me."

Bronus placed his heavy hands on Ethan's shoulders. "Clean yourself up, fetch this girl I've heard so little about and enjoy the queen's ball. If I have need of you, then you will be close by." Bronus kissed the top of Ethan's head.

"I will."

"Good. Now take a knee."

Ethan hesitated. His kneeling days were in his past.

"I have something for you, son. Take a knee." Bronus smiled proudly.

Ethan complied, uncertain what Bronus was doing, but his father seemed in better spirits, and he didn't want to spoil it.

"You have given your brother your birthright, your throne, and the House of Blagen. I will not see you bereft of all my gifts." Bronus drew his sword from its plain black scabbard, lowering it to Ethan with one hand upon the blade and the other beneath the hilt.

"Your sword? Dad, that is the sword of the king. I have no right—"

"It is not the sword of the king. It is the sword of Bronus Blagen, and I bequeath it to my son, Ethanos, a son I am proud of, a son that I love. Take the blade, Ethan and do not argue with your father."

Ethan took the sword into his hands. It was called the Sword of Starlight, forged ages past by the sky lords of old. The blood of dragons was mixed with the blue steel and folded time and again, strengthening its blade to unbreakable perfection. Its azure shaft glistened in the dim light. It truly was the sword of a king. It was not just the sword his father was giving him, it was his heart. Ethan took the blade for his own. Bronus clasped Ethan's forearm, helping him to his feet.

Ethan looked into his father's gray eyes and thought of the burdens that weighed upon him. The throne was an anchor about his neck, strangling what life was left to him.

"Father, what joy is there in being king?"

Bronus thought for a moment. It was something he never contemplated. He was often too busy to ponder such possibilities. He was the king and carried the duty with steel determination.

"When justice is served, I feel joy, son. As for the feeling of being king, only men of petty minds and cruel hearts take joy from such power. Their reigns are remembered only with shame and infamy."

"Then why rule until your life is at its end? Pass the throne to Tristan and *live*. Come with me. See the world. Come across the barrier and meet Sheriff Thorton. Sail the Aqualania Sea. Feel the wind in your face and the sun on your back. Lay down your burdens and live life to its fullest."

"Men of conscience are burdened wherever they travel, son. Are you so free of burdens in this life you now live? I doubt you are. Why else would you risk your life in the Mage Bane to rescue this Vellesian girl? Or to kneel to her queen to gain her freedom?"

"You know that I traveled to the Mage Bane?" Ethan couldn't stay the alarm in his voice.

"I know. Your mother does not or else you would feel wrath I would tremble to contemplate. It would be the same wrath she would rain down upon me if I took your offer and joined you on your adventures."

"How did you know?"

"You think me blind, boy? I have sources throughout Elaria that could not help discover when a certain former crown prince travels the Aqualania Sea and enters the Mage Bane with reckless abandon. That story is already widely known. It won't be long before your mother knows it as well."

"I had a good reason."

"Yes, this girl that I haven't been properly introduced to as yet."

"You'll meet her."

"Aye, son, I shall. She'll receive my second dance after your mother, of course. I wish to meet the woman that has manifested such change in my mule-headed firstborn."

"I'll tell Allie that she owes the Astarian king a dance." Ethan smiled.

"If you're to fulfill that pledge you best hurry. It's not wise to keep a maiden waiting, Ethan."

"I'm going," Ethan stopped at the door and turned back to his father. "How did you know that I left Astaris this morning?"

"Several saw you depart, Sergeant Porlis, Captain Brenna, and Sir Thovan, to name a few."

That didn't make sense. Porlis was fast asleep when Ethan left, and Captain Brenna was posted at the queen's tower. Perhaps his father was mistaken.

*****

Ethan found a basin tub filled with warm bath water when he entered his chamber. Wondering who managed to haul such a monstrosity into his bedchamber, he stripped off his wet clothes and stepped in. He would have spent a day sitting in the tub, but time was short, and he quickly bathed. He found a silver tunic and hose laid out upon his bed. Whoever set them out didn't know him very well. He put on his black trousers, boots, and pullover shirt. He retrieved his single holster gun belt from his chest and fastened a sword sheath to its left side, opposite his Colt .45. He ran his fingers through his thickening hair. He needed to cut it as it was driving him crazy.

Tomorrow, he reminded himself. *I'll cut it first thing tomorrow.*

*****

"Does this meet your satisfaction?" Allie asked as he entered her chamber. Ethan was speechless. She wore a glistening gown with flickering hues of blue and silver. The thick folds of her ebony hair cascaded like a waterfall of obsidian. Her bright golden eyes sparkled, and her flush olive skin shone smooth and flawless. The gown's tight bodice enhanced the swell of her ample bosom, and the skirt swayed with her every move. She was the most beautiful woman he had ever seen or imagined. If he were not immune to magic, he would wager his life that the image before him was a fabrication, a cruel mage projected vision to beguile him. But this was the true Allie. Had she been of higher birth, every prince in the seven mage realms would kill one another to win her hand.

"Oh, you meet my satisfaction all right. I think you might look a little *too* good."

"How so?" She smiled with a tilt of her head.

"All the single men at the ball will be clawing each other, and me, to get close to you. All the suitors that your princess rejected will quickly forget her once they lay eyes on you."

Allie stepped close, placing her hands upon his cheeks. "There is only one man I will dance with tonight. This is a night we shall never forget." She pressed her moist lips to his.

*****

The great hall of the inner palace was decorated with holly and evergreen. Scented torches lined the cavernous azure chamber. Mage lanterns rotated above, casting rays of crimson, emerald, and gold upon the ceiling and stone walls above. Musicians armed with harps, flutes, and mandolins played soft tuned melodies upon a wooden circle dais in the chamber's center. Circled dining tables were placed on one half of the great hall, while the other half was open for dancing, with the musicians' dais dividing the chamber. The guests were seated in accordance with position. The kings and queens of the seven mage kingdoms sat behind a long raised table on the chamber's far wall, overlooking the guests seated before them. Queen Gabrielle presided over the gala, seated in the center of the long table with King Bronus upon her left and Queen Valera upon her right. It had taken nearly two hours for Lord Celembar, the steward of Astaris, to introduce each guest and her escort as they entered the great hall. Ethan wished they could've just snuck in, but Allie's face lit like the sun as she passed under the stone archway of the great hall with Ethan on her arm. Ethan hoped to be sitting with his sisters and grandfather, but etiquette at the queen's ball dictated that couples sit with the woman's family or friends. Allie chose to sit at a table of Vellesian delegates and mages. The other eight guests at their table were mostly women of middle age. Their gowns were simple black or gold. Not one of them smiled or acknowledged their presence in any way. He recognized several that attended the queen two nights ago. He wondered which was Allie's mother. She was certain to introduce her properly once the guests entered, and the queen gave her remarks to open the ball. If he wasn't to sit with his family, Ethan hoped to sit as far from the mage kings' table as possible, but they were placed just one row back.

"This music is dreadful," Ethan whispered in her ear. The musicians' tune was methodic and serene. Ethan would've volunteered to sing himself if he could play "The Yellow Rose of Texas" or "The Streets of Laredo," but his mother would strangle him if he did.

Allie smiled at him and placed her left forefinger over his lips to quiet him.

"All right, I'll shut up," he said. He found the others seated at the table unsettling. They stared at their queen as if waiting for her cue for some unknown purpose. Something felt amiss, and he suspected treachery afoot. He casually lowered his right hand to the grip of his pistol, preparing for anything that might come.

Allie placed her left hand over his right and slowly put it back upon the table. She squeezed his hand tightly and whispered in his ear. "You won't need that tonight. I'll keep you safe."

Ethan gave her a strange look. He then thought she was just adamant about having a joyous evening that she didn't want to imagine anything going awry. "Maybe you're right. The greatest danger tonight might be that we die of boredom."

She placed her slender finger over his lips again. "Shh. The queen is about to speak."

Ethan wished he were somewhere else. He'd rather be chopping wood or fishing—or swimming Shark's Bay.

Queen Gabrielle rose gracefully to her feet as the crowd quieted. All the guests had been introduced and seated, save for the Vellesian princess and her escort.

"My honored guests and loyal subjects. The queen's ball is an honored tradition in Astaria celebrated before the winter solstice. It is the one festival where maidenhood and motherhood are honored for the vital roles they play in the circle of life. It is the one night where the maidens of the realm can shed their feminine subtleties and declare their romantic aspirations without prejudice. I believe our men enjoy this tradition more than the ladies. Especially the obtuse among them who are ignorant of our feminine proclivities." She stared directly at Ethan as a smile pushed at the corners of her mouth. She noted the girl beside him, finally able to see her face. Gabrielle was taken aback by her beauty. It was strange that she hadn't noticed her before this night. A woman of such beauty would surely stand out. *The boy is not blind, that much is certain,* she mused.

As Gabrielle continued her speech, Ethan examined the room. He found it odd that the mage kings' personal guards stood further off, standing post near the entrance, clustered in their respective groups. The guard of Evor Ectus, with their bright mail and leggings with a leaping fish emblazoned upon their capes, contrasted with Queen Valera's royal guard clad in silver breastplates over white tunics. He noted the Gorgencians, Sarcosans, and Relusians standing in disciplined ranks behind their captains. If there was to be a mage attack this night, then who would be its architect? At this range, Ethan had a clear shot at any of the mage kings and Queen Valera. Any attack upon the House of Blagen would mean certain death to the other mage kings. There were also no armies waiting beyond the city walls. What was bothering him then? A grim thought suddenly struck him, Dragos. Could Dragos's vision come to pass tonight? He tried to remember the vision, but the only part he could see was the red-scaled creature itself. Dragos saw everything else. The way Dragos described what he saw made Ethan believe that attack would take place in summer, not the winter solstice.

"And to introduce our most honored guest, I present Queen Valera, mage queen of Vellesia!" Gabrielle finished, deferring to Valera, who rose gracefully to her feet as Gabrielle sat down.

Ethan gazed at Valera with guarded optimism. She looked stunning with rich black hair framing her sweetly feminine face. Her deep-olive skin was taut and youthful despite her years, which no one could rightly discern. She wore a dark-purple gown that clung to her frame with easy grace. She was tall as well, and Ethan surmised she was at least sixty-nine inches if not more. She towered over all women and most men.

"I wish to offer my gratitude to our hosts, Queen Gabrielle and King Bronus. You have opened your ancestral home to the rulers of the seven mage kingdoms during a time that you would rather spend with your family. In an age where kingdoms rise against kingdoms over trivial matters, we were able to come together after the direst of incidents to reach a peaceful accord and compromise. By offering a treasured son of Astaria to the Vellesian crown, you have bonded our realms through *blood*. To those gathered in this great hall, let it be known that our compromise was mutually agreed upon and sealed with the magic of the monarchs of all seven mage realms. We agreed that the crown princess of Vellesia would choose her consort by asking him to attend her at the queen's ball. The young man could either accept the invitation or not, the choice being his and *his* alone. The crown princess has made her choice, and the young man has accepted her invitation. There is an empty place at the table before us," Valera emphasized with an open hand to the two places at the table below the dais.

"We shall now welcome my daughter, Princess Amanda and her escort, the nephew of King Bronus, Geoff Jarvo," Valera introduced them.

Amanda and Geoff entered the great hall, making their way through the cheering guests. Ethan observed them suspiciously for he correctly predicted her choice. Geoff was the closest male heir to the throne that she could have chosen. The princess did not look well. She seemed ill at ease despite the fake smile she offered those around her. Her eyes caught sight of his as they scanned the chamber. She held his gaze for a brief moment before passing on.

The hairs on the back of Ethan's neck rose in alarm. *She knows something!* He panicked, shifting uneasily in his chair, turning his head to his left and right, but nothing else seemed out of place. His heart raced. He was in danger and could feel it. His instincts urged him to run away, but he remained frozen as Valera continued.

"You have all come to know my beautiful daughter Amanda, but with profound pride and joy, I would like you to formally welcome my *firstborn* daughter and the crown princess of Vellesia, *Alesha* Loria!"

Allie released Ethan's hand as she gracefully rose to her feet. Every eye shifted to her beautiful form standing in the center of the chamber, as if truly seeing her for the first time. Queen Gabrielle and King Bronus's eyes grew wide in alarm. Amanda was not the crown princess, this girl was. The remaining guests were suddenly struck by her profound beauty, for her charms that were well masked through magic were now revealed in their true glory. Only Ethan had been able to see what she truly looked like, but now everyone was equally privileged.

"Allie, what's she talking about?" Ethan asked as his eyes shifted warily between Valera and Allie.

She simply smiled at him before returning her gaze to her mother.

"Alesha!" Queen Valera declared with icy authority. "I ask for you to state the name of the man who accepted your invitation to the queen's ball?"

Alesha stepped forth, skirting her table to stand halfway between the king's table and her own. She turned, her golden eyes fixed to Ethan's dumbfounded gaze.

"Prince Ethanos Blagen!" she declared.

CHAPTER 28

The great hall grew quiet as a tomb as every eye and ear fixed upon Alesha. Ethan slowly gained his feet, skirting the table that separated him from Alesha. With his gaze fixed upon her, he did not see the guests following his every step or his grandfather and sisters nearby. He did not see the Mage Kings seated side by side, outwardly gloating or hiding their glee. He did not see his father's growing ire or hear his mother's racing heart. All he could see were Allie's golden eyes staring back at him. Yet they were no longer the eyes of a friend or the woman he thought to love; they were the eyes of a stranger.

"She's your mother?" Ethan asked, pointing his right forefinger past Allie's head toward Valera as he stopped but inches from her face.

"Yes, Ethan, Queen Valera is my mother," she answered with serene confidence as if her explanation should simply be accepted, though her heart pounded emphatically, wondering if he would ever forgive her.

"You lied to me, Allie." He lowered his hand, his voice echoing a deep sadness and hurt rather than anger.

"I never lied to you, Ethan. I never denied being the crown princess of Vellesia."

"You let me believe you were a simple mage healer. Letting someone believe a falsehood is the same as lying, just as you told me, remember?" he asked, wondering why she would do this.

She simply smiled as she tilted her head, looking at him as if she hadn't heard a word he said. Her cold facade masked the pounding of her heart. She played the role expected of her, never believing it could be so hard.

"No answer? How many other falsehoods have you let me believe? You said your queen was a cold, merciless tyrant!" he said with festering anger.

"She is," Alesha said as her eyes followed the length of his body as if examining him for purchase, though in truth she needed to avert her eyes from his. All he could see was her betrayal.

Ethan nearly threw his arms up in exasperation. He might as well be asking questions to his horse. She would not admit guilt or shame, so he might as well get to the point. "So what does this…" He spread his arms out to the spectacle around them. "What does this all mean?"

"My dear Ethanos, you have accepted Princess Alesha's offer of consort." Queen Valera smiled, her words laced with condensation. Alesha winced inwardly with her mother's tone. This was not what she intended. Ethan was always supposed to fall into her trap, but it always played better in her mind. This was harsher, crueler, more brutal.

A few moments before, the thought of spending the rest of his life with Allie seemed most pleasant. Now he only felt anger and betrayal. Her eyes were colder now, like a predator that just ate its prey.

"I'm not marrying her," he declared, turning his eyes to Valera.

"That choice is passed, child. When you accepted her invite to the queen's ball and entered this hall in her company, your choice was sealed. It is a pact bound in magic," Valera said.

"I'm immune to magic, witch, and don't call me child. I've had enough of these games. Go find another candidate to bed your daughter." He turned to leave when her voice stopped him before his first step.

"If you fail to obey your commitment, then House Blagen shall pay in *blood*!" Valera warned with ice in her voice.

"What blood?" He turned back to face her.

Valera smiled wickedly. "Your father's life shall be forfeit if you fail to obey."

The color drained from his face. He looked to his father, who came swiftly to his feet. Alesha winced at her mother's venom, but Ethan needed to be brought to heel, and his father's life was the leverage they held.

"*Enough!*" Bronus declared. "This…" He spread his hands to the gathered host. "This farce shall not stand, Valera. Ethanos was never one of our agreed-upon suitors."

"The only *agreement*, Bronus, was that the crown princess would choose, and the candidate could accept or decline her offer."

"No one explained that to Ethan. He is not bound to an arrangement that he knew nothing of."

"His ignorance is no excuse. His actions are now bound in magic. If he refuses to *obey*, you shall die."

Ethan turned on Allie. "You would do this, Allie? I saved your life, and you would kill my father?"

"The choice is yours, Ethanos, not mine," she answered, though she hated the sound of her cold answer. She doubted if she would ever allow her mother to follow through with that deadly threat but needed Ethan to believe that she would.

"Do you think I'll ever love you if you do this?" His heart beat rapidly as he felt the walls close around him.

"Love is a base emotion with little bearing in the fate of kingdoms, Ethanos. We are *perfectly* matched and I desire you, love has little relevance." *But I do love you, Ethan*, she wanted to scream. She wanted to shout her affection aloud for all to hear, but what place would it have at such a time? He would merely dismiss it as the ranting of a madwoman who cheated him of his freedom. No, she had her role to play and must hold firm despite the leanings of her heart. Beyond that, the fate of her realm depended on her bringing Ethan to Elysia. She originally planned to claim him for the glory of her house but was now driven to stop a far darker path from claiming him.

He stared at her incredulously, not believing what he was hearing. Was this the same girl he had come to know? No. That girl never existed; she was merely an illusion. So much didn't make sense that he could barely think, his mind clouded with unanswered questions.

"This violates the intent of our agreement!" Bronus's voice boomed. "Your deception can be overruled by a majority of our council." He looked to his left and right at the other mage kings, but they sat in silence.

Ethan noticed a visible smirk on the lips of Gregor Vorhenz. The Gorgencian king's demeanor revealed the deeper truth. "Save your pleas, Father. They're all in on it, every one of them. They win either way, with your death or my removal."

"Is this true?" Bronus shouted as his hands began to crackle. Gabrielle placed her hands upon him, to stay his anger lest his temper lead to war with all the other mage realms.

"You would let this…woman, use my hospitality to steal my son from my home? What protection shall any of you hope to have if you allow this? Your children shall not be safe either. Have you no honor?"

"Our children shall never be safe until your son is caged like the animal he is!" Gregor Vorhenz snarled while rising to his feet. "And if he refuses his collar, then we shall be rid of Elaria's only lightning lord!"

Ethan dove under the king's table, wrapping his hands around Gregor's legs and yanking him from under the table, grasping his neck with one hand, and held him aloft. Gregor's personal guard rushed from their posts to protect their sovereign but were too far afield. Ethan threw the large monarch onto the table behind him, breaking it in half. The blow snapped several of his ribs and spine. He screamed in utter agony. The guests were startled by Ethan's strength. He was renowned for his immunity to magic, but many forgot his other impressive abilities. Gregor's guards' feet pounded heavily on the mirrored stone floor. They were an even dozen, dressed in dark mail with the stallion of Gorgencia emblazoned upon their crests. Ethan drew his pistol, his finger drawing back the trigger as he broke leather.

Alesha calmly reached out her left palm, sending a wave of energy bursting toward the Gorgencians, knocking all twelve from their feet. They toppled like top-heavy stones. The congregants were dumbstruck, awed by her display of a power they had never seen.

"King Gregor's guardians seem out of sorts. Detain them and hand them over to our Astarian hosts for safekeeping!" Alesha commanded the Vellesian queen's guard. They responded without hesitation, obedient to their crown princess's command. Their crimson capes fluttered behind them as they quickly bound the hapless Gorgencians. Ethan noticed their faces void of emotion. They seemed a joyless lot.

"Lower your pistol, Ethan. I told you I would keep you safe." Alesha smiled, hoping her defense of him would ease his rage.

"What was that?" he asked, holstering his pistol. "What else can you do?" he asked with waning confidence.

"I am more than a mage healer, Ethanos."

"Yes, I can see you are," he growled.

King Gregor's moans echoed painfully through the hall.

"Don't worry Gregor, your friend here is a very gifted healer," Ethan derided.

Alesha knelt beside the fallen king and placed a finger upon his forehead. Her finger glowed, emitting a soothing fiery glow for a brief moment, then she stood. It was all Gregor needed as his wounds instantly healed. Even the greatest of mage healers could never display such power with so little effort. He could only wonder how powerful she truly was?

"Prince Ethanos should be shackled for the safety of your guests before he starts a war," Valera advised with a cruel smile pushing the corners of her lips.

Bronus looked upon Ethan with profound pride. "I have listened to your babbling for the last time, *woman*! Ethan warned me time and again that you were a treacherous serpent. I should have listened to my son. I will not restrain him ever again. My greatest disappointment in life has been his forsaking the throne of Astaria. Perhaps he was right to do so. He has always lived with honor in everything he has done. I could not be prouder." He looked into Ethan's eyes with a heartfelt smile. "I stand among the very mage kings my son warned me about. There is no honor among them. They have no moral authority to rule their realms. They rule through power and power alone. When it fails, so shall they. Power without justice and law is the most fleeting of all. As far as my son, Valera, you shall *not* have him. Damn the magic, for it can take me. I will not live out my days, how few are left, if my son lives as your slave!"

"How soon do you need my answer?" Ethan asked Alesha.

"You have until the sun's apex on the morrow to take your vows before the magic consumes the king," she said.

"Very well. I won't sacrifice you, Father," Ethan regarded him. Before turning to leave, he caught sight of Princess Amanda. Her eyes betrayed her sorrow. She tried to warn him, but he did not listen. He gave her a brief smile, then walked out.

*****

Gabrielle Blagen stared into the mirror of her vanity. She felt so old. The queen's ball ended as quickly as it began. What should have been a joyous event felt like a funeral. It was times such as these she felt her years. The wrinkles spreading from her eyes were the scars of a mother's worries. Ethan was the cause of most of them. It wasn't always his fault, but he was often the indirect cause of it. She had left Bronus to deal with the guests and his guards. She did not wish to treat with anyone, not after what had transpired. She had looked forward to this night as the conclusion of their dealings with Valera and turning her focus to the holiday with her family. Now her holiday was ruined as well. She would either be widowed or have her son dragged away to an unclear fate.

"Queen Gabrielle," a soft soothing voice echoed behind her. No one should have entered her private quarters unannounced. She turned, her eyes catching the beautiful face of Princess Alesha lit by soft candlelight.

"How dare you enter my chamber unbidden?" She came abruptly to her feet.

"My apologies, Queen Gabrielle, but there are things you must know, and it would be unwise if others knew of our meet."

"How did you slip past my guards?"

"We all have our gifts. Stealth is one I have mastered." She smiled.

"It seems it is not the only gift you have mastered. You are a healer, you possess a kinetic power of some sort, and you are a *deceiver* of unprecedented boldness."

"I have allowed misperceptions to manifest for my benefit. That is true."

"Misperceptions? Is that what you call them in Vellesia? In Astaria we call them *lies*!"

"It is unfortunate you feel so, Queen Gabrielle, but you may take solace in our mutual interests."

"What mutual interests?"

"Ethanos."

"I fail to see how your plans to humiliate him are in any way aligned with mine," she said through narrow eyes and gritted teeth.

"His humiliation, as you name it, is only a necessity for my true intent—*keeping him safe*."

"Speak plainly, Alesha"

Alesha smiled that sweet, calming smile that Gabrielle had seen her mother use. "I promised Ethan I would not tell you where he has been unless you asked it of me."

"Where has he been?" Gabrielle gritted her teeth.

"You must be *specific*, for I shall not break my promise."

There was only one place she made him promise *not* to go. "Did he enter the Mage Bane?" Her heart pounded emphatically dreading the answer that she already knew.

"Yes."

Gabrielle's heart sank like a rock in water. A weakness overtook her and she sat down.

"Why? Why would he go there?" she asked dryly, her throat suddenly hoarse.

"It was his destiny. I know the reasons you feared him venturing there. The first was that the Mage Bane hinders his ability to regenerate. It renders him mortal. What you don't know is that *Earth* functions the same as the Mage Bane, but on a much larger scale."

Gabrielle's eyes darkened, shifting suddenly to Alesha's.

"He kept this truth from you as well, no doubt." Alesha sighed tiredly, releasing her arrows one after the other into the queen's heart.

"Do you know that he plans to return to Earth? Do you know he has asked his father to join him? Do you know that your husband knew that Earth functioned the same as the Mage Bane?"

Alesha could see the storm building behind Gabrielle's eyes.

"I also know the reason you forbade Ethan to enter the Mage Bane. It was your vision. What you don't know is what your father's vision revealed. Ethan knows. He saw dragons wreaking havoc upon Astaris, so he plans to deal with them himself after your winter festival. If he survives the dragons, which will impair his wondrous regenerative powers, he will return to Red Rock, where once again he shall be unable to heal himself. If he survives that, he plans to continue spreading his insurrection throughout the seven kingdoms *and* the Mage Bane."

"Why should I believe you?"

"Ask him yourself. He will not lie to you directly. Even if he does, you can read the lie in his eyes, we both know he is a lousy liar. If left to his own counsel, he will eventually push fate once too often. I do not see a long life for him. I doubt he shall live to see the next winter festival. *Only* I can save him. Only I can protect him from his greatest enemy—himself." She emptied her quiver.

"How? By using his father's life to make him your slave?"

"He would hardly be a slave. He would hold an honored place in House Loria."

"He won't see it that way. And why Ethan? Why not any of the other suitors who would give of themselves willingly?"

"The others were a poor offering. It had to be Ethan. His place is beside me, whether he accepts it or not."

"What gives you the right to take him?"

"It is how the queens of Vellesia have chosen our mates for centuries. It is our way."

"He saved your life, Alesha. Is that your real name, or is it Allie?"

"Allie was the shortened name my father called me. Alesha is my true name. And yes, Ethan saved my life because that was his destiny."

"Is that your answer, Alesha, it was his destiny? He saved your life. I assume that was his reason for entering the Mage Bane?"

"It was."

"And you would treat him thusly? You would use his father's life to forge his chains?"

"Would he acquiesce otherwise?" Alesha countered.

They both knew that answer.

"Why are you here, Alesha? What do you want of me?"

"Your blessing."

"My blessing?" She nearly burst into laughter. "Your audacity is without limit."

"You can counsel Ethan to choose wisely. If he does, I will reward you with the most precious of gifts."

"Ethan is a man, not a boy. The decision is his, and no bribe will turn my tongue to sway him. You can keep your gold."

"I was not offering gold, Queen Gabrielle. I was offering the gift you most strongly desire."

"What gift?" she asked warily.

"Grandchildren. I shall name our daughter Gabrielle, in honor of her paternal grandmother. She will rule Vellesia one day. Would that not bring you joy?"

Gabrielle sat quietly for a time, contemplating Alesha's offer. For so long, she dreamed of her children's' future and hoped for their happiness above all else and grandchildren were at the center of those dreams. Could she consign Ethan to a life of bondage to secure his future? Is his safety worth more than his spirit? She then reminded herself that Ethan would not be in this perilous position had he heeded her warning of not entering the Mage Bane. She lifted her weary emerald eyes to Alesha's golden hues. "If you desire my blessing, then answer me true—do you *love* my son?"

"I…" For the first time in her life, Alesha was dumbstruck. Love was a fallacy lauded by dreamers and fools her mother would claim, and Valera lived her life under that belief. But what of Alesha? "I don't know what love truly is, but what I feel about Ethan transcends such a simple explanation."

"But do you love him, Alesha?"

"Yes." She sighed.

"Then why are you doing this to him?"

"I have no choice, Queen Gabrielle. I am the heir of Vellesia and must fulfill my destiny. Ethan's destiny is interwoven with mine, and he must return with me." *And he will die if he doesn't*, she reflected desperately, consumed by her terrible dream that forced her to betray his trust. *My people will suffer as well*, she thought miserably.

*****

Amanda took a deep breath before entering her mother's chamber. With her apparent betrothal to Geoff ended, she was still a maiden. She wasn't sure if she was disappointed or relieved. She smoothed her shimmering gown and stepped within.

Queen Valera stood before her window with arms crossed as starlight painted the night sky.

"You dare tarry when I call for you?" she said while gazing out the window.

"No, Mother. I was detained with various guests. Because of this night's…events, it required a certain deftness."

"You exchanged a look of understanding with Prince Ethanos before he left the great hall. Do not deny it."

"I am sorry, Mother. I just felt empathy for him, that is all."

"Another lie. What did you tell him when you asked him to dance two nights past?'

"I just wanted to meet him, Mother. You have prepared for this day for all of our lives, and I was curious what sort of man would instill such passion in you and Alesha."

"Your sister is furious with you. She and I both know you did more than dance with him. You warned him, didn't you?" Valera turned from the window, her dark eyes glowing red as she conjured her clairvoyance to no avail. Amanda's mental gifts were too strong for her.

"I did not, Mother. I can avow." Amanda backed a step.

"You may have inherited your father's mental powers, but I know when you are lying, child. You're the same as your faithless father."

Amanda had to come up with a better lie than a simple denial. A lie her mother would believe.

"I am sorry, Mother. When I first saw Prince Ethanos at the tourney field, I wanted him for myself. I was very jealous of Alesha, and when the opportunity was given before his apology, I asked him to dance. It was just my excuse to be close to him. He told me how you had sought his hand for me when he was a child. He didn't know you actually meant to match him with Alesha."

His parents must have told him of my first attempt to claim him, Valera mused. When his father refused, she feigned disinterest, allowing them to believe it was because of the boy's immunity from magic. They never imagined that his immunity to magic was the very reason she valued him.

"If this is true, you risked everything I have labored toward for a jealous tryst. Raise your skirts."

Amanda swallowed past the lump in her throat, bracing for the pain to come. Valera's left palm glowed a fiery crimson, emitting a searing heat. Amanda's breath caught in the willowy narrows of her throat as her mother pressed her glowing palm upon her right thigh. Screams of agony pushed from her mouth into the muffled aura that Valera erected around them. No one in the palace would hear her cry.

"I shall heal this wound once Prince Ethanos takes his vows of allegiance. Pray he follows the path we have placed before him, or your wound may fester longer."

Amanda looked at her mother's blurry image through watery eyes. "I think we are making a grave mistake, Mother. Ethanos will not behave as you expect. He is wild, untamed and unpredictable," she sobbed.

Valera stared into her eyes with a cold, piercing gaze. "He will obey like a trained puppy. He will obey *every* command Alesha and I give him, no matter how trivial, or his father's life will be extinguished," she snapped her fingers to emphasize the point.

"But then your hold on him would be broken."

Valera smiled cruelly. "Once we cross into Vellesia, he shall never return. He is still just a man. A man surrounded by our legions. He is immune to our magic, not our swords."

*****

Bronus found Ethan sitting on the edge of his bed with his elbows on his knees and his face in his hands. He had never seen his son like this. Ethan's heart was crushed. He felt like powerful invisible hands were reaching through his chest and squeezing his lungs. He wanted to flee but was surrounded by walls closing around him. The chamber was mostly dark, lighted by a single candle bracketed to the far wall.

"I am sorry, son." Bronus placed a heavy hand on Ethan's head.

Ethan looked up with tired eyes. "King's don't have to apologize."

"I'm not your king, son. I'm your father, and fathers make mistakes."

"You didn't make a mistake, Dad, I did. I trusted her. I saved her miserable life from certain death and torture, and she rewards me like this. I bent my knee to that witch of a queen to gain her freedom. Why would she do that other than to humiliate me. She didn't need freedom from a throne, she had every intention to sit upon one day. She probably had a good laugh over that one. It was probably a test to see if I was stupid enough to do that than I'd be stupid enough to accept her invitation to the queen's ball." Ethan shook his head disgusted with the whole mess.

"You didn't know, son. We set the parameters of courtship for those we assumed were legitimate suitors and for Princess Amanda. There was no need to explain such details to anyone else. I am an old fool, for only now can I see her brilliance. Never once did Valera refer to Amanda as the crown princess. We just assumed that she was. It was a trick played upon us both."

"Every crown prince in the other mage kingdoms is a horse's ass. Every one. If any of them were in my place when she was taken captive in the Mage Bane, they would have let her rot without a debate in their mind. They would've simply let her die without care or conscience. Not me though. I risk my life and break a sworn promise to my mother to rescue her and how does she reward me? Like this." He threw up his hands. "If I can escape this trap, I vow to never help a stranger again. To hell with them all."

"Good deeds are rewarded by the righteous and punished by the wicked." Bronus sighed.

"I guess I know which one is Allie or Alesha or whatever her true name is."

"You had best learn it," Dragos's craggy voice echoed as he passed through the doorway, his azure robes swirling about him.

"What have you learned?" Bronus asked.

"Nothing. Yet nothing is something," he answered, raking his fingers through his beard.

"Speak straight, Dragos! I haven't the patience for riddles!" Bronus commanded.

"When I attempted to search the mind of Princess Alesha, I was given false memories or blank ones. She is able to not only shield her mind, just as Tristan can, but to create false memories and thoughts. This gives a false impression to seers and telepaths. If she simply shielded her mind to us, we would have been alerted to her true power. But by allowing us to see what was untrue, she was able to pass in our midst undetected. She dressed as a mage healer, and we read her mind as a mage healer."

Ethan's thoughts went to the purple-eyed enchantress he encountered in Cordova. She was able to move within Astaris undetected before she attempted to capture him in Cordova. He always wondered the coincidence of her attack just before Luke's raid, thinking they might be related. But having seen her before in Astaris, he couldn't figure how her goals were linked to Luke's. They weren't; she was working for Alesha. The entire Vellesian errand of mercy to Cordova was really a plan to capture him, not heal the people of the isle. Looking back, he found it ironic that Luke's attack saved him from Allie's plot. "What of her mother?" Ethan asked, looking up at his grandfather from his bed.

"Her mother cannot create false memories or thoughts. She does have the ability to shield part or all her mind. She can shield whichever part she wants hidden and reveal whichever parts she wants us to see."

"That is more than nothing." Bronus rolled his eyes at Dragos's dramatics.

"*Ah!*" Dragos raised a finger to make his point. "It is as I said… nothing is something. By reading nothing I know they can shield their minds. By revealing something that I know to be false, I learn they are able to project that. And of course, they are able to read my thoughts as well. That is why they knew about the dragons in my vision."

"*Dragons?*" Bronus's voice rose in alarm. "Why have you not spoken of this before now?"

"Ethan actually saw the dragon. I have holes in my visions at times, caused by elements of anti-magic that are revealed in the visions. Ethan is able to see anything of this nature and filled in what I could not see. I hoped to wait until our guests departed before burdening you with one more worry, but alas, it is not to be."

"Blast! I thought after the Velo, our worries were well in hand, now the whole world is crashing around us," Bronus growled.

"Dragos, they did not read the dragons in your mind, I told Allie about them," Ethan confessed, feeling more the fool with every passing moment.

"Why would you tell her?" Dragos asked calmly.

"I had to tell her the truth so she would wait for me."

"Wait for what?" Bronus asked.

"I planned to go after the dragon myself after the winter holiday."

"*The wilds?*" Bronus growled. "Are you daft, Ethan?"

"You have grown quite bold if you think you can kill a dragon, Ethan," Dragos said.

"If you could not heal yourself, I swear you were hit on the head once too often, boy!" Bronus scolded him.

"I had to try, Dad. Dragos's vision showed the damn thing destroying Astaria. *All* of Astaria. Who else is going to challenge it? It doesn't matter anyway if I have to bend my knee to Allie."

"You're not. That woman will not have my son. I will not allow it!" Bronus declared.

"I might have a way to avoid it, but not that way. I will not sacrifice you, Dad. This whole scheme of theirs was either to neutralize you or me. If they take me, I can come back. If it's you, I can't bring you back from the dead."

"You are not bending your knee to this Vellesian princess. For once you will do as I say. You will help your brother fight in my absence."

"*No!*" a harsh feminine voice countered his command.

They turned toward the door as Queen Gabrielle passed within.

"Ethan shall take his vows tomorrow just as Valera commands!" Gabrielle's eyes glowed like embers as she stared down the three of them.

"It may come to that, Gaby, but we must—" Dragos began to explain before she cut him off.

"*No! He will* take his vows!" She stormed across the room and struck Ethan across his face. She had never raised a hand to her children until now.

Blood pushed to the surface of his lip before rapidly healing, the pain of the blow abating just as quick. "Mom, I—" Ethan uttered, unsettled by her anger.

"*Do not call me that.* I am your *mother*. You shall never speak so informally to me again, Ethanos. You lied to me, Ethanos. You broke your sworn promise to me. I have always indulged your rebellious nature. Tell me true, did you enter the Mage Bane?" she asked, standing over him with her hands on her hips.

"I did," he confessed quietly, looking into her eyes. "I didn't mean to go, I went to—"

"I know why you went. I hope she was worth it, for you will pay the price of sparing her life. I warned you about the Mage Bane. I made you promise never to enter it for a reason. I also know about Earth. It acts the same as the Mage Bane, doesn't it?"

He nodded.

"And you planned to go back?"

He nodded yes again.

"And the wilds, you planned to go there searching for dragons?"

He acknowledged that as well.

She slapped him again.

"You ungrateful child. You were born with such wondrous gifts, and you simply throw them away like worthless trifles. First, the throne of Astaria and your birthright. Now you risk your power to heal yourself. Do you care to wonder what it is like being your mother? Do you know how many nights I lie beside your father, denying him the affection he is due as my husband because I am crying over you? I care more about your life than you do. I wonder if you care if you live or die at all, do you?" she asked with her anger damming her tears.

"I want to live, Mother, but I can't turn my eyes from obvious dangers. I entered the Mage Bane to save her. I didn't know who she was, only that she was a mage healer. If Arian were in peril, wouldn't you hope someone would come to her aid? I didn't have the luxury of knowing her heart. As far as the wilds, I didn't plan to go there until I saw the dragon in Grandfather's vision destroying Astaria. What would you have me do, sit back, and let it happen, hoping someone else would find a way to stop it? I'm the only one who could hope to face a dragon. It's not how I wish things were but how they are. How did you come to know this? Did Allie tell you?"

"Does it matter?"

"Yes. She twists the truth to gain what she wants. She can't be trusted."

"Neither can you," she said, turning from him to direct her ire upon Bronus. "And you!" She slapped his thick head.

"What was that for?" Bronus growled indignantly.

"You knew he went to the Mage Bane. You knew that his healing powers were impaired on Earth. Yet you never told me. You would have let him go back, wouldn't you?"

"Now, Gaby, you mustn't get angry with him. Bronus was only—" Dragos tried to explain before she slapped him too.

"You knew as well, didn't you, Father? You are most culpable of all. You discovered the barrier and helped Ethan across it. That led us to where we are now. And your visions of dragons, that you could trust to Ethan but not your *king* and *queen*, when did you plan to tell us?"

The three men had nothing to say. They exchanged pained looks of shame and embarrassment, each avoiding looking her in the eye.

"My father, my husband, and my son…*idiots!*" she declared, turning away from them as she stepped toward the door. She paused at the entryway, craning her neck over her shoulder to look at them before stepping without. "I will treat with Queen Valera and inform her that we have agreed to her terms. Ethanos shall be presented to the Vellesian crown princess at the appointed time. I have posted guards outside your chamber, Ethan. They will accompany you everywhere you go. You are *forbidden* to leave the citadel. Your whole life you have resented the restraints we placed upon your wandering nature. I fear your Vellesian princess will not be as tolerant." She stepped without, wiping her tears once she was clear.

*****

The two queens met in Valera's chamber without aides or retainers. Each sat in soft, high-backed chairs, facing each other before the glowing hearth.

"It is agreed." Valera smiled. "Astaria has a wise queen."

"I am weary of false compliments, Valera. I doubt you would be as magnanimous if it were I who was stealing your firstborn."

"If my firstborn forsook her throne I would offer her up to you with much enthusiasm. You must be very disappointed in the boy?"

"I am proud of him. I doubt you can understand that. All I care is that he is safe, and I have your sworn vow that he shall."

"My dear Gabrielle, I have promised you that I shall treat Ethanos as my own child. He shall be *very* safe in my keeping. There is no possibility for him to ever again venture beyond Vellesia, let alone the Mage Bane, the wilds or across the barrier as he is wont to do. As agreed, you or any in your house may visit him as you wish."

"I do not wish him to suffer."

"Gabrielle, do you believe I shall whip Ethanos once he is in my keeping? I shan't torture the boy if that is foremost in your mind." She stifled a laugh.

"You do not know what you are asking of him. He hates rules and confinement. He loathes protocol, pomp, and formalities. I know my son, and I fear he will always hate you and Alesha for what you have done to him. You must be cognizant that he gave up the throne of Astaria for his freedom. Now you are taking that from him. It is soul-crushing." Gabrielle held Valera's gaze with great intensity.

"Then we shall grant him enough freedom to sate his thirst and spare him from the protocols of court as much as we can."

"Must you humiliate him tomorrow?"

"The ceremony tomorrow is a show of state. It is not something we take pleasure from but is merely a demonstration of Alesha's authority. Ethan need only perform as he is expected."

"Ethan never does anything as expected."

*****

"Come along, son," Bronus commanded as they walked side by side through the bluestone corridors of Astaris.

"Where are we going?" Ethan asked.

"We, my boy, are going to do what I did the night before I wed your mother."

"And what was that?" Ethan struggled to keep pace with his father's lively steps.

"We are going to get drunk. I want to see your princess's face when you show up for her big day, hungover and stinking of ale, hah." Bronus grinned.

Ethan laughed. His father rarely let his guard down, especially around him, lest it embolden Ethan's rebellious spirit even more.

"Mom won't be so pleased either," Ethan said.

"Bah! Women are always looking for an excise not to meet their wifely duties. You'll find that out soon enough."

"It doesn't matter anyway because Allie knows I can't get drunk. I can only pretend to be drunk, and she'll know I am just faking," Ethan confessed.

Bronus stopped in midstride. "What do you mean you can't get drunk?" A suspicious eyebrow rose over a gray eye.

Ethan cringed at the slip of his tongue. He stopped beside his father and lowered his head realizing what he had said. This was turning out to be one of *those* days. Everything was turning to crap before his very eyes. "I can't get drunk unless I'm in the Mage Bane or Earth."

"Are you saying all these years that we went drinking you were faking the whole time?"

Ethan lifted his eyes to face his father in the dim light. "Sorry." He shrugged.

"All those drinking games we played with your brother, Dragos and all the knights, lords, and soldiers in the palace, you always won. You drank me under many a table. So…you cheated?"

"It wasn't *really* cheating since I did drink all that ale." Ethan squirmed with his answer.

"Hah! You still cheated. You are the only man to ever best me at drinking and now I know why. My son the cheater," Bronus boasted.

"What was I supposed to do, tell the truth? None of the men would want me around. In a tavern full of drunks, no one likes the sober man."

"So to fit in you *stole* my title of hardest drinking man in the kingdom. Every soldier, knight, and mage lord in Astaria gives me grief about being bested by you."

"I'm certain you'll tell them the truth and restore your place among the gods of inebriation." Ethan laughed.

"You're damn right I will. Come along…cheater."

*****

"Now that my son, my beloved firstborn, is a confessed cheater, I reclaim my rightful title as the best drinker in Astaria. Does any man here wish to challenge my claim?" Bronus stood atop the bar overlooking the crowd. The tavern was cavernous, built in the subterranean levels of the inner palace. Dim torchlight lined the dark stone walls. Dozens of solid oak circled tables were spread across the floor. The bar was massive, running the length of the east and south walls. Wide stone steps descended from the west wall, which led through a wide tunnel to the ground level of the palace. A narrower tunnel in the southeast corner descended to the lower cellars, where hundreds of casks were stored. Barmaids in tight bodices and brief skirts circulated the floor, filling goblets and suffering the amorous advances of the patrons, most of which were soldiers, knights, craftsmen, and mages of varying castes.

"I do!" Every man shouted back to the king, accepting his challenge.

"Very well, bring up a hundred casks, barkeep. I have been challenged!" Bronus ordered.

Ethan stood at the bar, shaking his head as his father climbed down to stand beside him.

"Fill it up," Ethan handed his tall wooden cup to the barkeep.

The barkeep grinned, filling his cup with a white liquid.

"What's this?" Ethan made a face after taking a careful sip.

"Sorry, Ethan, but you only get milk. King's orders." The barkeep grinned as those gathered around him burst into laughter, his father especially.

"Where did you get this milk, from a dead cow?" Ethan pushed the cup away.

"We can't be wasting good ale on a lad who can't get drunk, boy. You stick with your milk and leave the good stuff to the men." Bronus slapped him on the back while downing a second goblet. Bronus was enjoying his restored status of drinking champion way too much.

"If that milk is not to your liking, Ethan, I know a wet nurse who would gladly give you a taste of hers," Lorgon Chartes, second son of Lord Corvan Chartes, said. He stood to Ethan's left with his green cape draping to the floor and the dancing flame of House Chartes sewn upon his gold tunic. Lorgon's dog sat upon the bar, lapping ale from his master's goblet. The canine was Jorster bred, with fat ears and a diminutive body, weighing little more than five pounds and no larger than a man's foot.

"Tell your sister I'm too busy for that because I'm trying to decipher if that is a small dog or a cat that barks," Ethan gave as good as he got. Everyone within earshot slapped Lorgon on the back, blowing half-swallowed ale into the air as they laughed. Lorgon was a good sport and laughed as well.

"Sire, I believe Ethan has earned a cup of ale after the day he has had," Lorgon asked of the king.

"Aye, I think the lad has suffered enough, Your Grace," Sergeant Mullar of the citadel guard seconded.

"Here is a toast to Ethan Blagen, the finest son of Astaria!" Vancel Torrent shouted over the crowd, raising his goblet into the air.

"To Ethan Blagen. Freemen of Astaria!" the men shouted their salute.

"To Ethan Blagen, my son and freeman of the seven kingdoms. He kneels to no man and no man kneels to him!" King Bronus downed his third goblet.

The barkeep passed Ethan a tall cup of ale and he paused before drinking. "I kneel to no one…until tomorrow," he said quietly before taking a drink.

"Not if you don't want to, Ethan," Bronus said. "I stand by what I said. They can take my life if you will stand with your brother."

"I could never do that." Ethan looked into his father's gray eyes.

"Valera wants you for a reason, Ethan, and it is more than warming her daughter's bed."

Ethan once thought that Valera would select Geoff Jarvo because he was the king's closest male relative beside Tristan and himself. He thought Valera sought a blood connection in order to sire a lightning lord of her own. But why choose him? He was immune to magic and was a threat to *all* mages, especially her. If she wanted him dead, why did she not have her men kill him while he was in the Mage Bane? It didn't make sense. Any offspring of Alesha and Ethan might be born void of magic. He might find the answer if he had time, but time was an asset he had little of. He looked at the cup of ale in his right hand, wondering if he would ever have another. He did not know what rules Allie would place on him. His lasting memory of her was when he left her in the great hall. Her eyes, which were always soft and inviting, were cruel and harsh. She seemed to think he should be honored that she chose him and was offended by his resistance. He couldn't believe she was doing this to him after he saved her life. He saved her life. He saved her *life!* Ethan suddenly sat upright, a smile playing along his lips. *There is a way*, he thought excitedly.

"*Sire!*" He heard someone call out to his father, breaking his train of thought. Drexer Torlis, commander of the garrison of Astaris, stood before the king with his silver mail and black cape. He was a bullnecked man with tints of gray in his dark mane.

"Commander, what troubles you this night?" Bronus set his sixth drink down upon the bar, turning to the commander.

"Sire, Captain Marco's patrol is long overdue. I sent a second patrol four hours past, and no word has returned on them as well. Before I send another, I thought you should be advised."

"Which direction did Marco scout?" Ethan asked, stepping close.

"To the east," Commander Torlis answered.

"I'll go after them. I don't have to be back until midday tomorrow to meet my jailer," Ethan said.

"You're going to do as your mother told you for once, son. You see those dozen palace guards standing post at the entrance? They are tasked with keeping you here." Bronus doubted any twelve men could make Ethan do anything he didn't want to do.

"It is my fault Marco is out there. He went on my counsel," Ethan pleaded.

"Marco is one of *my* captains. I will see to his safe return. Stay here, Ethan, and for once do as I command!" Bronus said as he excused himself with Commander Torlis following in his wake.

*****

The queen's guard shadowed his every step as he moved throughout the palace. Ethan watched his father depart with a dozen mages and two score of cavalry for his escort. Vancel and Xavier were among them. Ethan made his way to the queen's tower where the Vellesian delegation was quartered. Allie was no longer in the chamber that Ethan provided her, but in the royal apartments designated for royal guests of Astaris. He knew the way, and his escort followed close behind, cautioning him not to enter the corridors assigned the

Vellesian royal family. Ethan ignored their counsel. He would see Allie on his terms even if it killed him. He wanted to talk with her with no one else around, just the two of them. He was met with drawn swords and spear tips leveled as he turned into the Vellesian corridor. A half-dozen guards with silver breastplates and white kilted tunics blocked his way.

"Hold!" one commanded.

"I'm here to visit, Alesha," Ethan declared with steel in his voice.

The guards bristled at his informal reference to their crown princess.

"Be gone! Return at daylight and with proper deference for our crown princess," their Sergeant replied through clenched teeth.

"I have enough bullets chambered to put two into each of you. I will kill you if I have to, and you can't stop me. Therefore, you can't protect your princess, so I suggest you fetch her and tell her that Ethan Blagen is here to speak with her."

"The *crown princess* is sleeping," the sergeant answered, betraying no concern for Ethan's threat.

"Then wake her up or I *will!*"

"I am awake," Alesha's sultry voice echoed. She stood in the doorway of her chamber with a fur cloak around her shoulders.

"Your Highness, Ethan Blagen desires an audience. He refuses to depart. Shall we slay him?" the sergeant asked.

"Let him pass, Sergeant Bourvelle," Alesha said with her arms folded.

Ethan's escort remained in the outer corridor with the Vellesian guards as Alesha stepped aside, allowing Ethan to enter her chamber before closing the door behind them.

"You should be resting, Ethan. Tomorrow shall be a taxing day." She spoke calmly as he walked across the chamber and sat upon the wide sill of the window. He sat there a moment, glaring at her through narrow eyes.

"Rest, Allie? How can I rest with what you are doing? Why? Why are you doing this? And don't speak of destiny or desire or any of that crap. Did I wrong you in some way that I'm not aware?"

She stepped closer with the moonlight filtering through the window, lighting her face. "It is not that complicated, Ethan. Remember when we were in the Mage Bane? We spoke of finding the one person who matches our heart like a missing piece to a jagged puzzle? You are my missing piece. You are as my own flesh. Without you, I cannot be whole."

"Allie, I offered you all that I had. I would've married you. I never felt that way about anyone. What more do you want?"

"You offered me your corpse, Ethan. Marriage? Your way would have me a widow in a year's time. With Earth, the Mage Bane, the wilds, and any other danger you could conjure. I refuse your *offer*." She needn't say that she foresaw his death if he did not come. She kept that vision from his mother as well, doubting they would head her counsel at this time.

"If I'm so awful, Allie, then why pursue this scheme of yours? You see, I don't believe you. Your mother tried to trade a kingdom of gold for me when I was a child. Now you are doing the same but with my father's life as the payment. Valera acted disinterested once my immunity to magic was revealed, but now I know differently. You both want me *because* I am immune to magic. Why were you in Cordova? It wasn't a mission of charity to heal the sick, was it? You were after me, but Luke Crawford interfered and dragged you away to the Mage Bane. Am I right?"

She stepped nigh, her breath close enough to heat his face. "My mother desires your gifts."

"And you?"

She pressed her lips to his, fierce and savage, consumed with a lustful hunger. He didn't return her passion, nor did he resist. The feel of her flesh and the scent of her hair stirred longings that he had never known before her. After a moment, she withdrew, staring into his sea-blue eyes with the moon shining behind him.

"Is that your reason? I doubt it," he said.

"My reason was the same as my mother's. But then…I met you. I know you feel much the same. I see it in your eyes, Ethan." She ran her fingers over his chest. "I feel it in your touch. The only difference between us is that you forsook your duty to Astaria and I *embrace* mine to Vellesia."

We'll see about that. He smiled inwardly. "Tell me the truth, Allie."

"Alesha," she corrected him.

"You told me your name was Allie, so I will call you Allie." He smiled.

She stifled her annoyance, knowing that his insolence would cease once he took his vows.

"So, Allie, tell me the truth. Why did you have me beg your mother for your freedom when you had no intention of forsaking your throne?" he growled, unable to suppress the anger that festered like poison.

"You were entitled to a royal request for saving my life, Ethan. I couldn't have you using it to free your father or yourself. It was another unfortunate necessity brought about by Luke Crawford's interference," she explained.

"So that was why." He sighed.

"That was why." She shrugged, her answer seeming to deflate his ire.

She placed her right palm upon his cheek. He slapped her hand and pushed her away.

"Don't touch me!"

Fear crossed her eyes as she quickly withdrew her hand as if he might bite it off.

"You had me beg on my knees to Valera to win your freedom, when all I was doing was forging my own chains. I saved your life, Allie, and you are stealing mine. You speak simply about your hopes and desires, but what about mine? You think I wanted to go to the Mage Bane? Or to the wilds? If I don't find a way to stop the dragons, then Astaria is doomed. No one else will go. No one else can go, just me. And you curse me for it. What if it was Vellesia that held such a fate and only you could stop it. Then imagine I dragged you back to Astaria while your kingdom fell. Tell me, Allie, how would you feel?"

"You cannot defeat a dragon, Ethan. You shall only perish in the attempt. I am taking you to protect you from your greatest danger—

yourself. If you must hate me for keeping you safe, then your hate is a price I am willing to pay." She didn't say what her vision of Vellesia revealed if he didn't return with her. Her own land was doomed without him, though she could not see the nature of the threat or how Ethan could prevent it.

"You sound like my mother. What did you tell her to turn her against me?"

"Mothers have ways of finding the truth, Ethan. She asked if you went to the Mage Bane, and I answered."

"That's not all you told her. Dragos's vision, the wilds, how Earth impairs my mage power—she didn't conjure these answers so quickly without your help. What did you offer her?"

"What all mothers desire, Ethan, their children's safety and grandchildren."

"Grandchildren? She actually believed you? I would wager all the gold in Astaria that as soon as we return to Vellesia, your mother will have my heart ripped out of me to extract my power."

Alesha was stunned. How could he think that of her? Did he truly believe she would conspire to murder him? "Ethan…I swear by the throne of Vellesia and the blood of my house that your life shall be safe in Vellesia."

"Then why have the mage kings enlisted your help to remove me from my father's side? They will settle for nothing short of my death. If I ever get free of your leash, I will kill them all. Every. Last. One. They feared I would start a revolution in their lands, but now I will. I will see the power of mage rule broken forever. If any mage thinks of placing a crown upon their head, I'll lop it off."

"And you wonder why they fear you and wish you dead?" she said, growing weary of his argument. The mage kings were but insects beneath their feet. They held no power over anything but their decrepit realms. She was not accustomed to anyone speaking to her in such a manner. By midday on the morrow, he would not argue with her ever again, she reminded herself.

"I should have killed that Gorgencian prince the other day at the smithy. We would then have our war with Gorgencia when we are strongest, and I wouldn't have walked into your trap," he thought aloud.

"You are the one that speaks of killing this or that person, Ethan. Does that ease your shame of being bested by a *woman*? Perhaps if you imagine yourself cutting down the mage kings who offend you so, it will help you forget that come midday tomorrow, you *will* bend your knee before me. Then you will swear your loyalty to Vellesia and your obedience to *me*!" She hissed, her eyes darkened in fury. She had grown weary of his venom and returned some of her own.

He looked at her for a long moment, bereft of words that matched his thoughts. "I will never be what you want me to be, Allie. You're better off killing me."

She wanted to slap him but held her rage in check. "You *will* do what I command or your father's life will be forfeit. I know what he means to you. It is one of the many things I learned during my time with you. Remember Ethan that his life means *nothing* to me. His life from this time on is but a candle in the wind. If you do not obey me in all things, no matter how trivial they may seem, I will snuff out that narrow flame." Why did she say that? She cringed inwardly with her harsh words but felt her self-control off-kilter whenever in his presence. His anger only fueled hers, and she couldn't help but lose control. She wished no harm to his father, but what other leverage had she? He would die if left to his own devices, and she vowed not to let that happen. Her people would die. They had always planned to seize Ethan for the fulfillment of their prophecies, but she wondered if she cared as much for that anymore. Since she had come to know Ethan, she dreaded doing what must be done for his safety and the glory of her house.

"You do that, Allie, and you lose your hold over me. Then there is nothing to protect you from me," he warned.

She sighed, weary of this argument. "You may have the strength of three men or more, Ethan, but we have chains strong enough to hold ten. Do not forget your place."

Ethan smiled.

"Why are you smiling?" She lifted a dark brow.

"Because you have finally shown some emotion, Allie or Alesha or whatever your real name is."

"Are you satisfied?" she asked darkly, tired of their argument.

"Yes. You revealed quite a lot. You make my decision an easy one now."

"What do you mean?" she asked suspiciously.

"Well, if you're going to kill my father at the slightest sign of my disobedience, there is little point in my agreeing to terms that I can't possibly live up to."

"You will be told what orders must be obeyed, Ethan. You will have a fair warning. I promise they will be neither numerous or petty. Does that satisfy you?"

"Nothing you say satisfies me, Alesha," he said, blending her two names to mock her lies.

This was not going as she had hoped. She didn't wish to threaten him or provoke him, but she couldn't help herself. He brought her darker side to surface with such ease that she struggled to suppress it. She ignored his taunt and attempted a different tact. "I care for you, Ethan. I care more about you than anything else in this world. I do not wish to fight with you. I want you by my side, is that so terrible? You should be flattered. I went through a great ordeal to bring us to this juncture. Of all the men in Greater Elaria to share my bed, I chose you. Does this not satisfy you? You did claim that I was the most beautiful woman you had ever seen. Does that not ease your mind? You have said that women care only about power. You said they desired you when you were their crown prince but ignore you now that you are not. I don't desire you for your royal birth. I find it more a hindrance to me than an asset. Men, however, favor beauty in women above all else. Is this not so? I am beautiful, Ethan. I am perfectly matched for you."

"Your beauty only resides on the surface. Inside." He jabbed a thumb toward his heart. "Inside you are as cruel and evil as your mother. I fell in love with you, Alesha," he called her by her true name. "I fell in love with a girl who stood by me in the Mage Bane, who spoke out against her evil queen, who cared for the sick. I fell in love with a girl that dreamed of being free. You know what saddens me most, Alesha?"

"What?" she asked softly.

"The place I took you yesterday, overlooking the falls, I was going to build a house there for us. We could have lived away from the palace with no one near to disturb us. We could raise a family with no cares or worries other than ourselves."

"It is pleasant to ponder such possibilities, Ethan, but they are simple daydreams that have no basis in reality. You speak fondly of living a simple life, but what do you know of it? What trade could you ply to support a family? A farmer? A woodcutter? A fisherman? You are a warrior, Ethanos Blagen. That is what you are. That is the asset that you sell to earn your way in the world. You have no equal in that vocation. You are not a farmer, and I will not be a farmer's wife. I will be the queen of Vellesia, and *our* daughter will be as well."

"Is that what you want from me, a child?"

"It is the primary duty of a Vellesian consort, though there are others."

"If that is really all you need, then why not compromise? We can wed tomorrow, sharing vows before our houses. We can pledge our firstborn daughter to Vellesia and our sons can be free to choose their own path, like me. I promise not to leave your side until we provide the heir your mother requires. Then I can deal with Dragos's dragons, Cordova, and visit my family whenever I wish," he said, hopeful that she might be open to his suggestion.

She wanted to place her hand upon his cheek to ease her answer but feared he would slap it away again. "It is not possible, Ethan. The crown princess of Vellesia must be sired by a consort sworn to the Vellesian throne. The loyalties of the future queen cannot be divided between realms. I know this pains you, Ethan, but you *must* swear fealty to the Vellesian throne. There is no other way."

Ethan sat upon her bed with his face in his hands, defeated. He sat for a time, his world spinning apart. Alesha sat beside him, unsure if he would snap as he did before, but she felt this was different. She could read the defeat in his posture as she touched his shoulder. She needed him resigned to the fact that he must surrender, but she did not wish to see him suffer. It was a paradox her mother could never understand.

"Ethan?" she whispered. "Are you well?"

"I'm tired, Alesha, tired of fighting, tired of arguing, with you, my mother, my father, the mage kings, everyone. I will do as you ask. I'll take the vows you demand of me. You can have my life for what little it is worth. You have already taken everything I care about, so help yourself to whatever is left." He turned, facing her with lifeless, tired eyes. "But I will never love you again, Alesha, not after this."

His words cut like a knife to her heart. She sat there for a time, wondering what she might say. She never cared what others thought or felt, consigning their sentiments to irrelevance. So why did it bother her so how Ethan felt? Was this not their destiny? Was this not what she had planned since time immortal? Even her recent misgivings were set aside once her vision revealed his fate if she did not claim him. She never imagined this to be so hard.

She ran her fingers through his hair and down his neck. "You have given me so much, Ethan. What you have not given, I have taken. Let me give you something in return." She kissed the tips of her fingers and pressed them to his lips. Lowering her hands to his waist, she lifted his black shirt over his head and tossed it upon the floor. Then she pushed him onto his back, kissing his chest while running her hands over the muscled contours of his torso.

Ethan lay there while she applied her ministrations, conflicted by hatred and lust. She was impossibly beautiful, and he lacked the power to resist her, as if another force had taken possession of him. She threw off her robes, revealing herself to him for the first time. The swell of her breasts hovered teasingly close. The tautness of her belly contrasted the fullness of her hips and the smooth musculature of her thighs. Should he allow her to proceed after all she had done to him this night? As she unholstered his gun belt and removed his boots, trousers, and loin garment, he realized what she was really doing. This was a promise of what life with her would be like. If he followed the path she placed before him, he would be thusly rewarded. But once she had what she wanted, nights such as these would be precious few. No, he would make her desire this more than he. He grabbed her by the waist and flipped her underneath him, pinning her to the bed. Then he kissed her, working his way over the mysteries of her flesh. He took his time, savoring the seconds as minutes and the minutes as hours.

They made love with the luminous light of the waxing moon filtering throughout the chamber. Within the proximity of his aura, her mage powers were bound as if stripped away, rendering her vulnerable. Without her mage powers, she felt naked before him, mentally as well as physically. She yielded time and again with each climax. No man had ever touched her as her body was a temple for her consort only, but Ethan would be that consort. She planned to seduce him, driving his desire for her flesh to the apex of his thoughts. With the pleasure of this night fresh in his mind, he would be more malleable to the role she appointed him. Valera told her men are driven by their carnal urges. When all else fails, a woman can bend a man's will with the promise of sexual reward. It was a vital piece of her plan to guarantee that Ethan bent the knee on the morrow. He must weigh his father's life, his mother's ire, and his lust for her against his freedom. He should be driven mad with desire. But Ethan was not following her plan. It was she who was left breathless and wanting more as each climax rippled over her flesh.

"Don't stop," she begged. "Don't ever stop."

"I didn't plan to." He smiled, looking down into her golden eyes.

She gazed into the depths of his sea-blue eyes as she felt another shudder running the length of her. This was not going as she planned. She was supposed to seduce him, bringing him to his knees with a mad desire, yet he stared down at her with a slight smile, betraying little sign of lustful submission, calmly observing her helpless surrender. He continued for what seemed eternity until she lay spent and flush before releasing himself into her. Even then he showed little emotion other than a warm smile as he gently moved her hair from her glowing face.

"Alesha?"

"Yes," she said, opening her eyes.

"You're glowing." He pulled back, looking down as her skin glowed bright crimson and gold.

"So are you," she said as his muscular build emitted hues of blue and green.

Ethan lifted his hand before his face, his eyes wide as he took in his glowing digits. "What is wrong with us?"

"It is a reaction of our conflicting powers, my mage power and your anti-magic."

"You knew this would happen?"

"I knew something *might* happen, but I didn't know how it would manifest."

"Is there anything else you haven't told me?" he asked, knowing the litany of things she had not yet revealed were too numerous to recite.

She nodded, staring at him as if for the first time. The glow of their flesh dulled as he climbed off the bed. He reached down for his undergarment and trousers. He then buckled his pistol belt around his waist.

"Where are you going?" she asked, hoping he might stay longer.

"Back to my own bed. I have to get some sleep before morning. Perhaps a little rest will refresh my brain so I can think of some way of saving my father without bowing to your damn throne," he said, not unkindly as he pulled on his shirt and tied down his holster to his thigh.

"You wouldn't be the man I admire if you didn't try." She smiled. "Though you shall soon find there is no other way."

"I may have a few surprises left in me, Princess."

"I'm sure you do."

He turned to leave before she discovered how she affected him. He concealed his desire as best he could, feigning mild interest when she drove his lust to the brink. He pushed such thoughts aside, needing to push her away. He turned back at the door, looking at her over his shoulder. "Next time I share your bed, Alesha, try to put a little more effort into it so I might find it pleasurable as well. Good night," he said and slipped through the doorway.

A kinetic force erupted from Alesha's fingertips, striking the thick oak door as Ethan closed it. Her face shaded crimson with fury as the door broke asunder.

Ethan looked behind him at the ruined door and smiled. The guards in the corridor backed away, giving him room to leave.

"Tell your princess that guests are responsible for their damages." He walked away with his escort following in his wake.

CHAPTER 29

The morning came swiftly. The sun broke through his window, casting a bright light that played irritably across his eyes, stirring him awake. Ethan rested poorly, his mind a storm of a thousand worries. How could he rest knowing the night might be his last, or at least his last of freedom. The coming dawn drew him closer to his rendezvous with Allie in the great hall. Time was slipping away like water through his hands. He dreaded facing her again. The pain of her betrayal and the thought of his hard-won freedom being stripped away, constricted his chest painfully.

Ethan pulled on a pair of cotton breeches and stepped toward his window. Resting his hand upon the wall, he stared at the activity in the courtyard below. He wondered if his father had returned yet. He had not been informed either way. With his mother's mood, he couldn't rely on his guards to tell him anything.

"Prince Ethanos," a woman's stern voice echoed behind him. Standing in the doorway was a woman he recognized as one of Valera's ministers. She was tall, though not as statuesque as Alesha or Valera. Her red hair was swept up in a tall coiffure twisted high upon her head. Her face had a harsh beauty that matched the stern nature of her voice and demeanor. She had the look of a woman younger than her true age, which was likely in her fourth decade. She wore a long purple gown that was tight-fitting across its bodice and loose below the hips. She was accompanied by two younger women of similar disposition and dress.

"Who are you?" Ethan asked, irritated by their uninvited intrusion.

"I am Leora Mattiese, steward of Elysia and chief minister of Vellesia. I am the queen's right hand and first councilor." She spoke with an air of authority as if he were a child.

"You could just say you're Valera's lapdog and save yourself rattling of all those meaningless titles."

"I am not shaken by your coarse tongue or boyish insults, Prince Ethanos. You can save your childish wit for those who find them more insulting than irritating," she said with a humorless frown.

"I bet your charming personality fits in perfectly with Valera's court. Now Leora, why are you here? I don't think Alesha would be pleased to find three women in my bedchamber. Of course, if things don't go as she plans, I may be a freeman this evening if you care to come back. You're not too bad looking for an older woman." Leora's countenance darkened as the two younger women lowered their eyes, blushing in embarrassment.

"I was warned about you, Prince Ethanos," Leora said as calmly as she could manage.

"I'm sure you were."

"We are here to prepare you for your nuptials and school you on the proper etiquette of a royal consort. I see that you are clean-shaven. That is splendid for our queen does not favor facial hair among members of the royal court."

"*Proper* etiquette?" Ethan crossed his arms over his bare chest. He leaned his head close to hear her explain.

"The standards of conduct and comportment of a royal consort are *exceedingly* high. We shall instruct you on Princess Alesha's expectations."

"And what are Alesha's expectations?"

"Princess Alesha is *never* to be addressed so informally, Prince Ethanos!" Leora admonished. "She is the crown princess of Vellesia, and you shall show her proper respect."

"My name is Ethan. I am not a prince. As far as Alesha is concerned, she isn't my crown princess. Hell, she isn't even my wife... yet. Until last night, she told me her name was Allie, so don't scold me about *respect*." He rolled his eyes.

"Once you take your vows, your dedication to the crown princess must be your sole focus. Your petty resentments and dissatisfaction with your new status will not be tolerated once you pledge your fidelity to Vellesia and the crown princess."

"Petty resentments? You're stealing my life you conceited wench! Do you expect me to happily accept that?"

Leora's eyes narrowed coolly, matching her darkening mood. If she could cast fire at him, she would have already done so. "We are here to help you, Prince Ethanos. We are short of time and will focus our preparations on the things you must know for today's ceremony. We shall have ample time after this day to continue your instruction."

"What is there to know? All I have to do is take a knee and declare how much I love Vellesia."

Leora's nostrils flared with indignation. "It is hardly so simplistic, Prince Ethanos—"

"Ethan, just Ethan." He smiled at her. If he was going to be miserable, he might as well have a little fun with this insufferable woman. He was enjoying seeing her twist her words politely. He knew she was struggling to control her temper and loved nothing more than poking her with his verbal barbs.

"If it is your wish that I refer to you as Ethan for the next few hours, I shall comply with your request. After the ceremony, however, you shall be addressed as Consort Ethanos Loria, husband of Crown Princess Alesha Loria."

"Ethanos Loria?" Ethan raised an angry eyebrow. "My name is Ethan Blagen."

"Part of your vows requires you to forsake all loyalties to your father's house. When you kneel to the crown princess, you shall swear your loyalty to House Loria. This is one of many things you must learn. Now, may we continue?"

Ethan's anger was quickly trumping reason as he took in Leora's explanation like sour milk.

"The first protocol you must learn is how to perform a proper bow to Vellesian royalty. Whether you are presenting your person to the crown princess, the queen daughter, or the queen mother, you must kneel with both knees. Though kneeling upon one knee is acceptable in Astaria, kneeling with both knees is required in Vellesia."

Queen daughter? Queen mother? Ethan wondered what she was referring to.

"You can save your breath, Leora, I've heard enough. Each time I think the role of Alesha's consort can't possibly get any worse, it gets worse."

"We are not here to upset you, Ethan. These protocols are not meant to humiliate you. They are merely an acknowledgment of authority. We each play our role for the stability of the realm. Before we continue, perhaps we should get you dressed?"

"Get me dressed?" He did not like the sound of that at all. He was starting to think that Alesha sent these women here just to spite him for his cruel remark last night.

"Yes. Queen Valera has selected the outfit she desires you to wear for the crown princess. The clothing you wore the past several days is highly inappropriate for any interaction with a crown princess of Vellesia."

Anyone telling him what to wear was a sore point with Ethan. Bitter memories from his childhood when his mother forced him to wear the most ridiculous of costumes surfaced in his brain. He felt captive to whatever grotesque adornments Alesha might conjure.

The two younger women accompanying Leora presented him with a white tunic with a pleated kilt that overlapped sparkling silver folds. The hem would fall above the knee, and Ethan would never be caught dead in such a garment. A black sword belt and brown leather sandals with straps that crisscrossed over his calves, completed the outfit. Ethan stepped away as if they presented him with poison.

"I understand the men in your realm do not wear such revealing garments, Ethan, but Vellesian men wear such raiment to display their physical assets. The crown princess speaks highly of your physical attributes and desires that you tastefully display them for your nuptials."

"You can tell Alesha I'm not her slave yet. Until then I will dress myself." He grabbed Leora by her arm and dragged her to the door, pushing her into the outer corridor.

"Prince Ethanos!" Leora protested his rough handling. "Your mother, the queen, shall hear of this!" she warned.

"Ladies," Ethan waved his open hand to the outer corridor, directing the two younger women to follow Leora.

They each bobbed a curtsy to Ethan before stepping without.

"Tell Alesha that outfit would look much nicer on her," he said, closing the door.

Ethan shook his head as he returned to his window to survey the happenings below. No matter how he tried to think of his father, Dragos, Cordova, or Red Rock, visions of Alesha forced themselves upon him. The memories of sharing her bed consumed him. He regretted what he last said to her, for it was a lie. She did give him much pleasure, and his words were his way of hurting her like she hurt him. When she wasn't raising his ire, she was filling his mind with lustful thoughts that could never be sated with a thousand life-times. He tried to shake her image from his memory but to no avail. Since the moment of their physical consummation, it felt as if they were joined by invisible bonds. He was overcome by an irresistible urge to go to her as if the slack in those bonds were ever-tightening, drawing them together.

How is she doing this? he asked himself, believing Alesha was using some sort of enchantment to weaken his resolve. He was immune to magic unless she found a way around his power. The thought of her able to strip away his magical immunity made his blood run cold. She had his heart, but not his brain. Could his mind counter the lustful need filling his heart that drew him to her? It was clearly some sort of love spell, but they always took the mind first and the heart after. If he could keep his wits about him, he had two chances to free himself from her chains. Once free of her, he assumed the longings would be weakened with her absence.

The sound of horns broke the silent morning air as scores of mounted warriors flooded the gray stone courtyard. Ethan stared intently as his father's tall black destrier bore him through the main gate. There beside him sat a hunched, tired fellow wearing well used black trousers, dented gray mail, and a dented helm. The man lifted his face enough for Ethan to see his countenance clearly in the morning light.

"Tristan."

*****

Ethan donned his buckskin breeches and shirt. They were the last set he had that was not covered with stitches from the countless arrows and swords cuts he had received. They were inappropriate for the great hall, but he didn't care. He laced his moccasin boots with their leather-braided sides and buckled his single pistol belt and tied down the holster on his right side with the Sword of Starlight sheathed upon his left. He placed his Stetson low on his brow while digging through the chest at the end of his bed, retrieving the small smooth stone that glowed greenish blue whenever he touched it. He stuffed into a pouch tied to his pistol belt. He wrapped his twin pistol holster in his left hand and carried his Winchester in his right as he stepped without to seek out his brother.

*****

"I need to speak with Ethan, Mother," Tristan protested as Gabrielle ordered him out of his wet, ragged clothes. A young maid gathered his soiled clothing and hurried off, leaving the king and queen alone with their son in his bedchamber.

"Your brother can wait. You need to warm yourself and don dry clothing," she ordered. The hearth in his chamber was invitingly warm, and the trays of freshly cooked meat and bread sitting atop his side table would quickly tame his hunger, but Tristan needed to talk with Ethan before he enjoyed such indulgences.

"What I have to say cannot wait!" Tristan half shivered and half pleaded, staring at his parents' dumbfounded expressions as they stood before him.

"Then spit it out, boy!" Bronus growled. "You're as bad as your brother."

"I cannot tell either of you what I have learned, only the urgency of my message for my brother. Had I not been delayed by the storm, I could have saved him from his fate. I failed him." They could see the pained look upon his face.

"He failed himself," Gabrielle said through clenched teeth.

"It is a poor time to cast judgment on Ethan, my love. He broke his promise to you for the lives of others. Is there not honor in that?" Bronus asked of her.

"He should have let her perish. I warned him that no good would come of it. His mercy has cost him his freedom and perhaps his life, for I cannot truly know Alesha's intent," Gabrielle said.

"She will not kill him, Mother. Her intent for Ethan is as she claims. He will be her mate," Tristan assured her.

"Then what vexes you, Tristan? The thought of Ethan safe even in a life not of his choosing shall ease my troubled sleep," Gabrielle asked.

"I'm glad to hear that my chains will bring you comfort, Mom," Ethan said, entering the chamber.

"Mind your tongue when speaking to your mother, Ethan. I love you, boy, but I'll break your neck if you dare pay her the slightest disrespect," Bronus warned.

"I haven't disrespected my mother. I just hope she can forgive me for not easily accepting my fate. I still have a fair chance of escaping the *safe* life Alesha has promised her."

Gabrielle gave her son a disapproving look. "Time is short, Ethan. Your brother wishes to give you counsel on matters he will not reveal to us. Do not tarry for the Vellesian crown princess awaits you soon in the great hall," Gabrielle said before she and Bronus stepped without.

Once they were alone, Tristan embraced his brother fiercely.

"You look well-worn, little brother. It must've been a long ride." Ethan smirked as they parted.

"I would be dead had Marco not found me adrift in the blinding snow. I had been set upon by packs of wolves, which stripped my two mounts. I slew scores of the beasts with fire, but they would not relent. It was by mere chance that Marco found me. I owe you for that, as I'm told you were the one that sent out the patrols."

"Remind Mom of that if you can. Not all of my instincts end in disaster."

"She loves you, Ethan. She fears for you endlessly. You never see it for you are rarely here."

"I know," Ethan lowered his head. "But what choice have I had?"

"You could have kept the throne. I certainly don't favor it."

"That's why you should be king, Tristan, you will rule with reason and Justice as your guide, not petty selfishness. Any man who craves the power of the throne would make a terrible king."

"You would have ruled the same, Ethan, so your argument is false."

"No." Ethan shook his head. "You are far wiser than I, and you're more suited to be king. Now tell me what news you have for me, little brother?"

"I rode as fast as I could to warn you about Alesha, but fate is a fickle mistress that favors the Vellesian princess."

"Who warned you about her?" Ethan asked intently.

"I dare not say aloud, for her ears are everywhere and may be attuned to our presence."

"You think she can hear us?"

"Yes. Her powers are far beyond your imagining. Our Vellesian queen and crown princess have mastered every mage gift that we know and many more that we don't. They are nearly invincible. There are some powers that the princess possesses that her mother does not. They could strike down the entire host of mage kings and their attending lords with relative ease."

The color drained from Ethan's face. "Even Father? I thought they wanted a male from our house to sire a lightning lord."

"Lightning? Lightning is a power their line mastered ages ago. It is a trifle and barely worth their notice. There is only *one* obstacle to their supreme ascendancy."

"Me," Ethan answered somberly, finally cognizant of their interest in him.

"Yes, you, brother. You are the final piece to achieving their broader aims."

"Why am I such a threat to them? I may be immune to magic, but they have armies to protect them, and I can't protect anyone, save myself."

"I don't fully understand the nature of your power in relation to theirs, but there is more than you simply being immune to their mage power."

"If I agree to Alesha's terms, then they will take me where they can safely dispose of me, then the world is theirs."

"No. They want you alive and…obedient."

"For what purpose?"

Tristan leaned close, his voice but a whisper. "It is the magic of House Loria, passed down through the ages through the female line. The firstborn of the royal house is always female and inherits *all* the powers of her parents, *both* parents. Even physical traits that are to her benefit are passed on. Their stature and physical beauty are so inherited. For ages they have taken as their mates those who possessed mage gifts that they lacked, slowly strengthening their house with each mage gift added upon the last. They hold the power to topple the seven mage realms, but they bide their time, searching for the final power that will gain them dominion over the Mage Bane and the wilds as well. *You* are that power, Ethan. From you, Alesha's heir will be protected from all forms of magic. From Alesha, she will wield unchecked power, a power once coupled with your own that shall extend beyond the seven kingdoms, or so Valera believes."

And his great-grandfather thought he was the Free Born, destined to bring freedom to the masses. If what Tristan said was true, he was the catalyst that would bring about the absolute enslavement of every person in Elaria.

"Why not just take me? Why all the pretense?"

"The magic of Astaria prevented them from just taking you. It is an age-old magic that bound House Loria from ever directly interfering with House Blagen or Astaria. It is wrapped in the prophecies that have guided their house since its founding. They have long foretold the birth of one immune to magic with the power to self-heal and possessing great strength. They knew him to be the firstborn of a lightning lord. When father was born, House Loria knew their wait was nearly over. Their prophecy that shielded Astaria from their interference was the reason why no houses of our two kingdoms were ever joined through marriage. It was ancient magic that protected your eventual birth."

"Why would ancient magic of their house protect Astaria when my birth will guarantee its end?"

"Their ancient magic was designed to protect you from their interference, which might have prevented your birth. There have been many Vellesian queens like Valera that longed to intervene and seize control of Astaria, ever anxious for the prophecy to transpire. Their interference would have prevented what they desired to come to pass. When you were born, Valera desperately sought to seize you and raise you in her household, but when Father refused, the magic prevented it. She managed to have her agents dwell in Astaria to oversee her interests. They interfered with your betrothal to Elenna by creating a previous betrothal that was likely fabricated."

"Where is Elenna now?"

"She is wed to a Vellesian lord. That is all I know, and my benefactor had little time to share irrelevant news such as her place in Vellesia."

Ethan could ill imagine Elenna's fate if what he knew of Valera's vindictive nature were true.

"You mentioned Valera's agents in Astaris, did they have purple eyes?"

"Yes," Tristan said. "There were two that I know of, sisters of House Menau named Sarella and Selendra. Their house is nearly as ancient as House Loria. They are the second greatest House of Vellesia, and like our own house, their bloodlines were kept pure from House Loria until the appointed time of their union. Their brother was Valera's consort and Alesha's father. It was from House Menau that Alesha inherited the vast mental abilities that her mother lacks. Unlike House Loria, which passes all the gifts of both parents to the eldest daughter, House Menau passes on all their mental powers to each of their children. No children born of House Loria, other than the firstborn daughter, inherited more than a handful of their mother's powers. They were always relegated to obscurity, wed to lesser vassals as they held no importance for the greater goals of their house. But Valera's other children, Princess Amanda and Prince Raymar, inherited all the vast mental powers of House Menau through their father."

"And what powers do they possess?"

"They have the power to mask their appearance to others by manipulating what others see rather than changing their appearance. They can enchant multiple subjects simultaneously. Their powers of foresight, prophecy, and telepathy are far beyond even grandfather's astute prowess. They can project false memories, allowing them to pass among us without even a master seer able to detect their presence."

"Yeah, I had a run-in with Alesha's aunts in Cordova. They pitted at least forty free swords on me. I almost captured one of them, but she got away. I recognized her from Astaris."

"That was Selendra. Once you forsook the throne, the magic of Astaria no longer protected you from House Loria, and Valera and Alesha had you followed to Cordova, where they planned to seize you. Alesha led their mage healers to that Port to first observe you, then ordered her Aunt to take you back to Vellesia. Their disastrous attempt, coupled with your actions that followed, convinced Alesha that you were impossible to cage without your consent. Also, their prophecies were clear that you had to be bound to the throne through sacred vows, vows that Alesha knew you would never swear on your own accord. Your rescue of Alesha further complicated her plans by entitling you to a royal request, which you could easily exchange for your freedom if you were ever taken. They, therefore, needed a way to bind you to their will. They arranged the incident at Talesia, destroying their own vessel in our port, which led Father into the treaty, which led to the queen's ball in which you unwittingly accepted Alesha's invitation. Once you did that, Father was bound by her magic, which stripped away our protection that was afforded us by their ancient magic. Father will remain safe as long as you obey their will."

"Can I kill them?"

"You could, but Father will die, and many more of us as well. Their powers are nearly without limit, and though you may slay them, everyone else will likely die in the attempt."

"Maybe not." Ethan smiled as he drew the glowing stone from his pouch. He held it aloft for Tristan to see.

"What is it?"

"I think it will protect you from magic. It's like a smaller version of me. If I give this to Father, then Valera's magic can't touch him. Then I will kill her before she thinks of shifting her ire elsewhere."

"It's not her magic that will kill him, Ethan. His own magic is sworn to the pact he made. Once he parts with your stone, his own magic will consume him. And with the stone he will be powerless. We are doomed if you do this. Even if you kill all the mage kings and their retainers that are gathered here, their armies are all aligned to invade Astaria from each direction. The magic that protects us from the Relusians and Meltorians will be removed by our breach of sacred mage law. Valera has bound all the mage kings to her cause. They promise to attack Astaria if Father fails to deliver you into her hands. She paid them in gold sums so vast it dazzles the mind. After your fell deeds at the Velo, *all* the mage kings grew fearful of you. Valera promised to remove you to Vellesia in exchange for their aid. The sums of gold only further enticed them. If you violate the pact that Father agreed to, then the armies of the six other kingdoms shall swarm over Astaria like locust upon a ripened crop. Even if you slay Valera and Alesha, you could not stay the wrath of the might arrayed against us. The Gorgencians alone have amassed hundreds of thousands to our east. The Sarcosans have equal numbers to our southeast. Estasa has vast armadas prepared to strike our coast, while Relusia and Meltoria have reconstituted their armies with untold legions to our west. No, Ethan, there is no escaping your fate unless you have a peaceful means that appeases the magic that binds our father."

"But if I do as you say and bend the knee to Alesha, then we are doomed."

"Yes, but it will take time. In that time, we may find another way."

"As soon as I give Alesha her heir, they will likely dispose of me."

"If it was Valera's decision perhaps, but the queen mother believes differently. She follows the oldest prophecies that clearly state that the one born immune to magic must be forever bound to the Vellesian throne. Why this is so, none can know for certain, but the wording is clear, they need you alive and in service to their realm. This goes beyond siring Alesha's heir."

"Who is this queen mother you mentioned? I thought Valera was—"

"Vellesia is always ruled by two queens, a queen mother and a queen daughter. The queen daughter rules the affairs of state and represents Vellesia in the eyes of Elaria. The queen mother rules over House Loria and her heir, the queen daughter. Valera is the Vellesian queen daughter, while her mother, Corella, is the queen mother and the true authority in Vellesia. It is Corella that says you must be brought to Vellesia and kept safe so that you might serve the throne until the end of your days. Once Alesha bears the future heir, then she will become the queen daughter and Valera the queen mother. At such a time, Corella shall join with the still living matriarchs of House Loria in their coven. The coven guides the queen mother and are revered by her," Tristan explained. "It is always possible that Valera would dispose of you, but not against the counsel of her coven and Alesha."

"I don't know which is worse."

"Death is worse, Ethan. With life, there is hope, hope that we can bring you home."

The hour of decision was drawing nigh, and Ethan had to go. "Who was it that warned you?"

"I dare not even whisper his name."

"I'm immune to magic, Tristan. That immunity carries a few feet around me. If you whisper in my ear, your secret will be safe."

Tristan thought for a moment before drawing his lips to his brother's ear. "Raymar Loria, son of Valera."

Ethan gave him a doubting look. All of Tristan's knowledge of Alesha and Valera was drawn from a Vellesian prince. Could such a source be trusted? If it was a trick by Valera, what hope did she have that it would be believed? Perhaps it was a lie, a lie to make them seem invincible and force Ethan into their hands. Ethan doubted that Valera and Alesha wielded such power that Tristan described, yet Tristan risked his life bringing him this news, and he would have warned him about Valera if he arrived in time. Of course, this Prince Raymar might have told him sooner and saved Ethan his plight. Too much made little sense. Ethan wasn't sure of Raymar's loyalties.

"I will keep your secret safe," he assured him. "This is for you, Tristan." He set his double holster with the twin Colts upon his bed.

"Your pistols?"

"I would rather you have them than anyone else. Take care, little brother, I'll see you in the great hall." He hugged him fiercely then stepped without.

*****

Queen Gabrielle's guard shadowed Ethan wherever he went. He walked slowly through the courtyard, taking in the sights of Astaris and committing them to memory. He beheld the dark-gray stone of the courtyard grounds, the arched entrance with its stone pillars and the azure stone citadels that towered over the outer city from their airy heights.

Ethan found Bull in his stall and grabbed a brush to comb his old friend. Sir Blackar had the stable attendants groom the palomino thoroughly the morning before, when Ethan took him on the long patrol. He hardly needed much attention, but Ethan loved taking care of his mount himself. He combed out the hay that clung to his side that he slept on. As he smoothed his hand down Bull's face, the horse licked Ethan's chin.

"I love you too, boy." Ethan smiled sadly. He set the brush down and threw a blanket over Bull's back, followed by his saddle before fixing his bridle. He slid his rifle into its saddle sheath and tied his pack onto the back along with his guitar. Leading Bull out of the stable, he mounted up and rode through the courtyard. Every soldier, citizen, and servant stopped and stared as Ethan Blagen rode through their midst. He projected a strange image with his odd hat, buckskin trousers, leather moccasins, and pistol belt. The queen's guard rushed along his flanks on foot, while half their contingent stood post at the pillars that half circled the entrance to the outer citadel. He rode slowly to the inner palace that divided the tower of the king to the west from the tower of the queen to the east. The gathering crowd lined to either side, giving Ethan a wide berth. He stopped short of the wide stone steps that ascended to the arched gated doors of the palace. Ethan dismounted and called out a young servant boy from the crowd. He handed the boy a silver coin to hold Bull's reins while he was within. The boy held the coin dearly for it was a tidy sum for so little effort. He would wait for Ethan all day if need be.

Ethan climbed the seven steps that led to the large open doors of the central palace. He took a deep breath and entered.

*****

The palace corridors were eerily quiet as Ethan's moccasin clad feet walked quietly over the bluestone floor. Other than the guards standing post along the wide halls, not another soul was in sight. The walk filled Ethan with a grim disquiet as if passing through a cavernous tomb. Though he was relatively early, he assumed many would still be making their way to the great hall. Perhaps only the Vellesians would meet him once he passed into that appointed chamber. He couldn't imagine many others eager to bear witness to what might come. The soldiers guarding the entrance to the great hall opened the doors as he approached. They averted their eyes, none wishing to stare at the fierce gaze that transfixed his face. Any notion that it would be a small affair died upon his entrance.

A thousand pairs of eyes greeted Ethan as he entered the great hall. Nary a whisper escaped their lips as every eye fixed on the son of Bronus entering their midst. They were serried in close ranks, leaving him a narrow path to the chamber's center. The lords and ladies of all the great houses of Astaria were congregated among the gathered host. Mages, counselors, and commanders of rank mixed with courtiers to witness the spectacle. At the chamber's far end, a single throne rested upon the raised dais where the king's table resided the night before. Seated upon the throne was Queen Valera. As agreed with the council of kings, her throne represented the Kingdom of Vellesia, upon whose authority was given the use of the great hall during these proceedings. She wore a long purple gown whose skirts draped over the base of her throne like the cascading falls of an amethyst river. A golden crown lined with gems graced her head. Her eyes looked akin to burning embers and fixed sternly on his approaching form. Behind her stood her entourage, each dressed in black gowns with steel countenances that stared soulless into Ethan's eyes. He noticed Princess Amanda standing patiently to Valera's left. She wore a dull silver gown. Her soft golden eyes looked upon Ethan with obvious empathy.

King Bronus sat upon a similar throne on the opposing side of the hall, with the members of his house behind him. Queen Gabrielle, Prince Tristan, and Princesses Ceresta, Arian, and Felicia all stood, awaiting the fate of their son and brother.

Between the opposing thrones stood the mage kings of the other five mage realms, each surrounded by their personal guards and houses, and aligned to either side of the open space between the thrones. Ethan noticed his grandfather standing in the fore ranks, between the entourage of King Evor and the house of King Delmarin. He had asked Dragos to be nearby if he needed his knowledge of mage law, and the seer did not disappoint. Dragos gave Ethan a reassuring smile and a wink, assuaging the boy's apprehension.

Ethan stepped forth, standing before Valera's throne, fixing his eyes to hers. He did not see Alesha among the queen's retinue and wondered if she were still sore with his parting remarks when last they spoke.

"Where's Alesha?" he asked. The crowd gasped at his informality in addressing the crown princess so informally. Queen Valera's expression held, betraying only indifference to Ethan's ill manners.

"Now that you are here, we may begin," she stated firmly.

"Yes. Let's move this along. I have a dragon hunt to undertake and no time to waste, so hurry this along if you can, Valera." He hooked his left thumb in his holster belt, striking a relaxed posture as if nothing of note was about to transpire.

Valera ignored his bluster, her face a mask of trained indifference. He recalled Sheriff Thorton teaching him cards and how to use a poker face. He could picture Valera giving the sheriff a run for his money in that regard; the woman had a face of stone.

Alesha entered the great hall, marching forth with long powerful strides, closing quickly upon Ethan's rear. He felt her approach as she circled him, her eyes examining him head to foot. She wore dark-gray leather trousers and boots with dark mail. A slender sword of ancient steel graced her left hip, and a helm shaped crown rested upon her bound black hair. She looked every part a warrior queen. Her golden eyes locked with his, projecting a predatory gaze that tried to unnerve him.

"You certainly look…different," he said. Her countenance revealed nothing of the conflict within. She hadn't slept since their parting as thoughts of Ethan consumed her, just as thoughts of her consumed him. Her mind balanced rage and desire, anger, and lust. She mourned the loss of kind affection he had always shown her, but her betrayal in his eyes destroyed that bond, perhaps forever. Though she preferred that he love her, it was far more important that she possess him. She had a lifetime to tame his heart, once the formalities of this day were concluded. There was such a savage innocence to Ethan that stirred something deep within her. Part of her regretted having to do this to him, but she knew it was necessary. If left to his own devices, he would die, if not in the Mage Bane, then in the wilds or Earth. He needed protection from himself, even if she had to cage him. She recognized that look in his eye and knew he was up to something. If she learned anything about Ethanos Blagen in all her time with him, it was to never underestimate him. Though he was unpredictable, she knew he would not sacrifice his father, nor would he attempt to kill her, not after their intimate union. Despite the hurtful words he had said, she knew he desired her as strongly as she desired him. But what was he up to? Then she noted something different that she hadn't before, a way was open to his mind that his power had always blocked. She entered that narrow path that no one had ever followed, pushing to enter his thoughts with the totality of her power.

Ethan staggered back, a searing pain coursing his mind as if an invisible force attempted to enter. He fought to not reveal the pain the probing caused. *This shouldn't be happening*, he thought painfully. He was immune to magic. First, Alesha had placed a love spell upon him to some success, and now she was pressing into his mind. He finally halted her advance while coping with the pain until he stood unmoved.

Amanda noted her sister's probe and Ethan's struggle. Something was amiss.

Alesha relented, smiling inwardly with recognition. The stone in Ethan's pouch was an unexpected boon. Where did he find it? It was not large enough to touch him with her powers, but it was a start. She would reap rich rewards this day. She stepped away, climbing the three steps atop the dais to take her place at her mother's right.

"Prince Ethanos Blagen!" Queen Valera declared.

"Ethan Blagen," he corrected her.

"Ethan." She smiled poorly. "Step forward, child!"

"I'm fine where I stand, Valera."

"Are you now?" she sneered. "The time is at hand for you to choose. Step forth and kneel before Crown Princess Alesha or your father's life is forfeit."

"Alesha is *not* the crown princess. Amanda is." He smiled with his answer.

Alesha bristled at such a notion.

"No one from House Loria ever claimed Amanda to be the crown princess. I fear your statement is but a clumsy attempt to talk your way out of your decision," Valera said.

"I'm not talking about your deception pretending Amanda was your true heir. When I rescued Crown Princess Alesha in the Mage Bane, I *earned* a royal request."

"Which you were granted!"

"No. You made me beg for a royal request that was mine by right. You knew I had rescued your crown princess, but I did not."

"It matters not if you knew. Your actions warranted a royal request, and a *royal request* you were granted."

"And that request I used to release Alesha from her bond to Vellesia. If she is not bound to Vellesia, then clearly, she cannot be your crown princess. That title now falls to Princess Amanda. Now that we have settled that, you can welcome Geoff Jarvo into your house as the rightful consort to your crown princess. I hope you enjoy the rest of your stay in Astaris, but if you'll excuse me, I must be on my way." He turned to leave as Valera's cold laugh echoed through the hall.

"You stupid, stupid boy. Do you think you can cheat me with such poor logic? A Vellesian crown princess cannot forsake her title unless she does so before her queen. Alesha, do you accept Prince Ethanos's gift? Do you forsake the throne of Vellesia and your birthright?"

"No, my queen. I refuse his offer!" Alesha declared sadly.

"Then step forth, Ethanos, and kneel before the crown princess to take your vows!" Valera commanded.

Ethan just smiled.

"If Alesha refuses my gift, then by the ancient mage laws of Astaria, I can grant my gift to another."

"What ancient law?" Alesha asked suspiciously.

"Dragos, am I correct?" Ethan asked his grandfather.

"You are, Ethan," Dragos answered from his place among the assemblage.

"I am well-schooled in *all* mage laws created since the dawn of mage rule four thousand years ago. There is no such law!" Valera said icily.

"There is no such law in Vellesia, but there is in Astaria. I know a great deal about royal requests, Valera. That is how I won my freedom from the throne, through great deeds *and* great knowledge."

"It is irrelevant, Ethanos. I granted you a royal request under Vellesian law, not Astarian," Valera said.

"You granted me a royal request upon Astarian soil. That makes my request bound by the mage laws of Astaria."

"Let the council of kings decide if you are entitled to your royal request!" Valera snapped, unable to curb her anger.

"If the mage kings rule against the sacred laws of Astaria, then *all* bonds of magic protecting them within these walls as well as the bond upon King Bronus shall be severed!" Dragos declared, stepping to Ethan's side.

"With no knife at my father's throat, then I can put a bullet in your brain, Valera, and there's nothing you can do about it. With all the power that courses your veins, you are helpless against me."

Uncertainty and fear crossed her face. She had never been as vulnerable as she was now.

"You are entitled to your royal request, Ethanos. But I remind you that I granted you a royal request to free a subject of Vellesia. You accepted your royal request upon those terms and those terms shall remain," Valera stated carefully.

Alesha held her breath as all her plans rested on the brink.

"Why, thank you, Your Highness. Since I have to be a Vellesian subject in order to free myself, I will use my request *after* I take my vows."

"You are mistaken, Ethanos." Valera smiled. "I offered you a request to free a *current* subject of Vellesia, not a future one." Valera knew she had to play this carefully.

"You made no such distinction, Valera," Ethan countered.

"Of course I did, child. Royal requests are never granted lightly and are never meant to be used at a later convenience. They are given and they are *used*. If you doubt me, then let the council of mage kings decide the matter." She waved her open hands to her fellow monarchs assembled before them. This was a matter they could decide to her favor without unraveling the magic that bound Bronus.

"Mage kings that you bribed with gold and promises to place me in chains!" Ethan growled.

"What says the council?" Valera's voice carried loudly through the hall. "Is Ethanos's request bound to current or future subjects of Vellesia?"

One by one, the five mage kings answered. All five answered current. Bronus came to his feet, his eyes bearing a deadly feral gaze. The mage kings had broken all bonds of hospitality. He held his tongue with great difficulty.

"The time is drawing nigh, Ethanos. Choose a Vellesian subject to free from their oath. If they refuse your gift, then your royal request is thus spent." Valera smiled triumphantly.

Ethan sighed dejectedly. This was his only peaceful avenue of escape, but the way was now blocked. He felt Valera's noose tighten about his throat.

"They hang horse thieves in West Texas, but in Vellesia they put crowns on their heads." He stared intently into Valera's cold eyes. "That's all you really are, Valera, a thief."

"Choose a subject to free or forsake your royal request!" Valera's face flushed with indignation.

The apex of the sun was drawing nigh, and he had to decide. If he couldn't free himself from Valera's vile clutches, he might at least free another. But he didn't know any of her attendants. They were all emotionless statues bound to her will. When they did speak with him, like her chief minister, they were as pompous and condescending as their queen. Anyone he chose would have to accept his offer, and even then, their families would feel the queen's wrath. There was only one among them that ever showed him the slightest kindness. She was the one who warned him to leave. She was the only one among them who looked pained from this spectacle.

"Do you swear by your magic that whomever I choose, as well as their descendants, shall be protected from your wrath or the judgment of your house to the end of their days?"

"Yes," Valera said impatiently.

"Then I choose Princess Amanda."

Valera sprang to her feet in heated fury. "You assume much, Ethanos!" she roared.

"I *accept*!" Amanda ran to Ethan's side. She turned back toward her mother. "I renounce my oath and bond to House Loria and Vellesia. I choose freedom!" She turned back to Ethan, looking up into his kind blue eyes and kissed his lips fiercely.

Lightning erupted from Alesha's fingers, streaming forth upon her sister's narrow silhouette before dissipating into Ethan's aura that engulfed Amanda within its protective shadow. Alesha's eyes blazed a fiery crimson as her jealous heart raged. The thought of another woman touching Ethan drove her to the brink of madness.

"Remove yourself from him!" she shouted.

The gathered host gasped. Alesha could wield lightning just as Tristan had said. Doubt filled the hearts of the mage kings. They always feared Bronus and the power he wielded. Though great, they knew the limits of Bronus's power. With Alesha, they knew almost nothing.

"Alesha, be still your hands!" Valera commanded. After a long moment, she did so, but the damage was done for all the seven kingdoms now knew some of the vast power they held. Any furtherance of Alesha's attack could constitute a hostile attack upon Astaria and thus negate the agreement that bound Bronus.

Amanda parted from Ethan's embrace to again look into his eyes. "Thank you, Prince Ethanos."

"Ethan. Just Ethan," he told her.

She shook her head no. "You are a prince whether you claim the title or not, the only prince worthy of the name."

"My brother is worthy of the name."

"I stand corrected. The House of Blagen is the only royal house worthy of their name. Might I ask one more favor of you, Ethan?"

"If I can grant it, I will."

"You must have a small stone that glows ere you touch it. Give it to your sire, lest my sister claim it when she claims you."

"How do you know—"

"It's anti-magic, the same as you. If it were larger than they could use it to touch you with their power. That was the cause of your headache when Alesha entered therein," she whispered.

Ethan drew the stone from its pouch and placed the glowing rock into her hand. The glow faded as she took possession of it. A tear rolled down her cheek as she looked at him with gratitude and pity. "I fear for you, Ethan. Do as she asks of you, for the thought of her hurting you is…" She couldn't finish, her throat tightened as she struggled to dam her eyes.

He wiped the tear from her cheek. "I'll be all right. Go to my father and ask for sanctuary in House Blagen."

Amanda hugged him tightly and then turned upon her mother and sister for the last time. "May the fates curse you for your cruelty!" She stepped gingerly for the painful burn still afflicted her thigh.

"Take the freedom Ethanos has granted you, my ungrateful child, and step away," Valera snarled.

Amanda backed away as Ethan caught her by the arm. "What's wrong with your leg?"

"Mother burned me with her hands as punishment for warning you," she said.

"My sister will heal you. Go!" He looked at Valera with disgust.

Amanda stopped before the mage kings, looking intently into each of their eyes. "You fools! Do you know what you have done? He was the only hope you had of facing my mother and you deliver him into her hands. There is little hope for you. You shall each bend your knees to Alesha's spawn or perish with your defiance."

"You dare speak to us with such regard, wench!" Gregor Vorhenz growled, stepping forth as if you to strike her.

"Step back, Gregor!" Bronus warned. "Any threat upon any of my guests and the laws of host and hospitality shall not protect you."

Gregor checked his anger and sheepishly withdrew.

"Come, Princess!" Bronus beckoned the girl hither.

Amanda walked softly across the chamber. Stopping short of his throne, she dropped to her knees and bowed her head. "I offer myself into your service, King Bronus."

Tristan descended his father's dais, circling behind the princess. He noted her beauty and courage. Her brother told him much of her kindness and spirit as they worked to hinder their mother's plans. Unclasping his gray cloak, he wrapped it around her shoulders and helped her to her feet.

"You are welcome in my house, Princess Amanda," Bronus answered her.

"Just Amanda, Your Grace. I am no longer a princess of Vellesia or a member of House Loria."

"Of course you're not a princess of Vellesia, you're a princess of Astaria. So shall you serve in the House of Blagen!" Bronus declared.

"Thank you, my king," she whispered wordlessly, tears flooding her eyes. She stepped forth, holding out the stone that Ethan had gifted her. She stopped again at the base of the dais, knelt, and offered the stone to the king.

"What is this?" Bronus asked.

"It is anti-magic, my king. It is more precious than all the wealth of Astaris. My mother must never have it, no matter how small of a measure it is." She set it upon his palm as he wrapped his fingers around it.

"Take your place in my house, Amanda." He kissed her forehead as Tristan led her up the dais to stand with House Blagen.

All eyes then fell to Ethan standing before the scowling Vellesian queen. Alesha stood to her right, her eyes fixed sternly upon him. The sun was at its apex, and the time of decision was at hand.

"Kneel, Ethanos!" Valera hissed, pointing to the floor before Alesha's feet. Her eyes glowed with hatred. She would be leaving Astaris sans her daughter and the precious stone, but she would have him.

Ethan looked into her eyes with open contempt before stepping toward Alesha. He found her eyes a strange maelstrom of sorrow, triumph, and longing. The racing of his heart was too rapid to quell. Closing his eyes, he sank to his knees.

"Remove that thing from your head!" Valera commanded.

Ethan opened his eyes and lifted his Stetson from his head.

"Lower your eyes," Valera ordered.

He did so. Alesha felt sick within at the sight of him so humbled. She had planned for this day all her life, often believing it to be the pinnacle of her destiny, but now it felt bittersweet. Why did she care so if he were humbled? Was that not the destiny of her chosen consort? But this was more than a mere vessel of her house's ascension, this was her one true friend, and she betrayed him, at least in his eyes.

"Let us begin!" Valera declared, sitting back down upon her throne while Ethan knelt before Alesha to her right.

"You shall first forsake all bonds to Astaria! Avow it, Ethanos!"

"I…I forsake all bonds to Astaria," he barely whispered.

"Avow it for all to hear, Ethanos!" Valera commanded.

"I forsake all bonds to Astaria!"

"Forsake the bonds and loyalty to House Blagen!"

The words came hard as his throat tightened.

"Avow it, Ethan," Alesha said not unkindly.

"I forsake all bonds and loyalty to House Blagen!"

Across the chamber upon the dais and behind the king, tears sprang from his sisters' eyes. Amanda pressed her head into Tristan's shoulder, unable to witness anymore.

"Forsake the name *Blagen*!" Valera smiled with this command.

"I forsake the name Blagen."

"Now you shall take your vows of affirmation. Your first vow is submission to the throne of Vellesia!"

"I pledge my service to the throne of Vellesia. I pledge my life to the throne of Vellesia. I pledge my honor to the throne of Vellesia!"

"Acknowledge Queen Valera as your monarch!" Valera commanded.

"I acknowledge Queen Valera as my sovereign and queen."

"Vow your obedience to your queen!"

"I vow to obey Queen Valera!"

"Vow to serve your queen in *all* things!"

"I vow to serve Queen Valera in all things."

"Vow to Crown Princess Alesha to serve faithfully as her consort!"

"I vow to serve Crown Princess Alesha faithfully as her consort."

Alesha cringed inwardly, never fully contemplating what this day would entail for Ethan. He might never forgive her, and that troubled her deeply.

"Vow to obey Crown Princess Alesha in all things!"

"I vow to obey Crown Princess Alesha in all things."

"Vow on your honor to never look upon any other than Crown Princess Alesha with lustful desire or infidelity!"

"I vow upon my honor to never look upon any other than Crown Princess Alesha with lust or infidelity."

"Vow to always speak with deference and respect to your queen, your crown princess, and the ministers of my court!"

"I vow to always speak with deference and respect to my queen, to my crown princess and to the ministers of the Vellesian court."

Leora Mattiese masked her glee with a veil of indifference. She enjoyed watching her queen squeeze the arrogance out of Ethanos like a washerwoman wrings water from a wet stocking. She looked forward to dealing with a more compliant and respectful Ethanos when next they speak.

"Vow your fidelity to House Loria!" Valera commanded.

"I vow my fidelity to House Loria." Ethan was dying within. He could feel the eyes of Valera's courtiers looking down upon him gleefully with smug satisfaction. Each affirmed vow felt like a dagger twisting his innards. *How many more vows must I make?* he thought bitterly, wishing for this day to mercifully end.

"Thus concludes the vows of affirmation. Crown Princess Alesha!" Valera commanded of her.

"Yes, my queen," Alesha answered, not taking her eyes from Ethan kneeling before her. After all the years of planning, she finally had him. She resigned herself to the necessity of the ceremony to bind him to the Vellesian throne, but her pity for Ethan robbed her of her expected glee. The ceremony was nearly complete, and then she could take her leave of Astaria and return to the comfort of Elysia, and thankfully be done with this day.

"Do you accept this offering from House Blagen?" Valera asked.

"I accept the former crown prince of Astaria, the firstborn of King Bronus, the one kneeling before me, the one named Ethanos as my consort!" she declared.

With those words, the queen's steward and chief minister, Leora Mattiese, stepped forth, carrying an item wrapped in gold silk. She knelt to Alesha's left and presented the silk-wrapped object in her outstretched hands. Alesha froze, her eyes shooting to her mother's as she understood all too well what lies beneath the silken folds. She told her mother that this was unnecessary and thought they were agreed upon that point, but it seemed her mother had altered those plans.

"Mother, I don't—"

"Proceed, Alesha. That is the word of your queen!" Valera regarded her coolly, weary of Alesha's affection for the insolent Astarian prince.

Alesha unfolded the silk, revealing a collar of gold. She lifted it reverently from the cloth and turned to Ethan.

"Raise your head, Ethanos," she said.

Ethan paled as he beheld the item in her fingers. He flinched as she leaned close, drawing his head away.

"Be still," she commanded softly.

"*Valera!*" Bronus shouted angrily, marching forth across the mirrored stone floor.

Alesha froze, her eyes shifting to the Astarian king striding forth with his cape billowing behind him and a savage look in his gray eyes.

"King Bronus." Valera smiled sweetly.

"You *never* spoke of collaring him! You dare insult *my blood* with this humiliation?"

"No insult is intended, my dear king. It is Vellesian custom and law that the consort of a crown princess or queen wear a golden collar so that all may know their station. It is a symbolic warning for any who gaze upon him with lustful intent shall do so under pain of death," Valera explained. What she did not say was that such collars were always bound in magic that bound the wearer's mage powers, rendering them magically impaired for the rest of their lives, unless they could remove that adornment from their necks. Alesha's father had never worn one as his house had insisted upon that condition of their betrothal, but every other consort had done so for over a thousand years. Ethan was immune to such magical impairments, and his wearing the collar would be merely symbolic, but Valera would not forsake tradition for his feelings.

"You will not collar my son!"

"He is no longer your son. He is Alesha's consort!" Valera countered, establishing her claim.

"Ethan, get up! Damn the magic. No son of mine will suffer this insult upon our house!" Bronus commanded, his fingers beginning to crackle with electricity.

Ethan did not move.

"Damn it, boy, get off your knees!"

Ethan looked over his shoulder to his father's crimson face.

"My queen, may I speak with my father but a moment?"

"Of course, my child." Valera eyed Bronus carefully. The king of Astaria was on the brink of madness and could easily undo all her labor if he ended his own life. Only Ethan could bring him back from the precipice.

Ethan gained his feet and approached his father. "You must not interfere," Ethan said, placing a hand upon his father's shoulder.

"No son of mine will suffer—"

"Father, you cannot do this. It is more than your own life you would be sacrificing."

"What are you implying, Ethan?" Bronus's eyes narrowed.

"I cannot tell you, lest my queen learn what I know. Ask Amanda. She will tell you. If I don't go, then Mother, Tristan, Ceresta, and all of them will perish. We can't win this battle. We must hope for another day when the odds are better than certain death."

Bronus looked into Ethan's eyes with profound sorrow and pride. He took him in his arms, hugging him as tightly as he could, his eyes moist with dammed tears.

"Go," Bronus relented as they parted.

Ethan returned to Alesha, kneeling before her as he looked into the depths of her golden eyes.

She sighed, placing the collar about his throat. The smooth round collar had a narrow hinge on one side and interlocking arms upon the other. There was no keyhole or visible means of unlocking the device. Once fastened, it was never to be removed.

Click.

The finality of that sound sickened Ethan's stomach. He gazed into those golden eyes that stared down upon him with unbearable intensity.

Alesha released a measured breath. It was done. She extended her hand to him, raising him to his feet. She stepped nigh, placing her slender fingers upon his cheeks, and kissed him. She savored the warmth of his lips as if they were sweet wine. He returned her affection as was expected. His heart pounded emphatically, matching the rhythm of her own. His instincts were driving him mad with desire, but his brain despised her. The love spell he felt he was under was waxing in strength, weakening his repulsion of her touch. As their lips parted, she smiled lasciviously, but her elation quickly waned as she beheld his cold indifference, or was it hate she saw in his eyes? She knew he was angry, but she told herself he would acquiesce to the role she appointed him in time. She believed he would eventually be content serving as her mate. Now she was not as certain and those insecurities attempted to burrow into her thoughts.

"Lower your eyes!" she commanded, unable to bear his gaze any longer.

"Yes, Your Highness." His words were lifeless, and he didn't want to look at her anyway. Her proper title sounded unnatural and off-putting coming from his lips, and part of her would always wish that she could still be Allie in his eyes. Alas, those days were now passed.

"Let us celebrate the union of Crown Princess Alesha and her chosen consort, Ethanos Loria!" Valera declared.

A mild cheer emitted from the visiting mage kings and a louder cheer from the Vellesian contingent, but the host of Astaria stood in stone silence.

Bronus and Dragos stood side by side in the chamber's center, their eyes fixed on the Vellesian queen with heated glares.

"Valera!" Bronus's harsh voice quieted the festive part of the crowd.

"King Bronus." She smiled, answering him properly, which contrasted his rude appellation of her name.

"If you hurt my son in any way, there is no power in this world that shall stop me from killing you and burning your wretched kingdom to ash."

Fool, she thought. *Your power to mine is as an insect to a tiger.* She could kill him in so many countless ways. She found his bluster amusing. Men who were ignorant of her power often boasted to do her great harm as if she were but a weak, frightened woman quivering before their masculine magnificence. She recalled other men who threatened her with similar bluster. She fondly recalled their tortured screams as she peeled their flesh. She would heal them enough to ensure they linger in their endless torment. Some she would finish in weeks, some months, and others languished for years, their minds but wretched shells of their former glory. Two she kept for many years, allowing them to serve as the meanest of slaves, begging to please her in the basest of ways, ever fearful of her terrible ministrations. She thought Bronus fortunate to be Ethan's father, lest she subject him to such treatment. She found the vision of Bronus begging for death most humorous. How she would delight in his ruination, the greatest of the mage kings would be nothing more than a nameless drone toiling under a Vellesian lash. Yet he was still a handsome man despite starting his fifth decade. Though Ethan was boyishly handsome and large of build, Bronus was slightly larger with the manliest face she had beheld. It had been long since her husband passed and her bed was warmed. She wondered what it might be like to bed the father while Alesha bedded the son. She pondered what might have been had she not inherited the power of lightning from her mother. She would probably have ensnared Bronus as Alesha had Ethan. Alas, it mattered not now. Bronus needed to be safe in Astaria to ensure Ethan's obedience, but once he was secure in Vellesia, the world of possibilities seemed endless.

"Ethan is *my* child now, King Bronus. No harm shall befall him in Vellesia." She smiled sweetly.

"He has a mother, and you're not her!" Bronus growled.

"Every member of House Loria is my child, King Bronus. Come!" she commanded her entourage as she stepped past the Astarian king.

Alesha followed next.

"You will follow two paces behind me at all times, unless I call you forth!" she commanded Ethan before stepping forth. She loathed speaking to him thusly, but he needed to understand his proper place in the protocols of court.

"Yes, Princess Alesha," Ethan answered. He paused as he came to his father.

Bronus placed a hand upon his shoulder as they looked one last time at each other.

"You've already shared your farewells, Ethanos! Follow as I have ordered!" Alesha admonished him.

They continued across the great hall with heads held high like highborn ladies walking amid peasants. Valera paused before the Astarian throne, regarding Queen Gabrielle centered amid her children.

"Queen Gabrielle, Ethanos has words left unspoken between you," Valera said.

Gabrielle gave her a cool regard.

"Ethanos, come hither!" Valera commanded.

Ethan closed his eyes and nodded in disgust before stepping forth to attend his queen's bidding.

"My queen," he answered quietly.

Valera stepped nigh, softly stroking his face with her right hand. "You are to kneel before the queen of Astaria and beg of her forgiveness for the lies you told her. We must never *lie* to our queen or our mothers, child," Valera backed a step and swept an open arm toward the dais.

Before Gabrielle realized what Valera had asked him, Ethan ascended the dais and knelt before his mother, keeping his eyes to her feet.

"Queen Gabrielle, I beg your forgiveness for lying to you. I entered the Mage Bane, breaking my oath to you, then denying that I did so by omission. I allowed you to believe falsehoods regarding the barrier. I planned to enter the wilds, even though I knew you would object. I beg your forgiveness for forsaking the throne for my personal freedom. I beg your forgiveness for my repeated insults of your guests through these recent days."

Gabrielle nearly broke in tears. *He thinks I betrayed him!* she thought in alarm. She desperately wanted to touch him but resisted.

"Lift your eyes to mine, Ethan," she said.

"Queen Gabrielle," he acknowledged her as their eyes met.

Never had that appellation sounded so horrid coming from his lips.

"Are you truly sorry, Ethan, or are you merely obeying Queen Valera's instructions? You must tell me the truth, son?"

Ethan had to answer carefully, for he was caught between angering Valera or again lying to his mother.

"My feelings are irrelevant, Queen Gabrielle. May I have your leave? My queen is anxious to depart."

He hates *me!* her thoughts screamed. She wanted to burst into tears but would not give Valera the satisfaction. She wanted to tell him that Alesha would protect him from her terrible vision of his suffering but doubted he would believe her. "Go, my son," were the only words she could muster.

Ethan was dying inside, but the look in his mother's eyes was heartbreaking. She warned him repeatedly to not enter the Mage Bane, and here was the result. Perhaps he deserved her ire. He couldn't leave with this between them. He gained his feet and hugged her tightly as she squeezed him desperately.

"I'm sorry," he whispered in her ear before drawing away.

With his hat in his hands, he took his place behind Alesha, following her out of the great hall.

*****

The midday sun broke through the gray winter sky, bathing the courtyard in ethereal light as Valera descended the palace steps. Dozens of Vellesian knights flooded the courtyard clad in armor of crimson and gold with bloodred capes draping from their shoulders. Their eyes peered intently through the narrow slits of their visors. Amid their assemblage was the queen's carriage with its gold plating and silver inlays. It was six meters in length and three abreast, drawn by six bronze coated horses, with four footmen. Scores of the queen's personal guards stood post to either side of the carriage, uniformed in silver breastplates, helms, and shin armor over snow-white tunics with pleated kilts. The interior of the carriage was covered with soft pillows and cushioned seats for the queen's comfort. The smaller carriages that carried Valera's ministers bond courtiers waited behind in the large column.

"Here's your horse, Ethan," a young boy's voice greeted him as he descended the palace steps, following Alesha at the proper distance.

Ethan had forgotten that he paid the boy to watch Bull while he was within. The boy was some meters away, his path blocked by the queen's guards.

"It's all right, the boy was holding my horse for me," Ethan told the guards as he stepped toward the boy. The guards ignored Ethan's explanation and stood unmoved, refusing the boy's advance.

Alesha turned back, visibly annoyed with Ethan's independence, though she heard his entire conversation. "The boy has your horse, Ethanos?" she asked.

"Yes," he answered.

"When I address you in public, you are to kneel and reply with the proper appellation!" she firmly reminded him. *Please do not make me admonish you in public, Ethan,* she thought wearily, not wishing to humiliate him any more than necessary.

Ethan stared at her incredulously, his temper nearing to explode. How could he endure a lifetime of this humiliation? He lowered his eyes and knelt. "Princess Alesha, I hired the boy to attend Bull during the ceremony."

She inwardly sighed with relief with his obedience. "And you already paid the boy his coin?" she asked.

"Yes, Your Highness."

"Very well. Retrieve your mount and follow me."

She watched as he came to his feet and approached the boy, the guards parted as he neared. She could see him speak kindly to the child and fetch an object from his saddle pack to give the boy. The object had a long shinning blade with a wooden handle—a knife, a beautifully crafted knife that Ethan had brought with him from across the barrier. The boy held it tightly to his chest as Ethan rubbed his head affectionately. The boy hugged him in return with tears pouring from his eyes. It was this quality in Ethan that set him apart from so many others. On his worst day, his kindness and generosity still shone through. Alesha smiled, recalling the tenderness he had shown her on so many occasions. She wished this day to end and for their journey to Vellesia to be complete, so she could return some of the kindness Ethan had given her. She was more relieved than joyous with the conclusion of the ceremony. She hoped he would forgive her in time and wondered why she cared if he did? Her bonding with Ethan was nothing like her mother had prepared her for. Her mother thought she should not concern herself with Ethan's happiness, so long as he obeyed, but she did care. She regretted that she was not yet finished with breaking his spirit and hoped to expunge any thoughts he might harbor of resisting her will. Once that was done, she could go about restoring his spirit and happiness, if only by the smallest of measures to begin with. The boy finally separated from Ethan and disappeared into the gathering crowd.

Ethan led Bull between the guards and followed Alesha to her mother's carriage. The carriage driver bowed as Valera approached. He was a young man with boyish features that Ethan thought looked entirely too pretty to be a man. The driver wore a silk hat, short puffed pantaloons with green hose and a waistcoat. He spoke not a word as he rose and opened the carriage door for his queen.

"Are you riding with me, Alesha?" Valera asked.

"No, Mother," she answered, tilting her head toward the white palfrey awaiting her beside the carriage. The mare was impeccable, flush and flawless in its equine perfection.

"Glynderelle," Alesha summoned the horse hither. The beautiful white palfrey trotted forth, obedient to her will.

"How lovely," Valera marveled. The horse had no equal in all of Valera's stables. "Where did you find her?"

"She was a gift from Ethanos." She gently stroked the horse's face. "He said I needed a mount that matched my beauty." She gifted him a mischievous grin.

"That was thoughtful of the boy." Valera said as she climbed into her carriage.

Ethan's blood boiled in rage as he recalled the effort he expended, finding that horse for Allie. It now represented the mockery of every affection he had for her. The saddle he bought for her horse was now replaced with a black leather rig with gold inlays with the golden rose of Vellesia emblazoned upon its flanks. Alesha climbed atop her mount.

"Come, Ethan. We shall lead our column through the city."

Ethan mounted up. He put on his Stetson and followed as Alesha's horse trotted forth through the pillars that guarded the citadel's entrance.

"Ride beside me, Ethan!"

"As you wish, Princess," he answered quietly, pushing Bull up beside her.

Alesha rode with her head high as they rode through the palace green and through the main gate and into the outer city, before riding into the wide central avenue of Astaris. Crowds gathered thickly to either side of the streets, watching as they passed at the head the Vellesian column.

"Riding at your side and not behind you? I am honored." Ethan rolled his eyes.

"It is a gift to your people, so they might bid their beloved prince farewell."

"I doubt I'm so beloved, Princess. I'm the son of the mage born, what love could they have for our kind that's not forced?"

"Oh, Ethan." She smiled. "It is those very beliefs you hold that they love you for. You represent a hope in all of them that mage rule might one day end. My gift to them is to see you ride through these wide avenues leading this great column of Vellesians forth of your own volition."

"Pardon me, Alesha, but they can see this damned collar around my neck. I'm not leading anything. You're dragging me along like a dog on a leash!" he snarled. "Oh, sorry, I meant to say that you're dragging me along like a dog on a leash, *Your Highness*!" He bowed with mock deference.

"You may forgo such titles when we are alone, Ethan, as long as you maintain an expected level of civility. The kneeling, bowing, and flowered courtesies are for the eyes and ears of others to demonstrate the power and prestige of the Vellesian throne. You may call me Alesha when we are alone."

"That's very kind of you, Your Highness."

She ignored his jibe for he was behaving better than she expected.

Ethan figured if he only had to bow and kiss her posterior while in her or Valera's presence, he would try to find something to occupy his time as far from them as his leash would allow.

"I know you hoped this day would unfold differently, Ethan. Be glad that it didn't. Even if you found a means for your father to escape the magic, I would have gone to war anyway to secure your person."

"I'm not that special, Alesha. I was stupid enough to believe all the crap you told me and stupid enough to walk into your trap."

"You should be proud, Ethan. No Vellesian consort was so difficult to collar as was you. You managed to elude us for years. You evaded me in Cordova and then earned a royal request in the Mage Bane. Even after we tricked you into using your request to free me, you still managed to trick my mother into releasing Amanda from our house. She is furious with you for that, by the way."

"Well, yippee for me. I'm still wearing this damned collar of yours, so *what* difference does it make."

She laughed. No other mage-born prince was so self-effacing. He was always calling himself clumsy or stupid or ugly when he was none of those things. She knew he was brave and intelligent and so very handsome. She loved his laugh, his smile, his confidence, his face—she loved everything about him. According to her house's prophecy, his destiny was ever tied to hers, and all her life his only importance was in that fulfillment. But then she met him, and in that time, she came to desire him so fiercely that she often forgot about the prophecy altogether. Though she loved everything about him, did she love *him*? She didn't believe in love as romantics dreamed of it. They mistook desire, lust, and affection for the ambiguity called *love*. She only knew that she desired him, that she lusted for him, and that she felt strong affection for him. But since he now belonged to her, what did it matter if she loved him or not. But he must learn to fear her, and it was time for her to demonstrate her power.

"Do you see that old man dancing, Ethan?" Alesha asked him, pointing to the crowd lining his side of the avenue.

Ethan shifted his stare to where she indicated. The road was serried with thousands of onlookers lining the broad avenues. The people crowded scores of rows deep throughout the length of their route of travel, from the inner palace to the outermost gate of the city. The entire city had emptied into the streets to see the procession. Ethan didn't remember this many of Astaris's citizens lining the streets to celebrate his victory at the Velo. But this wasn't a celebratory crowd; it felt more like a funeral. The citizens of Astaris stared wide-eyed as they passed, but he didn't see anyone dancing.

"I don't see anything?"

Alesha reached out her mind to an old, stick-thin man with gray straw hair and wearing a loose tunic that swallowed his emaciated form. The man took a step forward into the street, moving his feet in little circles while his arms and legs flailed like a puppet on a string.

After a moment of confusion, Ethan realized Alesha was making the man act against his will. "Alesha, stop!"

"I told you when we were alone that you could use my name sans title, Ethan, but you must keep your tongue civil. You are to never *demand* of me anything. It does not amuse me to make that old man dance. It is a mere demonstration!" With that she released him, and the old man crumbled to the ground as if his bones were jelly. Several men stepped forward to drag the man back into the crowd.

Alesha descried dozens of sparrows lining the branches of an ancient oak along her side of the avenue. She called them forth, the flock of dark feathered birds sped forth to obey their mistress's will. They circled overhead before descending before them. They took the shapes of letters, forming one word after another for Ethan's benefit.

Hail. Princess. Alesha. We. Honor. Your. Victory. Safe. Journeys.

The sparrows returned to their perch high atop the towering oak as Alesha gifted Ethan a mischievous smile.

"So you can talk little birdies into doing your bidding." Ethan shrugged, though they both knew she could just as easily have commanded packs of wolves or herds of mastodons to do similar tasks.

Alesha drew her hands together, drawing droplets of water from the air around them. The water spun rapidly, forming a large circle before them. The water solidified into ice, then Alesha shot streams of fire from her fingertips through the icy circle. Her left palm pushed outward, forcing the circle further away. She clapped her hands, and the circle of ice turned to water and rained upon the road before them. She summoned the wind, drawing it close in spirals of dust rising from the roadway to form dozens of narrow funnels that drifted before them. She sent them one after the other toward Ethan, where they broke apart ere touching his protective aura.

"If you were not immune to magic, I could have the wind whisper to you."

"And what would you have it say?" he asked, annoyed with her demonstration.

She ignored his tone and continued. "There was a Vellesian knight named Rodero Dougaris. He was handsome, tall, and brave. Many a Vellesian maiden gazed upon him with lovesick eyes, but he was promised to Lady Teresa Mattiese."

"Is she any relation to your kind-hearted Chief Minister Leora?" He asked.

"Her daughter," Alesha answered. "They were promised to each other when Teresa was born."

"How romantic." He tried not to roll his eyes.

"Romantic?" She raised an eyebrow. "They were suitably matched, and their parents desired a union of their houses. It came to my mother's knowledge that our young and dashing Sir Dougaris had found favor with another maiden of Vellesia. She was the beautiful daughter of a wealthy wine merchant named Melana Phortess. They would visit one another in the forest outside the city, always careful not to be followed. Of course, our handsome young knight could not hide his thoughts from my mother or myself. We discovered his indiscretion and cleared his mind of such complications."

"Was he married to the girl Teresa?" Ethan asked.

"They were promised but not then wed."

"Then why concern yourself with his life. Let him choose who he wants to be with."

"He was promised to Teresa. Such a rift might have caused undue friction within the Vellesian court. Perhaps you should meet Sir Dougaris."

"Why should I care to meet him?"

A Vellesian knight rode quickly up on Ethan's side. He was clad in crimson and gold armor from head to foot, and only the knight's face could be seen through his raised visor.

"Princess." He bowed his head, regarding her. Sir Dougaris struck a handsome posture with green eyes, square jaw, and a lean build.

"Sir Dougaris, are you familiar with a wine merchant's daughter named Melana Phortess?" Alesha asked.

Sir Dougaris struggled recalling the name. "My apologies, Your Highness, I do not know that name."

"That is well. Please tell my consort of the most beautiful woman in the world?"

"Your Grace is the most beautiful woman in the world, but my eyes favor Lady Teresa Mattiese."

"She is your betrothed, and it is well that you feel so. You may return to your post, Sir Dougaris."

The knight tilted his head to his princess and turned about, galloping back to his position in the column.

"What did you do to him?" Ethan gave her a look of revulsion.

"I cleansed him of the memories that would only cause him pain, Ethan. And I magnified the feelings he harbored for Lady Teresa. So you see, all is for the best?"

"Why show me this?" Dark thoughts crept into his consciousness, for he knew she had a reason for everything she did.

They were nearing the main gate of the city. The guards stepped back as if pushed aside by a strong gale. With a flick of her finger, the heavy beam barring the gate was thrown off and the massive doors pulled open. From the corner of his eyes, Ethan noticed an auburn-haired woman standing near the gate, wearing a long yellow gown, richly detailed with full sleeves and drooping neckline. She approached them quickly on foot, her eyes locked on Alesha. A realization struck him for the girl was Jennifer Murtado.

Jennifer hurried nigh; her eyes fixed upon Alesha as if she were her dearest friend.

"Princess Alesha!" she greeted her, ignoring all that her eyes beheld save for Alesha sitting atop her snow-white mare.

"Jennifer, are you well?" Alesha asked.

"Yes, Princess. I have so enjoyed myself during the festivities, you were most helpful in introducing me to the Estasan Prince," Jennifer thanked her.

"It was my great pleasure, Jennifer. You both make a lovely couple."

"Jennifer," Ethan greeted, but she seemed to not notice him.

"Princess Alesha, I hope your journey fares thee well." Jennifer smiled.

"I am in good company, Lady Murtado. Please let us part with fond regards."

Jennifer bobbed a curtsy and withdrew, never sparing Ethan the slightest glance.

"What did you do to her?" Ethan regarded Alesha warily.

"I merely altered her memories of you."

"What gives you the right to do that?" he growled.

"Does she mean so much to you, Ethanos?" she asked suspiciously as Jennifer disappeared into the crowd.

"She is a friend," he said.

"I may not be able to read your thoughts or your heart, but I can read hers. She was more than a friend, Ethan. When I first arrived in Astaris, I read her memories, memories that were filled with *you*. How many times have you kissed her? Too many to count, I presume. She expected you to wed her once you returned to Astaris. Since I can't read your thoughts, I must assume hers were true." The very thought of Ethan kissing another woman filled Alesha's mouth with bile.

"I can't control what others think or feel, Alesha. To punish others for any feeling they once harbored is petty. Are you so vindictive? Should I punish any of the young lords in your court who had similar fantasies about you? If you held men to that same standard, you would have a kingdom of widows. Men think erotic thoughts about women every other moment."

"I know the depravity of the male mind, Ethan. That is the purpose of this demonstration. I need not read your thoughts to know your mind. I am merely severing you from your past. Jennifer Murtado no longer remembers you as before. She can acknowledge your presence, but her more intimate memories have been expunged. I was forced to do the same for many of the ladies in the great houses of Astaris. You were the fancy of many a young maid's dreams, Ethan."

"You stole their memories?" he asked. He never heard of such a mage power. To read minds was one thing, but to shape thoughts was far more. He recalled the rude reception he had received from many of the maidens of Astaria when he returned a few days past. They ignored him because she erased him from their memories.

"It is a simple skill that I have mastered. It works quite well on those born without mage power and those of lesser mage skills. Mage kings, of course, are immune to such power, but their houses are not."

The veiled threat to his family did not escape him. "Did you twist my mother's mind with this power?"

"Your actions are what turned your mother against you, Ethan, not I. Besides, your mother is a master seer. I can read her thoughts, but even I cannot shape them."

"You would have if you could."

"No. I respect your mother and your house. I would not do that."

"You respect my house?" He turned in his saddle to fully face her. "You are threatening my father's life unless I'm your obedient slave. You threaten to erase the memories from my family's minds and you make a girl I know fall in love with another just to teach me a lesson. You respect no one, Allie. You care only for yourself. Once the novelty of my capture wears off, I'm sure you'll dispose of me."

"Respect, Ethan? What respect had you ever shown Lady Murtado? You never intended to wed her. You allowed her to believe in false hopes of a life with you, robbing her of years that she might have used to find another. Which is crueler, what I have done or you? And to speak of disposing of you? Oh no, Ethan. You are bound to me for life. All that I've shown you is a mere warning to never *betray me* in matters of state and matters of the heart."

"Betray *you*! You betrayed me. You lied to me so often I don't know how you kept it all in straight in your head. I saved your life, Allie! And this is the thanks I get." He tapped his collar. "I hate to think how you treat your enemies if this is how you treat your friends!"

"Friends? You are my lover, Ethanos, not my friend. There are no friends in love or war, only victors and the vanquished. I am unlike any opponent you have ever faced, Ethan. The others were simple. They waged war directly, and you defeated them. I never revealed my true self until you were already beaten. I won. You lost. You now belong to me. I will forgo punishing you for this outburst for you are new to the collar, but you will do well to remember your place." She hated her words the moment they escaped her lips, but he tested her emotions in ways she never thought possible.

"My place? My rightful place is where I choose, that is the natural right of any man. I belong in Red Rock, not here!"

"Your place is beside me, Ethan. If left to your own counsel, you would be dead in a year. You care nothing of your own life, so it falls to others to safeguard your destiny. Hate me for what I have done, but I would do anything to keep you safe, even taking away your precious freedom. My destiny cannot be fulfilled without you."

"What virtue is there in a destiny that enslaves the world?"

She gave him a dark look. "Is that what you believe? Tell me true, Ethan, what virtue is born from the world you envision? Freedom? In your idyllic world, all men are free, free to kill one another, free to starve, and free to indulge in the vilest inclinations of their hearts. Careful what you wish to foist upon the world. My goal is to usher in a golden age where the power of Vellesia can safeguard the lives, health, and bounty of every man, woman, and child in all of Elaria. The peasants you claim to care so much for would suffer under your ideal governance. Our daughter will bend hunger and war throughout the mage realms, the Mage Bane, and the wilds. *That* is true virtue. *That* is peace."

"Peace is not the absence of war, but the preservation of liberty."

She regarded him curiously, wondering why the fates instilled such opposing passions in two people that destiny drew together?

****

Within Valera's carriage she sat, her amethyst eyes hidden beneath her cowl as she faced the Vellesian queen. Her time in Astaris was at its end. With Amanda's betrayal, Sarella's subterfuge would be exposed. It mattered not for her purpose was complete; Ethanos was delivered into their keeping by his own hand.

"You have done well, Sarella." Valera's satisfaction barely touched her lips, forcing the tightest of smiles.

"I am overjoyed that you are pleased, Your Grace," Sarella said demurely. The cowl shielded her still youthful face from those who might see through the mage spells she projected to mask her countenance, especially from those who would know her origin by merely noting the hue of her eyes.

Sarella served Queen Valera from the day her eldest brother wed the Vellesian queen, a union that bound House Menau to the throne through their magic and their blood. Just as her sister, Sarella Menau, possessed the mage power to alter the appearance of memories, thus fooling even master seers and telepaths of a person's true identity. This skill, coupled with her powers of enchantment, allowed her to dwell for years in the Astarian capital undetected along with her sister, Selendra, watching over Valera's interests, especially Ethanos. It was Sarella that informed the queen of Ethan's betrothal to lady Elenna and advised how it might come undone. It was Sarella that pushed Lady Lucia to advise Ethan about royal requests. It was Sarella and Selendra that followed Ethanos to Cordova, hoping to finally deliver him into their hands. Though Sarella advised against a physical confrontation with Ethanos, Valera ordered his seizure. The plan went quickly awry with Ethan slaying dozens of enchanted free swords and nearly capturing Selendra before Sarella intervened, enchanting the fleeing men to reengage Ethanos and allowing her sister to escape. With Selendra's identity compromised, they fled Cordova. Before they could formulate a new plan to seize Ethanos, Palacian corsairs attacked Cordova and seized the Vellesian mage healers, including Crown Princess Alesha, who planned to seize Ethanos herself after their failed attempt.

Despite Alesha's vast powers, Sarella doubted she would have any more success in caging him than she did. Once Alesha was captured, all the Vellesian efforts were shifted from capturing the Astarian crown prince to rescuing their own crown princess.

In her time watching Ethanos from the shadows of Astaris, Sarella learned to expect the unexpected from the Astarian crown prince. This was never more apparent than when Ethanos rescued Alesha from the Mage Bane. The irony of Alesha being rescued by the man she was sent to capture never ceased to amuse Sarella. Of course, Ethanos's spontaneity caused the Vellesians grievous apprehension when he disappeared across the boundary during his time in Red Rock. They knew he would return as their prophecies remained unchanged, though Valera arranged the Meltorian and Relusian invasion of Astaria to force Ethan's return. The events in Cordova and the Mage Bane were fortuitous, for only Ethan's intervention could have saved Alesha, and it persuaded the Vellesian crown princess that brute force and mage craft would most likely fail in binding Ethan to the Vellesian throne. They needed to find a way for Ethan to bind himself to the Vellesian crown.

Upon her rescue, Alesha conceived the plan that would eventually chain Ethanos to her without war. Sarella returned alone to Cordova and then Astaris thereafter, helping to move the Astarian king toward diplomacy with Vellesia following Valera's feigned indignation after her envoy ship was destroyed in Talesia.

"I assume you shall now return to your father's house, Sarella?" Valera asked.

"Indeed. I look fondly to return to my ancestral home."

"Your lord father and lady mother will be pleased to see you, no doubt. You have fulfilled the destiny of House Menau."

"Yes, but the legacy of House Menau has ever been the fulfillment of House Loria's destiny, my queen. Our ancestors were of a single mind in that regard. Just as your ancestral line passed on all the positive traits of either parent to your firstborn daughters, gathering every mage power under your dominion, so my house similarly passed on every mage gift of the mind."

"Your family's power of persuasion is well known, Sarella. What else could explain their influence upon House Loria over the millennia? No Lorian queen demanded a consort of your line until my mother arranged my nuptials to your brother," Valera said sweetly, masking the venom of her nature. How she loathed her deceased husband, the smug fool who drowned under all-too-mysterious circumstances. His mental prowess afforded him the ability to hide his thoughts from her, making Valera ever suspicious of what he kept hidden within his mind. Any limits upon her dominion ever frustrated her. Such was the nature of Vellesian queens' insatiable hunger for power. This insatiable hunger for mage powers they did not possess, caused them to resent their mates for possessing a power that they could never have, even though the power would pass onto their daughters. Most Vellesian queens broke their mates by the cruelest of means, yet Valera's queen mother denied her such pleasure, insisting the son of House Menau be afforded the respect his house had earned for their service to House Loria. The joining of their houses was long foretold to precede the final joining to the prince born of House Blagen, the son of a lightning lord and immune to magic.

It was House Menau's influence upon the Vellesian throne that counseled that Ethanos must bind himself to House Loria by his own hand, rather than taking him by force. They believed he held great import for Vellesia and Alesha beyond siring the future queen.

"My house is ever loyal, Your Grace, and we have joined our mage gifts to the throne as we have long foretold," Sarella reminded the queen of their loyalty, and that Alesha now possessed all the mage powers of her father's house. "We have aided in delivering Prince Ethanos into your hands, ensuring the dominion of House Loria over all of Elaria. Within a generation, all of the mage realms, the Mage Bane, and the wilds shall fall under your sway. Is this not a time of rejoice?"

"Rejoice?" Valera hissed. "The insults I endured from that *boy* pains me even now. I despise taking possession of him through such trickery as Alesha has done. Nay, I would have been better served leveling this wretched kingdom to its foundation and dragging the royal family of Blagen to Vellesia in chains. And if that brat refused to bend the knee to me, then I'd cut his family's throats one by one. That, my dear Sarella, is how I envisioned taking Ethanos. But alas, the ancient magic of my house prevented any such assault upon the wretched House of Blagen."

"And he would've refused you, Your Grace, and fought you to his dying breath. The magic protecting Astaria from your house is now lifted, but by allowing Astaria to yet stand, Ethan's sacrifice of his freedom is not done in vain. He shall serve as you desire as long as this is so," Sarella wisely counseled. "Thus, he rem—"

"The boy tests me!" Valera snarled. "I would see him broken. Only then can he serve as you envision!"

"As you wish, my queen, though that decision rests with Alesha as he is *her* consort," Sarella sagely opined. *You yet fear he is Free Born,* Sarella mused. *As well you should.* She smiled wickedly to herself. *If you only knew what the Free Born prophecy truly meant? Oh, how I shall savor the moment you finally learn the truth, you wretched creature.*

*****

They passed through the outer gates of Astaris, the late day sun shining brightly in the clear sky, a harbinger of victory for Alesha and despair for Ethan. They rode for a time in silence, side by side and far in front of the trailing host. Turning sharply to the east, they continued without speaking until the azure walls of Astaris disappeared to the west. Ethan found it odd that a crown princess would lead a procession through a foreign land with her guards nowhere near to lend aid if attacked, but then he realized how little she needed protection. She need only to step away from him and cast lightning, fire, ice, or any other calamity upon a witless attacker. Whenever she wished to demonstrate another of her apparent limitless magical powers, she simply drew away a few paces and showed him. She called fist-sized rocks to her before crushing them with her bare hands. She levitated above her saddle, following her mount from above as she floated through the air. She tore trees from the ground with their roots, tossing then aside with her telekinetic power. And so it went, with Alesha displaying many powers he had never seen as well as *every* power that he had. When she appeared to finish, she drew her mount closer to his, appraising him with a curious smile.

"Shall I continue?" she asked.

"If you wish." He shrugged, dismissing her smile as he stared ahead.

"Look at me, Ethan!" she commanded sternly with a tone that brokered no compromise. When she spoke thusly, she meant to be obeyed.

He obeyed, the hardness of his eyes betraying his rage.

She stared into his sea-blue eyes, strangely annoyed with his bitterness. Why did she care if he were unhappy? He belonged to her now; is that not what she sought since time immortal? His whining was unbecoming one of his character, and she tired of it. He was constantly testing her patience, and she still wondered why she cared for his happiness?

"I loved you, Allie," he said with sadness rather than spite. It was a simple declaration of what was but was no more. He vowed to shut his heart to her for all time, but was that even possible? She vexed him in ways that seemed unnatural, binding his heart with mysterious tendrils that wove themselves through every fiber of his being.

"And you still do," she declared as if stating a fact rather than an opinion.

"No, I don't," he said tiredly, not wishing to discuss the matter, especially with her.

"Deny it if you wish, Ethan, but you cannot help loving me. It is your destiny."

"I thought you didn't believe in love?"

"I don't for me. I am beyond the simple affections that plague the hearts of my lessers. Lust, attraction, and reciprocity are the lifeblood of the primitive emotion you call *love*. You are not above its trappings, Ethan. It binds your heart to me even now, after all I have done to you. I need not read your thoughts to see the conflict within. You are torn by your affection and hatred of me, each vying for dominion."

"You're awful sure of yourself, Alesha, and I thought your mother was conceited. She's a humble little dove next to you."

"Conceited?" She lifted a brow over a dangerous eye. "Conceit is an overvaluation of self-worth. I am the amalgamation of millennia-long culmination of power. There has never been born one such as me. I am the apex of mage power in all of Elaria and beyond. Conceit is a pompous trait to those who *believe* they are better, I simply *am*. This is not conceit but an acknowledgment of fact. I am superior to my mother before me, just as she was superior to hers, and so forth through the ages of House Loria. Just as one day, my daughter shall be superior to me. It shall be her destiny to rule all of Elaria. Every king shall bow and every mage born and common born shall call her queen, forever raising House Loria to its proper place. All my future daughter lacks is her father's immunity to magic. Such is your place in her destiny, Ethan. We have waited ages for your coming, and it is time for you to fulfill the role appointed you."

"Destiny is a two-edged sword, Alesha, it cuts both ways," he warned.

"Ah, you are referring to your great-grandsire's Free Born prophecy. It is irrelevant now. You must remember that your grandfather's prophetic mage gift was but a poor version of my own. Our prophecies and visions were clear that you were born to complete the ascension of House Loria. It is your destiny. If you were Free Born, you could not achieve that which my forebears have foreseen for hundreds of years. You were not born to bring freedom to the pitiful masses, Ethanos. You were born to complete the dominion of House Loria for all time."

She paused, appraising him for his reaction. For one immune to magic, she was often surprised how easy it was for her to read his thoughts as if she had known him all her life. It was strange that he claimed that she enchanted him, binding his heart with a power that could never penetrate his magical immunity. Stranger still was her unease whenever he was absent from her side. The more time that they spent in each other's company, the stronger the bond linking them. She could not confess this truth to her mother, for fear of her reaction. Vellesian crown princesses were never bound to their consorts; their consorts were bound to them. If Valera discovered that Ethanos held such power over her heir, how would she react? Their prophecies and visions spoke not of this unnatural bond that joined them. Ethan's great-grandsire believed him to be Free Born, a living catalyst to bring true freedom to the masses. She knew this to be rubbish. Had her mother believed that, she would have discovered some way to seize Ethan when he was a child, taken him to the Mage Bane, and killed him. She cringed at the thought of him dying. Why did it bother her so? Once she gives birth to their daughter, then his destiny is fulfilled, yet even then, she could not imagine a world without him. Was there more to their prophecy than they knew? Was there more to their destiny than just the joining of their powers?

Alesha gasped, her mind awash with the thoughts of those trailing them hundreds of paces behind. She could suddenly hear them despite her nearness to Ethan, as if the mage-less void surrounding him was no longer a hindrance to her power.

"Alesha, are you all right?" he asked, visibly concerned as she brought Glynderelle to a halt. He circled Bull in front of her, passing to her other side as they faced opposite directions.

"I'm fine," she said elatedly, her eyes alit with overwhelming joy as she stared intently into his sea-blue eyes.

"What's wrong?" He made a face, unnerved by her sudden gaiety.

She crooked a finger, ordering him to lean close with the most inviting smile he had ever seen. He thought to disobey her, to pull away just to spite her but was drawn to her for some reason only the fates must know.

"Close your eyes," she commanded with a seductive whisper as he drew nigh.

No sooner had he closed his eyes than she was upon him, her lips pressed to his, devouring him with savage passion.

Aw, hell. Ethan sighed, deciding to give in. He wasn't made of stone, no matter how hard he tried to refuse her, kissing her back with equal ferocity.

Alesha reached her hands around his neck, releasing small streams of lightning, fire, and ice into the air behind him before turning it upon his back. The mage powered elements dissipated above his flesh, proving he was still immune to magic, but his immunity no longer hindered hers. Had it been so throughout the morn? Had she been merely unaware that his aura no longer suppressed her powers? What had changed? Then it dawned on her like the morning sun breaking the dawn—their physical union the night before. She knew the moment when his seed took root.

Her heart sang. Her *baby*, her child of prophecy and destiny grew within, extending its magical immunity to her as its life source. Her lips lingered upon his for a time, savoring this triumphant moment. She lowered her hands to his collar, unlocking it with her magic, the audible click ringing distinctly in their ears. She tucked the collar in her saddle. He opened his mouth to ask why, but she pushed a finger to his lips.

"My mother has had her revenge. I'll not have you further humiliated, not without purpose." Besides, she couldn't bear to see his sad eyes. She gifted the most beautiful smile she could manage before kissing him again.

After a time, they parted, neither saying a word as she regarded him with wonder. Despite what her mother claimed that he served no purpose beyond their physical joining, she knew that she needed him beside her for all time.

Ethan started to question her sudden elation but thought it wiser to keep quiet.

"Come, we have far to travel, my love," she commanded.

"Love? You said that was a primitive emotion?"

"Oh, shut up and follow me," she said.

"Why should I?" he challenged.

"Because you are sworn to obey me, and—"

"And what?"

"And because I love you." With that, she winked and kicked her heels, urging her mount onward and following the road east toward Vellesia and their destiny.

Ben Thorton sat in front of the jail, his chair leaning against the wall with his boots resting on the porch post. It was a warm and windy early winter day, the dry wind blowing tumbleweeds down the dusty avenue. Red Rock was a peaceful town for over a year, and the good townsfolk were thankful for the reprieve. There had been no sign or word of Luke Crawford since Ethan left. Perhaps the outlaw thought it best to stay clear since all of Texas wanted him dead. Ben lit his cigar, blowing lazy puffs into the air with his Henry rifle across his lap. Just another quiet day in Red Rock, and he wondered when George Adams would cross the street to talk his fool head off as he did every day since he could remember. He caught sight of a different character making his way toward the jail from the other end of the street—Judge Donovan. His large, boisterous, loud-spoken friend ambled up to the jail.

"Afternoon, Judge," Ben touched a finger to his Stetson, saluting his friend.

"Ben," the judge greeted. "Quiet day?"

"I suppose," Ben said, taking another puff on his cigar.

The judge grinned wryly; his old friend never was one for lengthy responses. Ben seemed more ornery as late, though most folks couldn't tell the difference as he was never one to smile without good reason. Hell, Ben often had less charm than a snake bit grizzly. As the local schoolmaster, the judge sent the kids home early as it was the last day of school before Christmas. He figured on spending his free afternoon with Ben and took a chair from inside the jail and joined him on the porch, lighting his own cigar with his feet up on the railing.

"Before George Adams makes his way across the street and talks our ears off, Ben, mayhap you'll tell me what burr has crawled up your britches? You've been in a sour mood for several days now," the judge asked.

"Ethan's in trouble."

"Ethan? Thought he was back in Ohio with his kinfolk?"

"He ain't from Ohio, Judge."

"Pennsylvania?"

"Nope."

"Then where?" The judge made a face at Ben's cryptic tone.

"I didn't raise a liar."

"A liar? What in tarnation are you talking about, Ben?"

"Sometime after Ethan and Krixan left, Jake came to me with a strange tale. So strange in fact, I knew it had to be true because even a liar couldn't come up with the story he told."

"This story is about Ethan?"

"Yep. The strangest part is how it all makes sense." Ben reflected on all the odd details in Ethan and Krixan's stories and mannerisms and how Jake's explanation connected the various parts of their intricate puzzle.

"You aren't makin' much sense, Ben. You mind telling me what Jake said?"

Ben told the judge everything, how Ethan and Krixan came across the barrier, how they saved Jake, and why Jake was hurt. He explained how Ethan was some sort of prince in a feudal society that Jake only briefly glimpsed, and how Ethan was the key to opening the way to that world. He went on, explaining every detail that he was privy too, speaking more in that time than he probably said in years. At the conclusion, Judge Donovan took a deep puff on his cigar, thinking the sheriff must be touched in the head believing such a tale, but strange as it was, he believed it too.

"I've heard some strange things, Ben, but that story takes top prize. You must be a fool for believing it, but I'm a bigger fool for believing it too."

"You believe it?" Ben looked at him with a raised brow.

"I reckon I do for two reasons. One is Jake. His word is gold to me. The other is Ethan. Anyone that can shoot like him, think like him, hell, even play guitar like him ain't from our world. Throw in the fact that he's so good at all that, but plays poker like my Great Aunt Bessy who had the shakes, and I'll believe just about anything." The judge took another puff, blowing smoke rings in the air. "So if Ethan is in this other place, how do you know he's in trouble?"

"It's what I sense, not what I know. It's the same feeling I used to get when I was a Texas ranger and a Comanche was sneaking up my backside."

"I'll take your word for it, Ben, but what are you going to do about it?"

"There ain't nothing we can do unless Ethan can find a way to open the barrier. Until then, we just have to wait."

OTHER BOOKS BY AUTHOR

Free Born Saga

Book 1 Free Born
Book 2 Elysia coming 2023
Book 3 Dragon Wars (in production)

Chronicles of Arax

Book 1 Of War and Heroes
Book 2 The Siege of Corell
Book 3 The Battle of Yatin
Book 4 The Making of a King
Book 5 Battle of Torry North (late 2023)
Book 6 Fall of Empires (2024)

ABOUT THE AUTHOR

Ben Sanford grew up in western New York State, enjoying the great outdoors. He has traveled throughout the United States and abroad. He is currently living in the mid-Atlantic states with his family.

www.ingramcontent.com/pod-product-compliance
Lightning Source LLC
Chambersburg PA
CBHW022009300726

48970CB00003B/810